Henry Thomas Riley

Chronica Monasterii S. Albani. Thomae Walsingham, Quondam Monachi S. Albani, Historia Anglicana

Vol. 2. A. D. 1381-1422

SALZWASSER VERLAG

Henry Thomas Riley

Chronica Monasterii S. Albani. Thomae Walsingham, Quondam Monachi S. Albani, Historia Anglicana

Vol. 2. A. D. 1381-1422

Reprint of the original, first published in 1864.

1st Edition 2022 | ISBN: 978-3-75259-173-6

Verlag (Publisher): Salzwasser Verlag GmbH, Zeilweg 44, 60439 Frankfurt, Deutschland
Vertretungsberechtigt (Authorized to represent): E. Roepke, Zeilweg 44, 60439 Frankfurt, Deutschland
Druck (Print): Books on Demand GmbH, In de Tarpen 42, 22848 Norderstedt, Deutschland

CHRONICA MONASTERII S. ALBANI.

THOMÆ WALSINGHAM,

QUONDAM MONACHI S. ALBANI,

HISTORIA ANGLICANA.

EDITED

BY

HENRY THOMAS RILEY, M.A.,

OF CORPUS CHRISTI COLLEGE, CAMBRIDGE;

AND OF THE INNER TEMPLE, BARRISTER-AT-LAW.

VOL. II.

A.D. 1381—1422.

LONDON

1864.

CONTENTS.

INTRODUCTION.

INTRODUCTION TO VOLUME II.

THE present Volume contains the concluding portion of the *English History* attributed to Thomas Walsingham, A.D. 1381 to A.D. 1422, the end of the reign of Henry the Fifth.

Source of the earlier part of Walsingham's *History*.

The fact has been already noticed, in the Introduction to the First Volume, that the earlier portion of Walsingham's *History* is immediately derived from an older compilation, once belonging to the Abbey of St. Alban's, and now forming part (fols. 177–326) of the manuscript Volume 13 E. ix. in the King's Library at the British Museum.

Source of the latter part of the *History*.

Description of the Corpus Christi MS. No. vii.

At the beginning of the last page (folio 326 b) of this Manuscript, as given in the [1] Museum Volume, it is abandoned by the compiler of the *History*, who passes on to another source, from which he derives his matter down to the end of the work. This source is to be found in the Manuscript No. vii. in the Library of Corpus Christi College, Cambridge; a volume which bears internal evidence of having been compiled in the Abbey of St. Alban's, and which is incorrectly described in Nasmith's [2] *Catalogue* (1777) as containing no less

[1] An additional leaf of this MS., which has been found by the Editor in the Corpus Christi MS. Volume, No. vii., will be mentioned more fully in the sequel.

[2] The *Catalogue* (1777) gives the following incorrect list of the Contents of this Volume: 1. *Hist. Angliæ ab anno* 1377 *ad annum* 1400. 2. *Hist. Angliæ ab anno* 1404 *ad annum* 1409. 3.—*ab anno* 1393 *ad annum* 1403. 4.—*ab anno* 1400 *ad annum* 1406. 5.—*ab anno* 1393 *ad annum* 1422. *Hæc historia semper fere concordat cum Thoma de Walsingham, etsi nonnulla habeat codex noster quæ ipse omisit.* Nasmith then refers to the words of Tyrrell, in his *History of England*, Vol. iii. *Introd.*, p. xi., in reference to this

than five different MS. Histories of England; whereas, in fact it contains but three such Histories, in addition to a Register-Book of the Benefactors of St. Alban's, which occupies the latter part of the Volume, a large folio of 264 pages.

The Corpus Christi MS. No. vii., the source of the *History*. A.D. 1392–1422.

Of these three Manuscripts, those, the commencing portions of which are marked (1) and (5) in Nasmith's *Catalogue*, are the sources from which the *History*, between A.D. 1392 and 1422, is immediately derived; the second being little else than a revise or second edition of the first, down to the year [1] 1405 (p. 271 of this Volume), where MS. (1) abruptly terminates. After this date, MS. (5) is the sole source borrowed from by the compiler down to the [2] end of the *History*, A.D. 1422.

---

volume: — "There is still pre- "served in the Library of Bennet "College in Cambridge a large "Leiger Book, that once belonged "to St. Alban's Abbey, of which "our Author (Walsingham) was a "monk; wherein, among divers "particulars relating to that Mo- "nastery, there is also intermixed "(by way of Annals) a great deal "of Civil History, especially re- "lating to the reign of this Prince, "and from whence I find our Au- "thor to have borrowed most of "his matter, though he had digested "it into a much better style and "order." The volume appears to have been in this fragmentary condition as early as the middle of the 15th century; for at the foot of the first page we find the following Note:—"*Hunc librum cronicalem* "*tam gestorum regum quam abbatum,* "*post mortem Dompni Willelmi* "*Wyntershylle, in quaternis de-* "*relictum, connecti fecit Dompnus* "*Robertus Ware; et licet diversæ* "*materiei diversa sunt, propter de-* "*fectus quaternorum, non consonan-* "*tia, studeat tamen lector flores mel-* "*lifluos et coloribus amaricatos,* "*prout tempora fuerunt, degustare,* "*timere et refutare.*" Robert Ware, monk of St. Alban's, was present at the re-election of John Whethamstede, as Abbot, in 1451.

[1] As already remarked, MS. (1) is incorrectly described in the Catalogue, as to the date of its conclusion.

[2] At page 181 of the volume, the concluding page of MS. (5), the following is written in a hand of Elizabeth's time: "*Hiis istis verbis* "*finitur Historia Thomæ de Wal-* "*singham,—qui ex hoc opere suam* "*Historiam compilavit,*"—the last seven words being in a somewhat later hand. MS. (5), it should be remarked, is a Continuation of an earlier Chronicle (not identical with Walsingham's *History*) of which only a small fragment is preserved in the volume prior to A.D. 1393.

These Manuscript *Histories* (or other MSS., from which they have been transcribed) have been evidently employed also by Walsingham in that portion of his *Ypodigma Neustriæ*, which extends from A.D. 1393 to its conclusion in 1419.

The Corpus Christi MSS. employed also in Walsingham's *Ypodigma Neustriæ*.

From A.D. 1393 to 1404 in that work, Walsingham mostly adopts the text of MS. (5); occasionally inserting passages to be found in it that are omitted in the *History*, and at other times omitting matter which the compiler of the *History* has retained. Sometimes again, though rarely, he inserts matter from MS. (1) that has not been retained in MS. (5), while on other occasions he gives facts that are not to be found in either of those Manuscripts, but are derived by him from other sources. From A.D. 1404 to the conclusion of the *Ypodigma*, Walsingham has almost implicitly followed the text of MS. (5).

The Corpus Christi MSS. No. vii., (1) and (5). probably not compiled by Walsingham.

It is of course within the limits of possibility that either MS. (1) or (5) Corp, Chr. vii., or even both of them, may have been compilations by Walsingham's own hand; but if, as will be suggested in the sequel, the compiler of Bibl. Reg. 13 E. ix. (A.D. 1272–1392) was no other than Walsingham himself, this will be found to be improbable in a high degree. The style, diction, and treatment of the subjects, in these Manuscripts (especially MS. 5), the abrupt manner in which matters of high interest and great political importance are disposed of, and the comparatively numerous inaccuracies in reference to persons and facts, all go towards shewing that the compilers of Bibl. Reg. 13 E. ix. and the Corpus Christi MSS. were, in all probability, different persons. There cannot, perhaps, be a stronger proof of this than the fact, that whereas the compiler of MS. Bibl. Reg. 13 E. ix. is never tired of narrating the prowess, and repeating the praises, of Sir Hugh Calverley, one of the most eminent commanders of his day, and who appears as one of his most prominent heroes, the compiler or compilers of the Corpus Christi MSS. have never even named Sir Hugh, and, on reaching A.D. 1394, have not so much as mentioned his death, which took place on the 23rd of April in that year, while the deaths of individuals of less note and celebrity are not unfrequently recorded.

As the *Ypodigma Neustriæ* was compiled by Walsingham in or about A.D. 1419, and certainly concluded in that year, as we learn from the Dedication, the final [1] three years of (5) MS. Corp. Chr. vii. (A.D. 1419–1422), supposing Walsingham to have employed it in his compilation, must have been added at a somewhat later date.

Probable date at which Walsingham flourished.

As to the identity of the Compiler of MS. Bibl. Reg. 13 E. ix.—Bale and Pits assert that Thomas Walsingham flourished (*claruit*) A.D. 1440, in the reign of Henry the Sixth. This is to all appearance an error, as we learn from undoubted [2] authority that in the time of Abbot Thomas de la Mare, who died in 1396, Walsingham was already high in station in the Abbey of St. Alban's, holding the offices of *Præcentor* and *Scriptorarius;* and from other [3] authorities we find that he sat in the capacity of Prior of the Cell of Wymundham at the election of Abbot John de la Moot, on the 9th of October in that year; to which office of Prior he had been promoted in [4] 1394; facts that would tend to shew that even then he was advanced in life, so far advanced, at least, as to render it highly improbable that he was flourishing at a later date by six and forty years.

[1] From "*Die Lunæ*," p. 330 in this Volume, to "*sunt commissa*" in p. 346.

[2] The *Register-Book of Benefactors* of St. Alban's; being the Fourth (Sixth in Nasmith's *Catalogue*) Manuscript in the Corpus Christi Volume No. vii.

[3] Cited in Newcome's *History of St. Alban's*.

[4] Blomefield's *History of Norfolk*, ii. p. 519. He was appointed 4 Sept. 1394, *Reg. Norw.* vi. 195.

Probable date of the compilation of MS. Bibl. Reg. 13 E. ix.

As already remarked in the Introduction to Vol. I. (p. x.), the Manuscript Bibl. Reg. 13 E. ix. was most probably compiled in or soon after A.D. 1394, inasmuch as the writer seems to allude (Vol. I. p. 372, and *infra*, p. 89) to Sir Hugh Calverley as then being but recently dead, and he died on the 23rd of April in that year. That it was compiled by some one who was a member of the Abbey of St. Alban's there are internal evidences in the Manuscript in abundance, both in its contents and its style of penmanship. The Compiler too must have been a man who had passed his youth, for he speaks of himself — unless indeed he is heedlessly borrowing the language of some other writer, which there seems no reason to believe,—as having conversed (I. p. 435) with Sir John Philipott, Alderman of London, in the year 1380, or, at all events, between that year and 1384, in which year Philipott died (*infra*, p. 115); and in another place he states that he had heard certain language used in the year 1385 (*infra*, p. 140) by a knight in reference to the contemplated spoliation of the Abbey of St. Alban's.

Walsingham a compiler before A.D. 1394.

Previously to the year 1394, to about which date the Editor would be inclined to assign the compilation of the Manuscript Bibl. Reg. 13 E. ix., we have the best reason for believing that Walsingham had been for some time engaged in the work of authorship or compilation, for in the *Gesta Abbatum* of St. Alban's (MS. Claudius E. iv., in the Cotton Collection) there is a Note, in rubric, at the foot of folio 189 a, to the following effect; — "*Exhinc usque ad obitum Thomæ* "*Abbatis ex studio Fratris Thomæ de Walsigham* [sic] "*præcentoris;*" which Note (from the style of penmanship, added, no doubt, very shortly after the Volume was completed), while informing us that Walsingham was the compiler of the [1] latter part of it, is certainly

The latter part of the *Gesta Abbatum*, (MS. Claudius, E. iv.) compiled by Walsingham.

[1] After the accession of Abbot Hugh de Eversdon in 1308. The earlier part is attributed to Matthew Paris.

erroneous in other respects. We have already seen that he had ceased to be Præcentor two years before the death of Abbot Thomas de la Mare in [1] 1396, and as the very latest date to be found in the contents of the *Gesta Abbatum* appears to be the 14th of Richard II., 1390-91 (some years before the death of Abbot Thomas), the strong probability is, that it was compiled between 1391 and the time of Walsingham's removal to Wymundham in 1394. In size (large folio), penmanship, and style of illumination, it may be pronounced the exact counterpart of the Manuscript Volume Bibl. Reg. 13 E. ix.

Walsingham probably the compiler of MS. Bibl. Reg. 13 E. ix.; which has been erroneously considered as a Continuation of Higden's *Polychronicon*.

These facts combined, render it quite possible that the Compiler of the MS. Bibl. Reg. 13 E. ix. may have been no other than Thomas Walsingham, to whom the entire compilation, known as the *History*, has been hitherto attributed: but there is still further evidence at hand, which would appear to render it probable that such was the fact, in the highest degree. From the *Centuriæ* of John Bale we learn, as quoted by Camden, in his *Anglica, Normannica, etc.* (Pref. p. vi., *Authorum Vita*), that Walsingham compiled—"*De Gestis Anglorum,—* "*Historiam Breviorem,—Auctuarium Polychronici,*" —evidently considered by Camden, or his Editor, to mean three separate works,—"The Deeds of the English,"— "A Shorter History," and—"A Continuation of the "*Polychronicon*;" whereas, in reality, the passage undoubtedly bears reference to but one [2] work, and means that Walsingham compiled "a Shorter History, "on the Deeds of the English, a Continuation of (Hig- "den's) *Polychronicon*;" the Longer History being no doubt his *Ypodigma Neustriæ*, which extends from the ninth century to A.D. 1419, while the "*Auctuarium*"

[1] At which date Richard Beaver was Præcentor, and voted as such at the election of Abbot John de la Moot.

[2] Pits says, in reference to this work:—"*Adjecit præterea Auctuarium ad Polychronicon Ranulphi* "*Monachi Cestrensis, incipiens ab* "A.D. 1342 *et finiens ad ann.* "1417."

is stated, in the above quotation in Camden's *Anglica, etc.*, to begin A.D. 1342, and to end in 1417.

The same work is also alluded to in Bishop Tanner's *Biblioth. Brit. Hib.* p. 752. (Note);—"*Scripsit etiam* "*Auctuarium Polychronici ab anno* MCCCXLII. ad "MCCCXVII., *lib.* I.—'*Hoc anno quinto die Junii*'— "*MS. in Coll. Gonvill. et Caii Cant. Ita ex nota* "*præfixa MS. Wharton. Y II. in Bibl. Lambeth.*

In the Bodleian Manuscript, No. 462, (15th cent.), which is evidently, to a great extent, a [1] close transcript of MS. Bibl. Reg. 13 E. ix., at fol. 140, after the word [2] "*Edmundus*", (A.D. 1341), we find the following passage inserted,—"*Hic finivit Ranulphus Cestrensis* "*opus suum; sequentia scripsit Frater T. W. Præ*-"*centor Sancti Albani;*" and at fol. 150, where, through an oversight on part of the compiler, the year 1341 is again reverted to, the same statement is repeated, though in somewhat different language,—"*Hic finivit* "*Ranulphus Cestrensis opus suum. Cronica Fratris* "*T. de Walsingham.*" We here see, apparently, the same statement made as that in Bale,—that Walsingham wrote a Continuation of Higden's *Polychronicon* from 1342. No work of Walsingham's, it may safely

Proofs of his having been such Compiler.

[1] In one instance, where Bodl. 462 does not follow the context of Bibl. Reg. 13 E. ix., it seems probable, almost beyond a doubt, that the latter is the volume referred to, in the following words, in reference to Wat Tyler's Insurrection in 1381:—"*Si quem scire delectat horum ma*-"*lorum nomina incentorum, sive* "*ductorum, communium, una cum* "*opinionibus cur hæc mala diversis* "*provinciis uno eodem tempore hiis*-"*dem fere diebus infra Octabas* "*festi Corporis Christi specialius* "*acciderunt, in Cronicis Majoribus* "*fratris Thomæ de Walsingham* "*apud Sanctum Albanum poterit* "*reperire.*" The names of the malefactors and the opinions referred to, are to be found in sequence in MS. Bibl. Reg. 13 E. ix. (p. 11 of the present Volume). The work is probably called the *Chronica Majora* of Walsingham, either on account of the large folio size of the volume, or from the fact of its details being more full than those of his other Chronicle, the *Ypodigma Neustriæ*. In Tanner (p. 752) the above passage is given as from the *Chronicle of Tynemouth.*

[2] See Vol. I. of this *History*, p. 253.

be asserted, is known to exist, that purports to be a Continuation of the *Polychronicon*. On turning, however, to folio 225 b. of MS. Bibl. Reg. 13 E. ix., we find satisfactory evidence how the mistake originated. The text, from the beginning of the narrative, at folio 177, down to folio 225, neither is that of the *Polychronicon* nor bears any [1] resemblance to it. On the reverse, however, of the last-mentioned folio, after the word [2] "*Edmundus*," we find a Note inserted in large modern Gothic characters to the following effect:—[3] "*Hic finivit Ranulphus Cestrensis opus suum*,"—but with no allusion to Walsingham's authorship of the work. This, there can be little doubt, has misled subsequent transcribers from the Manuscript; and aware probably that Walsingham had been connected with the compilation, they have fallen into the error of supposing that the earlier part of the Manuscript must have been the composition of Ranulph Higden, attributing only the latter portion of it (A.D. 1342–1392) to Walsingham.

Probable origin of the error, in taking MS. Bibl. Reg. 13 E. ix. (ff. 177–326) to be a Continuation of Higden's *Polychronicon*.

Probable results of the preceding enquiries.

The original of Walsingham's so-called *Auctuarium* of Higden's *Polychronicon* is then in all probability identical with the Manuscript Bibl. Reg. 13 E. ix. (fol. 177–326); and, if such is the case, in the absence of materials for coming to any positive conclusion, we arrive at the following probable results:—That the MS. Arundel vii., hitherto known as the [4] "*English History*

[1] The *Polychronicon* devotes but a few pages to all the Edwards, and has extremely little in common with the preceding part (A.D. 1272–1341) of MS. Bibl. Reg. 13 E. ix.

[2] See Vol. i. p. 253 of this *History*.

[3] It can only have been inserted as being a fact of some interest to the compiler, and occurring to him at the moment he had penned the preceding passage.

[4] Or the "*Historia Brevis*;" so called, in all probability, either from its having been confounded with the supposed *Auctuarium*, extending only from 1342 to 1392; or from the fact of the period embraced in it extending from 1272 to 1392, while that of the *Ypodigma* embraces from the ninth century to 1419. There is a transcript (of the latter part of the 16th century) of the Arundel MS. No. vii. in MS. Harl. 136, in which the *History* is intituled the "*Historia Magna*" of Thomas Walsingham.

"of Thomas Walsingham," is in reality not a compilation made by Walsingham, but by some other writer in the earlier half of the 15th century. That it is derived from two principal sources; one of which is the *English History* (A.D. 1272–1392) found in MS. Bibl. Reg. 13 E. ix. fol. 177–326, which we are justified by evidence, both internal and external, in supposing to be the *Auctuarium Polychronici* of the old writers, a compilation by the hand of Walsingham. That the other source from which it is compiled is the MS. (5) Corp. Chr. vii., (which, in its turn, is partly derived from MS. (1) Corp. Chr. vii.); to which Manuscripts Walsingham has also had recourse for the latter portion (A.D. 1393–1419) of his *Ypodigma Neustriæ*. As stated in the Introduction to the First Volume (p. xviii.), the Compiler of the Arundel Manuscript has temporarily abandoned the St. Alban's Chronicle between the years 1327 and 1343 (Vol. I. pp. 191–253), though reverting to it from time to time. The various authorities from which he has borrowed his matter on such occasions, will be found set forth in the inner margin of the page.

The first 15 years of Richard II. probably the part of the *History* more especially the composition of Walsingham.

The earlier part of the compilation being derived from known sources, the portion of this *History* which may probably be regarded as more especially the composition of Walsingham, is that which extends from A.D. 1377 to 1392 (Vol. I. p. 329 to p. 211 *infra*), the first fifteen years of the reign of Richard the Second; being at once the most important part of the work, and having the negative merit of being disfigured by comparatively few of those petty but striking inaccuracies with which the latter part of the *History*, derived from MS. (5) Corp. Chr. vii., so [1] plentifully abounds. In these fifteen

[1] One especial reason why the compilation of the Corpus Christi Manuscripts can hardly be ascribed to Walsingham, supposing him to have been the compiler of MS. Bibl. Reg. 13. E. ix. Among the more striking of these errors, the following may be enumerated:—The name of Brentingham, Bishop of Exeter, was *Thomas*, not *William*, as in p. 218

years we recognize by far the most valuable portion of the whole compilation, though put together, probably, not until, or shortly after, the close of that period, and from diverse and apparently discordant materials; in witness of which, we need only refer, through the aid of the Index, to the conflicting opinions stated during the course of those fifteen years in reference to the character and conduct of King Richard, and his uncle, John of Gaunt, the Duke of Lancaster; the former of whom, for example, is in one place (*infra*, p. 148) represented as in all probability defiled by the most abominable of vices, while elsewhere, though certainly he is mostly spoken of in terms of [1] censure, he is mentioned with words of commendation, extending almost to praise.

Conflicting opinions in the *History*, in the course of those 15 years.

The more striking points of value and interest in this

The more striking

of this Volume, and he died in 1394, not 1395; Wakefield, Bishop of Worcester, died in 1394, not 1395 (p. 218); *John* Beaufort, not *Thomas*, was created Earl of Somerset (p. 223); *William* de Bottlesham, not *John*, died in 1400, not 1401, as stated in p. 248; Roger de Waldene was Bishop of London for rather *more* than a year, not *less*, as stated in p. 273; *Edmund*, not *Thomas*, Earl of Kent, was slain in 1407, not 1408 (p. 279); *John* Beaufort, Earl of Somerset, died in 1410, and there was no such person as *Thomas* Beaufort, Earl of *Surrey*, who is stated (p. 283) to have died in that year; Archbishop Arundel died in February 1413, and not in 1414 (p. 300); Stephen de Patryngton became Bishop of St. David's in 1415, not 1414 (p. 300). The siege of Rouen and other matters are omitted (p. 329), and the narrative leaps from the middle of August 1418 to the 1st of August 1419, the surprise of Pontoise,—an error which, if not originating with Walsingham, has been implicitly followed by him in the *Ypodigma Neustriæ*. Among errors peculiar to MS. (1) Corp. Chr. may be mentioned the alleged death (p. 420) of a Bishop of Lincoln in 1404, no such event having happened in that year; and the alleged death of the King of France in that year (p. 422), which is equally remote from the truth. The errors as to chronology and events in the reign of Edward II., noticed in the Introducion to Vol. I. (p. xvii.), are mostly to be attributed to Trokelowe, from whose Chronicle the account is derived.

[1] Note the sneer (*infra*, p. 103) at his meanness in borrowing the Abbot's palfrey, which he took care never to return; also the account (*infra*, p. 199) of his exacting from the Abbey of St. Alban's a horse worth 24 marks, and then demanding of the Abbot a loan of 500 marks.

points in this portion of the *History*.

history of these fifteen years, may be thus briefly enumerated :—A singularly full account of the Coronation of Richard the Second, and of the [1] circumstances preceding it; the relations during this period between the King and his uncles, the Dukes of Lancaster and Gloucester; full particulars in reference to the naval enterprises of the English, communicated, it seems not unlikely, down to 1384, the year of his death, by Sir John Philipott, Alderman of London, and the most eminent financier of his day; who, indeed, in one instance (I. p. 435) is cited by the writer as his informant; various particulars relative to the trade, commerce, and general affairs, of the City of London, derived probably from the same source to a considerable extent, not omitting the story of the quack physician and soothsayer, and his singular [2] punishment (*infra*, p. 63); the numerous attacks made by the French during this period on our southern coasts; the proceedings against John [3] Wyclif, A.D. 1377 and 1378; the exploits of Sir Hugh Calverley against the French; the pollution of Westminster Abbey by the

---

[1] A most important passage in reference to these circumstances, which had been omitted in the former editions of the *History*, will be found restored in these pages, from MS. Bibl. Reg. 13 E. ix. See Vol. I. p. 331 and *infra*, pp. 383–387, including an account of the singular quarrel between the Londoners and Chief Justice Belknappe, and of their curious way of revenging the slight which he had put upon them.

[2] A similar account of his punishment is given in *Letter-Book H*, fol. 145, preserved in the Record Room at Guildhall; but his offence is there described as being of a different character.

[3] The corrected text in the present edition (Vol. I. p. 357, for example) will probably be found to throw light upon some passages in the *Fasciculi Zizaniorum* of Netter of Walden, most ably edited by the Rev. W. Waddington Shirley in the present Series; the text of which work, in the editing of this portion of Walsingham, has always been carefully kept in view. The utter worthlessness of the text of Walsingham's *History*, as given in Parker's and Camden's Editions, is perhaps nowhere more strikingly seen, than in the portion which bears reference to the proceedings against Wyclif in 1378. Indeed, it seems quite incomprehensible how Archbishop Parker or William Camden could have given the sanction of his name to such a mass of perversion and absolute nonsense.

murder of Robert Haule there, and the implied complicity of the Duke of Lancaster therein; inroads upon the North of England by the Scots; the great Pestilence there in 1379; the confinement of John Mercer the Elder in the Castle of [1] Cherbourg, and the capture of English ships by the younger Mercer in retaliation, with his own ultimate discomfiture through the spirit and patriotism of the London Alderman, Sir John Philipott; the sacrilege and cruelties committed by Sir John Arundel and his comrades,—an account not to be found in the pages of Froissart (who styles Arundel "a valiant and enterprising knight"), where he narrates the disasters which ultimately befell them; the remarkable duel between Sir John Annesley and Thomas Katrington; an account of the Insurrection in 1381 of Wat Tyler and his followers, John Straw and John [2] Wraw in the number; the active part taken in the insurrection by the townsmen of St. Alban's, William Grindecobbe at their head; the serious danger threatened to the Abbey, and the flight of several of the monks thereupon; the doctrines and singular Letter of John Ball, which differs almost wholly from the copy given by Knighton; the rivalry between the Duke of Lancaster and the Earl of Northumberland; the Propositions and Conclusions of John Wyclif issued in 1382, and the proceedings thereupon; the extensive adoption of the doctrines of Wyclif by the Londoners; full particulars—though inferior, perhaps, in interest, to those given in the narrative of Froissart—of the Crusade

[1] The Editors of the *Pictorial History of England* (i. p. 783) have taken the word "*Scarbourgh*" (*Hist.* I. p. 369) to mean "Scarborough."

[2] This individual seems to have held as eminent a place among the insurgents of the East of England as his almost namesake, John Straw, in London and its vicinity. The Editors of Parker's and Camden's texts have confused the names, probably considering the name "*Wrawe*" to be a mistake for "*Strawe*;" but that they were really different persons there cannot be a doubt: the execution of Straw is mentioned at page 10 of this Volume, that of Wrawe at page 63. He is perhaps the Eastern insurgent who is called "*Vaquier*" by Froissart.

in Flanders against the [1] Clementists, under Henry Spencer, the warlike Bishop of Norwich;—all which particulars were not improbably derived by the writer from Sir John Philipott, to whom appears to have been mainly entrusted the fitting-out of the expedition, and who himself had been deprived of his Aldermanry by the Mayor of London, John Comberton, or John de Northampton, shortly before; the obstinate persecution of the fishmongers of London by the same John Comberton, the result of which was, that fish was made cheaper in London, but dearer in the [2] country, than theretofore; the proceedings in 1387 of Walter Disse, Peter Patteshulle, and the leaders of the Lollards; the King's strenuous support of his favourites, Robert De Vere, Earl of Oxford, successively Marquis of Dublin and Duke of Ireland, and Michael de la Pole, Earl of Suffolk, against the Duke of Gloucester and the Earls of Arundel and Warwick; the punishment of Sir Nicholas Brembre, or Brambre, late Mayor of London, one great [3] charge against whom, as we learn from the restored reading in the present Edition (*infra*, p. 174) was, that he intended to change the name of the City of London to that of "New Troy," and designed to have himself created Duke by that title:—such are some among the more prominent subjects treated of in these pages under the first fifteen years of Richard the Second, decidedly the most valuable portion of the compilation that has come down to us as Walsingham's *English History*.

---

[1] As Froissart remarks, the Flemings in reality were not Clementists, but Urbanists, like the English. It was alleged, however, that Flanders was then in the hands of the French, who *were* Clementists.

[2] This subject would in all probability be of especial interest to the monks of St. Alban's, as we learn from *Liber Albus* (p. 384), that the Abbot of that house enjoyed singular privileges in the London fish-market.

[3] He would no doubt have the less sympathy from the populace, from the fact, as to which we are informed by Froissart, that he gave active and energetic assistance against the London insurgents under Wat Tyler in 1381.

As to Walsingham himself, who has been mentioned in the preceding pages as most probably the Compiler, not of the entire *History*, but of the St. Alban's Chronicle, MS. Bibl. Reg. 13 E. ix. (fols. 177–326), its primary and most important source, but very little seems to be known, and, with the exception of one or two ascertained facts, his biography is wholly a matter of uncertainty.

But few particulars known relative to Thomas Walsingham.

From his name and the assertion of the [1] old writers, we may conclude that he was a native of the County of Norfolk. In a passage (I. p. 345) where he laments the degeneracy of the University of Oxford and its laxity as to heresy, he speaks of it in such terms as to leave no doubt that he was [2] educated there, unless indeed, which is just possible, the passage is derived from some other [3] source, and consequently applicable to some other person. As already noticed, during the rule of Abbot Thomas de la Mare, at St. Alban's, who died in 1396, he held the offices of [4] *Præcentor* and *Scriptorarius*, or chief copyist, and from the *Register of Benefactors* in the Corpus Christi Manuscript, previously quoted, we learn that a new *Scriptorium*, or Copying-room, was erected by Abbot Thomas at his suggestion. In 1394 he became Prior of Wymundham, as already stated; and voted as such at the election of Abbot John de la Moote in 1396. In 1400 he ceased to be Prior of that place, and probably returned to St. Alban's, John Savage being appointed to the office of Prior. About the year 1419, probably, he compiled his

---

[1] Bale and Pits. Leland is in total ignorance about him.

[2] "*Ne materna videar ubera decer-* "*pere dentibus.*"

[3] This fact, perhaps, would make but little difference in the estimation of the compiler. Roger de Hoveden not only borrows from Henry of Huntingdon without acknowledgment, but copies a passage (*s. a.* 1144) in which Huntingdon states himself to have been eye-witness of a certain miracle, in such a manner as to lead the reader to suppose that Hoveden himself had been the witness.

[4] Pits calls him "Regius Pro- "fessor of History" at St. Alban's; but upon what authority, does not appear.

[1] *Ypodigma Neustriæ*, which he dedicated to Henry the Fifth, by way of compliment upon his recent conquests in Normandy. The sources from which the latter part of the *Ypodigma* is derived, have been already [2] indicated; the earlier portion is a compilation from the works of William de Jumieges, Ralph de Diceto, Rishanger, and the work which has been hypothetically attributed to Walsingham in the preceding pages, the Manuscript Bibl. Reg. 13 E. ix. (ff. 177–326). After the probable date of the Dedication of the *Ypodigma*, A.D. 1419, the Editor has failed to meet with any further mention of Walsingham, beyond the vague and apparently improbable assertion of the old writers, who state, as already mentioned, that he flourished (*claruit*) in 1440. Bale attributes to him a work intituled "*Acta Regis Henrici Sexti;*" perhaps incorrectly, but if not, it does not seem now to be known. Bishop Tanner (*Bibl. Brit. Hib.* p. 752), makes mention of a Manuscript in the Library of St. John's College, Oxford, containing a work by Thomas Walsingham—"*De Generatione et Natura Deorum.*"

Other works attributed to Walsingham.

Chronology of the earlier part of the *History*.

Rishanger, from whose Chronicle the earlier part of the Manuscript Bibl. Reg. 13 E. ix. is derived, has given A.D. 1273 as being the first year of the reign of Edward I.; whereas in reality his first year was from the [3] 20th of November 1272, to the 20th of November 1273. Walsingham, (supposing him to have been the Compiler of MS. Bibl. Reg. 13 E. ix.), with singular perverseness, it would seem, has added one year to Rishanger's numbers throughout, thus making Henry the Third to have died (16th November) 1273, and 1274 to have been the first year of the reign of Edward

[1] Which he explains as meaning, "Demonstration of events in Normandy;" though, in reality, the affairs of Normandy occupy but a small proportion of the entire work.

[2] In pp. ix. x. *ante*.

[3] Four days after his father's death; who died 16th November 1272.

the First. In some instances the regnal years of our early sovereigns were dated from the day of their Coronation; but Walsingham cannot have had this in view, as he makes Edward to have been crowned in [1] 1275, which he calls the second year of that reign. In Vol. I. this faulty Chronology of Walsingham, which has been followed in the Arundel Manuscript, has been corrected in the margin throughout the reign of Edward the First.

Purview of Contents of the Appendices.

The Appendices have been added to the present Edition, with the view of presenting to the reader all matter which may be legitimately considered as more or less nearly connected with the *English History*, attributed to Thomas Walsingham.

As stated in the Introduction to the First Volume, the present edition of the *History* is derived from the Arundel MS., No. vii., now preserved at the College of Arms; and [2] which, in all probability, was employed by Archbishop Parker and Camden in the preparation of their respective editions of the work. These editions, however, (as remarked in that Introduction, [3] p. xviii.) abandon the Arundel MS. in the earlier part of the reign of Edward III., and adopt a different text. The text thus introduced in these editions, to the exclusion of that of the Arundel MS., will be found in Appendix (A.) pp. 349–359, in the present Volume; consequently, in the present edition, no part of Walsingham's *History*, as hitherto printed, has been omitted.

The compiler of the Arundel Manuscript, while deriving his matter mainly from the St. Alban's Chronicle,

---

[1] He was really crowned on the 19th of August 1274.

[2] Or else a very close copy of it. See Introd. to Vol. I. p. xi.

[3] See also p. xvii. of the Introduction, as to a passage peculiar to the printed editions, relative to the marriage and Coronation of Edward II.; given in App. (A.) p. 349 of this Volume.

Bibl. Reg. 13 E. ix., has in various places rejected considerable portions of its text; more especially in the earlier part of the reign of Edward III., as noticed in the Introduction to Vol. I., pp. xviii. xix. All the passages in the St. Alban's Manuscript thus omitted have been carefully extracted, and will be found—some of them of considerable interest,—in Appendix (B.) pp. 360–406.

The fact has been previously [1] noticed that in the Corpus Christi Manuscript No. vii., a leaf has been found, which evidently, from the similarity of the illumination and the writing in the first dozen lines, was originally the concluding folio of the St. Alban's Chronicle, Bibl. Reg. 13 E. ix.; and which (continued in a different hand) now forms the first leaf of another Continuation of the St. Alban's Chronicle, being MS. (3) in the Corpus Christi Volume. The contents of this leaf are given in Appendix (C.) pp. 407–410.

It has been already stated that the latter part of this *History* (A.D. 1392–1422) is mainly derived from the Manuscript (5) Corp. Chr. vii.; which, in its turn, is derived from (1) Corp. Chr. vii., down to [2] A.D. 1405. The passages in the last named of these Manuscripts that have been omitted in the compilation of the *History*, will be found in Appendix (D.) pp. 411–424.

It has been remarked (p. ix. *ante*) that in the *Ypodigma Neustriæ* (A.D. 1393–1419) Walsingham, to a great extent, has followed the same text as that employed in the compilation of the *History* under those years. The more important of the Various Readings found in the *Ypodigma* (Camden's Edition) are set forth in Appendix (E.). Though, in general, the printed text of the *Ypodigma* is incorrect in the extreme, most of the readings here selected will be found to be improvements of the text of the *History*.

---

[1] In page vii. *ante*, Note 1.

[2] P. 271 of this Volume.

In conclusion, the Editor feels that he is discharging a duty, as pleasing as it is imperative, in acknowledging his obligations to the following gentlemen:—to T. Duffus Hardy, Esq., Deputy-Keeper of the Public Records, for many valuable suggestions made to him in reference to Walsingham's *History*, and the sources from which it is derived: to Sir Charles George Young, Garter King at Arms, for facilities courteously and kindly afforded him for consulting the Arundel Manuscript of this *History*; and to William Courthope, Esq., Somerset Herald, for the hospitable manner in which, by placing his chambers, in the College of Arms, at the Editor's service, he gave him the most ample opportunity, extending through many months, of enjoying those facilities. The Editor's best thanks are also due to the Rev. W. Middleton Snell, Fellow and Bursar of Corpus Christi College, Cambridge, for good offices and most cordial hospitality extended to him, during his prolonged examination of several volumes in the Parker Collection of Manuscripts, in the Library of that College.

H. T. R

CORRIGENDA.

Page 38, Side note, line 19, *for* "only" *read* "duly."
Page 115, " lines 4, 5, *for* "Duke of Gloucester" *read* "Earl of "Buckingham."
Page 221, Text, line 25, *for* "plenas" *read* "plenos."
Page 242, " line 29, *for* "defluenda" *read* "deflenda."
Page 245, Side note, line 4, *for* "Holland" *read* Huntingdon."
Page 249, " line 32, *for* "Dunbury" *read* Danbury."
Page 254, Text, line 29, *for* "resposita" *read* "reposita."
Page 255, " line 27, *for* "æmulatiorum" *read* "æmulatorum."
Page 258, " line 10, *for* "partes" *read* "partis."
Page 262, Note 1, line 1, *for* "(5) MS. Corp. Chr. vii." *read* "(1) MS. "Corp. Chr. vii."
Page 284, Note 1, line 19, *for* "magum" *read* "magnum."
Page 329, " line 1, *for* "crudelissim" *read* "crudelissime."
Page 442, Col. 1, line 23, *for* "sent to Boulogne" *read* "sent to Bre-"tagne."

In Vol. I.

Page 131, Text, line 1, *for* "Thoma" *read* "Thomæ."

THOMÆ WALSINGHAM,

QUONDAM MONACHI S. ALBANI,

HISTORIA ANGLICANA.

THOMÆ WALSINGHAM,

QUONDAM MONACHI S. ALBANI,

HISTORIA ANGLICANA.

[Continuatio de Tempore Regis Ricardi Secundi.]

Furia acta in Northfolcia.

MS. Bibl. Reg. 13 E. ix.

A.D. 1381.

The confusion that universally prevailed.

Exigit historiæ confusum ordinem confusio rerum in locis plurimis [1]perpetratarum, et vix, pro varietate locorum et diversitate facinorum, uno tempore commissorum, servari potest ordo scribendi. Ecce enim! dum magna et nimis magna facinora scribo, diebus Veneris atque Sabbati gesta Londoniis, vix eorum explicare possum tragœdiam, quin eisdem diebus occurrunt scribenda similia apud Sanctum Albanum, ut prætactum est. Necdum apud Sanctum Albanum exarare possum commissam miseriam, antequam se offerat alibi aliquod par, aut magis execrabile, seu notabile, nefas.

The insurrection in Norfolk and Suffolk.

Enormities committed there.

Eodem die Sabbati, ut generalis esse videretur ista tempestas, in partes Southfolchiæ et Northfolchiæ misit Deus iram indignationis suæ, indignationem et iram, et tribulationum immissiones per angelos malos, quosdam videlicet perfidis Estsexcensibus periculosiores, [2]angelis Sathanæ, qui informarent populum in quiete degentem, populum innocentem, ad tumultuationem superioribus similem, et [3]converterent in suos dominos corda servorum. Qui confestim, efficientes magis quam proficientes, duce quodam sceleratissimo presbytero, dicto

[1] *perpetrata* in the printed texts.
[2] *angelos* in the printed texts.
[3] *connecterent* in orig. and the printed texts. Corrected from Bibl. Reg. 13 E. ix.

A.D. 1381. [1]"Johannes [2]Wraw," qui et ipse Londoniis fuerat pridie, et instructus a ganeone præfato, Waltero Tylere, de facili congregaverunt turbam, cujus numerus excedebat, ut ferunt, quinquaginta millia plebanorum. Hii autem, juxta [3]morem eorum qui Londoniis furuerunt, in universis furentes, domos et prædia magnorum virorum, legisperitorum, prostraverunt, legis apprenticios occiderunt, et Dominum Johannem Cavendische, Justiciarium regni Principalem, interceptum decollaverunt; et super collistrigium in foro villæ Sancti Edmundi de Bury [4][caput ejus, in opprobrium, posuerunt. Priorem insuper Sancti Edmundi de Bury], Dominum Johannem de Cantebriggia, virum industrium et solertem, Orpheum Thracem, Neronem Romanum, [5]Belgabred Britannum, vocis dulcedine, pariter et cantus scientia, superantem, dum a facie eorum fugere niteretur, repente captum, crudeliter capitis truncatione peremerunt. Causa mortis ejus satis nota est; quia, cum esset circumspectus et prudens, causas domus suæ suscepit tuendas. Et quia fideliter decertavit contra villanos de Bury pro jure Monasterii, accepit, ut diximus, sententiam capitalem prope villam de Mildenhale, quæ ad jus ejusdem Monasterii pertinere dinoscitur; non tam villanorum prædictæ villæ de Bury, suorum adversariorum, sed propriorum servorum et nativorum, arbitrio simul et judicio, addictus morti. Corpus ejus fuit usque ad staminum nudatum, et femoralia; in aperto campo sub divo jacuit inhumatum quinque diebus, nemine præsumente illud vel auferre, vel naturæ debitum illi [6]munus impendere, propter [7]sævitiam rusticorum.

MS. Bibl. Reg. 13 E. ix.

Sir John Cavendisch, and Sir John de Cambridge put to death.

Cause of the violent death of the latter.

Nota—De Johanne Wraw, ductore plebis.

Disturbances at Bury Saint Edmund's.

Perpetrato prædicto piaculo, proceres perfidiæ, cum plebe perfida, dictus scilicet Johannes [8]Wraw, cum præfata turba, ad villam de Bury properant, et, nemine resistente, subintrant, caputque Prioris prænominati in conspectu villarum, tanquam

[1] *Johanne* in the printed texts; *Johannes* in Bibl. Reg. 13 E. ix.

[2] Thus written in orig. and in Bibl. Reg. 13 E. ix.; apparently by mistake for *Straw*, as in the printed texts. The anonymous author, however, of the *Hist. Ricardi II.*, published by Hearne (Oxon., 1729) in p. 29, makes "John Wraw" and "Jak Straw," to be two different personages.

[3] *majorem* in orig. and the printed texts; corrected from Bibl. Reg. 13 E. ix.

[4] Omitted in orig. and the printed texts; supplied from Bibl. Reg. 13 E. ix.

[5] *Bledgabred* in Bibl. Reg. 13 E. ix.

[6] *minus* in orig. and the printed texts. Corrected from Bibl. Reg. 13 E. ix.

[7] *sententiam* in the printed texts.

[8] Sic in orig. and Bibl. Reg. 13 E. ix.; *Straw* in the printed texts.

MS. Bibl. Reg. 13 E. ix.

processionaliter circumeundo, [1]in edito super lanceam perferentes, donec ad collistrigium pervenirent: quo cum accessissent, in signum antehabitæ [2]amicitiæ inter Priorem et Johannem Cavendich, et derisionem utriusque personæ, capita, modo velut ad auriculandum, jam quasi ad osculandum, invicem super summitates lancearum cum maxima [3]ineptia conjunxerunt. Postremo, cum talibus saturati fuissent ludibriis, utriusque caput iterum super collistrigium posuerunt. Deinde mox, in odium Prioris, quamdam domum quam ædificaverat et a fundamentis de novo construxerat, diruerunt. Quibus perpetratis, claustra ingressi Monasterii, Dominum Johannem de Lakynghuythe, custodem Baroniæ, illis tradi jusserunt, comminantes incendium Monasterio, nisi traderetur. Cumque staret inter illos, mirum dictu, nulli eorum nota fuit persona sua. Sed hæc omnia perfecerunt instinctu villanorum, qui ad hæc eos, ut facile erit probare ex sequentibus, occulte conduxerant, ipsis se a turba subtrahentibus, ut vel sic a tantis sceleribus esse viderentur immunes. Igitur præfatus Johannes, cavens domus suæ periculo, respondit se esse quem quærebant, interrogans ad quid a communibus peteretur: ad quem illi "Ad mortem," inquiunt, "proditor, te modo "quærimus; non [4]enim diutius vitam protelabis." Quibus ille, "Ad mortem quidem paratus sum, quam et libenter "amplector; ita duntaxat, ut istud Monasterium nullum causa "mei detrimentum patiatur." Moxque tractus ab eis, cum ingenti vociferatione quod invenissent [5]falsum monachum, adduxissent proditorem, in foro publice decollatus est, octies percussus antequam caput esset a corpore separatum. Cujus caput illico super collistrigium capiti Prioris sociaverunt. Nec hiis contenti, quemdam alium monachum, videlicet Walterum Todyngtone, ad consimilem mortis pœnam quæsierunt: sed is occultatus diligentissime, cum non posset inveniri, mortis periculum evitavit.

A.D. 1381.

Atrocities committed there,

and at the Monastery.

Murder of John de Lakynghuythe.

Escape of Walter Todyngtone.

Post hæc, evocatis cunctis monachis, dixerunt eos jam diuturno tempore per potentiam oppressisse consocios eorum, burgenses villæ de Bury; quapropter voluerunt, ut in conspectu communium modo redderent obligationes, quibus obligati fuerant Regi et Monasterio, si contigisset eos aliqua tentasse contra Abbathiam; necnon et chartas libertatum villæ, quas Cnuto, fun-

[1] *inditum* in the printed texts.

[2] *victoriæ amicitiæ* in orig.; *victoriæ et amicitiæ* in the printed texts. In Bibl. Reg. 13 E. ix., *victoriæ* has an expunctory mark beneath, being inserted by mistake.

[3] *amentia* in the printed texts.

[4] *nondum enim* in orig.; *non jam enim* in the printed texts: corrected from Bibl. Reg. 13 E. ix.

[5] *filium* in orig. and the printed texts.; *flm* in Bibl. Reg. 13 E. ix.

A.D. 1381. dator Monasterii, quondam concesserat; et quas successores sui Reges, usque in præsens, ad firmamentum Monasterii concesserunt. Monachi vero, sibi et suæ domui metuentes, si non parerent voluntati communium, omnia quæ petebantur, quæ scilicet vel villanorum firmamento vel illorum detrimento esse poterant, in forum coram omnibus protulerunt, jurantes inveniri non posse plures chartas, quæ villanorum commodo cedere possint, apud eos. Communes autem fidem dictis eorum vix dare volebant; sed vocatis villanis, qui simulabant in istis tristitiam, tanquam displicerent quæ gesta sunt, præceperunt eis ut diligenti scrutatione superviderent obligationes et chartas præfatas, et si ex hiis non possent consequi veteres libertates, edicerent, quibus gaudere solebant. Et Abbas, qui in carcere tenebatur apud Notyngham, Edmundus Brounfeld, quem deliberare proposuerant, ut in sequenti festo Johannes Baptistæ in suo Monasterio solemniter divina celebrare deberet, post quadragesimum diem adventus ejus exinde confectam chartam sigillo suo muniret, et Conventus idem facere sigillo suo communi non differret.

MS. Bibl. Reg. 13 E. ix.

Charters and deeds extorted from the Monks of Bury.

The jewels of the house delivered to the townsmen of Bury; to be returned on certain conditions.

Placuit hæc oratio monachis extrema metuentibus, et compellentibus communibus, et ita faciendum esse dictantibus: jocalia domus maxima, quamdam crucem auream, et unum calicem de fulvo [1] metallo pretiosum, aliaque nonnulla jocalia elata de Monasterio, quorum pretium excedebat mille libras monetæ, tradiderunt vice pignoris manibus villanorum; ea videlicet conditione, ut si Edmundus Brounfeld, ut præmittitur, deliberatus a carcere gauderet ibidem Abbatis honore, sigillum apponeret proprium, una cum consensu communi et sigillo Conventus, infra tempus limitatum libertatibus eorundem. Quod si conditio prædicta non esset impleta, remanerent prædicta jocalia in perpetuum penes villanos. Et ita quidem apud Bury res se habebant, mirum in modum, communibus petentibus pro villanis quæ ad eos minime pertinebant. De quibus rebus etiam scire non poterant, qualia quoque facere non debebant, nisi informatione et instigatione villanorum. Quis unquam crederet communes quemquam ex monachis, eis invisum, incognitum, innocentem, ad mortem petisse; quem insuper, eis astantem, non cognoscebant, si ad hæc minime inducti per alios extitissent? Quid ad eos pertinuit libertates exquirere pro villanis, [2] [qui villam minime incolebant? Vel si villanis] hæc omnia displicebant, cur recedentibus communibus, et pace reddita, ablata restituere distulerunt? Inexcusabiles prorsus mihi videntur, ut ex posteris clarius apparebit.

---

[1] *metalla* in orig., by inadvertence.

[2] Supplied from Bibl. Reg. 13 E. ix.; omitted in the printed texts.

MS. Bibl. Reg. 13 E. ix.

Consimilia facta in Comitatu Cantabrigiæ et in Insula Eliensi.

A.D. 1381.

Similar atrocities committed in Cambridgeshire and the Isle of Ely.

Exaratis pro parte, quæ apud Burgum Sancti Edmundi contigerunt, prætermissis facinoribus apud Cantebriggiam perpetratis, et in Comitatu Cantebriggiæ, necnon in Insula Eliensi, quæ non fuere disparia, sed omnino similia sceleribus, in mortibus hominum et locorum demolitionibus, cæteris quoque malis quæ docuimus alibi perpetrata, ad ea quæ in Northfolchia gesta sunt transeamus.

Sedition of John Littestere, of Norwich.

Igitur, conglomerata ibidem communium turba non modica, duce quodam tinctore de Norwico, cujus nomen erat "Johannes Littestere," cœperunt, ut ubique locorum alii fecerant, et ipsi facere, nihil prætermittentes ex omnibus quæ audierant communes in aliis locis egisse; sed majora insuper præsumentes, ad rapinas cœperunt extendere manus suas. Igitur nullus pene locus tutus ab hiis esse poterat, quorum omnium conspiraverat ad mala consensus. Et quoniam parva videbatur eis ad tanta mala facienda auctoritas propria, Comitem Southfolchiæ, Dominum Willelmum Ufforde, duxerunt adhibendum turbæ communium, ut si contingeret inferiores impeti pro talibus causis inposterum, exhibere possent majorem, et parem, sub cujus umbra vel conniventia hæc fecissent. Sed Comes, præmunitus de eorum adventu, repente surrexit a cœna ad quam consederat; iter faciens per [1] deserta, per loca ultra citraque [2] posita, semper declinans turbas communium, pervenit ad Sanctum Albanum; et ita pervenit ad Regem, garcionem Domini Rogeri de Boys se simulans, manticamque post tergum ducens. Communes autem, eo frustrati, subito loca quorundam aliorum militum occupantes, et eos in eisdem invenientes, compulerunt in sua vota jurare, ac pro majori cautela cum ipsis per patriam equitare. Quod nisi fecissent, confestim morti turpissimæ succubuissent. Nomina militum qui eos sequi compulsi sunt, fuere, Dominus de Scales, Dominus Willelmus de Morlee, Dominus Johannes de Brewes, Dominus Stephanus de Hales, Dominus Robertus de Salle; qui Robertus non diu vivus permansit inter eos, quia dissimulare nescivit, ut cæteri, sed cœpit eorum facta condemnare publice, et horrere; ob quam causam, a quodam rustico repente

The Earl of Suffolk escapes to Saint Alban's.

A number of knights seized by the insurgents.

Murder of Sir Robert de Salle.

---

[1] The word *pu͞ua* follows this word in orig., and in Bibl. Reg. 13 E. ix.; meaning, perhaps, *pervia*: *desertas patrias* in the printed texts.

[2] *proposita* in orig. and the printed texts; corrected from Bibl. Reg. 13 E. ix.

A.D. 1381. percussus in cerebro, nativo scilicet proprio, expiravit; miles, qui mille ex eis solus terruisset, si contigisset eum aperto Marte pugnasse contra eos. Cæteri vero, cernentes vel esse dissimulandum vel turpiter moriendum, casu consimili, et periculo docti præfati militis, decreverunt universa laudanda quæ ipsi laudarent, et vituperanda quæ eis displicerent. Unde contigit, ut in gratiam recepti dicti nebulonis, Johannis Littestere, qui se "Regem Communium" appellabat, mererentur prægustatores effici ciborum ejus et potuum, et flexis genibus ei obsequi, in prandio residenti. Nempe Dominum Stephanum de Hales, quia miles honorabilis fuerat, ad scindendum coram eo præelegit, et prægustandum cibaria quæ sumpturus erat; cæteris quoque alia officia designavit.

MS. Bibl. Reg. 13 E. ix.

Insolence displayed by Littestere towards the knights.

The insurgents send two knights, to make terms for them with the King.

Cumque jam fatigari communes cœpissent, et multi dies pertransissent, consilium inierunt, ut mitterent duos ex militibus, Dominum scilicet Willelmum de Morlee, et Dominum Johannem Brewes, cum tribus in quibus fidebant ex communibus, ad Regem Londonias, vel ubicunque posset inveniri, pro charta manumissionis et remissionis obtinenda; quæ ut specialior esset cæteris chartis, aliis Comitatibus concessis aut concedendis, magnam summam pecuniæ quam ceperant de civibus Northwicensibus, sub obtentu salvandæ urbis a cædibus, incendiis, et rapinis, præfatis nunciis tradiderunt, ut videlicet pacem et libertatem, quam ipsi non meruerant, pecunia impetraret.

Animositas Episcopi Norwicensis.

The knights are met by the Bishop of Norwich.

Milites ergo, acceptis comitibus de comitiva communium, ad exequendum properant injunctum mandatum; et cum pervenissent ad villam de [1]Igingham, quæ [2]non multum distat a villa quæ dicitur "Novum Forum," inopinate fit eis obviam Episcopus Northwicensis, Dominus Henricus le Spencer, vir idoneus satis armis gerendis bellicis, et ipse armatus ad unguem. Audierat namque famam, cum moraretur apud manerium suum de Burlee, prope castellum Regis de Okam, in partibus Stanfordiæ, tumultuationis Northfolkensium; quare proposuit illuc descendere, ad videndum utrum clamorem opere compleverint, vel complevissent. Habebat tunc in comitatu suo non plures quam octo lanceas, et sagittariorum numerum perexilem. Videns autem milites et quosdam [3]e communibus, præcepit,

---

[1] *Ickingham* in the printed texts.

[2] *nondum* in orig. and the printed texts; corrected from Bibl. Reg. 13 E. ix.

[3] *a* in orig.; corrected from the printed texts.

MS. Bibl. Reg. 13 E. ix.

A.D. 1381.

sub ligeantia sua, militibus, ut edicerent, si [1] qui ex proditoribus Regis præsentes essent cum illis. Milites vero, quos dudum rusticalis timor absorbuerat, dissimulabant respondere, æstimantes Episcopum, quia juvenis erat et audax, inconsulte talia verba protulisse, nec habere qui adjuvarent, si proditores prodidissent. Episcopus autem, cernens et considerans rem, ut erat, hortabatur eos ut confidenter agerent, et, si qui adessent, traderent proditores. Tunc milites, detersa ignavia et sumpta audacia, responderunt, duos ex maximis concitatoribus inter eos adesse, tertium, pro eorum coemendo prandio, alibi concessisse; sed et causam eorum itineris per ordinem narraverunt. Episcopus ergo statim illos duos decapitari fecit, et tertium ipsemet requirere studuit; ovem suam, quæ videlicet perierat, et dum a regia fide desciverat, et quæ peritura fuerat, tunc episcopali decreto capite punienda. Fixis ergo capitibus eorundem apud Novum Forum, Episcopus cum militibus properat festinanter versus Northfolchiam, ad North Walsham videlicet, locum in quo communes expectasse decreverant responsum regium et reditum sociorum. In pertranseundo ergo patriam, semper numerus episcopalis augebatur, quia de ordine militari et plures e patria generosi, qui delitescebant timore communium, videntes Episcopum militem induisse, et galeam assumpsisse metallicam, et loricam duram, quam non possent penetrare sagittæ, necnon gladium materialem ancipitem arripuisse, ejus lateri se junxerunt.

The knights deliver up two of the insurgents; who are beheaded.

The Bishop moves on to Norfolk, and the gentry take courage.

Episcopus itaque, cum pervenisset ad locum præfatum, stipatus turba decenti, reperit rusticos, more bellatorum, fossata circumcinxisse locum in quem convenerant, et super fossam tabulas, fenestras, et ostia, cum palis, in defensionem sui fixisse. A tergo autem conspicit eorum cariagium et carectas locatas, tanquam de fuga minime cogitarent. Nec mora, Episcopus Martius, aperto Marte pugnaturus, commotus super audacia nebulonum, jubet tubicinibus et [2] clarigatoribus suis canere; et ipse, arrepta dextra manu lancea, urget cornipedem acutis calcaribus, et tanta animositate, tanta audacia, [3] efferatur in eos, ut cursu velocissimo fossam præoccuparet, citatior sagittis suis; nec erat opus arcitenentibus sagittariis, cum res jam manu ad manum comminus ageretur. Antistes ergo belliger, velut aper frendens dentibus, sibi nec hostibus suis

The insurgents make a stand at North Walsham.

They are attacked by the Bishop, and defeated.

[1] *quis* in orig. and Bibl. Reg. 13 E. ix., by inadvertence; *qui* in the printed texts.

[2] Sic in orig. and Bibl. Reg. 13 E. ix.; *clangatoribus* in the printed texts.

[3] *effertur* in the printed texts.

A.D. 1381. parcens, ubi [1]majus conspicit esse periculum, dirigit [2]tentum suum, [3]et, hunc perforando, illum dejiciendo, alium vulnerando, non cessat lædere vehementer, donec omnis turba quæ eum secuta fuerat, nacta fossa, ad confligendum parata foret: idcirco pugnatum est acriter ab episcopalibus, nec secus a communibus, donec, ut assolet, infirmior [4]conscientia partem terreret injustam, et animum ab audacia et voluntate subtraheret moriendi. Nihil est infelicius quam bella gerere cauteriata conscientia, qua timor et confusio semper solent ingeri, nunquam victoria provenire. Fugiunt idcirco meticulosi plebani, et quia nulla alia restabat via ultra carectas suas et cariagia, quæ retulimus eos a tergo suo locasse, per saltus iter facere elaborant. Sed Præsul, imperatoris circumspecti ubique gerens officium, hos conatus elidit, et fugere meditantes cædendo impedit, impediendo cædit; donec captis majoribus turbæ concitatoribus, et ipso eorum rege, Johanne Littestere, [5][et quot volebat occisis e communibus], et quot volebat ad vitam reservatis, plena victoria potiretur.

MS. Bibl Reg. 13 E. ix.

Littestere is taken prisoner.

Finis Johannis Littestere, Regis Northfolciæ.

And is hanged.

Episcopus itaque præfatum Johannem, idolum Northfolkorum, [6]addixit tractioni et suspendio, necnon decapitationi. Quem, auditum et absolutum virtute officii, ipsemet prosecbatur ad furcas, demonstrans in eo, quanquam vicisset eum, opus mansuetudinis et pietatis, sustentans videlicet caput ejus, ne collideretur a terra, dum ad [7]suspendendum traheretur. Quibus ita gestis, nondum quievit Episcopus, donec, perscrutatis per totam patriam malefactoribus, justitia fieret de eisdem. Sicque pacem peperit regioni, et indicibile toti regno commodum, laudanda probitas et audacia commendanda Pontificis bellicosi.

Capitulum probans eos in Ecclesiæ et fidei Christianæ, necnon Regis, destructionem conspirasse.

Expeditis paucis quæ in Northfolchia gesta fuerunt, supersedeo scribere quæ mala in Northfolchia, quot [8]damna in

[1] *manus* in the printed texts.
[2] *robur* in the printed texts.
[3] *et* omitted in the printed texts.
[4] *conscia* in the printed texts.
[5] Supplied from Bibl. Reg. 13 E. ix.: omitted in the printed texts.
[6] *adduxit* in the printed texts.
[7] *suspendium* in the printed texts.
[8] *dampnis* in orig.; apparently, *dampna* in Bibl. Reg. 13 E. ix.; *damn a* in the printed texts.

MS. Bibl. Reg. 13 E. ix.

reliquis Comitatibus, per viros diabolicos, in turbationem totius regni sunt expleta: nisi enim dæmoniis pleni fuissent, nequaquam in destructionem Sacrosanctæ Ecclesiæ et Christianæ fidei, necnon in regni exterminium, conspirassent. Probant hæc eorum opera, probant confessiones quorundam qui expost capti sunt, quæ narrabimus loco suo. Ex operibus quippe judicandi sunt, quia patrem totius cleri et caput Ecclesiæ Anglicanæ, Archiepiscopum Cantuariensem, occiderunt. In fidei quoque detrimentum quid fecerunt? Magistros scholarum grammaticalium jurare compulerunt, se nunquam parvulos instructuros in arte præfata. Amplius quid fecerunt? Munimenta vetera studuerunt dare flammis; et [1] ne de novo quis reperiri valeret qui vetera [2] sive nova de cætero posset, vel nosset, commendare memoriæ, hujusmodi trucidabant. Periculosum erat agnosci pro clerico, sed multo periculosius, si ad latus alicujus atramentarium inventum fuisset; nam tales vix aut nunquam ab eorum manibus evaserunt.

A.D. 1381. The evil designs of the insurgents.

Atrocities committed by them upon the learned.

Quid in regni destructionem cogitaverant, probat confessio Johannis Straw, qui fuit, post Walterum Tylere, maximus inter illos. Hic cum captus, et Londoniis, Majore dictante sententiam, capite privandus esset, Major Londoniarum, postquam damnatus fuisset, publice eum taliter est allocutus:—"Johannes," inquit, "ecce! mors tua instat absque dubio, et nullam sperare potes viam evadendi. Quapropter, in adjutorium tui exitus, et pro salute animæ tuæ, absque mendacio narra nobis propositum quod inter vos concepistis, ad quem finem turbam communium commovistis." Cumque aliquandiu hæsitaret, et differret loqui, Major subjunxit:—"Scias firmissime, O Johannes, quæ præcipio, si hiis parueris, in animæ tuæ commodum conversura; sed et ego in adjutorium animæ tuæ plures [3] tricennales Missas faciam celebrari;" multique, qui aderant ex civibus, idem promiserunt, unusquisque pro persona. Ipse vero, jam animatus tam pulchris pollicitationibus, ita cœpit:—

John Straw interrogated by the Mayor of London.

Confessio Johannis Strawe.

"Jam," ait, "mentiri non expedit, nec fas est falsa proferre; præsertim cum per ea noverim spiritum meum tormentis artioribus deputandum, et quia duplex spero commodum ex veritate dicenda; primo, quia reipublicæ

Confession of John Straw, as to the designs of the insurgents.

[1] *ne* omitted in the printed texts.
[2] *sine* in the printed texts.
[3] *tircennales* in orig.; *triennales* in the printed texts: *tricennales* in Bibl. Reg. 13 E. ix.

A.D. 1381. "profectura sunt quæ dicam, et postea, juxta promissa "vestra, post mortem vestris suffragiis adjuvari, sine "fuco eloquar falsitatis. Eo tempore,"—inquit,—"quo ad "le Blakehethe convenimus, quando pro accersendo Rege des- "tinavimus, propositi nostri fuerat, cunctos milites, armi- "geros, et cæteros generosos, qui cum eo venissent, morti "subito tradidisse; ipsum quoque Regem, inter nos regaliter "exhibitum in universis, nobiscum de loco ad locum tra- "duxisse, ut, eo viso, omnes, et præcipue commune vulgus, "ad nos et nostram turbam transmigrare debuissent audacius, "qui viderent ipsum Regem esse velut auctorem nostræ com- "motionis. Cumque innumerabilem turbam conflassemus per "omnes patrias communis plebis, repente dominos mortifi- "cassemus, in quibus consilium contra nos, vel resistentia, "esse potuisset; et primo et principaliter, destructioni Hospi- "talariorum vacassemus. Postremo, Regem occidissemus, et "cunctos possessionatos, episcopos, monachos, canonicos, rec- "tores insuper ecclesiarum, de terra delevissemus. Soli "Mendicantes vixissent super terram, qui suffecissent pro "sacris celebrandis aut conferendis universæ terræ. Cum "vero nullus major, nullus fortior, nullus scientior, nobis "superfuisset, leges condidissemus ad [1]placitum, quibus sub- "jecti regulati fuissent. Nam et reges creassemus, Walterum "Tylere in Cancia, et in cæteris Comitatibus singulos, præ- "fecissemus. Sed quia istud nostrum propositum impeditum "fuit per Archiepiscopum, majori odio exarsimus contra eum, "et citius studuimus tradere eum morti. Rursum, eo die "[2]advesperascente quo occisus est Walterus Tylere, propo- "suimus, quia commune vulgus Londoniensium nobis favebat, "et præcipue pauperiores, injectis ignibus in quatuor partibus "Civitatis, urbem repente cremasse, et omnia pretiosa re- "perta inter nos pro libito divisisse." Et addidit;—"Hæc "fuerunt in nostro proposito, sicut Deus me adjuvet in exitu "vitæ meæ." MS. Bibl. Reg. 13 E. ix.

John Straw is beheaded.

Post hanc confessionem factam, decapitatus est, et caput ejus positum super Pontem Londoniis, juxta caput collegæ sui, Walteri Tylere. Ecce! hic edocuimus, qualiter in regni destructionem conspiraverunt. Ne autem insufficiens videnda fuerat ista unius confessio, confessi sunt eadem, vel omnino similia, plures alii, dum mortem adesse præ oculis cernerent, qui expost capti sunt.

A similar confession made by many others.

---

[1] *palatium* in orig.; corrected from the printed texts.

[2] *advesperante* in orig. and the printed texts; corrected from Bibl. Reg. 13 E. ix.

MS. Bibl. Reg. 13 E. ix.

A.D. 1381.

Nomina Ductorum Communium.

Names of the leaders of the insurgents.

Si [1] quidem scire delectat nomina eorum, qui incentores et ductores fuere communium, inveniet hic inserta pro parte. Primus et principalis dicebatur "Walterus Tylere," vel, ut quidam dicunt, "Walterus Helyer;" secundus "Johannes "Straw;" tertius, "Johannes Kyrkeby;" quartus, "Alanus "Threder;" quintus, "Thomas Scot;" sextus, "Radulphus "Rugge;" hic multos multis possessionibus investivit, tempore ducatus sui. Hii et plures alii, ductores Kentensium et Estsaxonum extiterunt.

Eorum qui apud Mildenhale et Burgum Sancti Edmundi insanierunt, Robertus Westbrom, qui se regem fecerat, nominatissimus fuit post Johannem [2] Wrawe; qui, quoniam presbyter erat, ut diximus, coronam apponere [3] noluit super coronam; sed contentus una corona, quæ erat ei satis competens, sacerdotali videlicet, nomen regium, et coronam, si placeret, dereliquit præfato Roberto. Apud North [4] Walsham, præfatus Johannes Littestere et nomen et potestatem, ut præmittitur, regiam exercebat.

Opiniones cur hæc mala acciderunt.

Various opinions as to the causes of these disturbances.

Acciderunt hæc mala omnia [5] diversis provinciis uno [6] eodem tempore, iisdem fere diebus, quanquam itinere longissimo loca distarent, infra Octavas videlicet festi Corporis Christi: multis opinantibus propter remissam [7] curam Archiepiscopi, cæterorumque comprovincialium Episcoporum, hujus rei præcipue, quam curasse debuerant, qua fides et stabilimentum Christianæ religionis consistit. Nempe cum novissent indigne agere filios suos, Johannem Wyclif et ejus sequaces, dogmatizando perversam et damnatam doctrinam Berengarii, de Sacramento corporis et sanguinis [8] Christi, et, longe lateque per patrias populum maculando, suam prædicationem dilatasse;

Alleged laxity of the Bishops.

---

[1] *quis* in the printed texts.

[2] *Wrawe* in orig., Bibl. Reg. 13 E. ix., and Camden's text; *Straw* in Parker's text.

[3] *voluit* in orig. and the printed texts; *noluit* in Bibl. Reg. 13 E. ix.

[4] *Waham* in orig.; *Walham* in the printed texts; *Walsham* in Bibl. Reg. 13 E. ix.

[5] *adversis* in orig. and the printed texts; corrected from Bibl. Reg. 13 E. ix.

[6] *eodemque* in the printed texts.

[7] *curiam* in orig. and Parker's text; corrected from Bibl. Reg. 13 E. ix. and Camden's text.

[8] *Christiani* in the printed texts.

A.D. 1381. ita ut pene majores provinciarum eorum sequerentur errorem, quia sciebant quod, MS. Bibl. Reg. 13 E. ix.

"Mobile versatur semper cum principe vulgus,"

et majorum exempla minores sequerentur; nec fuit ullus cornutus qui volebat, vel audebat, tantis malis occurrere, et filios perfidos correptione debita castigare; misisse creditur a multis [1] Dominum tribulationem præfatam, eo præcipue tempore quo specialem de [2] transubstantiatione Corporis Christi facit Sacrosancta Ecclesia mentionem; Archiepiscopum vero, quanquam credibile est eum martyrio finisse vitam, tamen propter teporem curæ quam adhibuisse debuerat in hac parte, horrenda mortis passione punisse, videlicet [3] spiritui pie consulens, ut si quid hac occasione purgandum in eo fuerat, aut ex alia levi culpa, quia sine peccato in carne ista non vivitur, quia, dicente Sapiente, [4] "Septies in die cadit "justus et resurgit," tam terribili, tamque gravi, et tam aspera, passione in hac vita penitus purgaretur.

Alleged infidelity of the nobles.

Alii peccatis dominorum ascribebant causam malorum, qui in Deum erant fictæ fidei; nam quidam illorum credebant, [5] [ut] asseritur, nullum Deum esse, nihil esse Sacramentum altaris, nullam post mortem resurrectionem; sed, ut jumentum moritur, ita et hominem finire. Erant præterea in subditos tyranni, et in pares [6] tumidi, invicem suspecti, vivendo incesti, violatores conjugii, Ecclesiæ destructores.

Alleged criminality of the general public.

Alii imputandum esse communis vulgi facinoribus dicebant esse, quod accidit, quia in pace degentes bono pacis abutebantur, dominorum facta rodentes, noctes insomnes in potationibus, ebrietatibus, et perjuriis transigentes; vivebant in terra pacis sine pace, rixando, litigando, cum proximis contendendo, fraudes et falsitates jugiter [7] meditando, libidini dediti, fornicationibus assueti, adulteriis maculati, [8] "unusquis- "que post uxorem proximi sui hinniebat." Et super hæc omnia, in fide et fidei articulis plurimi claudicabant. Quare non immerito opinatum est iram Dei descendisse in filios diffidentiæ.

---

[1] *Domini* in the printed texts.

[2] *translatione* in the printed texts.

[3] *spiritum* in the printed texts.

[4] *Prov.* xxiv. 16.

[5] Supplied from Bibl. Reg. 13 E. ix., and the printed texts.

[6] Intended for *inimici*, to all appearance, in orig.; *diversi* in the printed texts; an abbreviation of *timidi*, or *tumidi*, in Bibl. Reg. 13 E. ix.

[7] *meditanda* in orig.; corrected from the printed texts.

[8] *Jerem.* v. 8.

MS. Bibl. Reg. 13 E. ix.

Nota—Contra Fratres Mendicantes.

A.D. 1381.

The writer's own impression as to the shortcomings of the Mendicant Orders.

Mihi quoque videtur, tempora mala non [1] tantum istis imputanda, sed generaliter cunctorum habitatorum terræ peccatis, [2] inclusive Ordines sumendo Mendicantium, ad cumulandum causas malorum. Qui, suæ professionis immemores, obliti sunt etiam, ad quid ipsorum Ordines instituti sunt; quia pauperes, et omnino expeditos a rerum temporalium possessionibus, eorum legislatores, viri sanctissimi, eos esse ideo voluerunt, ut pro dicenda veritate non haberent quod [3] amittere formidarent. Sed jam [4] possessionatis invidentes, procerum crimina approbantes, commune vulgus in errore foventes, et utrorumque peccata [5] commendantes, pro possessionibus acquirendis, qui possessionibus renunciaverant, pro pecuniis congregandis, qui in paupertate perseverare juraverant, dicunt bonum malum et malum bonum, seducentes principes adulationibus, plebem mendaciis, et utrosque secum in devium pertrahentes. In tantum etenim illam veritatis professionem suam perverse vivendo macularunt, ut in diebus istis in ore cujuslibet bonum sit argumentum, tenens tam de forma quam de materia,—"Hic est Frater, ergo mendax;" sicut et illud,—"Hoc est "album, ergo coloratum."

Sed ne videamur livore scripsisse præsentia, fateamur nos omnes in culpa, et emendemus in melius quæ scienter peccavimus; et Deum pacis et dilectionis deprecemur attentius, ut fiat pax et veritas in diebus nostris.

Rex colligit exercitum magnum valde contra Kentenses.

Scripsimus, non sine labore, in præcedentibus historiam tragicam, ad posterorum notitiam et cautelam, de dominatione rusticorum, [6] et debacchatione communium, [7] insania nativorum. Modo redeundum recte videtur ad enumerandum quos fructus collegerint viarum suarum, Regis et nobilium dominio respirante.

Further concessions made by the King.

Occiso, ut præmittitur, superbissimo nebulone Waltero Tylere, corruit spes et fiducia rusticorum; sed quia adhuc fluctuabant animi Regis et regalium, [8] concernentes plebem pronam esse

---

[1] *tamen* in the printed texts.

[2] *inclusione* in orig.; corrected from the printed texts.

[3] *admittere* in orig. and the printed texts; corrected from Bibl. Reg. 13 E. ix.

[4] *possessionatus* in orig.; corrected from the printed texts.

[5] *comedentes* in orig., Bibl. Reg. 13 E. ix., and the printed texts.

[6] *et* omitted in Bibl. Reg. 13 E. ix. and the printed texts.

[7] *et insania* in the printed texts.

[8] *conspicientes* in the printed texts.

A.D. 1381. ad malum, concesserunt eis chartas manumissionis, ut diximus, et remissionis forisfacturæ, et eorum quæ sequuntur, et abire permiserunt. MS. Bibl. Reg. 13 E. ix.

The King levies a great army. Quibus gestis, congregari fecit Rex exercitum de Londoniis, et misit per patrias, ut qui diligerent Regem et honorem regium, accelerarent ad eum Londoniis, armis instructi et equis vecti; nullus veniret inermis, nullus pedes, et qui non habebant arma remanerent domi; et consimiliter, quibus equi defuerunt. Et factum est, ut infra triduum numeraret circa se quadraginta millia equitum, decentissime armatorum. Exibat cotidie ad le Blakeheth, ad recensendum numerum adventantium, ipse Rex, inprimis inter armatos [1][armatus] equitans dextrarium grandem; et vexillum ante faciem ejus portabatur: in exercitu gaudebat conspici, et ab hominibus suis dominus [2]recognosci. Cum ergo tantus coactus esset exercitus, quantus nunquam in Anglia fuit ante conspectus, audivit Rex Kentenses iterum conspirasse, iterum impiam familiam in totius regni perniciem congregasse. [3]Quid multa? Indignatur Rex, excandescit exercitus, et extemplo in Kanciam [4]proficisci, et totum illud germen Kentensium et [5]Juttorum statuerunt de terra viventium [6]explanare. Sed procerum et majorum Kanciæ interventu, qui fidejussere pro communibus, placatus factus est, et qui cum eo erant, super malignitate quam dixerant facere toti populo imperito. Et tunc primo missi sunt Justiciarii ad sedendum et inquirendum de malefactoribus, et eis principaliter, qui auctores, incentores, et concitatores fuere turbarum in Kancia; et siluit terra illa in conspectu eorum, et timuerunt valde.

His indignation against the Kentish insurgents.

Justiciars sent to make inquisition in Kent.

The Mayor of London inflicts capital punishment on many of the insurgents. Tunc Major Londoniarum, et ipse sedens pro tribunali, cepit tam urbis illius malefactores quam cunctos qui comprehendi [7][potuerunt] de Cancia, Estsexia, Southsexia, Northfolchia, et Sowthfolchia, et cæteris Comitatibus ubi communes fuerunt, infra libertatem civitatis Londoniarum, ad judicium audacter trahere publicum, et universos quos reperit respersos præfata perfidia decollare.

Decollatio Ductorum Communium Londoniis.

Leaders of the in- Tunc Johannes Straw, Johannes Kyrkeby, Alanus Tredere, ductores communium, decollati sunt. Tunc etiam Johannes

[1] Supplied from Bibl. Reg. 13 E. ix.

[2] *recognossi* in orig.

[3] *Quod* in orig.; corrected from the printed texts.

[4] *proficissi* in orig.

[5] *junctorum* in the printed texts.

[6] *eradicare* in the printed texts.

[7] Omitted in orig. and Bibl. Reg. 13 E. ix. Inserted from the printed texts.

MS. Bibl. Reg. 13 E. ix.

Starlyng de Estsexia, qui gloriabatur se Archiepiscopum decollasse, et ipse decollatus est. Iste, mox post illud perpetratum facinus, arreptus a diabolo, insanire cœpit, et, domum veniens, nudum gladium a collo suo suspendit ante pectus suum, et cultellum, (quem "*daggere*" dicimus) etiam evaginatum, suspendit ad tergum; et ita vesanus circuibat per plateas et vicos, clamans et protestans se cum eis Archiepiscopum occidisse. Et cum per dies aliquot domi moram fecisset, rediit Londonias, affirmans se mercedem accepturum ibidem illius facti. Quo cum pervenisset, et constanter fateretur se Archiepiscopum decollasse, recepit capitalem sententiam pro mercede. Sed et hoc advertendum, quod cuncti de Cancia vel Estsexia, qui manus apposuerunt noxias super Archiepiscopum, consimili modo confessi sunt, quanquam inviti, sponte tamen venientes, qui in eum commiserant, et Londoniis pro majori parte decollati sunt.

A.D. 1381. surgents beheaded at London.

The murderers of the Archbishop are put to death.

Nota—De Villanis Sancti Albani.

Tunc quoque accidit et villanis de Sancto Albano prognosticum futurorum malorum in eadem urbe. Nam cum quidam illorum conducti et missi fuissent per Abbatem in supplementum regalis exercitus, noluerunt tamen, — dubium an pro malitia aut pro superbia,—fateri eos missos ad Regem per Abbatem, sed velut propria venissent auctoritate jactitare. Accidit tunc Ricardum [1] Perers, quemdam ex armigeris Archiepiscopi, qui in obsequio etiam erat Abbatis et ad robas ejus, eos in urbe videre, et recognoscere quod quidam eorum malefactores fuerunt, et incentores malorum gestorum apud Sanctum Albanum. Quos sine mora, adhibitis ballivis, trahi fecit ad carcerem, in crastino proculdubio capitibus puniendos, nisi citatum remedium per Abbatis adjutorium affuisset. Nempe carceri mancipati, nullo modo alio speravere salutem, nisi [2] ut, missis nunciis ad convicaneos suos villanos, edicerent quibus periculis constituti essent, et eisdem exponerent, quod nisi ipsi jam adire curarent Abbatem pro salvatione eorundem, in crastino, sine ulla dubitatione, fuerant puniendi. Acciderunt hæc in Vigilia Passionis Sancti Albani, octavo videlicet die ab illo die Veneris quo cœperunt primo contra Martyrem calcitrare.

The townsmen of Saint Alban's accused of taking part in the London riots.

Quid plura? Venerunt lugubres majores villæ, tempore Matutinarum, quæ solemnes erant in honore Passionis dicti Martyris, dum Conventus hymnum laudis cantabat, scilicet

The intercession of the Abbot is invoked

[1] *Peeres* in the printed texts. | [2] *ut* omitted in Camden's text.

A.D. 1381.

"Te Deum laudamus," quæsituri remedium proximis suis, et acceptori ab Abbate. Cumque, finitis Laudibus Matutinis, exposuissent hæc omnia coram Abbate, ingemuit Abbas vehementer, et, ultra modum tristis effectus, maledixit armigero suo, qui causa fuerat miseriæ prædictorum, jurans se maluisse trajectum fuisse gladio, quam talia audivisse; præsertim cum ipse eos illuc misisset, et [1] ascribenda esset sibi calamitas quam patiebantur. Nec mora, accersito quodam ex commonachis suis, jussit ut festinantissime Londonias properaret, non parcendo cornipedi, nec dimittendo, donec incarceratos liberos abire vidisset: qui, non segniter jussa complendo, sine somno nocte perdurans Londonias properavit. Injunctum est ergo præfato Ricardo, ut desisteret ab inceptis, sicut diligeret honorem Abbatis; et juratum coram Majore, eos missos fuisse per Abbatem ad incrementum exercitus regii. Et sic demum, post magnos timores, ipso die Sancti Albani dimissi sunt, præstito prius juramento, ut fideles essent Domino Ricardo Regi, et domino eorundem, Abbati Sancti Albani. Et hoc initium malorum quæ contigerunt illis.

(Margin: in their behalf. — MS. Bibl. Reg. 13 E. ix. — The Abbot intercedes in their favour. — After taking the oath of fealty, they are liberated.)

Nec fuerunt [2] Albanenses villani absque terroribus, cunctis feriis sextis et Sabbatis expost sequentibus, usque ad illam sextam feriam qua Rex, ut dicemus, venit ad Sanctum Albanum, ad ulciscendum injurias Martyris exasperati per eos. Sed hæc plenius dicemus suis locis, interim scribendo acta Regis usque ad tempus prænotatum.

(Margin: Continued terrors of the townsmen of Saint Alban's.)

Rex ergo interea modo Londoniis, modo ad Waltham, morabatur, cum turba plurima, cogitans quid agendum pro communi regni commodo et quiete. Placuit tandem Regis Consilio hujuscemodi litteras per patrias destinare:—

Commissio Regis pro resistendo pacis regni perturbatoribus.

(Margin: Writ enjoining resistance to the insurgents.)

"Ricardus, Dei gratia, Rex Angliæ et Franciæ, et Dominus
"Hiberniæ, universis et singulis Vicecomitibus, Majoribus,
"[3] ballivis, et aliis fidelibus nostris Comitatus N. salutem.
"Quia datum est nobis intelligi, quod diversi subditi nostri,
"qui, contra pacem nostram, et in turbationem populi, in
"diversis Comitatibus regni nostri Angliæ se levarunt, et in
"diversis conventiculis et congregationibus se posuerunt, et,
"damna plurima fidelibus nostris perpetrando, populo nostro
"Comitatuum prædictorum dant intelligi, et affirmant, se

[1] *ascribendi* in orig.; corrected from the printed texts.

[2] *Abbanenses* in orig.

[3] *et ballivis* in the printed texts.

MS Bibl. Reg. 13 E. ix.

dictas congregationes et levationes ex nostris voluntate et auctoritate fecisse et facere, ac damna perpetrare.—Vobis innotescimus per præsentes, quod hujusmodi levationes, congregationes, et damna, ex nostra voluntate seu auctoritate minime processerunt, prout nec procedere aut fieri debent; sed inde, quantum plus potest, nobis displicet in immensum, et ea in nostri maximum vituperium, et coronæ præjudicium, et totius regni nostri damnum et turbationem, redundare sentimus. Et ideo vobis, et cuilibet vestrum, injungimus et mandamus, quod hoc in locis ubi melius et celerius pro pace nostra in hac parte conservanda vobis videbitur faciendum, publice proclamari, et pro resistentia quorumcunque contra pacem nostram, ut prædictum est, levantium, manu forti [1] et pro toto posse vestro, si necesse fuerit, taliter ordinari faciatis, quod, pro defectu hujusmodi proclamationis et resistentiæ, damna [2] vel mala aliqua in Comitatibus prædictis per hujusmodi congregationes seu levationes, vel alio modo, minime fiant seu perpetrentur; et sub forisfactura omnium quæ nobis forisfacere poteritis, nullatenus omittatis: præcipientes universis et singulis ligeis et subditis nostris, quod ab hujusmodi congregationibus, et levationibus, et damnis, penitus desistentes, ad propria se trahant, et ibidem in pace morentur, sub forisfactura vitæ et membrorum, et omnium aliorum quæ nobis forisfacere poterunt. Teste meipso, apud Londonias, [3] octavo decimo die Junii, anno regni nostri quarto."

Good effects resulting from the writ.

Hæc commissio fideles Regis et regni plurimum confortavit, et perfidos, nec immerito, conturbavit. Compulsi sunt igitur quærere latebras, qui antea videri appetebant, et ausi sunt de cavernis egredi juristæ, et qui primitus a facie furoris fugiebant. [4] Illi sub silentio jam expectabant, trementes judicium et justitiam in eos statuenda; isti, detersa formidine, gaudentes erigebantur ad injurias suas vindicandas. Attamen non in omni parte ad similem timorem rustici sunt perducti; quin, ubi primum pullulavit insania, in Estsexia, rustici, recollecta nova multitudine, ad Billerica, quæ est villa prope villam de Hatfeld Peverel, sic nuncupata, nimis fidentes suis viribus, propria decepti superbia, decreverunt, vel extorta libertate gaudere, vel pro eadem pugnando mori.

[1] *et* omitted in the printed texts.

[2] *et mala* in orig.; corrected from the printed texts.

[3] 17 *die* in the printed texts; xviii° in orig. and Bibl. Reg. 13 E. ix.

[4] *Ibi* in orig., Bibl. Reg. 13 E. ix., and the printed texts: evidently an error of the transcriber.

Mittuntur nuncii per Rusticos ad Regem, de Estsexia, pro libertate.

Messengers sent by the insurgents of Essex, to make certain enquiries of the King.

MS. Bibl. Reg. 13 E. ix.

Mittuntur ergo ad Regem, qui tunc ad Waltham morabatur, qui sciscitarentur ab eo, si cogitaret permittere eos præmissa libertate gaudere; et amplius peterent, ut essent in libertate pares dominis, et quod non essent cogendi ad curias, nisi tantummodo ad visum franciplegii bis in anno. Rex autem et Consilium, quod tunc aderat, super tanta temeritate rusticorum admirantur quam maxime; et aliquandiu hæsitatum est quale responsum reportarent; donec Rex in persona propria taliter respondisset :—" O," inquit " miseri, et odibiles " terræ marique, nec vivere quidem digni, petitis dominis " comparari. Morte turpissima multandi fuissetis procul- " dubio, si non decreta nunciis observasse statuissemus. " Sed quia more nunciorum advenistis, non in præsenti " moriemini, sed vita gaudebitis, quatenus nostra responsa " vestris consociis narratione veridica nuncietis. Proferte " ergo ista collegis ex parte Regis. Rustici quidem fuistis " et estis; in bondagio permanebitis, non ut hactenus, sed " incomparabiliter viliori. Nam ad hoc dum vivimus, et " regno, Deo dante, præfuerimus, sensu, viribus, et catallis " nostris, elaborabimus vos suppeditare, taliter ut exemplum " sit posteris vestræ servitutis offensum, et habeant præsentes " et futuri vobis similes semper coram oculis, et tanquam " pro speculo vestram miseriam, et vobis maledicendi mate- " riam, et timorem vobis similia perpetrandi. Vos autem, qui " nuncii advenistis, expleto nostro mandato et vestræ lega- " tionis officio, si ad nos redire decernitis, et in nostra per- " severare fidelitate et ligeantia, vitam [1] vivetis. Jam ergo " eligite quod melius judicabitis, cum ad [2] vestros socios per- " veneritis, et consummaveritis nostra mandata."

Rebuke administered to them by the King.

An armed force sent into Essex.

Cumque abissent prædicti nuncii, missi sunt in Estsexiam e vestigio, cum armata manu, Dominus Thomas Wodestoke Comes Bukynghamiæ, et Dominus Thomas Percy, frater Comitis Northumbrorum, ad prædictorum comprimendum audaciam rusticorum. Rustici vero, ut prædiximus in superioribus Northfolkos fecisse, per omnia se munierant in fossatis, [3] palis, et carriagio, præterquam isti fruebantur majori sylvarum et nemorum tutamento. Qui quamvis fuisset eorum magnus

---

[1] *vevetis* in orig.; by inadvertence.

[2] *viros* in orig.; *vros* in Bibl. Reg. 13 E. ix.; *vestros* in the printed texts.

[3] *plagis* in orig. and the printed texts; corrected from Bibl. Reg. 13 E. ix.

MS. Bibl. Reg. 13 E. ix.

numerus, levi negotio dissipati sunt a decem tantum (ut usu vulgari loquar) [1]lanceis, qui præcesserunt dominos supradictos.

Occisio Rusticorum.

The Essex insurgents are put to flight.

Domini itaque, cum vidissent eos fusos tali modo, sepserunt sylvas, ne ullus quidem [2]ex eis evaderet; licet periculosum fuisset eos persequi intra sylvas. Et factum est ut occiderentur a viris utriusque [3]ævi diversis in locis quingenti, cæteris beneficio nemorum protectis et salvatis. Cesseruntque ibidem in usus militum octingenti equi, quos rustici secum duxerant, pro sarcinis trahendis aut portandis. Sed nondum statim finis post istam victoriam malitiæ nebulonum. Ausi sunt, qui evadere poterant tantam cladem, iterum calcitrare, iterum malignari. Nempe recollecti, qui dispersi fuerant, ad Colcestriam properaverunt, et oppidanos sollicitare cœperunt ad novam tumultuationem et vesaniam similem, summis precibus, magnis minis, pluribus argumentis; sed cum nihil profecissent, ad Sudburiam commigrarunt. Cognoscentes autem eorum transitum Dominus Fitz-Water et Dominus Johannes Harlestone, subsecuti sunt eos cum viris armatis, et repente, cum proclamationes solitas facerent ex parte communium, inopinate irruerunt super eos, et quot placuit occiderunt, et reliquos vel ad vitam dimiserunt vel carceribus recluserunt.

They gather again at Colchester and Sudbury.

Are again dispersed.

Rex pergit ad Havering in Essexia.

Rebus ita se habentibus in Estsexia et Southfolchia, Dominus Rex, volens Estsexiam sua justificare præsentia, se contulit ad prædium suum, quod dicitur [4]"Haveryng atte Boure," deinde ad villam de Chelmesforde; ubi constituit Dominum Robertum Tresilian Justiciarium, ut sederet et inquireret de malefactoribus et turbatoribus patriæ, et, secundum regni consuetudines, puniret delinquentes. Cum ergo viderent Estsaxones fortunam adversam, et librarent mala imminentia, supplices venerunt ad Regem quingenti, et eo amplius, viri, nudatis pedibus et discoopertis capitibus, veniam ab eo, et misericor-

Sir Robert Tresilian is appointed Justiciar, to make inquisition in Essex.

[1] *lances* in orig.; by inadvertence.

[2] *ex eis* omitted in the printed texts.

[3] This is perhaps the meaning of *eui* in orig. and Bibl. Reg. 13 E. ix: it is omitted in the printed texts.

[4] *Havering at the Boure*, in the printed texts.

diam, petituri. Quibus ea conditione concessa est venia, ut malefactores majores et concitatores præfatæ turbationis proderent, et traderent ipsi Regi. Factum est ergo, ut multi custodiæ traderentur, super quibus deliberandis vel occidendis, Justiciarius oneravit viginti quatuor homines in eorum conscientiis, ut, nulli parcendo favorabiliter, nec quenquam propter odium persequendo, de eorum factis et moribus dicerent veritatem. Et factum est ut plures, dictante duodena, [1] tractione et suspendio interirent, aliquando suspensis super [2] unam trabem decem et novem. MS. Bibl. Reg. 13 E. ix.

The leaders of the Essex insurgents are delivered up, tried, and punished.

[3] Usi sunt tamen prius judices, qui sederunt in Estsexia, Kancia, et Londoniis, propter multitudinem perimendorum, decollationibus rusticorum, donec visum fuisset pœnam capitalem non correspondere tantis tamque facinoribus manifestis; quia quodammodo erat nimis secreta punitio tam evidenti delicto. Ob quam causam, expost, juxta regni consuetudines, decreverunt omnes [4] repertos [5] sceleratiores, ut diximus, [6] protractione, suspensione, punire: et in Estsexia res utique taliter se habebant.

Change in the mode of executing the insurgents.

Interea placuit Regi, Regisque Consilio, has litteras diversis provinciis demandare.—

Litteræ [7] revocationis libertatum.

King's Letter, recalling the grant of liberties.

"Ricardus, Dei gratia, Rex Angliæ et Franciæ, et Dominus "Hiberniæ, omnibus ad quos præsentes litteræ pervenerint, "salutem. Licet nuper, in turbatione detestabili, per quosdam "ligeos et subditos nostros, contra pacem nostram insurgentes, "horribiliter facta, certæ litteræ nostræ patentes, ad [8] ipsorum "insurgentium instantiam importunam, factæ fuissent, continentes, quod nos universos ligeos nostros et subditos, communes "et alios, cæterorum Comitatuum regni nostri Angliæ, manumisimus, et ipsos et eorum quemlibet ab omni bondagio et "servitio exuimus et quietos fecimus. Ac etiam, quod perdonavimus eisdem ligeis et subditis nostris omnimodas in-"surrectiones, per ipsos contra nos factas, equitando et eundo "per diversa loca in regno nostro, cum hominibus armatis, "sagittariis, et aliis viis manu armata, cum vexillis, penni-

New Rymer IV. [not published] p. 126.

---

[1] *traxione* in orig. and Bibl. Reg. 13 E. ix.

[2] *una trabe* in the printed texts.

[3] Apparently written *Visi* in orig.; partly erased in Bibl. Reg. 13 E. ix.; *Usi* in the printed texts.

[4] *expertos* in orig. and in the printed texts: corrected from Bibl. Reg. 13 E. ix.

[5] *sceleratos* in Bibl. Reg. 13 E. ix.

[6] *protraxione* in orig.

[7] *renovationis* in orig. and Bibl. Reg. 13 E. ix.; incorrectly.

[8] *ipsum* in the printed texts.

MS. Bibl. Reg. 13 E. ix.
New Rymer.

cellis displicatis; ac etiam omnimodas proditiones, felonias, transgressiones, et extortiones, per ipsos vel aliquos ipsorum factas sive perpetratas, ac etiam utlegariam et utlegarias, si qua vel quæ in ipsos, vel aliquem ipsorum, fuerint, vel fuerit, hiis occasionibus promulgata, vel promulgatæ, [1] vel firmam pacem nostram eis et cuilibet eorum concessimus. Quodque voluimus, quod iidem ligei nostri et subditi nostri liberi essent ad emendum et vendendum in quibuscunque civitatibus, burgis, villis mercatoriis, et aliis locis, infra regnum Angliæ; et quod nulla acra terræ in Comitatibus prædictis, quæ in bondagio vel servitio [2] tenetur, altius quam ad quatuor denarios haberetur: et si qua minus antea tenta fuisset, in posterum non exaltaretur. Nos tamen, pro eo quod dictæ litteræ de curia nostra, absque matura deliberatione, et indebite, emanarunt, perpendentes concessionem litterarum prædictarum in nostri et coronæ nostræ maximum præjudicium, ac tam in nostri, et prælatorum, procerum, et magnatum, dicti regni nostri, quam Sacrosanctæ Ecclesiæ Anglicanæ, exhæredationem, necnon dispendium et incommodum reipublicæ, tendere manifeste, dictas litteras, et quicquid exinde fuerit subsecutum, de avisiamento Concilii nostri, revocavimus, cassavimus, irritavimus [3] et adnullavimus, et de facto revocamus, cassamus, irritamus, et penitus adnullamus; nolentes quod aliquis, cujuscunque status seu conditionis fuerit, libertatem sive commodum aliquid de prædictis litteris quomodolibet habeat seu reportet. Volumus enim, et intentionis nostræ existit, talem gratiam singulis subditis nostris, quamvis enormiter [4] [contra] ligeantiam suam forisfecerint, de avisiamento sani consilii nostri, in posterum impertiri, quæ Deo placabilis, nobisque et regno nostro utilis, fuerit, et unde fideles nostri subditi reputabunt rationabiliter se contentos; et hæc omnibus, quorum interest, [5] innotescimus per præsentes. Damus autem, tam universis et singulis dominis, magnatibus, et aliis fidelibus, ligeis et subditis nostris, [6] quam Vicecomitibus, et aliis ministris nostris Comitatus N., [7] tenore præsentium, firmiter in mandatis, quod ipsi præsentes litteras nostras in singulis civitatibus, burgis, et aliis villis et locis in Comitatu prædicto, tam infra libertates quam extra, ubi expediens fore viderint, et necesse,

[1] *et* in Rymer.

[2] Written "*tenns*" in orig.

[3] From this word down to *irritamus*, the context is omitted in the printed texts.

[4] Supplied from Rymer.

[5] *innotissimus* in orig.

[6] *quam* omitted in the printed texts.

[7] *tenere* in the printed texts.

"ex parte nostra publice proclamari faciant; ulterius districte "præcipiendo, quod omnes et singuli, tam liberi quam nativi, "opera, consuetudines, et servitia, quæ ipsi nobis aut aliis "dominis suis facere debent, et ante turbationem prædictam "facere consueverunt, absque contradictione, murmure, resis-"tentia, seu difficultate, faciant aliquali, prout ante solebant. "Insuper inhibendo eisdem, ne ipsi opera, consuetudines, et "servitia sua prædicta, istis turbationum temporibus, magis "solito retrahant, seu nobis aut prædictis dominis suis facere "ullo colore retardent; nec aliqua alia libertates sive privi-"legia exigant, vindicent, sive clament, quam ante turba-"tionem prædictam rationabiliter habuerunt. Et quod ipsi, "qui prædictas litteras nostras manumissionis et perdonationis "penes se habent et custodiunt, eas statim penes nos et "Consilium nostrum deferant et restituant, cancellandas, sub "fide et ligeantia quibus nobis tenentur, et sub forisfactura "omnium quæ nobis forisfacere poterunt in futurum. In "cujus rei testimonium has litteras nostras fieri fecimus "patentes. Teste meipso, apud Chelmesforde, secundo die "Julii, anno regni nostri quinto."[1]

MS. Bibl. Reg. 13 E. ix. New Rymer.

Hæc in Estsexia, ut ante docuimus, facta sunt; ubi erat Rex moram trahens. Jam redeundum est ad scribendum processum factum apud Sanctum Albanum, ut eo discant posteri villanorum dolos magis feliciter præcavere, quoniam,—

"Felix quem faciunt aliena pericula cautum."

Processus factus apud Sanctum Albanum per Walterum At Le, militem.

The King proposes to visit Saint Alban's, and punish the insurgents there.

Cum itaque Rex in Estsexia aliquandiu moram traxisset, et multorum relatione didicisset, quas injurias et damna villani de Sancto Albano non tam procurassent quam irrogassent Monasterio, proposuit cum omni turba sua, quæ erat copiosa valde, personaliter locum adire, de transgressoribus justitiam rectam facturus. Sed huic proposito obstitit toto nisu Dominus Walterus Atte Lee miles, quia de patria illa fuerat, timens videlicet patriæ destructionem, si tantus [2]illic populus advenisset. Ob quam causam persuasit Regi et Consilio, se facturum bonam pacem inter villanos et Abbatem Monasterii Sancti Albani, si placeret eis sibi committere causam istam. Qui, fidem adhibentes verbis ejus, dant commissionem, sociantes

A commission finally granted to

[1] The words "*per ipsum Regem*" follow in Bibl. Reg. 13 E. ix.

[2] *illuc* in the printed texts.

MS. Bibl. Reg. 13 E. ix.

eidem Edwardum Benstude et Galfridum Stuklo, et quosdam alios, quorum nomina non occurrunt.

Sir Walter Atte Lee.

Feria ergo sexta in Vigilia Apostolorum Petri et Pauli, ut non deessent eis miseriæ illa die in qua ipsi immisericorditer miseros, ut retulimus per ante, afflixerant, cognoscentes villani prædictum Walterum cum armata manu in crastino adventurum, factis propriis torti, et conscientiis male consciis fatigati, cœperunt pavere et tædere. Jam jamque multi fugam inissent, nisi obstitisset improba animositas Willelmi Grindecobbe, quem inter oppidanos supra retulimus magnum fuisse. Hic namque perfidos in infidelitate confortavit, dicens:—"Estote "viri cordati, locupletes enim sumus; non deerunt nobis "auxilia, quamdiu non defuerit nostra pecunia. Ecce! villæ "circumjacentes nobis fœderantur, quæ nobis erunt adjutorio, "si oportuerit. Egrediamur mane, velut homines, in obviam "militis extra villam, equis vecti, et [1]inquiramus, antequam "appropinquet villæ nostræ, utrum pacificus sit adventus ejus. "Qui si non fuerit, fugabimus eum verberibus a villa nostra."

The townsmen are alarmed, but are encouraged by William Grindecobbe.

Placuit ergo stultus sermo stultis, et mane, juxta verbum ejus, egressi sunt. Militem vero latuit causa hujus obviationis pro tunc. Qui tamen benigne postquam obviassent sibi, ut videbatur, salutatus ab eis et resalutavit eos, et conduxerunt eum ad villam honorifice more suo. Habebat autem secum miles quinquaginta [2]lanceas, et arcitenentium undecunque collectorum magnum numerum; qui forsitan, si militi aliquod periculum contigisset, quia de patria fuerant quidam, et villanis fœderati, in primis restitissent eidem. Mox itaque post adventum suum ad villam, in ipso festo Apostolorum Petri et Pauli, fecit proclamari, ut omnes villani, et qui citati fuerant ad compariendum de villis vicinis coram eo, convenirent in campum de Derfold, voluntatem et mandatum regium audituri, post horam nonam. Convenerunt ergo omnes ad horam et locum præfatum, et ipse, una cum eis, stipatus armatorum multitudine, pariter est egressus. Cumque locasset se, et armatos circa eum, sub sylva de Derfold, et cunctum populum stare disposuisset coram eo, ad modum arcus cœlestis, ad eos sermonem hujuscemodi peroravit:—

They escort Sir Walter atte Le into the town.

They are summoned to meet him in the Derfold Wood.

Oratio Militis habita ad Villanos.

"Domini,"—inquit,—"et amici, qui citati convenistis ad "hunc locum, antequam quicquam aggrediar, causam adventus "mei vobis exponere conveniens reputavi. Nostis enim

Speech made by Sir Walter to the townsmen.

---

[1] *inquirimus* in orig.

[2] *lanceis* in the printed texts.

"quam graviter pacis perturbatores regiam majestatem offenderint. Ob quam causam Dominus Rex modo in partibus Estsexiæ exercet judicia maxima et [1] manum gravem super patriam universam et habitatores ejus, [2] et jugum eorum aggravat vehementer. Qui audiens de perturbationibus, et damnis, et injuriis factis in hac villa et [3] præsenti Monasterio, cujus patronus est et advocatus, ultra quam credi potest indoluit, et, vindicari cupiens in transgressores, statuit personaliter, cum exercitu qui cum ipso est, huc adventasse; qui si venisset cum ea turba quam ibidem retinet, proculdubio omnes fructus, cuncta blada patriæ, necessario devastasset. Tantus nimirum est cum eo exercitus, quod per quinque milliaria in eorum circuitu, non fœnum, non blada aliqua, non fructus terræ novi, non antiqui, supersunt, sed omnia consumpta et conculcata sunt. Condolens ergo [4] tantis damnis patriæ meæ proventuris, præcavens et compatiens convicinis, [5] elaboravi in hac parte Regis enervare propositum, et impedire adventum, assumens quidem pro patriotis onus grave super humeros, sed tamen voluntarium: quia speravi aliquid patriæ tali occasione conferre. Commissa est ergo mihi potestas, licet non sine difficultate, ad precum mearum instantiam, patriam justificandi, vice Regis, cui non extranei, non incogniti, sed proximi vestri et amici, in commissione sunt juncti. Agite igitur quod expediat, et alacriter principales concitatores turbarum tradatis, et Abbati hujus Monasterii satisfacere studeatis, quem [6] invenietis, ut reor, satis rationabilem, quia vir sanctus et justus esse dinoscitur; et regiam benevolentiam et tranquillam recuperabitis tali facto." MS. Bibl. Reg. 13 E. ix.

He charges a jury of the townsmen.

Finitis hiis sermonibus, applaudunt multi, et ejus consiliis se velle parere promittunt. Tunc miles, convocata duodena de villanis, onerat ut, in crastino venientes, juxta formam juramenti edicant quoscunque reos sciverint in hac causa; et sic, ea die dimissa turba, et ipse ad hospitium est reversus. In crastino autem, quia proposuerat malefactores, quos judicandos putavit per præfatam duodenam, sine strepitu apprehendisse, vocavit viros duodenæ ad cameram suam, ut sciret quos [7] indictassent. Qui cum venissent, responderunt se

[1] *magnum gravamen* in the printed texts.

[2] *ut* in orig. and the printed texts: corrected from Bibl. Reg. 13 E. ix.

[3] *præsenti* omitted in the printed texts.

[4] *elaboravi in his tantis* in the printed texts.

[5] *elaboravi in hac* omitted in the printed texts.

[6] *invenitis* in the printed texts.

[7] *judicassent* in orig. and the printed texts; corrected from Bibl. Reg. 13 E. ix.

MS. Bibl. Reg. 13 E. ix.

neminem indictare posse, neminem accusare velle; omnes esse bonos et fideles Regis, neminem alium nosse inter eos. Quibus auditis, et cognito quorsum intentio eorundem vergeret, quod videlicet pejorando mallebant suas conscientias maculare quam quemlibet ex proximis accusare, miles conticuit, arte artem delusurus. Post auditam Missam, monuit eos reddere chartas quas extorserant de Monasterio, dicens ex tali facto eis non modicum commodum proventurum. Illi vero pro tunc promiserunt se sursum post nonam chartas præfatas reddituros. Cum vero post nonam revenissent ad cameram Abbatis, ubi comederat dictus miles, excusationes novas prætendentes, innuebant se chartas reddere non valere, propter metum communitatis, et maxime, quia non sciebant pro certo quis eas in custodia detinebat. Miles igitur commotus, nec immerito, juravit quod exirent de præsentia sua, donec chartas reddidissent. Ob quam causam, mendaces et falsi, expost dixerunt se [1] imprisonatos fuisse in camera Abbatis injuste. Abbas autem, ne materiam vel occasionem haberent male loquendi, quos [2] scivit pronos ad mendacia, intercessit pro eis penes militem; dicens se tantum in eorum confidere conscientia, quod non esset opus alio mediatore inter ipsos, præter eosdem et semet ipsum. Quibus verbis miles mitigatus, dimisit eos.

The jury refuses to indict.

Sir Walter demands that the Abbey Charters shall be returned.

Excuses are made by the townsmen thereon.

The Abbot intercedes successfully in their behalf.

Hiis itaque gestis, miles omnem turbam jussit convenire ad le Barnet Wode; ubi parum aut nihil agens, propter metum villanorum, qui aggregaverant illuc prope trecentos sagittarios de villis circumjacentibus, inter quos præcipui fuerunt Barnetenses et viri de Berkhamstede; qui omnes, si aggressus fuisset aliquam publicam justitiam facere in eo loco, ut credebatur, insurrexissent in eum; et hii fortassis qui cum eo venerant, eo relicto, aliis adhæsissent; nihil pro tunc aliud decrevit aperte, nisi monere eos de satisfaciendo Abbati, et chartis reddendis. [3] Secrete vero seorsim convocatis ballivis et constabulariis, jussit, ex parte Regis, ut mox, post subtractionem turbæ quæ ad villam convenerat, elaborarent circa captionem Willelmi Grindecobbe, Willelmi Cadindone, et Johannis Barbitonsoris, (qui videlicet, ut supra retulimus, petras molares abstulerat de locutorii pavimento,) et quorundam aliorum, quos dixit ita aperte accusatos de tam manifestis maleficiis, quod oportebat omnino, pro honore villæ et salvatione villanorum, eos ad tempus artari. In-

Sir Walter again convenes them at Barnet Wode, and advises them as to restoration of the Charters.

He takes measures for the arrest of Grindecobbe and others.

[1] *imprisonatas* in the printed texts.

[2] *sciunt* in the printed texts.

[3] *Secretis* in orig. and the printed texts: corrected from Bibl. Reg. 13 E. ix.

junxit insuper, ut apprehensos adducerent Hertfordiam in crastino, hora tertia, coram eo. MS. Bibl. Reg. 13 E. ix.

He proceeds to Hertford.

Post hæc, repente ascenso [1] sonipede, cum omnibus qui cum eo venerant, Hertfordiam festinavit. Et factum est post recessum ejus, magnanimitate, diligentia, et probitate armigerorum, qui tunc in obsequio Abbatis erant, scilicet Ricardi [2] Perers, Johannis Chival, Thomæ Eydon, Willelmi Eccleshale, [3] ut ballivi, quanquam inviti, inducerentur ad capiendum præfatos viros: et capti sunt eadem nocte tres nominati superius, et in prisona positi apud portam.

The three persons named are arrested,

Captivi ducti ad prisonam.

And are taken to Hertford.

In crastino vero, juxta præceptum militis, Herthfordiam sunt deducti, comitantibus eos majoribus et valentioribus villæ Sancti Albani, et cunctis armigeris et valectis Abbatis, decenter armatis; sic enim præceperat miles ut venirent, ad fortificandum eum, qui justitiam et judicium eo die erat facturus.

Threats of the populace at Saint Alban's.

Post quorum recessum, cœpit turbari universa villa, et ampullosa verba fundere, et juramenta supervacua [4] miscere; quod videlicet centum pro uno occiderentur, si contingeret quemquam ex proximis eorum occidi. Hinc cœperunt eodem die a villanis frequentari consilia, congregari conventicula, non tamen in villa, sed in campis, sylvis, et extra villam locis; unde credebatur, quod ipsa die immisissent ignem in Abbathiam, quia nullus domi [5] [erat] qui defenderet; vel hostili more Monasterium obsidione vallassent. Ex qua causa, Abbas et commonachi, in timore maximo constituti, miserunt pro quibusdam generosis de patria, qui locum tuerentur si necessitas accidisset. Abbas etiam, cum cognovisset quo abissent armigeri sui, et quod intendebant prædictos captivos ad mortem insequi, confestim misit ad [6] illos litteraliter, præcipiens ut, dimissis omnibus, festinantissime remearent ad eum, pro præcavendis periculis quæ sibi de novo emerserant [7] insperate. Erant, cum ad eos hæc nova perlata fuissent, stantes coram judice, et constanter prædictos captivos accusantes, et de eis, secundum jura regni, judicium fieri postulantes. Viderant autem in quosdam eis similes capitis [8] punitione

Fears entertained of their vengeance.

The Abbot commands his esquires to return home.

---

[1] *compede* in orig. and the printed texts; corrected from Bibl. Reg. 13 E. ix.

[2] *Peeres* in the printed texts.

[3] *et* in orig. and the printed texts; corrected from Bibl. Reg. 13 E. ix.

[4] *missere* in orig.

[5] Omitted in orig. and Bibl. Reg. 13 E. ix.; supplied from the printed texts.

[6] *eos* in the printed texts.

[7] *insperato* in the printed texts.

[8] *punitionis* in the printed texts.

MS. Bibl. Reg. 13 E. ix.

animadversum ibidem, unde conceperant spem eos consimiliter puniendi. Visis ergo litteris Abbatis, armigeri vehementer doluerunt, eo quod compellendi erant ad recedendum antequam vidissent finem de prædictis. Qui si expectassent, proculdubio eo die vidissent eosdem decollatos. Redierunt idcirco, notificata prius militi legatione domini sui, cum summa celeritate, quia ignorabant causas tam repentinæ revocationis. Quibus recedentibus, insteterunt villani de Sancto Albano, qui ibidem erant, pro manucaptione dictorum; sed duobus detentis in carcere, tertius, scilicet Willelmus Gryndecobbe, deliberatur eisdem, obligantibus se pro eisdem tribus de vicinis suis in trecentis libris, singulis etiam [1] [in] integra summa obligatis, quod eum carceri restituerent die Sabbati proximo sequente, (nam tunc erat dies Lunæ in Octavis Sancti Johannis Baptistæ,) nisi contingerent eos inire concordiam cum Abbate infra dictos dies. Revertuntur igitur cum Willelmo, sua æstimatione laudabiles quod manucapere poterant pro amico, nisi timor surrepsisset de fuga Willèlmi; quæ si contingeret, semetipsos æstimabant perituros. Tractant interea cum vicinis super deliberatione Willelmi, affirmantes unum e duobus necessarium, aut Abbati, restitutis chartis, satisfacere, aut eundem Willelmum in suo reditu capite privari, et plures forsitan ex vicinis consimili pœna percelli.

They unwillingly obey.

Grindecobbe is released at Hertford, on bail.

His sureties fear that he may take to flight.

Cumque intrarent et responsa suspenderent, Willelmus Gryndecobbe, cujus cor jam induratum in malo fuerat, ita ait; —"Concives, quos jamdudum parca libertas de oppressione "diutina relevavit; state modo, dum stare licebit, et de mea "multatione minime timeatis; qui in causa liberatis acquisitæ "moriar, si nunc contingat occumbere, felicem me reputans "per tale posse martyrium vitam finire. Agite hoc in tempore, "ut facere debuissetis, si Hertfordiæ hesterno decollatus "fuissem. Nam nihil obstabat quin finem vidissem vitæ, "si non Abbas armigeros suos tempestivius revocasset. Nempe "ipsi me in multis accusaverant, et judicem favorabilem eis "habebant, et in sanguinem meum pronum."

They deliberate, and Grindecobbe addresses them.

Quid multa? Indurantur et villani, et jurant se nondum libertates recuperatas dimissuros; quin potius æstimant se infortunatos et vecordes, qui cum tantam turbam eis faventem habuissent, quod caput militis, qui in [2] burgum eorum et burgenses tanta præsumpserat, ad terrorem ubique terrarum judicum et falsorum Justiciariorum, [3] humaniter amputassent, et

Resolutions taken by the townsmen.

[1] Supplied from Bibl. Reg. 13 E. ix.: omitted in the printed texts.

[2] *burgo* in orig. and Bibl. Reg. 13 E. ix.: corrected from the printed texts.

[3] *viriliter amputassent* in the printed texts.

super collistrigium collocassent. Pœnituit tamen Willelmum Gryndecobbe, sed sero, stultitiæ suæ, quia vicinos, elatos in superbiam, et cum vellet, non potuit a stultitia revocare. MS. Bibl. Reg. 13 E. ix.

Grindecobbe is taken back to prison at Hertford.

Adveniente ergo Sabbato, ut diebus Sabbati innovaretur tribulatio eis qui eo die multos conturbaverant, reductus est ad carcerem, per eos qui pro eo fidejusserant, Willelmus antedictus, et ibidem custoditus usque ad tempus illud quo reductus est ad Sanctum Albanum, ad judicium subeundum in adventu Regis, ut expost dicetur.

News reaches Saint Alban's, of the approach of the Earl of Warwick and Lord Thomas Percy.

Interea non cessabant conjurationes, [1][comminationes], elationes inter villanos per illam hebdomadam usque in diem Veneris; quo die Willelmus Gryndecobbe misit illis nova multum displicentia, de adventu Comitis Warwici et Domini Thomæ Percy, qui mittendi fuerant in favorem Abbatis, ad judicium exercendum in eos cum mille viris armatis. Nam et ipse Willelmus fratrem habuit, qui ad intercedendum pro eo Curiam Regis adiverat Chelmesfordam, et ibidem audiens talia, prædicto Willelmo, fratri suo, [2]nunciare curavit, et Willelmus vicinis suis. Tunc mœror et luctus iterum, tremor et [3]horribilatio, invaserunt perfidos, superbos, elatos villanos. Tunc de novo tractare cœperunt de chartis Abbatis reddendis, de novis fœderibus feriendis de concordia ineunda. Venerunt idcirco in crastino, id est, die Sabbati in Octavis Apostolorum [4]Petri et Pauli, hora Completorii, ad reddendum chartas et quemdam librum, in quo veteres placitæ, inter Abbathiam et villanos habitæ, continebantur; quem quidem librum abstulerant in die furoris sui; sed Abbas non reputavit illam horam idoneam ad tractandum cum illis super re tam ardua. Quapropter misit ad illos fratrem Willelmum Kyllingworth, Priorem de Wymundham, qui librum ab eis reciperet, sed chartas reacceptare differret, et ducentas libras quas pro emendis faciendis obtulerant, usque in [5]crastinum [6][ad] horam primam.

The townsmen offer to restore the Charters; but the offer is not accepted.

The Earl of Warwick is obliged to return home.

Accidit autem ut Comes [7]Warwici, cui causa Monasterii commissa [8]fuerit justificanda, eodem tempore audiret a referentibus in partibus sui dominii gravem turbationem exortam esse; quare, causis extrinsecis omnino dimissis, oportebat eum ad sua quantocius festinare. Missis ergo qui eum excu-

---

[1] Supplied from Bibl. Reg. 13 E. ix.: omitted in the printed texts.

[2] *nunciari* in the printed texts.

[3] *horror* in the printed texts.

[4] These three words are omitted in Bibl. Reg. 13 E. ix., and their place is occupied by an hiatus.

[5] *crastinam* in the printed texts.

[6] Supplied from Bibl. Reg. 13 E. ix.: omitted in the printed texts

[7] *Warwicy* in orig.

[8] *fuerat* in the printed texts; *fuerit* in Bibl. Reg. 13 E. ix.

MS. Bibl. Reg. 13 E. ix.

sarent, de suis militibus ad Abbatem, et eum confortarent, ne concideret vultus ejus pro dilatione adventus sui, abiit in viam suam. Cum vero in crastino cognovissent villani pro certo Comitem non esse venturum, in derisiones dissolvuntur, et sannas, ad invicem garrulantes;—"Quid est quod timebamus? "Quare a verbis mendacibus formidavimus? [1]Non putandum "est exercitum hic fuisse contrahendum ad preces Abbatis. "Stulti sumus; [2]inepte credidimus, ut fatui operati sumus. "Nunquam de cætero est offerenda pecunia, nunquam chartæ "reddendæ. Et [3]si reddendæ chartæ forent, quare nos primi "meticulose in perniciosum exemplum inciperemus? Non "contingat hoc dedecus in persona nostra; salliat interim "Abbas carnes quas mactavit, ne putrescant; et vendat "cervisiam quam pandoxavit, ne acescat; et panes quos "pinsuit, ne indurescant aut muscidi fiant, aut a muribus "corrodantur."

The townsmen again take heart.

Hujuscemodi verbis per singulos dies improperabant Abbati et famulis de Abbathia, donec quidam ex armigeris Abbatis, zelo ducti, Domino Regi tantas molestias indicassent. Qui cum audisset talia, commotus et ipse nimirum, juravit se accessurum personaliter ad tantas insolentias compescendas. Villani vero, ut videbatur, interim de pace reformanda minime cogitabant. Requisiti autem cur chartas non redderent, responderunt se timore Barnotensium, et Watfordensium, et cæterarum villarum, differre; qui incendium villæ comminati fuerant, et eis exterminium, si ipsi primo id attentare præsumerent; sed falsi quidem locuti sunt falsa, ut rerum exitus comprobavit. Nam Barnotenses et cæterarum conterminarum viri villarum, priusquam illi et chartas humiliter reddiderunt, et se in misericordia domini posuerunt; et se paratos esse ad pugnandum cum eis dixerunt, videlicet cum singulis singuli, aut cum decem totidem, aut cum omnibus omnes, in hac causa, quod scilicet mendose de eis talia protulissent. Sed de hiis hactenus; jam ad superiora revertamur.

The King determines personally to take cognizance of their insolence.

Frivolous excuses made by the townsmen, as to the Charters.

Dum igitur hæc agerentur, [4]allati sunt rumores flebiles ad Sanctum Albanum, quod Rex adventare disponeret, et ibidem judicia præsentialiter exercere. Doluit idcirco Abbas, [5]quia timuit per tantum populum patriam [6]devastandam. Doluerunt villani, sed dispariter; quia metuebant subire judicium debitum maleficiis eorundem. Abbas, [7]quem reipublicæ caritas

Alarm caused by the contemplated arrival of the King.

[1] *Num* in the printed texts.

[2] *inepti* in the printed texts.

[3] *sibi* in orig.; corrected from the printed texts.

[4] *allate* in orig. and Bibl. Reg. 13 E. ix.; corrected from the printed texts.

[5] *qui* in the printed texts.

[6] *devastandum* in the printed texts.

[7] *quam* in orig., by inadvertence.

The Abbot attempts, but vainly, to prevent it.

MS. Bibl. Reg. 13 E. ix.

detinebat, [1]et aliis satis benigne præcavere cupiens, misit Londonias ad Dominum Hugonem Segrave, Senescallum, amicum suum, et alios amicos et notos quos habebat in Curia, rogans et efflagitans ut Regis impedirent adventum, si quoquomodo possent. Monachus vero, qui hæc executurus exiverat, cum nihil omnino proficere posset ille, vel amici præfati, rediit infecto negotio, narrans Abbati Regem pro nullo velle mutare propositum, quin omnino accederet infra duos dies.

The Abbot is defamed by the townsmen, in reference thereto.

Tristatus est ergo Abbas ultra quam credi potest, non pro se, sed pro miseris oppidanis Sancti Albani, necnon pro patria convicina, quibus scivit per adventum regium proventurum maximum detrimentum; quanquam iidem villani expost, mendacia fabricantes, asseveraverunt Abbatem Regi contulisse mille libras, ut in excidium eorum properaret. Sed fallax turba, gens perfida, populus dolosus, viri mendaces, homines fraudulenti, proximi vicini invidi, beneficiis semper ingrati, talia confinxerunt ad diffamandum eorum, velint nolint, dominum et patrem spiritualem, ut vere iniquitatis filii, patrem totius ingratitudinis et mendacii, diabolum, imitantes. Hii cum audissent Regem proculdubio adventurum, conducunt quemdam militem causidicum, scilicet Willelmum Croyser, magno pretio, quia ipsimet propter malificia sua, juxta opinionem propriam, non merebantur audiri, ad intercedendum et proloquendum pro eis, si forte Abbas, pro reverentia mediatoris, induci posset ad ignoscendum eis. [2]Non erat apud Abbatem [3]labor iste difficilis, quin ignosceret deprecantibus, ita tamen ut damna resarcirent Ecclesiæ, quæ intulerant perturbatione præfata. Convenit igitur inter Abbatem et villanos, mediante præfato milite, et timore adventus regii, ut eo die post nonam quo die Rex erat venturus, reportarent tot molarum manualium lapides, quot [4]asportaverant de pavimento ostii locutorii forinseci, et restaurarent propriis sumptibus domum quam diruerant; præter id, quod Abbas concessit eis meremium quod remansit de domo præfata; et quod solverent eidem Abbati, vel successoribus suis, pro damnis et injuriis illatis sibi, pariter et expensis suis, ducentas libras argenti bonæ et legalis monetæ, citra festum Sancti Michaelis Archangeli proximo sequentis; ad quam summam solvendam obligaverunt se plures de majoribus, appositis sigillis suis, sub pœna duplici. Et quod Abbas nullam deponeret querimoniam penes Regem pro illatis per illos injuriis; sed si contingeret eos impeti per Regem pro factis suis in turbatione præfata,

They employ a pleader, to intercede for them with the Abbot.

Terms are made between them and the Abbot.

[1] *et* omitted in Bibl. Reg. 13 E. ix. and the printed texts.

[2] *Noverat apud* in the printed texts.

[3] *laborem hunc facilem qui* in the printed texts.

[4] *asportarunt* in the printed texts.

MS. Bibl. Reg. 13. E. ix.

idem [[1] Abbas] apponeret diligentiam suam pro adquietatione eorundem et gratia obtinenda. Quibus [2] repromisit Abbas, se nullam querimoniam depositurum de eis, si condicta servarent; penes Regem vero se intercedere velle pro posse promisit, siquidem ejus preces possent exaudiri; cæterum se nolle promittere eis veniam, publice protestatus est, quæ tantummodo esset de regia gratia processura, quia ignorabat si id impetrare posset. Quod verbum acceperunt de ore ejus majores pariter et communes, asserentes illis sufficere bonam voluntatem Abbatis; cum Rege autem se optime conventuros de hiis quæ spectant ad regiam dignitatem. Et ita pro tunc solutum est Consilium, et dimissa.

The Abbot promises to intercede in their favour.

Circa horam Vesperarum allati sunt lapides molares sex, quot videlicet asportaverant, et ministerio villanorum positi juxta locum de quo alii fuere levati. Chartas insuper et obligationes quas extorserant, timore ducti, suppliciter veniam deprecati sunt, et chartas redonaverunt; et quamplures se obligaverunt ad satisfaciendum juxta quantitatem delictorum suorum. Et ista, utique eo die quo Rex erat venturus, facta sunt.

The promises of the townsmen are fulfilled.

Finitis Vesperis, cum processione solemni obviam Regi processum est ab Abbate et Conventu ad Occidentale ostium Monasterii; [3] acceptusque est honorifice, cum pulsationibus [4] campanarum, cantuque tam debito quam devoto. Advenerunt autem cum eo ad millia arcitenentium et armatorum; inter quos Dominus Robertus Trysilyan, miles, Justiciarius peritissimus, vir multum habens pectoris, et prudentiæ serpentinæ. Hic, in crastino sedens pro tribunali in villa apud le Moot-Halle, accersiri jussit ex Hertfordia Willelmum Gryndecobbe, Willelmum Cadyndone, et Johannem Barbitonsorem; quem supra retulimus pavimentum locutorii confregisse, et molares abstulisse et comminuisse, in spiritu furoris sui. Cum ergo venissent ad Sanctum Albanum, jussit eos in custodia conservari usque in diem Lunæ; quo videlicet die jurati, qui onerati fuerant primo die Sessionum ad prodendum malefactores qui regiam pacem perturbaverant, dicturi erant veredictum onerationis eorundem. Erat autem primus dies quo eum sedisse descripsimus, dies Sabbati, et primus dies Canicularium; qui expost infausti fuere villanis.

The King arrives at Saint Alban's.

Sir Robert Tresilian sits in judgment upon the insurgents.

[1] Supplied from Bibl. Reg. 13 E. ix.: omitted in the printed texts.

[2] *promisit* in the printed texts.

[3] *exceptusque* in orig. and Bibl. Reg. 13 E. ix.; *acceptusque* in the printed texts.

[4] *campanorum* in orig. and the printed texts; corrected from Bibl. Reg. 13 E. ix.

De Johanne Balle, Presbytero.

John Balle brought to Saint Alban's, and sentenced to death.

MS. Bibl. Reg. 13 E. ix.

Hoc die præterea, Johannem Balle, presbyterum, captum a viris Coventrensibus, et pridie ductum ad Sanctum Albanum et Regis præsentiam, cujus majestatem convictus est læsisse enormiter, auditum et confessum turpissima scelera, tractioni, suspendio, decollationi, exentrationi, et quarterizationi, [1]ut usu vulgari loquar, idem Robertus adjudicavit; cujus mors dilationem accepit usque in diem Lunæ, interventu Domini Willelmi, Londoniensis Episcopi, qui, circa salutem sollicitus suæ animæ, illud ei spatium pœnitentiæ impetravit. Hic per viginti annos, et amplius, semper prædicans in diversis locis ea quæ scivit vulgo placentia, detrahens tam personis ecclesiasticis quam dominis sæcularibus, benevolentiam magis communis populi quam meritum penes Deum captabat. Docuit nempe plebem decimas non esse dandas curato, nisi is qui daturus esset foret ditior quam vicarius qui acciperet, sive rector. Docuit etiam decimas et oblationes subtrahendas curatis, si constaret [2]subjectum aut parochianum melioris vitæ fore quam curatum suum. Docuit etiam neminem aptum regno Dei, qui non in matrimonio natus fuisset. Docuit et perversa dogmata perfidi Johannis Wiclyf, et opiniones quas tenuit, et insanias falsas, et plura quæ longum foret recitare: propter quæ, prohibitus ab Episcopis in, quorum parochiis hæc præsumpsit, ne in ecclesiis de cætero prædicaret, concessit in plateas et vicos, vel in campos, ad prædicandum. Nec defuerunt ei de communibus auditores, quos semper studuit per detractiones prælatorum, et placentia verba, allicere ad sermonem. Postremo excommunicatus, cum nec desisteret, carceri mancipatur, ubi prædixit se deliberandum per viginti millia amicorum. Quod postea evenit in turbatione regni præfata, cum [3]communes omnes carceres confregerunt, et incarceratos abire compulerunt. Cumque taliter deliberatus fuisset, eos secutus est, instigans ad plura mala perpetranda, et prædicans ita omnino fore faciendum. Et ut sua doctrina plures inficeret, ad le Blakheth, ubi ducenta millia hominum communium fuere simul congregata, hujuscemodi sermonem est exorsus:—

Account of Balle's doctrines.

He preaches the doctrines of Wyclif, and is excommunicated.

The text of his Sermon at Blackheath.

"*Whan Adam dalf, and Eve span,*
"*Wo was thanne a gentilman?*"

---

[1] *in* in orig.: corrected from the printed texts.

[2] *a* inserted in orig., by inadvertence: it is found in Bibl. Reg. 13 E. ix., but with an expunctory mark beneath.

[3] *omnes homines carceres* in the printed texts; *omnes homines omnes carceres* in orig.: corrected from Bibl. Reg. 13 E. ix.

MS. Bibl. Reg. 13 E. ix.

A.D. 1381.

Continuansque sermonem inceptum, nitebatur, per verba proverbii quod pro themate sumpserat, introducere et probare, ab initio omnes pares creatos a natura, servitutem per injustam oppressionem nequam hominum introductam, contra Dei voluntatem; quia, si Deo placuisset servos creasse, utique in principio mundi constituisset quis servus, quisve dominus, futurus fuisset. Considerarent igitur jam tempus a Deo datum eis, in quo, deposito servitutis jugo [1] diutinæ, possent, si vellent, libertate diu concupita gaudere. Quapropter monuit ut essent viri cordati, et amore boni patrisfamilias excolentis agrum suum, et extirpantis ac resecantis noxia gramina quæ fruges solent opprimere, et ipsi in præsenti facere festinarent.—Primo, majores regni dominos occidendo; deinde, juridicos, justiciarios, et juratores patriæ, perimendo; postremo, quoscunque scirent in posterum communitati nocivos, tollerent de terra sua; sic demum et pacem sibimet parerent et securitatem in futurum, si, sublatis majoribus, esset inter eos æqua libertas, eadem nobilitas, [2] par dignitas, similisque potestas.

His text enlarged upon, in reference to the natural equality of mankind.

And consequent advice.

Cum hæc et plura alia deliramenta prædicasset, commune vulgus eum tanto favore prosequitur, ut acclamarent eum Archiepiscopum futurum, et regni Cancellarium; solum eum dignum Archipræsulatus honore; Archiepiscopum, qui tunc superstes erat, communium et regni proditorem fuisse, et idcirco decapitandum, ubicunque posset in Anglia comprehendi.

His doctrines gain the applause of the multitude.

Miserat insuper ductoribus communibus in Estsexia quamdam litteram ænigmatibus plenam, ad hortandum eos ut incepta perficerent; quæ expost inventa est in manica cujusdam suspendendi pro turbatione præfata, cujus tenor talis est:—

Letter sent by John Balle to the Commons of Essex.

[3] *Littera Johannis Balle, missa Communibus Essexiæ.*

"*John Schep, som tyme Seynt Marie prest of Ȝorke, and*
"*nowe of Colchestre, greteth welle Johan Nameles, and Johan*

[1] *diutius* in the printed texts.

[2] *pari* in orig.; by inadvertence; arising from the peculiar form of the *r* in *par*, in Bibl. Reg. 13 E. ix.

[3] In Camden's Edition, the orthography of this document is somewhat varied:—

"*John Schep, sometime Seint*
"*Mary priest of Yorkn, and now*
"*of Colchester, græteth well John*
"*Namelesse, and John the Miller,*
"*and John Carter, and biddeth them*
"*that they beware of guyle in*
"*borough, and stand together in*
"*Gods name, and biddeth Piers*
"*Ploweman goe to his werke, and*
"*chastise well Hob the robber, and*
"*take with you John Trewman, and*
"*all his fellows, and no moe.*

["*John*

A.D. 1381. "*the Mullere, and Johan Cartere, and biddeth hem that thei* MS. Bibl. Reg. 13 E. ix.
"*ware of gyle in borugh, and stondeth togiddir in Goddis* "*name, and biddeth Peres Plouȝman go to his werke, and* "*chastise welle Hobbe the robber, and taketh with ȝou Johan* "*Trewman, and alle his felawe, and no mo,* [1][*and loke* "*scharpe ȝou to on heued, and no mo*].

"*Johan the Muller hath ygrownde smal, smal, smal;*
"*The Kyngis sone of hevene shalle pay for alle.*
"*Be ware or ye be wo,*
"*Knoweth ȝour frende fro ȝoure foo,*
"*Haveth ynowe, and seythe 'Hoo:'*
"*And do welle and bettre, and fleth synne,*
"*And seketh pees, and holde therynne.*
"*And so biddeth Johan Trewman and alle his felawes.*"

The ultimate punishment of Balle.

Hanc litteram idem Johannes Balle confessus est [2]scripsisse, et communibus transmisisse, et plura alia fatebatur et fecit; propter quæ, ut diximus, tractus, suspensus, et decollatus, apud Sanctum Albanum Idibus Julii, præsente Rege; et cadaver ejus quadripartitum quatuor regni civitatibus missum est.

"*John the Miller hath yground*
"*smal, small, small;*
"*The kings sonne of heaven shal*
"*pay for all.*
"*Beware or ye be woe,*
"*Know your frende fro your foe,*
"*Have ynough, and say 'Hoe':*
"*And do wel and better, and flee*
"*sinne,*
"*And seeke peace, and holde you*
"*therin,*
"*And so biddeth John Trewman*
"*and all his fellowes.*"

The following is the earliest version, that in Bibl. Reg. 13 E. ix. fol. 287 a:—

"*I Johon Schep, som tyme Seynte* "*Marie prest of Ȝork, and now of* "*Colchestre, greteth wel Johan* "*Nameles, and Johan the Mullere,* "*and Johon Cartere, and biddeth* "*hem that thei bee war of gyle in* "*borughe, and stondeth to gidedre* "*in Godes name, and biddeth Peres* "*Plouȝman go to his werk, and* "*chastise wel Hobbe the robbere,* "*and taketh with ȝow Johan Trew-* "*man and alle hiis felawes, and no* "*mo, and loke scharpe ȝou to on* "*heued, and no mo.*

"*Johan the Mullere hathe y*
"*grounde smal, smal, smal;*
"*The kynges sone of hevene schal*
"*paye for al.*
"*Be war or ye be wo,*
"*Knoweth ȝour freend fro ȝour foo,*
"*Haveth ynow, and seith 'Hoo':*
"*And do wel and bettre, and*
"*fleth synne.*
"*And seketh pees and hold ȝou*
"*therinne.*
"*And so biddeth Johan Trewman*
"*and alle his felawes.*"

[1] Omitted in orig. and the printed texts: supplied from the version in Bibl. Reg. 13 E. ix., given herewith.

[2] *se scripsisse* in the printed texts.

Comitia celebrantur apud Sanctum Albanum.

MS. Bibl. Reg. 13 E. ix.

Robertus Trysilian, Justiciarius, Idibus Octobris apud Sanctum Albanum convocari fecit duodenam, quam tridie oneraverat ad indictandum et prodendum malefactores et pacis regiæ turbatores. Venerunt igitur jurati de villa, et dixerunt se nullum talem scire, nullum indictare juste posse, cunctos fideles et obsequentes Regi fore, semperque fuisse. Videns autem Justiciarius quo tendebat ista responsio, ut erat vir sapiens et profundæ intelligentiæ, præcepit ut redirent, et memores essent verbi illius dicti ex parte Regis, quando suppliciter egressi in obviam Regi, misericordiam et veniam postulabant; in hoc videlicet et perdonationem et veniam consecuturos, si incentores et auctores turbationis regni tradidissent; sin alias, juxta sermonem Regis, eos subituros prædixit eandem pœnam quam pertulissent iidem malefactores, si deprehensi fuissent.

A.D. 1381. The jurors of Saint Alban's refuse to indict, and are rebuked by the Justiciar.

Regressi sunt igitur dicti jurati, quos e vestigio secutus est Justiciarius ad [1]locum [2]quo erant de præmissis tractaturi; et proferens de sua manica [3]quemdam rotulum, in quo et nomina plurimorum, et malefacta, continebantur, [4]ait eis; "En," [5]inquiens, "deposita proximorum vestrorum scelera "per bonos viros et fideles patriæ, quæ neminem pene latent; "et vos putatis nos omnes deludere vestro silentio, vel excæ"care? Nequaquam fiet quod putatis, cum in promptu ha"beamus et nomina et facta sceleratorum, quos vos justos "monstrare velletis. Agite propterea quæ vobis expediunt, "et vitam vestram servare satagite, ne, dum nimis inutiliter "cavetis proximis, vobismet periculum [6]excitetis."

His ultimate advice to them.

Turbati ergo villani, æstimaverunt salubrius indictare reos vicinos, quam in semetipsos dicta mala congerere. [7]Indictaverunt quamplures, tam de patria quam de villa.

The jurors indict several persons.

Tunc Justiciarius, convocata seorsum alia duodena, demonstravit eis et nomina et indictamenta personarum per primam duodenam (ut præmittitur) [8]exarata, interrogans quid illi vellent dicere de personis prædictis, si illi onerati essent super præmissis. Viri autem de secunda duodena, cernen-

The justiciar, by stratagem, obtains an indictment by three juries of twelve.

---

[1] *lacum* in orig.; by inadvertence.

[2] *in quo* in the printed texts.

[3] *quandam rotulam . . . qua* in the printed texts.

[4] *ante eos* in the printed texts.

[5] *inquit* in the printed texts.

[6] *exitetis* in orig. and Bibl. Reg. 13 E. ix.

[7] *et indictaverunt* in the printed texts.

[8] *exaratra* in orig.; by inadvertence.

A.D. 1381. tes cuncta fore vera, quæ per primam duodenam fuere scripta, responderunt se eo modo fecisse quo illi, si fuissent onerati. Igitur hanc duodenam servavit judex, ad dicendum veredictum de præfatis personis; quæ nullo modo potuit aliter dicere in reddendo veredicto quam dixerant cum interrogarentur de præmissis; sed oportuit [1] illis, vellent nollent, damnare eos quos antea fatebantur se voluisse indictasse de prædictis sceleribus, vel cum rubore falsi apparere. Et hoc commento Justiciarius induxit eos, quanquam falsi esse maluissent, ad dicendam veritatem. Oneravit nihilominus et tertiam duodenam super eadem re; quæ cum vidisset primæ duodenæ deposita, eadem deposuit quæ prima descripsit, ita ut nullus damnaretur, nisi per ora triginta sex virorum; sed secunda duodena, ut diximus, semper servabatur pro veredicto dicendo, postquam prima et tertia duodena indictamenta fecissent.

MS. Bibl. Reg. 13 E. ix.

Executio Malefactorum.

Some of the insurgents at Saint Alban's are executed, others imprisoned.

Tunc damnatus est Willelmus Gryndecobbe, Willelmus Cadyndon, Johannes Barbitonsor, et quidam alii malefactores, pro turbatione pacis regiæ; et tracti sunt et suspensi, ad numerum decem et quinque virorum. [2] Incarceratique sunt de majoribus villæ, ad sectam Regis, suis convicinis eosdem indictantibus, Ricardus Walyngforde, Johannes Garlek, Willelmus [3] Berewik, Thomas Putor, et plures alii mediocres. De patria vero [4] commendati sunt custodiæ carcerali ad numerum octoginta personarum; qui expost Regis indulgentia sunt dimissi.

Accusantur Abbas et Conventus Sancti Albani de perturbatione et commotione prædicta.

The Abbot and Convent are accused by the townsmen, of causing the commotion.

[5] Interea villani, ut nullum lateret eorum malitia, quanquam Dominus Abbas sæpius pro eis intercessisset Domino Regi, et pro salute et vita supplicasset eorundem, et frequenter ob id iram regiam metuisset, quia proclamatum fuerat nullum debere pro quoquam preces fundere, non onerati, non jussi, non coacti, sed sponte, in Abbatem [6] et Conventum dolum cogitantes, et

---

[1] *illos* in the printed texts; *illis* in Bibl. Reg. 13 E. ix.

[2] *Incarcerati* in orig. and the printed texts; corrected from Bibl. Reg. 13 E. ix.

[3] *Berewil* in orig.; *Berewill* in the printed texts: *Berewik* in Bibl. Reg. 13 E. ix.

[4] *commendato* in orig.; corrected from the printed texts.

[5] *Interim* in the printed texts.

[6] The words *et Conventum* are erroneously placed after *cogitantes* in orig., and in Bibl. Reg. 13 E. ix.: corrected in the printed texts.

MS. Bibl. Reg. 13 E. ix.

A.D. 1381.

mendacia fabricantes, eosdem indictaverunt de prima commotione villanorum; quod scilicet Abbas jussisset et coegisset eos egredi ad turbam quæ erat Londoniis congregata, cum villani parum aut nihil de talibus cogitassent; quare asseveraverunt Abbatem et Conventum, et famulos eorundem, incitatores, [1][concitatores], et auctores primos fuisse turbationis quæ in villa postea contingebat; et insuper, eos direxisse in adjutorium inimicorum Regis et regni.

The Justiciar charges them, on their oath, thereon.

Cumque Justiciarius hæc audisset et vidisset, abhorrens nimium, et execrans, tantam tamque manifestam villanorum malitiam, dixit eis:—"Dicatis," ait, "O perfidi, in animabus "vestris, hoc quod creditis; utrum Abbas ista fecerit tanquam "Regis et regni proditor, vel pro meliori, id est, pro periculo "præcavendo, ne turba veniens, quæ furebat, damna tam vobis "quam sibi inferret. Edicite si sibi et vobis optavit exitium, "aut si intentionis ejus fuerat, ut revertentes cum tanto nu- "mero inferretis damna quæ sibi et vicinis vestris intulistis. "Dicatis per juramentum vestrum, si reus est Abbas horum "quæ numeravimus in præsenti."

The townsmen at length admit the falsehood of their charges.

Illi autem confusi in astutia propria, nec habentes quid responderent, aliquandiu conticuerunt. [2]Urgebat autem Justiciarius vehementer ut dicerent quid sentirent. Tandem verecundi compulsi sunt dicere veritatem, asserentes Abbatem satis fidelem tam Regi quam regno fore, et hæc omnia juxta intentionem suam pro meliori fecisse. Tunc Judex detestatus est eorum perfidiam coram multis, et increpavit eos asperrime, præcipiens ut sine mora ipsimet manibus suis indictamentum prædictum confringerent, et cassarent. Quod et villani, licet cum mala voluntate, fecerunt.

The indictment is quashed.

Slanders circulated by the townsmen, in reference to the Abbot.

Considerantes vero quod fraudati fuerant suo nequam desiderio in hac parte, cogitaverunt qualiter Abbatem molestare possent per alias adinventiones. Hospites namque suos, milites et armigeros de Regis familia, qui apud eosdem copiose hospitati fuerant, fictis insimulationibus credere compulerunt Abbatem fore hypocritam, et, per speciem sanctitatis quam foris monstrabat, plerosque dominorum regnique magnatum deludendo decipere; unde contigit, ut, eorum fultus patrociniis, tyrannides impune exercere, et injuste subjectos opprimere, non timeret. Asserebant insuper eundem Abbatem burgensium Sancti Albani jura et libertates avitas nequiter per falsa commenta surripuisse, et eosdem, liberos homines, tanta oppressione contrivisse, ut nemini liceret in domo sua molam

[1] Supplied from Bibl. Reg. 13 E. ix.; omitted in the printed texts.

[2] *Ugebat* in orig.; by inadvertence.

A.D. 1381. manualem erigere, sed, more nativorum, cuncti compellerentur molere ad ipsius Abbatis molendina. Dicebant etiam eum [1]infinitam auri quantitatem Regi dedisse, ut adveniens, secundum quod accidit, concives eos suspendi juberet. Persuadebant præterea muneribus, ubi verba defuerunt, ut quoquo pacto regales inducerent ad male loquendum de Abbate, si saltem mala irrogare actualiter non valerent. Suadebant et mulieres eorum quod viri non valebant; quæ satis communes fuerunt eisdem, tempore hospitalitatis eorum. Sicque factum est, ut tot excrescerent maliloqui, quod pene cunctos amicos Monasterii conturbarent, licet proclamaretur publice viros suspendendos qui Abbatem accusare false præsumerent, et fœminas concremandas. Et hæc quidem erat retributio villanorum, quam retribuerunt Abbati; qui reddere mala pro bonis festinabant, et odium pro dilectione sua, ac pro eo [2]ut eundem diligerent detrahebant sibi. MS. Bibl. Reg 13 E. ix.

Measures taken by the King and his Council, in behalf of the Abbot.

Cum Dominus Rex jam fuisset octo dies apud Sanctum Albanum, intelligens et prænoscens ejus Consilium, quod tunc aderat, nativorum et servorum Monasterii corda non recta futura cum suis dominis, id est, cum Abbate et Conventu, in posterum, nisi cautius ageretur cum eisdem, jussu Regis remedium apponere statuerunt hujusmodi malis futuris, Magno Regis Sigillo firmatum. Nam Regis Cancellaria tunc tenebatur in Domo Capitulari, unde facilius consequi potuit idem Abbas quæ volebat.—

Commissio ad inquirendum, ut omnes tenentes Sancti Albani reddant servitia consueta Abbati prædicto.

Commission for enquiry as to services due from the tenants to the Abbot; and injunction that the same shall be only performed.

"Ricardus, Dei gratia, Rex Angliæ et Franciæ, et Dominus "Hiberniæ, dilectis sibi Johanni Lodewyk, Johanni West "Wycombe, Johanni Kentyng, Ricardo Perers, Waltero Graun- "ford, Ricardo Gyffard, Thomæ Eydon, et Willelmo Eccles- "hale, salutem. Mandamus vobis, et cuilibet vestrum, firmi- "ter injungentes, quod statim visis præsentibus, quacunque "excusatione cessante, in singulis villis et locis in Comi- "tatibus Hertfordiæ et Bokynghamiæ, tam infra libertates "quam extra, ubi expediens fore videritis et necesse, ex parte "nostra faciatis publice proclamari, quod omnes et singuli "tenentes dilecti nobis in Christo Abbatis de Sancto Albano, "tam liberi quam nativi, opera, consuetudines, et servitia, quæ "ipsi prædicto Abbati facere debent, et ab antiquo, ante tur-

[1] *infinitatam* in orig.; by inadvertence.

[2] *quod eundem* in the printed texts.

MS. Bibl. Reg. 13 E. ix. "bationem in diversis Comitatibus regni nostri Angliæ jam "noviter exortam, facere consueverunt, absque contradictione, "murmure, resistentia, seu difficultate aliquali, faciant, prout "antea facere solebant. Et ulterius, ex parte nostra districte "inhibeatis, quod iidem tenentes aut nativi, seu alii qui- "cunque, opera, consuetudines, aut servitia sua prædicta, "istis turbationum temporibus magis solito non retrahant; "sed nec ea prædicto Abbati facere ullo colore retardent, nec "aliqua libertates sive privilegia exigant, vendicent, sive cla- "ment, quam ante præsentem turbationem habuerunt, sub "fide et ligeantia quibus nobis tenentur, et sub forisfactura "omnium quæ nobis forisfacere poterunt in futurum. Et "omnes illos, quos, post proclamationem et inhibitionem præ- "dictas, contrarios inveneritis seu rebelles, arestetis et capiatis, "et [1] ipsos in prisonis nostris mancipetis, in eisdem moraturos, "quousque de eorum punitione aliter duxerimus demandan- "dum; et hoc, sicut nos et honorem nostrum, ac salvationem "[2] jurium regni nostri, diligitis, nullatenus omittatis. Teste "meipso, apud villam de Sancto Albano, quinto-decimo die "Julii, anno regni nostri quinto." A.D. 1381.

Homines de Comitatu Hertfordiæ præstant fidelitatem Regi.

The men of the County of Hertford do fealty to the King, who then leaves Saint Alban's.

In die Sanctæ Margaretæ Virginis, post refectionem, Dominus Rex, transiturus ad castellum de Berkhamstede, in Magna Curia Abbathiæ apud Sanctum Albanum fidelitatem suscepit de hominibus Comitatus Hertfordiæ, qui summoniti fuerant ut ibi comparerent coram eo; cuncti videlicet qui erant inter quintum-decimum et sexagesimum ætatis annum. Qui omnes simul, data fide, jurarunt se de cætero fideles domino suo Regi futuros, et nunquam iterum contra pacem surrecturos, sed citius morituros quam regni turbatoribus parituros; et eosdem regni turbatores pro viribus comprehensuros, et carceribus adducturos, opera et servitia consueta facturos fideliter. Et si qui inter eos essent qui ductores, concitatores, turbarum fuerant, continuo captos Regi monstraturos. Post quod juramentum dimissi sunt in sua, Rege ad Berkhamstede properante; ubi cum aliquandiu moratus fuisset, transivit venandi gratia ad villam de [3] Esthamstede, quo in loco relatum est sibi,

[1] *ipso* in orig. and Bibl. Reg. 13 E. ix.; corrected from the printed texts.

[2] *jurii* in orig.; *juris* in the printed texts: corrected from Bibl. Reg. 13 E. ix.

[3] Originally written *Berkhamstede* in orig. (from Bibl. Reg. 13 E. ix.), but corrected to *Esthamstede* in a later hand: *Esthamstede* in the printed texts.

A.D. 1381. [1]suspensos apud Sanctum Albanum fuisse depositos, et a furcis longius fuisse remotos. Dominus autem multum miratus super tanta audacia, et commotus immodice propter contumeliam in hac parte sibimet irrogatam, illico breve suum misit ballivis villæ de Sancto Albano, in hæc verba:— MS. Bibl. Reg. 13 E. ix.

The bodies of those executed are privily removed from the gibbets.

Corpora Proditorum, jussu regio, ferreis catenis ad furcas suspensa sunt.

Order by the King, that the bodies shall be replaced.

"Ricardus, Dei gratia, Rex Angliæ et Franciæ, et Dominus Hiberniæ, ballivis villæ de Sancto Albano salutem. "Quia certitudinaliter informati sumus quod diversi malefactores, timore nostræ regiæ majestati abjecto, corpora diversorum proditorum et felonum apud villam prædictam, qui, "pro eorum maleficiis, in præsenti perturbatione contra nos "et ligeantiam suam factis, ut suspenderentur, et penderent, "quamdiu possent durare, adjudicati fuissent, prædictis proditoribus et felonibus juxta judicium prædictum suspensis, "a furcis ubi pendebant ceperunt et asportaverunt, in nostri "vituperium et contemptum, ac contra judicium supradictum; "unde quamplurimum commovemur, nec immerito conturbamur.—Vobis igitur, in fide et ligeantia quibus nobis "tenemini, præcipimus, firmiter injungentes, quod statim "visis præsentibus, catenas ferreas fieri, et corpora prædictorum suspensorum, ubicunque inventa fuerint, ad furcas "prædictas reduci, et ea cum eisdem catenis resuspendi, "faciatis ibidem, quamdiu durare poterunt; pensura, juxta "formam judicii supradicti. Et hoc, sub forisfactura omnium "quæ nobis forisfacere poteritis, nullatenus omittatis. Teste "meipso, apud Esthamstede, tertio die Augusti, anno regni "nostri quinto."[2]

Villani, regio mandato coacti, cives suos resuspendunt.

The townsmen of Saint Alban's are compelled, with their own hands, to replace the bodies.

Hoc mandatum villanos de Sancto Albano, jamdudum pro libertate tumultuantes, turpis et abominabilis servitutis servos effecit, dum, non habentes qui hujusmodi obsequium pro eisdem vellet agere, compulsi sunt propriis manibus suos concives resuspendere catenis ferreis; quorum jam corpora, tabe fluentia, scatentia vermibus, [3]putrida et fœtentia, odorem

---

[1] *suspensus* in orig.; *suspensos* in the printed texts.

[2] The words "*Per ipsum Regem*" are added in Bibl. Reg. 13 E. ix.

[3] *putida* in the printed texts.

MS. Bibl. Reg. 13 E. ix.

A.D. 1381.

ipsis teterrimum refundebant. Et quidem merito hoc erat fœdum officium virorum usurpantium minus juste nomen civium, ut apte vocarentur, et essent, suspensores hominum, ipso facto incurrentes opprobrium [1][quod non delebitur, opprobrium] sempiternum. Et qui veritatem reticere et pejorare maluerant, quam sibi similes proditores prodere, non temere ipsos eosdem suspendere sunt coacti. Consecuti quoque sunt canes eorum quod domini non merebantur; dum per dominos, detractis catenis quibus ligati fuerant, libertati donati sunt, ipsis catenis [2]cedentibus in usus suspendendorum hominum, et [3]magistris eorundem canium [4]suspendium, ut præfertur, ministrantibus, ac per hoc, ut dicitur, in turpissima morantibus servitute. Quia videlicet par erat, ut perjuri et Deo odibiles detractatores canibus, Dei judicio, monstrarentur pejores, dum, canibus eorum dimissis liberis, ipsi necterentur tam execrandæ servitutis obsequiis. Et hæc quidem apud Sanctum Albanum gesta sunt, circa festum Inventionis ejusdem Martyris; quem probati sunt peccabiliter offendisse, et in multiplices miserias corruisse.

Treugæ biennales inter Anglos et Scotos.

The Duke of Lancaster, in alarm, hastens to make peace with the Scots.

Dux Lancastriæ Johannes, quia parum ante prædictæ tumultuationis tempus, pro Die Marchiæ, prout moris est, tenenda inter Anglos et Scotos annis singulis, in partes concesserat Boreales, cum audisset de dominatione servili, et quid rustici nebulones, tempore quod datum eis fuerat prævalere, vel in dominos vel æquales illis perpetraverant, consternatus est valde; et præcavens in futurum, utile judicavit sub festinatione pacem facere cum gente Scotorum, ne si pervenissent rumores tam flebiles ad aures eorum, non solum illis afferrent insperatum gaudium, verum [5]sed audaciam inculcarent, refutatis pacis conditionibus, in nostram regionem hostiliter irruendi.

A truce for two years concluded with the Scots.

Et factum est, Deo volente, ut firmarentur treugæ ad instantiam Ducis prædicti, antequam notitia facti daretur Scotis; concessis prius eisdem certis terrarum spatiis, quibus per plures annos non fuerant ante gavisi. Sed nimietatem hujus

[1] Supplied from Bibl. Reg. 13 E. ix.: omitted in the printed texts.

[2] *sedentibus* in orig, Bibl. Reg. 13 E. ix., and the printed texts.

[3] *magistros* in the printed texts.

[4] *suspendendum* in the printed texts.

[5] *etiam audaciam* in the printed texts.

A.D. 1381. concessionis excusat nimietas supradictæ turbationis, quæ quemlibet etiam constantissimum turbasse et terruisse merito potuisset. Scoti vero, cum juramento firmassent biennales treugas se fideliter servaturos, et earum formam, in chartas redactam, sub chirographorum signis munissent, audierunt a suis exploratoribus de turbatione præfata, qualiter vel Regi dominabantur et Turrim Londoniarum occupaverant, vel Cancellarium seu Thesaurarium regni decollaverant, et cætera per ordinem quæ facta sunt hiis diebus.

MS. Bibl. Reg. 13 E. ix.

The Scots repent of the treaty, but offer to give assistance to the Duke.

Tunc primum dolere cœperunt, se tam cito condescendisse pacis conditionibus; quia miscuisse se desiderabant tantis turbationibus, et terram replesse cædibus et rapinis. Tamen, quia turpe videbatur eisdem tam cito notari perjurio, Ducem confortare cœperunt, et ei suadere, [1]ut acceptis viginti millibus bellatorum de gente Scotorum, quos ei concederent animo liberali, ad Angliam properaret, vindicaturus, eorum ope et auxilio, communes dominorum injurias, et emendas accepturus de damnis et dehonestationibus illatis irreverenter personæ suæ.

The Duke gives his reasons for declining the offer.

Sed renuit plane Dux promissa, dicens, proculdubio si id attentarent, futurum quod bellum contra eos paratum reperirent satis asperum, antequam ad Eboracum pervenirent, etiamsi cum eis contraherent potestatem gentis Scotorum. Noscere se dixit multitudinem, fortitudinem quoque, necnon audaciam, Anglicorum, qui nihil minus quam bellum timebant; quibus asseveravit Scotos in brevi fore ludibrio, etsi in duplo major numerus eorum esset. Tamen, quia dubiam cernebat fidem multorum quos fideles sibi reperisse putaverat, puta Comitis Northumbrorum, aliorum quoque militum qui in illis partibus habebant custodias castellorum, insuper et suorum militum commensalium, necnon totius pene suæ familiæ, quippe a facie formidinis prædictæ tumultuationis contabuerant, in tantum ut vix pauci cum eo starent,—audierant nempe Regem, timore ductum, corpus domini sui, Ducis, donasse communibus id petentibus,—rogavit Scotos Dux, ut si eum diligerent, ut dicebant, concederent ei salvum conductum in terras eorum, et facultatem morandi, quamdiu sibi placeret, inter illos, necnon emittendi in Angliam quoscunque de suis vellet, et eos vel alios admittendi, qui ad eum ex Anglia pacifice venire vellent, ac etiam potestatem, quandocunque sibimet hoc placeret, sine impediment ad Angliam remeandi.

He askes leave to retire into Scotland.

And obtains it.

Scoti vero cuncta petita liberaliter

[1] *tot* in orig., by inadvertence; probably from its slight indistinctness in Bibl. Reg. 13 E. ix.: *ut* in the printed texts.

MS. Bibl. Reg. 13 E. ix. concesserunt, et eum venientem honorifice susceperunt, et longo tempore confoverunt. A.D. 1381.

Discordia inter Ducem Lancastriæ et Comitem Northumbrorum.

Dissension between the Duke of Lancaster and the Earl of Northumberland.

Talibus occasionibus orta est discordia gravis inter Ducem et Comitem Northumbrorum, quæ, [1][ut] expost dicetur, totam Angliam deterrebat. Comes etenim, audiens tam horrenda mirabilia, [2]aperte Duci parere vel timebat, vel, ut quidam asserunt, contemnebat. Cujus exemplum comprovinciales secuti, Duci non parvum timorem imprimebant. Quod factum postea non solum Comitis inobedientiæ, sed ingratitudini, Dux ascripsit. Et quoniam scriptum est—"[3]Vexatio tantum dabit intellectum auditui," tunc primo Dux ipse, conversus ad religionem, cœpit accusare vitam suam pristinam, non solum privatis sed publicis confessionibus: tunc suis peccatis ascribere causas malorum quæ contigerant; tunc sibimet imputare mortes, non solum nobilium, sed reliquorum, qui illo tempore manu impia strati sunt; tunc illius Katerinæ Swynford consortium abhorrere, vel potius abjurare: et fletibus ac singultu facere videbatur pœnitentiæ dignos fructus; quibus commentis, ut creditur, iram Domini complacuit.

The Duke repents of his past transgressions.

Igitur [4]regioni [5]data pace, et oppressis vel occultatis malefactoribus, cœpit Dux de reditu cogitare. Tamen ante regressum suum, ut se Regi regnoque monstraret humiliatum usquequaque, præmisit qui nunciarent Regi ejus fugam, et fugæ causas, quam maluit ipsemet "migrationem "in Scotiam" nominare. Nunciarent etiam, si placeret res, et id opus expeteret, se velle reverti, cum ingenti Scotorum multitudine, ad comprimendos rebelles, vel, si hoc displiceret, cum propria familia quam recollegerat, et illucescente pace, de latebris ad eundem emerserat, quæ satis fortis erat ad obviandum cunctis rusticis regionis. Quod si nec sic placeret adventus ejus, vel si multitudo [6]venientium cum eodem [7]eum Regi sive Regis Consilio suspectum redderet, deter-

The Duke thinks of returning, and sends a dutiful message to the King.

[1] Omitted in orig. and Bibl. Reg. 13 E. ix.; supplied from the printed texts.

[2] *a parte* in the printed texts.

[3] *Isaiah* xxviii. 19.

[4] *regione pacificata* in the printed texts.

[5] *daturo* in orig.; *data* (somewhat indistinct) in Bibl. Reg. 13 E. ix.

[6] *viventium* in orig. and the printed texts: corrected from Bibl. Reg. 13 E. ix.

[7] *eum* is repeated before *multitudo* in orig. and the printed texts; erroneously.

A.D. 1381. minaret Rex, cum Consilio assistente, personas quas, vel quot, placeret eisdem; et ipse, dimissis reliquis, paratus erat ad Regem venire, etiamsi contingeret determinari solum tres personas, militem, armigerum, et valettum. Si vero nec ista Regi placerent, et ipse ita invisus esset vel proceribus vel communibus regionis, ut putarent per eum vel regnum turbandum vel pacem minuendam, paratus erat, si Dominus Rex id dictaret, regno discedere, velut exul; Angliam denuo non visurus, dummodo pacem consequeretur Rex, et regnum ejus. Rex autem et proceres, compatientes afflicto, renunciarunt sibi, ut, dimissa gente Scotorum, confidenter rediret cum tota familia propria; quæ si [1] numero non præstaret, assumeret de unaquaque villa per quam transiturus erat, certum numerum ad conducendum eum usque ad villam aliam pro tutela, donec veniret ad Regem. Et factum est ita, Rege præbente sibi commissionem; veniensque ad dominum suum, Regem, honorifice susceptus est.

MS. Bibl. Reg. 13 E. ix.

The King assents to his proposal, and he returns.

Post paucos dies deposuit querimoniam contra Comitem Northumbrorum, quod non solum inobediens, sed infidelis et ingratus, extitisset ei, [2] prout præmittitur, turbationis generalis tempestate. Ob quam causam vocatus est Comes ad Berkhamstede, ubi congregati fuerunt, ad interessendum Consilio, pene cuncti Comites totius regni: ubi cum Dux plura dixisset contra eum, Comes impatiens, (more gentis suæ), contra prohibitionem regiam, in verba contumeliosa est resolutus; cum tamen Dux, tacere jussus, ad primam jubentis vocem satis humiliter tacuisset. Cujus inobedientiæ occasione, Comes tanquam reus læsæ majestatis regiæ protinus arestatur; sed fidejubentibus pro se Comitibus Warwici et Sowthfolchiæ, quod veniret ad proximum Parliamentum, et suam præsentiam exhiberet, dimissus est, et Consilium resolutum.

The Duke and the Earl of Northumberland are summoned before the Council.

The Earl is arrested, but soon released.

Parliamentum Londoni.

Parliament at London: attendance of the Duke and Earl with great numbers of their retainers.

Circa festum Omnium Sanctorum, convenerunt ad Parliamentum Londonias Barones regnique communitas; ad quod Dux cum tanta copia convenit armatorum, ut facile dinumerari non posset. Contraxit et Comes de partibus Borealibus non inferiorem numerum, et Londonias usque pervenit. Sed Dux,

[1] Apparently written *uno* in orig.; omitted in the printed texts: an abbreviated form of *numero* in Bibl. Reg. 13 E. ix.

[2] *prout ut præmittitur* in orig. and the printed texts; corrected from Bibl. Reg. 13 E. ix.

MS. Bibl. Reg. 13 E ix.

A.D. 1381.

The Earl receives great favour at the hands of the Londoners.

suspectam putans fidem Londoniensium, propter inveteratum odium, non æstimavit tutum [1] Londoniis hospitari. Comes vero ad Civitatem fiducialiter cum suis accessit; qui protinus a civibus acceptus est cum favore, illis obviam in equis procedentibus, illis [2] exennia opipara præmittentibus, hospitia [3] suæ genti præbentibus, et pasturas, quas in circuitu Civitatis possidebant, armentis quæ secum duxerat, pro tanta familia copiosa nimis, commodantibus, et eidem, si oporteret, promittentibus fidele juvamen. Erat igitur Comes tunc multum auctus et numero et favore Londoniensium, et jam multo fortior partibus Ducis pars ejus existere videbatur.

Dangerous results arising from this rivalry.

Erat interea cernere miserandum spectaculum, regnum, quod olim pacis tranquillitate præ cunctis regnis gavisum fuerat, undique, versa vice, turbationis fluctibus agitari, hinc seditione communium, illinc diversis factionibus optimatum. Revera viri [4] diversæ partis Ducis et Comitis armati, contra regni consuetudinem, ad Westmonasterium diebus aliquot convenere, inusitatum de semetipsis incolis præbentes spectaculum, sed sapientioribus non modicum tali facto inculcantes metum. Expectabatur tot diebus a pacis perturbatoribus, ut ignis conceptus arderet in publicum, et furor dominorum procerum libere prodiret ad actum. Nutans commune vulgus non curabat quem illorum magnatum sequeretur ad pugnam, dum tali occasione, sicut prius turbationis tempore, irrefrænatas discursandi possidere posset habenas, et materiam vindicandi suorum complicium proditorum decollationes, tractiones, et suspensiones, factas per Regem et fideles regni. Totus clerus autem, pluresque de populo, quorum Deus corda tetigerat, interim constituti erant in timore magno et expectatione, propter mala quæ superventura erant universo orbi Britanniæ, occasione dissensionis eorundem, si effutire pararent odium præconceptum: unde fiebant in clero orationes publicæ et privatæ, ut Deus, cujus natura est bonitas, inter illos spirare concederet auram pacis. Tandem, cum diu Parliamentum protelatum fuisset inaniter, propter dissensionem supradictum, intercurrentibus regni proceribus, cepit Rex querelas eorum in manus suas, ne, propter Dominorum discordiam, cuncta regni negotia non solum paterentur impedimentum, sed et irrecuperabile detrimentum. Sicque soluta sunt a metu corda fidelium, Domino miserante.

The King takes the matter in hand.

[1] *Londonias* in the printed texts.

[2] *xenia* in the printed texts.

[3] *sua præbentibus* in the printed texts.

[4] *diversi* in orig. and the printed texts; corrected from Bibl. Reg. 13 E. ix.

Dissolvitur Parliamentum. Soror Regis Boemiæ honorifice suscipitur.

A.D. 1381. Arrival at Calais, of the intended Queen, sister of the King of Bohemia.

MS. Bibl. Reg. 13 E. ix.

Processum est perinde ad tractandum de regni Regisque negotiis in Parliamento præsenti; sed immoratum est inaniter in eodem diu, nec ad aliquem effectum quicquam productum, quamvis non sine magnis fuisset ibidem sumptibus demoratum. Et cum jam effectus aliquis successisse putaretur, supervenere nova de adventu novæ Reginæ Calesiam, sororis videlicet Regis Boemiæ, Wynceslai, filii quondam Regis Boemiæ et Imperatoris, qui et ipse expectavit in Imperatorem coronari, et se Imperatorem ubique litteraliter nominavit. Hanc igitur magno pretio, multisque [1] coemptam laboribus, habendam Rex præelegerat, quanquam cum inæstimabili auri summa oblata fuisset ei filia Domini Mediolanensis Barnabonis. Audito igitur, ut retulimus, de adventu Reginæ futuræ, solvitur Parliamentum, reincipiendum post regales nuptias et Natale Dominicum. Et insuper laborat unusquisque pro viribus tantas nuptias honorare muneribus, insuper et obsequiis favore dignis. Missum est ergo in obviam tantæ virgini, et conducitur cum omni gloria mundi ad portum usque Doveriæ, comitantibus eam multis nobilibus, tam suæ patriæ quam istius terræ.

King Richard refuses the daughter of the Duke of Milan.

Dissolution of Parliament, and preparations for the marriage.

Marvellous occurrence on the landing of the Princess at Dover.

Accidit illo die mirabile cunctis auspicium, juxta multorum opinionem, favorem Dei, felicia fata terræ affutura præmonstrans. Nam cum pedem terræ intulisset e navi, et salvo cunctis egressis, navigio reliquo, secuta est e vestigio tanta maris commotio, quanta diu ante visa non fuerat; et ipsas naves in portu constitutas adeo agitavit, ut dissiparentur subito et colliderentur, navi prius, in qua Regina consederat, dissoluta, et in multas partes horribiliter comminuta.

Varying opinions concerning it.

Quidam vero aliter interpretati sunt supradicta, putantes esse futurum, ut regnum turbaretur per eam, vel regioni incommodum aliquod eveniret. Sed istius dubiæ perplexitatis obscuritatem gesta sequentia declarabunt.

Dux Britanniæ, comminatus a Britonibus, dimittit Anglos.

A.D. 1382. Anno Dominicæ Incarnationis millesimo trecentesimo octogesimo secundo, qui est annus regni Ricardi Regis, a Conquæstu Secundi, quintus,—circa præsens tempus Britones in Armorica Britannia, indignati quod Anglici in tanto con-

[1] *peremptam* in orig. and the printed texts; corrected from Bibl. Reg. 13 E. ix.

MS. Bibl. Reg. 13 E. ix.

A.D. 1382.

stituti essent honore penes dominum suum, Ducem Britanniæ, versi in seditionem, convenerunt adversus dominum eorundem; imperiose mandarunt, ut, dimissis a suo famulatu cunctis Anglicis, tantummodo gauderet ipsorum obsequiis, scilicet Britonum; vel mortem inferrent eisdem, insuper et ab ejus obsequiis cuncti Britones [1]desciverent. Igitur Dux, in arcto constitutus, convocatis de familia sua Anglicis, enarrat dolenter instans periculum, et, licet [2]invitus, a sua terra quantocius universos jubet abire. Conturbati vero et conterriti super audita Angli, cum omni festinatione parant indemnes abscedere, ne fortassis eis queant deteriora contingere incolarum malitia dictæ terræ.

The Bretons demand of their Duke the dismissal of the English in his service.

Audiens Anglorum recessum repentinum Dominus de Clisson, et causam diligenter inquirens et agnoscens, nam et ipse reconciliatus erat Duci, vehementer irascitur contra auctores recessus Anglorum, et, convocatis tam militibus quam armigeris, cæteris quoque quos novit in hac causa peccasse, quærit cujusmodi auctoritate id efficere præsumpserunt, ut a Duce, suo domino, removerent viros domino suo fidelissimos, et qui ultra nationes alias suis dominis decenter obsequi et placere sciverunt, et eis reverentiam omnem impendere [3][et] commodum providere. "Nullus," inquit, "vestrum tanto honore dominum suum colere, affectu tanto diligere, tantæ humanitatis obsecundatione venerari, novit, ut Anglici, quos invidia pleni, in vituperium domini vestri, atque dedecus, abjecistis. Quapropter redire sinatis ad domini vestri solatium, quos, ad ejus tædium, amovistis, et eidem eos pacifice deservire permittite; aut, Deum testor, superbissimos e vobis faciemus suspendio [4]strangulari." Quibus dictis, mittit qui revocarent familiam ejectam, præhabitis officiis iterum gavisuram; sed frustra, quia jam plures ad Angliam transfretaverant, et relicti fuerunt pauci admodum, qui, deficiente navigio sive vento, post socios remanserunt: quos revocatos iterum restituit Curiæ domini sui Ducis.

De Clisson interferes on behalf of the English.

Most of the English take their departure, but some few of them are recalled.

Regales Nuptiæ.

Post festum Epiphaniæ convenit Londonias universa regni nobilitas, ad interessendum regalibus nuptiis, et obsequium

---

[1] *disciverent* in orig.

[2] *invitis* in the printed texts.

[3] Supplied from Bibl. Reg 13 E. ix.; omitted in the printed texts.

[4] *strangulari* in orig. and the printed texts; corrected from Bibl. Reg. 13 E. ix.

A.D. 1382. deferendum juxta consuetudinem a quolibet antiquitus usitatam. Benedicitur apud Westmonasterium Imperialis puella in sponsatam regiam; a Domino Cantuariensi Archiepiscopo in Reginam cum gloria et honore coronatur. MS. Bibl. Reg. 13 E. ix.

Celebration of the royal nuptials; and Coronation of the Queen.

Hastiludia quoque fiunt pro magnificentia tantæ celebritatis, per dies aliquot; in quibus et Angli et virtutem suam, et patriotæ Reginæ suam probitatem, publice demonstrarent. In quibus, non sine damno personarum utriusque partis, laus est acquisita, et rei commendatio militaris.

Parliamentum nuper solutum incipitur.

Parliament resumes its sittings.

Expletis nuptiarum solemniis, incipitur Parliamentum, quod omissum prædiximus propter causas præmissas; in quo plures articuli sunt propositi et decreti, videlicet, de extraneis admittendis ad vendendum personaliter, sine impedimento mercatorum Angliæ, libere sua mercimonia: de abrogatione pelluræ et apparatus argenti in zonis etc., a communibus status inferioris: de pretio [1] vinis apposito, videlicet [2] quod dolium non [3] excederet sex marcas. Multa sunt et alia, quæ statuta sunt ibidem. Sed quid juvant Statuta Parliamentorum, cum penitus expost nullum sortiantur effectum? Rex nempe, cum Privato Consilio, cuncta vel mutare vel delere solebat, quæ in Parliamentis antehabitis tota regni non solum communitas, sed et ipsa nobilitas, statuebat.

The King changes or abrogates the decrees of Parliament.

Statute to empower the summary arrest of insurgents.

Editum est et ibi Statutum contra communitatem in posterum insurgentem, ut, non expectato alieno suffragio, videlicet brevi regio, fideles regni, ubicunque viderent rusticos vel communes [4] accitare suspecta consiliabula, senos aut septenos, eos capere foret eis licitum, et in custodia detinere.

Comes Suthfolciæ obiit morte repentina.

Sudden death of William Ufforde, Earl of Suffolk.

Comes Sowthfolciæ, Willelmus Ufforde, in isto præsenti Parliamento, dum a militibus Comitatuum fuisset electus ad pronunciandum ex parte illorum negotia reipublicæ, die et hora quibus executus fuisset susceptum negotium, cum gradus ascendere incepisset ducentes ad cameram in qua regni nobilitas tota concesserat, repente corruit, et inter suorum manus illico spiritum exhalavit; quamvis jocundus et nihil mali sentiens Aulam Westmonasterii

[1] *vini sic apposito* in orig. and the printed texts; corrected from Bibl. Reg. 13 E. ix.

[2] *quod* omitted in the printed texts.

[3] *excedere* in the printed texts.

[4] *excitare* in the printed texts.

MS. Bibl. Reg. 13 E. ix.

A.D. 1382.

parum ante, et velut immediate, subintrasset. De cujus morte subitanea non parum consternati sunt, non tantum cuncti regni proceres, sed et omnes mediocres et pauperes, quia cunctis se in omni vita amabilem exhibuerat. Post cujus mortem, finis est impositus Parliamento; postquam mercatores Angliæ concessissent Regi pro subsidio consuetudines lanarum iterum, quas "*maltot*" vulgares appellant, per quadriennium expost sequens. Ordinatus est etiam in hoc Parliamento, petentibus hoc magnatibus et communibus, Ricardus Scrop, miles, Cancellarius, utpote vir qui spectabili scientia et inflexibili justitia non haberet ex sua fortuna parem in regno. Ad officium vero Thesaurarii Dominus Hugo Segrave, miles, subrogatur.

Consternation caused thereby.

Richard Scrop appointed Chancellor, and Hugh Segrave Treasurer.

Per idem tempus Comes Marchiæ, Dominus Edmundus de Mortuo Mari, in Hibernia concessit in fata, postquam illam terram totam pene perduxisset ad pacem, et nobilissime et sapientissime gubernasset.

Death of the Earl of March.

Circa dies istos, Magister Willelmus Courtenay, Episcopus Londoniensis, transfertur ad Archiepiscopatum Cantuariensem, et Magister Robertus Braybrok effectus est Londoniensis.

Ecclesiastical preferments.

Carolus coronatur a Papa in Regem Neapolis.

Circa tempus illud, Karolus de Pace, de quo superius pauca præstrinximus, post coronatus est a Domino Papa in Regem Terræ Laboris, [1][id est], Neapolis, [2]intravit in manu forti, possessurus terram illam, et, nemine resistente, pervenit in pace Neapolim, civitatem metropolitanam regni, ubi cum honore decenti a civibus est susceptus; et, ut successus corresponderent ei juxta Domini Papæ vaticinium, dicentis in quodam Sermone habito ad populum ejusdem Karoli Pacis;—"Est tibi, fili carissime, non [3]abs re cognomen [4]indictum, "quoniam proficisceris in pace, et pax erit tibi in ingressu tuo, "pax in progressu, et pacis successione gaudebis,"—in terra illa redditæ sunt ei pacifice, sine cujusquam belli tumultu vel dispendio, urbes Gaietana, Capua, Beneventum, Aversana, et plures aliæ, quarum nomina non tenemus. Et illa meretrix magna quæ sedit super aquas multas, et vocabatur "Regina "Neapolis," a facie formidinis Karoli et ejus exercitus, fugit in castellum urbis ejusdem, quod vocatur "Castrum "Novum;" quam mox Karolus obsidere curavit, et protelavit obsidionem quadraginta et duobus diebus. Igitur quadra-

Charles of Durazzo takes possession of the throne of Naples.

Queen Joanna takes to flight.

---

[1] Supplied from Bibl. Reg. 13 E. ix.: omitted in the printed texts.

[2] *quam intravit* in the printed texts.

[3] *ab* in orig; *abs* in the printed texts.

[4] *inditum* in the printed texts.

A.D. 1382.

MS. Bibl. Reg. 13 E. ix.

gesimo [1] [secundo] die obsidionis præfatæ, insultum fecit asperrimum ad castellum. Et cum maxime desudaret ipse, et suus exercitus, ad perturbandum castellanos, et castellum violenter occupandum, repente supervenit, a tergo Karoli et ipsius exercitus intromissus in urbem, mediante proditione, Dominus Otto de Brouneswiche, maritus prædictæ Reginæ, cum Marco de Monte Ferrando et armatorum copiosa turba, ad irruendum in Karolum, et succurrendum Reginæ.

Otho of Brunswick, and others, hasten to her rescue.

Erat tunc in exercitu Karoli quidam miles, dictus "Jomitus," qui et ipse princeps erat exercitus, vir utique et in bellis providus et manu promptus. Hic repente sentiens dolum proditorum et periculum quod imminebat, partem exercitus locat ad muros, quæ castellanos prohiberet ab irruptionibus, dum manus consereret pars exercitus altera cum Ottone; cui mox obviatum est cum audacia a Karolo et Jomito, et pugnatum est atrocissime, donec hostilis exercitus dissipatus et victus est, plurimis occisis et multis captis. In qua pugna peremptus est Marcus de Monte Ferrando, et Otto de Brouneswiche letaliter vulneratus et captus. Quem confestim Reginæ monstrantes, minabantur in machina positum projecturos ad illam in castellum, nisi mox reddere vellet illud. Sed tamen, nocte superveniente, non fecerunt ita. Igitur Regina, nocte illa tractatum cum suis faciens, in crastino se reddidit, et castellum, in quo repertæ sunt divitiæ infinitæ. Capta autem in custodia servabatur, donec Karolus, cum Domini Papæ consilio, deliberaret quid agendum esset de persona sua. Captus est in eodem castello, cum Regina, Comes Cancellarius, cum Comite Camberlano et multis aliis, quos longum foret per singulos nominare. Hoc modo parata est pax Karolo de Pace, et paratum est regnum in conspectu ejus.

They are defeated.

Joanna is taken prisoner.

Report that Joanna had become a nun.

[2] Ferunt quidam, quod Regina, post captionem suam, mediantibus utriusque partis amicis, Papa sic volente et Karolo permittente, ingressa sit religionem monialium quæ de Ordine Sancti Francisci sunt, et "Minorissæ" vocantur; quæ si consecutura sit de tanta perfectione meritum, novit Deus, cui omne cor patet.

Propositiones Septem Magistri Johannis Wicliff.

Adversarius fidei Christianæ, hæresiarcha recordationis execrabilis, Johannes Wiclif, sollicitus pervertere tam majores quam minores regionis incolas suis nequam adinventionibus,

[1] Supplied from Bibl. Reg. 13 E. ix.; omitted in the printed texts.

[2] *Fuerunt* in Camden's text. In reality, Joanna was put to death, in 1382.

MS. Bibl. Reg. 13 E. ix.

suas damnabiles opiniones, modo per se, modo per sequaces suos, modo scriptis, modo prædicationibus, per totum tempus illud dilatare contendit. Et quia minus satisfaciebat ejus affectui, prædicationibus in vulgari plebe inexecrabiliter declamatis, scribit ad dominos et magnates, qui, circa festum Sancti Johannis ante Portam Latinam, Londonias ad Parliamentum coadunati fuerant, machinationes novas, quibus et illos allicere [1] possit, et in errorem trahere, sub hiis verbis. Modum ponemus præmissum, ut in ejus sedula scribitur. Erat nempe ista præscriptio:— A.D. 1382.

Wyclif addresses certain Propositions to the Lords of England.

"*Magistri Johannis Wiclif Septem Interpretationes, ad tutelam regni Angliæ per ejus proceres exequendæ.*—

The Seven Propositions, so addressed.

1. "Quod Rex aut regnum nulli sedi vel prælato obediat, " nisi de quanto ex fide Scripturæ sonat in obedientiam Jesu " Christo. Patet,—quia aliter [2] præponeretur Christo in " obedientia Antichristus; omnis enim obedientia quæ non fit " Christo, fit Antichristo; quia Lucæ [3] Secundo, 'Qui non est " 'mecum, etc.'"

2. "Quod nec Curiæ Romanæ, nec Avinonicæ, nec alicui " exteræ, emittatur regni pecunia, nisi doceatur hoc esse " debitum ex Scriptura Sacra. Patet,—quia aliter foret " rapina lupi rapacis. [4] Quia Christus [5] Matthæo dicit esse a " fructibus [6] cognoscendam.

3. "Quod nec [7] Cardinalis, nec alius, habeat fructum " ecclesiæ vel præbendæ de Anglia, nisi vel rite resideat, " vel occupetur legitime in causa regni a proceribus rationa- " biliter approbata. Patet,—quia aliter non intraret per " Christum, sed aliunde ascenderet, ut Antichristi discipulus, " et per traditiones sæculi tanquam latro prædaretur reg- " num in subjectis pauperibus, sine æquivalentia pecuniæ " recompensæ.

4. "Quod Rex et regnum tenentur destruere regni prodi- " tores, et suos a ferocibus inimicis defendere.

5. "Quod regni communitas non oneretur tallagiis insuetis, " antequam totum patrimonium, quo clerus dotatur, deficiat.

[1] *posset* in the printed texts.

[2] *proponetur* in the printed texts.

[3] Apparently a wrong reference, *Matt.* xii. 30, being the passage alluded to.

[4] *Quam Christus Matthæi* in orig.; *quam Christi Matth.* in the printed texts: corrected from Bibl. Reg. 13 E. ix.

[5] *Matt.* vii. 16, 20.

[6] *cognoscendum* in the printed texts. The passage seems to be imperfect.

[7] *Cardinales* in orig.; corrected from the printed texts.

A.D. 1382. "Patet,—quia omnia ista sunt bona pauperum, caritative exponenda ad eorum [1]egentiam, vivente clero in perfectione primariæ paupertatis. MS. Bibl. Reg. 13 E. ix.

6. "Quod quocunque Episcopo vel curato dotato de Anglia "in contemptum Dei notorie incidente, nedum liceat Regi, "sed teneatur, sua temporalia confiscare. Patet,—quia aliter "regnum postponeret [2]Christianum, Regis, domini temporalis, "contemptum ponderans plus quam [3]Christi.

7. "Quod Rex nullum Episcopum vel curatum mancipiet "suo ministerio sæculari. Patet,—tam Rex quam clerus foret "proditor [4]Domini Jesu Christi."

Aliæ Propositiones Johannis Wicliff.

Other Propositions of Wyclif.

"Quod Rex nullum, propter moram in excommunicatione, "incarceret, antequam secundum legem Dei mora ista sit "docta esse illicita. Patet,—quia sæpe excommunicantur "multi improvide, ubi, secundum legem Dei et Ecclesiæ, "debeant excommunicationes perpetue tolerare: auctorizare "incarcerationem hominis propter hoc quod facit, [5]ut debet, "[6]foret opus dæmonii meridiani. Contraria autem istorum, "licet sint insensibilia non curata, tamen nimis confundunt "rempublicam, quia res insensibiles parvipensæ sunt maximæ "in vigore.

And other Conclusions.

Ut autem periculosius haberet auditores suos, scripsit eo tempore, et publicavit, [7]et alias Conclusiones, ab omni Ecclesia anathematizandas; et sunt [8]istæ:—

"[9]Substantia panis manet post consecrationem, et substantia "panis post consecrationem est corpus Christi.

"Deus de potentia sua absoluta non potest facere quod in "Sacramento altaris essent accidentia sine subjecto.

"[10]Nulla hæresis vel falsitas in tota doctrina Magistri "Johannis Wiclif poterit probari.

"Deus debet obedire diabolo.

---

[1] *agentiam* in orig. and the printed texts: corrected from Bibl. Reg. 13 E. ix.

[2] *Christum* in the printed texts.

[3] *viginti* in orig. and the printed texts; from ignorance of the meaning of the abbreviation in Bibl. Reg. 13 E. ix.

[4] *Domini* omitted in the printed texts.

[5] *et* in orig. and the printed texts; corrected from Bibl. Reg. 13 E. ix.

[6] *fore* in the printed texts. The meaning of this passage is anything but obvious.

[7] *et* omitted in the printed texts.

[8] *isti* in orig, by inadvertence.

[9] See the *Fasciculi Zizaniorum*, p. 203.

[10] This Conclusion is omitted in the printed texts.

MS. Bibl. Reg. 13 E. ix.

A.D. 1382

"Papa plus tenetur Imperatori quam e converso.

"Omnes monachi de Ordine Sancti Benedicti, nolentes labore "manuum victum adquirere, non solum [1] non sunt apostatæ "ab Ordine Sancti Benedicti, sed, quod verius est, a discipu-"latu Christi.

"Nullus est dominus [2] civilis, nullus Episcopus, nullus est "Prælatus, dum est in peccato mortali.

"Si Ordines Fratrum essent certi, et in Christo fundati, "non quærerent confirmationem a Papa.

"Ubi leges humanæ non fundantur in Scriptura Sacra, sub-"diti non tenentur obedire."

Emissaries sent forth by Wyclif to preach his doctrines.

Has delirationes execrabiles posuit idem Johannes ea vice; sed, ad damnationis suæ cumulum, emisit viros apostatas, de fide Catholica pessime sentientes, ad dogmatizandum et prædicandum et alias Conclusiones periculosissimas, quas audiens quisque fidelis, merito tinnirent aures ejus. Inter quos erat quidam vultum et habitum præferens heremitæ, veniens equidem in vestimentis ovium, sed intrinsecus erat lupus rapax. Hic, emissus per dictum Johannem, publice prædicavit Leycestriæ, Dominica in Ramis Palmarum, abominationes istas.—

[3] *Conclusiones Johannis Wicliff.*

Conclusions of Wyclif promulgated at Leicester.

"Prima Conclusio. Quod homines qui dimittunt audire "verbum Dei et Evangelium prædicatum, propter excommuni-"cationes hominum, sunt excommunicati, et in die judicii tra-"ditores Dei habebuntur; et etiam illi qui dimittunt prædicare "propter talem excommunicationem.

2. "Excommunicatio, quæ datur ad impediendum homines "audire verbum Dei, excommunicatio Antichristi est, et non "Christiani.

3. "Quod nullus Prælatus debet excommunicare aliquem, "nisi prius sciat ipsum excommunicatum a Deo; et si quis "aliter aliquem excommunicaverit, ipse excommunicatus est, "et hæreticus.

4. "Nullus debet aliquem excommunicare, nisi ex caritate, "et pro salute animæ suæ.

---

[1] This word is evidently inserted erroneously; but it appears in Bibl. Reg. 13 E. ix., and the printed texts.

[2] *simul* in orig. and the printed texts; corrected from Bibl. Reg. 13 E. ix.

[3] In place of this, the rubric in Bibl. Reg. 13 E. ix. is as follows:— "*Conclusiones quas publice prædicavit Willelmus Swynderby Leycestriæ.*"

A.D. 1382. 5. "Prælatus excommunicans clericum, qui appellat ad "Regem et Consilium regni, eo ipso traditor Dei est, et regis, "[1][et] regni. MS. Bibl. Reg. 13 E. ix.

6. "Prælati Ecclesiæ adquirunt beneficia sua per aurum, "et sic sunt simoniaci et hæretici.

7. "Contra antiquam legem est, et etiam contra novam, "quod viri ecclesiastici habeant possessiones temporales.

8. "Nunquam erit bona pax et plenaria in regno isto, quo-"usque ista temporalia auferantur a viris ecclesiasticis."—Et ideo rogabat populum, manibus extensis, ut unusquisque adjuvaret in ista materia, quantum posset.

9. "Quod viri ecclesiastici, dummodo vixerint in divitiis "et voluptatibus, sicut jam vivitur, sunt inhabiles ad orandum "pro populo, pro quo fine fuerunt principaliter ordinati.

10. "Si Rex haberet in manu sua temporalia ecclesiasti-"corum, non oporteret eum tunc accipere tallagia, nec com-"munitatem regni spoliare.

11. "Beatus Paulus adquisivit victum pro se et discipulis "suis, suis manibus; et sic deberent religiosi manibus suis "laborare, et non publice mendicare.

12. "Quod [2]istæ novæ sectæ, quæ quasi hesterno die vene-"runt, asserunt vitam suam perfectiorem quam religionem "Christi communem, et Apostolorum, et volunt sic facere "Christum fatuum.

13. "Quod Sacramentum altaris, post consecrationem, est "verus panis et verum corpus Christi; et illa rotunditas quæ "videtur, et albedo, et hujusmodi, sunt panis; et hæc est sen-"tentia Apostoli, Doctorum antiquorum, et Sanctorum, et in "ista materia Doctores novelli vel contradicunt inter se, vel "non dant sufficientem hujus Sacramenti descriptionem.

14. "Religiosi prædicantes, qui nolunt dicere populo et "scribere veram descriptionem hujus Sacramenti, et fidem "fundatam in Evangelio et Sacra Scriptura, sunt excommuni-"cati et hæretici; et si quis talibus eleemosynam suam de-"derit, ipse est fautor illorum, et cum ipsis excommunicatus; "et quod fratres verecundantur dicere fidem suam de Sacra-"mento Altaris."

Confirmatione autem omnium dictorum suorum, dixit quod hæc est fides quam debent habere ex Evangelio et dictis Apostolorum; et si quis oppositum prædictorum diceret vel prædicaret, quod nullo modo esset ei credendum.

Hæc et multa alia erronea dixit publice, et prædicavit idem

---

[1] Supplied from Bibl. Reg. 13 E. ix.; omitted in the printed texts.

[2] *si istæ* in Camden's text.

MS. Bibl. Reg. 13 E. ix.

A.D. 1382.

zizaniæ seminator, in detrimentum Ecclesiæ et fidei orthodoxæ. Nec suffecit huic [1]Diei malitia sua, nisi ut et apponeret iterum in die Sanctæ Parasceues prædicare nequitiam inauditam in eodem loco, rectoribus ecclesiarum non valentibus prohibere eum, [2]ob favorem popularem; qui libentissime eum audiebant, et se periculo malebant exponere pro eodem, antequam vel prohiberetur prædicare, aut quicquam contra eum per viam juris tentaretur. Revera loquebatur eis placentia, et quicquid proferre noverat in derogationem prælatorum, detractionem magnatum; quæ vulgus commune solet libenter audire, lingua protulit venenata, captans per singula verba sermonis sui favorem, laudem quoque vulgi; callide commentis talibus seducens et decipiens populum imprudentem.

Further proceedings of Wyclif's emissary (Swynderby) at Leicester.

Unde postea contigit, cum Episcopus Lincolniensis eum correxisse parasset, et ab eo facultatem prædicandi tulisse, sæviens turba demens Episcopum adeo deterrebat, ut nihil auderet agere contra eum. Ad notitiam igitur posterorum, ut cognoscant quantum nostris temporibus prævaleret inimicus, et impune debacchatus fuerit, Conclusiones, vel potius "Abu-"siones," quas in Die Parasceues, ubi supra, proclamavit, huic paginæ inseremus.—

Manifestations of the populace in his favour.

[3] *Conclusiones in Die Parasceues.*

Conclusions promulgated at Leicester, on the Parasceve (Good Friday).

1. "Quod si parochiani sciverint curatum eorum incon-"tinentem esse, et malum, debent subtrahere ab eo decimas; "et alias, sunt fautores criminis, et consentientes ejus malis "operibus.

2. "Quod decimæ sunt puræ eleemosynæ, et in casu quo "curati fuerint mali, possunt licite eas aliis conferre.

3. "Quod homines possunt debita ex caritate petere, sed "nullo modo propter debita aliquem incarcerare.

4. "Quod curatus malus subditos excommunicans pro deci-"marum detentione, non est nisi pecuniam ab eis indebite et "male extorqueri.

5. "Si aliquis capellanus, vel compatres aut commatres "infantium puerorum, temporibus quibus hujusmodi pueros "seu infantes baptizaverunt et levaverunt de sacro fonte, "fuerint in aliquo mortali peccato detenti, infans hujusmodi,

---

[1] *dei* in orig., by inadvertence; corrected from the printed texts.

[2] *ad* in orig.: corrected from the printed texts.

[3] "*Abominationes quas idem in* "*eodem loco proclamavit, in die Pa*-"*rasceues.*"—Rubric in Bibl. Reg. 13 E. ix.

A.D. 1382. "sive puer, non est baptizatus, nec [1] recipit tempore hujusmodi "Sacramentum baptismi. MS. Bibl. Reg. 13 E. ix.

6. "Quicunque Episcopus conferens alicui sacros ordines "presbyteratus,—hujusmodi [2] persona taliter ordinata non est "presbyter ratione collationis hujusmodi sibi factæ, nisi sit "[3] [et esset electus] a Deo."

7. Item, idem dixit publice et expresse, in prædicatione sua coram Majori Leycestriæ et multis aliis, quod Deus nunquam constituit Missam celebrari; et quod bonum esset istis temporibus ut pauciores Missæ celebrarentur quam celebrantur.

8. Item dixit publice et expresse, coram Vicario de [4] Frisby, Decano de Gosecote, et multis aliis, in prædicatione sua, quod quicunque parochianus dans decimas suo curato, sciens ipsum in mortali peccato, vel tenere aliquam mulierem suspectam publice vel occulte, quod ipse conferens decimas hujusmodi curato suo, manutenet ipsum in peccato suo hujusmodi, et est particeps criminis ejusdem.

9. Item dixit, quod sacræ Canones sunt traditiones humanæ.

10. Item, idem Willelmus dixit publice et expresse in prædicatione sua Leycestriæ, quod scivit bene quod illud quod tractabatur in altari, fuit Corpus Dominicum; sed, ut asseruit, scivit plus dixisse de ista materia, si voluisset: et sic per hujusmodi verba sua, per eum prolata, nequiter et perplexe indicata simplici populo Christiano, eosdem Christi fideles fecit per sua erronea multipliciter deviare, et de fide Catholica desperare; et, quod deterius est, omnes laicos de ipsa patria a tramite justitiæ et veritatis quasi penitus declinare; Diœcesano, ut retulimus, timore turbæ, cui quam maxime complacuere sermones ejus, quicquam contra eum agere non audente.

N. Hertford et quidam Canonicus Leicestriæ, discipuli et sequaces Johannis Wicliff.

Supporters of Wyclif in the University of Oxford, and elsewhere.

Fuerunt eo tempore et plures alii hujus nefandæ doctrinæ sequaces et discipuli; qui prædicaverunt et ista et plura alia magis enormia, non in quibuscunque villis aut civitatibus, sed in ipsa Universitate Oxoniæ, profestis diebus, Cancellario pro tunc, [5] [Magistro Roberto Rugge, favente, et hujus sectæ discipulo

[1] *recepit* in orig. and in the printed texts: corrected from Bibl. Reg. 13 E. ix.

[2] *personaliter ordinata* in orig., *personaliter ordinatus* in the printed texts; corrected from Bibl. Reg. 13 E. ix.

[3] *et cesset a Deo* in orig., *sit electus a Deo* in the printed texts: corrected from Bibl. Reg. 13 E. ix.

[4] *Fusby* in the printed texts.

[5] Supplied from Bibl. Reg. 13 E. ix.: omitted in the printed texts.

MS. Bibl. Reg. 13 E. ix.

A.D. 1382.

existente. Inter quos plus fuere notabiles,] Magister Nicholaus Herford, acerrimus sectator Johannis Wiclif, et quidam Canonicus Leycestriæ, et alii qui non ascenderant per ostium in ovile scholarum, sed aliunde, potestate magnatum, contra fratrum suorum et Abbatis proprii voluntatem.

Other doctrines promulgated by them.

Hii omnes, et plures alii ex eorum complicibus, peccatum suum, quasi Sodoma, prædicaverunt, nec absconderunt; nec suffecit [1] eis solis male sentire de fide Catholica, aut de cæteris in quibus errabant Articulis, nisi publicis prædicationibus traherent in suæ pravitatis devium Christi fideles. Ex quibus ille Canonicus Leycestriæ, ut pateret quam imperfecte vivendi normam [2] didicerat ex doctrina Sanctorum, asseruit in quadam prædicatione, [3] se solummodo laudare suum Ordinem, ex hoc quod cæteris Ordinibus erat propior et conformior vitæ sæculari. Qui ut erat in cæremoniis propior, optabat ut [4] et in habitu conformis esset; hoc solum eis deesse ad gradum perfectionis asseruit, quod in habitu essent sæcularibus disconformes. Monachorum vitam et aliorum religiosorum [5] imperfectiorem esse dicebat, quod pluribus observantiis astringebantur.

Archiepiscopus rem agit cum Coepiscopis de Conclusionibus Wicleff.

The Archbishop of Canterbury takes cognizance of the doctrines of Wyclif.

Hiis clamoribus excitatus Dominus Cantuariensis, Magister Willelmus Çourtenay, ut erat vir, ut creditur, spiritu Dei plenus, non passus est tantas nequitias habenas liberas possidere, sed mox, ut erat in Christum Domini consecratus, ut doceret sibi non justitiam [6] Phinees, sed facultatem, hactenus defuisse, in refrænandis animis irruentibus et [7] infrænatis, convocatis fratribus suis Suffraganeis, tractat de malitia temporis, edicit miseriam, et conqueritur de filiis [8] perditionis, qui, sinu foti Matris Ecclesiæ, conantur discerpere matrem suam. Tandem post tractatum habitum, auditis quorundam super ista re sententiis, deliberat penes se vel tot enormitates ad rectam regulam retorquere, vel caput exponere pro causa Dei. Disposuit ergo primum, adhibitis quibusdam Coepiscopis, qui post Baalim non abierunt, et pluribus de Sacræ Paginæ Professoribus, diversitates lepræ

---

[1] *scholis male* in the printed texts.

[2] *didiceret* in orig., by inadvertence.

[3] *sua se* in the printed texts.

[4] *et* omitted in Camden's text.

[5] *imperfectionem* in the printed texts.

[6] *Finees* in orig. and Bibl. Reg. 13 E. ix. The allusion is, probably, to *Psalm* cvi. 30.

[7] *infrunitis* in orig. and Bibl. Reg. 13. E. ix: *infrænatis* in the printed texts.

[8] *proditionis* in the printed texts.

A.D. 1382. discutere, [1]quia [2]respersæ erant oves erraticæ, et, diligenter inspectis opinionibus infirmis, discernere inter lepram et lepram. Igitur aperiuntur in medium tantæ fœditatis ulcera, pastoris palpanda manibus, ejusque ministerio anathematis ignibus consumenda. Quæ seorsim singillatim ponemus, prout damnari meruerunt.— MS. Bibl. Reg. 13 E. ix.

Articuli Johannis Wicliff ab Archiepiscopo, etc., damnati.

Doctrines of Wyclif condemned by the Archbishop of Canterbury.

1. [3]"Quod substantia panis materialis et vini maneat post "consecrationem in [4]Sacramento altaris.

2. "Quod accidentia non maneant sine subjecto post consecrationem in eodem [4]Sacramento.

3. "Quod Christus non sit in [4]Sacramento altaris identice, "vere, et realiter, in propria præsentia corporali.

4. "Quod si Episcopus, vel sacerdos, existat in peccato mortali, non ordinat, conficit, nec baptizat.

5. "Quod si homo fuerit debite contritus, omnis confessio "exterior est sibi superflua vel inutilis.

6. [5]Quod pertinaciter asserere "non esse fundatum in Evan-"gelio quod Christus Missam ordinaverit."

7. [6]"Quod [[7]Deus] debeat obedire diabolo.

8. "Quod si Papa sit [8]præscitus et malus homo, ac, per "consequens, membrum diaboli, non habet potestatem supra "fideles Christi ab aliquo sibi datam, nisi forte a Cæsare.

9. "Quod post Urbanum Sextum non est aliquis recipiendus "in Papam, sed vivendum est more Græcorum sub propriis "legibus."

10. Asserere "quod est contra Sacram Scripturam, quod "viri ecclesiastici habeant possessiones temporales."

Notatis gravioribus culpis, Dominus Archiepiscopus consequenter descendit ad minores, ut evellat et destruat, dissipet

---

[1] *quia* in orig.; *quibus* in the printed texts: corrected from Bibl. Reg. 13 E. ix.

[2] *respersi* in orig., by inadvertence.

[3] See the *Fasciculi Zizaniorum*, p. 493.

[4] *sacrosancto* in orig. and the printed texts; corrected from Bibl. Reg. 13 E. ix., the abbreviation in which is evidently meant for "*sacramento*."

[5] This word is superfluous; it is omitted in the printed texts, but is found in Bibl. Reg. 13 E. ix.

[6] *Quod debent* in orig. and the printed texts.

[7] Supplied from Bibl. Reg. 13 E. ix.; omitted in the printed texts.

[8] *præstitis* in orig.; *præstigiator* in the printed texts; *præscitus* in Bibl. Reg. 13 E. ix., and *Fasc. Zizan.* p. 494.

MS. Bibl. Reg. 13. E. ix.

A.D. 1382.

Doctrines of minor importance so condemned.

et disperdat, quæ filius perditionis seminaverat omnia scandala in regno Dei; quæ partim hic inferius annotantur.—

1. "Quod nullus Prælatus debet aliquem excommunicare, "nisi prius sciat ipsum excommunicatum a Deo.

2. "Item, quod sic excommunicans, ex hoc sit hæreticus "vel excommunicatus.

3. "Quod Prælatus excommunicans clericum, qui appellavit "ad Regem et Consilium regni, eo ipso traditor est Dei, et "regis, et [1] regni.

4. "Item, qui dimittunt prædicare, seu audire, verbum Dei, "vel Evangelium prædicatum, propter excommunicationem "hominum, sunt excommunicati, et in die judicii traditores "Dei habebuntur."

5. Asserere quod "licet alicui, diacono vel presbytero, prædicare verbum Dei absque auctoritate Sedis Apostolicæ, vel "Episcopi Catholici, seu alia de qua sufficienter constet.

6. [2] "Quod domini temporales possunt, ad arbitrium eorum, "auferre bona temporalia ab ecclesiasticis habitualiter delin-"quentibus; vel quod populares possunt, ad arbitrium eorum, "delinquentes corrigere.

7. "Quod decimæ sunt puræ eleemosynæ, et quod paro-"chiani possunt, propter peccata suorum curatorum, eas "detinere, et ad libitum aliis conferre.

8. "Quod speciales orationes applicatæ uni personæ per "prælatos vel religiosos, non plus prosint eidem personæ, "quam generales orationes eidem, cæteris paribus.

9. "Eo ipso quod aliquis ingreditur religionem privatam "quamcunque, redditur ineptior et inhabilior ad observantiam "mandatorum Dei.

10. "Quod Sancti instituentes religiones quascunque pri-"vatas, tam possessionatorum quam mendicantium, in sic "instituendo peccaverunt.

11. "Quod religiosi viventes in religionibus privatis, non "sunt de religione Christiana.

12. "Quod fratres teneantur per laborem manuum, et non "per mendicationem, victum suum adquirere."—Error damnatus ab Alexandro Papa Quarto.[3]

---

[1] *regem* in orig.; corrected from the printed texts.

[2] A Conclusion, as given in the *Fascic. Zizan.*, is omitted here:—"*Quod nullus est dominus civilis,* "*nullus est Episcopus, nullus est Prælatus, dum est in mortali peccato.*"

[3] Another Conclusion, according to the *Fascic. Zizan.* (p. 497) is omitted here:—"*Quod conferens* "*eleemosynam Fratribus, vel Fratri* "*Prædicanti, est excommunicatus, et* "*recipiens.*"

Archiepiscopus Cantuariensis mittit mandatum suum Cancellario Oxoniensi contra Articulos prædictos.

A.D. 1382. The Archbishop sends a mandate thereupon to the Chancellor of Oxford, who disregards it.

MS. Bibl. Reg. 13 E. ix.

Damnatis prædictis Conclusionibus hæreticis et erroneis a Domino Archiepiscopo et cœtu sapientium, consequenter idem Archiepiscopus mandatum mittit Cancellario Oxoniæ, Roberto Rugge, in quo declaravit damnationem, et mandavit, ut per se, vel per alium, easdem esse damnatas faceret publice declarari. Prohiberet insuper hæc, et cætera talia, vel in scholis communicari, vel in prædicationibus attrectari, de cætero; et eo effectualius [1]elaboraret in executione mandati sibi directi, quo Dominus Archiepiscopus posset aperte cognoscere eum nullatenus talibus erroribus maculatum, aut talium prædicatoribus adhærere. Sed dissimulari non potuit malitia præconcepta in corde suo, quin patenter foris ostenderet venenum quod in ejus animo firmaverat sibi sedem. Revera diebus solemnioribus, quibus ejus incumbebat officio sermones in populo facere, commisit onus verbi hiis quos scivit acerrimos Johannis Wiclif sectatores, spreto vel parvipenso Archipontificali mandato. Et quidem Philippo Rypyndone, præfato Canonico de Leycestria, sermonem dicendum assignavit in festo Corporis Christi; in quo sermone, inter multa quæ dixit abusiva, talia peroravit:—"In doctrina autem speculativa cujusmodi est "materia de Sacramento altaris, ponam," inquit, "custodiam ori "meo, donec Deus aliter illustraverit, sive instruxerit, corda "cleri." Factumque est, ut non [2][ad] emendationem malorum, sed augmentationem, idem Cancellarius mandato Archipræsulis uteretur, et ad irritationem paternæ patientiæ et lenitatis.

Philip Rypyndone's Sermon at Oxford.

The Chancellor, and others, are compelled to acknowledge their heresies and errors.

Quibus rebus nimirum Archiepiscopus exacerbatus, iterum recollecto cœtu Magistrorum, citari fecit expost prædictum Cancellarium, et cæteros [3]superius nominatos, ad respondendum de tanto contemptu coram eis publice, et declarandum quid de præmissis damnatis Articulis ipsi sentirent. Qui tandem, post multas tergiversationes, imponendo duplicem sensum in eisdem, et cavillationes diversas, coacti sunt, licet inviti, simpliciter proferre sentire suum de præmissis, facta prius protestatione, quod vellent et intenderent esse humiles et fideles filii, et Ecclesiæ in omnibus obedire, etc. Concesserunt igitur cunctas præmissas Conclusiones, intelligendo eas, prout verba sonant, fore vel hæreticas vel erroneas, juxta

---

[1] *laboraret* in the printed texts.

[2] Supplied from Bibl. Reg. 13 E. ix.: omitted in the printed texts.

[3] *superios* in orig., by inadvertence.

MS. Bibl. Reg. 13 E. ix. quod Dominus Archiepiscopus et Magistrorum cœtus, ut ante retulimus, plena deliberatione diffinierant de eisdem. A.D. 1382.

Comes Flandriæ expellitur de terra sua.

Comes Flandriæ circa dies istos expellitur cum dedecore grandi de terra sua; qui dum plus studet falsitati quam veritati, injustitiæ quam æquitati, sentit repente manum Domini aggravatum super eum. The Count of Flanders is expelled from his territories.

Revera Gandavenses, cum jam nullatenus eum fidem erga eos servaturum agnoscerent, nec eis more domini debito præfuturum, postquam multa mala eis latenter et aperte irrogasset, vindicari statuunt in eum et adhærentes sibi, si fortuna permittat. Quapropter in Die Inventionis Sanctæ Crucis, qui est dies celeberrimus in tota Flandria, dicti Gandavenses, latenter congregatis innumeris de communibus et stipendiariis [1] Selondensibus [2] et Estlondensibus, necnon [3] Brabantinis, et quibusdam Anglicis, hostiliter egressi sunt, et pene subito ad tertium milliarium a villa de Burges pervenerunt; ductore quodam Philippo den Arthfeld,—(Arta Villa,)—qui quondam consanguineus extitit Anglorum Reginæ Philippæ. Comes ergo, audiens de adventu Gandavensium, repente cum multis obviam est egressus. Bellum igitur est commissum inter eos atrocissimum, et cadunt hinc vicissim plurimi. Sed Burgenses [4] sensere totum pene dispendium, prostratis in brevi septem millibus ex eisdem. Cernens autem Comes partem suam totaliter infirmatam, et animos deficere reliquorum, concidit et ipse animo, et timide fugiendo festinat ad Burges; quem Gandavenses e vestigio insecuti sunt ad villam usque de Burges, et portas violenter effregerunt, et fossas, aqua repletas, levi negotio transierunt. Nam villa non munitur muro, sed [5] præ optimis fossis circumdatur, et profundis: et sic in villam velociter irruperunt. Impedimento erat eis paulisper fossarum transilitio, quibusdam de villa repugnantibus; cum interim qui in villa fuere, quinque bella licenter ordinaverunt contra eos, et intra villam locaverunt. Quæ pene sine difficultate vicerunt, dissipaverunt, et occiderunt, et Comitem in Franciam fugere compulerunt.

He is defeated by the people of Ghent and others.

He takes refuge in Bruges; which is captured.

The Count takes refuge in France.

---

[1] *Zelandensibus* in the printed texts.

[2] These two words are omitted in the printed texts.

[3] *Brabantis* in the printed texts.

[4] *censere* in orig. and Bibl. Reg. 13 E. ix.: *sensere* in the printed texts.

[5] *præ* omitted in the printed texts.

A.D. 1382. Bruges is sacked.

MS. Bibl. Reg. 13 E. ix.

Peracta tandem strage belli, ad cædes civium convertuntur. Discurrentes ergo per totam villam, scrutantur ubicunque locorum frequentatores istarum artium, videlicet piscariorum, pellipariorum, carnificum, et eorum quos "*macleres*" vocant lingua sua, qui mercedes recipiunt ex utraque parte pro negotiis expediendis: de quibus quosque repertos in ore gladii peremerunt. Excrevit autem numerus occisorum ad decem et septem millia virorum de Burges. Nonaginta vero de majoribus villæ de Burges captos Gandavum transmiserunt; veruntamen nulli mercatori extraneo nocuerunt, vel quicquam molestiæ intulerunt. Sed et Anglicis præcipue pepercerunt, adeo ut si quis convinceretur de bonis cujusquam Anglìci aliquid rapuisse, mox sine respectu misericordiæ capite plectebatur. Et cum cujusdam Anglici compotorium, quod [1] "*countour*" vocamus, esset confractum in prædicta deprædatione, et idem Anglicus de hoc deposuisset querelam capitaneo eorundem, cum interrogatus nesciret dicere quis hoc fecisset, capitaneus dedit ei equum suum, præcipiens ne de hac re ulterius quereretur; pro quo dictus Anglicus mox recepisse potuit octoginta florenos, cum resarcire damnum suum potuisset minus quam decem marcis.

Peculiar favour is shown to the English there.

Order is restored at Bruges.

Hiis itaque gestis, Gandavenses tam prudenter disposuerunt pro villa de Burges, ut infra triduum omnia mercimonia et mercata ibidem, quod mirum dictu est, non minus aperte et quiete tenerentur et frequentarentur, quam triduo vel quatriduo tenebantur ante conflictum. [2] Disposita villa more suo, Gandavenses regressi sunt Gandavum [3] cum multis spoliis et triumpho, mittentes ex eis qui sequerentur et obsiderent eos qui ad munitionem de Udenarde confugerant, et [4] eandem contra eos præsumpserant detinere. Fuerunt equidem nobiliores et valentiores milites et armigeri totius Flandriæ, et putabant, tum pro fortitudine loci, tum quia contigua est illa [5] munitio provinciis Galliarum, unde auxilium eis de facili ferri posse credebant, ibidem se fore salvandos. Igitur obsidione disposita, circumsederunt locum per totum tempus æstivale: quibus Comes Flandriæ, apud Sanctum Audomarum commorans, plura damna pluries irrogavit, ut subvenire posset obsessis.

Audenarde is besieged by the people of Ghent.

---

[1] *comitor* in orig. and the printed texts; *countour* in Bibl. Reg. 13. E. ix.

[2] *Deposita* in orig. and the printed texts; corrected from Bibl. Reg. 13 E. ix.

[3] *in multis* in the printed texts.

[4] *andem* in orig., by inadvertence.

[5] *inimico* in orig. and the printed texts: corrected from Bibl. Reg. 13 E. ix.

Parliamentum Lon̄dini.

MS. Bibl. Reg. 13 E. ix.

Circa festum Sancti Johannis ante Portam Latinam, convocati sunt ad Parliamentum Londonias cuncti majores regni, et qui de consuetudine vocari solebant, quamvis in Quadragesima præcedente factum fuisset aliud Parliamentum, prout supra scripsi. In quo, petitione militum Comitatuum, Johannes [1]Wraw, presbyter, qui ductor fuit eorum qui insurrexerant apud Bury et Mildenhale, tractioni et suspensioni adjudicatur; licet multi putassent eum fuisse [2]pecunia redimendum.

A.D. 1382. Parliament at London. John Wraw is condemned and executed.

Quidem nebulo Physicus, equo impositus, recepit mendacii mercedem.

Londoniis eo tempore, quidam nebulo, prætendens [3]se physicum et astrologum, proclamari per urbem fecerat, ne quisquam in Vigilia Dominicæ Ascensionis cubiculum suum exire præsumeret, antequam dixisset quinquies Orationem Dominicam, et comedendo solvisset jejunium, propter nebulam pestilentem quæ eo die superventura fuit. Rogaverat insuper se servari interim, et pœna plecti, fidens forte in fatuitate civium, si ipsum suum vaticinium fefellisset. Nam prædixit omnes subito morituros, qui secus quam ipse consulerat facturi essent. Plures igitur, parentes consilio ganeonis, eique credentes, eo die nec ad Missas audiendas processerunt, nec egredi voluerunt, priusquam illius diei jejunium violassent.

Punishment of an impostor, at London.

In crastino, cum mendacium latere non posset, captus est et equo impositus; equinaque cauda commissa suis manibus loco fræni, et duæ ollæ, quas "*jordanes*" vulgo vocamus, ad ejus collum colligantur, cum cote, in signum quod illam mentiendo promeruit; et ita circumductus est per omnem civitatem, in conspectu cunctorum physicorum et cirurgiorum, digna dehonestamenta recipiens pro mercede.

Anglici navem Falconem, a piratis diripiunt.

Prope tempus istud, nostrates, cum quibusdam viris de Rya, et nonnulli de patria, sunt egressi ad lustrandum mare et [4]purgandum ab incursu piratarum, cum ecce! repente vident

A vessel, captured by the enemy, is

[1] *Straw* in the printed texts: *Wraw* in orig. and Bibl. Reg. 13 E. ix.

[2] *pecuniam* in orig., by inadvertence.

[3] *se* omitted in the printed texts.

[4] *pugnandum* in orig. and the printed texts; corrected from Bibl. Reg. 13 E. ix.

A.D. 1382. quasdam naves hostiles; inter quas conspiciunt unam navem quæ quondam fuerat Domini Thomæ de Latimer, et vocabatur "Falco," propter insigne falconis quod positum erat ad cognitionem dictæ navis. Hæc dudum, prævalentibus hostibus, capta fuit, et per eosdem abducta. Hanc igitur cum nostri vidissent, et, ad Anglorum dedecus, ampliatam, et insigne pristinum superpositum, in vituperium Anglicorum, se periculo cuncti devovent, et statuunt extrema quæque pati, nisi eam victoriose recuperare valerent. Præmissis ergo, qui suaderent hostibus qui in ea erant, ut eam pacifice redderent, cum nihil præter cachinnos recepissent, ad conflictum se præparant hinc et inde; et post diuturnum belli congressum, nostris prævalentibus, reddita est navis, occisis prius in ea, et sex aliis vasis [1] captis cum eadem, trecentis viris. Regressi sunt quoque nostri cum victoria commendanda, ducentes secum prædicta vasa onusta multis bonis, puta vino, cera, et diversi generis mercibus, non parum incolis profuturis.[2]

Retaken by the English.

MS. Bibl. Reg. 13 E. ix.

Dux Andegaviæ coronatur in Regem Neapolis.

The Duke of Anjou is crowned by the Anti-Pope King of Naples.

Dux Andegaviæ, coronatus ab Antipapa Avinione in Regem Neapolis, circa dies istos carpit iter versus Neapolim, cum magna turba dominorum Galliæ et Comite de Saveya, ad deponendum Karolum, quem supra diximus a Papa coronatum in Regem dicti regni, et [3] qui, Regina victa, jure conquæstus occupaverat regnum illud. Fertur autem Dux præfatus traxisse cum eo tria millia hominum [4] de armis, et mille balistarios, præter illos qui Comitem de Saveya secuti sunt; quorum numerus, ut usu vulgari loquar, ad sexcentas lanceas ascendebat; et præter triginta galeyas per mare destinatas, armatas optime, et ad usum prœlii præparatas. Præmisit autem ante faciem suam in Italiam, gentibus quæ in Lumbardia et Tuscania commorantur, tres solemnes nuncios, ad manifestandum adventum suum; et adventus causam innuens, videlicet, se venturum ad succurrendum et juvandum, ac recuperandum Johannæ Reginæ, quam Karolus deposuerat, regnum illud. Et hæc quidem erant verba monstrata deforis ad omnes dominos et communes Italiæ, per nuncios supradictos.

He prepares an expedition in support of the rights of Queen Joanna.

---

[1] *captus* in orig., by inadvertence.

[2] A passage in Bibl. Reg. 13. E. ix. is omitted here.

[3] *quia* in the printed texts.

[4] *armatorum* in the printed texts.

Perturbatio per Londinenses.

MS. Bibl. Reg. 13 E. ix.

A.D. 1382.

The Londoners usurp certain Episcopal rights, in reference to persons detected in fornication or adultery.

Londonienses isto tempore cœperunt ultra modum insolescere, in perniciosum exemplum urbium aliarum. Revera freti Majoris illius anni, Johannis de Northamtone, auctoritate superciliosa, præsumpserant episcopalia jura, multas dehonestationes inferentes, in fornicationibus vel adulteriis deprehensis. Captas nempe mulieres in prisona quæ vocatur "Dolium," apud eos, primo seclusas incarcerarunt: postremo, productas ad conspectum publicum, descissa cæsarie ad modum furum, quos "appella-"tores" dicimus, circumduci fecerunt in conspectu cunctorum inhabitantium civitatem, præcedentibus tubicinis et fistulatoribus, ut latius innotescerent personæ earundem; nec minus hujusmodi hominibus pepercerunt, sed eos injuriis multis et opprobriis affecerunt. Animati etenim erant per Johannem Wiclif et sequaces ejus ad hujusmodi perpetrandum, in reprobationem Prælatorum. Dicebant quoque se abominari curatorum non solum negligentiam, sed et detestari avaritiam; qui studentes pecuniæ, omissis pœnis a jure limitatis, et receptis nummis, reos fornicationis et incestus favorabiliter in suis criminibus vivere permiserunt. Dicebant se utique pertimescere, ne propter talia peccata in urbe perpetrata, sed dissimulata, tota civitas, quandoque Deo ulciscente, ruinam pateretur. Quapropter, velle se purgationem facere civitatis ab hujusmodi inquinamentis, ne [1] forte accideret eis pestis aut gladius, vel certe absorberet eos tellus. Erat autem Major eorum homo duri cordis et astutus, elatus propter divitias et superbus, [2] qui nec inferioribus adquiescere, nec superiorum allegationibus sive monitis flecti, valeret, quin quod inceperat proprio ingenio, torvo proposito ad quemcunque finem perducere niteretur. Habebat plane totius communitatis assensum ad nova moliendum, quia,

They adopt certain of the opinions of Wyclif.

Perverseness of the Mayor of London.

"Mobile versatur semper cum principe vulgus,"—

et quo rarius audita vel visa tentaret, eo avidius eum sequi ad hujusmodi negotia festinaret.

The multitude impede the trial of John Astone.

Factumque est ut curatus eorum, Episcopus Londoniensis, veritus indisciplinatum, cum capite, vulgus, et malitiam temporis, contra eos procedere non auderet. Sed et ipsum Archiepiscopum [3] irreverens turba præsumpsit in civitate sedentem impedire, cum processum [4] fecisset contra quemdam Johannem

[1] *fore* in orig.; corrected from the printed texts.

[2] *quoniam* in orig. and the printed texts; corrected from Bibl. Reg. 13 E. ix.

[3] *irreverenter* in the printed texts.

[4] *fuisset* in the printed texts.

A.D. 1382. Astone, Magistrum in Artibus, et artissimum sequacem Johannis Wyclif; effractis foribus conclavis in quo idem Archiepiscopus sedit, cum turba Theologiæ et Juris Professorum. MS. Bibl. Reg. 13 E. ix.

The Mayor of London persecutes the craft of the Fishmongers.

Nec suffecere eis ista, quin apponeret Major supranominatus, adjutorio et favore communis plebis, omnes piscarios civitatis ad tantam miseriam illo anno [1]perducere, [2]ut melioris conditionis esset extraneus quisque piscator, quam illi qui civilitatem urbis vel hæreditarie vel emptione possidebant. Revera cuilibet licebat forinseco suos pisces in propria persona infra civitatem vendere, cum piscariis civitatis adempta facultas fuisset ita facere, sub magna forisfactura, corporibus eorum nihilominus [3]carceri detrudendis, si contravenire tentarent. Quid plura? In tantum artavit eosdem piscarios, ut compulsi faterentur aperte, artem quam hactenus exercuerant non esse artem, nec pro arte computandam, aut nominandam inter cæteras artes civitatis; effecitque ut qui antea superiores in civitate fuerant, vix inferiores esse permitterentur. Eos autem, qui perante banniti fuerant, et quibus interdictum est, ne consiliis et tractatibus civitatis interessent de cætero, ad gradum pristinum revocavit; quorum consilio et ordinationi subjecta est tota communitas, cum ipsa civitate; qui studentes quomodo quam maxime communibus complacere possent, et Major eorum eis fieri valeret acceptior, nullum permiserunt forinsecum piscatorem transire per urbem ad [4]deferendum patriæ victualia; sed omnes expectare fecerunt ibidem, et communibus vendere pisces suos, apposito pretio juxta voluntatem Majoris. Commune vulgus igitur, cernens forum venalium emendatum, usque ad sidera Majorem extollunt; et jam habentes odio concives suos piscarios, eos exterminare, si id oporteat et Majori placeat, sunt parati. Sed de patria convicina in hiis omnibus nihil cogitarunt; quæ de eorum abundantia summam patiebantur inopiam, dum nihil patriæ inferre permiserunt. Enimvero illis viluit pretium marinorum piscium, patriæ autem non tantum carum, sed omnino [5]rarum, factum est, illis impedientibus commeatum. Contigit ergo, ut unde Major urbanorum favorem meruit, inde maledictionem incurrit, et odium, totius patriæ convicinæ. Et Londoniis quidem eo tempore res ita se habebant.

Fish is made cheaper thereby in London, and dearer in the country.

---

[1] *producere* in orig. and the printed texts; corrected from Bibl. Reg. 13 E. ix.

[2] *et* in orig., by inadvertence.

[3] *carcerari* in orig., by inadvertence.

[4] *differendum* in orig. and the printed texts; corrected from Bibl. Reg. 13 E. ix.

[5] *carum* in orig. and the printed texts; corrected from Bibl. Reg. 13 E. ix.

Terræ-motus.

MS. Bibl. Reg. 13 E. ix.

A.D. 1382. An earthquake in England.

Hac æstate, in Anglia [1]terræ-motus est magnus, ubi raro cernitur vel auditur, duodecimo Kalendas Junii, hora nona, multorum mortalium corda deterrens. In Cancia tamen vehementius terra tremuit, in tantum, ut ecclesias quasdam concuteret et dirueret solo tenus. Secutus est et alius terræ-motus nono Kalendas ejusdem mensis, summo mane ante solis exortum; sed non ita terribilis sicut prior.

Cardinales perterriti a Romanis.

Insurrection at Rome.

Romani eo tempore, seditiosi et inquieti, insurgere contra Papam et Cardinales cœperunt, et tantum terrorem Cardinalibus incusserunt, ut pene fugerent universi, vel diverticula quærentes et latebras, quibus salvari possent a facie furoris crudelis et indisciplinatæ plebis. Sed Dominum Papam, in sua justitia confidentem, et adjutorio sperantem Altissimi, non [2]plebs armata, non clamor horribilis, non discursus inordinatus vulgi, perterruit, quin confidenter, assumpta cruce sua manibus, egrederetur ad eos, hujusmodi verba faciens ad eosdem;—"Quid est," inquiens, "filii? Quid molimini? Subvertere nitimini amicos vestros? Quid in vos peccavit Collegium fratrum meorum? Quare exarsit ira vestra in eos qui vos diligunt? Aut certe, si me quæritis, cur moramini caput meum tollere? Ecce! caput [3]meum in manibus vestris est; si placet, tollite, ut pax reformetur: si tamen hoc opus habetis."

Pope Urban addresses the insurgents.

The insurgents sue for pardon.

Videntes autem Romani tantam in viro constantiam, tanquam telo trabali percussi, cuncti protinus corruerunt ad terram, indulgentiam implorantes flebiliter de commissis, et paternam benedictionem humiliter postulantes. Quibus Dominus Papa, elevata manu, libenter benedictionem impertitus est, monens unumquemque cum pace ad propria remeare, et a talibus tumultibus et seditionibus in posterum temperare. Qui parentes paternis monitionibus, non sine grandi miraculo, deposita suæ ferocitatis malitia, ad propria sunt reversi.

---

[1] There are poems of this period still in existence, in which this earthquake is referred to. See Wright's *Political Poems and Songs* (printed in the present Series), Vol. I. pp. 250, 253, 254.

[2] *plebe* in orig., by inadvertence; corrected from the printed texts.

[3] *meum* omitted in the printed texts.

Papa confirmat Johannem Tymworth in Abbatem Sancti Edmundi; sed non sine pecunia.

A.D. 1382. The Pope confirms the election of John Tymworthe to the Abbacy of Bury, on certain terms.

MS. Bibl. Reg. 13 E. ix.

Dominus Papa, sub istis temporibus, postquam distulisset per amplius quam biennium electionem factam de Johanne Tymworthe apud Bury confirmare, tandem regalibus et procerum litteris pulsatus frequentibus, Edmundum Brounfeld, cui contulerat Abbathiam de Bury, transtulit ad Abbathiatum cujusdam monasterii in Wasconia; si tamen Regi placeret eundem Edmundum a diutina, quam pertulerat, carceris custodia liberare; Johanni vero Tymworth non confirmando electionem de ipso factam: sed per provisionem concessit Abbathiam, ita duntaxat, ut solveret Romanæ Curiæ duplicis vacationis censum, videlicet pro Johanne Brinclee et Edmundo Brounfeld; et ita videbatur novissimus error esse pejor priori.

The King and Council disapprove of this assertion of the Papal prerogative.

Fratres tamen Monasterii, tamdiu paterno destituti solatio, ad hanc formam consenserunt, non considerantes quod eundem Edmundum, prius provisionaliter eis datum, abegerant, et quanta pro tuitione causæ suæ profuderant, ne videlicet electio facta per eosdem locum non haberet. Regi vero regioque Consilio non placuit ista forma Papalis collationis; tum quia credebant electiones in futurum faciendas, per eandem, si admitteretur, periclitari; tum quia turpe videbatur eis flecti de causa, [1] quam tam diu, dictante conscientia, defenderant studio pertinaci. Et ita videbatur amor juris et æquitatis dilectio inter monachos quodammodo dormitare, inter sæculares et laicos vigilare.

Appearance of a comet.

Hoc anno, mense Decembri, stella cometa apparuit in Occidente, amplius quam per quindenam.

Ricardus Scrop, Miles, privatur officio Cancellarii.

Sir Richard Scrop opposes the King's extravagance, and is deprived of the Chancellorship.

Dominus Ricardus Scrop, miles, quem supra docuimus, per regni communitatem et assensum Dominorum, electum in regni Cancellarium, per dies istos dejicitur de officio [2] Cancellariæ, quod laudabiliter administraverat et prudenter. Causa dejectionis ejus extitit pertinax resistentia regiæ voluntati, qui desiderabat semetipsum exinanire, ut forinsecos exalteret. Enimvero post mortem Edmundi de Mortuo Mari, Comitis Marchiæ, aliorumque Dominorum qui nuper in fata concesserant, accedentes ambitiosi, tam milites quam armigeri, et

---

[1] *quantam diu* in orig. and the printed texts; corrected from Bibl. Reg. 13 E. ix.

[2] *Cancellarii* in the printed texts.

MS. Bibl. Reg. 13 E. ix. inferioris gradus famuli, ad Regem, postulabant ab eo certas terras et dominia mortuorum sibi concedi, pro tempore quo, de regni consuetudine, Rex deberet ea in manibus tenere. Quibus Rex, utpote puer, nil moratus, postulata concessit, et mittens eos ad Cancellarium, jussit ut eisdem chartas, Sigillo Magno signatas, contraderet, juxta arbitrium voluntatis eorum. A.D. 1382.

Cancellarius autem, qui cupiebat ardenter regni profectum, Regis quoque commodum, negavit [1]eis plane petita, asserens Regem, ære alieno [2]multimodo prægravatum, opus habere talia contingentia penes se detinere, ut per ea debita sua possit in parte debitoribus restituere. Ipsos autem, qui noverunt quibus debitis Rex obligatus erat, non esse fideles Regi, dum magis suæ consulerent avaritiæ, quam utilitati regiæ, emolumenta talia postulantes et privata commoda publicis necessitatibus præponentes. Quapropter desisterent ab hujusmodi postulationibus, et contenti essent superioribus Regis largitionibus, quæ satis erant competentes eis; scientes proculdubio, ipsum nullas chartas confirmatorias eisdem facturum aut sigillaturum de hujuscemodi Regis donationibus, qui nondum pueriles annos excesserat; ne forte malas ab eodem grates reciperet in futurum.

Ricardus Scrop Sigillum Regi dat: Londoniensis Episcopus Cancellarii officium suscipit.

Igitur reversi [3]vacui qui a Cancellario talia venerant petituri, renunciant Regi obstinatum esse animum Cancellarii, et nihil eum [4]velle facere ad Regis imperium, sed contemnere potius regale mandatum; Regem cum severitate debita tam effrænatam inobedientiam debere celeriter coercere, aut cito futurum esse ut Regis honor vilesceret apud suos, et imperium non valeret. Rex ergo, qui sapiebat ut parvulus, plus attendens delatorum falsas machinationes quam sui Cancellarii fideles allegationes, in furoris spiritu mittit qui Sigillum suum expeterent ab eodem, et sibi deferrent. Et cum iterum atque iterum misisset Rex per solemnes nuncios [5][et solemniores,] ut Sigillum sibi remitteret, Cancellarius [6]tandem ita respondit: — "Sigillum," inquit, "paratus sum resignare, "non vobis, sed ipsi qui mihi illud servandum tradidit; nec

Particulars of Sir Richard Scrop's deprivation.

---

[1] *eos* in orig.; corrected from the printed texts.

[2] *multum* in the printed texts.

[3] *vacui* omitted in the printed texts.

[4] *vellere* in orig., by inadvertence.

[5] Supplied from Bibl. Reg. 13 E. ix.: omitted in the printed texts.

[6] *tandem* omitted in the printed texts.

A.D. 1382. "erit medius portitor inter me et illum, sed ego restituam "illud manibus suis, qui mihi propriis, non alienis, manibus "commisit illud." Et ita pergens ad Regem, Sigillum [1] quidem retradidit, et se fidelem Regi, sicut hactenus, fore repromisit. Officiarium tamen se futurum sub illo in posterum, denegavit. Et ita Rex, recepto Sigillo, multis diebus quicquid libuit faciebat, donec Magister Robertus Braybrok, Londoniensis Episcopus, officium Cancellarii suscepisset.

MS. Bibl. Reg. 13 E. ix.

Robert Braybrok appointed Chancellor.

Public indignation at the dismissal of Scrop.

Audientes igitur non solum magnates regni, sed et ipsa communitas, Regem, contra regni consuetudinem, Cancellarium deposuisse [2] capitose, quem tota regni nobilitas, cum suffragio totius vulgi, delegerat, indignati sunt valde. Nemo tamen audebat aliquid palam loqui de materia, propter malitiam Regi assistentium, et ipsius Regis irrationabilem juventutem. Et ita Regis regnique commoda suppeditata sunt a facie insipientiæ Regis, et a malitia inhabitantium cum eodem.

Conspiratio inter homines de Northfolcia.

A rising in Norfolk.

Circa festum Beati Michaelis Archangeli, quidam in Northfolchia, dæmone agitati, quos non castigaverant aliena pericula, mortes aut tormenta non terruerant aliorum, facta conspiratione, congregaverunt iniquitatem sibi, et firmiter statuerunt, si fortuna faveret, Episcopum Northwicensem et cunctos majores patriæ, interceptos, inopinato necare; et, ut majori fulcirentur potentia, nundinas apud Sanctam Fidem adire latenter decreverunt, et cunctos congregatos ibidem cogere vel in sua vota jurare, vel sine dilatione trucidare. Quibus ad effectum productis, cogitaverunt occulte præoccupare Abbathiam Sancti Benedicti de Hulmo, quod fortis munitio videbatur eis futura, si aliquid periculi contra eosdem perfidos immineret. Sed hæc omnia, antequam ad effectum perduci possent, compressa sunt, uno de conjuratis prodente consilium reliquorum; unde contigit, ut inopinato caperentur conspiratores, et dignam malitiæ suæ apud Northwicum subirent pœnam, capitibus amputatis.

It is quelled.

Parliamentum, ad quod venerunt Flandrenses.

A Parliament summoned.

Circa idem tempus, vocati sunt ad Parliamentum, prout moris est, majores regni, et quorum intererat de consuetudine

[1] *quid* in orig.; corrected from the printed texts.

[2] *captiose* in the printed texts.

MS. Bibl. Reg. 13 E. ix.

A.D. 1382.

interesse. Ad quos venerunt majores de Flandrensibus, missi de Flandria per concives suos, ad supponendum se et terram suam [1] dominio Regis Angliæ; eorum domino naturali, scilicet, Comite Flandriæ, abdicato. Et quoniam minus sufficiens esse videbatur ista legatio, remissi sunt ad reducendum cum eis quosdam de singulis villis Flandriæ, qui majoris reputationis essent et famæ; de quibus merito constaret, quod potestatem haberent tractatum hujusmodi facere, et pactum firmare super præmissis. Quorum adventum simul et petitiones, ac responsa quæ ceperunt, cum locus et tempus se [2] ingesserint, describemus.

A deputation of Flemings offer to accept King Richard as their lord.

They are sent back for more extended powers.

In isto Parliamento, Major Londoniarum, cum magna parte communitatis, facta suggestione Regi et Consilio de fraude ac deceptione, quam, ut asserebat, exercuerant piscarii in distractione victualium, impetraverunt ne de cætero ullus eorum, vel reliquorum qui victualia distrahunt, puta vinum, carnes, aut qui de numero sunt apothecariorum, eligantur in Majores civitatis. Et ita indies elaboratum est per Majorem, ne unquam piscarii occasionem possent habere ad gradum [3] pristinum aspirandi; adempto ipsis tantæ dignitatis honore. Considerans insuper Major Domini Johannis Philipot auctoritatem in civitate plurimum prævalere, et cognoscens quod amicus erat hiis quibus Major ipse invidebat, abdicari fecit eum, ne de cætero tractatibus secretis civitatis et consiliis interesset; virum videlicet, qui plus cunctis pro libertatibus civitatis laboraverat, et honore. Alios autem, ut præmittitur, qui quondam falsi reperti fuerant, et propter hoc abdicati, ad tractatus urbis et consilia revocavit:—

Petition of the Mayor of London against the fishmongers.

John Philipot is forced to resign his Aldermanry.

[4] "Dans veniam corvis, vexans censura columbas."

Bulla Papalis, Episcopo Norwicensi directa, et quibusdam cum eo in Franciam volentibus proficisci, ad destructionem Antipapæ.

Episcopus Northwicensis, Dominus Henricus le Spencer, parum ante istud tempus receperat Bullas a Domino Papa sibi directas, ad Cruce-signandum quoscunque volentes cum eo proficisci in Franciam, ad destructionem Antipapæ, qui se

The Bishop of Norwich receives a Bull, empowering

---

[1] *Domino Regi Angliæ* in the printed texts.

[2] *ingresserunt* in orig.; corrected from the printed texts.

[3] *pistrinum* in orig.; by inadvertence.

[4] An unskilful adaptation of a well-known line of Juvenal

A.D. 1382. "Clementem" appellavit, et sanctificandum bellum contra quoslibet adhærentes sibi. Quas Bullas, quia ei magnam contulerant potestatem, fecit in Parliamento publicari, et earum exemplaria fecit dirigi circumquaque, et in ostiis ecclesiarum et in [1] portis monasteriorum publico [2] conspectui jussit affigi. Bullam præterea, quam Papa sibi misit, et jus suum, et injuriam quam irrogaverant ei [3] Antipapales, declarantem, publicavit ibidem; cujus tenorem non de verbo ad verbum, sed effectum, præsentibus inseremus.—

him to act against the adherents of Clement, the Anti-Pope.

MS. Bibl. Reg. 13 E. ix.

Effectus prædictæ Bullæ.

Purview of the Bull so received.

Bulla Papalis, in qua Papa conqueritur de filiis, quos exaltaverat Romana Ecclesia, qui, versa vice, conati matrem suam viperinis conatibus laniare. Unde Dominus Papa, de suorum confratrum consilio, decrevit exsurgere contra eos, et adhærentes eis et faventes, qui colligationes, conspirationes, et machinationes diversas facientes, in Ecclesia Dei schisma et divisionem ponere, et civitatem Anagnum et castellum Sancti Angeli de Urbe, et nonnulla alia castra, terras, et loca [4] Papalia occupare, præsumpserunt; et insuper venire fecerunt ad Civitatem, et alias terras provinciæ suæ Campaniæ violenter occupandas, multitudinem gentium armigerorum, quæ "Britones "Vascones" nuncupantur; qui ibidem plura homicidia, sacrilegia, rapinas, depopulationes, et alia mala, ac damna et scelera, perpetrarunt. Et cum exhortasset eos ut ad cor redirent, per Petrum Episcopum Portuensem, aliosque duos Cardinales, et multos honorabiles et probos viros, ac etiam per litteras suas iteratis vicibus, et ipsi nihilominus contempsissent ejus monitis obedire, quem dudum in Urbe per ipsos et alios, ad quos spectabat, in Papam elegerant, ac, debitis et consuetis solemnitatibus observatis, intronizaverant, ac publice coronaverant, et quem tanquam Papam, Summum Pontificem, in Missarum solemniis et Consistoriis publicatis et privatis, consulendo et ordinando de statu Romanæ Ecclesiæ ac Reipublicæ, per plures dies tractaverant, recipiendo ab eodem ecclesiastica Sacramenta, ac dignitates et beneficia ecclesiastica, pro se et aliis, ab eo impetrando, diversos libellos diffamatorios fecerunt, et illos ad diversos prælatos et mundi principes transmiserunt, per quos asserebant eum non verum Papam fore; ac multa

[1] *pratis* in the printed texts.
[2] *conspectu* in the printed texts.
[3] *aut Papales* in orig. and the printed texts; corrected from Bibl. Reg. 13 E. ix.
[4] *Puchalia* in orig.; *Paschalia* in the printed texts: corrected from Bibl. Reg. 13 E. ix.

MS. Bibl. Reg. 13 E. ix.

A.D. 1382.

alia et enormia de ipso dicere præsumpserunt, et tandem, cum quibusdam aliis, quos cum eorum suggestionibus ad eorum impium propositum attraxerant, congregati in domo iniquitatis filii Honorati [1] Gaietani, olim Comitis Fundorum, cum ipsius Honorati auxilio et favore, Robertum olim Basilicæ Duodecim Apostolorum, vulgariter dictum Gebenensem, Johannes [2] titulo Sancti Clementis vulgariter dictus, Majoris Monasterii Presbyter Cardinalis, et Petrus olim [3] titulo Sancti Eustachii Diaconus Cardinalis, temere eligendo Antipapam fecerunt, ipsumque ausu sacrilego Papam nominare præsumpserunt, et præsumunt; ipseque Robertus se Papam nominare, ausu temerario, non erubuit. Præterea, cum etiam iniquitatis alumnus, Petrus, olim Archiepiscopus Arelatensis, et Camerarius ejusdem Domini Papæ, diabolico spiritu instigatus, de urbe prædicta, ubi cum eo erat, absque licentia sua et quasi furtive recessit, et de Camera Papæ quamplura jocalia et alias res magni valoris et pretiosa, ad Dominum Papam et Romanam Ecclesiam pertinentia, secum asportavit, et ad dictam civitatem Anagnum se conferens, cum [4] præfatis sceleratis diversas conspirationes et colligationes ordinare et facere, et ad conducendum dictas gentes armigeros ad dictam civitatem Anagnum, consilium, auxilium, et favorem, præbere. Et tam ipsi quam [5] proditionis filii, Jacobus olim Patriarcha Constantinopolitanus, Nicholaus olim Archiepiscopus [6] Cusencensis, Petrus olim [7] [Urbecretanus, Guillerus olim] Urbinas, Petrus olim [8] Montis Flasconiæ, Johannes olim Gebenensis, et Franciscus olim [9] Gaietensis, Episcopi; Bertrandus Rasun, olim Clericus Cameræ Apostolicæ, et Matellus Casillii, olim rector Ecclesiæ Sanctæ Mariæ Pedisgriptæ, prope Neapolim; ac etiam iniquitatis filii, Honoratus prædictus, Antonius olim Comes Casertanus, Franciscus de Vico, olim [10] Præfectus Urbis, Johannes de Malastret, Nicho-

---

[1] *Gaitani* in orig. and Bibl. Reg. 13 E. ix; *Caietani* in the printed texts.

[2] Written *t⁹t⁹* in orig.; interpreted as "*Carter*" in the printed texts.

[3] The same abbreviation; interpreted as "*Tarter*" in the printed texts. From Migne's *Index of Cardinals* it appears that there was a Cardinal *Peter de Tartaris* about this period; but his title seems not to be known.

[4] *prælatis* in the printed texts.

[5] *prohibitionis* in the printed texts.

[6] *Censensen* in orig. and the printed texts; corrected from Bibl. Reg. 13 E. ix.

[7] Supplied from Bibl. Reg. 13 E. ix.: omitted in the printed texts.

[8] *Axutis* in the printed texts; to which the word bears a singular resemblance in orig.

[9] *Gaiciens* in orig. and the printed texts; corrected from Bibl. Reg. 13 E. ix.

[10] *præfatus* in orig., but corrected in the margin in a somewhat later hand.

A.D. 1382. laus Spinellus de Jumenatio, alias dictus "de Neapoli," Silvester Bude, Bernardus de Lasala, [1][Petrus de Lasaga,] milites, et Guilhonetus de Lasala, domicellus, præfato Roberto adhærere, credere, ac favere, et eum Papam prædicare et prædicari facere, non verentur; ipsumque Dominum nostrum Papam non fore Papam, nec Romanum Pontificem, eorum falsis et confictis mendaciis asseverant; ac Franciscus de Vico civitatem Domini Papæ Viterbiensem, et Johannes de Malestrett, Silvester Bernardus, Petrus de Lasaga, et Guilhonetus, cum eorum complicibus, dictam civitatem Anagnum et alias terras Papæ occupare, et occupantibus favorem præbere, præsumpserunt, crimen hæresis, [2]schismatis, læsæ majestatis, et apostasiæ, damnabiliter incurrendo. Cumque hujusmodi excessus et scelera essent adeo notoria, quod nulla possent tergiversatione celari, Dominus Papa, ad majorem certitudinem eorundem, Johanni [3]titulo Sanctæ Sabinæ, et Guillelmo titulo Sancti Eusebii, Presbyteris Cardinalibus, successive et indivisim commisit, [4]ut se de prædictis informarent; qui informationem hujusmodi, per eos debite receptam, Domino Papæ in Consistorio retulerunt, prædicta excessus et scelera fuisse et esse notoria, et esse manifesta. Et tandem Dominus Papa, nequiens absque gravi offensa Christi, et [5]remorsu conscientiæ, tot et tantos excessus amplius tolerare, adversus præfatos sceleratos viros in virtute Altissimi, de dictorum fratrum consilio, ut præmittitur, exsurgere dignum duxit, et contra ipsos procedere, justitia mediante. Ipsis igitur ad hoc legitime citatis, et aliis debitis juris solemnitatibus observatis, per Papalem diffinitivam sententiam, decrevit et declaravit prædictos Robertum, Johannem, Geraldum, Petrum, olim Cardinales, necnon Jacobum olim Patriarcham, Petrum olim Arelatensem etc., fuisse et esse schismaticos, et contra Papam conspiratores et blasphemos, et tanquam hæreticos puniendos, et reos criminis læsæ majestatis; ipsosque pariter excommunicatos et anathematizatos, et incidisse in pœnas et sententias tam a jure quam ab homine in talia perpetrantes inflictas et promulgatas, etc. Ac etiam declaravit dictos Robertum [6][etc.] fuisse et esse depositos, et ab omnibus beneficiis ecclesiasticis quibuscunque fuisse

MS. Bibl. Reg. 13 E. ix.

---

[1] Supplied from Bibl. Reg. 13 E. ix.: omitted in the printed texts.

[2] *scismaticis* in orig.; *schismatici* in the printed texts; corrected from Bibl. Reg. 13 E. ix.

[3] $t^o t^o$, the same abbreviation as mentioned in p. 73, Note 2.

[4] *et* in orig. and Bibl. Reg. 13 E. ix.; corrected from the printed texts.

[5] *remorsi* in orig.; corrected from the printed texts.

[6] Supplied from Bibl. Reg. 13 E. ix. and the printed texts.

MS. Bibl. Reg. 13 E. ix. et esse privatos et inhabiles; et inhabilitavit etiam ad habenda. A.D. 1382. Declaravit etiam prædictos Patriarcham, et Archiepiscopos, et Episcopos, depositos ab omnibus dignitatibus Pontificalibus, etc.; necnon prædictum [1] Honoratum etc., deposuit Dominus Papa ab omnibus dignitatibus et honoribus, et gradu militiæ et cingulo militari privavit. Ac etiam declaravit tam prædictorum olim Cardinalium, quam etiam omnium aliorum superius nominatorum, bona et immobilia, ac jura et jurisdictiones, fuisse et esse confiscata, et personas eoram detestabiles fuisse et esse exponendas, et eas exposuit, a Christi fidelibus capiendas; ut sic captæ, si absque eorum fuga et evasionis periculo fieri posset, eidem Papæ indilate transmitterentur, alioquin [2] in artis carceribus traderentur, et sub fida custodia detinerentur, donec aliud super hoc ipse mandaret. Credentes præterea, receptatores, et defensores eorum, et fautores, excommunicationis sententia innodavit, absolutione ipsorum, præterquam in mortis articulo, Romano Pontifici reservata. Decrevit insuper, quod quicunque aliquem ipsorum scienter præsumerent ecclesiasticæ tradere sepulturæ, excommunicationis sententiæ subjacerent, a qua absolvi, præterquam in mortis articulo, non possent, nisi prius propriis manibus extumularent, et procul ejicerent ab ecclesiastica sepultura, corpora eorundem. Et subsequenter inhibuit omnibus Christi fidelibus etc., ne in locis suis aliquem prædictorum scienter reciperent, seu eis ad illa loca in quibus prædicti damnati, vel aliquis illorum, habitarent vel moram traherent, blada, vinum, carnes, pannos, ligna, vel ulla victualia, ad eorum usum utilia, portare, mittere, seu portari, mitti, [3] aut deferre, præsumerent, si hoc prohibere possent. Prohibuit insuper Dominus Papa, ne quis impedire præsumeret quovismodo, quominus prædicti Robertus etc., caperentur, detinerentur, et ad eum transmitterentur: præcepit quoque, ut quilibet auxilium præstaret ad captionem eorundem. Qui vero contra præmissa facerent, seu qui præfatum Robertum, qui se "Clementem Papam" nominat, scienter Papam nominarent vel tenerent, vel ipsum Papam crederent vel prædicarent, si persona singularis, excommunicationis, si vero communitas vel universitas [4] esset, [5] interdicti sententias incurrerent, et civitates ac terræ eorum aliorum carerent commercio civitatum, locorum, atque terrarum; ac civitates ipsæ se noscerent pontificali dignitate privandas,

[1] *Honeratum* in orig.

[2] *in* omitted in the printed texts.

[3] *aud* in orig. and Bibl. Reg. 13 E. ix.

[4] *ēē* in orig.; *ēnt* in Bibl. Reg. 13 E. ix.; *esset* in the printed texts.

[5] *ut interdicti* in orig. and the printed texts.

A.D. 1382. et quod [1][ab] hujusmodi excommunicationis sententia nullus ab alio quam a Romano Pontifice, præterquam in mortis articulo, absolvi, nec interdictum hujusmodi per alium possit quam per eundem Romanum Pontificem relaxari. Inhabilitavit insuper omnes, qui a præfato Roberto quælibet beneficia acceptarent. MS. Bibl. Reg. 13 E. ix.

Dedit deinde præfato Northwycensi Episcopo potestatem publicandi, per se vel per alios, omnia præmissa, et contra præfatos damnatos procedendi, etc.

Indulgences granted to the supporters of the Bishop of Norwich against the Anti-Pope.

Concessit præterea Dominus Papa omnibus vere pœnitentibus et confessis, qui præfatum Robertum Antipapam et alios damnatos prædictos, et eorum complices, expugnabunt in personis propriis vel alienis, et super hoc per unum annum, incipiendum a die quo Episcopus Northwicensis duxerit ordinandum, continue, vel interpolatum, in [2]expugnatione hujusmodi laborabunt, Ecclesiæ sequendo vexillum, tam clericis quam laicis, et eis insuper, qui eis duntaxat expensas, juxta quantitates et facultates suas, destinabunt, vel Episcopo, vel alteri deputando per eum, ministrabunt sufficientia stipendia [3]ut destinare valeat idoneos bellatores per dictum tempus bellaturos, et moraturos ibidem, illam indulgentiam quæ concedi consuevit proficiscentibus in subsidium Terræ Sanctæ.

Privilegia concessa a Papa Episcopo Norwicensi pro executione præmissorum.

Privileges granted by Pope Urban to the Bishop of Norwich, in reference thereto.

Privilegia per Sanctissimum in Christo patrem et Dominum, [4]Dominum Urbanum, Divina Providentia Papam, Sextum, Domino Henrico, Northwicensi Episcopo, conceduntur.—

Inprimis, quod dictus Episcopus possit exequi [5]capitula contra Antipapam et ei adhærentes, fautores, et consiliarios, ubicunque locorum, cum manu forti.

Item, habet potestatem publicandi processus contra Antipapam et ei adhærentes, et quoscunque alios, per dictum Dominum Romanum Pontificem contra ipsos, et ipsorum singulos, fulminatos.

Item, habet potestatem inquirendi summario, et de plano, de omnibus et singulis schismaticis, et ipsos incarcerandi, et ipsorum bona mobilia et immobilia confiscandi.

---

[1] Supplied from Bibl. Reg. 13 E. ix.: omitted in the printed texts.

[2] *executione* in the printed texts.

[3] *et* in the printed texts.

[4] *Dominum* omitted in the printed texts.

[5] *capitulia* in the printed texts.

MS. Bibl. Reg. 13 E. ix. Item, habet potestatem privandi aicos schismaticos quibuscunque officiis sæcularibus, ipsaque officia conferendi aliis personis idoneis. A.D. 1382.

Item, habet potestatem privandi, et privatos declarandi, quoscunque schismaticos clericos in hac parte, ipsorum beneficia, cum cura vel sine cura, dignitates, personatus, vel officia, conferendi aliis personis idoneis.

Item, habet potestatem in personis exemptis, laicis et clericis, sæcularibus et regularibus, etiamsi fuerint fratres de Ordine Mendicantium, seu Præceptores, aut aliarum professi domorum, vel Hospitalis Sancti Johannis Ierosolomitanæ, aut Beatæ Mariæ [1] Theotonicorum, vel cujuscunque, [2] [seu quorumcunque] aliorum Ordinum professores.

Item, habet potestatem dispensandi cum quibuscunque clericis sæcularibus beneficiatis, cum cura vel sine cura, etiam [3] dignitates, personatus, vel officia, habentibus, etiam regularibus, exemptis vel non exemptis, quod ipsorum singuli poterunt secum abesse de ipsis beneficiis, dignitatibus, etc., sub vexillo Crucis, sine licentia ipsorum prælatorum obtenta, cum integra perceptione fructuum beneficiorum suorum, acsi personaliter residerent.

Item, conceditur omnibus transeuntibus suis propriis sumptibus et expensis, vel etiam alicujus expensis, plena remissio peccatorum, et tot privilegia conceduntur secum transeuntibus, [4] [sicut transeuntibus] in Terræ Sanctæ subsidium [5] conceduntur.

Item, illi qui propriis bonis et facultatibus ministrabunt sufficientia stipendia idoneis bellatoribus, juxta discretionem dicti Domini Episcopi, vel alterius deputandi per eum, licet ipsimet personaliter non interfuerint in executione negotii prædicti, consimilem habebunt remissionem peccatorum, ut supra, et indulgentiam, sicut secum personaliter interessent.

Item, hujus remissionis sunt participes omnes, qui ad expugnationem dictorum schismaticorum dicto Episcopo de bonis suis congrue ministrabunt.

Item, si aliquem sequendo vexillum per iter arreptum mori contigerit, vel interim ipsum negotium congrua terminatione compleri, integre percipiet ipsam gratiam, et erit particeps indulgentiæ et remissionis memoratæ.

Item, habet potestatem excommunicandi, suspendendi, interdicendi, quascunque personas rebelles, seu impedientes ipsum

---

[1] *Thotonicorum* in orig., by inadvertence.

[2] Supplied from Bibl. Reg. 13 E. ix.: omitted in the printed texts.

[3] *dignitatibus* in the printed texts.

[4] Supplied from Bibl. Reg. 13 E. ix.: omitted in the printed texts.

[5] Omitted in the printed texts.

A.D. 1382. exercere potestatem sibi commissam, cujuscunque dignitatis, status, gradus, præeminentiæ, ordinis, loci, conditionis, extiterint, etiamsi regali, aut reginali, [1] vel imperiali, seu quavis alia ecclesiastica vel mundana, præfulgeant dignitate. MS. Bibl. Reg. 13. E. ix.

Item, habet potestatem compellendi quoscunque religiosos, etiam de Ordine Mendicantium professores, si sibi videbitur expediens destinare seu transmittere pro executione prædictorum.[2]

Mandatum Episcopi Norwicensis Clericis et Rectoribus, ad publicandum Bullam prædictam.

Mandate of the Bishop of Norwich, for publication of the aforesaid Bull.

"Henricus, permissione divina Northwicensis Episcopus, "Sedis Apostolicæ Nuncius, dilectis nobis in Christo, omnibus "et singulis rectoribus, vicariis, et capellanis parochialibus "per Civitatem et Diœcesim Eborum constitutis, salutem in "Domino. Licet vobis omnibus singulis auctoritate Apostolica "in Domino exhortavimus, et districte præcipiendo manda-"vimus, quatenus vestris parochianis Cruciatam nobis commis-"sam, et ejus virtutem, pro tempore et loco magis opportunis "publicaretis, cujus sustentatores, fautores, et auxiliatores, se-"cundum nostram, seu nostrorum deputatorum, discretionem, "plena conceditur remissio peccatorum, [3] et tanta indulgentia "quæ concedi consuevit transeuntibus in Terræ Sanctæ subsi-"dium; et ultra hoc, salutis æternæ pollicetur augmentum, "prout in litteris Apostolicis, per [4] totam Angliam legitime "publicatis, plenius continetur. Et quia, ex relatione fide-"dignorum facta, sentimus quod exhortatio nostra et manda-"tum nullum, aut modicum, sortiuntur effectum, maxime, ut "creditur, propter negligentiam curatorum, in diminutionem "fidei Catholicæ et periculum animarum, quæ faciliter, con-"silio et exhortatione vestra, præfata privilegia et gratiam "consequi [5] poterunt sempiternam.—Quapropter nos, anima-"rum salutem et profectum affectantes, [6] vobis omnibus et "singulis, sub intestatione divini judicii, ut pluries, præci-"piendo mandavimus, ne hujusmodi gratiæ spiritualis et "insolitæ pretiosum munus, seu vestra potestas, aliquem paro-

---

[1] *aut* in the printed texts.

[2] A Bull of Indulgence to the Hospital of Saint Mary at Leicester, given in Bibl. Reg. 13 E. ix., is omitted here.

[3] From this word down to "*subsi-*" *dium*," the context is omitted in the printed texts.

[4] *totum* in orig., by inadvertence.

[5] *potuerunt* in orig. and the printed texts; corrected from Bibl. Reg. 13 E. ix.

[6] From this word down to "*man-*" *davimus*," the context is omitted in the printed texts.

MS. Bibl. Reg. 13 E. ix.

A.D. 1382.

"chianum vestrum, quantum in nobis est, lateat in futurum; "nomina autem singulorum parochianorum vestrorum scribi "faciatis, summas et donationes solventium super ipsorum "nomina signando, et non solventes de diebus in dies, quotiens "[1] et quando plus expedit, non solum divites sed pauperes, "ad similitudinem [2] paupercula viduæ, sanos et valetudinarios "maxime, in confessionibus prudenter tractetis et inducatis, "ut hujusmodi sancto viagio, in destructionem et exterminium "hæreticorum modernorum, manus apponant adjutrices, ut "meriti et præmii in hac parte indultorum valeant esse partici-"pes, et vos ex hoc ab onere curæ vestræ plurimum relevari. "Insuper hujus viagii sancti [3] perturbatores, seu nostris man-"datis, verius Apostolicis, rebelles, schismatis moderni fau-"tores, citetis, seu citet aliquis vestrum, peremptorie, quod "certo termino, per vos vel aliquem vestrum præfigendo, "compareant personaliter coram nobis, vel Commissariis "nostris, in Ecclesia Cathedrali Sancti Pauli Londoniæ, "ostensuri et propositori, pro termino præciso et peremp-"torio, quare in censuras, contra talia perpetrantes fulmi-"natas, pronunciari non debeant incidisse; ulteriusque fac-"turi et recepturi, quod justitia suadebit. De nominibus et "quantitate eleemosynam in hac parte conferentium, necnon "de diebus citationis vestræ, modo et forma ejusdem, nos vel "nostros Commissarios discrete et prudenter certificetis, seu "certificet aliquis vestrum. De quibus omnibus et singulis, et "cujuslibet vestrum conscientiam oneramus, vobis, in virtute "obedientiæ, qua Sedi Apostolicæ tenemini, firmiter injun-"gentes, quatenus præsentes litteras nostras inter parochianos "vestros publicatas, copiis penes vos retentis, ipsas ad cura-"tum proximum in Diœcesi præfata celeriter transmittatis. "In cujus rei testimonium, sigillum Cruciatæ, quo in hac "parte utimur, præsentibus apposuimus. Data in hospitio "nostro apud [4] Charryngge, juxta Westmonasterium, nono die "mensis Februarii, anno Domini millesimo trecentesimo octo-"gesimo secundo, et consecrationis nostræ tertio-decimo."

Forma Absolutionis.

Form of Absolution.

"Auctoritate Apostolica, mihi in hac parte commissa, te "A. [5] [de] B. ab omnibus peccatis tuis, ore confessis et corde

---

[1] *et* omitted in the printed texts.

[2] *Mark* xii. 41–43; *Luke* xxi. 1–8.

[3] *perturbatoris* in the printed texts.

[4] *Charyngu* in the printed texts.

[5] Supplied from Bibl. Reg. 13 E. ix.; omitted in the printed texts.

A.D. 1382. "contritis, et de quibus confiteri velles, si tuæ occurrerent memoriæ, absolvimus, et plenariam tuorum peccatorum remissionem indulgemus, et retributionem justorum ac salutis æternæ pollicemur augmentum, et tot privilegia, quæ in Terræ Sanctæ subsidium proficiscentibus conceduntur, tibi concedimus; ac [1]sanctæ et universalis Synodi, et Ecclesiæ Sanctæ Catholicæ, orationum et beneficiorum suffragia tibi impertimur." MS. Bibl. Reg. 13 E. ix.

[2]*Solutio Obsidionis villæ de Owdenarde; magna confusio Flandrensium.*

Raising of the siege of Audenarde, and death of Philip Van Arteveldt.

Vix Parliamento terminato, lugubria nova feruntur e Flandria de solutione obsidionis villæ de Owdenarde, et de morte Philippi den Artfelde, et confusione magna Flandrensium per bellum Britonum et Francorum.

Enimvero Rex Franciæ, cum omni [3]militia suæ terræ, et quibuscunque quos poterat de externis regionibus in auxilium evocare, Flandriam est ingressus; quibus Gandavenses incunctanter obviam exierunt, sperantes in auxilio sociarum civitatum et villarum Flandriæ; quod fuit eis causa magnæ ruinæ. Revera cum ad bellum perventum esset, et jam inclinari cœpisset status belli de parte Francorum, supervenit multitudo maxima de villa de Bruges et partibus adjacentibus, quasi ad auxilium ferendum Gandavensibus; [4]quæ tamen eosdem prodere cogitabat. Igitur Gandavenses, nihil doli metuentes, sed instanter et animose pugnantes, concives proprii de Bruges aggressi sunt a tergo, hostibus afferentes auxilium; et illis ante, istis retro, cædentibus, Gandavenses, inopinato perterriti, pugnandi animos dimiserunt; sicque factum est, ut levi negotio vincerentur, occisis in eo bello viginti quinque millibus Gandavensium et sociorum.

Treachery of the people of Bruges.

Galli Villanos de Burges e suis Laribus detrudunt.

The people of Ghent retire to their own city.

Hoc ergo bellum Francis animum attulit, et Gandavensibus ademit spem resistendi, donec iterato novo suffragio fulti, vel in Francos vel in patriotas injurias suas ulcisci valerent.

---

[1] *Ecclesiæ universalis Synodi* in orig. and the printed texts: corrected from Bibl. Reg. 13 E. ix.

[2] A passage, of considerable length, in Bibl. Reg. 13 E. ix., is omitted here.

[3] *malitia* in orig.; corrected from the printed texts.

[4] *quem* in the printed texts.

MS. Bibl. Reg. 13 E. ix.

A.D. 1382.

Gandavenses idcirco compulsi fugere, propriam villam [1] petierunt; sed injustitiam deficientium sociorum mox ultio justa secuta est.

The French oppress their own allies, the people of Bruges.

Nam Brugenses et cæteri eorum complices, qui malitiose suos prodiderant, quos adjuvisse debuerant, subito senserunt semetipsos in gravibus miseriis constitutos. Quia Gallici, nullam fidem aut gratiam illis pro tali facto debentes, ingressi villam de Bruges et omnes alias villas provinciæ, expulerunt e suis propriis Laribus proditores, et quæque pretiosa diripientes, ad Gallias transmiserunt, et ipsos proditores vectigales esse Regi Franciæ statuerunt. Itaque factum est, ut conditio Gandavensium superatorum multo melior esset quam Brugensium proditiose victorum. Quia illis et propria civitas libertasque remansit, istis nihil omnino, neque civitas, neque libertas, nec possessiones, remanserunt. [2] Speraverant utique Brugenses, si, [3] desertis sociis, opem ferrent Gallicis, Francos a direptione rerum suarum temperaturos post victoriam. Sed secus accidit quam sperabant. Nempe Gallici ex insperato omnes villas et loca eorum, qui eis detestandum tulerunt auxilium, armatis hominibus munierunt, et inter eos degentes ipsos diris servitiis oppresserunt.

The English merchants at Bruges are plundered.

Sensit et Anglia hujus incommodi grave damnum. Nam sicut per antea in conflictu inter Gandavenses et Brugenses, mercatores Anglici sunt salvati, et in rebus suis nil mali passi, ita, versa vice, modo prævalentibus Gallicis, externis mercatoribus cunctis impunitate gaudentibus, solummodo Anglicorum bona direpta sunt, et Regis Francorum usibus confiscata, occisis apprenticiis Anglicis obvíam illis factis.

The return of the Flemish envoys to England is delayed.

Igitur in Anglia hiis auditis rumoribus, nunciis, de quibus supra retulimus, redeundi timor incutitur, et ipsorum responsum ad tempus suspenditur, donec Consilium regium tempus plus conveniens ipsis non solum respondendi, sed et opem ferendi, providisset.

Crudelitas Regis Franciæ in Parisianos sibi resistentes.

Cruelties exercised by the King of France

Hiis ita se habentibus in Flandria, regressus est Rex Franciæ arrogans et superbus Parisius pro victoria memorata; sed tamen in patria propria reperit resistentes. Communitas siqui-

[1] *petierant* in the printed texts.

[2] *Superaverant*, erroneously, in orig. and in the printed texts: corrected from Bibl. Reg. 13 E. ix.

[3] *non tulissent desertis* in the printed texts, and *ferrent* omitted; the context being altered to adapt the sense to *superaverant*.

A.D. 1382. against the insurgents at Paris. MS. Bibl. Reg. 13 E. ix.

dem Parisiorum portas claudere, muros munire contra eum, et arma sumere, moliebatur. Statuit ergo Rex violenter, collecta multitudine obsidentium, civitatem effregisse. Sed tamen, visa numerositate intus repugnantium, divertit ab hoc proposito, et locutus est eis verba pacifica in dolo; et crediderunt ei, permiseruntque intrare cum omni turba secum essentium bellatorum. Astu itaque civitatem ingressus, illico rupit pactum, et mentitus est eis, faciens nobiliores urbis contemptibiliter comprehendi, et quosdam ex eis suspendi, quosdam decollari. Eis vero qui arma tulerant contra eum, brachia dextra abscindi, et, in signum opprobrii sempiterni, ad illorum colla suspendi fecit ipsa brachia amputata. Omnes autem Portas urbis fecit dirui, præter Portam Sancti Antonii, in qua Rex ipse possidet domicilium speciale. Ipsam vero civitatem omni armatura et vasis bellicis spoliavit, ne habitatores illius vel occasionem minimam habere possent in posterum rebellandi. Insuper et nova graviaque tributa illis imposuit, violenter, si nollent voluntarie, exigenda. Et hæc quidem Parisius gesta sunt.

Comes Cantabrigiæ rediit e Portugalia.

The Earl of Cambridge returns from Portugal.

Dominus Edmundus, Cantebrigiæ Comes, Domini Regis avunculus, et quos supra docuimus missos Portyngaliam, hoc tempore, post expertam maris sævam fortunam, et quorundam bonorum amissionem, Angliam redierunt. Missi siquidem, ut diximus, fuerant ad ferendum auxilium Regi Portyngaliæ contra Bastardum Hispanniæ, qui se "Regem" dixit, quique multis injuriis affecerat Regem Portyngaliæ, et pene contrivisset, si non juvamen ex Anglia sibi maturius affuisset. Post annalem [1]moram nostratum in regno Portyngaliæ, et plures irruptiones in Hispanniam, et quarundam munitionum captionem, placuit Hispanis hostiliter campum petere contra Regem Portyngaliæ et exercitum Anglicanum. Nec segnius Rex, cum nostratibus, illis occurrit, pugnaturus si fortuna permitteret, et, ut sperabatur, victor futurus.

Intrigues of the Spaniards to ensure the departure of the English.

Cujus animositatem, simul et nostrorum probitatem, timentes Hispani, tractare cum Rege Portyngaliæ petierunt; ita duntaxat, ne Comes Cantebrigiæ aut ullus Anglicus suis consiliis interesset. Annuit ipse Rex petitis, et ad tractatum accessit. In quo, tam Hispanis quam Portyngalibus cupide pacem desi-

[1] *qui* occurs here in orig., by inadvertence; from misapprehension of an abbreviation in Bibl. Reg. 13 E. ix. written on an erasure; perhaps for *vero*.

MS. Bibl. Reg. 13 E. ix.

derantibus, cito conventum est ad hoc, quod utrisque placeret; et, illis Regi Portyngaliæ, et ipsis, salvo utrorumque jure, concedentibus quæ volebant, pax clanculo est firmata; ita tamen, ut Rex Portyngaliæ regnum suis Anglicis vacuaret. Et ne iidem Anglici prætenderent navigium sibi deesse, Rex Hispanniæ de suis illis concessit navigium, et Rex Portyngaliæ naulum et quæ necessaria esse navigantibus viderentur. Timebant nempe Hispani Anglicorum audaciam, et jam iidem Anglici Portyngalibus facti sunt onerosi; quia quos contutandos contra hostes susceperant, ipsi viliori servitio deprimebant, non tamen bona diripientes eorundem, sed et uxores et filias execrabiliter opprimentes; quare suis hospitibus odibiles sunt effecti. Rex vero Portyngaliæ, de dicto tractatu rediens, indixit communiter suis et nostratibus, ut domum redeuntes arma deponerent, et quod in pacem redisset cum Hispanis, omnibus intimavit. Oportebat ergo nostrates, vellent nollent, ejus parere mandatis: et ita campum, cum magna mentis amaritudine, deseruerunt, eo quod non est permissum [1] eos confligere cum Hispanis. Ab illo ergo die non tantum præparati, quantum coacti, sunt ad reditum, donec omnis Portyngalia Anglicis vacuaretur.

A.D. 1382.

Bad conduct of the English towards the Portuguese.

Rediit igitur, ut prædiximus, cum suis Comes, reducens secum uxorem suam, quondam Petri, Regis Castellæ, filiam juniorem, et filium ex ea susceptum per annos aliquot antequam Angliam exivisset. Quem quidem, tempore moræ quam fecit in Portyngalia, desponsavit filia Regis Portyngaliæ, cum solemnitate congruente. Sed quia timebat dubiam fidem illius regionis hominum, noluit eum post se relinquere, quanquam Rex Portyngaliæ id petisset; nec Rex filiam suam voluit in Angliam cum Comite destinare. Et hoc quidem modo eo tempore in Portyngalia negotium se habebat.

Marriage of the Earl's son to the daughter of the King of Portugal; who will not allow her to come to England.

Navis Carika applicuit apud Sandwicum.

Anno Domini trecentesimo octogesimo tertio, qui est annus Regis Ricardi Secundi sextus,[2]—[3] eodem tempore venit in magna tempestate ad Sandewici portum navis; [4] quidem dicunt "carika,"[5]—et magnitudinis, plena divitiis, quæ facile inopiam

A.D. 1383.

A carack arrives at Sandwich, with a

[1] *eis* in the printed texts.

[2] A long passage in Bibl. Reg. 13 E. ix. is omitted here.

[3] This word is preceded by *fuit* in orig. and in Bibl. Reg. 13 E. ix.

[4] *quam dicunt* in the printed texts.

[5] *miræ magnitudinis* in the printed texts. The apparent hiatus in orig. is caused by an omission of the previous passage in Bibl. Reg. 13 E. ix. in reference to another carack, wrecked on the coast.

A.D. 1383. Cargo of great value. Through the agency of the London merchants, the Genoese are induced to depart.

totius terræ relevare potuisset, si incolarum invidia permisisset. Sed mercatores, ut fertur, Londonienses, habentes domi plura mercimonia, non nova sed vetera, puta, fructus, species diversi generis, oleum, et cætera talia, et ea, ne, novis supervenientibus, projicerentur, vendere cupientes, facta pactione cum Januensibus, eorum portum relinquere et Flandriam velificare fecerunt; et ita, propter paucorum avaritiam, magnum dispendium sensit totum regnum.

MS. Bibl. Reg. 13. E. ix.

Parliamentum Londini, in quo tractatur de potestate concessa Episcopo Norwicensi.

The powers granted to the Bishop of Norwich are discussed in Parliament.

Diebus Quadragesimalibus factum est Parliamentum Londoniis, in quo per plures dies tractatum fuit de potestate concessa per Summum Pontificem Episcopo Nortwicensi, et de profectione sua contra schismaticos; et factus est ibi motus varius animorum. Nam pars, quorum corda Deus tetigerat, volebat eum proficisci, tanquam Ecclesiæ pugilem, contra hostes Christi; pars adversa repugnabat, asserens non esse tutum committere plebem Regis et regni presbytero inexperto; et schisma erat inter eos. Ob quam causam Pontificale negotium, simulque totius Ecclesiæ, protelatum est usque ad Sabbatum, quo de Passione Cruceque Dominica in universali Ecclesia fit mentio specialis. Tandem, post multas tergiversationes per duces regni factas, post plures altercationes interpositas per Comites, Barones, et magnates terræ, plurimos, sed omnino, Dei virtute, et laudabili constantia militum Parliamentalium, conquassatas, ipsa die Sabbati, [1]horaque quibus Sancta Ecclesia vexilla Crucis prodisse decantat, omnis repente turba quæ illi Consilio, vel Parliamento, interfuit, et quæ maxime steterat contra Crucis negotium, Crucisque fidei promotionem, consentit, tanquam perculsa tonitruo solemnis illius Antiphonæ, "Ecce! Crucem Domini, fugite, partes adversæ," decrevitque pro votis Episcopi [2]Cruce-signati.

All opposition thereto is finally overcome.

Grants made by Parliament.

Assignatur ergo sibi, per commune decretum, quintadecima Regi præconcessa in superiori Parliamento pro bellatoribus conducendis. Decima vero, Oxoniis præconcessa per Episcopos, Regi remanere statuitur pro maris custodia, dum Episcopus agere deberet in remotis. Quibus ita se habentibus, misit Episcopus litteras, sigillo suo munitas, per omnes regni provincias, committens rectoribus et vicariis, aliisque curatis per universam Angliam constitutis, potestatem audiendi suorum

Powers granted to rectors and vicars by

---

[1] *oraque* in orig.

[2] *Cruce-signari* in Camden's text.

MS. Bibl. Reg. 13 E. ix.

A.D. 1383. the Bishop's Letters.

confessiones parochianorum, eisque qui de bonis a Deo sibi collatis aliquid erogarent, unde negotium Cruce-signatorum promoveri posset, absolutionis beneficium, pariter et remissionis, auctoritate Apostolica impendendi, juxta formam Bullæ prænotatæ. Igitur regni totius incolæ, audita tantæ benedictionis dulcedine Anglicis advenisse, tantam gratiam nec abjicere, [1] nec in vacuum prorsus suscipere, voluerunt, sed devotionis fideique calore succensi, qui bello se reputaverunt idoneos, ad proficiscendum se cum omni festinatione præparabant; qui vero profectioni videbantur inhabiles, juxta consilia confessorum, de bonis suis liberaliter ad opus proficiscentium erogarunt, ut tantæ remissionis et indulgentiæ esse participes mererentur. Et ita generaliter, Deo volente, sunt accensa devotioni corda cunctorum, ut pene nullus in tam spatioso regno reperiretur, qui non vel semetipsum offerret dicto negotio, vel de bonis suis aliquid erogaret. Factumque est, ut in brevi magnæ pecuniarum summæ, ex multis regni partibus acervatæ, Episcopo deferrentur, ut jam incepit videri possibile, quod per ante Regis [2] consiliariis, vel hujusmodi profectionis adversariis, impossibile visum fuit, unde videlicet Episcopo, et inter Episcopos regni pauperrimo, substantia tantæ profectioni necessaria ministraretur. Episcopus autem non Dominos præpotentes, nec eos qui in incerto divitiarum suarum sperant, elegit in consodales sibi, sed mediocres, et qui sine strepitu vel sine pompa disponere bellum scirent, et regere bellatores.

Great preparations made in England, in support of the Bishop's contemplated expedition.

Primus et principalis illorum erat Dominus Hugo de Calverlee, vir ab antiquo exercitatus in armis, et qui in cunctis locis opera militaria laudabiliter et prudenter adimpleverat, et jam pulchrum sibi videbatur bellando bella Dominica finem imponere operi militari. Secundus vero dicebatur "Dominus "Willelmus de Faringdone," sane vir prudens et callidus, sed cujus opera non responderent ultima primis; quia quod laudabiliter inchoavit, expost perfidia maculavit. Hic primo, ut apparuit, minas judicum non timuit, nec a facie Ducum, superciliosa verba nectantium, formidavit, quando pene cuncti magnates regni Crucis negotio restiterunt; sed constanter atque prudenter pro Episcopo Cruce-signato disseruit, et ipsius [3] provectionem non solum Sacrosanctæ Ecclesiæ promotionem futuram, sed totius regni provectionem, palam argumentis evidentissimis allegavit. Sed tamen more Cayphæ [4] prophetavit, ut posterius elucebit.

Names of the principal leaders of the expedition.

Advocacy of the cause by Sir William de Faringdone.

[1] *nec* omitted in the printed texts.
[2] *consiliarios* in orig., erroneously.
[3] Apparently *provectioni* in orig.; *provectionem* in Bibl. Reg. 13 E. ix.; *profectionem* in the printed texts.
[4] In allusion to *John* xi. 51.

A.D. 1383.

Other leaders enumerated.

Habuit Episcopus secum et alios nominis non parvi milites, puta, Dominum Willelmum [1] Elmham et Dominum Thomam Trivet, et plures quos longum foret inserere. Quibus Deus proculdubio dedisset bene expediendi gratiam in rebus militaribus, ultra quam meruerunt Duces et Marchiones Angliæ, [2] qui multis annis elapsis bella Gallica frequentarunt, si eodem anno eadem intentione iter illud arripuissent, quibus Episcopus, et simplicioris conditionis homines qui profecti sunt cum eo: sed inerat eis, ut expost apparuit, mens invidia corrupta, [3] animus obsessus avaritia, et cor proditionis felle toxicatum; ut ex sequentibus apparebit.

MS. Bibl. Reg. 13 E. ix.

Evil results of the want of principle on their part.

Piscatores Londonienses libertatibus restituti.

The liberties of the fishmongers of London are restored by Parliament.

Piscatores Londonienses,—quos supra docuimus suis consuetudinibus et dignitatibus exutos fuisse, non tantum causa transgressionum factarum per eosdem quantum malitia Majoris Londoniarum, et ejus complicium eisdem invidentium,—in hoc Parliamento suis consuetudinibus, per chartam Regis patentem, restituuntur; excepto quod Curias inter semetipsos, ut hactenus, non tenebunt; sed transgressiones per eosdem factæ in Curia publica civitatis emendabuntur, ad libitum Majoris, prout de aliis artibus urbis fieri consuevit.

The Mayor of London persists in his persecution of the Londoners, in spite thereof.

Major vero civitatis, veteri nondum digesta invidia, quam gerebat contra eos, quanquam demonstrassent chartam regiam de libertatibus reconcessis eisdem, et allegassent esse voluntatis regiæ, simul et totius Parliamenti decretum, quod prædictis gauderent libertatibus, acquiescere noluit eorum assertionibus, nec quovismodo chartam regiam acceptare; sed permanens in sua malitia eos violenter oppressit. Quod ut liberius facere prævaleret, data fulvi metalli inæstimabili summa suis fautoribus et eis qui de Consilio Regis erant, ipsos in partem suam traxit. Piscatores autem, videntes se nihil proficere in hiis omnibus, usque ad tempus tacere decernunt. Et quidem erga piscatores ita se res habebat.

Gandavenses tributum collectum in usum Regis Franciæ hostiliter diripiunt.

The people of Ghent seize the tribute-

Hoc pene tempore qui de villa de Bruges et de Ypres erant, et omnes de Occidentali Marchia Flandriæ, vectigales effecti Regi Franciæ, tributum collectum a semetipsis Regi Franciæ,

[1] *Elinham* in orig. and the printed texts; *Elmham* in Bibl. Reg. 13E.ix

[2] *quia* in the printed texts.

[3] *animis* in orig.; by inadvertence.

MS. Bibl. Reg. 13. E. ix.

A.D. 1383.

juxta condictum, per suos mittere disponebant; qui, ut securiorem possiderent transitum, adhibuerunt armatos qui conducerent vectigal portantes, et suffragia ferrent, si contingeret hostes adesse. Quibus omnibus cognitis per exploratores, Gandavenses se præparant ad auferendum tributum nunciis supradictis, vel certe, si contra vota contingeret, moriendum. Igitur dispositis in itinere turmis Gandavensium, sed latenter, [1]ex insperato veniunt ad manus hostiles tam Gallici quam Flandrenses, cum pecunia memorata. Et quia fuit impar manus Gallicorum, Gandavenses sine difficultate vicerunt, et Gallicis, et qui cum eis venerant, non tantum vitam sed et vectigal, [2]surripuerunt, et Gandavum, sine magna suorum civium læsione, cum spoliis [3][remearunt].

Money sent to the French by the people of Bruges and Ypres.

Comes de Saveye, Antiochi more percussus, obiit.

Circa tempus Paschale, Comes de Saveye, qui cum viginti [4]octo [5]militibus profectus fuerat, cum Duce Andegaviæ, contra Papam et Karolum de Pace, cum diutinam moram fecisset in illis partibus, sed damnosam, agnovit manum Domini contra eum missam: nam qui in patria sua subdi Deo noluit, et communem mundi patrem [6]venerari, sed potius, dimissa quiete qua diu gavisus fuerat, statuit persequi in remotis, justo Dei judicio, miserabiliter percussus, Antiochi more, periit in terra peregrina, contestatus prius quod justum est subditum esse Deo, ejusque vero Vicario, quodque peccavit enormiter patrem, filius, persequendo. Quapropter, filio suo et hæredi dedit mandata salutaria, ne Urbanum Papam, exemplo paterno, persequeretur. Et si quid forte contra eum tentasset, celeri satisfactione corrigere niteretur, ac ad unitatem Ecclesiæ se conferret. Augebant autem non solum dolorem suum, sed et pœnitentiam ejus, mortes infandæ suorum militum quos conduxerat, qui omnes præter octo ante ipsum dysenteria perierunt: talique fine consummatus est Comes et pene cuncti sui milites; Duci Andegaviæ, si fuisset in gratia, manifestum resipiscendi relinquentes exemplum; sed superba mens ejus, quamvis hæc omnia cerneret, renuit tamen humiliari. Induratum erat nempe cor ejus contra Dominum, et contra Christum ejus.

The Count of Savoy, a supporter of the Anti-Pope, comes to a violent end.

---

[1] *et* in the printed texts.

[2] *surrupuerunt* in orig.

[3] Supplied from Bibl. Reg. 13 E. ix. : omitted in the printed texts.

[4] *octoginta* in orig. and Bibl. Reg. 13 E. ix. : *octo* in the printed texts.

[5] *millibus* in the printed texts.

[6] *venereri* in orig., by inadvertence.

Episcopus Norwicensis, cum suis, properat versus mare.

A.D. 1383.

The Bishop of Norwich proceeds towards the sea-coast.

MS. Bibl. Reg. 13. E. ix.

Circa festum Trinitatis, quod evenit hoc anno in medio [1] mense Maio, Episcopus Northwicensis Cruce-signatus, cum quibusdam de exercitu conducto per eum, arripuit iter versus mare, et festinato perveniens Kanciam, ad manerium Abbatis Sancti Augustini, vocatum "Northbourne," divertit, præstolaturus ibidem auram secundam; apud quem locum dum adhuc moram protrahit, [2] accipit breve regium, in quo jubetur redire ad alloquendum Regem, et ejus cognoscendum voluntatem. Episcopus ergo, timens si reverteretur ad Regem, mandatum remanendi susciperet, et sic omnis labor, omnis apparatus ejus, non sine risionibus, deperiret, eligit exponere se fortunæ, cum parva manu quam præsentem habebat, citius quam remanendo effici proverbium æmulorum. Igitur renunciari Regi fecit, se jam paratum ad procinctum profectionis, non expedire ut modo impediretur per ullum colloquium, quod forsitan parvi vel nullius esset ponderis; sed oportere potius ut iter acceptum maturaret, tam ad Dei quam ad Regis honorem. Et concito convocatis quos secum habuit, adjutorio Domini Johannis Philipot, militis et mercatoris Londoniarum, qui navigium procurabat, cum illis Calesiam est transvectus, recordatus illius Poetæ consilii qui sic jubet,—

He is summoned by the King, to return; but refuses, and crosses over to Calais.

[3] "Tolle moras, semper nocuit differre paratis."

Calesiæ igitur commoratus paucis diebus, donec advectus esset exercitus qui primam aciem facere debuisset: quo adunato, mox egressus de Calesia, vexillum Sanctæ Crucis erexit, et ad villam de [4] Gravenynge, muris fortibus circumcinctam, bellatoribusque ex Francia et Britannia contractis munitam, audacter accessit. Quam non obsidere, sed [5] insilire, maluit, dum adhuc Anglici vigere viribus viderentur. Nec segnius qui in villa erant ad defensionem sui se paraverunt, sed alacriter ad muros cucurrerunt, et modo plumbum, modo ferrum, modo calcem vivum, modo lapides et quicquid erat necessarium defensioni, super Anglicos projecerunt. Nostri vero, vexillum Sanctæ Crucis habentes præ oculis, et ad causam suæ Cruce-signationis, pariter et absolutionis, dirigentes intuitum, vincere quidem gloriam in hac causa, sed mori lucrum, reputabant; quapropter, contemptis periculis, vulneribus parvipensis, spreta morte, muros invadunt, cum hostibus comminus

He approaches the town of Gravenynge in hostile form.

The town is assaulted.

[1] *mensis Maii* in the printed texts.
[2] *accepit* in the printed texts.
[3] A quotation from Lucan.
[4] *Graveling* in the printed texts.
[5] *inspicere* in the printed texts.

MS. Bibl. Reg. 13 E. ix.

A.D. 1383.

bella committunt, et [1]modo repellunt, modo repelluntur, vulnerant et vulnerantur, prosternunt et prosternuntur, donec ex utraque parte intereunt multi mortales.

Interea Britones et Gallici, qui in villa erant, villanos animant ad resistendum fortius, pugnandum acrius, asserentes superventuros Gallicos, qui præsentes Anglicos, inopes, imbelles, et mendicos, in ore gladii, tanquam ignis stipulam, devorabunt. Parte vero nostra, Episcopus et Dominus Hugo Calverlee, cujus memoria in benedictione est, nostris audaciam monitis et persuasionibus ingerunt, monstrantes causam Dei esse et totius Ecclesiæ, quam tuendam susceperant, prædicantes martyres futuros, quotquot discedere contingeret in hac causa. Quapropter rogant, hortantur, adjurant, ut, omni metu deposito, hostes Crucis invadant, non minus recepturi meritum de dictorum canum mortibus, quam si tot de gente Judaica vel Saracenica peremissent. Talibus monitis animata juventus vires colligit, et hostes acrius invadendo cædit, retrocedere cogit, donec rarus super muros defensor appareret. Occupant idcirco muros nostri viriliter, et in villam desiliendo descendunt, et hostes intra muros comprimunt et coartant, donec pavefacti arma projiciunt, et latibula fugiendo requirunt. Nostrates autem, cernentes jam rem correspondere, ardent Crucis opprobria vindicare, necnon et proprias ulcisci injurias, insolenter ab habitatoribus villæ illius die præcedente acceptas, cum primo applicarent ad muros. Dixerant nempe multa convitia in nostrates, quæ illos, nec immerito, molestarent. Ob quam causam modo nostri hostes scrutantur per latibula, et eos contumeliose extrahunt, et pollutos spiritus compellunt emittere violenter. [2]Percurrentes itaque villam, nulli parcunt, sed eos usque ad unum delere laborant; sicque Crucis beneficio factum, ut Cruce-signati et villa gloriose potirentur, et hostes Crucis ita delerent, quod unus ex eis non remansit. Nec occulte muris ruinam molientes, aut dolose hostes circumvenientes, sed aperto Marte pugnantes, hanc victoriam sunt adepti, a meridie diei præcedentis, per totam noctem, usque ad meridiem diei sequentis fortunam variam tolerantes. In portu villæ prædictæ captæ sunt tres magnæ naves, in quibus habebantur ducenta dolia vino plena, et carnes multæ salitæ, frumentum quoque, simul et ferrum; quæ omnia fuerant advecta instaurationi villæ memoratæ. Captæ sunt insuper ibi duæ bargiæ, quibus non facile [3]reperirentur ex tota Gallia

The English enter the town,

And gain possession of it.

Spoils of victory captured there.

---

[1] These two words are omitted in the printed texts.

[2] *Præcurrentes* in orig. and the printed texts: corrected from Bibl. Reg. 13 E. ix.

[3] *reperientur* in the printed texts.

A.D. 1383. meliores. Duæ præterea galeæ, cum scaphis piscatoriis sexdecim, interceptæ sunt ibidem. Equi etiam multi nobiles et alacres in eadem villa reperti sunt, quos Gallici præmiserant ad illam villam, quia [1] disposuerant interfuisse bello quod expost gestum est, ut dicemus, et, obtenta victoria quam sine dubio sperabant, Episcopum fugientem cum suis intercepisse: sed evenit aliter quam sperabant, quia quicquid ipsi disponebant ad dolum, hoc Divinitas suis convertit in bonum, et dedit eis prius præoccupare præfatam villam quam Gallici crediderunt. MS. Bibl. Reg. 13 E. ix.

Intentions of the French, in case of success.

Great number of horses taken there.

Factum est ergo ut nostri tantis proventibus plurimum confortarentur, quia plurimi qui pedites venerant ex insperato equites sunt effecti. Nam fuit ibidem equorum tanta copia, ut equus uno solido venderetur. Et ad villam de [2] Gravenynge hæc quidem gesta sunt.

Prœlium inter Cruce-signatos et Flandrenses, etc.

The Bishop of Norwich proceeds to Dunkirke, and captures it.

Protractis diebus paucis apud villam de [2] Gravenynge, quibus Episcopus et Dominus Hugo de Kalverlee dictum oppidum munierunt, et custodes statuerunt ibidem, assumpsit commanipulares suos, et ad villam de Dunkirke, pulchram valde, fossis latis circumdatam, portis et seris firmam, profectus est. Audierat utique villanos de Dunkirke nuper nocte [3] peremisse de nostris viris nauticis ad triginta septem; unde offensus eis, mortes patriotarum in illos statuit vindicare. Quam quidem villam sine grandi labore cepit, et quibus voluit in illa vicem reddens, quibusdam vero parcens, totum exercitum suum in dictam villam traxit.

The Flemings and French raise a great army.

Interea Flandrenses et Gallici, Britones et alii conductitii, exercitum grandem comparaverant, ducibus Bastard Flandriæ, quem "*Hasam*" lingua sua vocant, et Domino de Dixemuth, ac quodam Johanne Mytteneye, qui et ipse parum ante in Anglia fuerat, et Episcopo auxilium fidele promiserat venienti; sed prævaricatus est pactum, in omnibus mentiendo.

Hii ergo, contractis amplius quam triginta millibus balistariorum et virorum bellicosorum, sed tamen occulte, statuerunt repente super Episcopum improvisum irruisse, et eum de sub cœlo, cum toto suo exercitu, delevisse. Sed hiis conatibus restitit Dominus, fortis et potens, Dominus potens in prœlio,

---

[1] *deposuerant* in orig. and the printed texts; corrected from Bibl. Reg. 13 E. ix.

[2] *Graveling* in the printed texts.

[3] *pervenisse* in the printed texts.

MS. Bibl. Reg. 13 E. ix. et dolos eorum tali occasione Episcopo patefecit. Egressi siquidem fuerant garciones ad pabulandum super velocissimos magistrorum suorum equos; qui inopinato conspiciunt exercitum magnum et fortem, armis fulgentem, et pene superficiem terræ replentem. Et existimantes, prout erant, hostes videlicet eos esse, urgentes equos calcaribus, festinanter fugerunt, et Episcopo, cœnanti apud villam de Dunkirk, universa quæ viderant nunciarunt. Nec mora, Episcopus, dejectis mensis et sumptis armis, villam egreditur, illico pugnaturus, quamvis nonnulli laudarent socios ex Anglia superventuros, qui plures extiterant, expectandos. Dominus Hugo de Kalverlee, videns animositatem Episcopi, et hostes adesse prope sentiens, hortatur socios ut etiam nunc viriliter agant, et de Dei adjutorio ne diffidant, qui eis tam læta principia contulit, qualia ipsi sperare vix poterant, antequam [1] denique illis infudisset [2] tota gratiæ plenitudo.—"Quis enim vestrum credidisset," inquit, "tam fortem villam, tot fortibus custoditam, a tam paucis "potuisse subjici; ubi nec instrumenta bellica, nec multitudo "repugnantium, defuerunt, nisi Dominus adjuvisset nos, nisi "manus Domini fecisset hæc omnia. Cogitate," ait, "vos "modo non esse pugnaturos contra muros lapideos, contra "vallum fossasque de [3] Gravenynge, sed leviorem instare "pugnam, contra Flandrenses imbelles, schismaticos, Crucis "hostes; et quia nec usum pugnandi contra Anglicos hactenus habuerunt, ideo leviori negotio superandos."

A.D. 1383.

The Bishop is warned of the approach of the enemy to Dunkirk.

Sir Hugh de Calverlee addresses the troops.

Exhortatione facta, disposuit aciem, collocat certis stationibus arcitenentes, [4] et quemlibet rudem instruit de pugnandi forma. Hostes vero, videntes nostros jam obviam processisse, occurrunt cum clamore. Sed ne propius accederent, repulsi sunt sagittis, donec manus armata parata esset ad congrediendum cum ipsis. Igitur accedentibus comminus armatis, cernere erat durus conflictus, hostibus gladiis, lanceis, et cudibus ferro ligatis, rem agentibus, Anglicis vero securibus duris et acutis contra stantes, more pecudum, prosternentibus. Ibi rectores et vicarii, quos beneficium absolutionis illexerat, periculis expositi, gustaverunt quam dulcis est domus propria, monachi et canonici cognoverunt quam bona sit obedientia, Fratres Mendicantes senserunt quanto levius sit stipem postulare inter notos et in patria. Nam, ut ita dicam, erat ex parte

The battle commences.

Resolution of the clergy in the English ranks.

---

[1] *Deus* in the printed texts. In Bibl. Reg. 13 E. ix. the word is doubtful, but has the appearance of meaning "*semel.*"

[2] *totam . . . plenitudinem* in the printed texts.

[3] *Graveling* in the printed texts.

[4] *in* in orig. and Bibl. Reg. 13 E. ix., by inadvertence: corrected from the printed texts.

A.D. 1383. nostra nisi manipulus hominum, videlicet quinque millia majorum et minorum, oppositorum triginta millibus bellatorum. Quare merito viri de rebus bellicis [1]expertes, deliciose educati, in pace requieque nutriti, animo poterant concidisse, nisi affuisset illis spiritus Domini, spiritus consilii et fortitudinis, et audaciam infudisset. Sed accidit ea hora, cooperante Divinitate, quod viri, [2]ut usu transacto loquar, [3]requieti, viribus et pulchris facinoribus demonstrarent, quia multum illis profuit requies [4]diuturna. Namque compertum est quosdam ex religiosis sexdecim homines in ipso conflictu peremisse, et tanto alios in fortitudine præcessisse, quanto constabat eos claustralibus otiis diutius senuisse; de qualibus olim Poeta sic ait;— MS. Bibl. Reg. 13 E. ix.

[5]"Da requiem, requietus ager bene credita reddet."

—Ita isti, de requie ad laborem repente translati, fructum quietis et otii nobiliter reddiderunt.

Skill of the English archers.

Sed inter omnes, et præ omnibus, arcitenentes nostri laudem ibidem merebantur, et gloriam, qui hostes sic a sagitta volante percusserunt, ut non plus in armis illorum morarentur quam si nudos feriissent ipsæ sagittæ; tanta itaque erat densitas sagittarum volantium, ut aer, tanquam a nube nigra, obscuraretur, et tam crebræ hostibus mittebantur, ut vultus erigere non auderent. Quia quicunque in sublime suspicere nitebatur, hic repente vel amissum oculum [6]per sagittam, vel perforatum cerebrum, deploravit. Fuerunt multi, qui dum manus armatas apponunt frontibus, subito sagitta perveniens utramque configit. Perforabantur [7]corpora, non obstante lorica, sauciabantur pectora, nil resistente lamina, transfigebantur capita, nihil juvante galea, manus tenentes lanceas sive sudes ipsis instrumentis suis sunt affixa, non proficientes [8]chirotheca. Et, ut utamur brevibus, tanta erat pugnantium ibi diversitas, ut hinc homines paratos ad occidendum cerneres, illinc pecudes ad moriendum.

Franci igitur et Britones qui affuerunt, quorum numerus ad mille nongentos se extendit, videntes tantam stragem Flan-

---

[1] *experti* in Bibl. Reg. 13 E. ix.: *ex parte* in orig. and the printed texts.

[2] *et* in orig., by inadvertence; corrected from the printed texts.

[3] *irrequieti* in the printed texts.

[4] *diurna* in the printed texts.

[5] Ovid, *Ars Am.* ii. 351.

[6] *vel sagittam* in orig. and the printed texts: corrected from Bibl. Reg. 13 E. ix.

[7] From this word down to *transfigebantur* the context is omitted in the printed texts.

[8] *chirothecæ* in the printed texts.

MS. Bibl. Reg. 13 E. ix.

drensium, horrore nimio sunt [1] perculsi. Hii nempe anteposuerunt Flandrenses in dicto bello, duabus quidem causis; quarum una fuit, quia suspectam habebant fidem Flandrensium, et ideo, ne de bello fugerent, cum instaret necessitas, eos primis periculis exposuerunt. Alia causa fuit, ut si contingeret Anglicos esse victores, ipsi haberent majorem copiam fugiendi. Igitur Gallici, considerata, prout diximus, tanta pernicie, obriguerunt omnes, timore perterriti, et festinant, terga vertentes; fugerunt post quos mox omnis reliqua multitudo. Quod videntes Anglici, confestim hostes insequi maturabant; cædebant ergo comprehensos fugientes ante faciem suam, necnon a dextris et a sinistris, et cadebant in denso numero jugulati. Ut autem nulli veniret in dubium hanc victoriam divinitus procuratam, fiebant in hora pugnæ præfatæ horrida fulgura, tremenda tonitrua, quæ, sicut Anglicis famulabantur, sic in perniciem hostium ferebantur. Nam et in bello et in fuga, [2] [hostes] per crebra fulgura, in suos oculos emissa, cæcabantur, prosternebantur, et necabantur. Anglici vero, sentientes hæc esse divina beneficia, confortabantur, exhilarabantur; ut æstimare merito valerent illud [3] Claudiani fuisse eorum cuilibet applicatum:—

A.D. 1383.

The Flemings are placed in the front of the battle.

The French take to flight.

A storm of thunder and lightning, greatly in aid of the English.

" Te propter, gelidis Aquilo de monte procellis
" [4] O venit adversas acies, revolutaque tela
" Vertit in auctores, et turbine repulit hastas.
" O nimium dilecte Deo, [5] qui fundit ab antris
" Æolus [6] armatas hyemes; cui militat æther,
" Et conjurati veniunt ad classica venti!"

[7] Interfecta sunt autem in loco pugnæ et in fuga duodecim millia inimicorum, de nostris vero tantum septem viri ceciderunt, ut cunctis sæculis eluceret hanc victoriam de cœlis fuisse collatam.

Amount of the slain on both sides.

Commissum est dictum bellum octavo Kalendas Junii, die videlicet quo facit Sancta Ecclesia de [8] Beato Urbano, Papa et Martyre, mentionem; ita omnia concurrebant, ut istam profectionem Deo placere nullus hominum dubitaret. Expleta pugna, Episcopus, cum suis, in villam de Dunkirke se recepit.

The Bishop retires to Dunkirke.

---

[1] *proculsi* in orig. and Bibl. Reg. 13 E. ix.; *percussi* in the printed texts

[2] Supplied from Bibl. Reg. 13 E. ix.; omitted in the printed texts.

[3] *De III. Consul. Honorii*, ll. 93–98.

[4] Sic in orig., Bibl. Reg. 13 E. ix., and the printed texts. The correct reading is " *Obruit.*"

[5] Sic in orig., Bibl. Reg. 13 E. ix. and the printed texts: correctly *cui*.

[6] *armatos* in orig., Bibl. Reg. 13 E. ix., and the printed texts.

[7] *Interfecti* in the printed texts.

[8] *bono* in the printed texts.

Quid Rex Franciæ fecerit post hoc bellum.

A.D. 1383. Auditis rumoribus de præfata victoria, [1]et Episcopi continuatis successibus in Galliis, concidit vultus adversariorum, et timuerunt valde. Quamobrem Rex et tota nobilitas Franciæ, deliberato consilio, statuerunt universos amicos et notos, prope positos, ad ferendum auxilium contra tam infestos hostes evocare; quod et factum est, Rege interim in valle Suessionensi expectante venturos, et ibidem suos Gallicos adjuvante: nam regio illa multorum capax erat et fertilis, ac victualibus cunctis abundans. Illic descenderunt ad Regem Duces septem, cum suis exercitibus, Comites quidem decem, quidam ligeantia astricti, quidam precario advocati, cum multis aliis dominis et viris magni nominis et potestatis; [2]absque militibus et armigeris, valettis et civibus, necnon et communi vulgo, quorum numerus centum millia excedebat. Sed horum omnium congregationem Episcopus parvipendens, statuit interea subjicere patriam sibi vicinam, donec et ipse suos conductitios, qui nondum mare transierant, recepisset; conduxerat siquidem multos viros exercitatos in armis et bello aptos, si fideles fuisse maluissent. Quorum unus erat Willelmus de Bello [3]Campo, frater Comitis Warwici, scilicet Domini Thomæ de Bello Campo. Hic quingentas marcas suscepit ab Episcopo pro sua sola persona; sed quia non ante solutum erat ei de totidem quas habuisset ex pacto antequam transfretaret, pecuniam quidem sibi retinuit, et nihilominus domi remansit, cum imprecatione sinistra totius vulgi. Dominus Thomas Trivet, et ipse conductus, nondum suos secum profecturos congregaverat, non ante paratus et ipse fuerat, sed, more mulieris jacentis in puerperio, jacebat ad mare; nescio quid expectans. Ob quam causam, Londonienses et quidam ex amicis Episcopi comminati sunt ei mortem, nisi maturius transfretaret, cunctis acclamantibus eum proditionis causa remorari. Quibus aculeis stimulatus mare transiit, et ad Episcopum festinanter pervenit; sed nihil profecit adventus ejus Episcopo, [4][sicut ex sequentibus cognoscetur]. Igitur Episcopus, ut præfati sumus, affectans subjugare provinciam, de villa de Dunkirke profectus est; a facie [5]cujus mox tota vicina turbabatur. Et recordantes quanta fecerit apud [6]Grave-

MS. Bibl. Reg. 13 E. ix.

The King of France collects a great force.

The Bishop awaits fresh troops from England.

William de Beauchamp violates his engagement, and Sir Thomas Trivet shews remissness.

The latter joins the Bishop; who now leaves Dunkirke.

---

[1] *vel* in orig. and the printed texts: corrected from Bibl. Reg. 13 E. ix.

[2] *non absque* in the printed texts.

[3] *Campi* in orig., by inadvertence.

[4] Supplied from Bibl. Reg. 13 E. ix.: omitted in the printed texts.

[5] *cui* in orig.; *unde* in the printed texts: corrected from Bibl. Reg. 13 E. ix.

[6] *Graveling* in the printed texts.

MS. Bibl. Reg. 13 E. ix.

A.D. 1383.

nynge, quanta per post apud Dunkirke, sine resistentia se reddere maluerunt, quam resistendo perdere villas et vitas. Villas ergo de Newport, de Burburgh, de [1]Braw, et de Poperyngge, sine conflictu recepit, et multas alias adjacentes.

The Bishop captures several towns.

De nova profectione Cruce-signatorum.

Effect of the news of these victories in England.

Cum igitur in Anglia tam læta nova fuissent cognita, per quosdam qui interfuerunt captioni villarum de [2]Gravenynge et de Dunkirke, qui, in testimonium fidelis relationis, de præda equos et equas, boves et [3]multam supellectilem, domum secum contraxerant, confestim omnis patria, spe prædæ illecta, commota est ad proficiscendum. Et sine majori deliberatione de Londoniis multi apprenticii, plures servi, sumptis albis caputiis et rubeis crucibus in parte dextera, rubeis quoque gladiorum vaginis in sinistra, invitis magistris et dominis, sunt profecti. Quod exemplum secuti [4]alii de tota pene Anglia, relictis parentibus et cognatis, carisque famulatibus, inermes præter gladios, arcus, et sagittas, sunt egressi; et non tantum sæculares viri ista fecerunt, sed religiosi sectæ cujuslibet eodem animo, petita licentia, licet non obtenta, illud iter arripere præsumpserunt, in magnum personarum suarum dedecus et detrimentum; quia non propter Jesum tantum peregrinare decreverunt, sed ut patriam mundumque viderent. Currebatur itaque [5][per omnes vias], per omnes semitas, a plebe inexperta et gente rustica, donec perveniretur ad mare; ubi Dominus Johannes Philipot, sollicitus pro Episcopo, navigium providebat. Ibi fuerunt multi, qui præter navium nullas habebant expensas; eo quod æstimabant, si mare transissent, nihil eis omnino defuturum, sed [6]affutura cuncta pro votis; transpositi sunt ergo multi, et ad Episcopum festinabant, qui, tunc ulterius progressus, ad villam de Ypres pervenerat cum exercitu, divitiis plenam, ædificiis inclytam, bellatoribus communitam. [7]Ibi ergo quamvis invitus, quamvis protestans non esse suæ voluntatis obsidionem ponere, sed Franciam, tam in causa Domini Papæ quam Regis, intrare, compellitur per milites, Dominum Thomam Trivet, Willelmum de Elmham, et Willelmum Faryndone, residere, velit nolit, invitus; qui omnes

Numbers of recruits from England join the Bishop at Ypres.

---

[1] *Barw* in Bibl. Reg. 13 E. ix.

[2] *Graveling* in the printed texts.

[3] *multum* in orig. and the printed texts.

[4] Repeated in orig. and Bibl. Reg. 13 E. ix.

[5] Supplied from Bibl. Reg. 13 E. ix.: omitted in the printed texts.

[6] *futura* in the printed texts.

[7] These two words are omitted in the printed texts.

A.D. 1383. unanimiter affirmabant se nolle ulterius sequi eum, donec dictam villam hostiliter effregissent, licet in Franciam ire vellet. Asseverebant etiam Gandavenses affuturos in adjutorium, et non esse modo difficile Anglicis et Gandavensibus, simul [1]junctis, villam effringere, cum tantummodo Gandavenses, sine externo suffragio, eodem anno villam eandem vi et armis cepissent. Videns ergo Episcopus se nihil proficere, tacere decrevit, et eorum ad tempus obsequi voluntati; maxime quia pro certo cognovit Gandavenses obsidionis socios et laboris. MS. Bibl. Reg. 13. E. ix.

By persuasion of his officers, the Bishop resolves to besiege Ypres.

De Obsidione villæ de Ypres.

The Bishop and the people of Ghent lay siege to Ypres.

Igitur villam de Ypres Episcopus et Cruce-signati, ex una parte, et triginta millia Gandavensium, ex altera parte, circumsederunt. Venerunt idcirco catervatim ex Anglia ad obsidionem,—quos supra diximus illectos spe prædæ,—et jam tantus effectus est numerus accurrentium, ut sexaginta millia numerarentur ex Anglicis advenisse. Igitur perpendens Episcopus tantum populum advenisse, qui nec exercitatus esset in armis, nec arma quidem possideret, doluit, et mittens ad Dominum Johannem Philipot, rogavit ne permitteret quemquam de cætero mare transire, nisi valentes; et ait ad eos qui inermes venerant;—"Ut quid ergo venistis? Ad consumendum victum, qui vix sufficiet bellaturis? Vos [2]'numerus estis, 'fruges consumere nati;' melius fuisset vobis domi sine cura [3]super ollas carnium resedisse." Ob quam causam vulgus indignabatur, et jam quisque cœpit Episcopo detrahere; occulte tamen, propter metum ejus.

His complaints as to unarmed recruits resorting to his standard.

Indignation against him.

Rex Angliæ circuit per Abbathias.

The King and Queen visit the Abbeys of England.

Dum hæc aguntur in Flandria, Rex Angliæ et Regina, cum suis Boemiis, Abbathias regni circueunt visitando; quibus tanto tristior fuit eorum adventus, quanto gravior; quia et accesserunt in excessivo numero, et non "offerre," sed "auferre," venerunt. Sensit hoc Abbathia de Bury, quæ in eum et Reginam, ipsorumque familiam, per decem dies quibus moram fecerunt ibidem, expendit octingentas marcas; tanquam non suffecissent eis pastoris viduatio per quadriennium, damna

---

[1] *victus* in orig.; *victis* in the printed texts: corrected from Bibl. Reg. 13 E. ix.

[2] An adaptation from Horace, *Epist.* I. 2. 27.

[3] In allusion to *Exod.* xvi. 3.

MS. Bibl. Reg. 13 E. ix. — A.D. 1383.

irrestaurabilia per insurrectionem communium, pecuniarum largæ [1]profusiones pro recuperatione suorum jurium, tam in Romana Curia quam in ista terra.

The King ratifies the election of John Tymworth as Abbot.

Ut videretur tamen Rex adventu suo eidem Monasterio aliquid contulisse, fecit ut novissima illius fierent pejora prioribus, admittendo provisionem factam per Dominum Papam de Johanne Tymworth; qui paulo ante juraverat se nunquam consensurum ut gauderet honore pastorali, nisi simpliciter Papa vellet confirmare electionem de ipso factam. Insuper et dudum Papæ rescripserat in eadem verba, sed vix ambassiatores sui [2]Romam pervenerant, antequam, pueriliter mutato proposito, eundem Johannem Tymworthe benedici fecit a Confessore suo, Episcopo Landavensi; quo facto inconstantia Regis, ejusque Consilii, longe lateque innotuit, et sicut Ecclesiæ Anglicanæ detrimentum, ita Papæ et Curialibus magnam peperit materiam [3]insolescendi.

Consequences of the King's irresoluteness.

Expletis diebus moræ dispendiosæ apud Bury, recte ad Thetford properat, et sic ad Northwicum, ubique [4]munera tam a religiosis quam a sæcularibus [5]scienter accipiens; ubi duo mala concurrere videbantur. Non enim Regi magna donaria suffecerunt, nisi et Reginæ æqualia præberentur; nec, cum populo grave visum fuisset ejus honoris intuitu exhibuisse perampla donaria, si ad usum eorum prudenter conservata fuissent. Sed quicquid hausit eorum manus avida, mox alienigenis de gente Reginæ, scilicet Boemiis, prodigaliter erogavit, unde contigit ut, post regni circuitionem, magis inopes reverterentur quam egressi fuerant; ut cunctis verum esse constaret illud proverbium Sapientis; "[6]Væ terræ, "cujus rex puer est."

Extortions practised on behalf of the Queen, as well as the King.

The monies so gained all lavished on the Queen's countrymen.

Tædet recordationis tot nugarum, et [7]ideo placet melius silere quam loqui. Jam ergo ad [8]Flandrense bellum stylum vertamus.

---

[1] *profusionis* in orig and Bibl. Reg. 13 E. ix.; corrected from the printed texts.

[2] *Romani* in orig. and in the printed texts: corrected from Bibl. Reg. 13 E. ix.

[3] *insoluendi* in orig.; *insolendi* in Bibl. Reg. 13 E. ix.: corrected from the printed texts.

[4] *multa* in the printed texts; imperfectly written in orig.: but *munera* in Bibl. Reg. 13 E. ix.

[5] Apparently *satienter* in Bibl. Reg. 13 E. ix.

[6] *Eccles.* x. 16.

[7] *idcirco* in the printed texts.

[8] *Flandrenses bellum* in orig.; *Flandrensium bella* in the printed texts: *Flandrense bellum* in Bibl. Reg. 13 E. ix.

Proditio quorundam.

A.D. 1383. Remissness of the English, at the siege of Ypres. Sedente igitur Episcopo, suisque complicibus, in obsidione villæ de Ypres, in ipso fervore dierum, Yprenses, considerantes obsessores esse remissos otiisque vacare, villam firmare, ruinas reficere, arma et utensilia bellica, quibus hostes arceri deberent, fabricare, continue satagebant. Gandavenses vero, qui alteram partem villæ obsidebant, comportare aggerem, implere fossam, ut facilior esset aditus ad conserendum cum villanis, totis viribus laborabant. Sed nostris militibus non placuit insilire villam, experiri fortunam, aut appropinquare muris, propter pericula quæ possent emergere, sed [1] opperiri tempus deditionis voluntariæ; quod sciebant nunquam fore futurum, nam [2] intus carnibus et tritico, et diversi generis potibus, abundabant. MS. Bibl. Reg. 13 E. ix.

Charge of treachery against Sir Thomas Tryvet and others. Fuerunt qui dixerint Thomam Tryvet, et quosdam ex militibus reliquis, utres [3] plenos auro de villanis cepisse, et in villam sæpissime introisse, ac, tam private quam publice, cum illis tractatus multotiens habuisse; unde non solum plebs communis [4] suspicabatur eos esse proditores, sed clamando publice testabatur. Factum est itaque ut, per moram inutilem quam traxerunt, pejor esset conditio obsidentium quam obsessorum, quia et illis inter se inerat multa concordia et victus abundantia, nostris suspicio et discordia, ac panis et aquæ penuria; unde contigit pestis mortifera inter nostros, et cotidie plures dysenteria perierunt. Furtive igitur e castris recedendo, nostri cotidie mare petunt, et Angliam venientes, [5] quæ viderant vel audierant de dictis militibus referebant. Videns ergo Episcopus indies numerum suorum minui, instat apud milites, qui jam non ejus subditi, sed magistri, fuerunt effecti, ut contra villam suas vires experiantur, antequam turba nimis vel peste vel discessione minuatur.

Distressed state of the besiegers.

The Bishop gives orders for the attack.

Insultus ad villam de Ypres.

Cui petitioni vix tandem consentientes, [6] [circa Vigiliam Sancti Laurentii applicant ad vallum; quod sentientes] [7] villani

---

[1] *operire* in the printed texts.

[2] *omnibus* in orig. and the printed texts: corrected from Bibl. Reg. 13 E. ix.

[3] *plenas* in orig. and Bibl. Reg. 13 E. ix. : corrected from the printed texts.

[4] *supplicabatur* in orig. ; corrected from the printed texts.

[5] *qui* in orig. ; corrected from the printed texts.

[6] Supplied from Bibl. Reg. 13 E. ix. : omitted in the printed texts.

[7] *villam occurrunt* in the printed texts.

MS. Bibl. Reg. 13 E. ix.

occurrunt totis animis, et cum lapidibus, lanceis, et sagittis, igne Græco, et [1] missilibus quæ "gunna" vocantur, nostros ubique repellunt. Fecerat autem Episcopus fieri quemdam pontem subtilissimum, per quem ad vallum facilis fuisset ascensus. Quem villani cernentes in magnam perniciem illorum esse compositum, emittunt [2] [de quadam] gunna grandem lapidem, qui percutiens pontem, sine difficultate confregit, et quosdam milites superstantes simul crudeliter interemit. Nec minora damna fiebant in locis aliis, propter quæ nostri sese retrahere, et insultum dimittere, cogebantur. Subtractis cunctis qui superfuerant, de loco periculi discessum est ad hospitia singulorum, et intra paucos dies obsidio dissoluta, Gandavensibus cum mœrore discedentibus, et falsitatem execrantibus Anglicorum; quia profecto, si fuisset tanta fides inter duces Anglicorum quanta fuit inter Gandavenses, villa de Ypres hodie non superesset.

A.D. 1383. The besiegers are repulsed.

The siege is raised.

Relinquentes autem obsidionem, quæ incendere poterant exurebant, ne hostibus essent ad solatium vel juvamen; vellent nollent, tamen reliquerunt ibidem quæ nec incendere, nec confringere, nec evehere, potuerunt, gunnas videlicet magnas, ingentis pretii et valoris. Plurimi vero nescientes tempus discessionis, quæque pretiosa et [3] parata per multos labores et pericula, subito migrare compulsi, dimiserunt ibidem. Sic finis et fructus obsidionis villæ de Ypres.

Implements of war left by the besiegers.

Milites contradicunt Episcopo, volenti ingredi Pykardiam.

Post obsidionis solutionem, cognoscens Episcopus per exploratores Regem Franciæ cum exercitu pervenisse ad civitatem Ambianensem, alloquitur suos milites, scilicet Dominum Thomam Tryvet et Willelmum de Elmham, cæterosque, dicens se velle Pikardiam ingredi, et contra Regem Franciæ uno die Martis experiri fortunam. Et cum multa allegasset quibus merito accendi potuissent ad profectionem, nihil tamen profecit, sed cum injuria etiam contumelias recepit ab eis, dicentibus eum temerarium et nescientem vires tantæ multitudinis, quæ centum habebat contra unum ex illis. Non fore tutum, nec discretioni consonum, sic tentare Deum, ubi nulla spes esset victoriæ, sed certitudo confusionis, nisi forte subito tam artam necessitatem incurrissent, de qua non possent effugere, nisi

The Bishop proposes to enter Picardy; but is opposed by his officers.

[1] *missibiles* in orig., by inadvertence.

[2] Supplied from Bibl. Reg. 13 E. ix.: omitted in the printed texts.

[3] *ptata* in orig.; *portata* in the printed texts: corrected from Bibl. Reg. 13 E. ix.

A.D. 1383. The officers retire to Burburgh. MS. Bibl. Reg. 13 E. ix.

pugnando. Quibus auditis, Episcopus valefecit eisdem, cum paucis admodum Pikardiam ingrediendo. Milites vero ad villam de Burburgh properant, quam munire [1] et custodire decreverunt contra Francos, si forte illuc eos contingeret advenisse.

The Bishop enters Picardy, and then returns to Gravenynge.

Cum ergo Episcopus prope partem exercitus Gallicorum [2] appropinquasset, demonstravit se suosque in campo explicatis vexillis; sed nemine audente conserere, quia nondum totus exercitus Gallicanus convenerat, Episcopus vexilla reflexit, et, sub omni festinatione, ad villam suam de [3] Gravenynge cepit iter, cum Domino Hugone de Kalverlee, qui ei semper fuerat in cunctis angustiis comes individuus, sociusque fidelis.

Episcopus revertitur ad Gravenynge, et Milites ad Burburgh.

The King of France marches against Burburgh.

Coadunatus suis exercitibus Rex Franciæ, et de nostrorum discessione non parum [4] elatus, ut agnovit quosdam villam de Burburgh ingressos fuisse, totum exercitum convertit ad locum, jurans se neminem illorum qui fuerunt ibidem, prece vel pretio, salvaturum, sed omnes vel ignibus crematurum, cum eadem villa, vel certe captos in ore gladii peremplurum. Quibus molitionibus Dux Britanniæ contravenit, asserens non ita futurum ut credebat; se nosse personas quæ in ea fuerunt, quod omnes essent viri fortes et scientes bellum, et sine gravi Gallorum dispendio [5] superare non posse.—"Non," inquit, "contra Flandrenses pugnaturi estis, sed contra Anglicos, "viros utique cordatos valde, et qui malunt mori quam "vinci." Rex autem, commotus ad hæc verba Ducis,—"Et "tu," inquit, "ex illis es, et ideo pro illis verba facis." Cui confestim Dux,—"Et ne æstimetis me," ait, "aut timore "vel eorum favore talia protulisse, videbitis me primum "cum meis hominibus insultum facere contra eos." Habebat siquidem virorum electissimorum ad duodecim millia, quos contraxerat ex omni ditione sua. Et illico, vexillis erectis, ad muros accessit. Erant autem in villa Dominus de Bemond et Thomas Tryvet, Willelmus [6] Elmham, et Willelmus de Faryndone, milites, et multi alii viri fortes, qui, [7] locatis in

Speech of the Duke of Bretagne to the King of France.

---

[1] These two words are omitted in the printed texts.

[2] *appropinquasse* in orig. and the printed texts: corrected from Bibl. Reg. 13 E. ix.

[3] *Graveling* in the printed texts.

[4] *elatis* in orig.; by inadvertence.

[5] *superari* in the printed texts.

[6] *Elmtham* in orig.; *Elintham* in the printed texts: corrected from Bibl. Reg. 13 E. ix.

[7] *locati* in orig., Bibl. Reg. 13 E. ix., and the printed texts.

MS. Bibl. Reg. 13 E. ix.

A.D. 1383.

circuitu [1] defensoribus, mox contra Britones dimicare parati, suas occupant stationes. Fit ergo pugna ingens, spectante Rege Franciæ cunctisque Gallicis, et in omni conatu Britones pejorem calculum reportabant. Fecerant autem nostri instrumenta ferrea et uncata, quibus attraherent appropinquantes et in villam ejicerent, vel certe pungendo repellerent, et in fossas cadere facerent luto [2] plenas. Attrahebantur itaque plures supra muros in villam, et more pecudum mox cadentes cum securibus excerebrabantur: multi autem a muro repulsi in cœno, quod in fossis erat, demergebantur. Insuper et vexillum Ducis Britanniæ, violenter extortum de manibus signiferi, raptum est in villam, cum signis pluribus aliorum. Cogebantur ergo Britones metu mortis a pugna quiescere, et se muris subtrahere cum pudore. Tunc Gallici, et ipsi præsumptuosi, accedere tentaverunt, sed suis periculis didicerunt Britones non se temere subtraxisse; nam mox ut appropinquaverunt, [3] candentibus verubus sunt repulsi; quibus apponere manus volentibus, et ad se contrahere, dum multi super unum veru manus mittunt, omnes parem [4] recepere mercedem, manibus eorum miserabiliter concrematis; unde confestim inutiles facti, dum manus solvunt, vel trahuntur in villam vel præcipitantur in fossam. Igitur interfecti sunt ex Gallicis in illo conflictu amplius quam quingenti, nostris pene nihil læsis, nisi quod per ignem Græcum, in villam emissum, tertia pars domorum, cum multis victualibus, est combusta.

The Bretons and French are repulsed.

Nocte superveniente, pugna dimissa, et Gallici se ad sua tentoria contulerunt, amissis signis Regis et plurium dominorum. Sub ipso noctis articulo, Dux Britanniæ venit ad Regem Franciæ, quærens quid sentiret de Anglicis, et si adhuc censeret plures insultus facere contra eos. Rex vero respondit eos esse dæmones, non homines, qui tam fraudulenta commenta adinvenissent adversus aliquos Christianos. Nihilominus dixit se non cessaturum, donec omnes eos cepisset manu forti. Cui Dux,—"Et ego," ait, "non laudo plures in-"sultus fieri, quia et ingeniosi et fortes sunt viri, et cotidie "novas contra adinventiones disperquirent; et si tales tres "dies fecerimus, perdendo contra eos, nostro numero immi-"nuto, ipsi satis fortes erunt quarto die, cum auxilio Epi-"scopi, qui tenet prope villam de [5] Gravenyng, ad exeundum "et pugnandum contra nos in campo; tunc non dubito quin

The Duke of Bretagne expostulates with the French King against renewing the attack.

[1] *ut defensores* in the printed texts.

[2] *plena* in the printed texts.

[3] *cadentibus* in Bibl. Reg. 13 E. ix; incorrectly.

[4] *recipere* in orig., Bibl. Reg. 13 E. ix., and in the printed texts.

[5] *Graveling* in the printed texts.

A.D. 1383. "plura perdemus quam prius amisimus." Rex igitur et sanior pars Gallorum, jam aliqualiter animo fracti, non de insultu, sed de tractatu, cum nostratibus cogitare cœperunt; angustiabant nempe eos tot mortes, non [1]plebeianorum, sed exercitatorum militum et armigerorum, tot læsiones dominorum, tam Britanniæ quam Gallorum. Nam et ibi Marescallus Franciæ fuit occisus, et Dominus de Clissone graviter vulneratus; ita ut in manibus asportaretur a muris. Propter quæ omnia reputantes Ducem Britanniæ jam [2]veridicum, decreverunt ut ipse alloqueretur eos ex parte Regis Franciæ, de reddenda villa; quia notus erat eis, et ipse peroptime novit eos. MS. Bibl. Reg. 13 E. ix.

The English officers surrender Burburgh on terms.

Agentes ergo tractatum Dux et nostrates, post plures altercationes, tandem in hanc sententiam consenserunt; ut villam redderent Regi Franciæ, et ipsi cum equis et armis, et cunctis servientibus, cunctis quoque bonis quæ de villa asportare placeret, indemnes exirent, et ad quemcunque locum vellent pergerent, sub conductu Regis Franciæ; ita tamen, ut versus Angliam properarent. Exeuntes autem, Calesiam pervenerunt, cum ipsis multa spolia deducentes; quod nimium Gallicos contristavit. Speraverant nempe ditati fuisse de eorum spoliis et exhilarati mortibus; sed tamen secus accidit quam credebant, ut prætactum est.

Rex Franciæ componit cum Episcopo, ut deserat villam de Gravenynge.

The surrender of Gravenynge is demanded by the French.

Post discessionem nostrorum de villa de Burburgh, convertit se exercitus Gallicanus, cum Rege suo, ad villam de [3]Gravenynge, ubi erant Dominus Hugo de Calverlee et Episcopus constituti. Quia ergo Gallici jam satis experti sunt quæ damna, quæ pericula, sequantur insultus, insultum facere de cætero metuebant. Idcirco mittunt ad Episcopum, enumerantes multitudinem Gallicorum, fortitudinem et animositatem Britonum, et qui cum illis erant, denunciantes ut reddat Regi Franciæ villam suam, quam injuste dinoscitur occupare. Et Episcopus ad hæc breviter respondebat, se, tam in causa Domini Papæ quam Regis Angliæ, lucratum fuisse villam prædictam, per multa pericula; insuper, et expost eandem reparasse ac fortificasse, fusa multa pecunia, nec se

---

[1] *plebeiũ* in orig. and Bibl. Reg. 13 E. ix.; *plebium* in the printed texts.

[2] *viridicum* in Camden's text.

[3] *Graveling* in the printed texts.

MS. Bibl. Reg. 13 E. ix.

A.D. 1383.

cognoscere quemquam habere juris titulum præter Regem Angliæ, vel semetipsum, in eam. Cum ergo Gallici hæc audissent, et diffiderent de redditione, remiserunt qui nunciarent Episcopo se velle quindecim millia marcarum dare, ita ut Episcopus eam deserat et complanet ad terram; et habeat facultatem Episcopus libere migrandi quocunque vellet, cum omnibus bonis suis et cunctis qui ibidem fuerunt cum eo. Ad hæc Episcopus petit inducias, ut responsum differat ad certum diem; et dantur ei. Qui statim misit in Angliam, nuncians Regi semet in arto positum, et Regem Franciæ cum innumerabili exercitu ante ipsum jacere; jam tempus esse, si unquam vellet congredi cum Rege Franciæ, properare, vel mittere qui cum eo auderent congredi; quia nisi in Angliam navigasse præsumpsisset, non potuisset propius accessisse, et ideo non erat difficile Anglicis ad succursum properare, cum nil in terra Franciæ morarentur, priusquam vel bellum haberent vel Regem Franciæ effugarent.

Terms are offered to the Bishop of Norwich, who communicates with his Sovereign.

Hiis auditis, Rex Angliæ, dum adhuc esset vagabundus, ut diximus, per patriam et domos religiosorum, et esset in cœna apud villam de Daventre, mox, expulsis tabulis, cum omni furia et festinatione surrexit, et apprehenso equo, cursu velocissimo noctem consumit equitando, multotiens equos mutando, tanquam ea nocte esset Regem Franciæ perempturus; venitque ad Sanctum Albanum nocte media, sed nil moraturus ibidem, nisi dum palefridum Abbatis mutuat, nunquam redditurus eundem. Confestim festinat ad Westmonasterium, sequentibus eum paucis; quo cum pervenisset, fatigatus a laboriosa equitatione et somno pressus, ibidem pernoctare decrevit. Cum autem dormisset, cernens requiem quod esset bona, statuit mitius agere cum hostibus suis, et alios mittere qui propulsarent eos. Sicque actum est, ut post grandia verba et pompam nimiam, ab ipso factum est nihil; qualibus illudens Poeta dicit,—

King Richard receives the communication at Daventre.

He departs in great haste for Westminster.

His ardour cools.

"Parturiunt montes, [1] exibit ridiculus mus."

Missum tamen est pro Duce [2] Lancastriæ, ut ipse usque ad locum properando festinet, et Episcopum liberet, et Gallicos arceat manu forti. Qui et ipse, tanquam continuo facturus, ita festinat ad mare, et expectat ibidem donec dies induciarum pertransissent. Videns ergo Episcopus ex Anglia nullam fidem, nullum evenire remedium, componit cum Gallicis, et villam destruit solo tenus, ut tenebatur ex pacto; sed pecuniam non recepit, quia hoc cognovit [3] consiliariis Regis displicere.

The Duke of Lancaster shows similar lukewarmness.

The Bishop makes terms, and destroys Gravenynge.

[1] Correctly "*nascetur*," in Horace, *De Arte Poet.* l. 139.

[2] Not in Bibl. Reg. 13 E. ix.

[3] *consolariis* in orig.

Galli revertuntur ad propria, infirmati.

A.D. 1383. The French army returns home, greatly lessened in numbers.

Post recessum Episcopi, et ipsi Gallici ad propria recesserunt, in parte tamen maxima imminuti; quia, ut supra diximus, ad villam de Burburgh plures valentes amiserunt, et cotidie in exercitu plures subito dysenteria et aliis variis infirmitatibus perierunt, ita ut multis diebus amplius quam trecenti in die spiritum exhalaverunt. Coacti revera fuerunt juvenes delicati, mercatorum et burgensium filii, nescientes arma, ignorantes vigilias, et per omnia inexperti, ad supplementum exercitus, qui mox ut consuetudinem mutare cœperunt, continuo infirmabantur, et repente juxta latus Regis, dum starent in armis, nil habentes [1] mali, prout visum fuit, mortui corruerunt. Quare, si qua fides, si appetitus gloriæ, si audacia, in nostris tunc militibus qui domi remanserant et hæc audierant, extitisset, profecto fuisset tempus acceptabile transfretandi et experiendi vires contra hostes, totiens in terra sua quæsitos. Nam multotiens quæsiti fuerant in regno Franciæ per Duces, per Comites, et alios dominos, sed tamen inveniri nequibant; jam præsentes fuerunt, non procul sed prope; non pauci, sed plures; non communes, sed potentes et divites; non exercitati, sed inexperti; non fortes, sed infirmi; et ecce! nostri, vel proditione detenti vel vecordia refrænati, non transeunt contra diu desideratos, sæpe quæsitos. Proh dolor! terra quæ olim generavit et produxit homines cunctis reverendos prope, et procul positis metuendos, effœminatos jam evomit, ridiculum hostibus, fabulam civibus: nam nullus vel rarus reperitur in ea, qui reipublicæ se devoveat, qui pro civibus laborem impendat, sed omnes sua lucra sectantur, propria commoda perscrutantur. Sed [2] ne lectores scandalizentur hujuscemodi verbis, plura de hiis scribere supersedemus. Ad materiam igitur superius memoratam revertamur.

MS. Bibl. Reg. 13 E. ix.

The writer laments the opportunity thus lost by the English, of humbling the French.

The Duke of Lancaster censures the Bishop of Norwich.

Igitur Episcopus, relinquens Gallias, Angliam est reversus; qui cito postquam terram attigit, Ducem adivit, qui adhuc jacebat illis in locis; qui Episcopum objurgans, quærens nodum in [3] scirpo, cito dimisit. Hugonem vero Calverlee aliquanto diutius secum detinuit, honorem ei exhibens, propter antiquam militiam approbatam. Hic ergo finis fuit profectionis et belli Pontificalis.

---

[1] *male* in orig.; corrected from the printed texts.

[2] *nec* in orig.; corrected from the printed texts.

[3] *cirpo* in orig. and Bibl. Reg. 13 E. ix. A classical proverb.

Scoti intrant Angliam.

MS. Bibl. Reg. 13 E. ix.

A.D. 1383.

The Scots invade the North of England.

Scoti per idem tempus occasionem nacti, eo quod plures fuissent cum Episcopo egressi, Northumbriam intraverunt, prout moris eorum est, cum superiores esse videntur; incolis damna irrogarunt, agentes prædas ubique, et captivos de suis domibus educentes et Scotiam pertrahentes. Ausi sunt insuper ad castellum quod vocatur "Werke," super flumen de Twede, cum multis armatis accedere, et captum ac deprædatum ignibus [1] conflagrare, nemine conatus eorum impediente, nec semet ipsorum insolentiis [2] opponere volente, propter metum quorundam qui tunc temporis a communi populo putabantur plus Scotis quam Anglicis favere. Ob quam causam, milites et armigeri, qui custodias castellorum vel munitionum habebant in [3] illa patria, venerunt ad Regem, et reddiderunt ea in manus suas, dicentes Scotos vehementer invaluisse, et Anglicos, qui in partibus illis erant, perpaucos esse ad resistendum illis, nisi Rex ipse manus apponeret adjutrices; qui responsum consolatorium acceperunt, ut dicemus in Capitulo de proximo Parliamento, quod scripturi sumus.

Application is made to the King for assistance against them; which is promised.

De Papa et Romanis.

The Pope takes measures to deceive the people of Rome.

Eodem fere tempore, Papa diffidens de fide Romanorum, simulata causa, velut puriorem aerem vellet haurire, urbem ad quoddam castellum non procul positum multotiens egrediebatur, et revertebatur, quandoque ad noctem; aliquando vero pernoctavit ibidem, et die secundo vel tertio est reversus. Ut autem tolleret omnem suspicionem a cordibus Romanorum, non procul a dicto loco [4] eo, quod amœnus esset et ibi locus, dixit se velle castellum forte construere, in quod sese posset secure recipere, si necessitas ulla urgeret. Unde gavisi Romani, jam libere permiserunt eum, sine suspicione vel exploratione, quotiens vellet, vel quando vellet, adire locum; pro eo maxime, quod noverunt eum [5] latomos et fabros plurimos conduxisse, et ad eum locum magnam materiam lapidum et lignorum comportasse.

He makes secret arrangements for his departure for Naples.

Jam ergo Papa, securus neminem ejus migrationem velle [6] scrutari, accito [7] clanculo quodam potenti domino, qui erat in illis partibus, componit cum eo, ut, certo die veniens cum armata manu, deducat eum in patriam suam ubi natus fuerat,

---

[1] *conflagare* in orig.

[2] *apponere* in orig. and the printed texts: corrected from Bibl. Reg. 13 E. ix.

[3] *villa* in Camden's text.

[4] *eo* omitted in the printed texts.

[5] *latamos* in orig.; *lutomos* in the printed texts.

[6] *perscrutari* in Bibl. Reg. 13 E. ix.

[7] *clanculum* in the printed texts.

A.D. 1383. scilicet in Neapolim; quia rebatur majorem fidem invenire inter suas patriotas quam Romanos, si contingeret indigere. Quod et factum est. MS. Bibl. Reg. 13 E. ix.

The people of Rome demand his return; but in vain.

Audientes autem Romani Papam repente fugisse, cum magno supercilio miserunt ad eum, mandantes ut revertatur; alioquin affirmabant eum velle deponere, et [1] quemquam de Cardinalibus, qui in urbe remanserant, in Papam eligere; vel certe revocare ejus adversarium, Antipapam, et ipsum intronizare. Ipse vero, parvipendens eorum minas, moram suam continuare disponit in dicta terra, quanquam ibidem multa adversa essent proventura; prout in sequentibus plenius, cum locus et tempus id postulaverint, edicetur.

De Navibus hostium captis.

Conquest of French ships of war, by the men of Portsmouth and Dartmouth.

Circa dies quibus Episcopus Northwicensis et Cruce-signati sederunt circa villam de Ypres, hostes armaverant quinque vasa bellica, qualia "balingarias" appellamus, ut arcerent et impedirent tam transitum versus eum quam versus Aquitanniam; quia et illuc dirigendi fuerant Cruce-signati, cum turba militum et armigerorum, ducibus Domino Britrigaldo de la Bret et nonnullis aliis [2] lectis ex Anglia viris bellicosis. Et cum plura mala fecissent in mari, non ferentes [3] hæc viri de Portesmutha [4] [et Dortesmutha], armaverunt ipsi naves suas [5] bellicas ad impediendum conatus eorum. Et progressi in obviam, commiserunt repente prœlium cruentum valde; sed tamen, adjutorio superno, nostri, superiores effecti, occiderunt omnes qui erant in eis, præter novem viros, et vasa et universa contenta diripiebant sibi, advehentes patriæ tam prædam quam pacem, per victoriam gloriosam.

Another naval victory.

[6] Eadem fere tempestate, navigium Anglicanum, dum liquidas observat in mari vias, octo naves grandes, refertas multis bonis, et [7] vinis præcipue, bellico jure [8] lucrantur; in quibus dicuntur fuisse mille et quingenta dolia boni vini. Et ita, licet per breves successus, [9] Anglia plurimum confortabatur.

---

[1] *aliquem* in the printed texts.
[2] *electis* in the printed texts.
[3] *hæ* in orig.
[4] Omitted in orig.; supplied from Bibl. Reg. 13 E. ix., and the printed texts.
[5] This and the four following words have a contemporary expunctory mark in Bibl. Reg. 13 E. ix.; and the context continues, —*videlicet, tres naves magnas bellicas, ad impediendum conatus eorum.*
[6] *Eidem* in orig.; by inadvertence.
[7] *unus* in orig.; *unam* in the printed texts: corrected from Bibl. Reg. 13 E. ix.
[8] *lucraturi* in orig.: corrected from the printed texts.
[9] *Angliam* in the printed texts.

Qualiter Gandavenses lucrati [1] *[sunt] villam de Owdenarde.*

MS. Bibl. Reg. 13 E. ix.

Postquam Cruce-signati e Flandria Angliam sunt [2] regressi, Gallici qui custodiebant villam de Owdenarde, quam superiori anno Gandavenses obsederant, a festo Inventionis Sanctæ Crucis usque ad Natale Domini, (quo tempore, ut superius scripsimus, Gandavenses ibidem victi fuerunt per Regem Franciæ, et Philippus den Artefeld interemptus, cum viginti quinque millibus Flandritarum); cœperunt Gallici crudele dominium exercere super cives illius villæ, opprimentes eos vehementer, et, non tantum bona diripientes eorum, sed etiam uxores vi rapientes, eis, pro suæ voluntatis arbitrio, abutebantur. Super quibus omnibus oppidani de Odenarde vehementer commoti, nec immerito, cum jam nullam spem cernerent correctionis Gallicorum, sed potius indies eorum scelera augeri viderent, miserunt secreto nuncios ad Gandavum, qui et eorum injurias civibus nunciarent, et auxilium rogarent ab eisdem; promittentes insuper, illos, quacunque nocte vellent, introducere in villam de Owdenarde; ut sic et dominio villæ potirentur, et acceptas frequenter injurias, sive damna, per Gallicos in ipsos viriliter vindicarent.

A.D. 1383. Excesses and cruelties of the French at Audenarde.

The citizens communicate with the people of Ghent.

Hiis auditis, Gandavenses non segnes accinguntur ad iter, et nocte pervenerunt ad villam, datisque signis ad invicem, qui in villa erant et qui extra villam, intromissi sunt Gandavenses. Oppidani igitur dictæ villæ, juncti Gandavensibus, scientes peroptime ubi hospitia Gallicorum fuere, domos repente irrumpunt, Gallicis dormientibus, et in ipsos subito irruentes, jugulant quotquot in villa fuere, multos valde, ita quod non superfuit unus ex eis. Et ita Gandavenses, villa potiti, etiam stragem magnam fecerunt in Flandrensibus, qui falsi fuerant suis civibus dictæ villæ. Ibi mercatores Anglici in parte recuperaverunt damna quæ pertulerant per ante in villa de Bruges, dum bona in dicta villa reperta a Gandavensibus pretio levi emunt; et non solum mobilia, sed etiam domos, et quæque [3] loca villæ. Post hæc, Gandavenses miserunt ad Regem Angliæ, nunciantes se lucratos dictam villam, quam vellent dare sibi, si vellet illuc ex Anglia custodes et auxilium destinare; alioquin detraherent illam solo tenus. Rex vero gratias agit illis, respondens se nolle illuc suos dirigere, propter instantia pericula quæ regno suo multis ex

With the aid of the people of Ghent, the French are destroyed.

The English merchants are recompensed for their former losses at Bruges.

Audenarde is offered to the King of England on

---

[1] Supplied from Bibl. Reg. 13 E. ix.

[2] *egressi* in the printed texts.

[3] *leta* in orig.; *læta* in the printed texts: corrected from Bibl. Reg. 13 E. ix.

A.D. 1383. partibus imminebant, et honoratos dictos nuncios, prout decuit, Gandavum remisit. Et hic finis Gallicorum, qui multa mala perpetraverant in villa de Owdenarde. MS. Bibl. Reg. 13 E. ix.

certain terms. The offer is declined.

Treasure of the Count of Flanders found there.

Nec silentio reticendum, quod in dicta villa repertus est infinitus thesaurus Comitis Flandriæ; qui merito et Gandavenses animaret ad continuandam werram, et Comitem [1] cogeret desperare.

De Parliamento facto Londoniis.

A grant made in Parliament, but a part is claimed by the Lords of the Northern parts.

Circa festum Omnium Sanctorum, factum est Parliamentum Londoniis; in [2] quo concessa est medietas quintæ-decimæ per laicos, et paulo post, medietas unius decimæ per clerum, Regi. Cujus pecuniæ portionem Domini partium Borealium petierunt, quia in hoc Parliamento fuerunt deputati ad custodiendum partes illas contra Scotorum irruptiones. Quibus responsum est per Dominum Willelmum Wykham, Episcopum Wintoniensem, quod ideo ex pauperibus effecti fuerant divites et Domini, ut Scotos liberius arcere possent, et ut Rex et Australium Domini partium minus gravarentur, dum alias oporteret eos omni anno comparare exercitus, populumque vexare, contrahendo versus partes illas. Nec esse difficile eis ibidem hostes repellere, qui Domini et magnates facti sunt, cum eorum antecessores, videlicet patres et avi, qui neque fuerunt Domini, ut ipsi, nec divitiis abundantes, potuerunt sua animositate et audacia hostibus, id est, Scotis, resistere, et de ipsis multotiens triumphare. Concessæ sunt tamen illis commissiones congregandi virtutem exercitus, et Scotis resistendi et damna pro damnis inferendi, quotiens contingeret Scotos irrumpere, vel hostili more partes illas intrare. Hæc autem facta sunt pro eo maxime, quia in ultimo die quo Dux Lankastriæ et ipsi convenerunt ad Diem Marchiæ, conventum fuit inter eos, pro commodo partis utriusque, ut de cætero ipsi, nec Anglici, vexarentur per tot labores et expensas, sed singulis annis certi utriusque partis destinarentur ad [3] Parliamentum regni utriusque, qui et injurias acceptas proferrent in medium, et emendas acciperent secundum quantitatem damnorum, per judicium Dominorum. [4] Quia vero Scoti supersederunt ad hoc Parliamentum venire, juxta condictum, et insuper damna interim plura Borealibus præsumpserunt inferre, ac etiam hostes ex Galliis, in nocumen-

Answer made to the demand, by the Bishop of Winchester.

---

[1] *cogere* in Camden's text.

[2] *qua* in orig., Bibl. Reg. 13 E. ix., and the printed texts.

[3] *Parliamento* in orig.; corrected from the printed texts.

[4] *Qui* in orig., Bibl. Reg. 13 E. ix., and the printed texts.

MS. Bibl. Reg. 13 E. ix.

A.D. 1383.

tum Anglorum, conducere; decretum est per Parliamentum ut [1] frangenti fidem, fides frangatur eidem, et ut potestas lecta ex Anglia mittatur illuc, sub ductore Domino Thoma de Wodestoke, videlicet mille lanceæ, et duo millia arcitenentium, ad compescendum conatus eorum. Quibus cognitis, Scoti valde timentes, in fine Parliamenti, supplices advenerunt; etiam de pace vel treuga tractare voluerunt. Sed Anglici, totiens eorum falsitatem experti, cum eis tractare nec componere [2] voluerunt, sed eos, [3] affectos contumeliis, ad propria redire præceperunt; denunciantes ut capita sua defenderent quam bene scirent, et sua jura tuerentur. Quibus regressis, ut præmisimus, Domini Boreales susceperunt patriam conservandam, donec Comes Bokynghamiæ, Dominus Thomas de Wodestoke prædictus, paratus esset ad accedendum cum potestate graviori.

Preparations being made to oppose the Scots, they sue for peace.

Their request is rejected.

In hoc Parliamento, Rex cepit temporalia Episcopi Northwicensis in manu sua, eo quod inobediens erat voci ejus, quando, ut præmisimus, revocavit eum per breve suum, cum paratus esset ad transfretandum, sed tamen Episcopus noluit revenire. Milites quoque, qui cum Episcopo fuerunt in Flandria, quia et ipsi Episcopo fuerunt inobedientes, et, quod pejus est, proditores, incarcerati sunt; sed mox manucapti sunt per amicos, redimendi fulvo metallo. Et hic finis et fructus Parliamenti præsentis.

The King takes possession of the temporalities of the Bishop of Norwich.

His disobedient officers are imprisoned.

Annalis Conclusio.

Transit annus iste frugifer et fructifer; sed in fructibus arborum suspicio multa fuit, eo quod per nebulas fœtentes, exhalationes, aerisque varias corruptiones, ipsi fructus, puta poma, pyra, et hujusmodi, sunt infecta; quorum esu multi mortales hoc anno, [4] vel pestem letalem, vel graves morbos et infirmitates, [5] incurrerunt. Fuit etiam annus iste Anglicis luctuosus, quia plures, tam in Flandria quam in patria, perierunt; Flandrensibus exitiosus, quia patria illa, cum suis habitatoribus, tam per suos quam alienos est vastata; Gallicis formidabilis et onerosus, quia nunquam per ante timuerunt quemquam ex [6] [Anglicis] ducibus, sicut Episcopum formida-

Diseases contracted in England, from eating unwholesome fruit.

[1] These five words are, not improbably, a quotation, intended for an Hexameter, though not in conformity with the laws of Prosody.

[2] *noluerunt* in the printed texts.

[3] *effectos* in orig. and the printed texts: corrected from Bibl. Reg. 13 E. ix.

[4] *ut* in Camden's text.

[5] *incurrunt* in the printed texts.

[6] Omitted in orig.; supplied from Bibl. Reg. 13 E. ix. and the printed texts.

A.D. 1383. bant; et onerosus, propter contractionem tanti exercitus quantum Rex Franciæ congregavit, et expensas quas in commune ad hoc negotium profuderunt. MS. Bibl. Reg. 13 E. ix.

De Treugis inter regna.

A.D. 1384. Anno Domini millesimo trecentesimo octogesimo quarto, qui est annus Regis Ricardi, a Conquæstu Secundi, septimus, fuit idem Rex ad Natale apud manerium suum de Eltham, et cum eo Regina Anna.

A truce with France is effected by the Duke of Lancaster.

Exactis diebus Natalitiis, Dux Lancastriæ, Johannes de Gandavo, qui ante Natale profectus fuerat in Franciam ad tractandum de pace inter regna, rediit in Angliam, ferens treugas usque ad festum Sancti Johannis Baptistæ; quo tempore rediturus erat ad tractandum iterum, et confirmandum pacem, si posset fieri inter Reges. Quæ treugæ quantum contulerunt utrique regno, regna manifeste suis commodis persenserunt. Nam Anglia per Gallicos, et maxime per Normannos, sequente Quadragesima referta est cunctis necessariis mercibus, puta vino, fructibus diversi generis, speciebus, atque piscibus; adeo affluenter, ut [1] admirationi foret incolis vilitas rerum venalium, præcipue in illis partibus ad quas accessus esse poterat Normannorum. Francia et Normannia [2] lætatæ sunt, quia argentum et [3] aurum prompte perceperunt ex Anglicis pro suis mercimoniis, et abundantius multo quam in suis partibus pro tantillo commercio percepissent. Unde ab utriusque regni incolis, et maxime communibus, pax est ardentissime concupita.

Benefits to both England and France, resulting therefrom.

De dissidio inter Londonienses pro Majoribus.

Disturbances in London, through the agency of John de Combertone, the late Mayor.

Eodem anno, in nocte Purificationis Beatæ Virginis, visa sunt ingentia fulgura et audita tonitrua, quæ corda mortalium non modice terruerunt: et non multo post, Johannes de Northamptonia, dictus alias "de Combertone," Major Londoniarum anno præcedente, qui suis seditionibus, juxta sui nominis etymologiam, civitatem Londoniarum seditionibus adimplevit, moliri nova tentavit, multis assentantibus quibus rapina [4] placebat. Nempe Majorem, electum juxta morem civitatis, turbare, et cum multitudine stipatorum incedere,

[1] *admirationem ferret* in the printed texts.

[2] *lætati* in the printed texts.

[3] *arum* in orig., by inadvertence.

[4] *placebit* in orig. and Bibl. Reg. 13 E. ix.; corrected from the printed texts.

MS. Bibl. Reg. 13 E. ix. non semel, sed pluries, ad plurimorum terrorem, quibus [1][pax] placebat, [2]ausus. Et cum jam Major illius anni, dictus "Dominus Nicholaus Brambre," miles, occurrere suis motibus paravisset, in tantam insaniam dicti Johannis Combertone amatores conversi sunt, ut quidam ex arte sutoria, qui Major æstimatione videbatur, publice communitatis suffragium expeteret et commoveret. Ob quam causam, consilio Domini Roberti Cnolles, militis, domo sua tractus et decollatus est, tanquam insurrectionis concitator et pacis regiæ perturbator. Quod factum pro tunc compescuit commotionem vulgi, insurrectionem populique sedavit, qui dicebatur eo tempore in necem Majoris electi et multorum valentium conspirasse.

A.D. 1384.

Punishment of one of the principal leaders of the sedition.

De profectione Ducis versus Scotiam.

Instante tempore Quadragesimali, Dux Lancastriæ Johannes, cum fratre suo, Thoma de Wodestoke, Comite Bokynghamiæ, et innumerabili pene turba militum, armigerorum, et arcitenentium, profectus est versus Scotiam, ut Scotis perfidis perfidiæ pœnas inferret. Cumque in partibus Borealibus perhendinasset, donec, incolarum destructis victualibus, plus damni irrogasset eisdem quam per ante intulerant ipsi Scoti, tandem, circa festum Paschæ, terram Scotorum intravit; ubi tanta erga eos usus est patientia, ut villanos de Edenburgh permitteret asportare de villa quæcunque vellent, et ultra mare Scoticum comportare; indicens interim exercitui, ne præsumerent, sub pœna mortis, versus eandem villam pedem movere. Jacebant ergo nostrates per totum triduum non procul a villa, id est, per tres leucas, dum potuissent adivisse prædictam villam, et Scotos asportatione rerum vel perturbasse, vel jure bellico ipsa bona occupasse. Sed asportatis quibuslibet rebus e villa, et Scotis fuga salvatis, signum dedit movendi exercitum penes villam. Ad quam cum venissent, nihil præter domos vacuas invenerunt, et non tantum vacuas, sed omne stramentum tectorum depositum propter incendium, et detractum. In nocte vero Paschæ fecit exercitum in paludibus, propter metum hostium, armatum pernoctare; sed superveniente nive, et intolerabili frigore, perdidisse fertur, ut taceam de hominibus exanimatis, per frigus amplius quingentis equis. Scoti vero, semper prudenter agentes, se subtraxerunt, et in nemoribus, vel ultra mare Scoticum, de-

The Duke of Lancaster and Earl of Buckingham invade Scotland.

Singular lenity shown by the Duke towards the Scots.

Hardships inflicted upon his own troops.

---

[1] Supplied from Bibl. Reg. 13 E. ix.; omitted in the printed texts.

[2] *usus* in orig. and the printed texts; corrected from Bibl. Reg. 13 E. ix.

A.D. 1384. lituerunt, nolentes bellum inferre nostratibus, sed experimentaliter cognoscentes nostros illis in locis, et illo tempore, sine gladio, sine certamine, frigore et inedia perituros. Quod et factum est; nam plures sine ferro perierunt, plures per irruptiones Scotorum vel [1] captivitatem vel mortem incurrerunt. MS. Bibl. Reg. 13 E. ix.

Great losses sustained by the English.

Rigorous treatment of the English foragers.

Ut viderentur ergo boni ductores, Dux et fráter ejus volentes pabulatum exire prohibuerunt; exeuntes, ascensis velocissimis equis, persecuti sunt, et cum lanceis præacutis, non plus parcentes eisdem quam hostibus, percusserunt, vulneraverunt, perforaverunt, et occiderunt, plures ex Anglicis quam hostibus perimentes. Tandem parum damni inferentes hostibus præter incensionem villarum paucarum, cum imprecatione cunctorum Borealium, id est, Northamhumbrensium, cum magno quidem supercilio ipsi Domini, sed mediocres egentes, angustiati, afflicti, redibant. Post quorum discessum, mox erumpentes Scoti, in partibus Borealibus [2] mox prædas egerunt, et plura damna per combustionem villarum fecerunt, quam nostrates intulerant ante illis. Et factum est, in hac expeditione non minus perderet et regnum in effusa pecunia, in turba virorum perdita, in amissa substantia, quam anteactis expeditionibus, per annos multos factis, noscitur perdidisse.

Fresh incursions of the Scots; and disastrous results of the expedition.

De Parliamento facto apud Salesbury.

Parliament at Salisbury.

Charges made by a Carmelite Monk against the Duke of Lancaster.

Exacto tempore Paschali, id est, post quindecim aut paulo plures dies post Pascha, convenere citati proceres apud Salesbury, ad Parliamentum celebrandum. [3] Quo quidam de Ordine Carmelitarum frater, Bacularius in Theologia, Hibernicus genere, infausta hora properavit. Hic namque quamdam cedulam dictaverat et conscripserat, in qua plura enormia machinamenta per Ducem Lancastriæ, ut asseruit, excogitata, fuerant exarata. Contenta siquidem in illa fuerunt, quod Dux statuerat Regem repente oppressisse, regnumque occupasse. Designavit tempus, locum, et cætera, quæ hujus rei facere possent argumentum. Obtentoque aditu ad regale colloquium, porrexit cedulam, jurans in Sacramento Corporis Christi, quod ipse eodem die celebrando confecerat, nullum verbum fore falsum quod in cedula scripserat [4] supradicta, [5] monuit[que] ne audirentur Ducis

[1] *capite* in orig.; the abbreviation being somewhat indistinct in Bibl. Reg. 13 E. ix., in consequence of an erasure; *captivitatem* in the printed texts.

[2] *mox* omitted in the printed texts.

[3] *Quo* omitted in the printed texts.

[4] *supradicta* omitted in the printed texts.

[5] *que* omitted in orig.: supplied from Bibl. Reg. 13 E. ix. and the printed texts.

MS. Bibl. Reg. 13. E. ix.

A.D. 1384

excusationes, "quia per subtilia," inquit, "verba, hac die quidem judicium differet, et si fugerit in spatio milliarii, populum [1] contrahet, et quo plus facultatis obtinuerit recedendi, tanto materiam obtinebit majorem fortitudinem congregandi; et ita efficietur vel hostis publicus, vel dolose reconciliabitur tibi Regi."

The King takes counsel,

Hiis auditis, Rex puer non Dominos, non pares regni, seu qui sensu vigebant in regno, sed consuetos consiliarios suos, duos videlicet Capellæ suæ clericos, Nicholaum Slake et quemdam alium, super tantis convenit negotiis, ut discernant quid in tali articulo sit agendum. Inter tractandum, more solito Dux intravit, nihil volvens adversi, omnino nesciens quid tractarent. Quem cum Rex torvo vultu respexisset, nec, ut solebat, honorem impenderet, Dux æstimans aliquid latere in mente Regis quod personam suam tangeret, se subtraxit. Interea duo dicti Regis consiliarii, fortassis metuentes Ducis dominationem, vel affectantes amorem, consulunt, ut omnibus viis et modis Ducem [2] accersat, et ipse eum conveniat super istis. Vocatus est tandem Dux a Rege, et cedula sibi tradita supradicta; quam ut perlegerat, suspirans ait ad Regem:—

And questions the Duke.

The Duke's answer, denying the charge.

"Heu," inquit, "Domine mi, cur fidem datis talibus delatoribus? Cur de mea persona talia opinamini? Nonne sum avunculus vester? Nonne tutor extiti? Nonne post vos principalis in regno? Quid mihi suaderet vos prodere vel certe necare, qui nihil lucri reciperem de vestra morte? Nunquid hostes vestri me ditiorem facerent in terra sua, quam effectus sum in terra vestra et in natali solo? Aut si regnum affectarem, credendumne est post vestram interfectionem, quod absit, Dominos hujus regni æquanimiter ferre me posse, Domini mei et patriæ proditorem? Desistite, si placet, fidem dare talia referentibus, quia paratus sum, more militis, contra quemcunque mundi mihi in hac causa adversantem pugnare, et meam innocentiam defendere, et purgare." Cumque hæc, et hiis similia plura, pro se dixisset, credidit Rex ipsi Duci et suscepit excusationes ejusdem.

The Friar is kept in safe custody, in charge of Sir John Holand.

Dux vero rogavit Regem, [3] ut Frater supradictus in custodia teneretur, usque ad diem quo causam diceret horum quæ proposuerat contra eum. Et rogavit specialiter, ut Dominus Johannes Holand ejus custodiam obtineret. Erat iste Johannes Holand frater Regis ex parte matris, filius scilicet quondam

[1] Written as *contra hec* in orig.; the word being so divided, without a hyphen, in Bibl. Reg. 13 E. ix.

[2] *accersiat* in orig. and Bibl. Reg. 13 E. ix.

[3] *et* in orig., by inadvertence.

A.D. 1384. Domini Thomæ Holand; qui libenter, propter amorem Ducis, Fratris custodiam acceptavit. MS. Bibl. Reg. 13 E. ix.

Interficitur Frater Carmelita.

The Friar is cruelly murdered.

In ipsa nocte quæ præcessit diem datum suæ responsioni, idem Johannes et quidam alius miles, dictus "Henricus "Grene," apprehendentes Fratrem, et mittentes funem in collo ejus, et eadem reste nectentes ejus genitalia, suspenderunt a terra, imponentes super ventrem ejus lapidem tantæ ponderositatis, qui et torqueret eum per districtionem verendorum, et ejus guttura suffocaret, confringeretque spinam dorsi ejus; ut non tantum uno supplicio, sed tribus tormentis, vitam finiret: qua injuria Frater occubuit superatus. In crastino fecerunt Fratris corpus exanime per villam detrahi, more proditoris, ut suspicionem tollerent illatæ sibi mortis injuste. Et mirandum, quod non armigeri, non valecti, non garciones, nec inferioris status viri, quicquam mali voluerunt inferre Fratri, sed milites hæc fecerunt. Ipsi judices, ipsi ministri, ipsi tortores, extiterunt!

Grant made by Parliament.

Sir William La Zouche is accused of inventing the charge against the Duke; but denies it.

Et hic fructus Parliamenti præsentis, excepto quod Rex petiit et obtinuit de laicis quidem medietatem unius, ut usu vulgari loquar, quintæ-decimæ, de clericis vero unius decimæ medietatem. Et præter hoc, quod Dominus Willelmus La Zouche, quamvis gravissima detineretur ægritudine, accersitus erat ad Parliamentum prædictum, ad standum judicio Regis et Dominorum, quia idem Frater eum velut inventorem, inceptorem, et incentorem, dixerat omnium quæ scripserat extitisse. Qui cum venisset, lectica delatus, quia propter guttam equitare non poterat, compulsus est, discinctus et discooperto capite, ad hæc omnia sibi objecta, more latronum vel proditorum, respondere. Qui viriliter negavit objecta, sacramento firmans hæc [1] se nunquam audisse, vel hujuscemodi cogitasse; et ita demum absolutus est, et domum redire permissus; factus non solum illius Ordinis, sed cunctorum Ordinum, Fratribus inimicus.

Alleged miracles, in reference to the body of the murdered Friar.

Sunt qui dicunt cratem sutam, super quam Fratris corpus tractum erat, reviruisse, floruisse, et folia produxisse, et quemdam cæcum ad eandem cratem lumen amissum recepisse; sed si vere id asseveraverint, vel amore vel odio personarum, nondum scitur. Ferunt etiam, quod Dominus Thomas de Wodestoke, frater Ducis, irruperit in cameram qua Rex erat, et terribiliter juraverit, se oppugnaturum vel occisurum

---

[1] *se* omitted in the printed texts.

MS. Bibl. Reg. 13. E. ix.

A.D. 1384.

quemlibet qui proditionem imponere vellet fratri suo Duci; nullum excipiens, non ipsum Regem quidem. Unde Rex turbatus, nec contra mutire quidem ausus est. Quod factum capitale fuisset, si Rex habenas regni rite rexisset.[1]

The King threatened by the Duke of Gloucester.

Irruptio Scotorum.

Circa idem tempus, quia Scoti varia damna Northumbrensibus inferre non cessabant, Comes Northumbriæ, Dominus Henricus Percy, Scotorum regnum parat ingredi, et damna pro damnis illis reddere, et injurias illatas suis patriotis ulcisci. Quibus ita gestis, cum reversus fuisset Comes et exercitum dimisisset, revertuntur Scoti, et, damna damnis in patria [2]cumulando, dictum Comitem multipliciter irritarunt. Eratque per totam æstatem utriusque gentis eventus varius, dum nunc illi, nunc nostri, propriis damnis addiscerent quanta mala pariat discordia, quanta pericula lis inter regna.

Incursions of the Scots.

Hac æstate Dominus Johannes Philipot, miles et civis Londoniarum, [3]nobilissime qui pro regno regnique commodo plus omnibus laboraverat, et expensis et affectu sæpius Regem regnumque relevaverat, concessit in fata; neminem in hujuscemodi affectibus relinquens superstitem sibi parem.

Death of Sir John Philipot.

Dux Lancastriæ Franciam proficiscitur pro treugis.

Prope mensis Augusti principium, Dux Lancastriæ profectus est in Gallias, ad tractandum cum Francis de pace vel treuga; [4]quorum tractatus semper [5]damnosi Anglicis, et promissiones [6]infructuosæ, fuerunt. Igitur Dux ibidem, cum [7]numeroso nobilium comitatu, diu perhendinans, cum jocunda nova patriæ putaretur afferre, reversus est cum denunciatione belli anno futuro, prima æstate; treugas tantum habens usque ad primum diem mensis Maii. Sicque reversus est in terram istam, postquam expendisset, ut dicitur, quinquaginta millia marcarum argenti.

The Duke of Lancaster visits France, and concludes a short truce with that country.

---

[1] A passage in Bibl. Reg. 13 E. ix. is omitted here.

[2] *cumulant, unde* in the printed texts.

[3] *nobilissimus* in orig. and the printed texts: corrected from Bibl. Reg. 13 E. ix.

[4] *quarum* in the printed texts.

[5] *damnosæ* in the printed texts.

[6] *infructuosi* in orig.; *infructuosæ* in the printed texts. The last letter is indistinct in Bibl. Reg. 13 E. ix.

[7] *universo* in orig.: corrected from the printed texts.

Processus et judicium in Johannem de Northamptone, olim Majorem Londoniæ.

A.D. 1384. John de Northampton, the late Mayor of London, is convicted of sedition.

MS. Bibl. Reg. 13 E. ix.

Eodem tempore, Rege vocante, congregati sunt multi de nobilibus regni apud Radyng, dum adhuc Dux ageret in remotis, ad compescendum seditiosos motus Johannis de Northamptonia, nuper Majoris Londoniarum, qui ingentia facinora nisus est; de quibus et convictus est ibidem, suo familiari clerico eum accusante, et molitiones plurimas per ipsum excogitatas, tam in damnum Regis quam totius civitatis Londoniarum, [1] [dilucidante]. Cumque sententia ferenda esset in eum, Rege præsente, reclamavit improbus, et asseruit tale judicium non debere fieri in absentia domini sui, Ducis. Quo verbo suscitavit suspicionem sinistram, tam vulgi quam procerum, contra Ducem. Tamen ex processu juris, Justiciarius hujusmodi verbis usus est:—"Johannes," inquit, "scelera "quæ tibi objiciuntur, debes duello refellere, vel, per jura "regni tractioni, suspensioni, et quarterizationi, subjacere:" cumque mutus staret, nec ullum verbum vellet edere, decretum est ut perpetuo carceri [2] traderetur, et ejus bona regiis usibus confiscarentur, et ut Londonias non appropinquaret per centum milliaria in vita sua.

He is banished to Cornwall, and his property is confiscated.

Destinatus est igitur ad castellum de Tyntagel, in finibus Cornubiæ constitutum; et interim ministri Regis, velut [3] Harpyiæ, bonis illius incubabant. Et hic finis pro tunc processus contra eum facti.[4]

De Miraculo facto in Die Sancti Oswini Regis.

A Miracle, on St. Oswin's Day, at Newcastle-on-Tyne.

Prope dies istos, id est, vicesima die mensis Augusti, quo die videlicet celebratur Passio Sancti Oswyni, Regis et Martyris, in Novo Castro super Tynam apparuit novum et inauditum nostris diebus prodigium. Duo nempe nautæ, ad resarciendum navem suam quoddam lignum [5] dolare satagentes, die prædicto, dum alter illorum securi dictum lignum percussisset, sanguinem repente de ligno prædicto, tanquam de pecude,

[1] Omitted in orig.; supplied from Bibl. Reg. 13 E. ix.: *objiciente* in the printed texts.

[2] *trudaretur* in orig. and Bibl. Reg. 13 E. ix.; *traderetur* in the printed texts.

[3] *arpie* in orig. and Bibl. Reg. 13 E. ix.

[4] A passage in Bibl. Reg. 13 E. ix. is omitted here.

[5] *dolore* in orig.

MS. Bibl. Reg. 13 E. ix. ubertim stupuit emanasse. Perculsus ergo formidine magna de tanta [1]rei novitate diu hæsit: tandem recordatus Diei Sancti Oswyni, cujus solemnitatem infestaverat, vovit se nihil ulterius eo die in æternum facturum operis manualis. Quod audiens ejus socius, et miraculum parvipendens, jurat se dolaturum dictum lignum, et eo die loco præordinato positurum. Cumque et ipse lignum percussisset, vidit sanguinem abundantius effluentem in parte percussa. [2]Induratus tamen lignum vertit, et insistit operi alia parte ligni; sed nec ibi defuit miraculum præostensum. Nam et ibi sanguis, tanquam e bove vel vacca, decurrit. Gyratur lignum ad quatuor partes; omni parte percutitur, omni parte fluit cruor. Quod cernens qui prius improbe signum contempsit, ad devotionem se convertit, et deinceps eo die ab omni opere [3]servili spondet [4][se] cessaturum. Istud miraculum, a multis visum, et quibus incumbebat approbatum, testimonium magnum reddit sanctitati et excellentiæ Martyris supradicti. A.D. 1384.

De Eclipsi Solis.

[5]Eodem anno, die sexta-decima mensis Augusti, sero et per noctem sequentem, audita sunt in Anglia perhorrenda tonitrua, et visa fulgura terribilia; quæ mortales multipliciter terruerunt. In crastino vero, post meridiem, quasi per horam facta est eclipsis solis, et conjunctio simul, aspicientibus eas multis. Thunder and lightning, and an eclipse of the sun.

De Parliamento Londini, et Duello in eodem, et condemnatione Comitis Northumbriæ.

Eodem anno, circa festum Sancti Martini, factum est Parliamentum Londoniis, in quo, prout jam a multis consuevit temporibus, nihil dignum memoria fuit actum, præter illud, quod [6]sedulo actitabatur extortio, videlicet pecuniæ de clero et communi plebe, ad sustentationem [7]inutilis werræ regalis; Extortionate grants made by Parliament.

---

[1] *re novitate* in Bibl. Reg. 13 E. ix. and the printed texts.

[2] *Induraturus* in orig. and the printed texts; corrected from Bibl. Reg. 13 E. ix.

[3] *steriali* in orig.; *manuali* in the printed texts: corrected from Bibl. Reg. 13 E. ix.

[4] Omitted in orig. and Bibl. Reg. 13 E. ix.; supplied from the printed texts.

[5] In Bibl. Reg. 13 E. ix. this passage precedes the Miracle at Newcastle.

[6] *cedulo* in orig. and Bibl. Reg. 13 E. ix.: *sedulo* in the printed texts.

[7] *militibus* in orig. and the printed texts; corrected from Bibl. Reg. 13 E. ix.

A.D. 1384. et præter hoc, quod duellum commissum est infra listas inter quemdam armigerum Anglicanum et quemdam de Navaria, qui accusaverat dictum armigerum, cujus nomen erat "Johannes Walshe," de proditione Regis et regni; effectualiter tamen, non erat proditor, sed invidebat sibi, eo quod cum esset idem Johannes subcapitaneus de Cherburgh, oppresserat uxorem dicti Navariensis; prout idem Navarus, expost superatus ab eodem, et moriturus, publice fatebatur. Ob quam causam idem Navarus regali judicio, qui ad spectaculum duelli, cum principibus regni sui, consederat, tractus et suspensus est; quanquam Regina et plures alii pro eo preces sedulas porrexissent.

MS. Bibl. Reg. 13 E. ix.

Duel between an English Esquire and a native of Navarre; in which the latter is defeated.

The Scots obtain Berwick Castle, by treachery.

Nondum Parliamentum finitum fuerat, cum nova de partibus Borealibus sunt allata de captione castelli de Berwico per Scotos, cujus custodiam Comes Northumbriæ, Dominus Henricus Percy, avito jure possedit. Scoti namque, mediante pecunia, de quodam, qui secundarie castri custodiam tunc habebat, introitum castelli dolose nacti sunt. Quibus Dux Johannes cognitis lætatus est valde, quod materiam jam invenerat nocendi dicto Comiti, prout fertur. Factum est ergo, Duce procurante, prout dicitur, ut pro perditione dicti castelli regalis Comes judicium qui aderant optimatum, et Regis sententiam damnationis, exciperet, in eum publice promulgatam. Cujus executionis vindicta per Regem postea cito relaxata fuit, quamvis id Duci, ut dicitur, displiceret. Acta sunt hæc decimo-quarto die Decembris in eodem Parliamento, non obstante quod idem Comes ad dictum Parliamentum vocatus fuerat per breve regium, et ad custodiam suæ patriæ morari maluisset. Hæc idcirco causa inter ipsum Ducem et Comitem postea iræ et odii fomitem ministravit.

The Earl of Northumberland is condemned for neglect of the Castle; but is pardoned, contrary to the wish of the Duke of Lancaster.

Comes Northumbriæ capit Castellum de Berwico.

The Earl of Northumberland recaptures Berwick Castle.

Comes Northumbrorum, taliter adjudicatus, sed indulgentia Regis vitæ possessionibusque restitutus, nullas moras nectens, omnem apparatum belli præparat ad obsidendum dictum castrum, et expugnandum eos qui in eo erant. Et cum populosum exercitum congregasset, et utensilia comportasset expugnationi necessaria, repente castrum obsidione vallavit. Tandem cum ibidem moram traxisset aliqualem, conventum est inter obsidentes et obsessos, ut ipsi obsessi castellum relinquerent, et vita gauderent et mobilibus bonis suis, et pro redditione castelli reciperent ab eodem Comite duo millia marcarum Anglicanæ monetæ. Et hoc modo recepit Comes castellum de Scotorum manibus, doctus prudentius in futurum sua fortalitia custodire.

Nota.—De Papa Urbano.

MS. Bibl. Reg. 13 E. ix.

A.D. 1384. Miserable death of the Duke of Anjou.

Hoc anno, Dux Andegaviæ, post longam et procul positam a patria peregrinationem, post opum indicibilium [1] et expensarum profusionem, post magnatum suorum morte pereuntium [2] amissionem, spe sua frustratus, decidit in lecto ægritudinis et simili [3] fortuna periit, in magna mentis amaritudine moriens in terra aliena. Sicque factum est, ut cui non placuit fortuna sua, dum ad dignitatem aspirat regiam, Ducatus amisit honorem, et, non solum ambitiosus moriens, sed etiam excommunicatus, vitam finivit. Qui remanserunt de ejus exercitu, vispiliones et latrones facti, non solum regnum Siciliæ, sed et alias regiones in gyro positas, impleverunt cædibus et rapinis. Et hic [4] factus et fructus totius apparatus Ducis Andegaviæ regnum Siciliæ meditantis conquirere, et Papam Urbanum suppeditare, conantis.

The remains of his army become marauders.

Transit annus iste, quoad Gallicos pacificus, sed Anglicis nocivus Scotorum irruptionibus; frugum fertilis, sed fructuum neque omnino sterilis neque fœcundus; in hac quidem terra seditionibus turbulentus, propter motus inordinatos Londoniensium, volentium Johannem de Combertone ad dignitatem pristinam revocare, et propter occultum odium inter Dominos suscitatum, prout in gestis sequentis anni patebit.

A.D. 1385. Shamelessness of the Queen's fellow-countrymen.

Anno Domini millesimo trecentesimo octogesimo quinto, qui est annus regni Regis Ricardi, a Conquæstu Secundi, octavus, fuit idem Rex ad Natale cum Anna Regina, quam raro vel nunquam lateri suo deesse permisit. Affuerunt et Boemi, patriotæ Reginæ, qui, gustata dulcedine terræ, propriæ regionis obliti, inverecundi et illæti hospites repatriare nolebant.

De morte Johannis Wicleff.

Death of John Wyclif.

Die Sancti Thomæ, Cantuariensis Archiepiscopi [5] et Martyris, organum diabolicum, hostis Ecclesiæ, confusio vulgi, hæreticorum idolum, hypocritarum speculum, schismatis incentor, odii seminator, mendacii fabricator, Johannes de Wiclif, dum in

---

[1] *ex* in orig.; by inadvertence.

[2] *amissione* in orig. and the printed texts; corrected from Bibl. Reg. 13 E. ix.

[3] *sorte* in Bibl. Reg. 13 E. ix.

[4] *fis* (for *finis*) in the margin of Bibl. Reg. 13 E. ix. in apparently a contemporary hand.

[5] *et* omitted in the printed texts.

A.D. 1385. Sanctum Thomam, ut dicitur, eodem die in sua prædicatione quam dicere præparaverat, [1] orationes et blasphemias vellet evomere, repente judicio Dei percussus, sensit paralysim omnia membra sua generaliter invasisse. Os nempe, quod contra Deum et Sanctos ejus, sive Sanctam Ecclesiam, ingentia locutum fuerat, a loco suo miserabiliter distortum, horrendum cernentibus spectaculum exhibebat: lingua effecta muta confitendi vel testandi copiam denegabat, caput tremulum maledictionem quam Divinitas in Cayn fulminaverat, in ipsum latam etiam patulo demonstrabat. Et ut nulli veniret in dubium eum Cayn consortio deputandum, ut ferunt hii qui affuerunt morienti, per signa forinseca moriens desperavit: et quidem totius malitiæ suæ conclusio talis erat.

MS. Bibl. Reg. 13 E. ix.

Alleged judgment inflicted on him at his death.

De Domino le Bourser, et ejus [2] necessitatibus apud Gandavum.

Sir Edward Le Bourser takes command of the people of Ghent.

Dominus Edwardus Le Bou[r]ser per hos dies missus est Gandavum cum armata manu, ut Gandavensibus præesset more capitanei; illis quidem a Rege hoc instanter petentibus, et sibi fidelitatem promittentibus sub jurisjurandi attestatione; ubi quam prudenter Gandavenses rexerit, quam circumspecte res belli tractaverit, et nobis silentibus, hostes sui, videlicet Gallici, fatebuntur. Nam in ipso adventus sui principio, ipso duce, Gandavenses tria millia Gallicorum devicerunt, et ex illis quosdam fugaverunt, nonnullos ceperunt, plurimos occiderunt, et, præter reliquam prædam, quadringentos equos hostium abduxerunt. Gallici proinde multipliciter exasperati cunctos captivos, quos inter se tenebant, enormiter mutilantes, effossis oculis et amputatis manibus, et variis modis læsis irrestaurabiliter, domum, ad commovendum corda Gandavensium, remiserunt. Quibus visis, Gandavenses commoti, voluerunt militibus et armigeris, quos de Francis, ut diximus, vivos ceperant, eadem supplicia irrogasse. Quibus conatibus obstitit Dominus le [3] Bourser, dicens, id non debere fieri viris, qui, jure belli capti, seipsos pro salvatione vitæ ipsorum fidei reddidissent; si vero in futurum quoscunque Gallicos possent violenter intercipere, hos dixit se bene permissurum tali modo mutilatos ut Gallias mitterent, et

His great success.

Cruelties practised by the French.

The people of Ghent are prevented by Le Bourser from retaliating on their prisoners.

---

[1] *actiones* in the printed texts; *oēs* in orig; *inexiones* in Bibl.Reg.13 E. ix.: probably for *invectiones*—"invectives."

[2] *successibus* in the Rubric in Bibl. Reg. 13 E. ix.

[3] *Bourses* in orig. and Bibl. Reg. 13 E. ix., by inadvertence: *Bourser* in the printed texts.

MS. Bibl. Reg. 13 E. ix. simili sorte Gallicos salutarent. Quod paulo [1][post] factum est, ipsis sibimet obviantibus, et Gandavensibus victoriam reportantibus, ipso duce. A.D. 1385.

De discordia inter Papam et Regem Siciliæ, et degradatione sex Cardinalium.

Sub præsenti tempore commota est universa Sicilia, commota est et tota Romana Curia, commotione magna, qualem per ante nunquam senserat vel toleraverat; cujus causam inferius describemus.

Cum Dominus Papa, ut supra retulimus, dulcedine natalis soli illectus, Romanos decepisset suo repentino recessu, et Neapolim appropinquasset, Karolus, Rex Hierusalem et [2]Siciliæ, qui vocatur a multis "Rex Neapolis," cepit [3]inopinate Papam in lecto suo, et per octo dies in privato loco secum tenuit, et [4]tam secrete servavit, ut ignoraretur a Papalibus famulis, quonam illorum dominus devenisset. Quam quidem detentionem Papa vocavit expost "incarcerationem." Hac ergo de causa, grandis dissensio crevit inter Papam et Regem; [5]etiam invaluit in alterutrum odium eorundem. Regina vero Neapolis, non mediocriter dolens de tanta dissensione, apposuit vires omnimodas pro pace reformanda et benevolentia redintegranda inter illos; ad cujus instantiam commendabilem, quamvis foret difficile, facta est pax, Rege juramentum edente, et obligationem faciente, de nunquam delinquendo contra Papam verbo vel facto.

Charles, King of Naples, seizes the Pope.

The Pope is liberated, and they are ultimately reconciled.

Ex parte vero Papæ, Cardinales cum Romanis obligaverunt se Regi pro Papa in centum millibus florenorum; quod videlicet Dominus Papa servaret conditiones factas inter illos; inter quas conventiones, conventum est inter Papam et Regem, quod Dominus Papa præstaret auxilium ad custodiendum civitatem Neapolim; quibus firmatis, Dominus Papa crucesignavit Regem suis manibus, et confortavit eum ad bellandum inimicos Ecclesiæ, et campum tenendum contra eos. Rex itaque progressus tenuit campum contra dictos adversarios per octo menses; sed mox post recessum Regis, Papa transtulit

The King takes the field against the Pope's adversaries.

---

[1] Supplied from Bibl. Reg. 13 E. ix. and the printed texts.

[2] *Silicia* in orig. and Bibl. Reg. 13 E. ix.; by inadvertence.

[3] *inopinato* in the printed texts.

[4] *a tam* in orig.; *a tam* in Bibl. Reg. 13 E. ix., with an expunctory mark under *a*.

[5] *et etiam* in the printed texts.

A.D. 1385. se, cum tota Curia sua, ad villam quæ "Luceria" nominatur, et infregit conventiones et pactum initum inter illos. Regina proinde Neapolis dedit mandatum civitatibus et castellis, vicis et villis, et omnis conditionis hominibus, sub pœna mortis, ne victualia Papæ aut Curialibus ferre præsumerent, et omnem illis ex omni parte interdixit commeatum. MS. Bibl. Reg. 13 E. ix.

The Pope breaks his compact with the King of Naples.

The Pope breaks his compact with the people of Rome.

Nec solum tunc inter Papam [1] et Siculos orta est discordia, sed inter ipsum et Romanos, propter pacta quæ pepigit et misit eisdem sub Bullis suis plumbo sigillatis. Juramento etiam firmaverat iisdem Romanis, et spoponderat, se [2] rediturum et moraturum inter eos; sed tamen nihil implevit ex omnibus quæ promisit. Quibus de causis Romani illum falsum reputabant, et publice proclamabant.

De discordia inter Papam et quosdam de Collegio.

The Pope accuses certain Cardinals of conspiring against him.

Eodem tempore, tertio Idus Januarii, orta est gravis dissensio inter Papam et quosdam de Collegio [3] Cardinales, qui intraverunt ipso die, prout moris erat, Papale Palatium, vocati prius ab eodem. Ignorantes siquidem intentionem Papæ, Consistorium sunt ingressi, ubi Papa [4] inopinate proposuit et objecit, in Conclavi, sex Cardinalibus conspirationem in mortem suam, et affirmavit eosdem triginta articulos hæresis voluisse sibimet imposuisse, et comprobasse eum [5] deprivatum fuisse hæretica pravitate. Cardinales mox attoniti, unus post alium, juraverunt se nunquam talia cogitasse. Papa nihilominus, sine processu facto, comprehendi fecit eosdem, et incarcerari, et expost quæstionibus contorqueri; quorum quidem nomina Cardinalium ista fuere:—

They are put to the question, and tortured.

Nomina Cardinalium degradatorum.

Names of the Cardinals so degraded.

Cardinalis de Venetia, Cardinalis de Anglia, Cardinalis de Janua; qui omnes erant viri venerabiles et religiosi, et maximæ opinionis in vulgo, et Sacræ Paginæ Professores. Trium reliquorum nomina fuere ista;—Cardinalis Zangro, Cardinalis Corfiensis, et Cardinalis [6] Tarentinus, qui fuerunt valentes et

---

[1] *sed* in orig., but corrected in the margin, in a later hand: *et* in the printed texts.

[2] *redditurum* in orig. and the printed texts.

[3] *Cardinalibus* in orig. and Bibl., Reg. 13 E. ix.; corrected from the printed texts.

[4] *inopinato* in the printed texts.

[5] *depravatum* in the printed texts.

[6] *Terrentinus* in orig. and Bibl. Reg. 13 E. ix.: corrected from the printed texts.

MS. Bibl. Reg. 13 E. ix.

A.D. 1385.

de magno genere, et ex eis duo Doctores Legum. Igitur, postquam torti fuissent, ut præfertur, dicti Cardinales confessi sunt, ut dicitur, delictum suum, sive conscientia stimulati, sive pro [1] carenda pœnarum acerbitate. Cardinalis tamen Angliæ nihil fatebatur præter id, quod dixisset Papam esse nimis superbum.

The Cardinals confess, with one exception.

Proximo die Dominico sequente, Papa compelli fecit Curiales et laicos de villa et casalibus in circuitu, ad veniendum in castellum; quibus ingressis, portas claudi fecit, ne quis exiret donec ipsemet prædicasset. Ascendit igitur turrim altissimam [2] [super] secundam portam; etiam prædicare cœpit, plebe sedente exterius super terram in magno frigore et esurie, donec esset fere hora Vesperarum: in qua prædicatione movit multas rationes, inter quas dixit quod Cardinales prædicti confessi fuissent se adinvenisse articulos supradictos, et conspirassent in mortem suam tali modo, videlicet quod Rex cum sua comitiva cepisset eum subito, et deposuisset, vel certe peremisset. Dixit etiam, quod ista omnia fuerunt demonstrata sibi revelatione divina. Longum est autem, et tædiosum, fabulas inserere quas narravit; inter quas dixit, quod Cardinalis Reatinus, quondam factus per eundem, sed diu ante depositus, fuit inceptor et inventor dictorum malorum contra eum; qui etiam diu ante fuit excommunicatus ab eo. Qui Reatinensis judicio populi vir sapiens et circumspectus reputabatur, et erat Doctor Legum apprime eruditus; et quamvis Papa privasset eum, erat tamen maximæ æstimationis in consilio, et inter Consiliarios Regis Karoli supradicti. Præterea, Papa retulit in illo Sermone, quanta fecit pro Rege dicto et Cardinalibus memoratis, et ut promoverit eos de pulvere et de terra, et quot gratitudines ostendisset Regi et Reginæ, et Cardinalibus sæpedictis. Post finem vero Sermonis, Papa, cum Cardinalibus non privatis, erecta cruce et accensis candelis, excommunicavit Regem Karolum et Reginam, Antipapam et Anticardinales, Abbatem Montis Cassini, quondam Reatinensem Cardinalem, et prædictos sex quondam Cardinales, et omnes consiliarios et adjutores, vel fautores eorum verbo vel facto, et omnes comedentes aut bibentes cum eisdem; et interdixit civitatem Neapolitanam, ne ibidem celebrarentur aut fierent Sacramentalia vel Sacramenta; et una cum hiis, extinxerunt candelas suas, et extra jecerunt inter plebes. Quibus

The Pope preaches before the people, on the enormity of the offence committed by the Cardinals.

The Pope excommunicates the King of Naples and others.

Naples placed under interdict.

[1] *carendo* in orig., Bibl. Reg. 13 E. ix., and the printed texts.

[2] Supplied from Bibl. Reg. 13 E. ix.: omitted in the printed texts, which read *secundum portam*.

A.D. 1385. expletis, tumultus magnus excrevit in tota Luceria, et patria in circuitu constituta; et malefactores discurrere cœperunt, et despoliare quoscunque poterant superare. MS. Bibl. Reg. 13 E. ix.

De malis quæ irrogaverunt Regales peregrinis, post datam sententiam.

An attack made upon foreigners at Luceria, and an Englishman slain.

Eodem die, post solis occasum, malefactores peremerunt quendam Anglicum, procuratorem et nuncium cujusdam clerici Regis Angliæ, dictum "Johannem Aleyn," dum ire disponeret ad hospitium suum; et despoliaverunt eum. Quapropter omnes, qui sequebantur Curiam, colligatis sarcinis, reliquerunt ibi esse, et ad villam quæ citra est constituta, dicta "Castel-"mare," properare cœperunt, viri amplius quam sexcenti: sed tamen deprædati fuerunt in ipso itinere, et amiserunt amplius quam quadraginta onera asinorum. Ut autem Papa cognovit tantum miseriam, et procinctum itineris peregrinorum et aliorum Curialium, summoneri fecit omnes Anglicos ad veniendum ad ejus colloquium, ut videlicet commorati fuissent in castello suo, et custodissent illud, sub pœna excommunicationis omnium beneficiorum suorum. Non tamen voluerunt ex Anglicis expectare cum eo viri aliqui nominati, præter Episcopum Bethleemensem, et Magistrum Henricum Bowet, et alios circa duodecim.

The English are invited by the Pope to remain, but, with a few exceptions, they refuse.

Redit Rex Carolus.

King Charles returns to Naples.

Septimo Kalendas Februarii, venit Karolus Rex Neapolim, stipatus turba magna; cui cives et milites exierunt obviam cum ingenti lætitia, et deduxerunt eum in castellum suum.

The deprived Cardinals are compelled to make a public confession.

Proximo die Sabbati subsequenti, Papa in publico Consistorio educi fecit dictos sex Cardinales privatos, ubi fatebantur publice dictos articulos et objecta de conspiratione contra Papam: sed tamen Cardinalis Angliæ nihil fatebatur, nisi sicut prius, scilicet quod intolerabilis erat fastus Papæ: credebatur tamen eos voluisse longe aliam fecisse confessionem, si fuissent e carcere liberati. Ibi tunc Papa iterum excommunicavit eosdem, et privavit, et Regem et Reginam.

The King of Naples sends a force to besiege Luceria.

Cumque Rex hæc universa cognovisset relatione veridica, iratus est valde, et quarto die sequenti misit illuc magnam turbam hominum bellatorum, quibus præposuit villæ Nocheum et Amiralium, cum tota potestate sua. Qui confestim cœperunt destruere casalia et villas in circuitu Luceriæ constitutas, et capere cunctos quos poterant qui cum Papa tenebant, aut cum Principe Capuano, qui erat consanguineus Papæ, et compellere

MS. Bibl. Reg. 13 E. ix. A.D. 1385.

eos ad redemptionem. Proxima sexta feria sequente, obsederunt villam de Luceria, et insultum fecerunt [1][tam villanis quam illis qui erant in castello; in quo insultu fuerunt] ex utraque parte plurimi vulnerati.

Convocatio Cleri Neapolis.

The clergy of Naples are consulted as to the Pope's Interdict.

In crastino, id est, die Sabbati, fecit Rex congregari totum Consilium cleri Neapolis, ad quærendum si Interdictum foret timendum; cui, post tractatum diuturnum, clerus respondit Interdictum non fuisse factum bono sensu et bona deliberatione, nec in jure Sacrosanctæ Ecclesiæ, sed potius [2]capitose; et ideo non fuerat metuendum. Die Lunæ proximo sequente, regalis exercitus cepit villam de Luceria, et concremavit illam. Cepit insuper ulteriorem Custodiam, quam "Wardam" vocant, castelli Papæ, et gardinum ejus. Tandem metuens sibi, Papa misit ad Regem nuncios pro concordia et pace reformanda. Sed Rex, multipliciter exasperatus, respondit Papam fore falsum, et semper conventiones factas inter eos infregisse, et nullum ex pactis omnibus custodisse; et ideo nolle se de cætero credere suis sponsionibus fraudulentis. Demum tamen, intercurrentibus viris [3]timoratis et bonis, concordati sunt Summus Pontifex et Rex magnus, et Papa dimissus propriæ libertati.

The King captures Luceria, and burns it.

The Pope sues for peace, which at length is granted to him.

Causa de Bury.

The dispute as to the Abbacy of Bury is finally settled; and the election of John Tymworth is confirmed.

Causa Monasterii Sancti Edmundi de Bury, pro qua multotiens multi versus Curiam Romanam laboraverant, hujuscemodi finem cepit. Papa, laudabili instantia ambassiatorum, concessit et permisit, ut, ad novam procedentes electionem, satagerent eligere Monasterio dignum patrem, quanquam jamdudum Johannes de Tymworth, per provisionem sibi factam, Abbathia aliquanto tempore fuisset gavisus. Misit ergo fratribus, [4]monens ut eundem Johannem Tymworth, si posset fieri, præ cæteris eligerent in pastorem; cujus conditiones perante Papæ commendaverant in immensum. [5]Cassavitque Papa tam benedictionem quam perceperat ab Episcopo Landavensi, quam electiones et provisiones de eo vel sibi factas, ut electio, juxta postulata, posset esse libera et quieta: delegationem vero, ad ratificandum quæ in hac parte secundum jura fierent, et munus

---

[1] Supplied from Bibl. Reg. 13 E. ix.; omitted in the printed texts.
[2] *captiose* in the printed texts.
[3] *illustribus* in the printed texts.
[4] *movens* in the printed texts.
[5] *Cessavitque* in Camden's text.

A.D. 1385. benedictionis impendendum electo, commisit Magistro Roberto Braybrok, Episcopo Londoniensi; qui, accedens ad locum, adimplevit officium, et ejusdem Johannis Tymworth, quem iterum Conventus elegerat in Abbatem, ratificavit electionem; et benedixit eundem in eadem ecclesia cum solemnitate magna, in Die Sancti Albani, Anglorum Protomartyris. MS. Bibl. Reg. 13 E. ix.

De discordia inter Regem et Ducem Lancastriæ orta.

Measures taken, with the King's sanction, for the arrest of the Duke of Lancaster.

The Duke is warned, and escapes.

The King and the Duke are reconciled, by the agency of the King's mother.

Per idem tempus in Anglia orta est Duci Lankastriæ inquietudo gravissima, juvene Rege et juvenibus ejus complicibus in mortem illius conspirantibus. Convenerunt nempe inter eos, ut eum, subito arestatum, judicio sisterent coram Justiciario Roberto Trysilian, qui manu-ceperat audacter in eum laturum sententiam, juxta qualitatem criminum sibimet objiciendorum. Sed Dux, præmunitus a quodam de Consilio, et propriæ salutis non negligens, prudenter se subtraxit, et ad castellum suum de Ponte Fracto quantocius properavit, quod et armis et victualibus affatim communivit; unde factum est, ut jam, non tantum occasione dissensionis hujus in privato, sed etiam in publico, invalesceret odium in alterutrum; et [1]jam timebatur affuturum quod communes diu affectaverant, discordia videlicet [2]inter eos, ac, per hanc, licentiam impune discursandi et grassandi, sicut olim quando communes non principati sunt, sed debacchati sunt. Sed tantum discrimen regni ferre non sustinens Domina Johanna, mater Regis, quamvis tenera foret et delicata, et, præ corporis sui sagina, semetipsam vix portare valeret, neglecta tamen corporis sui quietudine, laboriosum iter, nunc ad Regem, nunc ad Ducem, gratis assumpsit, nihil parcens expensis, nihil humilibus precibus, donec, voti compos effecta, inter eosdem pacem et concordiam reformasset.

Conjunctio Jovis et Saturni.

Conjunction of Jupiter and Saturn.

Eodem tempore conjunctio duarum [3]maximarum planetarum facta est, videlicet Jovis et [4]Saturni, mense Maio; quam secuta est maxima regnorum commotio, prout patebit inferius, cum attigerit stylus locum.

---

[1] *jamjam* in Bibl. Reg. 13 E. ix. and the printed texts.

[2] *inter magnates* in Bibl. Reg. 13 E. ix.

[3] *duorum maximorum* in orig. and Bibl. Reg. 13 E. ix.; corrected from the printed texts.

[4] *Saturnini* in orig., by inadvertence.

De apparatu Regis Franciæ, volentis Angliam invadere, et metu Anglicorum.

MS. Bibl. Reg. 13 E. ix.

Sub eadem tempestate Rex Franciæ, cum suis Gallicis, exitium quod Anglorum regno diu perante excogitaverat, effutire parat, et congregatis ratibus undecunque, atque conductis, apud Solusam in anchoris stare præcepit. Illuc ergo omnis ætas apta bello, jussa venire, equos adducit, arma comportat, victualia congerit, et cuncta necessaria tantæ profectioni deponit. Auditur in Anglia rumor iste, scilicet sexcentarum navium isthuc dirigendarum, cum exercitu infinito, qui totum regni solum, sicut locustæ, repleret; et illico, quasi nulla spes salutis esset, non solum plebani, sed et ipsi milites, olim exercitati, sed modo effœminati, olim animosi, sed modo meticulosi, olim cordati, sed nunc excordes et enervati, trepidare cœperunt, et non de resistentia, non de bello modo, sed de fuga vel deditione, tractabant. Missus est insuper Hertfordensis Episcopus, cum nonnullis aliis reverendis nunciis, ut cum Francis componat, vel certe dilationem belli reportet. Qui, derisus a Gallicis, treugas reportat non nobis utiles, [1] sed majus illis, bimestres videlicet, donec illi se possent commodius præparare, adjectis conditionibus, quod nec illi terram istam, nec nostrates terram suam, ingrederentur hostili modo per tempus prædictum. In mari tamen liceret eis nobisque prædas agere, hostiliter accitare. Videbatur interea Anglia respirare, quod non statim hostili gladio subjicienda foret.

A.D. 1385. The King of France prepares to invade England.

Universal alarm caused in England thereby.

An embassy is sent to France, and a short truce, with certain reservations, is agreed upon.

De vecordia nostratum in mari.

Interea præparatur navigium ex cunctis portubus Anglicanis, conducuntur bellatores copiosi, præficiuntur eisdem Ammiralli, Magister Hospitalis Sancti Johannis et Dominus Thomas Percy, frater scilicet Comitis Northumbrorum: qui per totum tempus æstivum observaturi maris semitas, videntes frequenter classem [2] Gallicam nunc eos prætereuntem, nunc etiam deridentem, nihil omnino contra eos qui in [3] illa erant agere statuerunt, impediti vel privata discordia, vel vecordia repercussi.

Remissness of the Admirals of the English fleet.

Sed non sic viri de Portesmouth et Dortemouthe, non sic, Energy

[1] *sed ad duos menses, videlicet,* in the printed texts.

[2] *Gallicum* in orig. and Bibl. Reg. 13 E. ix.: *Gallicam* in the printed texts.

[3] *illo* in orig. and the printed texts.

A.D. 1385. shown by the men of Portsmouth and Dartmouth; who make a successful descent upon the French coast.

MS. Bibl. Reg. 13 E. ix.

foriare decreverunt; quos nullus conduxerat, nullus coemerat, ad nocendum hostibus, sed virtus propria stimulaverat, probitas innata succenderat. Hii nempe, nihil metuentes a facie multitudinis navium, nihil formidantes occursus hostium, cum parva manu pertranseuntes [1]oceanum, in Sequanam navigarunt, ubi sine magna difficultate quatuor naves hostium demerserunt, alias quatuor abduxerunt, cum bargia Domini de Clissone, cui par non erat in Angliæ sive Franciæ regnis. In quibus [2]vina, ferrum, et prædam aliam, sunt lucrati, quæ merito avidissimi cujusque saturare posset avaritiam, et inopiam relevare.

An earthquake.

Hoc anno terræ-motus factus est ante mediam noctem præcedentem Diem Inventionis Sanctæ Crucis; significans fortassis commotionem magnam, et profectionem quæ postea cito facta est in terram Scotiæ per nostrates.

Indignatio Regis contra Cantuariensem [3]Archiepiscopum, et quosdam alios.

Disgrace of the Archbishop of Canterbury. The Chancellor and others, also incur the King's displeasure.

Eodem tempore, Rex, ob leves occasiones, in tantam exarsit iracundiam contra Cantuariensem Archiepiscopum, Dominum Willelmum de Courtenay, [4]ut ejus bona temporalia juberet auferri, et in manus suas seysiri; factumque fuisset ut jusserat, nisi Cancellarius regni, Dominus Michael de Poole, ejus conatibus laudabilius restitisset. Ob quam causam idem Cancellarius indignationem regiam vix evasit. Prætermitto, quia longum foret scribere, verba contumeliosa quæ Rex jecit in utrumque, quæ regale fastigium non decerent. Taceo probra et opprobria, quæ dixit in Dominum Thomam Trivet, quamvis, ut quidam [5]asserunt, verum dixerit, vocando eum publicum proditorem; taceo verba procacia et contumeliosa habita per eum contra Dominum Johannem Deveroux, militem generosum, qui [6]verba pro Archiepiscopo facere sunt conati. Archiepiscopus vero, ut a præsentia Regis est egressus, sumpta cruce sua, et consuta sub pannis [7]suis, ad pectus ejus, paucis consciis, latenter se subtraxit et latibula perquisivit, donec, intercurrentibus viris timoratis, pax est inter eosdem, et gratia, reformata.

---

[1] *octeanum* in orig. and Bibl. Reg. 13 E. ix.

[2] *una* in orig. and the printed texts; corrected from Bibl. Reg. 13 E. ix.

[3] *Archiepiscopos* in orig.

[4] *et* in orig.; corrected from the printed texts.

[5] *asseruit* in the printed texts.

[6] *verbo* in orig., by inadvertence.

[7] *ejus* in the printed texts.

De adventu Francorum in Scotiam, et profectione Regis contra illos.

MS. Bibl. Reg. 13 E. ix.

A.D. 1385.

A French army lands in Scotland.

Dominus Johannes de Vienna, stipendiarius Regis Franciæ, per idem tempus pervenit in Scotiam, cum magna multitudine navium et hominum bellatorum, ut pariter juncti Scotis totum regnum Angliæ infestarent, et ut, dum ipsi potentiam regni ad illas partes attraherent, et detinerent occupatam, Rex Franciæ, cum suo navigio et exercitu congregato, alias partes regni licentius posset ingredi, nemine videlicet, vel saltem paucis, domi dimissis, qui ejus introitum prohiberent. Comperto in Anglia dicti Johannis adventu et Scotorum ferocitate, qui, jam fulti Francorum subsidio, nihil illis obstare posse credebant, Rex et tota regni nobilitas se [1] præparant ad profectionem; expetunt servitia consueta, et nova non tam precantur quam timore potestatis extorquent. Fit concursus ad Regem, jam primo suos adversarios debellaturum, militum, armigerorum, et arcitenentium, nostris sæculis et regionibus [2] inauditus, ita ut equorum numerus ad summam excresceret trecentorum millium, prout æstimaverunt, quibus incumbit, servientes de armis. Lætatus est ergo Rex, ut veraciter lætari poterat, de tam valentis exercitus numero et effectu [3] penes eum, [4] gaudet de nobili apparatu suorum, et [5] divitiis, gaudet de animositate quam suis [6] cernit inesse.

A great force is raised by the King of England.

Sed privatum et publicum gaudium obnubilavit apud Eboracum cito ferocitas Domini Johannis Holond, fratris Regis; qui Dominum Radulphum de Stafford, filium Comitis de Stafford, occidit in via, dum pergeret ad Reginam, cujus familiaris erat miles, et ab eadem summa fuerat affectione dilectus. Erat non minus percarus ipsi Regi, utpote qui cum eo coaluerat, et sodalis ejusdem fuerat ab ætate primæva; quamobrem Rex indignatus statuit persequi dictum Johannem, non tam vindicare cupiens dolorem proprium, quam Comitis de Stafford, patris ejusdem juvenis, orbitatem. Confiscari fecit igitur bona Johannis de Holand, ut nulli veniret in dubium

Sir Ralph de Stafford is murdered by Sir John de Holand.

The king determines to punish him.

[1] *præparavit* in the printed texts.

[2] *inauditis* in orig. and the printed texts; corrected from Bibl. Reg. 13 E. ix.

[3] *penes eum* omitted in the printed texts.

[4] *gauderet* in orig., by inadvertence. The reading in the printed texts is "*effectu, ac etiam de tam* "*nobili.*"

[5] *diutius* in orig. and the printed texts.: corrected from Bibl. Reg. 13 E. ix.

[6] *terruit* in orig., an error for *cernit*, as in Bibl. Reg. 13 E. ix.: *vidit* in the printed texts.

A.D. 1385. eum ex animo vindicare velle mortem juvenis supradicti; quo facto sibimet conciliavit amorem Comitum de Stafford et de Warwyk, [1]Domini de Basset, et omnium qui ipsi juveni necessarii fuerant, vel affines. Ipse Johannes, jam fortunam mutatam intelligens, fugit Beverlacum, ut impunitate gauderet ejusdem loci. MS. Bibl. Reg. 13 E. ix.

Holand takes refuge at Beverley.

Causa mortis Matris Regis.

The King's mother, (who is also mother of Sir John de Holand) dies from grief.

Audiens Domina Johanna, mater Regis et ejusdem Johannis de Holand, et homicidium quod filius suus fecerat, et ut Rex eum subjiciendum legis rigori juraverat, mittit illico qui Regem adeant, maternas preces deferant, et filio pro fratre porrigant; exorent ne matris faciem pro tantilla petitione confundat, misereatur fratris, misereatur et matris, et ampliorem experiatur frater misericordiam quod frater suus sit. Sed cum nuncii redissent Walyngfordiam, et mater filiorum nullam in hac parte a Rege consecuta fuisset gratiam, [2]nimio profecto gravata dolore, lecto decumbit, et post quatuor aut quinque dies sæculo valefecit; cujus corpus, ceratis linteaminibus involutum, et plumbo impositum, conservatum est Walyngfordiæ, usque ad Regis regressum de Scotia, et tempus quo deberet Staunford, inter Fratres Minores, honorifice tumulari.[3]

De fulguris tonitruis, et terræ-motis.

A disastrous tempest of thunder and lightning.

Hoc anno, septimo die post Translationem Sancti Thomæ, Cantuariensis Archiepiscopi et Martyris, circa horam tertiam post nonam, audita sunt tonitrua, et visa fulgura et coruscationes, jugiter per unam horam, quæ multorum corda terruerunt; ex quorum ictibus quidam sunt mortui, quidam irremediabiliter læsi, multis in locis.

An earthquake.

Quarto die sequente dictam tempestatem, affuit terræ-motus circa secundam vigiliam noctis, præsignans forsitan inanem commotionem utriusque Regis, Angliæ videlicet et Franciæ, qui jam contraxerant inauditos exercitus, unus versus Scotiam, ut hostes arceret a regno, alter versus Angliam, ut adquireret sibi regnum.

[1] *Dominum* in the printed texts.

[2] *nimia* in orig., Bibl. Reg. 13 E. ix., and the printed texts.

[3] A passage in Bibl. Reg. 13 E. ix. is omitted here.

Rex Angliæ equitat per totam terram Scotiæ, et comburit loca diversa.

MS. Bibl. Reg. 13 E. ix.

Mense Augusti, Rex Angliæ, cum potenti manu, regnum Scotiæ est ingressus; cujus viribus Scoti et Gallici sese cernentes impares, divortia quærunt, nemora petunt, et ad latibula festinare contendunt. Ex quibus tamen frequentius latenter egressi, nostros, ignaros tam locorum quam insidiarum, ex [1] insperato invadunt, perimunt, captivos abducunt. Exercitus Anglicanus, quo nunquam pulchrior, nunquam fortior, numerosior, visus est, equitat per terram habitatoribus destitutam, animalibus vacuatam, carentem victualibus; quæ omnia Scoti, cum Francis, præscientes adventum nostratum, abegerant, abduxerant, et asportarant; in tantum enim desolata est terra, ut nostrates veraciter fatebantur, nec avem quidem se vidisse ibidem, bubonibus solummodo duntaxat exceptis; fruges tamen ibi pulcherrimas virides copiosas invenerunt, quos vel in equorum pabulis consumpserunt, vel equorum pedibus destruxerunt. Cæterum hostibus bellum subterfugientibus, nihil dignum relatu per nostrates actum est amplius, nisi ad Abbathiam de Mailros et villam de Edeneburgh, cum casalibus; quas obiter repererunt nostri, flammis dederunt.

A.D. 1385. The English invade Scotland; the Scots and French take to flight.

The country is laid waste, in every direction.

De discordia inter Regem et Ducem Lancastriæ, et reditu de Scotia.

Cum pervenisset exercitus noster ad Edeneburgh, deficientibus victualibus, cœperunt multi infirmari, [2] nonnulli fame periclitari. Ibi ergo [3] consuluit Rex quid melius videretur agendum. Dux Lancastriæ, qui inter magnos maximus post Regem aderat, fari taliter est exorsus:—"Domine mi Rex," inquit, "Deum laudandi, et multipliciter gaudendi, vobis se "ingessit occasio gratiosa. Primo, quod hostes, qui, sua "confisi potentia, existimabant regnum vestrum pessumdare, "a facie vestra veriti comparere non audent, sed fugiunt "cum dedecore. Secundo, quod adest vobis dominorum et "nobilium spectabilis numerus, bellatorum copiosus exercitus,

The English suffer from deficiency of provisions.

Advice given to the King by the Duke of Lancaster; that the

---

[1] *inspirato* in orig., by inadvertence.

[2] *nonnullū* in orig.; corrected from the printed texts.

[3] *consuluit* in Camden's text and Bibl. Reg. 13 E. ix.: *consulit* in orig. and Parker's text.

A.D. 1385.

English should cross the Scottish Sea (Frith of Forth) in pursuit of the enemy.

MS. Bibl. Reg. 13 E. ix.

"qualis antea in hiis regionibus nunquam visus est, pro "vobis dimicare paratus. Tertio, quod favor Divinitatis vos, "ut verisimiliter arbitror, comitatur, quia et æstas temperata "et aura serena votis nostris in tantum hactenus arriserunt, "quod non vento contrario, non imbre nocivo, fuimus impe-"diti quominus vel in diebus equitare, vel in noctibus sub "divo requiescere, valeremus. Consulo propterea, ut mare "Scoticum transeamus, quo constat hostes nostros confugisse, "præsertim cum facilis sit nobis transitus; et patriam flamma "ferroque destruamus, ut vel sic compellantur hostes ad pug-"nam, vel saltem ad dedecorosam fugam."

The King rejects his advice with insult and reproach.

Rex ad hæc, tanquam testem proditionis invenisset Ducis sententiam, exarsit in iram;—"Tu," inquit, "ubicunque loco-"rum cum exercitu devenisti, meos homines malo ductu, malo "consilio, mala patria, fame, siti, penuria, perdidisti; semper "tuis marsupiis consulens, meis nihil: et nunc, juxta morem "tuum, me cogis ad transitum maris Scotici, ut ego, cum "hominibus meis, fame peream, et inopia, et fiam hostibus "meis præda: ecce! nobis, in hoc loco constitutis, desunt "victualia, et multi de meis hominibus inedia perierunt, et "tu compellis ad transeundum remotius, quo nullus victus ad "me vel meos possit adduci? Nequaquam fiet ut cogitas. "Sed si tu velis transire cum tuis, mare transeas. Nunquam "enim [1]ante stipatus fuisti tanto numero tuorum hominum "quanto modo stiparis. Ego enim et mei homines reverte-"mur."

The King and Duke, with difficulty, are reconciled; and the English army returns home.

Ad hæc respondente Duce,—"Et ego homo vester sum," "Nequaquam," inquit Rex, [2]["non apparet ita;" cumque Rex] vehementer [3]turbaretur, et Dux [4]humiliaret se satis eidem, non ferentes Domini tantam discordiam, ingesserunt se et pacem reformaverunt, qualem poterant pro malitia temporis, inter illos. Et factum est ita, ut non procederent, sed reverterentur via qua venerant in terram suam. Et quidem tantæ profectionis in Scotiam iste fuit finis et fructus.

Scoti prædantur Angliam, Rege absente.

The Scots and French enter Eng-

Rege cum universo exercitu suo terram vastante Scotiæ, ingressi sunt in Angliam Scoti, cum Gallicis, et, villas cre-

---

[1] *antea* in the printed texts.

[2] Supplied from Bibl. Reg. 13 E. ix.; omitted in the printed texts.

[3] *turbatus* in the printed texts; to suit the omission.

[4] *humiliavit* in the printed texts.

MS. Bibl. Reg. 13 E. ix. mantes, prædas agentes, et captivos multos abducentes, reversi sunt in terram suam, et sic, ingressu suo furtivo, plus commodi perceperunt in Anglia, quam Rex cum imperiali exercitu retulit de terra sua. A.D. 1385. land, and ravage the country.

Rex Franciæ præparari fecit navigium contra Angliam.

Dum adhuc Anglicanus exercitus moraretur in Scotia, Rex Franciæ [1] præparare [2][fecit] navigium, [3] conduci populosum exercitum, instrumenta bellica [4] congregari, et victualia suæ profectioni necessaria [5] comportari ad Le Sclus, quia præcogitaverat intrasse regnum Angliæ, dum potestas regni, prout dictum est, in Scotia moraretur. Sed tantos sumptus, tantam astutiam, tantam prudentiam, tantum consilium, quia facta sunt contra Dominum, dissipavit in hora brevi Dominus, per captionem villæ de Le Dam in Flandria; quam ceperunt Gandavenses, habitatoribus illius villæ tradentibus eam ipsis, quia jam fessi de dominio Francorum, quod erat eis nimis superciliosum et importunum, magis expedire credebant se submittere suis proximis quam crudelibus dominis, id est, Francis. Et revera Gallici, ubi eos superiores esse et dominari contigerit, cum summa superbia et intolerabili injuria subditos suos tractare solent. Invenerunt ergo Gandavenses in dicta villa prædam magnam victualium diversorum, vinique præcipue, eo quod ibi erat cellarium vinorum Regis Franciæ; nempe mille et octingenta dolia inibi sunt reperta. Gandavenses, asportatis Gandavum quæ sibi necessaria videbantur, posuerunt in dicta villa præsidium hominum defensorum, et ad propria sunt reversi.

The King of France prepares a fleet for the invasion of England.

But is impeded, by reason of the capture of Le Dam by the people of Ghent.

Great stores of wine found there.

Obsidio villæ de Le Dam.

Audiens Rex Franciæ, cum suis magnatibus, quod Flandrenses qui in villa prædicta [6][erant], se tradidissent Gandavensibus, consternatus est, et jam primo desperans de regno Angliæ

---

[1] *præparavit* in the printed texts.

[2] Supplied from Bibl. Reg. 13 E. ix.: omitted in the printed texts.

[3] *conducit* in the printed texts.

[4] *congregat* in the printed texts.

[5] *comportat* in the printed texts.

[6] Omitted in orig. and Bibl. Reg. 13 E. ix.; supplied from the printed texts.

A.D. 1385.

The King of France employs his forces on the siege of Le Dam.

The French are repulsed.

MS. Bibl. Reg. 13 E. ix.

conquirendo, præmeditatum dimisit propositum, et cuncta quæ paraverat ad debellandum Angliam, contraxit ad [1]obsidendum prædictam villam. Collocatis ergo per gyrum suis exercitibus, signum datur insultum faciendi villæ, et fit insultus acerrimus, Francis nitentibus gloriose recuperare quod fradulenter amiserant, Flandrensibus contra certantibus conservare libertatem quam jam receperant, excusso jugo importabili Gallicorum. Quid multa? Repelluntur Gallici ferocitate Flandrensium, et recedunt; Flandrenses fessi in villam se recipiunt, et quiescunt. Cumque aliquotiens Franci insultus fecissent, nec tamen profecissent, ac per hoc videretur pars melior obsessorum, videntes tamen qui in villa erant jacula sibi deesse, et instrumenta repellendis hostibus necessaria, prudenti consilio tradunt villam quadam nocte conservandam mulieribus et senibus, affirmantes oportere eos facie tenus habere custodiam villæ per illam saltem noctem, qua oportuit eos, qui dimicaverant die præcedenti, membra reficere, somnum capere, corpora recreare. Dum ergo hii villam circueunt, vigilias noctis custodiunt, adversariorum irruptiones observant, omnes bello apti viri, nescientibus qui remanserant, villam furtivi egrediuntur, et Gandavum, nescientibus hostibus, perveniunt, sine rerum vel corporum læsione; confractis autem in egressum suum cunctorum doliorum capitibus, et effusis vinis et aliis liquoribus qui in eis erant, ne Gallicis cedere possent in adjutorium quovismodo. Sicque Rex Franciæ, dum villam se lucratum fuisse credidit, et adversarios subjugasse, dum villam intrat, cognoscit se delusum.

Stratagem of the besieged, for stealthy evacuation of the town.

Et quidem in Flandria res ita se habebant, et Anglia pro præsenti anno gratulata est hoc modo se ab hostibus liberatam.

Rex Portugaliæ vincit Hispanos.

The King of Portugal, with the aid of his English auxiliaries, defeats the Spaniards.

Circa tempus istud, Rex Portyngaliæ, congregatis quos poterat de terra sua pugnatoribus, una cum Anglicis qui sibi dudum missi fuerant in adjutorium, Marte favente, immo Domino Deo exercituum corda suis viresque præbente, de Castellanis Hispanensibus, habito congressu ferocissimo, gloriose triumphavit. Quod bellum sibi dedit requiem ab inimicis suis, et totum regnum Portyngaliæ suæ restituit ditioni. Nomina potentium peremptorum in prædicto bello duximus inserenda:—Comes de Mariorca, Comes Cariōn, Johannes Gandissaleyn, Prior Sancti Johannis de Castella, Consalpinus

[1] *obsidionem prædictam villam* in orig.; *obsidionem prædictæ villæ* in the printed texts: corrected from Bibl. Reg. 13 E. ix.

MS. Bibl. Reg. 13 E. ix. Galaci, Didacus Gomissixe, Magister de Galliaturna, Dominus Johannes Duke, Dominus Johannes Renulds, Comes de Dene, Didacus Avari et frater ejus, filius Mariaci de Willanor, Lupus de Rodynge, Lupus Gomossi de Lile, proditor. A.D. 1385.

Post dicti belli consummationem, Rex Portyngaliæ misit Regi Angliæ sex galeyas, ut adjuvarent eum, et essent illi solatio contra hostes suos; quæ, exceptæ cum favore, in brevi, beneficio Londoniensium et aliarum urbium, senserunt se non sine suo commodo in Angliam [1] remigasse.

The King of Portugal sends six galleys to the King of England.

Damna illata Regi Franciæ et suis, recedentibus de Flandria.

Rex Franciæ, post frustratum propositum, quo cogitaverat Angliam infestare, post dispendiosam moram factam circa villam de Le Dam, de qua cupiverat triumphare, post infructuosam adeptionem dictæ villæ, quam putavit bonis omnibus abundare, tristis, fessus, et illusus, ad propria remeavit, non sine magno suorum dispendio, in insultibus factis ad villam, ubi quinque valentiores primo perierunt, et in via versus patriam, ubi Gandavenses multos de suis ceperunt, et plurimos occiderunt. Nam, ut taceamus damna irrogata sibi per terrestrem viam, plura damna pertulit per campos liquidos, amissione tam hominum quam suarum rerum: affuit siquidem tempestas horrida, dum naves redirent de Le Sclus, quæ naves dispersit, allisit, confregit, et, invitis nautis, impulit in loca Regis Angliæ, Calesiam videlicet, et partes adjacentes. Revera, Die Exaltationis Sanctæ Crucis, duæ grandes galeyæ, et aliud genus ratis quod vocatur "*lyne*," et una bargia, et septem balingariæ, periclitatæ sunt ante villam de Calesia, et Calesienses captivos ceperunt quingentos de Gallicis et Normannis, qui, classe demersa, venerunt ad portum. Numerus captivorum, inter quos captus est Robertus Bremvile, homo prædives et potentissimus inter totius Neustriæ mercatores [2] .

Losses experienced by the King of France, in the siege of Le Dam.

His fleet suffers from a tempest.

Several vessels are taken by the people of Calais.

Tertio die sequente, septuaginta et duæ naves Francorum, redeuntes de Sclusa, pertransire Calesiam decertabant. Sed Calesienses, egressi, pugnaverunt contra eas, et lucrati sunt decem et octo naves, et quandam grandem bargiam, in qua fuerunt capti vel occisi armati homines sexaginta. Tertio itidem die sequente dictum conflictum, quadraginta et quinque naves maximæ, redeuntes de Sclusia, dum præterire vel-

Farther captures made from the French.

[1] *remigrasse* in the printed texts.

[2] The number of prisoners, (probably in the total), is apparently omitted.

A.D. 1385. lent Calesiam, per nostrates impeditæ sunt. Nempe Calesienses, et harum adventu cognito, armaverunt se contra eas, et pugnaverunt amplius quam per sex horas; tandem victoria cessit nostris, et fugerunt omnes illæ naves, præter duas et unum coggonem, in quibus capti sunt duo Admiralii Galliæ, cum multis bonis. Fuerunt autem duæ dictæ naves grandes adeo, quod apud Calesiam non valebant introduci; quamobrem ad Sandwicum missæ sunt. Harum majorem comparaverat Dominus de Clysson pro tribus millibus francorum, apud Sclusam, et erat navis nova utpote ipso anno facta. Prædictum vero coggonem de Estlondia Normanni conduxerant quinque millibus francorum, ut [1] fuisset eis ad tutelam et defensionem redeuntibus in terram suam; sed tamen, obsistentibus Anglicis, semetipsum defendere non valebat, quin caperetur et fieret Anglis præda. Capti sunt et occisi in dictis navibus de nautis et stipendiariis ducenti et viginti et sex; per omnia benedictus Deus!

MS. Bibl. Reg. 13 E. ix.

The larger vessels so captured, are sent to Sandwich.

Nostrates prædantur in Francia.

The English ravage the vicinity of Calais.

Die Sancti Dionysii, stipendiarii de Calesia, et fortalitiis Regis Angliæ illis in partibus constitutis, latenter exierunt in Franciam, et [2][prædam] quatuor [3] millium ovium et [4] trecentorum grossorum animalium versus sua municipia fugaverunt. Quod [5] cognoscens Dominus de Bambures, qui erat Capitaneus Boloniæ, cum armatis exiit contra nostros; qui, in primo congressu [6] acceptus lancea cujusdam Anglici, equo suo illico perturbatus est, et, levatus per suos in equum suum, non sustinuit ibidem diutius expectare, ne deterius sibi contingeret; sed urgens [7] sonipedem calcaribus præacutis, fuga sua nostris suam prædam abigendi liberam tribuit facultatem. Capti sunt per nostros in hac profectione plures quam centum [8] prisones.[9]

The Captain of Boulogne is wounded, and put to flight.

---

[1] *esset* in the printed texts.

[2] Supplied from Bibl. Reg. 13 E. ix.: omitted in the printed texts.

[3] *millia* in the printed texts.

[4] *trecenta grossa* in the printed texts.

[5] *cognoscentes* in orig. and the printed texts; corrected from Bibl. Reg. 13 E. ix.

[6] *exceptus* in orig. and Bibl. Reg. 13 E. ix.: *acceptus* in the printed texts.

[7] *compedem* in orig. and the printed texts: corrected from Bibl. Reg. 13 E. ix.

[8] *personæ* in the printed texts.

[9] A passage in Bibl. Reg. 13 E. ix. is omitted here.

De hiis quæ gesta sunt in Portugalia.

MS. Bibl. Reg. 13 E. ix.

A.D. 1383.

Præposterum petit ordinem posteritas nunciorum redeuntium a remotis, et me quandoque scribere quæ sunt prima novissime, et quæ novissime primo cogunt. Hinc est quod res Portyngalenses in hoc loco pono, quæ perante poni debuerant, si temporis ordinem conservassem.

(Ferdinand) King of Portugal, is poisoned by the Queen, who gives her daughter to the King of Castille.

Igitur, post decessum Domini Edmundi, Comitis Cantebriggiæ, de Portyngalia, Regina Portyngaliæ, prout dicunt, consensu cujusdam militis quem dilexit illicite, venenum Regi Portyngaliæ propinavit; cujus haustu letifero Rex in fata concessit. Regina, proinde considerans cuncta sibi licere quæ voluit, filiam suam, quæ desponsata fuerat filio Domini Edmundi Comitis Cantebriggiæ, vendidit Regi Castellæ, consilio militis supradicti. Rex ergo Castellæ, odium inveteratum, quod contra regnum Portyngaliæ diu conceperat, effutire gestiens, gaudio gavisus est quod occasionem quandam susceperat perdendi regnum sibi odibile diu ante. Et hac occasione villas et munitiones dicti regni suscepit in sua, parans proculdubio in futurum cunctos ibidem suos adversarios delere usque ad unum, immo destruere usque ad nullum. Proceres vero regni, rem tacite considerantes, quorsum hæc tenderent meditabantur; tandem videntes [1] [ad] regni desolationem [2] rem [3] parari, concito ad Regis defuncti fratrem, virum martium, fide perspicuum, sensu præditum, concurrerunt, incitantes eum ut se opponeret tantis malis. Erat ille Magister Hospitalis, vir tam religione quam potestate præstans cæteris, et habuit in temporalibus unde proferret nova et vetera pro defensione dicti regni. Hic ergo, pulsatus a civibus, castrum adiit manu forti, ubi Regina cum amasio moram traxit. Et quidem, pacificum prætendens ingressum, Reginam sibi fecit occurrere et eum eo ampliori honore suscipere, quo Regis defuncti frater, quo Magister Hospitalis, quo nominatissimus in regno, fuit. In primo itaque ingressu suo, Reginam cœpit convenire de fidefragio erga Comitem Cantebriggiæ, deinde de regimine pravo regni, per quod vacillabat regni [4] statura, ut præfertur. Quod

The nobles appeal to the brother of the late King, against the designs of the King of Castille.

He charges the Queen with perfidy.

---

[1] Supplied from Bibl. Reg. 13 E. ix.: omitted in the printed texts: *quod regni* in orig., by inadvertence.

[2] *rem* omitted in the printed texts.

[3] *præparari* in the printed texts.

[4] *statu* in orig.; *status* in the printed texts: corrected from Bibl. Reg. 13 E. ix.

A.D. 1383. audiens miles, quem prædiximus Reginam vitiasse, sine respectu reverentiæ tantæ personæ debitæ, insolentius respondit eidem, dicens nihil sibi competere de [1]regimine regni, quippe qui religiosus esse deberet, et suæ religioni potius indulgere quam regni gubernationi. Quo responso Magister Hospitalis agnovit militis assensum in præmissis minime defuisse; quapropter, illico extracto cultello, in proditorem irruit, et protinus interfecit. Reginam vero jussit apprehendi, et in eodem castello regaliter custodiri; corpus quoque militis interfecti jussit sepeliri; quo facto, tota regio adhæsit eidem. Cumque expost contra Regem Hispaniæ una vice et alia prospere dimicasset, totius vulgi favore electus est in Regem: reclamavit ipse tamen, dicens se, suæ religioni voto professionis astrictum, nec posse, nec debere, regni suscipere diadema. Instantibus, urgentibus, compellentibus, tandem illis, dixit se velle parere ipsorum quodammodo voluntati, dum dictum regnum administrare vellet usque ad adventum hæredis justi, filii videlicet Comitis Cantebriggiæ, cui filia fratris sui, Regis Portyngaliæ, ut præfertur, primo fuerat desponsata.

And slays her paramour.

MS. Bibl. Reg. 13 E. ix.

The Queen is imprisoned.

The King's brother accepts the crown, on certain conditions.

Et hoc quidem modo est regni consecutus honorem, Anglos multum diligens, acrius fovens qui erant in regno suo, propter illorum nimirum probitatem; per quos non dubitavit se superiorem manum semper in cunctis conflictibus reportasse.

Rex vero Castellæ, non ignorans per quos Rex Portyngaliæ triumphaverat, tentavit Anglos fulvo metallo corrumpere, quorum naturam didicit [2]indultam avaritiæ; transmittens aliqua, plura vero promittens, si prodere velint Regem cum gente. Erant revera duo armigeri, quorum virtute, discretione, prudentia, perante semper Portyngalensibus cessit victoria, Hispanis vero fuga. Hii, proh dolor! auri sacra fame coacti, consensere Regi Castellæ, præferentes pecuniam fidei, munera veritati; sed eorum internuncii, cujusdam Anglici illibata conscientia, Regi delati, et cito convicti; iidem armigeri capti sunt et carcerali custodiæ deputati, non sine magno totius suæ gentis opprobrio, et scandalo nationis. Hæc in Portyngalia gesta sunt, trans Neptunum.

The King of Castille bribes certain of the English auxiliaries of the King of Portugal.

---

[1] *regni regina* in orig.; *regni regimine* in the printed texts; *regimine regni* in Bibl. Reg. 13 E. ix.

[2] *indultum* in orig.; corrected from the printed texts.

Actus Papæ.

MS. Bibl. Reg. 13 E. ix.

Per idem tempus, [1]Papa Urbanus Sextus, cui nihil datum est diu dulce gustare, ejus nescio an adversariorum improbitate, iterum inimicitias renovatas agnovit inter ipsum et Karolum, Regem Siculorum; iterum nempe per ipsum Regem obsidionis contumelias, opprobria, damna, toleravit, usquequo pene ad desperationis articulum est perductus. Sed tandem, Januensium probitate, qui cuncta norunt facere propter quid, ereptus, libertati abductus, Januam usque perductus est; a qua civitate transmigrare non permittitur, donec inæstimabilem auri summam pro sua ereptione persolvisset Januensibus; qui plus propter nummum quam propter Deum ejus ereptioni intenderant, prout patet.

A.D. 1385. Renewed enmity between the Pope and King Charles.

The Genoese assist the Pope, but extort money for their assistance.

Electus Sancti Andreæ capitur.

Hiis diebus, Electus Sancti Andreæ in Scotia, dum proficisceretur cum multis militibus et armigeris versus Lugdunum, ut confirmaretur ab Antipapa, captus est: qui, quamvis unum tantum coggonem haberet, in quo ipse et sui consederant, septem tamen pene de nostris bargiis superavit; tanta vis armatorum nebulonum extitit in navi sua. Captus tandem est a duobus filiis Willelmi Ruscheby senioris, armigeris Comitis Northumbriæ, et eidem Comiti præsentatus. Qui, cogente tristitia, paulo post prætulit mortem vitæ, ingressus viam universæ carnis.

The Bishop Elect of St. Andrew's is captured, after a desperate resistance.

He dies soon after.

Parliamentum Londoniæ, et acta ejusdem.

Circa festum Sancti Martini, factum est Parliamentum Londoniis, in quo laici concesserunt Regi unam quintam-decimam et dimidiam, sub conditione tamen, quod clerus decimam et dimidiam daret eidem: cui conditioni obnixe restitit Archiepiscopus Cantuariensis, Dominus Willelmus de Courtenay, dicens hoc minime fore faciendum, præsertim cum Ecclesia debeat esse libera, et per laicos nullo modo taxanda; immo, citius caput exponeret pro hac causa, quam in tantum Sanctam

Attempt of the Parliament to tax the clergy, resisted by the Archbishop of Canterbury.

---

[1] *Papa* omitted in Camden's text.

A.D. 1385. Ecclesiam Anglicanam permitteret ancillari. Quæ responsio [1]tantum commovit turbam communium, ut milites Comitatuum, cum quibusdam ex proceribus regni, cum summa furia deprecarentur auferre temporalia ab ecclesiasticis, dicentes clerum ad tantam excrevisse superbiam, quod opus esset pietatis et eleemosynæ, per ablationem temporalium quæ ecclesiasticos extollebant, eos compellere ad humilius sapiendum. Hæc clamabant, hæc Regi in scriptis brevibus porrigebant; et tanta fuit eorum in hac parte vesania, quod hanc petitionem ad effectum posse perduci credebant. Inde cerneres milites lætari [2]Veneris, de hiis inter se conferre, et, velut totius Ecclesiæ temporalia eorum abusionibus jam deputata fuissent, hunc de hoc monasterio, alium de alio, sibimet blandiendo, promittere certam summam. Audivi egomet revera quemdam ex hujuscemodi militibus intense jurantem, se velle de domus Sancti Albani temporalibus annuatim [3]percipere mille marcas.

MS. Bibl. Reg. 13 E. ix.

Contemplated partition, by the laity, of the temporalities of the Church.

The King opposes these designs against the Church.

Sed tantæ delirationi non consensit Rex, sed auditis hinc inde, et horum, inordinatis clamoribus, et istorum justis responsis, præcepit deleri scripta et cessari inordinate petita, dicens se Ecclesiam Anglicanam in ejusdem status qualitate suis temporibus servaturum, qua ipsam cognoverat extitisse, cum regnum suscepisset, aut potius meliori: quo facto, et apud ecclesiasticos magna muneratione dignus censebatur, et apud bonos laicos hoc responsum maxime laudabatur. Archiepiscopus proinde, communicato cum clero consilio, Regem adiit, et dixit se, cum clero regni, unanimi voluntate, consensu spontaneo unam decimam Regis usibus providisse. Quam concessionem Rex tam læte audivit, tam grate suscepit, ut palam assereret se malle hanc ad præsens donationem liberam, quam alias quamcunque quadrupli valoris coactam; et ita pro tunc hostium Ecclesiæ aviditas insatiabilis est frustrata.

The clergy make a voluntary grant to the King.

The Earl of Oxford created Marquis of Dublin.

[4] Creata est in hoc Parliamento nova dignitas, Anglicis insueta; nempe Comes Oxoniæ, Dominus Robertus de Veer, appellatus et factus est Marchio Dubiliniæ in Hibernia; cæteris Comitibus hoc indigne ferentibus, quod viderent eum gradum celsiorem ipsis, Regis munere, percepisse, et præcipue, quia nec prudentia cæteris, nec armis, valentior videbatur.

Promotion of the King's uncles to the Dukedom with a grant of money.

Creati sunt insuper novi Duces; quanquam in procinctu Scotico Rex in campo donasset illos hiis nominibus; Dominus Thomas de Wodestoke, videlicet, Comes Bukyngamiæ, nomen Ducatus accepit, et vocatus est "Dux Gloverniæ," et Dominus

---

[1] *tamen* in the printed texts.

[2] *venerios* in the printed texts.

[3] *velle* repeated here in orig. and Bibl. Reg. 13 E. ix. by inadvertence.

MS. Bibl. Reg. 13 E. ix. Edmundus de Langeley, qui erat Comes Cantebriggiæ, vocatus est "Dux Eboraci;" quibus Rex de fisco regio summas dedit, propter honorem nominum, ne suscepisse tantum nomen inaniter viderentur. A.D. 1385.

Dominus Michael De le Pole, qui fuit regni Cancellarius, ibidem factus est Comes Southfolchiæ, datis ei annuatim de regio marsupio mille marcis; vir plus aptus mercimoniis quam militiæ, et qui [1]trapezetis in pace consenuerat, non armatis in bello.

Michael De la Pole, the Chancellor, made Earl of Suffolk.

Restitutio temporalium Episcopi Norwicensis.

Rex præterea in hoc Parliamento, mediatione sollicita Præsulis Eliensis, videlicet, Thomæ de Arundellia, restituit Episcopo Nortwicensi bona sua temporalia, quæ detinuerat per multos annos, ut superius exaravi, quamvis Cancellarius id fieri dissuaderet. Revera cum Dominus Eliensis rogasset Regem de re præmissa, Cancellarius, cum indignationis felle, respondit Eliensi, dicens:—" Quid est, Domine Præsul, quod " rogatis? Numquid tam leve Regi videtur Nortwicensis " temporalia modo dimittere, quæ per annum sibi præstant " amplius mille libris? Non indiget Rex talibus consiliariis; " non eget amicis hujuscemodi, qui eum multare cupiunt, " tantæ pecuniæ detrimento." Cui respondit illico Eliensis :— " Quid est quod loqueris, Domine Michael? Non de Rege " sua deposco, sed aliena, quæ minus justo detinet titulo, tuo " vel tibi similium inductus pravo consilio, sibi nunquam, " prout æstimo, profutura: et tu, si tantum Regis detrimenta " considerando ponderas, cur ab eo mille marcas [2]annuas tam " avide percepisti, cum te Comitem Southfolchiæ creavisset?" Cancellarius, cum id audisset, velut jaculo reverberatus, substitit, et amplius huic materiæ contradicere non præsumpsit. Et hic finis Parliamenti præsentis.

The temporalities of the Bishop of Norwich are restored, against the remonstrances of the Chancellor.

Answer of the Bishop of Ely to the Chancellor's objections.

[3][Transit hic annus ferax satis fructuum, mediocriter temperatus, sed Gallicis, propter expensas, damna, mortes, captivitates, tam virorum quam villæ de Le Dam, nimis infaustus; Anglicis mediocriter lætus; Scotis sumptuosus, formidabilis, et damnosus.]

---

[1] *trapazetis* in orig. and Bibl. Reg. 13 E. ix.

[2] *alnuas* in orig.; by inadvertence, arising from the peculiar form of the mark of contraction in Bibl. Reg. 13 E. ix.

[3] Omitted in orig. and the printed texts, evidently by inadvertence. Supplied from Bibl. Reg. 13 E. ix.

A.D. 1386. Visit of the King of Armenia, under pretext of making peace between the Kings of England and France.

MS. Bibl. Reg. 13 E. ix.

Anno Domini millesimo trecentesimo octogesimo sexto, qui est annus regni Regis Ricardi, a Conquæstu Secundi, nonus, tenuit Rex Natale apud Eltham, cum Anna Regina; quo pervenit ad eum Rex Armeniæ, sub prætextu pacis reformandæ inter Angliæ Reges et Franciæ: sed quid profecerit ejus adventus, ipse solus sensit. Nam præter innumera dona quæ de Rege regnique percepit proceribus, Rex concessit et dedit eidem chartam de mille libris, ad vitam suam percipiendum annuatim. Fuerat nempe, ut asseruit, fugatus a regno suo per Tartaros, et ob hanc causam multa a Regibus Christianis extorsit munera, in tantum ut felicior fuit illi fuga sua in aliena patria, quam dominium regni sui cum gente sua.

Carolus Neapolis moritur.

Death of Charles, King of Naples.

Per idem tempus moritur Karolus de Pace, Rex Siciliæ, qui multa damna Papæ irrogaverat, si injuste [1] nolumus diffinire; excommunicatus tamen a Papa discessit. Quo vindicandi genere Papa pro tunc contentus est, quia aliud vindictæ genus non occurrit. Nec est in ambiguo Papam voluisse seque severius et materialius vindicasse, si sibi potestas brachii sæcularis minime defuisset. Ferunt ipsum Karolum proditiose occisum a quodam milite, dum sederet ad mensam, die et hora quibus Papam proposuerat occidisse.

Report as to his assassination.

Gandavenses se reddunt Regi Franciæ.

The people of Ghent submit to the King of France.

Gandavenses hiis diebus, non expectato adjutorio quod illis Rex Angliæ, non sine magnis sumptibus, præparaverat, innato more genti suæ, [2] usi levi consilio, se Regi Franciæ dediderunt, manifeste monstrantes se non posse uni amico vel domino fidem diutius conservare. Igitur pars exercitus, cum quibusdam capitaneis, quæ Gandavum mittenda fuerat, ad villam de Berewico destinatur, ad retundendas irruptiones Scotorum, qui præparati erant ad inferenda damna nostratibus in hac plaga.[3]

The English army intended for their aid is sent to Berwick.

---

[1] *noluimus* in the printed texts.

[2] *usu* in orig.; *ut si* in Camden's text: *usi* in Bibl. Reg. 13 E. ix. and Parker's text.

[3] A passage in Bibl. Reg. 13, E. ix. is omitted here.

Dux Lancastriæ proficiscitur in regionem longinquam, Hispaniæ accipere sibi regnum.

MS. Bibl. Reg. 13 E. ix.

A.D. 1386.

Circa festum Paschæ, Dominus Johannes, Dux Lancastriæ, cum magna turba militum, armigerorum, et arcitenentium, se præparavit [1][ad iter Hispanicum, ut regnum] Hispaniæ, quod sibi debebatur hæreditario jure uxoris suæ, scilicet Dominæ Constantiæ, filiæ quondam Domini Petronis, Regis Castellæ et Legionis, vel cum incolarum pace [2]repeteret, vel jure bellico [3]vendicaret. Accessit ejus profectioni favor Papalis, et auctoritas, tribuens peccatorum veniam cunctis secum proficiscentibus, et omnibus ejus profectioni de bonis suis quicquam conferentibus; ut ipse quæstor ex principe effici videretur. Et revera cunctas dispensationes et singulas accepit a Papa, quas perante susceperat [4]Northwicensis Antistes, quando Crucesignatus erat contra Gallicos et Flandrenses: sed ipsa frequens veniæ et relaxationis concessio tantum viluit et sordebat in populo, ut pauci forent qui huic postremæ Cruce-signationi aliquid erogarent. Arripuit iter nihilominus, et ad mare cum pervenisset, expectare coactus est ventorum penuria, donec pene cuncta quæ sui comportaverant necessaria consumpsissent. Tandem cum humiliati fuissent sub potenti manu Dei, aspiravit aura quæ classem afflavit in Britanniam, prope castellum de Brest; contra quam patriotæ Britones erexerant duas munitiones ad arcendum castellanos, et prohibendum eorum egressum in terram suam. Erat tunc dicti castelli Capitaneus quidam miles, dictus "Johannes Roche," qui, cum deplorasset suam coartationem memoratam, laudabili probitate Domini Filii Walteri, et aliorum nobilium qui cum Duce erant, confortatus est: siquidem mox egressi contra munitiones prædictas, eas ceperunt, confregerunt, diruerunt, et magnam prædam, cum captivis, obtinuerunt ibidem, sed non sine suorum dispendio deplorando, quia perdiderunt illic viros quosdam validos atque fortes. Quibus patratis, surgente vento secundo, appulsi sunt in Hispanniam, in portum videlicet de Le Groyn, in Vigilia Sancti Laurentii, cum integra classe sua.

The Duke of Lancaster sets out for Spain, to claim the Spanish crown.

Certain immunities are granted to his supporters by the Pope; but are held in no esteem.

The Duke arrives in Bretagne, and relieves the Castle of Brest.

The Duke reaches Spain.

---

[1] Supplied from Bibl. Reg. 13 E. ix.: omitted in the printed texts.

[2] *repetere* in the printed texts.

[3] *vendicare* in the printed texts.

[4] *Northwicenses* in orig., by inadvertence.

De Henrico Percy, misso Calesiam.

A.D. 1386.

A force sent to Calais under Sir Henry Percy and others.

MS. Bibl. Reg. 13 E. ix.

Hac æstate increbuere rumores de proposito Regis Franciæ volentis obsidionem ponere circa villam de Calesia, et ad hoc exercitum comparantis; ad cujus impetus sustinendos, vel potius repellendos, cum multis victualibus missi sunt ex Anglia plures valentes; inter quos, Dominus Henricus Percy junior, [1] videlicet, Henrici Percy, Comitis Northumbriæ, destinatur, juvenis in quo totius probitatis et militiæ specimen elucebat. Qui cum aliquandiu apud Calesiam moram protraxissent in otio, indignatus Henricus Percy hujuscemodi quietes se odire professus est. Et revera perante, dum fuisset Custos villæ Berewici, gentem omnino inquietam, id est, Scotos, quiescere compulit, et sua alacri inquietudine multotiens fatigavit. Ob quam causam, illorum lingua ipsum Henricum [2] "Hatspore" vocaverunt, quod "calidum calcar" sonat.

Percy called "Hatspore" (Hotspur) from his alacrity in attacking the Scots.

After harassing the French, Percy returns to England.

Hic ergo Henricus, congregatis sociis, super Morinos et Pikardos facit expeditiones, prædas abducit, et actus exercet laudabiliter militares; et cum pluries ista [3] faceret, et nullus ei resisteret, insuper et cognovisset quod Rex Franciæ non proponeret obsidere Calesiam, sed potius invadere deliberaret Angliam, revertitur in hanc terram, ut hic ei occurreret quod volebat, bellum scilicet Gallicorum.

De his quæ contigerint in Austria.

The Duke of Austria exacts a tribute from Pilgrims resorting to the Papal Court.

Per id temporis, in Ducatu Austriæ sub brevi tempore fortuna vultus suos in diversa mutavit, modo se favorabilem præbens proceribus, modo semet ostendens adjutricem vulgaribus, versa vice. Nempe Dux Austriæ, vir vafer et cupidus, et Urbano Papæ contrarius, invidens peregrinis ad Papam confluentibus, imposuit tributum importabile per terram suam transituris, ut vel sic saltem arceret Catholicos a visitatione Papali. Unde factum est, ut per illam viam peregrini transire cessarent, præeligentes longiorem in circuitu peregrinationem suscipere, quam tot injustis exactionibus, contumeliis, et injuriis, lacessiri. Vulgares autem patriæ, cernentes vias desolatas, et [4] librantes damna quæ jamdudum perceperant, cum

---

[1] The word "*filius*," apparently, is omitted here, in all the texts.

[2] *Hotspor* in the printed texts: *Haatspore* in Bibl. Reg. 13 E. ix.

[3] *facerit* in orig.; from its indistinctness in Bibl. Reg. 13 E. ix.

[4] *laborantes* in orig.; corrected from the printed texts.

MS. Bibl. Reg. 13 E. ix.

A.D. 1386.

peregrini cessassent transire per illos, Ducem adeunt, oraturi ut, more solito, liceret peregrinis transire per illos; per quorum confluentiam non mediocre emolumentum perceperat tota terra: qui spreti, et superciliose a Duce repulsi, ad propria discesserunt, congregaturi communes regionis, ad vindicandum in Ducem superbum injurias præacceptas. Quorum cognitis molitionibus, Dux, cum suis generosis et dominis, pergit obviam turbæ vulgari. Et mox, commisso bello, cædit, prosternit, et captivat eosdem, et adductis morti [1] quot volebat, dimittit reliquos in domos suas; qui cum tanto damno ab eo digressi et amaro animo nimis effecti, jam tunc quidem cessare minis decreverunt, sed novum exercitum recolligere, de novo Ducem aggredi, statuerunt; quibus illico Dux occurrit, fidens in priori victoria perempturos omnes, si fortuna faveret. Sed aliter evenit quam sperabat; quia ipse, cum tota nobilitate et generosa gente Ducatus, coram eis corruit.

His people remonstrate, and rise against him, but are defeated.

He is finally defeated, and slain (at the Battle of Sempach.)

De timiditate Londinensium.

Londonienses, comperto pro vero quod Rex [2] Franciæ conduxisset navigium, comparasset exercitum, [3] fixisset propositum in Angliam veniendi, timidi velut lepores, meticulosi ut mures, requirunt hinc inde [4] divortia, perscrutantur latebras, et, velut jam capienda foret civitas, cœpere propriis diffidere viribus, et de resistentia desperare; et qui in pace [5] tumidi jactitabant se cunctos Gallicos [6] exsufflaturos [7] Anglia, audito jam licet inani rumore de adventu hostium, vix universam Angliam illos posse tutare putabant. Idcirco, velut a vino madidi, ad muros urbis currunt, contiguas domos dilacerant, deponunt, destruunt, et cuncta formidolose faciunt quæ in extremis necessitatibus positi facere consueverunt. Nondum ullus Gallicus in navem pedem posuerat, Neptunum nullus hostis intraverat, et Londonienses, acsi tota terra in circuitu victa conquisita fuisset, adeo metuunt, ita sollicitantur, velut ipsos hostes aspicerent ante fores. [8] Sic sic viri, qui in quiete

Alarm of the Londoners, on hearing rumours of the contemplated invasion.

---

[1] *quod* in orig.; *quos* in the printed texts: corrected from Bibl. Reg. 13 E. ix.

[2] *Franci* in the printed texts.

[3] *direxisset* in the printed texts.

[4] Altered from *divortia*, as in Bibl. Reg. 13 E. ix. and the printed texts, to *diverticula*, in a later hand.

[5] *timidi* in orig. and the printed texts: corrected from Bibl. Reg. 13 E. ix.

[6] *sufflaturos* in the printed texts.

[7] *ex Anglia* in the printed texts.

[8] This repetition occurs in all the texts.

A.D. 1386. fortes, in pace feroces, de semetipsis pulchrum præbent spectaculum, proferunt non sequendum exemplum quod acturi forent, si sentirent instare prœlium, [1]imminere periculum. MS. Bibl. Reg. 13 E. ix.

De Vasis captis, sed proditione liberatis.

Certain vessels are seized, as belonging to the enemy.

Sub hac tempestate, familia Regis, quæ constituta fuerat circa Doveriam et Sandewicum, ad resistendum Gallicis, si forte illic tentarent irrumpere, æquoris undas ingressa, duce Domino de Garsi, obviat [2]quinque magnis coggonibus et sex carricis refertis [3]vino, speciebus, pannis aureis et holosericis, auro et argento, et lapidibus pretiosis, et diversi generis mercibus exoticis; quæ cursum versus Sclusam in Flandria maturabant. [4]Quo cognito quod hostes essent, de [5]deditione requirit eos qui in illis erant. Januenses vero, videntes se impares tantæ virtuti, semetipsos sine magna resistentia reddiderunt. Nempe ipsa vasa, cum contentis, Januensium esse dicebant, attracta ad Sandewicum cœperunt ea exonerare multis rebus, qui ea lucrati fuerant. Januenses autem, non ignorantes ubi succurri deberet eisdem, mox festinant Londonias, Cancellarii regni, Domini Michaelis Atte Poole, Comitis Southfolchiæ, auxilium petituri; qui fuerat a pueritia magis mercimoniis, utpote mercator, mercatoris filius, quam militia, occupatus. Qui mox et illorum vicem doluit, et Regem circumvenit, ut scriberet hiis qui ceperunt eos, vetans ne quicquam præsumerent minorare de bonis eorum; restituerent insuper cuncta quæ cepissent. Cancellarius præterea jussit de thesauro regio eorum damna resarciri, ut, videlicet, pro cunctis quæ terra marique perdiderant post captionem suam, reciperent pecuniæ dignam summam; et ita Rex, circumquaque delusus, supplantatus, seductus est, et regnum thesauro debito vacuatum, et hostes sævissimi, infestissimi, crudelissimi, cum pace pecuniaque dimissi. Ipsi ergo, mox ut solverunt a littore, cursum versus Flandriam direxerunt, et portum de Sclusa subintraverunt.

Through the agency of the Chancellor, they are restored, and reparation made.

---

[1] *invenire* in the printed texts, and in Bibl. Reg. 13 E. ix.

[2] *quippe* in orig. and the printed texts: corrected from Bibl. Reg. 13 E. ix.

[3] *vini* in the printed texts.

[4] *Quo* in orig. and the printed texts: *Quæ* in Bibl. Reg. 13 E. ix. Probably, for *Qui*.

[5] *ditione* in orig. and the printed texts: corrected from Bibl. Reg. 13 E. ix.

Rex Franciæ parat invadere regnum Angliæ.

MS. Bibl. Reg. 13 E. ix.

A.D. 1386.

The King of France orders a wooden wall to be built, for the protection of his army.

Rex Franciæ, parans invadere regnum Angliæ, per illud tempus victoriam non armis sibi tantummodo proventuram credidit, sed muris ligneis æstimavit. Quamobrem congregatis ex multis locis fabris lignariis, quemdam murum ligneum, spissum atque densum, jussit fieri, altitudinis viginti pedum, qui semper ad duodecim passus haberet turrim capacem decem hominum, quæ foret altior subjecto muro per decem pedes; quem murum, ut fertur, erigere præfinivit in loco ubi applicaturus erat, ut per murum defenderetur a sagittis, et suos gunnarios protegeret, nostratibus plagas horribiles illaturos, et, cum opus esset, suum exercitum revocare posset [1] intra muri ambitum, ubi et fessi quiescere, et saucii recreari, valerent. Habebat murus ille, prout ferebatur, in longitudine tria millia passuum, et erat dispositus turribus firmis et crebris, ut præfertur.

Part of the wall, and its constructor, are captured by the English.

Eodem tempore, nostrates, qui in mari erant, obviant duabus navibus Regis Franciæ, sulcantibus campos liquidos, et iter carpentibus versus Sclusiam. Et illico conserta pugna, et naves illæ captæ et Sandewicum tractæ sunt; in quibus et pars muri et turrium prædictarum est reperta, et magister totius fabricæ interceptus, qui erat [2] Anglicus natione, sed quandoque bannitus. Captus est insuper ibi magister gunnarius, qui et ipse prius Anglicis famulabatur apud Calesiam, dum Dominus Hugo Calverlee Capitaneus ibi fuerat; et, cum hiis, diversæ machinæ ad jaciendum lapides et muros conterendum, et gunnæ plures, cum magna quantitate pulveris; cujus pretium prævaluit omnibus manubiis supradictis. Erecta est igitur illa pars muri apud Sandewicum, et quem contra nos hostes præparaverant, nos ereximus contra hostes.

As also, various munitions of war.

Parliamentum factum Londoniis; et immanis commotio regni.

Parliament at London.

Circa festum Sancti Michaelis Archangeli, citati sunt ad Parliamentum Londoniæ qui de jure [3] vel consuetudine [4] inesse Parliamento debebant. Per id temporis, Michael Atte Poole, dudum creatus Comes Southfolchiæ, et jam tunc regni Cancellarius, cui Rex plus debito credebat et favebat, convocari

---

[1] *ultra* in the printed texts.
[2] *Anglicanus* in the printed texts.
[3] *et* in orig.; corrected from the printed texts.
[4] *adesse* in the printed texts.

A.D. 1386. fecit pene de cunctis regni finibus [1] armatos et arcitenentes in Merciam, ut, prope Londonias existentes, parati forent ad repellendum Francos, cum Rege suo, si tamen verum esset quod dicebatur de eis, quia parati fuerunt cum ingenti multitudine navium ad regnum Angliæ invadendum. Adunatis igitur de diversis regni Comitatibus velut innumerabilibus, tam armatis quam arcitenentibus, perhendinaverunt prope Londonias viginti milliaria in circuitu, velut pro suis castris occupantes; ubi fuit cernere non secus quam hostilis recognitionis imaginem, dum plebs sic vocata, quæ et victu carebat et pecunia, cogebatur, sicut in hostili patria, pabulando vicinos spoliare, et cuncta, quæ fecissent inter hostes, in terra propria perpetrare; hoc excepto solummodo, quod ab incendiis abstinebant. Qui [2] cum diu moram, tam sibimet quam patriotis infructuosam, fecissent, jussi sunt ad propria remeare, et parati fore, cum Rex ipsos decerneret revocandos. Quorum plures, pro rei familiaris inopia, compellebantur revertentes exponere vel equos vel arma venditioni; quidam pro commeatu spoliis intendebant, et rapinis. Nondum finitum fuit Parliamentum, sed regressis ad sua vulgaribus, proceres Londoniis permanserunt, præstolantes rumores de Francorum adventu, qui cotidie dicebantur esse venturi.

MS. Bibl. Reg. 13 E. ix.

Great forces assembled in the neighbourhood of London, to oppose the French.

Great privations suffered by them, and disastrous results therefrom.

They are dismissed, in a state of great poverty.

The Earl of Oxford created Duke of Ireland.

Disgraceful reasons assigned for such favour.

Ubi ne Dominus Rex parum fecisse videretur, Dominum Robertum de Veer, quandoque Comitem Oxoniæ, sed nuper in ultimo Parliamento creatum Marchionem Dubliniæ, Ducem fecit Hiberniæ, facturus expost de Duce Regem, si fortuna faveret; tantum [3] afficiebatur eidem, tantum coluit et amavit eundem, non sine nota, prout fertur, familiaritatis obscœnæ; submurmurantibus cæteris nobilibus et baronibus, ac indigne ferentibus tantæ promotionis appetitum in viro tam mediocri, quem [4] non plus cæteris commendabant vel generis sui sublimitas vel reliquarum virtutum dotes.

Deposita in Parliamento contra Michaelem Atte Pole.

Per omne tempus istud duranto Parliamento, cotidie prædicabantur nova de Gallorum adventu, multis in magna tre-

[1] *armos* in Camden's text.

[2] *dum* in orig.; corrected from the printed texts.

[3] *efficiebatur* in orig.; *afficiebatur* in the printed texts, and Bibl. Reg. 13 E. ix.

[4] *in* in orig.; *nil* in the printed texts: corrected from Bibl. Reg. 13 E. ix.

MS. Bibl. Reg. 13 E. ix.

A.D. 1386. Accusations in Parliament against the Chancellor.

pidatione existentibus, quod viderent Barones in multis dissentire; unde putabant quidam de prudentibus magnum regno dispendium [1] affuturum, præcipue si mens non foret una Dominis, inter tot pericula quæ ab hostibus parabantur. Quia revera Rex infensus erat, non solum militibus Parliamentalibus, sed pene cunctis proceribus; quia favebant eisdem, proponentibus multos articulos falsitatis contra prædictum Michaelem Atte Poole, et instanter exorantibus judicium fieri de eodem. Convicerant eum nempe de multis fraudibus et quibusdam proditionibus in Regem, quos nequaquam inficiari nequibat; unde et cum responsis astaret, et objecta negare nequibat, Rex, pro ipso verecundatus, et rubore suffusus, caput agitans,—"Heu! heu!" inquit, "Michael, vide quid fecisti." De multis etenim objectis contra eum, hoc unum extitit, quod avarus existens et alienæ pecuniæ avidus, circumvenit Regem, ut concederet sibi firmam cunctorum quæstorum regni, qui cum indulgentiis circuire solent, et congregare pecuniam ad opus fraternitatis Sancti Antonii, daturus Regi viginti marcas de proventibus memoratis, de quibus singulis annis levasse videbatur [2] septingentas marcas. Hiis et multis aliis defectibus veridica ratione probatis contra ipsum, de officio Cancellariæ dejicitur, multandus pecunia, [3] scilicet [4] solvendis Regi, [5] et insuper, morte dignus [6] Parliamenti judicio diffinitur.

The King's sorrow thereat.

Particular charge against him, of overreaching the King.

He is deprived of the Chancellorship, and pronounced guilty of capital offences.

Responsum Regi fuit, ipsum non egere subjectorum tallagio, cum de tanta summa, ab eo qui juste debitor erat Regis, poterat merito provideri. Hæc autem omnia, quanquam summe Regi placuisse debuerant, maxime displicebant, adeo fidebat infideli, adeo coluit nebulonem. Factumque est ut, ejus amoris intuitu, non multo post infirmaret quicquid in Parliamento contra ipsum fuit statutum, et familiariorem haberet quam ante habuerat, non tantum in privato sed in publico, ita ut in convivio sequenti Natali in mensa sua recumbere faceret, non contentum communi procerum indumento, sed togatum; quod genus solis Regibus ab antiquo debetur. Et ne fieret in eum judicii executio, præelegit proditiose circumvenire suos accusatores, cum Duce Gloverniæ,

The King takes him back into his favour, and confers marks of high distinction upon him.

[1] *affecturum* in the printed texts.

[2] *septuaginta* in orig. and the printed texts: corrected from Bibl. Reg. 13 E. ix.

[3] *grandi, scilicet* in the printed texts.

[4] *solvenda* in the printed texts.

[5] This passage is omitted in the printed texts.

[6] *Parliamento indio diffiniturum* in orig., for which reason probably the passage is omitted in the printed texts. Corrected from Bibl. Reg. 13 E. ix.

A.D. 1386. qui maxima pars videbatur existere eorum qui pro regni commodo laborabant. Itaque provisum erat inter Regem et suos familiares, ut quidam de militibus Parliamentalibus qui plus obstiterant vel sibi potenti subsidium pecuniare, vel dicto Michaeli infesti fuerant, una cum Domino Thoma, Duce Gloverniæ, invitarentur ad cœnam in hospitio cujusdam Londoniis, et ibidem repente trucidarentur. Quorum morte solummodo æstimabat sibi cessurum arbitrium voluntatis. Sed non cepit effectum tantæ malignitatis commentum; quia et Dux de hiis omnibus [1] præmunitus fuit, et, ut caverent, cæteros [2] præmunuit, jubens ut cœnis essent contenti propriis, ne intricari valerent, ut præmittitur, alienis. Ferunt Dominum Nicholaum Brambre, qui Major Londoniarum fuerat anno præterito, huic assensum præbuisse consilio; sed laudabili constantia Ricardi Extone, Majoris anni præsentis, qui libere fatebatur, cum vocatus esset a Rege ad præbendum favorem tanto facinori, se nunquam consensurum in necem talium innocentium, dictum scelus est omissum. Et palam factum est verbum istud omnibus habitantibus in regione vicina [3] tua, ut extunc apud omnes odium cresceret talium consiliariorum, et amor Ducis et militum prædictorum. Non tamen omisit Dux, et milites, ea quæ vera sunt, regnoque fructuosa, loqui; sed majori constantia Regi petenti subsidia [4] restiterunt, sæpiusque illud [5] Susannicum inculcabat militibus, dicens,—"[6] Quia "melius est nobis incidere in manus hominum quam derelinquere legem Dei nostri." Tandem, propter improbitatem potentium, concessum tallagium, scilicet media pars unius decimæ, et media quintæ-decimæ, quod, non Regis arbitrio, sed procerum prædictorum judicio, pro regni commodo expenderetur. Recepit hanc pecuniam Comes Arundeliæ, profecturus ad mare, Duci Hiberniæ.

MS. Bibl. Reg. 13 E. IX.

A plot against the lives of the Chancellor's accusers.

The Duke of Gloucester and others, are warned in time.

The late Mayor of London, alleged to have assented to the plot, R. Extone, the present Mayor, dissenting therefrom.

Continued opposition of the Duke, and the Knights of Parliament, to the King's designs.

A grant made by Parliament.

Ad Regis instantiam, est provisum, ut hæredes Karoli de Bloys, qui vendicavit olim Ducatum Britanniæ Armoricæ, [7] venderent Francis pro triginta millibus marcarum; ut, hac [8] adjutus pecunia, dominium quod Rex sibi donaverat in Hibernia viriliter recuperaret; ea duntaxat conditione, ut citra proximum

Money raised by the King for support of the Duke of Ireland's claims.

[1] *præmonitus* in the printed texts.

[2] *præmonuit* in the printed texts.

[3] So in all the texts; qy. if not *sua?*

[4] *restituerunt* in orig. and the printed texts: corrected from Bibl. Reg. 13 E. ix.

[5] In allusion to *The Hist. of Susanna*, ver. 23.

[6] *Quin* in the printed texts.

[7] *venderet* in orig., Bibl. Reg. 13 E. ix., and Parker's text: *venderent* in Camden's text.

[8] *adductus* in orig. and the printed texts: corrected from Bibl. Reg. 13 E. ix.

MS. Bibl. Reg. 13. E. ix.

Pascha Hiberniam transfretaret. Tantum nempe proceres, tantum communes, ejus transitum affectabant, ut mallent regno carere tanto thesauro, quam ipsius habere præsentiam, Regem seducentis et infatuantis, in regno. A.D. 1386.

Regi Armeniæ denegatur conductus.

Per idem tempus, Rex Armeniæ, qui dudum expertus fuerat Regis liberalitatem, et procerum, mittit pro conductu, velut adventus ejus causa foret amor pacis reformandæ inter regna Angliæ et Franciæ; quorum unum jam omnino paratum fuerat ad reliquum invadendum. Sed revera plus desideravit dona quam pacem, plus pecuniam adamavit quam plebem, plus aurum regni quam Regem. Et licet Rex esset sibi benevolus, proceres tamen, librantes quod esset illusor, responderunt Regi se nolle tractare cum illo. Sicque impeditus est adventus ejus; qui sicut nec primo, nec quidem secundo, profuisset.

The King of Armenia is suspected by the English nobles, and is refused a safe-conduct.

Regis Franciæ adventus miraculose impeditur.

Rex interea Franciæ, [1] cum Ducum, Comitum, et aliorum procerum inaudita turba, moram traxit in Flandria, paratus ad diripiendum regnum Angliæ, si non Deus ejus conatibus obstitisset. Nempe per totum tempus quod fluxit a Kalendis Augusti usque ad Vigiliam Omnium Sanctorum, nunquam flavit aura sibi commoda per paucas horas. In ipsa vero Vigilia, surgente vento, prout putabat, sibi favente, turgidius, a longa statione dissolvit naves, et cum impetu portum de Sclusa reliquit. Cumque cunctæ rates fuissent egressæ, et jam profunda tenerent, essentque a portu remotæ quasi per viginti milliaria, ecce! ventus contrarius, obvius eis factus, omnes retrocedere compulit; et non tantum compulit, sed et impulit, naves, et allisit, ut quædam ex eis in introitu ipsius portus de Sclusa confringerentur. Hac occasione et Anglia metu liberata, et Rex Franciæ est regressus ad sua.

The King of France is prevented from invading England by contrary winds.

Some of his ships are lost, and he returns home.

Numerus classis Regis Franciæ mille [2] ducentæ naves; in hac comitiva fuere, Duces [3] quindecim, [4] Comites viginti sex, tria millia militum et sexcenti, centum millia pugnatorum.

Enumeration of his forces.

---

[1] *cum* omitted in the printed texts.

[2] *ducentes* in orig.; corrected from the printed texts.

[3] *sexdecim* in orig. and the printed texts: corrected from Bibl. Reg. 13 E. ix.

[4] From this word, down to *pugnatorum*, the context is supplied in orig. in a hand of the 17th century: it appears in the printed texts.

Processus in Michaelem Atte Pole.

A.D. 1386. Ad hoc usque tempus Parliamento continuato, licet Rex graviter ferret accusationes factas de Michaele Atte Pole cæterisque quos imprudenter amavit, compulsus est tamen, post multas tergiversationes, auditores et judicii diffinitores eligere, qui plenam haberent potestatem audiendi et judicium proferendi in dictum Michaelem, cæterosque quos milites accusaverant Parliamenti. Constituti sunt autem judices Dominus Thomas, [1] [Dux] Glovernïæ, et Dominus Ricardus, Comes Arundelliæ, [2] et ; qui non segniter injunctum negotium adimplebant, Rege ad alias partes digresso, quia noluit hiis judiciis, quamvis sibi forent proficua, interesse. Tandem, ut præfertur, dicto Michaele de multis sceleribus fraudibusque convicto, morte dignus judicatur, et ejus bona regio fisco cessura decernuntur. Ipse tamen manu-captus [3] [est], quibusdam divitibus pro eo in magna summa pecuniæ obligatis. Quem, ut diximus, Rex, mox finito Parliamento, recepit, et sibi cohabitare fecit, cum Duce Hiberniæ et Archiepiscopo Eboraci, Domino Alexandro Nevyle; qui extunc, quantum poterant, laborabant Regem contra Dominos commovere, diebus ac noctibus, et acta Parliamenti adnullare.

MS. Bibl. Reg. 13 E. ix.

Michael De la Pole is pronounced by his judges worthy of death, and his property is confiscated.

He is retained, with some others, in the King's favour.

The King's hatred of the Duke of Gloucester, and his party, increases.

Succrevit igitur indies Regi odium contra suos proceres naturales et fideles, istis susurrantibus Regem non in effectu fore Regem, sed umbratiliter, futurumque, ut nihil sui juris existeret, si Domini accepta potestate gauderent. Credebat itaque illis Rex, et idcirco de cætero proceres omnes [4] suspectos habebat; nihilominus tamen, dejecto Michaele Atte Pole de Cancellaria, subrogatus est Dominus Thomas Arundelle, Episcopus Eliensis, [5] [vir qui justitiam præferret auro, et æquitatem mundo obrizo. Depositus est insuper Dominus Johannes Fordam, Episcopus] Dunelmensis, de officio Thesaurarii, qui multum laboraverat, et expensas [6] fecerat, hujus dignitatis amore; et pro eo constitutus est frater Johannes Gilbert, de Ordine Prædicatorum, Episcopus Herefordensis, vir qui plus lingua quam fide vigebat. Et hic hujus Parliamenti finis.

The Bishop of Ely is appointed Chancellor.

A new Treasurer is also appointed.

---

[1] Supplied from Bibl. Reg. 13 E. ix. : omitted in the printed texts.

[2] *et* and the hiatus are omitted in the printed texts.

[3] Supplied from Bibl. Reg. 13 E. ix. : omitted in the printed texts.

[4] *suspecto* in the printed texts.

[5] Supplied from Bibl. Reg. 13 E. ix.; omitted in the printed texts.

[6] *fecerit* in orig., by inadvertence.

Annalis Conclusio.

MS. Bibl. Reg. 13 E. ix.

Transit annus iste frugifer, sed mediocriter fructifer; [1] Hispanis, propter adventum Ducis Lancastriæ, regnum vendicantis, sollicitus et suspectus; Austriæ, propter Ducem et nobiles interemptos a communibus, perniciosus; Franciæ, propter sumptus et apparatum quem fecerat ad Angliam invadendum, onerosus; Angliæ, propter graves rumores, sed Londoniensibus, propter muliebrem meticulositatem, maxime dedecorosus. A.D. 1386.

Anno Domini millesimo trecentesimo octogesimo septimo, qui est annus regni Regis Ricardi, Secundi a Conquæstu, decimus, fuit Rex ad Natale apud , cum Anna Regina et Boemiis suis. A.D. 1387.

Circa initium mensis Martii, juxta decretum Parliamenti, paraverunt se ad sulcandum liquentes campos Dominus Ricardus, Comes Arundeliæ, et Dominus Thomas Mounbray, Comes Notynghamiæ, quorum primus constitutus est Admiralius instantis termini; vir valde devotus et bonus, et qui probra quandoque desertæ militiæ, cum tunc Gallici circa Southsexiam oras infestarent maritimas, nunc abolere cupiens, curavit apponere totas vires.

The Earls of Arundel and Nottingham prepare to take command of the English forces.

Comes Arundeliæ proficiscitur ad mare.

Igitur profecturus ad mare, cum recensionem facturus esset in campo sui exercitus, cognovissetque Ducem Gloverniæ, cum multis nobilibus, velle videre collectam militiam, elaboravit ut bonos haberet et famosos, vitans conducere Londoniensium et aliarum civitatum sutores vel scissores, quales quidam ante conduxerant levi pretio, ut plus accresceret auri [2] suo marsupio. Et quidam alii sic agentes, non regni commodo, sed lucro proprio, militabant; unde factum est, ut a longo tempore regnum nihil aut parum [3] emolumenti perciperet, illis non hostes invadere, non experiri vires, sed inaniter tempus acceptum consumere, meditantibus, ut integra stipendia consequi prævalerent.

The Earl of Arundel strives to collect an efficient army.

Knavery recently practised by some of the English leaders, in this respect.

Comes, e contra, (ut diximus, non parcens expensis), valentiores quos novit, elegit, ut per hos posset magnum aliquid patriæ reportare. Dux [4] perinde Gloverniæ, cernens tam pul-

[1] *Hispaniæ* in the printed texts.

[2] *suo* omitted in the printed texts.

[3] *emolumentum* in the printed texts.

[4] *proinde* in the printed texts.

A.D. 1387. Energy shown by the Duke of Gloucester. chram, tam electam militiam, urgebat omnes, movebat singulos, ut maris undas intrarent, solutis morarum nexibus, multis se excusantibus quod oportebat [1]amicis valedicere, negotia disponere domus suæ; æstimabat nempe, prout erat, quosdam arma mutuo suscepisse pro dicto spectaculo, ut laudarentur a dominis tanquam sufficienter armati; quæ proculdubio, si divertendi copiam habuissent, reddituri suis erant possessoribus, et mare repetituri, velut inermes; quamobrem fuit verisimile quod minus audaces fuissent ad [2]adversarios invadendum. MS. Bibl. Reg. 13 E. ix.

Arms borrowed by some of the recruits, with a fraudulent design.

Ingressi sunt ergo mare, vellent nollent, cum cunctis utensilibus quæ habebant, fausta hora, quia non multum tempus effluxit antequam adversariis obviarent. Revera die Dominica in Vigilia Annunciationis Dominicæ, magna classis navium Flandriæ, Galliæ, et Hispanniæ, refertarum viris bellicis, [3]armatarum diversis machinis, de longe velificans, a [4]speculatore conspicitur; quæ mox Amiralio Comiti nunciata, ipsum et suos omnes hilaritate replevit. Adversarii vero, nihil tale suspicantes, quibus, ut fertur, promissum fuerat a quibusdam Angliæ proditoribus, (quibus regnum raro carebat), nostrum navigium [5]citra mensem Maium minime fore paratum, agebant per omnia magis secure, ventum pro vehiculo, et armatos pro tutela, tenentes. Cum autem nostratibus propinquassent, [6][obliquantes] vela, tanquam nostros vellent aggredi, nostri ex industria simulavere fugam, velut fuissent impares tantæ virtuti. Illi vero, plus securum transitum quam bellum cupientes, pertransibant, unde contigit, cum nostrates ventum percepissent ad vota, adversarios insequentes, irruerunt subito super eos, et conflictum atrocissimum commiserunt. Tandem victoria cessit nostris, captis octoginta navibus, et multis diversæ conditionis armatis, quampluribus quoque peremptis. Fugerunt tamen de conflictu quædam, quas biduo Comes Arundelliæ persequens, postremo cepit, et ad classem nostram traxit.

The Earl of Arundel defeats a large fleet of Flemings, French, and Spaniards.

Numerus navium captarum; numerus doliorum.

Number of vessels captured, Erant autem numero majores et minores rates centum, et eo amplius, quæ omnes vinis refertæ fuerunt. Numerus vero doliorum, ad decem et novem millia, aut plus, excrevit. Ipsa

[1] *amicus* in orig., by inadvertence.

[2] *diversarios* in orig., by inadvertence.

[3] *armatorum* in the printed texts.

[4] *spiculatore* in the printed texts.

[5] *circa* in the printed texts.

[6] Supplied from Bibl. Reg. 13 E. ix. : omitted in the printed texts.

MS. Bibl. Reg. 13 E. ix.

A.D. 1387.

And vast amount of tuns of wine.

vero vina, cum vasis, mox ad portum de Orwelle, et alios regni portus, destinata sunt, præter ea quæ Regis parti segregabantur; licet cives de Middelbourgh ad Comitem accessissent, et orassent ut liceret eis illa vina comparare, et dare mox pro singulis doliis centum solidos, eo quod amici nostri videbantur existere et vinis egere. Sed hiis respondit Admiralius, justius esse, [1]ut hii hiis gauderent vinis, qui expensas [2]fecerant pro sua profectione versus mare, scilicet communes Angliæ, [3]quam alii quicunque pro quocunque lucro ea auferrent.—"Attamen," inquit, "[4]quoniam estis amici, et de "longe venistis, dabimus vobis viginti dolia, ne omnino "vacui redisse videamini." Ipse vero Comes tanta liberalitate usus est, diversis conferens de parte sibi contingente, ut nec unum dolium sibimet remaneret, ut fertur. Accreverunt ergo laudes Comiti [5]in immensum a vulgaribus, quod postponens quæ sibimet [6]aggregasse poterat, vendens alienis direpta vina, præposuit communem utilitatem privato commodo; et eo maxime, quod vulgares in effectu senserant, non omnino deperisse quod penderant [7]profectioni suæ. Comes autem, volens hiis majora præstare patriæ, recollecto [8]præsarcitoque navigio, et conductis recentibus pro hiis qui læsi vel sauciati fuerant, sive deperempti, vela reflexit versus castellum de Brest, quod videtur [9]clavis esse Minoris Britanniæ; contra quod Gallici, sive Britones, jam duas munitiones erexerant, vel erecturi fuerant, majores et multo fortiores quam fuerunt illæ quas Dux Lancastriæ per suos debellaverat et destruxerat, versus Hispaniam proficiscens. Harum unam Admiralius, (debellatis qui intus erant), cepit, et quia videbatur fortis et necessaria castello, si nostri possiderent eam, posuit quosdam ex nostris in ea. Reliquam vero sumptuose paratam, [10][sed] nondum erectam, injecto igne cremavit; et sic Franci parvo tempore eodem in loco geminata damna cepere, primo per Ducis milites, secundo per Comitis hujus tirones.

Application of the people of Middleburgh; and the Earl's answer thereto.

Popularity of the Earl, for his disinterestedness.

He destroys the French fortifications at Brest.

Castellum insuper de Brest cunctis victualibus quæ suffi-

He returns

[1] *et* in orig.; corrected from the printed texts.

[2] *fuerant* in orig.; corrected from the printed texts.

[3] *quanquam* in orig.; corrected from the printed texts.

[4] *quia* in the printed texts.

[5] *et* in orig.; corrected from the printed texts.

[6] *aggragasse* in orig.; *aggerasse* in the printed texts.

[7] *perfectioni* in the printed texts.

[8] *resarcitoque* in the printed texts.

[9] *canis* in orig. and the printed texts: corrected from Bibl. Reg. 13 E. ix.

[10] Omitted in orig.; supplied from Bibl. Reg. 13 E. ix. and the printed texts.

A.D. 1387. home, after supplying the English garrison at Brest. cerent ad unum annum refecit, et castellanis vestes et calceamenta donavit: compositisque per omnia rebus, redivit in Angliam cum benedictione omnium plebanorum. MS. Bibl. Reg. 13 E. ix.

Envy of the King's favourites. Sed invidebant [1] tantæ probitati qui cum Rege erant, Dux Hiberniæ, Comes Southfolchiæ, et Symon de Burleya, cum Ricardo Styry; depravantes acta Comitis apud Regem, et dicentes eum nullum opus egregium [2] perpetrasse; quippe qui nonnisi mercatores invaserit, quorum fructuosius extitisset amorem servasse patriæ, quam odium [3] inexorabile concitasse.

Quidam invident factis Comitis.

Bad influence of the royal favourites upon the King. Et hii nimirum milites plures erant Veneris quam Bellonæ, plus valentes in thalamo quam in campo, plus lingua quam lancea præmuniti, ad dicendum vigiles, ad faciendum acta martia somnolenti. Hii igitur, circa Regem conversantes, nihil quod deceret tantum militem informare curabant, non dico tantum armorum usum, sed nec ea quæ maxime reges generosos decent in pace, videlicet, [4] venationem vel aucupationem, aut hiis similia, quibus [5] regius honor crescit. He repulses the Earl of Nottingham. Factumque est istorum instinctu, ut Rex tantum offenderetur hiis qui [6] in hoc negotio militaverant, quod venienti sibi Comiti Notynghamiæ, qui est Comes Marescallus, et Regis semper fuerat consodalis et coætaneus, et speranti magnas a Rege grates reportasse, Rex nullum bonum vultum faceret, sed omnino demissum. The Duke of Ireland shows jealousy of the Earls of Arundel and Nottingham. Dux autem Hiberniæ utrique Comiti non solum vultum subtraxit, sed colloquium; invidens fortassis probitati quam ipse assequi non valebat. Ipsi vero Comites, hæc cernentes, sed parvipendentes, ad propria discesserunt, victuri quietius quam cum Rege.[7]

Henricus Percy junior destinatur ad mare.

Insidious advice given by the royal favourites as to Sir Henry Percy. Interjecto post hæc parvo tempore, qui de Consilio Regis erant, monuerunt eum ut Henricus Percy, filius Comitis Northumbrorum, mitteretur ad mare, ad repellendum irruptiones hostium, qui dicebantur prompti, propter plagam quam dudum acceperant per Comitem Arundeliæ, ad irruptiones in

---

[1] *omnes tantæ* in the printed texts.

[2] *perpetrasset* in the printed texts.

[3] *exorabile* in the printed texts.

[4] *in venationem* in the printed texts.

[5] *regni* in the printed texts.

[6] *in* omitted in the printed texts.

[7] A passage in Bibl. Reg. 13 E ix. is omitted here.

MS. Bibl Reg. 13 E. ix.

A.D. 1387.

Angliam faciendum. Cui nec sufficientem manum delegaverunt, nec favorem, quem decuit, impenderunt; sed hæc fecerunt ei, invidentes, ut dicebatur, ejus indoli, eo quod jam nomen magnum propter probitatem, tam inter Scotos quam Anglicos, est adeptus. Sed ipse, quod ipsi [1]dolose machinati fuerant, vel nesciens, vel parvipendens, intrepide suscepit injunctum negotium, et animose strenueque peregit: et, expleto termino suæ militiæ, incolumis remeavit.

Percy shows his prowess, and frustrates their designs.

De potestate Fratris Walteri [2]Disse.

Per idem tempus erat quidem Frater in Anglia, de Carmelitarum secta, cui nomen erat "Walterus Disse;" qui dudum fuerat confessor Ducis Lancastriæ, sed cum eo, in Hispaniam tendenti, minime profectus est, sed domi remanserat, propter causam inferius declarandam.

Walter Disse, a Carmelite Friar.

Papa siquidem, Urbanus Sextus, agnoscens Hispaniæ regnum grande divitiisque refertum, et [3]librans, licet inaniter, quanta commoda sibi accrescerent, si Dux ejus dominio potiretur, præter privilegia quæ concesserat [4]profecturo, jam nova concessit profecto, per dictum Fratrem Walterum Disse postulantibus dispensanda, sed non sine pecunia adquirenda. Inter quæ privilegia sive potestates acceptas a Papa, fuit unum, ad quod adquirendum concurrebant, et grandes summas offerebant. Qui pronior existens plura proferentibus, eos Domini Papæ capellanos creavit, secundum formam [5]et juris consuetudinem in Romana Curia frequentatam. Concessit inter multas hanc libertatem cuidam Fratri de Ordine Augustinensium, dicto "Petro [6]Patteshulle;" qui exinde putans se omni libertati donatum, cœpit primo adhærere Wiclefensibus, (quos "Lollardos" [7]quidam vocant), qui, sui tenentes doctrinam magistri, jam examina multa suorum sequacium Londoniis fecerant, et plures doctrina polluerant sua prava. Igitur istorum se tradens informationi, [8]didicit quod bene fecerit privatam deserendo religionem, publicæ vitæ se conferens, quæ sanctior et perfectior, eminentior atque securior, esse videbatur.

He is entrusted with the sale of certain privileges, by the Pope.

He creates certain persons, Papal Chaplains, and, among them, Peter Patteshulle, a Lollard, but recently a Friar.

---

[1] *dolosi* in the printed texts.

[2] *Visse* in orig., by inadvertence.

[3] *liberans* in orig., by inadvertence.

[4] *profectura* in orig. and the printed texts; corrected from Bibl. Reg. 13 E. ix.

[5] *ut* in orig.: corrected from the printed texts.

[6] *Pareshull* in Camden's text.

[7] *quidem* in the printed texts.

[8] *dididit* in orig., by inadvertence.

A.D. 1387. Tandem, horum imbutus malitia, et propria exagitatus nequitia, hortantibus illis, coactus est prædicare, et publice vitia sui Ordinis propalare. Venit igitur ad ecclesiam Sancti Cristofori Londoniis, sequentibus eum pene centum de Lollardis, et ibidem tanta mala facinora in confratres quondam suos evomuit, ut horrori foret audientibus, et stupori. Interea, quidam accurrentes, hæc Augustinensibus nunciarunt. Quorum quidam mox egressi, scilicet ad numerum duodecim, majori animositate vigentium, venerunt ad locum, ubi adhuc flagitiosus ille tanta facinora declamabat. Et audientes quæ dicebantur, valde commoti sunt; unus autem, plus zelans pro religione, audacter astans contradixit hiis quæ nebulo proponebat. Quod cernentes Lollardi, surrexerunt cum impetu, et Fratrem contradictorem dejecerunt, laceraverunt, et conculcaverunt, et male verberibus tractaverunt. Sed et cunctos Fratres ejecerunt, et extra ecclesiam persecuti sunt, volentes eos perimere et eorum domos incendere, cum furore clamantes, et dicentes;—"Disperdamus homicidas, incendamus sodomitas, suspendamus Regis et Angliæ proditores." Cum isto itaque furoris clamore, currentes ignem in habitacula Fratrum injicere proponebant. Sed impediti tamen sunt humili oratione Fratris Thomæ Asshebourne et sodalis sui, qui ambo boni viri, ambo fuere Sacræ Paginæ Professores. Innuit insuper ad sedandum turbam furentem interventus cujusdam de Vicecomitibus Londoniarum, qui eos sua suasione mitigavit, et ad propria redire fecit.

MS. Bibl. Reg. 13 E. ix.

Patteshulle preaches against the evil lives of his late brethren, the Friars.

The Friars oppose him; and are attacked by the Lollards.

The tumult is with difficulty quelled.

Interea Lollardi, secum dictum Fratrem tenentes, hortabantur ut quia alias disturbatus in sermone fuerat, chartam conscriberet, in qua omnia præmissa, et si quæ plura nosceret, exararet. Qui, mox eorum adquiescens sceleratis consiliis, chartam [1] conficit, in qua quosdam Fratres suos accusat de diversorum confratrum suorum homicidio. Et ut major fides tribueretur dictis suis, edicit occisorum nomina et tortorum vocabula: necnon et loca designat in quibus occisi vel sepulti fuerant tali modo perempti. [2] Dicit insuper eos sodomitas existere, Regisque et regni traditores, et multa plura quæ dinumerare longum foret: confectamque chartam configit super fores ecclesiæ Sancti Pauli Londoniis, ut major confusio posset accrescere Fratribus memoratis. In cujus principio dicit, semet de nido egressum diaboli, et, per Dei gratiam, de malis et impuris hominibus evasisse ad vitam perfectissimam; ob quam causam, et quia erat veritatis assertor, dicit

Patteshulle reduces his charges of murder, and other enormities, to writing,

And fixes the paper upon the doors of Saint Paul's.

[1] *confecit* in the printed texts.

[2] *Dicebat* in orig.; the latter part of the word being written in a later hand.

MS. Bibl. Reg. 13 E. ix.

A.D. 1387.

plurima semet adversa passurum ab iisdem Fratribus, si comprehendere possent eum. Sed gratias agit Urbano Papæ, quod tantæ per eum libertati donatus sit, quod valeat, cum adjutorio amicorum, [[1] se] subtrahere de manibus æmulorum.

He thanks the Pope, for the privilege of the Chaplaincy.

Hanc chartam multi de [2] capuciatis militibus perlegentes, pro firmo prædicaverunt cuncta fore vera quæ scribebantur; unde et transcripta exinde sibi fecerunt, ut valerent suæ [3] malitiæ satisfacere in futurum.

Many Knights, of Lollard tendencies, adopt these charges.

Ruina Militum Lolardorum.

Principal supporters of the Lollards.

Erant autem milites qui hanc sectam coluerunt quam maxime et sustentaverunt, Willelmus Nevile, Lodowicus Clifford, Johannes Clanvowe, Ricardus Stiry, Thomas Latymer, et, inter cæteros major fatuus, Johannes Mountagu; qui in tantam lapsus est vesaniam, ut cunctas imagines, quas apud manerium de Schevele bonæ memoriæ quondam Johannes Aubrey, et expost Dominus Alanus Buxille, vel eorum antecessores, erexerant in capella sua, deponi faceret, et in locis abditis collocari: unum solummodo privilegium adepta est imago Beatæ Katerinæ, quam in [4] pistrinum suum deferri permisit, quia plures afficiebantur eidem. Hujus sacerdos, sectator acerrimus Lollardorum, cum pervenisset ad vitæ metam, et cognovisset se proculdubio moriturum, compunctus et pœnitens eorum quæ contra fidem commiserat, sacerdotem petiit [[5] cui confiteri valeret]. Cui quidam de familia, velut cum admiratione, responderunt:—"Quid est," inquiunt, "quod "quæritis? Quid quod desideratis? Nonne vos prædicastis "omnem confessionem extrinsecam, sacerdotibus faciendam, "supervacuam? Solummodo sufficere, ut quis soli Deo confi-"teatur?" Quibus ille,—"Erravi," inquit, "sed modo, precor, "indulgete mihi copiam sacerdotis." Accidit eo tempore, ut præsens esset Nicholaus Hereford, Doctoris Theologiæ gradum habens, sed seductoris sequens officium, quippe cui, post hæresiarcham Johannem Wyclef, omnes hujus sectæ viri maxime adhærebant. Hic ergo, cum ad presbyterum accessisset, et in voluntate confitendi positum cognovisset,—

Activity shown in behalf of their tenets, by Sir John Montagu.

Account of the death-bed repentance of a Lollard priest, in the household of Sir John Montagu.

---

[1] Supplied from Bibl. Reg. 13 E. ix. and the printed texts.

[2] "*Capuciati vocantur, quia ad* "*sacramentum altaris capucia non* "*deponebantur.*" A Rubric in Bibl. Reg. 13 E. ix.

[3] *militiæ* in the printed texts.

[4] *pristinum* in Camden's text.

[5] Omitted in orig.; supplied from Bibl. Reg. 13 E. ix. and the printed texts.

A.D. 1387. "Quid est," inquit, "quod agis, fatue? Quid turbaris? "Confitere Deo, qui potestatem ampliorem habet ligandi atque "solvendi quam habent laici sacerdotes, et sufficiet ista "confessio tua; tibi ipsi peccasti, non sacerdoti; ipse debet "remittere cui [1] fit offensa." Ille vero, persistens in petitione sua,—"In vobis," inquit, "sit peccati periculum, si sine "confessione viaticoque discedam, cui voluntas inest Catho- "lice moriendi, si mihi copia donaretur;" et, post pusillum, spiritum exhalavit. Cui credibile est suffragaturam voluntatem bonam confitendi, quam habuit moriendo. Et quia, pro majori facienda notitia hujus infandæ sectæ, paulisper digressi sumus a materia, ad continuandum inceptæ rei ordinem revertamur.

MS. Bibl. Reg. 13 E. ix.

Dux Hiberniæ repudiat [uxorem] suam, Regis [2] cognatam, et ducit Lancecron.

The Duke of Ireland repudiates his wife, of royal descent, and marries a woman of low station.

Accidit hiis diebus, ut Robertus de Veer, elatus de honoribus [3] quos Rex impendebat eidem, jugiter suam repudiaret uxorem, juvenculam nobilem atque pulchram, genitam de illustris Edwardi Regis filia, Isabella; et aliam duceret, quæ cum Regina Anna venerat de Boemia, ut fertur, cujusdam [4] sellarii filiam, ignobilem prorsus atque fœdam; ob quam causam magna surrepsit occasio scandalorum:—cujus nomen erat, in vulgari idiomate, "Launcecrona." Favebat sibi in hiis omnibus ipse Rex, nolens ipsum in aliquo contristare, vel potius, prout dicitur, non valens suis votis aliqualiter obviare, quia maleficiis cujusdam Fratris, qui cum dicto Roberto fuit, Rex impeditus, nequaquam quod bonum est, et honestum, cernere vel sectari valebat.

The King still shows his favour; which is attributed to magic spells.

Dux Gloverniæ indignatur.

Indignation of the Duke of Gloucester thereat.

Indignabantur proinde proceres, sed præcipue Dux Gloverniæ, avunculus præfatæ puellæ, qui etsi modo non valebat ulcisci tantas injurias illatas nepti suæ, omnia tamen conservabat in corde suo, usque in tempus retributionis futuræ. Ducem vero Hiberniæ præmissa non latebant, quamobrem et

Designs of the

---

[1] *fuit* in orig.: corrected from Bibl. Reg. 13 E. ix. and the printed texts.

[2] *natam* in orig.: corrected from Bibl. Reg. 13 E. ix.

[3] *quod* in orig.: corrected from the printed texts.

[4] *cellarii* in the printed texts.

MS. Bibl. Reg. 13 E. ix. sibi cavere statuit, et Ducem Gloverniæ, cum universis qui sibi favebant, de medio tollere meditatur. A.D. 1387. Duke of Ireland.

Jam Pascha transierat, jam tempus præterierat, [1] quo Dux Hiberniæ transfretaturus fuerat in Hiberniam, et adhuc eum, velut nihil de profectione cogitaret, Anglia retinebat. Sed ne tumultus foret nimius in regno inter proceres, Rex, velut deducturus eum ad naves, in Walliam proficiscitur cum eodem, non dimissurus eum, sed detenturus ibidem, ut illuc semoti quietius deliberare possent, qualiter Ducem Gloverniæ, Comites Arundeliæ, Warwici, Derbyæ, et Notynghamiæ, cum aliis [2] regno fidelibus, dolo tenerent et occiderent. Erant autem cum illis Comes Southfolchiæ, Michael Atte Pole, Robertus Tresilian, Justiciarius, et plures alii, qui, suæ pelli timentes, non segnius quam Rex et Dux Hiberniæ in necem prædictorum procerum conspirabant.

The King retires into Wales, with the Duke of Ireland.

Plot against the lives of the Duke of Gloucester and his supporters.

Emenso temporis magno [3] spatio, Rex in Cambria, velut profectio Ducis in Hiberniam oblivioni data esset cunctis qui remanserant in Anglia, redit cum Duce et suis traditoribus, ad castellum de Notyngham, tractaturus ibi finaliter de morte procerum prædictorum. Illuc igitur advocari fecit multos de Londoniis, quos novit contingentes ad utrumlibet, et cunctos regni Vicecomites et Justiciarios universos. [4] Hos Londonienses accersivit, quia mobiles erant ut arundo, et nunc cum Dominis, nunc cum Rege, sentiebant, nusquam stabiles, sed fallaces, quorum multi nuper de proditione in Regem confessi fuerant, sed tamen ejus gratiam consecuti, ut ipsi gratiam sibi pro gratia gratis rependerent; et Dominos indictarent de multis criminibus, quæ contra eos Rex, dum in remotis ageret, imaginatus fuerat cautelose. Vicecomites convenire fecit, ut sciret quantam potestatem possent contrahere in Regis negotium adversus Barones, et ut ipsi nullum [5] militem de pago vel schira permitterent eligi, nisi quem Rex et ejus Consilium [6] elegissent. Sed ad ista responsum est per Vicecomites, communes omnes favere Dominis, nec esse in potestate sua ad hanc causam exercitum [7] contrahendum. De militibus eligendis dixerunt similiter, communes velle tenere consuetudines usitatas, quæ volunt quod a communibus milites [8] eligantur.

The King and the Duke return into England, and take counsel at Nottingham.

Certain parties summoned in support of the King.

Answer of the Sheriffs to the King's enquiries.

---

[1] *quod* in the printed texts.

[2] *regni* in the printed texts.

[3] *spatio, e Cambria* in the printed texts.

[4] *Sed Londonienses* in the printed texts.

[5] *militum* in the printed texts.

[6] *elegisset* in orig. and the printed texts: corrected from Bibl. Reg. 13 E. ix.

[7] *contrahere* in the printed texts.

[8] *elegantur* in the printed texts.

A.D. 1387.

Certain Justiciars set their seals to the contemplated indictments.

MS. Bibl. Reg. 13 E. ix.

Vicecomites ergo, datis hiis responsis, dimissi sunt. Justiciarii sunt vocati, ut ipsi decernerent indictamenta fore legalia, et eisdem apponerent sua sigilla. Quod et tunc factum est [1]Roberto Tresilian, et Johanne Blake, juris apprenticio, quem Robertus Tresilian ad Curiam Regis ad dictum facinus introduxerat perpetrandum; expeditis ad vota indictamentis in sæpedictos proceres et multos alios, nobiles et barones, qui ad hoc vocati fuerant, sunt dimissi.

Rex conducit Bellatores.

The King raises troops in support of his cause.

Rex autem et Dux Hiberniæ, missis mox nunciis, conduci fecerunt quos poterant, ut cum illis starent, si oporteret, contra Dominos in die belli. Quorum multi responderunt se nec posse, nec velle, stare contra Dominos, quos pro certo sciebant intime Regem diligere, et omnia machinari, omnia studere, omnia facere, pro honore suo. Multi simpliciter putantes se conduci, promiserunt se ad [2]vocationem regiam fore paratos.

Sorrow of the Lords, on hearing this.

Interea rumor hujus facti pervenit ad Dominos, et eos magna replevit tristitia, eo quod, nullius culpæ conscii, tanto Regis odio turbarentur.

Dux Gloverniæ nititur Regem mitigare.

The Duke of Gloucester endeavours to assuage the King's anger.

Unde inprimis Regis patruus, Dominus Thomas, Dux Gloverniæ, ut Regis odium mitigaret, et animum ad concordiam pacemque reduceret, coram Episcopo Londoniensi et multis aliis regni nobilibus, tactis Sacrosanctis, juramentum edidit, se nunquam aliquid in Regis læsionem machinatum fuisse, sed omnia pro posse studuisse et perfecisse, quæ Regis honorem, commodum, et beneplacitum, prospectabant; excepto, quod Ducem Hiberniæ, quem Rex dilexit, lætis oculis non respexit, nec quidem in futurum respicere voluit; qui non tantum suam, sed Regis, consanguineam dehonestasset: [3]quam in eundem statuit firmiter vindicari.

Episcopus loquitur Michaëli Atte Pole.

Cum autem Episcopus Londoniensis ista, prout injunctum sibi [4]fuerat, Regi retulisset, et aliqualiter ad credendum Ducis

---

[1] *a Roberto* in the printed texts.
[2] *notationem* in the printed texts.
[3] *quamobrem* in the printed texts.
[4] *fuerant* in orig. and Bibl. Reg. 13 E. ix.: corrected from the printed texts.

MS. Bibl. Reg 13 E. ix.

A.D. 1387.

juramento inclinatus esset, Michael Atte Pole, timens, si Dux et Rex redissent in concordiam, sua affutura dispendia, verba fecit contra Ducem, quibus adversus eum Regis animum commoveret. Cui mox Episcopus,—"Sileas," inquit, "O Michael; "non decet enim te os de cætero aperire." "Quare," inquit Michael, "ita dicis?" [1]"Quoniam," inquit Episcopus, "damnatus fuisti in retroacto Parliamento, et non est nisi regia "gratia quod tu vivis." Ad hæc mox Rex iratus, præcepit Episcopo recedere, et ad suam ecclesiam remeare. Qui confestim discessit, et Duci quæ viderat, vel audierat, nunciavit.

De la Pole is rebuked by the Bishop of London.

The King enjoins silence upon the Bishop.

Hinc excrevit rancor et indignatio Duci, suisque [2]sodalibus, et Regi suisque nequam consiliariis odium inexorabile per omnes dies, [3]Duce Hiberniæ, Michaele Atte Pole, Roberto Trisilian, Alexandro Nevyle, Archiepiscopo Eboraci, et multis aliis, iram augentibus, concitantibus, et confirmantibus, contra Ducem.

Increased rancour of both parties.

Rex mittit ad capiendum Comitem Arundeliæ; sed evasit.

Qui considerans quorsum res tenderet, convocatis [4]secrete Comitibus Arundelliæ, Warwyci, et Derbeyæ, qui consimili damnationi subjicerent, si non [5]mature prospicerent sibi, denudat consilium, edicit periculum, quod omnes in commune tangebat. Qui, mox collectis exercitibus, statuerunt Regem convenire super præmissis, et favore quem præbuit, non tantum suis, sed publicis, proditoribus, necnon de periclitatione regni quæ imminebat, nisi maturius subveniretur [6]eisdem.

The Duke of Gloucester's supporters resolve to call the King to account.

E contra Rex, ex parte sua, agentibus proditoribus, deliberavit qualiter singulos præfatos tolleret, antequam munitis viribus sibimet subvenirent. Et primo misit ad castellum de Reygate, ubi Comes Arundeliæ morabatur, Comitem Northumbriæ, cum multis aliis, ad arestandum eum. Qui cernens animum Comitis exacerbatum, et militiæ magnam multitudinem circa ipsum, timens perficere commissum mandatum, negotio recessit infecto. Post quem missi sunt plures, qui noctanter eum interciperent, et præsentiæ Regis sisterent, vel certe perimerent,

The Earl of Northumberland is sent to arrest the Earl of Arundel; but hesitates to do so.

---

[1] *Quin* in the printed texts.

[2] This and the five following words are omitted in the printed texts.

[3] *Duci* in orig. and Bibl. Reg. 13 E. ix.: *Duce* in the printed texts.

[4] *secreto* in the printed texts.

[5] *nature* in orig.; corrected from the printed texts.

[6] *eidem* in the printed texts.

A.D. 1387. The Earl of Arundel escapes, and joins the Duke of Gloucester.

MS. Bibl. Reg. 13. E. ix.

si quo modo possent. Sed illorum adventum prævenit nuncius Ducis Glovernïæ, qui nocte tota illum equitare compulit, ita ut summo mane perveniret ad sylvam de Haryngeye, [1] transcursus [2] cum exercitu triginta [3] milliarium, non sine magno labore, ubi reperit congregatos Ducem Glovernïæ et Comitem Warwycensem, cum populo numeroso.

Rex proficiscitur Cantuariam.

Contemplated surrender by the King, of English possessions in France.

Eodem tempore, ut dicebatur, Rex versus Cantuariam se paraverat proficisci, non tantum ut vota redderet Beato Thomæ, sed ut promissa pacta firmaret transfretando Regi Franciæ, cui vendiderat Kalesiam, cum castello de Gynes, et universis fortilitiis quæ antecessores possederant in illis partibus, vel avito jure vel bellica adquisitione.

Proceres congregantur; Rex turbatur.

The King's departure for Canterbury prevented by the threatening movements of his opponents.

Sed hanc profectionem impedivit subito comperta congregatio Dominorum in sylva de Harynggeye, et Regem obstupescere multum fecit; unde convocatis familiaribus suis, scistabatur quid sibi vellet talis collectio inopinata. Et cum cognovisset propositum Dominorum, quod pro reducendo eum ad frugem melioris vitæ et regiminis commodioris convenerant, mox expavit, quærens quid agendum in tanta turbatione foret. Quidam autem censuerunt Dominos reconciliandos, et promittendum eis votivam executionem propositi sui. Alii

Divided counsels of the King's party.

laudaverunt Regis familiam congregandam, cum Londoniensibus, ad exeundum et obviandum proceribus, et [4] experiendam Martis fortunam. Et horum acerrimus erat Archiepiscopus Eboracensis. Sed dissuaserunt hoc prudentiores Conciliarii, asserentes Regi nullum proventurum commodum, licet vinceret, et magnum affuturum dedecus et dispendium, si vinceretur.

Ambiguous answer given to the King by a Knight,

Interea venit quidam miles exercitatus, sed sensu vacuus, Dominus Hugo de Lynne, qui eo quod stultus erat et sensum perdiderat, eleemosyna Dominorum plurium sustentabatur. Ab isto igitur Rex jocando quæsivit, quid acturus esset contra proceres, qui congregati dicebantur in prædicta sylva. Cui

[1] *transcursus* in Bibl. Reg. 13 E. ix.; *transcursis* in the printed texts.

[2] *cum exercitu* omitted in the printed texts; *celeritate* given in place thereof.

[3] *milliaribus* in the printed texts.

[4] *experiendum* in the printed texts.

MS. Bibl. Reg. 13 E. ix.

A.D. 1387.

mox Hugo, cum summa [1] melancholia, respondit:—" Exeas," inquit, " et aggrediamur eos, et cujuslibet matris filios peri- " mamus; et per oculos Dei, hoc completo, peremisti om- " nes fideles amicos quos habes in regno." Quod responsum, etsi stulte prolatum, sapientes quam maxime ponderant. *reputed to be a fool.*

Interea pacis mediatoribus intercurrentibus, res ad id [2] deducta est, ut Domini apud Westmonasterium coram Rege venirent, accepturi responsum de hiis, pro quibus commoti fuerant; Episcopo Eliensi, cum multis aliis fidedignis, sacramento firmantibus, pro parte Regis, quod nulla fraus, nulla deceptio, nullum periculum, pararetur, per quod ipsi Domini nec in vita vel membris sentirent dispendia quovismodo. Et si contingeret Regem, vel eos qui cum eo erant, ab isto pacto resilire, palam vel occulte, dicti mediatores Dominos inde præmunirent. Cum autem Domini se parassent ut Londonias, juxta condictum, convenirent, præfati pacis mediatores clam miserunt ad illos, nunciantes insidias tensas eis, in loco qui vocatur " Le Muwes," juxta Londonias; et ideo se nolle consulere ut venirent, nisi cum secura manu. Quod audientes Domini, suum distulerunt adventum. Unde transacta hora limitata, cum non affuissent, inquisivit Rex cur Domini pacta non servabant. Cui Episcopus Eliensis,—" Quia," inquit, " pa- " rantur insidiæ, mille vel amplius armatorum in tali loco, " contra pactum, et ideo nec veniunt nec reputant vos " fidelem." *The Lords arrange to hold a personal interview with the King; but being warned of treachery, decline to appear.*

Rex vero confestim motus, juravit se non esse conscium hujus rei, et ideo jussit [3] Vicecomitibus Londoniarum, ut, pergentes ad Le·Muwes, et omnia perscrutantes, interficerent si quos invenirent ob hanc causam congregatos ibidem: sed non latuit dolus ibi, sed apud Westmonasterium, factione Thomæ Tryvet et Nicholai Brambre, militum, qui, cognoscentes se deprehendendos, occulte dimiserunt armatos, et Londonias remiserunt. Misit ergo Rex iterum ad Dominos, promittens securum commeatum, si venirent. Qui mox ad Westmonasterium cum manu valida pervenerunt. *Enquiry made as to the alleged treachery. Names of the persons who had devised it. The Lords appear at Westminster.*

Acta apud Westmonasterium inter Regem et Dominos.

Rex vero, in adventu Dominorum, regalibus ornans se insigniis, [4] toga videlicet et sceptro, Aulam Westmonasterii est

[1] *malencolia* in orig.
[2] *deductum* in all the texts.
[3] *Vicecomites* in the printed texts.
[4] *tota* in orig.: corrected from the printed texts.

A.D. 1387. ingressus; pro quo Cancellarius, Episcopus Eliensis, verba fecit in hunc modum:—"Domini," inquit, "Dominus noster "Rex, audiens vos dudum congregatos in parco de Haryngeye "contra morem, non in vos irruere voluit; quod quidem sibi "fuisset facile, si non vobis cavisset, et hiis qui vobiscum "erant. Quia nulli dubium, si conflasset exercitum, multo "plures vobis habuisset, et fortassis multus hominum sanguis "effusus fuisset; quod constat Dominum nostrum Regem "quam maxime abhorrere; et ideo, patientiam sibi sumens, et "mansuetudinem, præelegit vos pacifice convenire, et causam "dicere, quare tot homines congregastis."

Speech made by the Chancellor to the Lords.

MS. Bibl. Reg. 13 E. ix.

The Lords avow their designs, and charge certain parties with treason.

Ad hæc Domini responderunt, ob Regis et regni utilitatem se convenisse, et ut proditores, quos secum jugiter detinebat, avellerent ab eodem. Proditores vero appellabant Robertum de Veer, Ducem Hiberniæ, Alexandrum Nevyle, Archiepiscopum Eboracensem, Michaelem Atte Pole, Comitem Southfolchiæ, Robertum Trisilian, falsum Justiciarium, Nicholaum Brambre, falsum militem Londoniensem. Et ut hanc appellationem veram fore monstrarent, projectis chirothecis, eam se velle duello prosequi juraverunt. Ad hæc Rex,—"Non," ait, "modo fiet "hoc, sed in proximo Parliamento, quod præfigimus in crastino Purificationis Beatæ Virginis, ad quod tam vos quam "ipsi venientes, recipietis, secundum juris exigentiam, quæ "ratio dictaverit universa. Et nunc ad vos, O Domini, meüs "sermo:—Quo modo, qua ratione, vel quali vos audacia præsumpsistis contra me insurgere in hac terra? Putastisne me "[1]terruisse cum tanta vestra præsumptione? An non armatos "habeo, si voluissem, qui vos circumseptos, ut pecudes, mactavissent? Profecto de vobis omnibus non plus in hac "parte reputo, quam de coquinæ meæ infimo garcione."

The Lords are directed by the King to postpone their challenge.

The King rebukes them for their audacity.

The King shows a friendly disposition to the Lords; and takes both parties under his protection.

Cum hæc et plura alia perorasset, levavit Ducem Gloverniæ, qui hactenus genuflexerat, et reliquis jussit ut se erigerent. Post hæc amicabiliter duxit illos in cameram, [2]ubi consederunt et pariter potaverunt; et finale responsum receperunt, quod cuncti, prout dictum est, ad Parliamentum convenirent, in quo fieret omnis justitia utrique parti. Et interim Rex recepit Ducem Hiberniæ et cæteros in suam protectionem, et Ducem Gloverniæ, cum suis sociis, pari modo, ut nulla pars interea noceret alteri, nec præsumeret congregationem facere usque ad diem tempusque præfixum: et sic istud Consilium

[1] *perterruisse* in the printed texts.

[2] *ubi consederunt* omitted in the printed texts.

MS. Bibl. Reg. 13 E. ix.

A.D. 1387.

est solutum. Hæc acta sunt in absentia [1]proditorum, quia non audebant comparere in Dominorum præsentia; quia profecto si comparuissent, tunc illico pœnas luissent, absque respectu regiæ majestatis.

Absence of the King's favourites at the meeting.

Dux Hiberniæ congregat exercitum ad extinguendum Dominos.

Recedentibus Dominis, non est visum eis tutum jam tunc disjungi, propter [2][Regis] [3]mobilitatem et proditorum notoriam falsitatem; quod eis expost magnæ sapientiæ loco fuit. Nam de conniventia Regis, Dux Hiberniæ in partibus Cestriæ Walliæ magnam turbam collegerat; quorum campiductor erat Cestriæ Constabularius, dictus "Thomas Moly- "newes," vir dives et audax, cujus nutum tota illa provincia expectabat. Non diu tamen Dominos latere potuit tantus dolus, sed [4]præmuniti de hiis omnibus, et quod Dux Hiberniæ Londonias properaret cum tanta turba, ut, junctus Londoniensibus, quasi invincibilem exercitum ex duobus faceret, extemplo suos armavit, et invicem cohortantur, ut jam non negligant salutem propriam, sed [5]festinent præoccupare vel extinguere qui in illorum necem conspiraverant fraudulenter.

The Duke of Ireland raises a force in Cheshire and the adjoining parts of Wales.

The Lords prepare to oppose him.

Domini exeunt obviam Duci Hiberniæ.

Igitur Duci Hiberniæ exeuntes obviam, sed occulte, dimiserunt turmas suas ab obsidendum omnes vias, quibus venturus sperabatur. Sed Dux Hiberniæ, cum sublimis et gloriosus equitaret, cum exercitu quem comparaverat, et nullum crederet ausurum obviare sibi, repente dirigens in [6]obliquum oculos, vidit Dominorum exercitum non procul ab eo distantem, et adventum ejus, in cujusdam vallis medio, præstolantem. Quo viso, cor ejus expavit, et dixit:—

The Duke of Ireland espies the army of his opponents.

---

[1] *prædictorum* in orig. and the printed texts: corrected from Bibl. Reg. 13 E. ix.

[2] Omitted in orig.; supplied from Bibl. Reg. 13 E. ix. and the printed texts.

[3] *nobilitatem* in orig.: corrected from the printed texts.

[4] *præmoniti* in the printed texts.

[5] *festinant* in orig. and Bibl. Reg. 13 E. ix.: corrected from the printed texts.

[6] *obsequium* in orig.: corrected from the printed texts.

Dux Hiberniæ verba facit ad suos.

A.D. 1387. Alleged speech of the Duke of Ireland to his own party; and subsequent flight.

"Amici," inquit, "ut cerno, mihi fugiendum est ad horam, "quia multo major fortitudo in adversa parte videtur quam "nostra: unde antequam sit manibus conserendum, me "subtraham et salvabo, si potero. Quia me solum quærunt, "contra vos autem nihil habent. Quamobrem, me dilapso, "vos de facili evadetis." Cui quidam ex militibus suis ait; —"Tu nos e patria exire compulisti, tu fidem nobis suasisti, "tu ad hoc iter nos coegisti; tecum ergo parati sumus dimi-"care, tecum vincere, si contingat, vel, si fortuna non faveat, "tecum mori viriliter." "Non," inquit, [1]"ita parati sumus "facietis," et mox, calcaribus urgens sonipedem, fugere [2]festinabat. Quare multi qui cum eo venerant, execrantes ejus meticulositatem, ad dandum dextras Dominis paraverunt.

MS. Bibl. Reg. 13 E. ix.

Thomas Mulinewes occiditur.

Violent death of Thomas Mulinewes, Constable of Chester, and one of the Duke's supporters.

Erat ibi tunc dictus Thomas Mulinewes, qui se præparavit ad pugnam, quia nondum Domini cuncti convenerant ad illum locum, sed unus tantum, filius Ducis Lancastriæ, Henricus, Comes Derbeyæ; qui, cum aliquandiu pugnasset, fessus et desperans flumen, quod prope erat, ingressus est. Inter multos vero, Thomas de Mortuo Mari, miles, hortabatur ut ascenderet, vel sine dubio eum in flumine sagittis perforaret. "Si," inquit Thomas, "ascendam, visne servare vitam meam?" "Non "hoc promitto," ait miles, "sed vel ascendas vel occumbes "mox." Cui ille,—"Si sic," inquit, "necesse est, sinas ut "ascendam [3]et tecum, vel quocunque vestrum, pugnem, ut "moriar sicut homo." In ascendendo autem cepit eum miles per cassidem, et de capite suo traxit, et mox, extracto cultello daggardo, ejus cerebrum perforavit.

The Duke of Ireland escapes by swimming across a river.

Interea, Dux Hiberniæ, fugiens pervenit ad flumen, sed cum transire ad pontem vellet, confractum reperit. Ad alium vero pontem dum pervenisset, arcitenentes invenit, qui ejus transitum prohiberent. Igitur divertens ab eis, et vadum

---

[1] *ita in præsentiarum facietis* in the printed texts. There is a lacuna after *ita* in Bibl. Reg. 13 E. ix.; and the passage is evidently imperfect.

[2] *æstimabat* in orig. and the printed texts; corrected from Bibl. Reg. 13 E. ix.

[3] *ut* in the printed texts.

MS. Bibl. Reg. 13 E. ix.

A.D. 1387.

quærens, equum compulit intrare flumen; in quo mox, ex equite natator factus, ad aliam ripam venit. Nox autem erat, et ideo non sunt secuti fugientem servi procerum, eo maxime, quod diverticula patriæ nesciebant. Equus tamen ejus, cum casside, et, cum chirothecis, pectorale, in sortem pervenit Dominorum. Unde expost magno tempore submersus fuisse putabatur. Quadrigam ejus insuper, cum clitellis, proceres interceperunt; in quibus plurima repererunt, et præcipue Regis ad ipsum litteras, in quibus continebatur, ut venire festinaret ad eum Londonias, cum potestate magna, et Rex paratus esset, et cor apponeret, ad vivendum et moriendum cum eo. Qui apices magnam fidem fecerunt Dominis de Regis inconstantia et mutabilitate.

The King's letters to the Duke fall into the hands of his opponents.

Acta Michaelis Atte Pole

Michael Atte Pole per idem tempus, timens animadversionem in eum futuram, latenter fugit Calesiam, ducente eo quodam milite Willelmo Atte Hoo. Quo cum pervenisset, mutato habitu et rasa barba, portabat altilia, velut ad vendendum, donec venisset ad fores castelli Calesiæ, cujus Capitaneus erat Dominus Edmundus Atte Pole, frater ejus: a quo, licet difficulter cognitus, propter vestem sordidam et rasam barbam, rogavit ut eum occultaret et tutaretur, narrans quod propter quosdam æmulos [1]quos timebat, Anglia excesserat. Cui ille,—"Frater meus es," ait, "sed noveris, quod pro ulla "consanguinitate nolo deprehendi falsus regno Angliæ, nec "te admittere sine scientia vel consilio Domini Willelmi de "Bello Campo, qui est Capitaneus hujus villæ; quia credo "et veraciter conjicio, quod sine magnis offensis non "fugisti."

Michael De la Pole escapes to Calais.

His brother refuses to admit him, without leave of the Captain of Calais.

Misit ergo ad Willelmum Beauchamp, nuncians fratrem ejus advenisse, non tam mirabiliter quam miserabiliter, et orans ut sibi liceret recipere eum et exhibere, donec idem Willelmus decerneret eum remittendum. Quod ita factum est; nam reductus ad Regem fuit, sed permisit illum Rex ire libere quocunque vellet, parvipendens verbum proprium, quo promiserat eum exhibendum cum cæteris Parliamento futuro.

He is finally admitted, and sent back to the King; who grants him his liberty.

Fugerunt eo tempore Archiepiscopus Eboracensis et Robertus Trisilian, iram, quam meruerant, procerum metuentes.

Flight of the Archbishop of York and R. Trisilian.

---

[1] *Anglia excesserat quos timebat* in orig. and Bibl. Reg. 13 E. ix.; the arrangement of the words being corrected in the printed texts.

A.D. 1387. Regressis Dominis a conflictu, qui fuit juxta Burford, prope Babbelake, ubi militibus qui convenerant cum Duce Hiberniæ, et armigeris, redonatis armis et equis, et secum detentis, sed plebanis equis, arcubus, sagittis spoliatis, et domum remissis, magna fiebat in communi vulgo lætitia de hostibus regni stratis. Sed hanc lætitiam temperavit evasio Ducis Hiberniæ, quia quid de eo fuit actum nesciebatur. MS. Bibl. Reg. 13 E. ix.

General rejoicing at the victory gained by the Lords.

Capitur nuncius Regis Francorum.

A messenger of the King of France is taken, with a copy of the compact made for surrender of the English possessions.

Accidit eo tempore, ut quidam nuncius Regis Franciæ caperetur, "Lustratus" nomine; qui detulerat apices, in quibus licentiavit Rex Franciæ Regem Angliæ et Ducem Hiberniæ, et quosdam alios, sub hominum certo numero, venire [1] Boloniam, ubi Rex Franciæ, collecto exercitu, adventum Regis præstolabatur, ut eum susciperet cum magna pompa, et ab eo reciperet possessionem in Calesia, et omnibus munitionibus quas Rex Angliæ in illis partibus possidebat; pro quibus omnibus Rex Franciæ [2] persolvisset; et Rex Angliæ pro Vasconia homo ligeus Regis Franciæ devenisset. Proceres autem hæc [3] reticentes, festinavere Londonias properare, ubi Rex Natale Dominicum celebraturus erat, non apud Westmonasterium, sed in Turri, quia putabat locum, si quid sinistri emergeret, se posse tueri. Collecto ergo exercitu prope ad quadraginta millium valentium bellatorum, eo libentius adventantium quo sperabant Londonienses spoliandos, in crastino Natalis Dominici Londonias pervenerunt, et se in [4] campis, ubi videri poterant a Turri, per bellicas acies demonstraverunt. Et quia res digessimus usque ad hoc tempus, hic erit elapsi finis anni.

The Lords raise a great army, and encamp in the fields near the Tower.

Transit annus iste frugifer, fructifer, et salubris mediocriter: Angliæ [5] turbulentus, præter id, quod vina capta per Comitem Arundeliæ [6] lætificarunt corda multorum: Hispanniæ lætus, de recessu Ducis regnum vendicantis, et suorum interitu miserando; Franciæ tristis et lugubris, propter non solum vina perdita, sed vasa, cum viris; Flandriæ mœstus, propter vina perdita cum bonis communiter Gallicorum.

---

[1] *in Boloniam* in Camden's text.

[2] The sum is omitted, with an hiatus, in Bibl. Reg. 13 E. ix.

[3] *retentes* in orig; corrected from the printed texts.

[4] *campos* in the printed texts.

[5] *turbulentur* in orig. from the peculiar form of the final *s* in Bibl. Reg. 13 E. ix.; *turbulenter* in the printed texts.

[6] In allusion probably to *Psalm* civ. 15.

Acta inter Regem et Londonienses.

MS. Bibl. Reg. 13 E. ix.

Anno Dominicæ Incarnationis millesimo trecentesimo octogesimo octavo, fuit Rex ad Natale Londoniis in Turri, ut præfertur,—hic est annus undecimus regni ejus,—ad quem locum collecti sunt proceres cum plebe sua; [1] [qui] [2] hospitati sunt in suburbiis, vitantes fallacias urbanorum. Erant tunc in magno metu Londonienses, librantes diversa pericula, scilicet Regis iram, si proceribus aperirent, si vero illos excluderent, indignationem indiscreti vulgi, quod cum illis venerat, et præsto fuit ad infringendum muros vel fores civitatis, si vel minime exacerbarentur. Restabat et aliud satis grave periculum; quia nisi majores Dominis aperirent, communes civitatis et pauperes, qui plus affectabant seditionem quam pacem, paraverunt se ad introducendum Dominos, cum plebe sua, et diripiendum [3] quicquid erat in domibus divitum pretiosum.

A.D. 1388.

Dilemma of the citizens of London as to the contending parties.

Habita tandem deliberatione, Major Londoniarum exiit, et Dominis hospitia intra urbem et omnia necessaria bona fide, si acceptare vellent, promisit, et vinum cum [4] cervisia, caseumque cum pane, distribuit in exercitu universis; quod non parvum commodum postea urbi fuit.

The Mayor offers quarters within the City to the Lords.

Rex interea, audiens et sciens hæc omnia, dissimulabat, tanquam collectam multitudinem parvipenderet, et Dominos non timeret, dicens Archiepiscopo Cantuariensi, et aliis qui intercurrebant pro pace facienda; — "Sinantur," inquit, "hic "jacere cum turba sua, donec expenderint omnia bona sua, "et tunc demum vacui revertentur, et egentes, in domos "suas, et tunc loquar cum eis judicium [5] singillatim."

The King affects to treat their movements with indifference.

Cum hæc audissent Domini, valde commoti, juraverunt se nunquam recessuros, donec cum eo, ore ad os, colloquium obtinerent. Et mox miserunt, qui fluvium [6] Tamensem custodirent, ne Rex [7] laberetur a manibus eorum, et postea subsannaret eos. Tunc videns Rex se undique circumclusum, nunciis loqui cœpit, et jussit renunciari Dominis, se velle tractare cum eis. Qui postulaverunt, ut in crastino veniret ad Westmonasterium,

Determination shown by the Lords.

---

[1] Supplied from Bibl. Reg. 13 E. ix.; omitted in the printed texts.

[2] *hospitatique* in the printed texts.

[3] *quicquam in domibus* in the printed texts.

[4] *servisia* in orig. and Bibl. Reg. 13 E. ix.

[5] *sigillatim* in the printed texts.

[6] *Tamesin* in the printed texts.

[7] *liberetur* in orig.; corrected from the printed texts.

A.D. 1388.

After due precaution taken against treachery, the Lords enter the Tower.

MS. Bibl. Reg. 13 E. ix.

ubi voluerunt sibi depromere vota sua. "Non," ait Rex, "volo "tractare cum eis apud Westmonasterium, sed hic in Turri." Cui Domini renunciaverunt, hunc locum suspectum fore, eo quod possent illic strui insidiæ, et eis pericula præparari. Ad hæc Rex,—"Mittant," inquit, "ducentos vel quot de suis voluerint, et prævideant cuncta, scrutentur universa, ne lateat "ullus dolus." Quod ita factum est. Tunc Dux Gloverniæ, cum sociis suis, [1]intravit Turrim, et habito palam cum Rege, sed brevi, colloquio, postulante Rege, cameram intraverunt, ubi coram eo ejus conspirationem qua indictati sunt, recitaverunt, et litteras ostenderunt quas miserat Duci Hiberniæ, ut exercitum congregaret in perniciem eorundem. Apices [2][quoque] Regis Franciæ, quas interceperant, exhibuerunt, quibus vel concessus fuit Regi conductus in Franciam veniendi, vel cætera firmandi, quibus ejus honor decresceret, potestas fatesceret, et fama periret.

They state their complaints to the King.

The King, in his alarm, promises to meet them at Westminster on the morrow.

Quid tunc Rex ageret, istis visis, [3]Rex nescivit, præcipue quia novit se notabiliter [4]deprehensum. Tandem confusum et lacrymantem, licentia tunc petita, reliquerunt, ea conditione ut [5]in crastino veniret ad Westmonasterium, auditurus plura, et tractaturus de necessariis negotiis regni sui. Quod ipse promisit, retinens secum, in pignus amoris, ad cœnam Comitem Derbensem; sed antequam iret cubitum, agentibus susurronibus, et dicentibus non esse decens Regi, tutum, nec honorificum, ut illic pergeret, propositum mutavit. Proceres, cum hæc novissent, tristes effecti et amaro animo, renunciaverunt ei, nisi venire maturaret, juxta condictum, quod eligerent alium sibi Regem, qui vellet, et deberet, obtemperare consiliis Dominorum. Quo telo Rex percussus, ad Westmonasterium in crastino remigavit. Cui, post paucos tractatus, dixerunt proceres, pro honore suo et regni sui commodo, oportere, ut proditores, susurrones, adulatores, et malefici detractatores, et inutiles, a suo palatio et comitiva eliminarentur; et alii substituerentur loco ipsorum, qui scirent, et vellent, sibi magis honorifice et fidelius famulari. Quod ubi Rex concessit, licet mœrens, censuerunt arcendos a Curia Alexandrum Nevile, Archiepiscopum Eboracensem, Johannem Fordam, Episcopum Dunelmensem, Fratrem Thomam Rushok, Regis Confessorem, de Ordine Prædicatorum, Episcopum Cicestrensem; sed ipse, sibi conscius, fugam iniit, et Eboracensis latebras requisivit. Ex-

He changes his design; but the Lords threaten to choose another King.

He meets the Lords at Westminster; where they state their demands.

Nobles banished from the Court, at their demand.

[1] *intrant* in the printed texts.

[2] Supplied from Bibl. Reg. 13 E. ix. and the printed texts.

[3] *Rex* omitted in the printed texts.

[4] *depressum* in the printed texts.

[5] *in* omitted in the printed texts.

MS. Bibl. Reg. 13 E. ix.

A.D. 1388.

pulerunt præterea Dominos de Souche, de Haringworthe, de Burnel, et de Bemond, Albredum de Veer, Baldewinum de Bereford, Ricardum Aderbury, Johannem Worth, Thomam Clifford, et Johannem Lovel, milites; non ut omnino dimissos, sed Parliamento proximo parituros. Expulsæ sunt et Dominæ, tanquam inutiles Curiæ, scilicet de Ponynges, quæ fuit uxor Domini Johannis Worth, de Mowen, et de Molyng, [1] quæ cunctæ manucaptæ sunt, objiciendis in proximo Parliamento responsuræ. Arestaverunt insuper Symonem Burley, Willelmum Elmham, Johannem Beuchamp de Holte, Regis Senescallum, Johannem Salesbury, Thomam Tryvet, Jacobum Berneys, Nicholaum Dagworth, et Nicholaum Brambre, milites. Ceperunt et clericos, Ricardum Clifford et Johannem Lyncolne, Ricardum [2] Mitford et Nicholaum [3] Solake, Decanum Capellæ Regis, cujus verba multa fiebant in Curia, et Johannem Blake, juris àpprenticium; quos omnes, milites et clericos, diversis carceribus transmiserunt, sub arta custodia conservandos usque ad Parliamentum futurum, quo suis astituri erant responsis.

Certain Ladies expelled from the Court.

Certain Knights arrested and imprisoned.

Clerks arrested and imprisoned.

Parliamentum Londoniæ.

Post festum Purificationis, inceptum est Parliamentum Londoniis, licet Rex voluisset omnino subterfugisse dictum Parliamentum ea vice. Ad quod proceres cum sufficienti convenerunt exercitu, ad compescendum, si emergerent, motus rebelles; et continuatum est istud Parliamentum usque ad festum Pentecostes, cum magna multorum sollicitudine et expectatione.

Parliament at London.

The Lords attend, with a strong force.

Capitur Robertus Trisilian.

In quo, primo captus est Robertus Trysilian; satis infortunate sibi, quia mox tractus [4] ad furcas suspensus [5] est. Consequenter, judicio Dominorum processum est contra Nicholaum Brambre, militem; qui eidem damnationi subjacuit, licet plures

Punishments inflicted on the adversaries of the Lords.

---

[1] *quæcunque manucaptæ* in Camden's text.

[2] *Motford* in the printed texts.

[3] *Lake* in the printed texts.

[4] *est ad* in orig. and the printed texts: corrected from Bibl. Reg. 13 E. ix.

[5] *est* omitted in the printed texts.

A.D. 1388. habuisset intercessores. Hic, ut fertur, nomen [1] Londoniarum delevisse meditatus fuerat, et apposuisse scilicet nomen [2] novum, scilicet Parvæ Trojæ; cujus urbis et nominis ipse Dux creari statuit, et nominari. Ad perducendum ad effectum facilius cogitata, [3] tabellas, sive rotulos, conscribi fecerat, in quibus plura millia nominum suorum civium exarata fuerant, quorum in hac parte resistentiam verebatur, qui omnes repente jugulati fuissent; sed tamen ante suspensus est, ut præfertur, quam ad effectum perduceret meditata.

Crime of Sir Nicholas Brambre; in proscribing many thousands of his fellow-citizens.

MS. Bibl. Reg. 13. E. ix.

Suspensio Militum.

Several other Knights are hanged.

Post hæc, Johannes Salesbury et Jacobus Berneys, ambo milites, ambo juvenes, sed ambo proditores, tracti sunt, Parliamenti judicio, et suspensi. Deinde Jacobus Beuchamp de Holte, Regis Senescallus, ab antiquo fallax et fraudulentus, et tam Domino Edwardo de Windeshore, Regi, quam filio suo Leonello, quondam Duci Clarentiæ, infidelis, ejusdem Parliamenti decreto tractus et suspensus [4] [est]. Suspensus est consequenter Johannes Blake, Scutifer, qui in Consilio apud Notyngham steterat contra Dominos, infausta hora.

Decollatus est Simon Burley.

Sir Simon Burley beheaded, against the expostulations of the Earl of Derby.

Novissime, decollatus est Symon Burley, quamvis Comes de Derby omnes vires apposuisset ejus ereptioni. Ob quam causam magna dissensio orta est inter eum et Ducem Gloverniæ; sed cito, laudes Deo, sopita. Hic, in cunctis locis ubi incedebat, non suæ fortunæ militem, sed in omni apparatu Ducem vel Principem seipsum exhibebat, eratque Custos castelli de Doveria, quod, ad nutum Regis, consenserat Gallicis vendidisse; fueratque intolerabiliter superbus et arrogans, oppressor pauperum, osor Ecclesiæ, mœchus et adulter.

His bad character.

Certain Justiciars condemned to exile.

Damnati sunt insuper, in præmisso Parliamento, Justiciarii, Robertus Belknappe, Johannes Holte, Rogerus Fulthorp, et Willelmus Burgh, exilio; concessa certa pecunia ad vitam singulis pro sustentatione sua cotidiana. Deinde exactum est

---

[1] From this word down to *novum*, the context is omitted in the printed texts.

[2] *novæ* in the printed texts.

[3] *tabellos* in the printed texts.

[4] Supplied from Bibl. Reg. 13 E. ix. and the printed texts.

MS. Bibl. Reg. 13 E. ix.

juramentum a Rege, ad standum regulationi procerum; et non solum a Rege, sed a cunctis regni incolis, idem juramentum est expetitum.

A.D. 1388. The King compelled to ratify these judgments.

Profectio Comitis Arundeliensis.

Victories gained at sea by the Earl of Arundel.

Post festum Pentecostes, Ricardus, Comes Arundeliæ, cum valentium turba, profectus est ad mare, et hinc inde velificans hostes ubique [1]quæsivit: tandem hostium rates reperiens, confligit et vincit, et naves octoginta vel mergit, vel capit, vel incendit. Insulam de [2]Beas ingreditur, quam despoliat et comburit. Insulas insuper de Us et de Ree, de Lemustre et de Rochele, de Olum et de Olorum,—ubi Leges Marinæ conduntur,—invadit, capit, et deprædatur, de quibusdam redemptionem percipiens, quasdam vero igne devastans; Gallicos sive Britones, qui resistentiam paravere, vincens, convertit in fugam; [3]peractoque cum summa felicitate negotio, redivit ad regnum.

Gallici ingressi terras Ducis de Gelre.

The French invade the territory of the Duke of Geldres, but are defeated.

Eodem tempore, Gallici, de pace fastidiosi, cum magno numero armatorum terras Ducis de Gelre sunt ingressi, ut ei inquietudinem suscitarent; eo maxime quod erat Anglis fidus amicus; sed mox Dux occurrens eis, cum quibusdam Anglicis, docuit quam periculosum fuerat excitare canem dormientem, occidens ex eis plurimos, multosque captivans, paucis per fugam dilapsis: sensitque in hoc conflictu damnum Francia, quantum non senserat a diebus antiquis.

The Flemings defeat the French, with great slaughter.

Flandrenses per idem tempus, et ipsi occurrentes Gallicis, magnam stragem fecerunt ex ipsis; nec immerito, [4]quia cum summa superbia gravique tyrannide Galli eos perante oppresserant et vexarant.

The Scots invade England, unprepared to oppose them.

Eodem anno Scoti, quietis nescii, considerantes Anglicos nihil moliri contra illos, præparaverunt se, ut mox, expirantibus treugis, essent omnes parati ad invadendum partes Boreales. Factumque est, ut cum grandi exercitu regnum intrarent, antequam Anglici quicquam disponerent contra eos. Igitur,

---

[1] Apparently written *quæ sunt* in orig.

[2] *Baas* in Bibl. Reg. 13 E. ix.

[3] *pactoque* in the printed texts.

[4] *quia* omitted in the printed texts.

A.D. 1388. nullo resistente, progressi, agebant cædes et rapinas ubique, multos captivantes, villasque conflagrantes quæ fuerunt in eorum itinere, nisi quas domini de eisdem pecunia redemissent. Perveneruntque cum magno fastu prope Novum Castrum super Tynam, [1] [et] non procul [2] sua tentoria posuerunt. Erat tunc in villa prædicta Henricus Percy junior, et Radulphus, frater suus, ambo milites, ambo gloriæ militaris cupidi, ambo Scotis infesti; sed Henricus præcipue, qui, pro suæ strenuitate personæ, a Scotis maxime timebatur. Hic Henricus, indigne ferens quod Scoti tam impune bacchabantur, et eo maxime quod provocatus fuisset ab eis ad pugnam, repromisit se proculdubio adventurum ad conserendum cum illis infra triduum, quamvis omnino foret impar [3] multitudini eorundem. Supervenit ergo repente, juxta condictum, irruens super eos in tentoriis constitutos, et magnam stragem faciens de eisdem.

MS. Bibl. Reg. 13 E. ix.

They encamp near Newcastle-on-Tyne.

Sir Henry Percy attacks them.

Duglas perimitur, et Henricus capitur.

(Battle of Otterburn)

Dux Scotorum præcipuus, Willelmus Duglas, qui et ipse fuit juvenis ambitiosus, videns [4] rem mille votis petitam, Henricum Percy, videlicet, intra castra, alacriter equitat contra eum. Erat ibidem cernere pulchrum spectaculum, duos tam præclaros juvenes manus conserere et pro gloria decertare; et quamvis neutri virilis deesset animus, tamen sors contulit Henrico victoriam, qui Scotum, Scotorum maximum, suis manibus interfecit. Supervenit [5] [tamen] Comes de Dunbare, cum excessivo Scotorum numero, et ipsum Henricum, cum fratre suo, cepit, occisis ex Anglicis ibidem multis; sed et ipsi Scoti damnum irrecuperabile perceperunt de suorum potentissimorum strage facta per Henricum, et paucos qui secuti sunt eum ad hanc pugnam.

William Douglas attacks Percy, and is slain.

Percy and his brother are taken prisoners.

Interea, dum proceres se disponunt ad obviandum Scotis, Scoti, humiliati per hoc dedecus illis illatum, de regno fugiunt, cum captivis quos ceperant, expectare adventum procerum non audentes; et sic unius Henrici videlicet probitate, licet captus esset, totum regnum fuit tam metu quam Scotis penitus vacuatum.

The Scots retire from England.

---

[1] Omitted in orig. and Bibl. Reg. 13 E. ix.: supplied from the printed texts.

[2] *inde sua* in the printed texts.

[3] *multitudinem* in orig.; corrected from the printed texts.

[4] *Anglos prævalere, Henricum* in the printed texts.

[5] Supplied from Bibl. Reg. 13 E. ix.; omitted in the printed texts.

Parliamentum Cantabrigiæ.

MS. Bibl. Reg. 13 E. ix.

Post festum Nativitatis [1] Beatæ Mariæ, factum est Parliamentum Cantebriggiæ, in quo nova Statuta sunt ordinata, de stipendiis famulorum; de [2] mendicis; de armis non portandis; de ludis non exercendis, præter ad arcum; de Stapula reducenda de Myddelbourghe ad Calesiam; de laboratoribus non recipiendis in aliena villa, nisi cum sigillo hundredi; de provisoribus, quod regnum non exeant ad adquirendum beneficia cum cura vel sine cura, nisi habeant ad hoc licentiam ex ore Regis; et si fecerint, eo ipso Rex excluderet eos a sua protectione. Multa fuerunt et alia ibidem statuta, quæ hic omitto scribere, propter id maxime, quod eadem perante sæpius sunt statuta, sed nullatenus observata. Tandem finis Parliamenti erat taxa levanda ad opus Regis, id est decima de clero, et quinta-decima de populo laicali.

A.D. 1388. A Parliament at Cambridge: Statutes enacted there.

Tempore Parliamentali, cum Dominus Thomas Tryvet cum Rege sublimis equitaret ad Regis hospitium, quod fuit apud Bernewelle, dum nimis urget equum calcaribus, equus cadit, et omnia pene interiora sessoris dirumpit: protelavit tamen vitam in crastinum; quod tempus, ut puto, datum fuit sibi ad pœnitentiam, si ille vellet acceptare. Facta est in ejus morte magna lætitia plurimorum, tum quia superciliosus nimis extiterat, tum quia, ut dicebatur, Norwycensi Episcopo infidus, in sua profectione cum [3] Cruciata, fuerat; et præcipue, quia contra proceres cum Rege steterat, consulens ut Rex eos perimeret, anno transacto.

Death of Sir Thomas Tryvet, during this Parliament. His unpopularity.

In eodem Parliamento, Dominus Johannes Holond, frater Regis [4] ex parte matris, qui nuper redierat de Hispannia, ubi Duci Lancastriæ militaverat, creatus est Comes Hontyndoniæ.

Sir J. Holand, the King's brother, made Earl of Huntingdon.

Abbas Montis Cassini prohibet transitum Papæ.

Per idem tempus, Urbanus Papa, ut erat semper varius, ad loca varia transtulit se frequenter; tandem, cum de Piisis latenter voluisset se transtulisse Neapolim, Romani cum armatis obviavere sibi, ut eum per vim violentiamque detinerent

Disagreement of the Pope with the people of Rome.

---

[1] *S.* for *Sanctæ*, in the printed texts.

[2] *mendicibus* in orig. and Bibl. Reg. 13 E. ix.; corrected from the printed texts.

[3] *cruce signatis* in the printed texts.

[4] *et* in orig., by inadvertence.

A.D. 1388. Romæ, si ibidem nollet morari sua sponte: sed cum [1]appropinquassent sibi, viderunt se multo inferiores militia quam ea quæ cum Papa venerat, et ideo, deposito verborum supercilio, eum pacifice salutarunt. Qui sciscitatus est ab eis, ad quid venerint cum tanta manu: qui mox finxerunt se venisse in ejus obsequium, ut, si sibi videretur expediens, eum deducerent quocunque vellet. Ipse vero commotus respondit, se non egere [2][eorum] conductu, quinimmo sub benedictione sua Romam remearent; illi autem, artem arte deludentes, accepta licentia regressi sunt. Sed mox adventum Papæ Abbati de Monte Cassino significare curarunt: hic erat quondam Cardinalis Reatinensis, ut præmittitur, sed degradatus fuerat per Papam præfatum. Hic illico, collecta manu militari, exploravit adventum Papæ, [3]quem oportuit omnino transire per illum. Qui cum venisset ad partes ejus, ei restitit, et ejus transitum prohibebat. Papa vero, [4][quem] nimius amor soli patriæ detinebat, confectis Bullis de restitutione sua ad Cardinalatus dignitatem, et gradum Doctoratus, necnon Abbathiæ Cassini Montis honorem, destinavit sibi hæc omnia; [5]tantum ut permitteret eum transire, revisere natale solum. Cui Abbas respondit, se quidem non egere Bullis suis ad restitutionem dignitatum [6]quibus gaudebat, quibus et donatus et investitus fuit a prædecessore suo; cujus temporibus non erat schisma in Ecclesia; qui et cognitus est universaliter pro Papa Romano, de isto vero dubium fuit si futurus esset Papa, vivente Clemente, suo adversario; et ideo remisit nuncios, cum Bullis Papalibus, injungens ut ei dicerent ex parte [7]sua, ut Romam rediret, mundi metropolim, et ibidem inter Romanos versaretur ut Papa Romanus; [8][quia] proculdubio non expediebat sub sua jurisdictione constitutis, eum quærere tam remote, ut ad Mare Magnum proficiscerentur, qui ejus perfrui benedictionibus affectabant. Rediit ergo Papa, vellet nollet, Romam; ubi a civibus summo cum honore receptus est.

MS. Bibl. Reg. 13. E. ix.

Opposition shown by the Abbot of Monte Cassino to the Pope.

The Pope ultimately returns to Rome.

[1] *propinquassent* in the printed texts.

[2] Omitted in orig.: supplied from Bibl. Reg. 13 E. ix. and the printed texts.

[3] *quam* in orig.; corrected from the printed texts.

[4] Omitted in orig: supplied from Bibl. Reg. 13 E. ix. and the printed texts.

[5] *tamen* in the printed texts.

[6] These two words are omitted in the printed texts.

[7] *suo* in orig. and Bibl. Reg. 13 E. ix.; *sua* in the printed texts.

[8] Omitted in orig.; supplied from Bibl. Reg. 13 E. ix. and the printed texts.

Translationes Episcoporum.

MS. Bibl. Reg. 13 E. ix.

Eodem anno Papa transtulit Dominum Thomam Arundel, Episcopum Eliensem, ad Archiepiscopatum Eboracensem, Alexandro Nevile, proditore et susurrone, translato ad Episcopatum Sancti Andreæ in Scotia; quanquam non habiturus esset eum, quia Scoti pro tunc fuere schismatici; Johannem vero Fordam de Dunelmensi fecit Episcopum Eliensem, Magistrum Walterum Skirlow de Batoniensi fecit Episcopum Dunelmensem, Magistrum Radulphum [1]Ergom de Sarum fecit Episcopum Bathoniensem, et [2]Johanni Waltham, Clerico de Privato Sigillo, per provisionem contulit Episcopatum Salisburiensem.

A.D. 1388. Episcopal promotions.

Annalis Conclusio.

Transit annus iste frugifer et fructifer abundanter; proditoribus lugubris; fidelibus regionis hilaris; Francis dispendiosus, propter vasa perdita invasione Comitis Arundeliæ; Hispanis quietus, tractantibus de pace; Scotis varius et infaustus, quanquam Henricum Percy eo tempore captivassent; Domino Papæ invisus et odibilis, quia non consecutus est arbitrium voluntatis.

Tractatus de treugis.

Anno Domini millesimo trecentesimo octogesimo nono, qui est annus regni Regis Ricardi, a Conquæstu Secundi, duodecimus, fuit idem Rex ad Natale cum Anna Regina apud [3][Westmonasterium].

A.D. 1389.

Hoc anno missi sunt nuncii, ex parte Regis Angliæ, pro pace, vel saltem treugis, petendis a Rege Franciæ, Magister Walterus Skirlow, Episcopus Dunelmensis, et Johannes Clambowe ac Nicholaus Dagworth, milites; qui diu perhendinantes Calesiæ, et nunc isthac, nunc illac, trans mare discurrentes, [4]pro nunciandis, vel accipiendis, treugarum conditionibus, tandem pro finali recepere responso, quod Gallici non consentirent ad treugas, nisi Hispani et Scoti [5]sub dictis treugis

The French refuse to make a truce, unless the Spaniards and Scots are included.

---

[1] *Ergon* in the printed texts.

[2] *Johannem* and *clericum* in orig., Bibl. Reg. 13 E. ix., and the printed texts.

[3] Omitted in orig., and Bibl. Reg. 13 E. ix., with a blank: supplied from the printed texts.

[4] *pro nunciandum vel accipiendum* in orig.; *in pronuntiandis vel accipiendis* in the printed texts: corrected from Bibl. Reg. 13 E. ix.

[5] *subditis* in orig.; corrected from the printed texts.

A.D. 1389. quiete simili congauderent. Diu igitur suspensum fuit pacis negotium, eo quod nostri affirmabant Scotos esse ligeos homines Regis Angliæ, qui pacem Regis sui enormiter conturbaverant, et ideo debere eos, ut transgressores legum, juxta voluntatem Regis et procerum regni puniri; nec fas esse ut Rex suis [1] subjectis, sed tamen transgressoribus, [2] tantum præstaret, ut absque vindicta cum eis taliter conveniret. Hac occasione treugæ dilatæ sunt; sed et Scoti, interim parvipendentes ampullosas minas nostras, irruperunt in Northumbriam, facientes magnam stragem ex hominibus, plures abducentes captivos, et prædas maximas in suam patriam revehentes.

MS. Bibl. Reg. 13 E. ix.

Arguments of the English against this proposition.

The Scots ravage Northumberland.

The Earl of Buckingham is sent against the Scots; with an insufficient force.

Eo tempore missus fuit, cum armata manu, Dominus Thomas Moubray Comes Bokynghamiæ, Marescallus, ut Scotorum obviaret improbitatibus: sed quia non erat par tantis exercitibus, nihil fecit; quippe qui non ultra quingentas lanceas secum duxit, contra triginta millia adversariorum.

Obiit Abbas Sancti Edmundi.

Death of J. Tymworth, Abbot of Bury St. Edmund's. He is succeeded by William de Stratfeld.

Circa dies istos obiit Dominus Johannes Tymworth, quondam Abbas Sancti Edmundi de Bury; cui successit, per electionem, Dominus Willelmus de Stratfeld, monachus ejusdem loci; qui, Romam pergens, confirmatus est a Papa, promissione prius petita, sed non concessa neque soluta, de certa pensione annua persolvenda de domo sua Edmundo de Brounfeld; per cujus ambitionem, ut præfertur, idem Monasterium varia sustinuit detrimenta.

Obiit Episcopus Roffensis.

Death of the Bishop of Rochester; and provision made by the Pope for Friar John

Eodem tempore, Dominus Thomas [3] Brunton, Roffensis Episcopus, concessit in fata; cujus morte comperta, mox Papa contulit Episcopatum illum Fratri Johanni [4] Boltesham, de Prædicatorum Ordine, qui fuit Episcopus Landafensis. Edmundum vero præfatum creavit Episcopum Landafensem: et sic exonerata est Domus de Bury de pensione petita, ratione videlicet beneficii sibi collati. Elegerant autem Roffenses in Episcopum unanimiter Magistrum Johannem de Barnet; sed

[1] *objectis* in the printed texts.
[2] *tamen* in the printed texts.
[3] *Bruton* in the printed texts.
[4] More generally, spelt as *Botlesham*; *Bottlesham* in Bibl. Reg. 13 E. ix.

MS. Bibl. Reg. 13 E. ix.

Papa, cupiens utrique personæ præstare gratiam, Johanni scilicet, quia secum permanserat in tentationibus suis, tempore quo apud Luceram fuit [1]obsessus, et Edmundo, eo quod carceres et damna sustinuerat in causa Papæ, quando sibi providit Abbathiam de Bury, [2]cassavit electionem factam de dicto Johanne Barnet, ut sic utrique [3]licentius provideret, Edmundo, videlicet, et Johanni.

A.D. 1389. Bottlesham, and Edmund de Brounfeld.

Rex vendicat liberam regni, jure hæreditario, dispositionem.

Eodem anno, Rex, ductus quorundam consilio susurronum, convocatis proceribus et multis regni valentibus, subito subintravit domum Consilii, ubi proceres ejus præstolabantur adventum, et sedens, requisivit ab eis, quot annos [4][ætatis] habebat. Responsum est, quod jam viginti annos peregisset.—"Ergo," inquit, "plenæ sum ætatis ad gubernandum domum et familiam, necnon regnum meum: injustum enim mihi videtur, ut conditio [5][in persona mea sit deterius quam conditio] minimi infra regnum. Nempe quilibet hæres regni mei, cum vicesimum [6]attigerit ætatis annum, defuncto parente, libere propria sua negotia tractare permittitur. Cur ergo mihi negatur, quod cuilibet alteri gradus inferioris jure conceditur?" Cumque Barones ad hæc attoniti responderent, nihil juris sibi debere subtrahi, sed eum habiturum regimen regni sui, sibi de jure debitum, ita ait;—"Ecce! nostis quod diu regulatus fuerim per tutores; nec licuit mihi quicquam, vel minimum, facere sine illis. Jam enim de cætero illos de Consilio meo amoveo, et, ut hæres ætatis legitimæ, quos voluero ad Consilium advocabo, et negotia propria pertractabo. Et ideo jubeo ut in primis Cancellarius Sigillum mihi resignet."

The King asserts, before his Council, his right to govern for himself.

The Council assent.

The Seal is demanded of the Chancellor, the Archbishop of York.

Cumque Eboracensis Archiepiscopus Sigillum reddidisset, Rex illud recollegit in sinum, et repente surrexit et exiit; et post pusillum rediit et resedit, tradiditque Sigillum Episcopo Wyntoniensi, Domino Willelmo Wykham, faciens eum Cancellarium, quamvis plurimum renitentem. Creavitque novos officiarios plurimos, antiquis depositis, in omnibus utens pro-

William Wykeham, Bishop of Winchester, is appointed Chancellor.

---

[1] *obcessus* in orig.

[2] *cessavit* in the printed texts.

[3] *liberius* in the printed texts.

[4] Omitted in orig.; supplied from Bibl. Reg. E. ix. and the printed texts.

[5] Supplied from Bibl. Reg. 13 E. ix.: omitted in the printed texts; which read, "*conditio mihi imponatur* "*infra regnum.*"

[6] *attigeret* in orig. and Bibl. Reg. 13 E. ix.: *attigerit* in the printed texts.

A.D. 1389. priis arbitrio et potestate; Ducemque Glorverniæ et Comitem Warwycensem, aliosque multos valentes, amovit a Consilio, adhibitis aliis qui suis oculis complacebant. Sub eodem tempore, Rex creavit Justiciarios novos quinque.[1] MS. Bibl. Reg. 13 E. ix.

The Duke of Gloucester and Earl of Warwick are removed from the Council.

Rex seducitur, et contra Ducem irascitur sine causa.

The Duke of Gloucester is maligned, but exculpates himself.

Interea quidam [2]detractores, Regem circumvenientes, tantum [3]dementaverunt, ut crederet avunculum suum, Ducem Gloverniæ, collegisse turbas ad infestandum eum; sed tandem Rex, accersito Duce, et comperta fama mendace, confusus erubuit. Aderant tunc præsentes quidam, qui hoc mendacium seminaverant, contra quos cum Dux loqui voluisset, et eorum perfidiam publice declarasse, rogavit Rex, sub obtestatione suæ dilectionis, ne ulterius procederet in materia prætaxata. Adquievit ergo Dux roganti, facilius, quod bene novit jam Regi suam innocentiam declaratam; sed cum recessisset ad sua, succrevit utrobique suspicio, susurronibus interponentibus partes suas.

The King still entertains suspicion against him.

Treugæ firmatæ.

A truce for three years is made with France.

Oaths of the Sovereigns exchanged.

Circa festum Nativitatis Sancti Johannis Baptistæ, firmatæ sunt treugæ triennales inter regna Angliæ et Franciæ; Johanne Clanbow, milite, et Ricardo Rouhale, clerico, suscipientibus in Francia juramentum ex parte Regis Franciæ; et paulo post, scilicet, circa festum Sancti Laurentii, venit in Angliam Comes Sancti Pauli, qui desponsaverat sororem Regis Angliæ [4]Matildem de Courtenay, cum aliis honorabilibus, ad suscipiendum juramentum de treugis servandis fideliter ex parte Regis Angliæ; qui cum honore maximo susceptus est.[5]

Nuncii destinantur ad Scotos.

The Scots have the option of being in-

Eo tempore, quidam ex nunciis qui de regno Francorum venerant, missi sunt in Scotiam, ad dandum Scotis [6]optionem sub certis conditionibus, vel includi inter treugas datas inter

[1] The word *videlicet* follows here in Bibl. Reg. 13 E. ix.; but the names are not given.

[2] *detractatores* in orig.: *detractores* in Bibl. Reg. 13 E. ix. and the printed texts.

[3] *profecerunt* in the printed texts.

[4] Correctly *Johannam*, "Joanna" being her name. See Vol. I. p. 430.

[5] A passage in Bibl. Reg. 13 E. ix. is omitted here.

[6] *opinionem* in Camden's text.

MS. Bibl. Reg. 13 E. ix.

A.D. 1389.

Reges, vel omnino de protectione Franciæ Regis excludi. Majores Scotorum responderunt, se libenter treugas et conditiones admissuros, sed tamen bene scire durum fore hæc communi vulgo persuaderi, cum jam parati essent iterum, cum abundantiori militia, Angliam ingredi, et sperarent de tali ingressu lucrum multum; præcipue cum jam antea, paucioribus qui audebat resistere, nullus fuit: et ut se monstrarent obedientes Regi Franciæ, rogaverunt ut nuncii cum illis accederent, et viderent simul et præparationem pugnæ quam Scoti fecerant, et audirent quæ communitas nunciis respondere vellet.

Cluded in the truce; but in consequence of their great preparations for invasion, they hesitate.

Gallorum ergo nuncii, cum venissent ad Scotorum exercitum, repererunt eos pulchre per turmas dispositos, fulgide et decenter armatos, et quasi ad procinctum prœlii præparatos. Quibus cum innotuisset causa adventus [1]nunciorum Franciæ, indisciplinatum vulgus reclamavit procaciter, se nolle tantum apparatum deserere, tantos sumptus perdere, quos ad regnum Angliæ invadendum comparasset; præcipue cum domos et pecunias, prædia et supellectiles, ad hunc finem invadiasset, et se multipliciter depauperasset. Nuncii nihilominus, hiis auditis, nunc minis et terroribus, nunc pollicitationibus et blanditiis, id egerunt cum populo, ut, armis depositis, [2]paci consentirent. Juvitque multum ad animos sedandos rebellium, et assertio procerum Scoticorum, qui omnino juraverunt, se nolle eis præbere ducatum in [3]Angliam, sed si omnino decernerent cœpta continuare, ipsi proprio periculo pergerent, et ex seipsis duces eligerent pro eisdem.

By persuasion of the French envoys, and of the Scottish nobles, the Scots at last assent to the truce.

Sicque factum est, ut improbi Scoti pacem susciperent, et treugis adquiescerent, non sine improperio Anglicorum.

Miraculum apud Ely.

Sub eisdem diebus, apud Ely Beata Etheldreda, Virgo perpetua et Regina, apparuit cuidam juveni, docens eum cavere pericula sibi imminentia, et instruens eum de periculis maximis quæ regno supervenirent, nisi pius Deus, placatus orationibus piis fidelium, manum suspenderet a vindicta. Quapropter monet, ut Priorem et monachos adeat, et eis mandata sua deferat, ut pro salute gentis exorent Dominum, et precentur ut avertat iram indignationis suæ a populo An-

Account of a Miracle at Ely.

[1] *judiciorum* in the printed texts.

[2] *pacem* in orig.; *in pacem* in the printed texts; corrected from Bibl. Reg. 13 E. ix.

[3] *Anglia* in the printed texts.

A.D. 1389. glicano. Spondetque Beata Virgo suas etiam preces oblaturam Domino pro causa præmissa: cunctanti vero juveni, nec audenti jussa perficere, signum dedit, dicens;—"Contractus et "claudus eris, et omnino inutilis, qui modo sanus et sospes "esse dinosceris, usque ad diem [1] festi Depositionis meæ. "Quo die deportatus ad meam memoriam, consequeris integram sanitatem."

MS. Bibl. Reg. 13 E. ix.

Prodit ergo juvenis quæcunque viderat, et ad credendum dictis suis suæ contractionis pœna multos invitat. Et ne fictum videretur, vel humano adinventum ingenio, quod in ipso factum fuerat, consumptis carnibus, tibiæ exinanitæ [2] [fuerant], ut tantum pellis hæreret ossibus, et [3] poplites ita constrictæ, ut tali natibus inseparabiliter jungerentur. Accurrerunt ergo multi, illecti fama facti, ferroque pungunt tibias seu pedes juvenis; sed caro consumpta, pellis mortua, nil sensere: tentant tibias contractas a tergo retrahere, sed minime profecere. Statuunt igitur opperiri diem præfixum, in quo vel fama mendax vel omnino vera probaretur.

Illabente Die gloriosæ Virginis et Reginæ, juvenis, ad ecclesiam deportatus, primo cœpit obdormire, et mox excitatus a somno resiliit. Audiebanturque nervorum crepitus, et sequebatur membrorum distensio, et juvenis exilire cœpit, et coram multis memoriam Sanctæ Virginis circuire. Et quia perante dictus juvenis multa, jussu Sanctæ Virginis Etheldredæ, secreta de multis prædixerat, quæ suo parochiali sacerdoti, sub sigillo confessionis, revelaverat, quæ omnia vera fuisse comperta sunt; fidem fecerunt indubitabilem de cunctis quæ ventura [4] fore prædixit.

Fulfilment of a prophecy of intense heat.

Prædixit enim plura pericula imminentia; inter quæ prophetavit æstatem fervidissimam affuturam, cujus fervor plumbum ecclesiarum liquefaceret, nisi Deus manus apponeret adjutrices. Fervorem utique sensimus, aliqualem intolerabiliorem [5] subituri, ut credimus, nisi preces fidelium obstitissent. Plumbum ecclesiarum per ignes cœlestes eo tempore liquefactum est; cum in Sowtsexia, in villa de Maunfeld, Ecclesia Collegialis Cantuariensis Archiepiscopi conflagrata est, cum omni pene villa; et quædam prædia in Estsexia, navesque, cum nautis, quibusdam in locis ictibus fulminum sunt consumpta.

Great damage caused by lightning.

[1] *festum* in the printed texts.

[2] Omitted in orig.: supplied from the printed texts.

[3] *poplices* in the printed texts; the form of *c* being used for *t* in the original, as in Bibl. Reg. 13 E. ix.

[4] *fore* omitted in the printed texts.

[5] *subdituri* in orig.: corrected from the printed texts.

Aliud miraculum.

MS. Bibl. Reg. 13 E. ix.

A.D. 1389. Another Miracle at Ely.

Fidem fecit hujus visionis et miraculi alia visio, cito subsecuta, manifestataque decrepitæ mulieri et octogenariæ; cui videbatur Beatam Reginam et Virginem Etheldredam astitisse sæpius, et eadem, vel plura, commemorasse superventura pericula, nisi devotis supplicationibus Omnipotens placaretur. Adjecitque Beata Virgo, se cum populo preces Domino porrexisse, ut malum subtraheret quod proposuit terræ immittere pro peccatis. Monuitque, ut Priori et Conventui, atque plebi, ex parte sua mandaret continuare processiones, multiplicare devotiones, facere incessanter orationes, ut Deus averteret gladium imminentem.—"Sciantque proculdubio," inquit Sancta, "quod ego precum mearum instantia minas varias et ruinas "ab eis averti." Jussitque gloriosa Domina, ut mulier hæc universa publice profiteretur, et in festo Sanctæ Mariæ Magdalenæ se deferri faceret ad ejus tumbam, ibidem contractionis et invaletudinis consecutura coram populo sanitatem. Nempe per triennium ita confecta fuerat tibiarum intolerabili passione, ut immobilis semper uno jaceret in loco, nisi quando, miseratione vicinorum compatientium, de uno loco ad alium portabatur.

Igitur in festo memorato, vetula in sporta ad feretrum Beatæ Etheldredæ defertur, ubi in somnum resoluta videt gloriosam Virginem [1]prodeuntem. Quæ accedens apprehendit ejus tibias, et in longum protraxit; nervique tibiarum, pluribus de populo assistente audientibus, crepuerunt; et mulier mox sana surrexit, quæ prius [2]ægra veterana fuerat, et contracta; tumbamque tribus perlustravit vicibus, illam devote deosculans, et agens Deo gratias et gloriosæ Dominæ Etheldredæ.

Mirabile de Corpore Christi, contingens Cantabrigiæ.

A Miracle at Cambridge.

Per idem tempus Cantebriggiæ, in festo Commemorationis Sancti Pauli, occurrebat et festum Dedicationis Sanctæ Mariæ ibidem; ad quod festum amplius honorandum, in processione per parochiam deferrebatur Corpus Dominicum, super [3]duorum humeros sacerdotum; in feretro non ponderoso, sed tam levi, ut a septenni puero, sine vexatione, portari tota machina po-

[1] *prodientem* in orig., Bibl. Reg. 13 E. ix., and the printed texts.

[2] *erga* in orig., by inadvertence.

[3] *duos* in the printed texts.

A.D. 1389. tuisset. Procedebant igitur, et præcedebant dicti presbyteri, supportantes Corpus Domini per dictam villam, donec venirent ante locum Fratrum Augustinensium, qui situati sunt juxta mercatum villæ; ubi repente feretrum, quod æqualiter utriusque humeris acclinis erat, se subrigens, nitebatur, quasi quadam virtute imperceptibili, ab eorum humeris resilire; efficiebaturque adeo ponderosum, ut sacerdotes vix neque possent sufferre tantum pondus, neque feretri fines humeros iterum detrahere et applicare; torquentur proinde, et sudant, et anhelant, præ labore nimio, laicorum auxilium flagitantes. Accurrunt laici, manus supponunt, sed, quod mirabile fuit, nihil ponderis persenserunt. [1]Duravit ista turbatio sacerdotum, quamdiu coram dictorum Fratrum habitaculo processerunt. Cumque pertransissent omnem loci situm dictorum Fratrum, feretrum iterum repente super illorum humeros æqualiter requievit. Sed tunc quidam ineptus et vere miser, incomposito motu corporis cœpit saltare, sive tripudiare, coram [2]Eucharistia; quem incontinenter apprehendit terribilis valde vindicta. Nam inter [3]jocandum repente corruit, et, post pusillum, spiritum exhalavit.

MS. Bibl. Reg. 13 E. ix.

[4]Horum causa mirabilium a multis multipliciter est interpretata; quam judicare nos prætermittimus, malentes aliis judicium derelinquere, quam de nobis incognitis inconsulte aliqua diffinire. Hoc tantum audemus adjicere, quod magna et formidabilis pestilentia extemplo subsecuta est Cantebrigiæ, qua homines subito, prout dicebatur, sospites, [5]invasi, mentis phrenesi moriebantur, sine viatico sive sensu.

Great pestilence at Cambridge.

Pugna inter Cinifes.

Appearance, at Shene, of vast clouds of gnats, and conflict among them.

Eodem tempore, in manerio regio de Schene, repente tot cinifes confluxerunt, ut ipsum [6]aerem obscurare viderentur; quæ mox, conflictum ineuntes, pugnam confecere durissimam, ita ut duæ partes illius innumerabilis multitudinis in terram caderent interfectæ; tertia vero pars, perfecto bello et consummata victoria, avolavit, dubium in quas partes. Tantaque fuit peremptorum copia, ut scopis [7]posset colligi, et ex illis plures

[1] The whole of this passage is omitted in the printed texts.

[2] *Eukaristia* in orig.

[3] *jocundum* in orig. and Bibl. Reg. 13 E. ix.; corrected from the printed texts.

[4] *Harum* in orig.; corrected from the printed texts.

[5] *correpti mentis* in the printed texts.

[6] *aere* in orig.; corrected from the printed texts.

[7] *possent* in the printed texts.

MS. Bibl. Reg. 13 E. ix. modii possent impleri. Quid significare velint, aliis [1] discutienda relinquo. A.D. 1389.

Fratres delirant.

Per idem tempus, in Francia Fratres Prædicatores, antiquam suam opinionem reassumentes de conceptu Beatæ Mariæ Virginis, et prædicantes illam fuisse in originali peccato conceptam, in tantam efferati sunt superbiam, ut Episcopis, [2] illis indicentibus hujus rei silentium, noluerunt obedire. Postremo nec Regi et proceribus, id jubentibus, parere volebant. Quapropter extra protectionem regiam facti sunt, et inhibiti circuire per patrias more solito, ne forte commune vulgus ducerent in ejusdem erroris devium, et seducerent innocentes; jussi sunt etiam intra propria se habitacula cohibere, de labore manuum suarum infra loca sua vivere, egredi nusquam præsumere, sub pœna capitali. Præceptumque est eis, ne de cætero quemquam ad Ordinem suum admitterent, vel reciperent, sub pœna præmissa; sed ipsimet ita facescerent, ut, post hos qui modo vivunt, nullus esset qui eorum Ordinem continuaret.

Heresy of the Friars Preachers, in France, as to the Conception of the Virgin Mary.

Restraints laid upon the Order.

Obiit Michael At[te] Poole.

Hac æstate, perfidiæ promptuarium, sentina avaritiæ, auriga proditionis, arca malitiæ, odii seminator, mendacii fabricator, susurro nequissimus, dolo præstantissimus, artificiosus detractor, patriæque delator, Michael Atte Pole, quondam Comes Sowthfolchiæ, regnique Cancellarius, sed nequam consiliarius, concessit in fata Parisius, merito perfidum evomens spiritum in terra peregrina. Cujus opes, quas sibi habuit, suo cessere collegæ, Roberto de Veer, quondam Duci Hiberniæ, qui illuc fugerat cum eodem.

Death of Michael de la Pole, Earl of Suffolk.

The Duke of Ireland succeeds to his property.

Papa constituit Jubilæum.

Dominus Papa, per id temporis considerans vires hominum, et ætates, imminutas, constituit Jubilæum fieri, qui inciperet a Natali sequente; et in æternum postea semper, revolutis tri-

The Pope appoints a Jubilee, to be held

---

[1] *discutiendam* in Parker's text; *discutiendum* in Camden's text; *discutienda* in Bibl. Reg. 13 E. ix.

[2] *illi* in the printed texts.

A.D. 1389. every three-and-thirty years. ginta tribus annis, cunctis Christianis volveretur, [1] indicans videlicet annos ætatis plenitudinis [2] [Christi] mysticos et idoneos ad renovandum Jubilæum. MS. Bibl. Reg. 13 E. ix.

Miraculum apud Sanctum Albanum.

A Miracle at St. Alban's. Eo tempore mulier quædam, "Agnes" nomine, de Londoniis, quam tristitia amentem effecerat, ita ut pene nulli, qui solebat frequentare Londonias, incognita foret ejus dementia, præ famositate sui clamoris et operum, admonita erat per visum Sanctum adire Albanum, Anglorum Protomartyrem, apud eum consecutura sanitatem et sensum. Quæ, mox ut paruit visioni, perfecte pristinæ est restituta saluti.

Lolardi Lolardos creant.

The Lollard priests claim the power of ordination. Lollardi, sequaces Johannis Wiclef, per idem tempus in errorem suum plurimos seduxerunt, et tantam præsumpserunt audaciam, ut eorum presbyteri, more pontificum, novos crearent presbyteros, asserentes, ut frequenter supra retulimus, quemlibet sacerdotem tantam consecutum potestatem ligandi atque solvendi, et cætera ecclesiastica ministrandi, quantam ipse Papa dat, vel dare potest: [3] practizaverunt autem istam perfidiam in Diœcesi Sarum. Et qui taliter ordinati sunt ab hæreticis, sibi cuncta licere putantes, Missas celebrare, divina tractare, et Sacramenta conferre, minime timuerunt. Prodita est hæc nequitia per quemdam ab eis ordinatum, qui, stimulatus conscientia, Episcopo Sarum confessus est errorem, apud manerium suum de Sunnyng.

Information of this given to the Bishop of Salisbury.

Pilgrimages are decried by the Lollards. Eodem tempore, dicti hæretici prædicaverunt peregrinationes non debere fieri, et præcipue apud Walsingham, et Crucem de *North Dore* apud Ecclesiam Sancti Pauli Londoniis; ubi nihil erat numinis, sed tantum putridæ stipites, scaturientes vermibus; per quas imperitum vulgus seductum idolatrare manifestissime cogebatur. Audierunt et viderunt, atque sciverunt, hæc universa Pontifices, sed abierunt, alius in villam suam, alius vero in negotiationem suam; dimiserunt oves expositas luporum rictibus, sed nullus erexit baculum ad abigendum. Jam plena erat omnis turba, non solum lupis, sed ipsis rapacibus, quorum morsus inevitabiliter virulenti atque letales;

Neglect by the Bishops of their proceedings.

---

[1] Or perhaps, *judicans*.

[2] Omitted in orig.: supplied from Bibl. Reg. 13 E. ix. and the printed texts.

[3] *exercuerunt* in the printed texts.

MS. Bibl. Reg. 13 E. ix.

sed nullus oblatrator, qui saltem voce terreret fures, præter Antistitem Northwycensem, sit nomen ejus benedictum in sæcula; quia non permisit plebem suam infici tanta labe. Juravit nempe, et non pœnitebit illum, quod si quisquam de secta [1] perversa prædicare præsumeret in Diœcesi sua, vel ignibus traderetur vel capite privaretur. Nullusque fuit de tanta sequela, qui, hiis cognitis, vellet ad martyrium properare; propter quod, in Episcopatu suo hactenus fides et religio inviolata permansit.

A.D. 1389. The Bishop of Norwich only excepted; who threatens them with death.

Miracula apud Wymundham.

Sub eodem tempore, (Divinitate procurante, ut putamus, ad confirmandum pie credentes, et confutandum hæreticos,) juxta Prioratum de Wymundham nova succrevere miracula, apud quandam crucem erectam in via publica; quæ merito et miracula dici possent, et credi.

Miracles at Wymundham.

Miracula de Brydlington.

Eo tempore, in Prioratu Canonicorum de Brydlingtone, qui est in Diœcesi Eboracensi, ad tumbam Johannis, quondam Prioris ibidem, tanta, namque manifestata, fiebant miracula, ut pene totam Angliam ducerent in stuporem; de quo ferunt, quod in vita sua super aquas ambulaverit, mortuum suscitaverit, et in horreis domus suæ tam [2] manifesta quam mirabilia per orationes frugum fecerit, ut quæ vix per mensem familiæ putabantur suffecturæ, prece sua sufficerent toto anno; prærogativa sanctitatis ejus, humilitas et misericordia super afflictos.

Miracles at Bridlington.

Marvellous powers attributed to John of Bridlington, in his lifetime.

Visitatio Archiepiscopi Cantuariensis.

Per id temporis, Archiepiscopus Cantuariensis, Magister Willelmus de Courtenay, suam Provinciam visitavit; qui, cum venisset [3] Oxonias, nisus est Nigrorum Monachorum habitationem visitare, misso prius mandato, quod omnes interessent die visitationi statuto. Sed dictum mandatum non fuit præ-

Claim of the Archbishop of Canterbury to visit the house, at

---

[1] This word is repeated in orig.

[2] *manifestata* in the printed texts.

[3] *Exonias* in the printed texts.

A.D. 1389. Oxford, of the Black Monks (Benedictines). Plan devised for defeating such claim.

MS. Bibl. Reg. 13 E. ix.

sentatum Priori [1]monachorum ibidem, ipso existente tunc Glastoniæ. Turbantur ergo scholares, de tam non exemptis Monasteriis quam exemptis, eo maxime quod nunquam viderant vel audierant simile mandatum visitationis.

Abbas ergo Westmonasterii, qui artius ista cepit cordi, deliberavit cum suo consilio, ut Abbas Sancti Albani, qui ab omnibus venerabatur, et colebatur præ cæteris Abbatibus Nigri Ordinis, destinaret litteram Magistro Symoni de Southerey, commonacho suo, Priori Nigrorum Monachorum ibidem, præceptoriam, in virtute obedientiæ, ut, omnibus postpositis, eo celerius quo posset, se transferret ad Monasterium suum, ad habendum colloquium cum Abbate suo, pro certis causis Monasterium concernentibus. Et quod ista littera præsentaretur coram testibus Magistro Symoni supradicto, pridie ante diem visitationis præfixæ, hora Vesperarum; et super istius litteræ præsentatione ac receptione fieret publicum instrumentum; et quod dictus Magister Symon, statim post receptionem litteræ sui Abbatis, constitueret procuratorem ad allegandum causam suæ absentiæ coram Archiepiscopo, vel ejus [2][Commissariis. Quo facto, discederet prædictus Magister Simon ad suum Monasterium; et adveniente die visitationis, Archiepiscopo vel ejus] Commissario sedente pro judicio, prædicto [3]Magistro Symone [4]præconizato et non comparente, procurator ipsius, non ut procurator, sed ut amicus duntaxat ejusdem, diceret quod prædictus Magister Symon mandatum Archiepiscopi non recepit, nec sibi fuit præsentatum. Qua quidem excusatione acceptata [5]et reputata pro vero, effectus dicti mandati totaliter expiraret. Et si tunc Archiepiscopus, vel ejus Commissarius, inquireret a cursore suo, in juramento sibi [6]præstito, si mandatum Archiepiscopi præsentavit præfato Symoni, et ille responderet quod sic, tunc oporteret probare contrarium per obliquum; et tunc si dicatur quod mandatum Archiepiscopi fuit sufficienter ostensum et promulgatum, tunc idem procurator, non ut procurator adhuc, sed ut amicus, allegabit, quod prædictus Magister Symon non potuit comparere dicto die statuto, propter præceptum sui Abbatis, in littera sua contentum; et si forte tunc Archi-

---

[1] From this word, down to *quam exemptis*, the context in the original is supplied in another, and apparently later, hand.

[2] Omitted in orig.; supplied from Bibl. Reg. 13 E. ix.; omitted in the printed texts.

[3] *Magistro* omitted in the printed texts.

[4] *per præconem citato, et* in the printed texts.

[5] *est* in orig.; corrected from the printed texts.

[6] *præfato* in the printed texts.

MS. Bibl. Reg. 13 E. ix.

A.D. 1389.

episcopus, vel ejus Commissarius, peteret quare responderet pro dicto Simone in judicio, imponendo sibi silentium, tunc primo diceret quod esset procurator ejus; et si oporteret, [1]demonstraret procuratorium; quo demonstrato, exhiberet litteram Domini Abbatis de Sancto Albano, per quam clareret quod dictus Magister Symon die statuto non potuit comparere coram Archiepiscopo, vel ejus Commissario. Et ita foret practica, sive Magister Symon mandatum Archiepiscopi recepisset, sive non, sive virtute illius mandati aliquos citasset, sive non: hoc tamen proviso, quod nullo modo litteras certificatorias exhiberet de mandato.

Provisum est etiam per eundem Dominum Abbatem Westmonasterii, et suum consilium, ut unus monachus studens Oxoniis provocaret pro se, et omnibus aliis sibi adhærere volentibus, pridie ante diem visitationis. Et ratio est, quia oporteret quod omnes sibi adhærere volentes, adhærerent infra decem dies, et quia bonum erat, ut eo minime [2]quo potuisset tempus curreret, ideo pridie ante diem visitationis provocaret pro se et aliis sibi adhærere volentibus: et hæc practica pro primo die, ad evacuandum mandatum; et si contingat quod Archiepiscopus novum mandatum dirigeret Priori studentium vel monacho singulari, provisum erat, ut mitteretur forma mandati festinanter ad Dominum Abbatem Westmonasterii, ad videndum quid deberet fieri quoad illud. Ista tamen nullius fuere valoris, quia non isto modo ad evacuandum visitationem processum est. Sed modo qui sequitur, Dominus Archiepiscopus ab executione visitationis sponte recessit.

This plan however is not put into execution.

Abbas Sancti Albani scripsit Domino Archiepiscopo, rogans et consulens ut a visitatione studentium desistere dignaretur, commemorans multa quæ tam sibi quam dictis scholaribus forent dispendio, si propositum suum exequendum putaret. Cujus litteras Dominus Archiepiscopus hilari vultu, lætoque corde, suscepit, et monachum Sancti Albani, litterarum bajulum, ad prandium humanissime invitavit. Et post prandium, ad se vocato monacho, asseruit quod pro Domino Abbate Sancti Albani, amico suo speciali, quicquid posset, salvo jure ecclesiæ suæ, libentissime faceret; veruntamen a visitatione Prioris et Nigrorum Monachorum Oxoniæ studentium dicebat se, salvo jure ecclesiæ suæ, nullo modo posse desistere, etiamsi Rex Angliæ pro prædictis instaret; et addidit,—"Ibi," inquit, "est

[1] *demonstrare* in orig. and the printed texts; corrected from Bibl. Reg. 13 E. ix.

[2] *infra id tempus* in the printed texts.

A.D. 1389. "Collegium; nunquid," ait, "non habetis Priorem, qui potest "tenere Capitulum? Et vivitis in communi?" MS. Bibl. Reg. 13 E. ix.

Ad hæc monachus Sancti Albani respondit, quod non fuit ibi Collegium, cum ibi morantes sigillum commune non habeant, nec locus sit [1]dotatus temporalibus et spiritualibus; et alia plura desint, quæ ad Collegium requiruntur. Cui Archiepiscopus,—"Volumus," inquit, "venire, et videre, et inquirere, "qualiter stat vobiscum." Ad hæc monachus,—"Domine," ait, "si veneritis ad illum locum, non habetis jurisdictionem "inquirendi de talibus, nisi in non exemptis, et ipsi sunt "visitati in propriis monasteriis per vos, ergo secunda vice "non sunt vistandi." Cui Archiepiscopus,—"Certum est," inquit, "quod in propriis monasteriis per me non fuerunt visi- "tati; immo, Abbates illorum excusaverunt eos, pro eo quod "fuerunt in scholis; quare in scholis eos intendimus visi- "tare."

Tunc quidam Doctor legisperitus, monachus Cantuariæ, qui cum Archiepiscopo venerat, volens ampliare jurisdictionem ejus, ait:—"Etiam Domine," ait, "potestis visitare exemptos, "quamdiu in scholis steterint, cum sunt ibi sub jurisdictione "Cancellarii, etc." Respondit Albanensis, quod exempti ibi ita sunt privilegiati, quod ubicunque fuerint, non sunt sub jurisdictione alicujus Episcopi, nisi Romani Pontificis, vel Legati a latere missi. Ad hæc Archiepiscopus benigne respondit, quod si ita foret, nec potuit, nec voluit, eos in aliquo molestare.

Die Sancti Bricii, Magister Simon de Sowthreye, monachus Sancti Albani, qui, dum hæc ageretur, absens fuerat, comparuit coram Archiepiscopo, supplicans ut a visitatione præmissa desisteret; sed Archiepiscopus noluit aliquo modo illud sibi concedere illa vice. Dominica vero sequente, præsentavit se dictus Simon, cum omnibus monachis, exemptis et non exemptis, post occasum solis, coram Archiepiscopo in ecclesia Sanctæ Fredeswidæ. Quos videns Dominus Archiepiscopus, petiit an ad submittendum semetipsos advenissent; cui responsum fuit, quod [2]non, [quod] ad captandum ejus benevolentiam advenerunt. Respondit benigne Dominus Archiepiscopus,—"Et ego vos habeo excusatos; nec unquam intendo "vos gravare:"—et hic finis negotii supratacti.[3]

The Archbishop ultimately abandons his design.

[1] *donatus* in Camden's text.

[2] *non quod* omitted in the printed texts; *quod* omitted in orig.: corrected from Bibl. Reg. 13 E. ix.

[3] A passage in Bibl. Reg. E. ix. is omitted here.

Obiit Urbanus Papa Sextus.

MS. Bibl. Reg. 13 E. ix.

Eodem anno, mense Octobris, Papa Urbanus Sextus diem clausit extremum; vir, cujus capitositas multis fuit exitio, et sibimet, ut ferunt, damno; arte tamen vivere dicebatur, ita ut mores [1] Carthusiensium, et consuetudines, quantum res patiebatur, imitaretur. Rigidus erat sibi, sed suis multo rigidior; ita ut delinquentibus nunquam ignosceret, aut eorum ærumnis aliquatenus compateretur. Probat hoc pœna suorum Cardinalium, ferociter inflicta, et æterna damnatio carceris subsecuta. A.D. 1389. Death of Pope Urban VI.

Cujus loco electus est a Cardinalibus Cardinalis dictus "Neapolitanus," qui "Bonefacius Nonus" est vocatus. Election of Pope Boniface IX.

Dux Lancastriæ rediit in Angliam.

Circa principium mensis Novembris, Dominus Johannes, Dux Lancastriæ, de partibus Wasconiæ in Angliam transfretavit, postquam in Hispannia et Acquitannia, sive Wasconia, moram fecisset triennalem; qui in Hispannia infortunia passus primo, postremo ad summam felicitatem perductus est, non viribus hominum, nec in numero bellatorum, sed manifesto divino favore. The Duke of Lancaster returns to England.

Enimvero cum primo pervenisset ad partes Hispanniæ, cum manu satis valida, deficientibus victualibus, cœpit plebs Anglicana, primo fame, postea dysenteria, interire, ita ut nonaginta milites famosi de exercitu miserabiliter morerentur. Quapropter residui, urgente necessitate, Ducem in campo deserentes, [2] transierunt ad exercitum Gallicorum, qui ibi aderat in adjutorium Regis Castellæ; obtento prius conductu ab exercitu memorato. Qui, eorum condolentes miseriis, humanissime eos tractaverunt, et de suis victualibus refecerunt. Nempe mos est utrique genti, Angliæ, scilicet, atque Galliæ, licet sibimet in propriis sint infesti regionibus, in remotis partibus tanquam fratres sibimet subvenire, et fidem ad invicem inviolabilem observare. Rex vero Portyngaliæ, qui tunc cum quatuor millibus bellatorum affuit, videns Anglos sic recessisse, allocutus est Ducem, dicens,—"Ecce!" ait, "Anglici vestri, qualiter te deserentes ad hostes recedunt; "qui, cum refocillati [3] fuerint, tibi et mihi infestissimi, ut Early misfortunes of the Duke in his Spanish campaign.

---

[1] *Cartusienciencium* in orig. and Bibl. Reg. 13 E. ix.

[2] *transirent* in orig.; corrected from the printed texts: the word is imperfectly written in Bibl. Reg. 13 E. ix.

[3] *fuerunt* in the printed texts.

A.D. 1389. "reor, erunt; vadam ergo, et manus conseram, et nullum ex "eis in vita relinquam." Cui Dux,—"Nequaquam, Domine "Rex, fiet ita; scio quod sola victus necessitate, et non ex "perfidia, hoc fecerunt." Et mox Dux, inclinans caput, ut erat [1] eques, amarissime flevit super equum, tacite fundens preces Omnipotenti Deo, commemorans in corde suo quod antea, in felicitate et rerum opulentia, nec Deum, ut debuit, cognovisset, nec, ut decuit, coluisset. Tacitus ergo, subortis suspiriis, implorat pro gratia, precatur pro misericordia, spondens in posterum correctionis vitæ practicam, et apud cordis oculos futuram jugem Dei sui notitiam; cujus videns lacrymas, Qui Mariæ peccatricis quondam suscepit suspiria, dedit ex insperato a die illo, et deinceps, sibi cuncta prospera, cuncta læta.

MS. Bibl. Reg. 13 E. ix.

Contrition of the Duke for his past life.

Terms as to the succession, entered into between the king of Castille and the Duke of Lancaster.

Nam adversarius suus, Rex Castellæ, non viribus humanis territus, nullius nisi Dei solius timore compulsus, quippe qui, inter suos securus habitans, et vidit et scivit nostratum miserias, tractare cœpit cum Duce [2] de forma pacis habendæ inter illos. Et ventum est ad istud, ut acciperet Rex Castellæ filio suo Ducis filiam in uxorem; quorum posteritas Hispanniæ regno gauderet. Et si nulli liberi provenirent inter illos, hæreditas volveretur ad filium Ducis Eboraci, qui frater erat Ducis Lancastriæ, et desponsaverat filiam Regis Castellæ, quondam Petronis, juniorem; et si contingeret eum discedere sine prole legitima, [3] jus regni revolveretur ad [4] sobolem inter Ducem Lancastriæ et Constantiam, filiam Petronis antedicti, procreatam. Quibus pactis firmatis, Dux accepit a Rege Castillæ [5] librarum pro tunc, et pro securitate solvendi residuum obsides nobilium filii dati sunt ei. In posterum vero, omni anno dum idem Dux viveret, pactus est Rex Castillæ sibi solvere decem millia librarum, et ejus uxori, Dominæ Constantiæ [6] ; pro qua pecunia solvenda fideliter, quatuor bonæ villæ assignatæ sunt Dominæ Constantiæ supradictæ.

Consilium apud Redinge.

A Council held at Reading.

Eo tempore apud Redyngum Rex Angliæ proceres ad Consilium convocavit; ad quod Dux Lancastriæ eo celerius properavit, quo percepit Regem non rectis oculis quosdam de

[1] *æquus* in the printed texts: *eques* in Bibl. Reg. 13 E. ix.

[2] *et* in orig.: corrected from the printed texts.

[3] *vis* in the printed texts.

[4] *sabolem* in orig.

[5] *pecuniam multam nimis pro tunc,* in the printed texts.

[6] *tantum, pro* in the printed texts.

MS. Bibl. Reg. 13 E. ix.

proceribus velle respicere, et metuit orituras eo tempore simultates, quas omnino sedare disposuit in adventu suo. Neque frustra quidem laboravit, sed id effecit, ut et pacem cordi Regis, pacemque magnatum pectoribus, infunderet gratiose; sicque dictum Consilium dissolutum fuit, et universi cum pace ad propria discesserunt.[1]

A.D. 1389. Efficacious intervention of the Duke of Lancaster.

Transit annus iste mediocriter [2]frugifer, sed satis abundanter fructifer; luctuosus Northumbrensibus, propter mala per Scotos illis illata; modeste lætus cæteris regni partibus, propter miracula renovata; regnis Angliæ et Franciæ satis commodus, pro treuga firmata; sed multis multum formidabilis, pro pestilentia provinciis diversis immissa.

Comes Pembrochiæ, ad hastiludium percussus, obiit.

A.D. 1390.

Anno gratiæ millesimo trecentesimo nonagesimo, qui est annus regni Regis Ricardi, a Conquæstu Secundi, tertiusdecimus, tenuit idem Rex Natale, cum Anna Regina, apud manerium suum de Wodestoke. Dux vero Lancastriæ fuit ad Natale in castello de Herthforde.

Death of John, Earl of Pembroke, at a tournament.

Sub eisdem diebus, Comes Penbrochiæ, dum ludum hastilium attentare cupit, percussus est in inguine a milite sibi occurrente, dicto "Johanne de Sancto Johanne;" quo videlicet ictu ejus viscera sunt dirupta, et mors est illico subsecuta. Cujus interitus luctum indicibilem, non tantum magnatibus, sed et cunctis communibus, generavit. Fuerat nempe liberalis, affabilis cunctis, humilis, et benignus, super omnes novellos dominos ejus ætatis qui fuerunt in regno. De cujus antecessoribus illud mirabile contigit, quod ab Eymero de Valence, Comite Penbrochiæ, qui fuit unus de assessoribus et judicibus super mortem Thomæ de Lancastria, usque ad istum Johannem de Hastyng, nullus unquam Comes Penbrochiæ patrem suum vidit, sed nec pater filii visione lætatus est.

Remarkable fatality as to the Earls of Pembroke.

Hoc quoque anno, Sanctus Thomas de Lancastria canonizatus est.

Thomas of Lancaster canonized.

Parliamentum Londini.

Die Lunæ proxima post festum Sancti Hillarii, factum est Parliamentum Londoniis; in quo constanter a communibus est petitum, ut signa Dominorum, quæ gestabant, et eorum famuli, deponerentur; eo quod jam tales per provincias qui

Parliament at London.

---

[1] A passage in Bibl. Reg. 13 E. ix is omitted here.

[2] *frugiter* in orig. and Bibl. Reg. 13 E. ix.: *frugifer* in the printed texts.

A.D. 1390. adepti fuerant signa talia, effecti fuere tyranni, malefactores, et malefactorum sustentatores: sed post multas altercationes, quia proceres noluerunt eorum signa deponere, saltem ad id consenserunt, ut nulli gestarent eorum signa, nisi qui forent de privata familia, et perciperent de magnatum marsupio certum aliquod annuatim.

MS. Bibl. Reg. 13 E. ix.

Regulations as to cognizances of peers.

Kentish insurgents executed.

In eodem Parliamento quidam novi insurrectores de Cancia, capti, tracti sunt et suspensi.

Statute of the said Parliament against Provisors.

Statutum est in eodem insuper Parliamento, ut de cætero nullus transfretaret ad obtinendum provisiones in ecclesiis, vel [1] ecclesia; et si quis contrarium faceret, si posset apprehendi, caperetur, ut Regi rebellis, et incarceraretur. Statutum est præterea, ut nullus occultus jugulator,—quales [2] "*mor-drerers*" appellant Anglici,—de cætero chartam de regia gratia obtineret; et si ullus Dux præsumeret pro hujusmodi preces facere, condemnabilis esset Regi in centum libris, si Comes, in centum marcis, si Archiepiscopus, in centum libris, si Episcopus, in centum marcis.

Grant on wool, made to the King.

Concessum est autem Regi in hoc Parliamento, ut habeat de quolibet sacco lanæ quadraginta solidos; de quibus quadraginta solidis, decem applicarentur in præsenti Regis usibus, et triginta servarentur in futurum in manibus thesaurariorum constituendorum per Parliamentum, non expendendi nisi cum [3] werræ necessitas instare videretur. Similiter Rex habebit de libra sex denarios, quatuor servandos ad usum præfatum per dictos thesaurarios, et duos jam percipiendos et expendendos ad voluntatem Regis.

Additional grant of sixpence in the pound.

Hoc anno Dominus Laurentius, quondam monachus de Bello, et expost Domini Papæ Pœnitentiarius, postremo Episcopus Assavensis, concessit in fata; cujus loco electus est [4] , qui mox virtute Statuti [5] Parliamentalis, postulavit ab Archiepiscopo Cantuariensi [6] consecrari.

Novus Dux Aquitaniæ.

John, Duke of Lancaster, created Duke of Acquitaine.

Eodem anno, in Parliamento præscripto, Dominus Johannes, Dux Lancastriæ, factus est Dux Aquitanniæ, per virgam et pileum, præbitis manu Regis.

---

[1] *ecclesiam* in the printed texts.

[2] *murderers* in the printed texts; *mordreres* in Bibl. Reg. 13 E. ix.

[3] *belli* in the printed texts.

[4] *alter* instead of the hiatus (as in orig. and Bibl. Reg. 13 E. ix.) in the printed texts. "*Alexander Bache*" was the Bishop's name, and his predecessor, Laurence Child, died in 1389.

[5] *Parliamentali* in the printed texts.

[6] *consecreri* in orig., by inadvertence.

MS. Bibl. Reg. 13 E. ix.

Eo tempore, filius et hæres Ducis Eboraci creatur Comes de Ruthland. A.D. 1390.

Quinto die Martii, ventus magnus, terribilis, atque nocivus, tecta [1]dilacerans, domos subvertens, animalia conterens, arbores prosternens, spiravit in Anglia, incommodo generali.[2]

A violent wind in England.

Hoc anno [3]magna pestis invaluit in hac terra, juvenum præcipue, et puerorum; qui passim moriebantur per civitates et villas, numero incredibili et excessivo. Quam epidemiam mox secuta est frugum [4]karistia, ita ut modius frumenti in quibusdam locis viginti tribus denariis venderetur.

A great mortality among young people. Dearth of corn.

Eodem tempore Dominus Adam, Cardinalis Anglicus, qui dedecorose depositus et privatus fuerat per Urbanum Papam, suo gradui per Bonefacium restituitur cum honore. Ferunt siquidem, quod cum Urbanus tyrannizare disponeret, hunc maxime, propter profunditatem sensus et scientiæ, plus cunctis metuerit; et ideo, ne per eum ejus conatus impedirentur, eum satis injuste comprehendit et extorsit, et [5]impure reclusit. Quod factum in morte sua satis [6]indoluit, publice pœnitendo, et protestando hunc reum nullius criminis extitisse.

Adam, the English Cardinal, is restored to his rank by Pope Boniface.

Declaratio Indulgentiæ.

Hujus adeo petitione, declaratum est per Papam Bonefacium, quod Bullæ de indulgentiis plenariis, concessæ quibuslibet in extremis, tantum valent eas obtinentibus in confessione quæ mortem immediate præcedit; qui licet multotiens propter [7]diversa pericula confiteantur et convaluerunt, usquo ad extremum articulum, nullum sortiuntur effectum.

Declaration of Pope Boniface as to Bulls of Plenary Indulgence

Gesta Henrici, Comitis de Derby.

Dominus Henricus, Comes de Derby, per idem tempus profectus est in Le Pruys; ubi, cum adjutorio Marescalli dictæ patriæ, et cujusdam Regis vocati "[8]Wytot," devicit

Exploits of Henry, Earl of Derby, in Lithuania.

---

[1] *delacerans* in orig.

[2] A passage in Bibl. Reg. 13 E. ix. is omitted here.

[3] The word *magno* is inserted here in orig. and in Bibl. Reg. 13 E. ix., by inadvertence.

[4] *caritas* in the printed texts.

[5] *in carcere* in the printed texts: *impure* in Bibl. Reg. 13 E. ix.

[6] *inde doluit* in orig. and the printed texts: corrected from Bibl. Reg. 13 E. ix.

[7] *divisa* in the printed texts.

[8] Meaning "*Witold*."

A.D. 1390. exercitum Regis de Lettowe, captis quatuor Ducibus, et tribus peremptis, et amplius quam trecentis de valentioribus exercitus supradicti pariter interemptis. Civitas quoque, [1] vocata "Wille," in cujus castellum Rex de Letowe, nomine "Skirgalle," confugerat, potenti virtute dicti Comitis maxime, atque suorum, capta est. Namque qui fuerunt de familia sua primi murum ascenderunt, et vexillum ejus super muros, cæteris vel torpentibus vel ignorantibus, posuerunt: captaque sunt ibi, vel occisa, quatuor millia plebanorum, fratre Regis de Poleyn, inter cæteros, ibi perempto, qui adversarius [2] noster fuit. Obsessumque fuit castrum dictæ civitatis per quinque hebdomadas; sed propter infirmitates quibus vexabatur exercitus, Magistri de Le Pruys et de Lifland noluerunt diutius expectare. Facti sunt Christiani de gente de Lettow octo, et Magister de Lifland duxit secum in suam patriam tria millia [3] prisonum.

MS. Bibl. Reg. 13 E. ix.

Transit annus iste, vernales opes reddens fraudulenter, quia nec copiam fructuum protulit, neque frugum; quamobrem sequens annus multo difficilior existebat. Odibilis erat hic annus non solum Romanis, Romanæque Curiæ, sed Anglicis infinitis, qui Curiam, propter provisiones et beneficia, sequebantur: suspectus prælatis et religiosis, quia metuebant censuras vel Interdictum regni futurum, propter Statutum præmissum factum contra Romanam Ecclesiam, quanquam ipsi prælati Parliamentum tunc exiverunt, et protestati fuerint se nihil commune sentire cum illis in hac parte, qui Statutum illud proponere voluerunt.

Adventus nuncii Regis Franciæ.

A.D. 1391. Anno gratiæ millesimo trecentesimo nonagesimo primo, qui est annus regni Regis Ricardi, a Conquæstu Secundi, quartusdecimus, fuit Rex ad Natale cum Anna Regina.

Propositions for peace made by the King of France.

Camberlanus Regis Franciæ, missus a Rege suo Francorumque proceribus, venit in Angliam, proferens pacem desiderabilem et diutissime concupitam. Post cujus recessum, missi sunt in Franciam de nostris quidam, ut rei veritatem certius explorarent. Qui, a Rege Franciæ cum honore suscepti, cum magnis muneribus sunt dimissi. Asserebant siquidem Gallici, se peroptime nosse fore insufficientes ad regnum Angliæ

---

[1] *vocatur* in the printed texts.
[2] *nostri* in the printed texts.
[3] *captivorum* in the printed texts.

MS. Bibl. Reg. 13 E. ix.

[1] conquirendum, et Anglicos nullatenus fore tam fortes ut Franciam subjugarent, et in talibus inutilibus expeditionibus utrumque regnum fore multipliciter [2] apporiatum. Quapropter dicunt se velle omnino dimittere, nec ulterius attentare quod constat eos nullatenus posse perducere ad effectum; et, altercationibus variis et damnosis postpositis, velle modis omnibus pacem quærere, pacem petere, pacem tenere, nisi per Anglicos [3] steterit quominus tantis commodis perfruantur; ut ergo pax stabilior, conditio firmior, tractatus [4] honorosior, habeatur, Rex Franciæ, tam per suos quam per nostros, petiit a Rege nostro colloquium personale, quod juxta Calesiam fieri postulavit.

A.D. 1391.

A conference near Calais requested.

Rex autem Angliæ, licet multis suspectus foret omnis tractatus Francorum, illuc proficisci decrevit. Et quia sublimis et honorabilis ibi apparere debuit, misit per singulas regni Abbathias pro equis nobilibus, quales Regem decuit insidere. Misit insuper ad eadem loca, ne minus [5] videretur equos dedisse Regi suo, pro magnis summis pecuniæ sibi mutuo concedendis, ne pacis negotium per religiosos impediri videretur, [6] [si] sibi quod Rex ab illis petiit negaretur. Ut autem de aliis taceam, de Monasterio Sancti Albani equum habuit, pretii viginti quatuor marcarum, et nihilominus ab Abbate petiit mutuo quingentas marcas. Quam summam quia pro tunc impossibile fuerat persolvisse, Dux Lancastriæ Johannes, caritatis intuitu, promisit thesaurariis se Regi velle satisfacere pro eisdem; ita duntaxat, ut Abbatem Sancti Albani quietum redderent in hac parte. Dederat nempe Regi mutuo quinque millia librarum parum ante, et ideo factus est audacior in nostra intercessione. Nec minus pepercit Rex civitatibus regni, sive burgis, qui a singulis peteret in hoc negotium singulas summas, et acciperet, quamvis plurimi murmurarent.[7]

The King of England demands horses and money of the Abbeys.

A demand made of the Abbey of Saint Alban's satisfied by intervention of the Duke of Lancaster.

Revocatio Anglicorum a Curia Romana.

Sub eisdem diebus, de consensu Regis, Regisque Consilii, proclamatio facta fuit Londoniis, ut omnes beneficiati existentes in Romana Curia, redirent in Angliam, citra festum Sancti

The English are recalled from the Roman Court.

---

[1] *devincendum* in the printed texts.

[2] *onerandum* in the printed texts.

[3] *steterat* in the printed texts.

[4] *honoratior* in the printed texts.

[5] *viderentur* in the printed texts.

[6] *si* omitted in orig.: supplied from Bibl. Reg. 13 E. ix. and the printed texts.

[7] A passage in Bibl. Reg. 13 E. ix. is omitted here.

A.D. 1391. Nicholai, sub pœna perditionis omnium beneficiorum suorum: et nondum beneficiati redirent per idem tempus, sub pœna forisfacturæ. Anglici, audito tanto tonitruo in remotis, metuentes ictum, deserta Curia, fugiunt ad natale solum. Papa vero, tanto sonitu [1]conturbatus, mittit nuncium sub celeritate, quendam Abbatem, videlicet, qui causas exploret harum rerum omnium, simul et Statuti Parliamentalis, nuper editi de Provisoribus, contra consuetudinem Ecclesiæ Romanæ.

MS. Bibl. Reg. 13 E. ix.

The Pope sends a Nuncio to England.

Expostulations on behalf of the Pope, against certain Statutes.

Adveniens dictus Abbas salutavit Regem ex parte Papæ, commendans Regis devotionem, et suorum prædecessorum, erga Ecclesiam, eo quod semper veris Summis Pontificibus adhæserunt. Deinde subintulit, quod Papa, percepto per litteras Regis quod Statuta sic edita fuerant, mirabatur, et, ut bonus pastor, salutem animarum desiderans, sæpius admonuerat et [2]excitatus fuerat statutarios, ut hujusmodi Statuta de medio tollerent, in quantum lædebant ecclesiasticam libertatem. Dixit etiam, quod Papa non intendit minuere coronam Regis, nec tollere, quin Statuta condere valeat, non facientia contra ecclesiasticam libertatem; quinimmo paratus est conservare, pro posse, Regis honorem, prout ad hoc se cognoscit multipliciter obligatum. Dixit etiam dictus nuncius, quod Papa, diutius expectans, non sensit obtemperatum fuisse suis monitis, et tamen, nihil innovando, nec processus aliquos faciendo, expressit quæ jura statuunt contra statuentes contra ecclesiasticam libertatem; et propulsatus a pluribus pronunciavit illa irrita fore, in quantum faciunt contra ecclesiasticam libertatem. Et quia Papa, si non sensit statuentium animas immutari, cum magna mentis amaritudine intelligens hæc in denigrationem famæ regiæ redundare, misit prædictum nuncium; per quem exhortatur, rogat, et requirit, quod Rex Statuta illa tolli, et de Capitularibus faciat aboleri maxime Statuta, "Quare impedit," et "Præmunire [3]facias," et hiis similia. Et Papa offert, quod si [4]statutarii velint conqueri de aliquo, si mittant ad Papam [5]ambassiatores, erit promptus, quantum cum Deo poterit, Regi et regno complacere. Et si statuentes non tollant etc., salvo honore Ecclesiæ et animarum salute, non potest illa dissimulare.

---

[1] *conturbato* in orig. and the printed texts: corrected from Bibl. Reg. 13 E. ix., the contraction in which somewhat resembles *conturbato*.

[2] *exitatus* in orig. and Bibl. Reg. 13 E. ix.: *obtestatus* in the printed texts.

[3] *facies* in orig. and the printed texts; abbreviated in Bibl. Reg. 13 E. ix.

[4] *statuarii* in orig.; corrected from the printed texts.

[5] *legatos* in the printed texts.

MS. Bibl. Reg. 13 E. ix.

A.D. 1391.

Alleged compact between the King of France and the Anti-Pope.

Item, Dominus Papa significat Regi, per prædictum nuncium, qualiter Rex Franciæ et Antipapa pacta inierunt hinc inde; videlicet, quod idem Rex, per fortitudinem Ducum [1] [Burgundiæ et Turoniæ, poni faciat Antipapam in Sedem Petri, et Antipapa promisit Regem Imperio coronare, et Duci] Burgundiæ magnalia, et investiet Ducem Turoniæ de omnibus terris Ecclesiæ in partibus Italiæ, et quendam alium promisit coronare Regem Tusciæ et Lumbardiæ, et Ducem [2] Andexaciæ firmare in regno Siciliæ. Quare Papa exhortatur et rogat, quod Rex ad defensionem fidei et Sanctæ Matris Ecclesiæ se exponat. Item, Papa exponit pericula, [3] si Antipapa et Rex Franciæ prævalerent; [4] quantum Papæ Gallici jura regni Angliæ conati sunt deprimere. Et si Gallici usurparent Imperium, consequenter totum mundum, et sic finaliter Angliam, usurparent. Ideo Papa consulit, quod Rex Angliæ videat et provideat de remedio opportuno. Item Papa significat, quod Gallici [5] tractant cum Anglicis, ut, concordia inita, possent liberius usurpare præmissa, et ut subtiliter, fractis tandem conventionibus, possint Angliam finaliter usurpare; quare Papa suadet, quod cum sint schismatici, ex nulla alia causa communicatio sit cum eis, nisi pro reducendo eos ad fidem et obedientiam debitam. Item, in casu quo tractatur de pace cum Gallicis, Papa hortatur et rogat, quod nulla fiat consensio, nisi pactio roboretur, pœnis vallata, quod Rex Franciæ non mittet gentes in Italiam, nec [6] permittet suos subjectos [7] illuc ire occasione præmissa, et de factis Romanæ Ecclesiæ, et Romani Imperii, vel Italiæ, nullatenus intromittet; et quod non favebit Antipapæ in partibus Italiæ, sub pœnis appositis, alias pax intelligatur esse fracta. Item, Papa desiderat quod Rex Angliæ mittat [8] ambassiatores ad Imperatorem, ut, pro honore Ecclesiæ et imperialis dignitatis, concurrat cum Rege Angliæ in præmissis. Item, quia dicitur quod gentes paratæ [9] [sint] ad invadendum, ut supra, Papa exhortatur et rogat, ut ad defensionem ipsius Rex Angliæ præstet subsidium, cum aliis subvenire volentibus, ad resistentiam Gallicorum.

Other representations made to the King of England, on behalf of the Pope.

---

[1] Omitted in orig. and the printed texts; where it runs,—" *per fortitudinem Ducem Burgundiæ expellet, et investiet, etc.*"

[2] So in all the texts. Evidently for *Andegaviæ*.

[3] *de* in orig.: corrected from the printed texts.

[4] *quantumque* in the printed texts.

[5] *tractabunt* in the printed texts.

[6] *permittat* in orig. and Bibl. Reg. 13 E. ix.; *permittet* in the printed texts.

[7] *illinc* in the printed texts.

[8] *legatos* in the printed texts.

[9] *sint* omitted in orig. and Bibl. Reg. 13 E. ix.: supplied from the printed texts.

A.D. 1391. Ex præmissis patet quantæ reverentiæ, quanti nominis, Rex noster pro tunc fuerit, cujus ope potissimum Papa se sperabat posse protegi et defendi. MS. Bibl. Reg. 13 E. ix.

Favourable answer given to the Nuncio by the King.

Rex noster, ut filius obedientiæ, auditis præmissis, et conceptis sensibiliter, subvenire decrevit, et parere, singulis [1] quæ expediebant maxime, vel licebant. Jussit ergo Papali nuncio, ut expectaret Parliamentum futurum, in quo, de communi consilio, responsum de singulis sibi daretur. Expectavit igitur non invitus, eo quod liberalitatem perante senserat Anglicorum.

Dux Gloverniæ iter arripuit, sed infaustum.

The Duke of Gloucester takes his departure for foreign parts.

Eodem tempore, Dux Gloverniæ, Dominus Thomas de Wodestoke, multis mœrentibus, iter [2] arripuit versus Le Spruys; quem non Londoniensium gemitus, non communis vulgi [3] mœror, retinere poterant, quin omnino proficisci vellet. [4] Nempe plebs communis, tam urbana quam rustica, metuebat quod, eo absente, aliquod novum detrimentum succresceret; quo præsente, nihil tale timebant; siquidem in eo spes et solatium totius patriæ reposita videbantur.

He is compelled, by adverse circumstances, to return to England.

Ipse vero, mox ut fines patriæ suæ transiit, illico, adversa agitatus fortuna, nunc hac, nunc illac, turbinibus procellosis circumfertur, et in tantum destituitur, ut de vita etiam desperaret. Tandem, post Daciam, post Northwagiam, post Scoticam barbariem, non sine mortis pavore transcursam, pervenit Northumbriam, et ad castellum se contulit de Tyniemutha, velut asylum antiquitus notum sibi; ubi per aliquot dies recreatus, iter assumpsit versus manerium suum de Plashi, magnum apportans gaudium toti regno, tam de ejus evasione quam de adventu suo.[5]

Mortalitas.

The sun obscured for several weeks.

Hoc anno, in æstate, septimo Idus Juliis, sol apparuit rubens per nebulas spissas [6] et fœtidas interpositas, et quasi nihil præstans luminis a meridie usque ad occasum. Et expost fere per sex hebdomadas nebulæ superabundabant temporibus meridianis. Quædam vero per totum diem et noctem durabant, nullatenus evanescentes.

[1] *quo* in the printed texts.
[2] *apparavit* in the printed texts.
[3] *moror* in orig.; corrected from the printed texts.
[4] *Nam* in the printed texts.
[5] A passage in Bibl. Reg. 13 E. ix. is omitted here.
[6] *et* omitted in the printed texts.

MS. Bibl. Reg. 13 E. ix.

A.D. 1391.

Eo tempore mortalitas tanta succrevit in Northfolchia et multis aliis Comitatibus, ut non impar magnis pestilentiis censeretur. Siquidem, ut de aliis civitatibus et villis taceam, apud Eboracum infra breve tempus undecim millia cadaverum sunt elata.

Great mortality in Norfolk and other Counties, and at York.

Eodem anno, Dominus Henricus Percy, Comes Northumbriæ, revocatus est de Calesia, et factus est Custos Marchiæ [1] Scotiæ, et Dominus Robertus Moumbray factus est Custos Calesiæ.

The Earl of Northumberland made Keeper of the March of Scotland.

Parliamentum Londini.

Sub eisdem diebus, scilicet feria sexta proxima sequente Commemorationem Animarum, inceptum est Parliamentum Londoniis; in quo tractatum est de Papali negotio, quoad Statutum nuper editum contra Provisores; et quanquam Rex ipse et Dux Lancastriæ viderentur Papæ deferre, tamen milites Parliamentales nullo modo consentire voluerunt, ut liceret Romipetis impune adquirere ibi beneficia, sicut prius; sed, ne viderentur nullum honorem Papæ vel Regi detulisse, hoc toleraverunt, ut, per Regis gratiam, liceret eis adquirere usque ad Parliamentum futurum.

Parliament at London.

Slight concession made by Parliament to the Pope's demands.

In hoc Parliamento, concessa fuit Regi dimidia decima, et dimidia quinta-decima; quæ pecunia deserviret tractatui habendo pro pace cum Gallicis; quem tractatum Dux Lancastriæ prosecuturus erat. Concessa est [2] etiam ipsi Regi conditionaliter plena decima, et integra quinta-decima, si videlicet ipso anno moveret expeditionem adversus Scotos: et hic finis et fructus Parliamenti prædicti.

Grants made by Parliament.

Annalis Conclusio.

Transit annus iste pauperibus et mediocribus multum durus et difficilis, propter [3] frugum caristiam, jam biennio continuatam; unde contigit ut, veniente tempore nucum, pomorum, et cæterorum hujuscemodi fructuum, plures pauperes, de eorum esu percepta dysenteria, morerentur. Fuissetque validior pestis ex fame, si non laudabilis diligentia Majoris Londoniarum communibus subvenisset. Qui jugi animo id providit, ut semper de transmarinis partibus frumenta Londonias deporta-

A dearth, followed by disease.

---

[1] *Socie* in orig. : *Stocie* in Bibl. Reg. 13 E. ix. ; by inadvertence.

[2] *etiam* omitted in the printed texts.

[3] *caritatem jam* in the printed texts.

A.D. 1391. rentur; alias sine dubio nec patria civitati, nec civitas patriæ, suffecisset. Autumnali tempore veniente.— MS. Bibl. Reg. 13 E. ix.

"Rus gaudens vario fundit munuscula fœtu,
"Cum bene vernales reddit et annus opes,"

cœpitque minorari pretium frumentorum.

Fuitque præsens annus multis in locis, ut prædicitur, pestilentialis; Angliæ et Franciæ quietus a bellis; sed Romanæ Curiæ, propter Anglorum revocationem, et statutariorum indurationem, odibilis et invisus.

A.D. 1392. Anno gratiæ millesimo trecentesimo nonagesimo secundo, qui est annus regni Regis Ricardi, a Conquæstu Secundi, quintusdecimus, tenuit Rex Natale magnificum, cum Anna Regina, et quatuor Episcopis, et tot Comitibus, et uno Duce, videlicet Eboraci, multisque proceribus et quindecim dominabus, apud Langley, juxta Sanctum Albanum.

A dolphin caught on Christmas Day, at London Bridge.

Ipso die Natalis, [1] delphinus, de mari veniens, lusit Londoniis in Tamisia, perveniens usque ad Pontem; præsagiens fortassis tempestates, quæ mox infra hebdomadam sequebantur. Qui a civibus visus et insecutus, sed [2] difficiliter interceptus, revectus est Londonias, multis præbens spectaculum de sui corporis vastitate, nempe qui habuit in longitudine decem pedes.

An account of the Dolphin.

[3] Sunt autem delphines marinæ belluæ, quæ voces hominum sequuntur, et gaudent cantibus tibiarum, et ad symphoniam solent gregatim advenire. Hii, quando præludunt in fluctibus saltu præcipiti, tempestates præsignant; quibus nihil velocius, nihil agilius, continent maria. Nam plerumque salientes transvolant vela navium. Cum coeunt, conjuges evagantur; catulos edunt. Decimus mensis mensuram partus facit, partum æstivus dies solvit; uberibus fœtus alunt teneros, et juvenes in faucibus receptant. Circa invalidos sollicitantur; usque ad tricesimum annum vivunt; quod exploratum est, in experimentum caudis amputatis. Ora habent loco quo cæteræ belluæ, sed in ventribus, contra naturam aquatilium, soli linguas suas movent; aculeatæ sunt pinnæ dorsales; cum irascuntur, inhorrescunt pinnæ, cum animi conquieverint, quibusdam receptaculis operiuntur. Spirare eos in aquis negant, sed vitales auras nonnisi in aere [4] superiore spirare dicunt; pro voce, gemitus est illis, similis humano. Certum

---

[1] *delphin* in the printed texts.
[2] *difficulter* in the printed texts.
[3] This lengthened account of the Dolphin is closely copied from Pliny's *Hist. Nat.*, B. ix. c. 8.
[4] *supero* in the printed texts.

MS. Bibl. Reg. 13 E. ix. A.D. 1392.

[1]habent vocabulum, quo accepto, vocantes sequuntur; nam proprie "Simones" vocantur. Voces hominum, cum ventus est in Aquilone, celerius audiunt; e contra, flante Austro, auditus illorum obstruuntur.

Sub Augusto Cæsare, puer quidam, primo fragmentis panis, delphinum allexit, et in tantum consuetudo valuit, ut ad manum pueri alendus veniret; mox puerilis audacia in tantum prorupit, ut super dorsum ejus ascenderet, et puerum delphinus per aquarum magna spatia vectitaret. Hoc tamen diu gestum est per annos plurimos, donec assiduo spectaculo desineret esse miraculum. Sed mox ut puer obiit, sub multorum oculis, desiderii mœrore delphinus interiit. Apud [2]Hipponem in Africa, delphinus a civibus pastus est, qui et se manibus tractandum præbuit, et multos dorso impositos frequenter gestavit. Apud Iassum, urbem [3]Babyloniæ, delphinus puerum adamavit. Quem, dum post assueta colludia, impatientius sequitur recedentem, [4]arenis invectus hæsit, ubi et mortuus est. Alium puerum, similiter insidentem dorsum delphini, cum undosior fluctus necavisset, delphinus ad terram revexit, et, velut fateretur reatum, pœnitentiam suam morte multavit, nec reverti voluit amplius in profunda.

Hæc de natura delphinorum curavimus isthic inserere, ut delectet quos latuit, et quos non latuit, non fastidiat.

De transfretatione Ducis Lancastriæ, et magnifica ejus susceptione per Regem Franciæ.

The Duke of Lancaster crosses over to France, to treat of peace.

Hoc anno, Johannes, Dux Lancastriæ, transfretavit in Franciam, ad colloquium Regis Franciæ, tractaturus de pace finali quam Rex Franciæ summopere affectavit; missus illuc videlicet per Regem Angliæ, totumque regni Consilium, pro negotio memorato. Cujus adventui Rex Franciæ non minora parari fecit, quam pro adventu Imperatoris cujusque maximi providisset. Nempe suis sumptibus suscepit eum et Episcopum [5]Dunelmensem, cum pene mille equis, et exhibuit a Calesia [6]usquedum perveniret ad civitatem Ambianensem;

Munificent reception of the Duke.

---

[1] *hoc* in the printed texts.

[2] *Ypponem* in orig.

[3] *Iasus* was an island and city of Caria, not Babylonia. The compiler has been led into the mistake, by his authority, Pliny, stating that Alexander the Great appointed this youth high priest of Neptune, at Babylon.

[4] *a renis* in orig. and the printed texts.

[5] *Undelmensem* in orig., by inadvertence.

[6] *insuper* in orig.: corrected from the printed texts.

A.D. 1392. nemine de Ducis vel Pontificis familia sollicitante de quibuslibet victualibus providendis, Regis Franciæ provisoribus et ministris cuncta comportantibus ad manus famulorum Ducis et Præsulis, quæ necessaria videbantur. MS. Bibl. Reg. 13 E. ix.

Interview with the King of France at Amiens.

Cumque ad Regis præsentiam Dux accessisset, Rex eum, ultra quam credi potest, honoravit, et gloriabundus semetipsum extulit, [1]quod colloquio Ducis sapientissimi, honorabilissimi, atque potentissimi, eum perfrui contigisset. Occurrerunt Ambianis, jussu Regis, ea vice, Duces illius regni, Comites, et Barones, ad deliberandum de tractatu et de pace componendum, ut, quo abundantior adesset in tractatu nobilium numerus, tanto rei felicior esset effectus. Tandem finito tractatu, Dux rediit [2]in Angliam, treugas unius anni reportans, ut per idem tempus deliberaret regni Angliæ collecta potestas, utrum expediret paci finali manus dare, potius quam negotia dubia belli tractare.

The Duke returns with a truce for one year.

Deliberation held by the Peers and Commons at Stamford.

Idcirco Stanfordiam accessere vocati, non solum regni Domini, sed et de qualibet civitate quidam, prout ad Parliamenta solent accedere; deliberaturi de tanto negotio [3]quid agendum. Sed tamen nihil profuit ea vice tanta collectio, præterquam quod treugas susceperunt, per anni circulum duraturas, ad quas servandas inviolabiliter uterque Rex, scilicet Franciæ [4]et Angliæ, corporale præstitit sacramentum; Seneschallo Franciæ huc accedente ad capiendum regium juramentum, et quibusdam de nostris militibus destinatis in Franciam, ad idem exigendum de Rege: quod et factum est.

The truce duly ratified by oath.

Adventus Ducis Gelriæ.

Advice given by the Duke of Gueldres to the King of England.

Eo tempore venit in Angliam Dux Gelriæ, cognatus Regis [5][Angliæ], vir [6]clarissimus in militia, Anglis honorabilis, et Francis formidabilis; qui strenue Francorum superbos motus compresserat in terra sua. Hic, magna animositate qua viguit, consulit Regi nostro, ne pacem cum Francis aut Scotis faceret, nisi quam deceret regiam majestatem, promittens se

[1] *et* in orig.; corrected from the printed texts.

[2] *in* omitted in the printed texts.

[3] *quod* in the printed texts.

[4] *et Angliæ* omitted in the printed texts.

[5] Omitted in orig. and the printed texts: supplied from Bibl. Reg. 13 E. ix.

[6] *clarissimus Angliæ unus in militia* in orig. and the printed texts; from the fact of the last syllables, *imus*, of *clarissimus* in Bibl. Reg. 13 E. ix. being in a separate line, and mistaken for *unus*; *Angliæ* also being inserted just before *imus* in the upper margin.

MS. Bibl. Reg. 13 E. ix.

paratum fore in auxilium Regis, (sive in Franciam transfretaret, sive in Scotiam arma moveret), cum nobiliori militia terræ suæ; quamobrem a Rege multipliciter honoratus, laudatus, muneribusque donatus, ac Ducibus Lancastriæ et Gloverniæ, regnique nobilitate, pari modo respectus, cum favore cunctorum permissus est ad propria remeare.

A.D. 1392. Proffer made of the Duke's services.

Adventus Comitis de Ostrinans.

Eodem tempore, sed non eodém anno, venit in terram istam Comes de [1] Ostrinans, tanquam amicus, pacisque mediator inter regna; qui, sarcinatus donis variis, cito recessit.

Visit of the Count of Ostrinans.

Hoc anno, Rex [2] Muritaniæ intravit terras magni Catayæ, et non modicam stragem fecit ibidem; et non multo post intravit terras Regis Hungariæ; sed ibi reperit obstaculum exercitatæ militiæ, Rege [3] vivaciter eum, cum suis omnibus, repellente.

Novum Festum Mariæ et Elizabethæ.

Circa diès istos, Dominus Papa, Bonefacius Nonus, ordinavit novum Festum celebrandum in Ecclesia, de Salutatione Beatæ Mariæ, qua salutavit Elizabeth, cognatam suam componens lectiones et historiam competentem, plenam mysteriis, refertam indulgentiis, excitativam devotionis. Nam et pares indulsit remissiones interessentibus divinis illis officiis, in Vigilia et in Die, ac infra Octavas, [4][et in Octavis], indulgentiis festo Corporis Christo præconcessis per Urbanum Quartum. Voluitque hunc diem haberi celebrem Septimo Kalendas Julii, id est, in crastino festi Nativitatis Sancti Johannis Baptistæ; quia eo tempore Sancta Maria mansit cum Elizabeth, et ministravit ei.

Feast of the Salutation of St. Mary, instituted by Pope Boniface the Ninth.

De transgressionibus Londinensium, et ira Regis.

Sub eodem tempore, misit Rex ad cives Londoniarum, petens ab eis mutuo mille libras; cui procaciter, et ultra quam

A loan to the King

[1] *Ostrians* in the printed texts: *Ostrinans* in Bibl. Reg. 13 E. ix.

[2] *Mauritaniæ* in the printed texts.

[3] *humaciter* in orig.; corrected from Bibl. Reg. 13 E. ix. and the printed texts.

[4] Omitted in orig.: supplied from Bibl. Reg. 13 E. ix. and the printed texts.

A.D. 1392. refused by the citizens of London. decuit, restiterunt, [1] et pecuniam se non posse præstare petitam unanimiter affirmaverunt; sed et quemdam Lumbardum, volentem accommodare Regi dictam summam, male tractaverunt, verberaverunt, et paulo minus occiderunt. Quæ cum Rex audisset, iratus est valde, et [2] convocans omnes regni pene majores, aperit proterviam civium Londoniarum, et de præsumptione conqueritur eorundem. Qui omnes infesti civibus, propter diversas causas, consulunt ut reprimatur citius eorum insolentia, et superbia destruatur. Erant quippe tunc inter omnes fere nationes gentium elatissimi, arrogantissimi, et avarissimi, ac male creduli in Deum et traditiones avitas, Lollardorum sustentatores, religiosorum detractores, decimarum detentores, et communis vulgi depauperatores. In tantumque excrevit eorum supercilium, ut auderent leges condere, quibus adventantes de circumjacentibus villis [3] et provinciis, contra rationem omnem humanam, Deum, et justitiam, molestarent, gravarent, et fatigarent. Prætereo eorum inhumanitatem, sileo rapacitatem, rēticeo infidelitatem, transeo malignitatem, quam indisciplinate in adventantes populos exercuerunt. Qui si vellem cuncta describere quæ perpetraverunt hoc tempore, [4] librum scriberem qui foret, [5] horresco.[6]

MS. Bibl Reg. 13 E. ix.

Anger manifested by the King thereat.

The bad character of the citizens enlarged upon.

Londinenses submittunt se Regis gratiæ.

The citizens resolve to submit themselves to the King's mercy.

Objecta sunt eis igitur quæ contra Regem fecerant, et [in] suæ majestatis notoriam læsionem; objecta sunt quæ in provinciales commiserant, ad Regis, ac Dominorum, regnique populi, detrimentum; quæ si vellent inficiari, præsto erant accusatores e patria, qui sacramento suo eorum probare cuperent acta prava. Londonienses ergo, in medio miseriarum subito constituti, et velut versati inter cudem et malleum, cum non esset locus excusationis, decreverunt se potius submittere Regis gratiæ, quam succumbere veredicto vel judicio duodenæ.

Major et Vicecomites arrestantur.

The Mayor and Sheriffs are arrested.

Regis ergo judicio arestatus est Major Londoniarum, et Vicecomites, cum quibusdam de majoribus, cæteris domum

---

[1] From this word down to *affirmaverunt*, the context is omitted in the printed texts.

[2] *convocatus* in orig.; corrected from the printed texts.

[3] *vel* in the printed texts.

[4] Instead of these words, the printed texts have—"*volumen credo maximum conficeret.*"

[5] In Bibl. Reg. 13 E. ix. this word has the appearance of "*horreste.*"

[6] A passage in Bibl. Reg. 13 E. ix. is omitted here.

MS. Bibl. Reg. 13 E. ix.

A.D. 1392.

redire permissis. Major autem missus est ad castellum de Wyndeshores, cæteri ad diversa castella destinata sunt, sub arta custodia conservandi, donec Rex cum Consilio deliberasset quid faceret de eisdem. Ibique decretum est, ne de cætero Londonienses Majorem eligerent vel haberent, sed Rex de suis militibus provideret aliquem qui rector foret, et "Custos Civitatis" vocaretur, et esset—quem alio nomine vocamus vulgariter "Gardianum"—ibi subsequenter: [1] et eorum sunt privilegia revocata, libertates annullatæ, et leges, quas vel condiderant vel a diebus [2] antiquis habuerant, abrogatæ.

The City of London is condemned to be deprived of its Mayor.

Tunc primo Rex constituit Custodem Civitatis, abrogato "Majoris" vocabulo, quemdam militem, dictum "Edwardum "de Dalyngrugge," qui et cives regeret et justitiæ cunctorum æque prospiceret; sed is cito fuit per Regem depositus, quia convictus est civibus fecisse juramentum vel de eorum consuetudinibus [3] contuendis, vel certe, pro posse suo, subtiliter revocandis. Fuerunt qui dicerent eum ex industria hoc fecisse, plusque Regis commodo quam civium in hac parte prospexisse. Quod cum Regi fuisset cognitum, pœnituit eum militem benevolum sic tractasse. Nihilominus Rex et alium militem loco suo constituit, nomine "Baldewynum de "Radyngtone," virum certe providum et discretum, qui sciret delinire mœrorem civium, et eorum mentes erigere ad spem bonam. Nam cives [4] pene præ tristitia contabuerant, et dolore.

The King appoints successive Wardens of the City.

Londinenses ad Windeshore vocantur.

Interea, [5] multis mediantibus, sed præcipue Duce Gloverniæ insistente, Rex, factus animi [6] æquior, paulatim discedit a sui rigore propositi, reducens ante mentis oculos honores varios quos per Londonienses acceperat, et magnifica dona per eos præstita; unde [7] decrevit mitius cum eis agere, et eos ad spem [8] qualisqualis gratiæ [9] evocare. Mittit nempe mandans Londoniensibus, ut ad castellum de Wyndeshore conveniant, de-

The King relents towards the Londoners.

He summons them

[1] *ut* in orig.: corrected from the printed texts.
[2] Omitted in the printed texts.
[3] *defendendis* in the printed texts.
[4] *pene* omitted in the printed texts.
[5] *milites* in orig.: corrected from the printed texts.
[6] *æquioris* in the printed texts.
[7] *decernit* in the printed texts.
[8] *aliqualis gratiæ* in the printed texts.
[9] *revocare* in the printed texts.

A.D. 1392. toWindsor, and makes certain provisions as to their liberties and privileges.

MS. Bibl. Reg. 13 E. ix.

monstraturi privilegia, libertates, ac jura civitatis, nova et vetera, coram eo, Consilio quoque suo, ut ibi decerneret quæ servanda forent in civitate, vel quæ penitus abolenda. Quibus ostensis, quædam ratificata, quædam permissa, quædam damnata, fuere; Majoris tamen nec personam nec dignitatem ea vice recuperavere, neque plenam Regis gratiam, donec satisfecissent Regi de damnis et injuriis quæ vel sibi vel Regis plebi antea intulissent. Equidem ea vice convenit inter Regem et Dominos, ne eorum satisfactionem acceptaret, nec cum eis quovismodo componeret, sine consilio Dominorum.

His intended measures against the citizens of London.

Nempe Rex, cum primo contra eos incanduisset, propter causas quas supra notavimus, meditatus est exercitum congregasse, et in civitatem irruisse cum impetu, et cives de sub cœlo delevisse. Quod tamen propositum Ducis Lancastriæ oratione mutatum est; qui [1]censuit eos, ut præmittitur, evocandos, et, ut præfertur, castigandos; vel, si obstinati fuissent, tunc juxta Regis propositum obsidendos, et de terra viventium disperdendos. Rex autem in hac collectione apud Wyndeshores, Dominos temporales regni cunctos, et Episcopos pene omnes, necnon exercitum talem contraxerat, qui merito terrori Londoniensium posset esse. In quos [2]omnes incredibiles fecit expensas, pro quibus certum erat Londonienses soluturos. Ipsi vero, non ignorantes quod horum finis esset expositio argenti et auri, submiserunt se et sua Regi voluntarie, ei decem millia librarum vadiantes; dimissi tamen sunt domum redire, incerti quid solverent, donec Regis Consilium et formam satisfaciendi et summam solvendi definisset.

They engage to find him a certain sum of money.

Rex accedit Londoniis.

The King resolves to comfort the citizens.

Cumque et cives regressi fuissent, et proceres qui cum Rege fuerant, ac reliquus populus, ad propria remeassent, Rex audiens Londonienses in tristitia constitutos et mente lapsos, ait suis;—"Vadam," inquit, "Londonias, et consolabor cives; "nec patiar eos ultra de mea gratia desperare." Quæ sententia, mox ut cognita fuit in civitate, incredibili jocunditate replevit omnes; unde omnes et singuli ei generaliter statuerunt occurrere, et non minores expensas facere in [3]exenniis et donativis quam fecerant in ejus Coronatione. Rex igitur, ut venit Londonias, tanta gloria, tanta pompa, tanta varietate

---

[1] *sensuit* in orig.

[2] Apparently written *onis* in orig.: *omnes* in Bibl. Reg. 13 E. ix. and the printed texts.

[3] *exinniis* in orig.; *xeniis* in the printed texts.

MS. Bibl. Reg. 13. E. ix.

A.D. 1392.

diversorum apparatuum, est susceptus, quanta suscipi decuisset aliquem regem triumphantem. Nam equos et phaleras, tabulas aureas et argenteas, pannos aureos et holosericos, pelves et lavatoria de fulvo metallo, aurum in pecunia, gemmas et monilia, tam ditia, tam nobilia, tam speciosa, donaverunt eidem, [1]ut cunctorum valor, et pretium, non posset facile æstimari.

Warmth and magnificence of his reception in the City.

Sicque recuperaverunt cives consuetudines et libertates antiquas, quæ saltem civitati possent esse [2]fulcimento, nec [3]extraneis detrimento. Indultumque fuit eisdem, ut Majorem possent eligere, sicut prius. Credebant autem Londonienses quod per hæc dona domigerium evasissent, et in posterum quieti fuissent; sed fefellit eos eorum opinio, quia coacti sunt expost solvere Regi decem millia librarum, de communitate collecta in amaritudine mentis magna. Proceres vero regni, qui Regis Consilio interfuerant, audientes quod Rex contra pactum indulsisset Londoniensibus, offensi sunt valde inter se, Regis levitatem et inconstantiam condemnantes. Nemo tamen palam Regem redarguit de præmissis, finemque cepit turba civium isto modo [4]quem delphinus præludens in Tamisia, die Natalis Domini ultimo præterito, forsan significavit eminus affuturam.

The citizens regain certain of their ancient liberties.

But are afterwards mulcted.

The nobles of the Council are offended at their restoration to the royal favour.

Dux Glovernicæ profectus in Hiberniam revocatur.

MS. Corp. Chr. vii. (1) & (5).

[5]Eodem tempore, cum Dux Glovernicæ recepisset pecuniam stipendiariam eundi cum exercitu in Hiberniam, cujus insulæ Rex dudum creaverat eum Ducem, et jam paratus et instructus esset ad proficiscendum, sine causa subito revocatus est, ad magnum tam Angliæ quam Hiberniæ detrimentum; nam adventus ejus fama cognita, cuncti pene reguli Hibernienses se ei deliberaverant submisisse; sed prævaluit penes

The Duke of Gloucester is recalled, when about to set out for Ireland.

[1] *et* in orig.; corrected from the printed texts.

[2] *fulcumento* in the printed texts.

[3] *extraneus* in orig.; corrected from the printed texts.

[4] *quam* in Bibl. Reg. 13 E. ix. and the printed texts.

[5] At this point, the last page (326 b.) of Bibl. Reg. 13 E. ix., the context of the latter, to the end of the year 1392, is abandoned by the compiler of the Arundel Manuscript. In the former the insanity of Charles VI., King of France, is spoken of as being *then* temporarily cured; whereas the text of the Arundel MS. speaks of him as *never* (evidently meaning, to the end of his life, A.D. 1422,) having fully recovered. Here also the compiler of the Arundel MS. is first indebted for his matter, and language, to (1) and (5) of the Corpus Chr. MS. No. vii.

A.D. 1392. Regem malignorum consilium, quod tamen, proh dolor! commodum impedivit. MS. Corp. Chr. vii. (1) & (5).

The King of France is attacked by madness, and never fully recovers.

Hoc anno Rex Franciæ, ut fertur, maleficatus incurrit amentiam, et phreneticus est effectus, dum expeditionem moveret contra Ducem Britanniæ, ut dicitur, minus justam; perduravitque in eo hæc infirmitas quamdiu duravit calor æstivus. Hyemali tempore mitigabatur passio, et ipse redditus suo sensui videbatur: nunquam tamen tam plene convaluit, quin expost semper eo anni tempore quo prius incurrerat istud incommodum, destitueretur sensu suo.

The Earl of Oxford dies at Louvain.

Eodem anno Robertus de Veer, quondam Comes [1] Oxoniæ, qui per multos gradus saltaverat ad nomen Ducatus Hiberniæ, in [2] Lovania diem clausit extremum, in mentis [3] anguria rerumque penuria miseranda. Qui equidem juvenis aptus fuerat ad cuncta probitatis officia, si in pueritia non defuit ei disciplina.

A.D. 1393. Parliament at Winchester. Intended embassy to France.

Anno Domini millesimo trecentesimo nonagesimo tertio, post Natale factum fuit Parliamentum Wyntoniæ, in quo concessum fuit Regi per clerum dimidia decima, et dimidia quintadecima per communes, pro expensis Ducum Lancastriæ et Gloverniæ, qui fuerant profecturi in Franciam, ad tractandum de pacis negotio inter regna.

The King of France narrowly escapes being burnt alive.

Eo tempore, Rex Franciæ, dum tripudiaret in aula sua cum quatuor militibus de familia, et esset [4] disfiguratus in sylvestrem hominem, habens strictum vestimentum resina [5] piceque linitum, ut lini stuppa, quæ fixa fuerat in veste stricta, hæreret tenacius et repræsentaret evidentius, fuisset repente in cineres combustus, nisi gratia affuisset, dolo fratris sui [6] Ducis, qui a tempore suæ infirmitatis aspiravit ad regnum. Nempe Rege, cum sociis, ducente choream, quidam ad hoc subrogatus, inclinato torticio, submisit ignem in stuppa [7] [vel] inusto quo corpora eorum fuere exterius cooperta, qui ardens usque ad vestimentum, quod strictum et consutum erat corpori, ubi invenit materiam picis et resinæ, inextinguibiliter arsit usque ad corpus: videns [8] tantum periculum, quædam domina accurrit, et Regem rapuit de chorea. Rex vero hoc

---

[1] *Exoniæ* in the printed texts.

[2] *Londonia* in orig. and the printed texts; *Lovania*, (meaning '*Louvain*') in Bibl. Reg. 13 E. ix.; *Lovonia* in (1) MS. Corp. Chr. vii.

[3] *angustia* in the printed texts; *angaria* in (1) MS, Corp. Chr. vii.

[4] *diffiguratus* in Camden's text.

[5] *piseque* in orig.

[6] There is an hiatus after this word in (1) MS. Corp. Chr. vii., with a side-note in an early hand, "*Aurelianensis.*"

[7] *vel* omitted in orig. and the printed texts; inserted from (1) MS. Corp. Chr. vii.

[8] *tamen* in the printed texts.

MS. Corp. Chr. vii. (1) & (5).

modo salvatus fuit, sed quatuor socii ejus nullo ingenio potuere salvari, donec semiustis pellibus atque carnibus expirassent. A.D. 1393

The King's Bench and Chancery removed from London to York. Brought back to London.

Hoc anno Bancus Regius et Cancellaria translata sunt de Londoniis Eboracum, vel odio Londoniensium, ut fertur, vel favore Eboracensium; eo quod Cancellarius, qui fuit Archiepiscopus Eboracensis, cuperet profectum civitatis suæ. Sed non longo tempore duravit hæc novitas, quia ea facilitate quæ transportabantur Eboracum, eadem Londoniis reportabantur.

Isto quoque anno Dominus [1] Albredus de Veer factus est Comes [2] Oxoniæ.

New appointments.

Eodem anno, in festo Cathedræ Sancti Petri, [3] [obiit] subito Johannes de Enros miles, Constabularius Doveriæ et Regis Senescallus; cui successit in officium Senescalli Dominus Thomas Percy, qui fuerat prius Sub-Camerarius Regis; in Constabulatum Doveriæ Dominus Thomas de Bemond successit; et Dominus Willelmus Scrop, Sub-Camerarius [4] efficitur, vir quo in humano genere de facili non inveniretur nequior aut crudelior.

William Scrope buys the Isle of Man.

Circa præsens tempus, idem Willelmus Scrop emit de Domino Willelmo de Monte Acuto, Comite de Sarum, insulam [5] Euboniæ, cum corona. Nempe dominus hujus insulæ "Rex" vocatur, cui etiam fas est corona aurea coronari. Hæc insula vocatur in vulgari "Insula de Man;" quæ inter Angliam et Hiberniam situatur.

Unsuccessful attempt to conclude peace with France.

Hoc anno Duces Lancastriæ et Gloverniæ transfretarunt in Franciam, pro fine faciendo treugarum prælocutarum, vel pacis finalis, inter regna. Sed tamen nondum finis, quia, Rege Franciæ iterum infirmato, non potuit finis esse.

H. Percy appointed Warden of Bordeaux.

Per idem tempus Dominus Henricus Percy, junior, constitutus est Custos [6] Burdegaliæ.

Damages done by thunder and lightning. Great inundations at Bury and Newmarket.

Mense Septembris, fulgura, coruscationes, et tonitrua, in multis regni partibus multa damna fecere, sed præcipue in Comitatu Cantebrigiæ, ubi domos et blada juxta Lolleworth, et in ipsa villa, terribiliter cremaverunt. Aquarum etiam inundantia non multo post irruit, quæ apud Bury aream implevit ecclesiæ, et apud Newmarket domorum parietes diruit, et viris illic ac mulieribus pene periculum demersionis intulit, mense Octobri.

Pestilence in Essex.

Eodem anno, multi moriebantur in Estsexia, ingruente pestilentia, [7] mense Septembri.

---

[1] *Albertus* in Camden's text.

[2] *Exoniæ*, incorrectly, in the printed texts.

[3] Omitted in orig., supplied from the printed texts.

[4] Omitted in the printed texts.

[5] Written as *eu bonis* in orig., by inadvertence.

[6] *Surdegaliæ* in orig. by inadvertence.

[7] *mensibus Septembris et Octobris*, in (1) MS. Corp. Chr. vii.

A.D. 1393. Cherbourg restored to the King of Navarre.

Ipso anno, dominium villæ de Cherburgh revolutum est ad pristinum possessorem, Regem Navariæ, quod [1] invadiatum fuerat Regi Angliæ per certos annos, [2] [pro viginti] duobus millibus marcarum, de Rege Angliæ mutuo susceptarum. MS. Corp. Chr. vii. (1) & (5).

Death of Thomas De Roos.

Eodem anno, Dominus [3] Thomas de Roos, dum reverteretur a Terra Sancta, [4] [in] insula de Cypro, civitate Papho, tactus [5] veris regionis incommodo, diem clausit extremum.

A.D. 1394. The Sultan of Turkey besieges Constantinople.

Anno Domini millesimo trecentesimo nonagesimo quarto,[6] [7] Morectus de Turkeya vallavit obsidione civitatem Constantinopolitanam; sed obsessorum probitate repulsus est.

Parliament at London.

In Octabis Sancti Hillarii factum fuit Parliamentum Londoniis, in quo petitum fuit Regi subsidium, volenti in Hiberniam proficisci; ubi clerus concessit ei plenam decimam, si transfretaret; si vero non laboraret, medietatem tantum decimæ concessit eidem.

Charge made by the Duke of Lancaster against the Earl of Arundel.

Tempore istius Parliamenti suborta est grandis discordia inter Ducem Lankastriæ et Comitem Arundeliæ: imposuit nempe Dux Comiti, quod circa festum Exaltationis Sanctæ Crucis, jacuerit cum armata manu in partibus Cestriæ, id est, in castello suo de Holte, eo tempore quo patria illa insurrexerit contra eum, Ducibus Nicholao de Cliftone, suisque complicibus, in subsidium rebellantium, ut putavit. Quod Comes negavit expresse, et se satis evidenter excusavit; sicque pro tempore tempestas magna cessavit.

The Earl clears himself.

Truce of four years concluded with France.

Circa festum Sancti Johannis Baptistæ, rediit e Francia Dux Lankastriæ, qui profectus ad tractatum fuerat mense Maio; reportans quatuor annorum treugas, in quibus et Scoti comprehendi debebant, si vellent subjici Regi Anglorum, ut de jure solebant.

Death of the Duchess of Lancaster; and the Countess of Derby.

Dum Dux agebat in Galliis, ut præfertur, obiit in Anglia conjux sua, Domina Constantia, Domini Petri, quondam Regis Castellæ, filia; mulier super fœminas innocens et devota. Et ne sola venirent funera lamentanda eo tempore, concessit in fata [8] Comitissa de Derby, uxor Domini Henrici Comitis de Derby, filii Ducis Lankastriæ supradicti.

---

[1] *Oppignoratum* in the printed texts.

[2] Supplied from (1) MS. Corp. vii. and the printed texts.

[3] Qy. *Johannes?* as in (1) MS. Corp. Chr. vii.

[4] Omitted in orig.; supplied from (1) MS. Corp. Chr. vii. and the printed texts.

[5] *aeris* in the printed texts.

[6] "*qui est annus regni Regis Ricardi, a Conquæstu Secundi, septimus decimus,*" inserted here in (1) MS. Corp. Chr. vii. and the printed texts.

[7] Bajazet is the sovereign here alluded to.

[8] *Maria Comitissa* in the printed texts.

MS. Corp. Chr. vii. (1) & (5).

A.D. 1394.

Death of Queen Anne, and burial at Westminster.

Obiit quoque Anna Regina, quæ apud Westmonasterium est sepulta. Cujus exequiæ quanto celebriores fuerunt in expensis, tanto notabiliores infamiis; quia Rex polluit locum sanguine Comitis Arundeliæ, in principio officii funeralis.

Death of the Duchess of York.

Eodem anno, obiit Domina Isabella, Ducissa Eboraci, soror uterina Ducissæ Lankastriæ, mulier mollis et delicata, sed in fine, ut fertur, satis pœnitens et conversa. Hæc sepulta est, jussu Regis, apud [1] Langle, suum manerium, inter Fratres.

Death of Sir John Hawkwood.

Hoc anno etiam obiit ille [2] toti mundo miles notissimus, Johannes Hawkwode, cujus gesta tractatum exigunt specialem.

The Irish in England are ordered to return to their own country.

Circa [3] mensem Augusti proclamatum est per totam Angliam, ut omnes Hibernici redirent ad terram propriam, [4] contra festum Nativitatis Beatæ Mariæ, præstolaturi in Hibernia adventum Regis, sub pœna capitali; dicebatur nempe quod [5] venerat in Angliam, spe lucri, tanta multitudo Hibernicorum, ut terra illa viris pene vacuaretur. Unde contigit quod [6] meri Hibernici, Anglicorum adversarii, partem insulæ quæ paruerat Regi Angliæ vastaverunt, nemine resistente. Cum vero Rex Angliæ illustris, Edwardus, Tertius a Conquæstu, illic posuisset Bankum suum atque Judices, cum Scaccario, percepit annuatim ad regalem [7] fiscum triginta millia librarum de terra illa: et modo, propter absentiam personarum et hostium potentiam irrefrænatam, nihil inde venit, sed per annos singulos de suo marsupio solvit triginta millia marcarum, ad sui dedecus et [8] cistæ detrimentum gravissimum.

Falling-off of the revenues from Ireland.

The King crosses over to Ireland.

Circa festum Nativitatis Sanctæ Mariæ, Rex Angliæ transfretavit in Hiberniam, et cum eo Dux Glovernię, Comitesque Marchiæ, Notynghamiæ, et Ruthlandiæ. [9] Hibernienses nimirum de tanto apparatu territi, quia palam non [10] audebant occurrere, clandestinis irruptionibus frequenter Regis exercitum fatigarunt. Coacti tamen, Anglicis prævalentibus, se Regi submittere plures reguli illius terræ, quorum quosdam Rex secum detinuit, ne nova aliqua molirentur; morabatur autem Rex in Hibernia usque post Pascha.

The rebellious Irish are compelled to submit.

The King is requested

Per idem tempus venerunt ad eum de Anglia Archiepiscopus Eboracensis et Episcopus Londoniensis, cum aliis nunciis

---

[1] *Langley* in the printed texts.

[2] *toto* in the printed texts.

[3] *Gulam* inserted in a smaller hand in (1) MS. Corp. Chr. vii.

[4] *citra* in (1) MS. Corp. Chr. vii.

[5] *venerant* in orig.: corrected from (1) MS. Corp. Chr. vii. and the printed texts.

[6] *mere* in (1) MS. Corp. Chr. vii.

[7] *regem* is inserted here in orig., by inadvertence.

[8] *fisci* in (1) MS. Corp. Chr. vii.

[9] *Hibernici de tanto* in the printed texts.

[10] *audiebant* in orig., by inadvertence.

A.D. 1394. missis per clerum, [1] rogantes ut [2] quantocius repatriare dignaretur, ad succurrendum fidei et Ecclesiæ, quæ jam per Lollardos, et eorum fautores, incredibiliter affligebatur. Nam ad hoc vacabant solummodo, ut imaginaretur qualiter totius Ecclesiæ [3] possessiones tollerent, et, quod pejus fuit, cunctas canonicas destruerent sanctiones. Hiis auditis, Rex inflammatus divino spiritu, quam cito potuit, in Angliam est reversus, arbitrans magis necessarium fidei periclitanti succurrere quam circa regna temporalia decertare.

to return, in consequence of the designs of the Lollards.

MS. Corp. Chr. vii. (1) & (5).

A.D. 1395. Anno Domini millesimo trecentesimo nonagesimo quinto,[4] Rex tenuit Natale in civitate Dubliniæ, Hiberniæ metropoli; et post Natale fecit Parliamentum ibidem, ad quod convenerunt tam [5] ligei [6] sui quam illi qui dudum submiserant se eidem.

Parliament at Dublin.

Parliament at London.

Eo tempore, post Octabas [7] Epiphaniæ, vocante Custode regni Angliæ, Domino Edmundo, Regis patruo, Duce Eboraci, factum est Parliamentum Londoniis; ad quod accessit, missus de Hibernia, Dux Gloverniæ; qui coram cunctis exposuit Regis necessitatem, qui jam [8] exhauserat thesauri sui inter Hibernicos facultatem. Cujus legatio tantum valuit, ut clerus unam decimam, et quintam-decimam [9] plebs communis [10] [daret], facta prius protestatione, quod ad hoc concedendum non tenebatur de stricto jure, sed sui Regis affectione.

Grant made to the King, for his expenses in Ireland.

The Lollards promulgate their doctrines.

Eo tempore Lollardi, cum suis fautoribus, in omnem malitiam efferati, fixerunt publice super ostia Ecclesiæ Sancti Pauli Londoniis, et Westmonasterii, abominabiles cleri accusationes, et hactenus inauditas Conclusiones, quibus nitebantur destruere personas ecclesiasticas et Ecclesiæ Sacramenta; animati, ut fertur, nimio favore quorundam procerum et militum Anglicorum. Inter quos campi-ductores fuerunt Ricardus Stury, Lodewicus [11] de Clifford, Thomas Latymer, Johannes de Monte Acuto, qui instigabant et confortabant hæreticos, ad confundendum, si posse daretur, præcipue religiosos.

Names of their principal supporters.

Rex igitur, ut præfertur, conceptis Lollardorum malitiis,

---

[1] *rogantes* omitted in the printed texts.

[2] *quam cito in patriam remeare* in the printed texts.

[3] *porcessiones* in orig., by inadvertence.

[4] "*qui est annus regni Regis Ricardi, a Conquæstu Secundi, octavus decimus,*"—inserted in the printed texts.

[5] *ligni* in orig., by inadvertence.

[6] *sui* omitted in the printed texts.

[7] *Ephiphaniæ* in orig.

[8] *exhausit* in the printed texts.

[9] *plebis* in orig., by inadvertence.

[10] Omitted in orig.; supplied from (1) MS. Corp. Chr. vii. and the printed texts.

[11] *de* omitted in the printed texts.

MS. Corp. Chr. vii. (1) & (5).

A.D. 1395.

The King returns to England, and threatens the supporters of the Lollards.

festinavit in Angliam, ut dissiparet ejus intuitu tanta mala. Quo cum pervenisset feliciter, quosdam de proceribus objurgavit acriter, comminans eis terribiliter, si de cætero Lollardis faverent, vel eos in aliquo confortarent. De Ricardo quoque Stury accepit juramentum, quod de cætero opiniones hujusmodi non teneret. Quo facto, dixit Rex, "Et ego juro tibi, si tu "unquam violaveris juramentum, morte turpissima morieris." Audientes cæteri tantum rugitum, cornua retraxerunt, et [1]hactenus delituerunt.

Prodigy at Laon.

Eo tempore, imago Crucifixi, cum stigmatibus sanguinolentis, apparuit in Gallia supra campanile Cathedralis Ecclesiæ Laudunensis, per mediam fere horam, cernentibus Episcopo, clero, et populo, manifeste.

Engagements between the Sultan of the Ottomans and the Christians.

Quo anno, [2]Morectus ille barbarus, cum trecentis quinquaginta millibus Paganorum, conflixit contra Priorem Sancti Johannis de Rodys, aliosque Christianos; sed Dei virtute convictus est, centum millibus de exercitu ejus [3]interfectis. Et quia fortuna non prævaluit sibi campestri prælio, navali bello statuit experiri fortunam. Sed Qui terræ marique dominatur, ejus conatus enervavit, et cum confusione maxima fugere compulit iterato. [4]Civitas quoque Constantinopolitana, quam supra diximus obsessam ejus exercitu velut infinito, superveniente Imperatore Constantinopolitano cum parvo Christianorum numero, liberatur, quingentis millibus de gente Pagana miraculose peremptis.

Piracy committed by subjects of the Queen of Denmark.

Misfortunes of the men of Norfolk.

Eo anno sensit Anglia grave damnum per piratas Reginæ Denemarchiæ, qui nautas et mercenarios deprædabantur; præcipue tamen viros de Norfolchia, qui ausi sunt, congregata multitudine, congredi cum eisdem; sed hostibus prævalentibus, multi perempti, plurimi vero ad redemptionem gravissimam sunt servati, amissis viginti millibus librarum, quas ad marcandizandum comportaverunt.

Extortionate demands of the Archbishop of Canterbury upon the clergy,

Eodem anno, Willelmus Cantuariensis Archiepiscopus, non considerata depressione ecclesiastica qua jugiter premebatur per talliagia pendenda Regi annis singulis, plus spectans [5]suo privato commodo quam communitatis [6]incommodo, impetravit

---

[1] *hatenus* in orig., by inadvertence.

[2] Bajazet, Sultan of the Ottomans, is meant. The allusion is, to the Battle of Nicopolis, fought A.D. 1396, in which he was not defeated, but gained a victory over the Christian army.

[3] *interfecit* in orig. and in the printed texts, incorrectly.

[4] *Comitas* in orig.; corrected from (1) MS. Corp. Chr. Camb. vii. and the printed texts.

[5] *suum privatum commodum* in the printed texts.

[6] *incommodum* in the printed texts.

A.D. 1395. Bullam ab Apostolico gratiosam, ut levaret per totam suam Provinciam quatuor denarios de qualibet libra omnium bonorum ecclesiasticorum, tam exemptorum quam [1][non] exemptorum, nulla prætensa causa vera nec legitima. Cujus Bullæ fuerunt constituti executores Archiepiscopus Eboracensis et Episcopus Londoniensis. Multi vero censuras [2]timentes tam sublimium executorum, maluerunt summam continuo solvere, quam dubiis litibus, cum jactura forsitan, subjicere; nonnulli [3]ad Sedem Apostolicam, tanquam a gravamine, appellantes, suam causam nitebantur defendere, et dictum subsidium, tanquam illegitimum, quomodolibet revocare; quorum animosiores et præcipue, fuere Lincolnienses: sed tantis motibus finem imposuit mors Archiepiscopi, cito postea subsecuta.

enforced by Papal Bull. — *MS. Corp. Chr. vii. (1) & (5).* — *The death of the Archbishop puts an end thereto.*

Obituary for the year.

Hoc anno obiit Johannes de Waltham, Episcopus Sarum et regni Thesaurarius; qui tantum Regi complacuerat, ut etiam, multis licet murmurantibus, Rege jubente, apud Westmonasterium inter Reges meruit sepulturam. Huic successit in officio Thesaurarii Dominus Rogerus Walden, prius Regis Secretarius et Calesiæ Thesaurarius; in Episcopatu vero [4]Dominus [5]J. de Mytforde, Cicestrensis Episcopus, ad cujus Episcopatum Dublinensis [6]Archiepiscopus est translatus, quia major Pontificatus in sæculari substantia minor erat.

Obiit etiam [7]Exoniensis Episcopus [8]Willelmus; [9]cui successit, Regis instantia, Magister Edmundus de Stafford, [10]Portitor Privati Sigilli. Obiit quoque Dominus [11]Henricus de Wakefeld, Episcopus Wigorniensis; cui successit, ad preces Regis, Papali permissione, quidam monachus [12]Cisterciensis, Regis physicus, dictus [13]["Robertus] Tydeman," spreta et cassata Magistri Johannis Grene electione legitima.

---

[1] Omitted in orig.; supplied from (1) MS. Corp. Chr. vii. and the printed texts.

[2] *tenentes* in orig., by inadvertence.

[3] *ad* omitted in the printed texts.

[4] *Dominus* omitted in the printed texts.

[5] Qy. if not *Ricardus?*

[6] Heylin and Beatson call this dignitary (Robert de Waldby) *Archdeacon* of Dublin; Le Neve styles him *Archbishop*, and the present passage proves that he is correct.

[7] *Oxoniensis* in orig.; corrected from the printed texts.

[8] *Thomas* Brentingham died 3rd Dec. 1394. "*Magister Thomas Bruntyngham*" is inserted in a somewhat later hand in (1) MS. Corp. Chr. vii.

[9] *post quem successit* in the printed texts.

[10] *Portator* in the printed texts.

[11] He died 11th March 1394.

[12] *Cistriciensis* in orig., *Cicestrensis* in the printed texts.

[13] Omitted in orig. and (1) MS. Corp. Chr. vii.; supplied from the printed texts.

MS. Corp. Chr. vii. (1) & (5).

A.D. 1395. The King orders the body of Robert de Vere to be buried at Colne, in Essex.

Hoc anno, mense Novembris, Rex Angliæ, apportato de [1] Lovania corpore quondam dilecti sui Roberti de Veer, quem creaverat Ducem Hiberniæ, — felicis quidem si non aspirasset ad gradus sublimes, sed propter extollentiam infelicitati subacti,—fecit apud Prioratum de Colne in Estsexia solemnes exequias, ibidem exhibens suam præsentiam, magnificans officium funerale. Curavitque thecam cypressinam, in qua corpus, balneo delibutum, jacebat, aperire, faciem considerare digitoque tractare, et publice monstrare dilectionem defuncto quam impenderat prius [2] vivo. Erant ibi, cum Rege, mater defuncti, Comitissa Oxoniæ, Archiepiscopus Cantuariæ, plurimique Episcopi, cum Abbatibus et Prioribus, aliisque religiosis; sed proceres pauci, quia nondum digestum erat odium quod conceperant contra illum.

Hatred of the nobles towards him.

A.D. 1396. The Duke of Lancaster recalled from Acquitaine.

Anno Domini millesimo trecentesimo nonagesimo sexto, Dux Lancastriæ, cui Rex donaverat Ducatum Aquitanniæ, cum jam inæstimabilem summam thesauri expendisset in illis partibus pro adipiscenda patriotarum benevolentia, consecutusque fuisset propositum, subito per mandatum regium revocatur. Qui nihilominus revocanti paruit, et redivit in Angliam, pervenitque Langleyam, ubi Rex Natale Domini tenuit isto anno. Susceptus est a Rege, prout decuit, cum honore, sed, ut [3] quidam asserunt, non amore. Licentiatus proinde a Rege, recessit a Curia et properavit Lincolniam, ubi Katerina de Swynford tunc morabatur; quam post Octabas Epiphaniæ, cunctis admirantibus facti miraculum, desponsavit, quia fortuna talis fœminæ (tantæ sublimitatis error) minime competebat.

He marries Katherine de Swynford.

The Pope requests the King's aid against the Lollards.

Hoc [4] anno, Papa scripsit Regi Angliæ, oravitque ut assisteret prælatis Ecclesiæ in causa Dei, et ipsius Regis et regni, contra Lollardos; quos declaravit non solum proditores Ecclesiæ, sed et ipsius Regis; rogavitque obnixius, ut quos prælati declarassent hæreticos condemnaret.

The religious recalled to their respective houses, who have received the Pope's chaplaincy.

Alias eo tempore direxit Bullas, ad revocandum religiosos qui capellanas obtinuerant vel ab ipso Papa, vel a quoquam alio, nuncio vel legato; quas Bullas, quasi munus gratissimum, amplexati sunt Ordines Mendicantium, sed Fratres Minores præcipue, qui confestim fratres suos, qui per exemptiones capellanatus ab eis segregati fuerant, rapere, capere, domumque reducere, satagebant.

Joy of the Mendicant Orders thereat.

---

[1] *Londonia* in orig. and the printed texts; corrected from (1) and (5) M.S. Corp. Chr. vii. See p. 212 *ante*, Note 2.

[2] The word *jacio* occurs before this word in orig.; *jacco* in the printed texts.

[3] *iidem* in the printed texts.

[4] *tempore* in (1) MS. Corp. Chr. vii.

A.D. 1396. Interview between the Kings of England and France.

MS. Corp. Chr. vii. (1) & (5).

Eo tempore, juxta pacta inter Reges Angliæ et Franciæ [1]prius firmata, convenerunt dicti Reges ad locum ultra Calesiam, eorum colloquio designatum, ubi ambo Regum tentoria magnifice fixa fuere. Qui ante tractatum, pro pacis veræ fidei securitate, corporale præstiterunt coram omnibus hujusmodi juramentum:—

Oath made by the King of France.

"Nos Karolus, Rex Franciæ, juramus in verbo regali, super "Evangelia, pro nobis et omnibus nobis subjectis, amicis, et "affinitate nobis junctis, et benevolentibus, quod non faciemus, "nec patiemur fieri, per nos nec per supra nominatos, dam-"num,[2] impetitionem, molestiam, arestationem, nec disturbati-"onem, ullo modo per tempus nostræ conventionis, nec per octo "dies ante conventionem, et septem dies sequentes, nostro filio "Regi Angliæ, nec alicui de suis subjectis, amicis, affinibus, "nec benevolis, ante dictum tempus. Et si casu aliquo inso-"lentia vel litigium per aliquos de nostris supradictis,—quod "absit,—emerserit, nos promittimus in verbo regali, et per "securitatem prædictam, quod faciemus hæc debite emendari, "et sine dilatione reformari; et juramus ulterius, super "securitate prædicta, quod si aliquis vel aliqui, [3]de qualicun-"que statu vel conditione extiterint, voluerit vel voluerint "contraire dictæ nostræ securitati, nos erimus in auxilium "nostri filii, pro nostro posse, ad resistendum malitiæ male-"factorum prædictorum, et conservandum nostrum dictum "filium et suos, per modum quem nos et nostri scimus. Et "ad tenendum omnia, et prosequendum, sine fraude vel malo "ingenio, ad hoc juramus et promittimus, ut supra."

Particulars of the interview.

Die vicesimo sexto mensis Octobris, Rex Angliæ equitavit de Calesia versus castrum suum de Gynes, et cum eo Dux de Berrey, qui missus fuerat ad recipiendum sacramentum Regis nostri. In crastino obviaverunt Reges pariter, ducentibus Regem Angliæ Dominis Franciæ; scilicet, quatuor Ducibus, de Berrey, Burgundiæ, Aurelianensis, et Burboniæ, Comite Santer, Vicecomite de [4]Maleyn, Episcopo de [5]Valenis, Domino de Buss'.

E contra, de parte nostra missi sunt ad conducendum Regem Franciæ [6]duo Duces, scilicet Lancastriæ et Gloverniæ, Comites

---

[1] *primus* in orig.; corrected from the printed texts.

[2] This and the next two words are omitted in the printed texts.

[3] *de* omitted in the printed texts.

[4] *Meleyn* in (1) MS. Corp. Chr. vii.; *Mileyn* in (5) MS. Corp. Chr. vii.

[5] *Vilainos* in (1) MS. Corp. Chr. vii.; *Vilaines* in (5) MS. Corp. Chr. vii.

[6] *ad suam papilionem* is inserted here in (1) MS. Corp. Chr. vii.

MS. Corp. Chr. vii. (1) & (5.)

A.D. 1396.

Derbyæ, et Ruthlondiæ, et Northumbriæ; habueruntque colloquium duo Reges, et assensu mutuo fuit ordinatum, ut construeretur in eodem loco, amborum sumptibus, in memoriam sempiternam una Capella; quæ "Capella Nostræ Dominæ de "Pace" vocaretur.

A Chapel to be erected on the site of the interview.

Die Sabbati in festo Apostolorum Symonis et Judæ, Rex Angliæ et Franciæ collocuti sunt de certis articulis tractatus sui; quo facto, jurati sunt [1] super Evangelia de pactis servandis. Tunc Rex Angliæ rogavit Regem Franciæ ut pranderet cum eo die sequente. Die Lunæ venit Rex Franciæ ad tentorium Regis Angliæ. Ea hora Regina fuit adducta ad tentoria Regis nostri. Rex Franciæ donavit eam Regi nostro; quam Rex noster cepit per manum, et osculabatur eam, regratiando patri suo, Regi Franciæ, de dono tam honorabili et gratioso; asserens se eam sub conditionibus accipere factis inter eos, ut [2] patet, per istam affinitatem possit uterque Rex vivere in pace et tranquillitate, et pervenire ad bonum finem et conclusionem pacis perpetuæ faciendæ inter regna, et ne sanguis Christianus effundatur, cujus effusio possit [3] verisimiliter evenire, si ista affinitas inter eos non fieret ista vice.

Visits interchanged between the Kings.

The daughter of the King of France given in marriage to the King of England.

Commendata est igitur Regina Duxissæ Lankastriæ et Glovernisæ, et Comitissis Huntyndoniæ et Staffordiæ, aliisque dominabus quæ aderant; quæ conduxerunt eam Calesiam, cum [4] maximo apparatu hominum et equorum, habuitque cum ea duodecim currus plenas dominabus et domicellis.

The Princess is conducted to Calais.

Quibus ita gestis, Reges accesserunt ad prandium in tentorio Regis Anglorum. Rex Franciæ consedit in dextera parte aulæ; cui servitum fuit regaliter more suæ patriæ, id est, de omnibus cibariis primi cursus simul in magna parapside, et de secundo cursu eodem modo. Regi vero Angliæ servitum fuit patriæ suæ more. Post prandium Reges osculati sunt pariter, et ascenderunt equos; duxitque Rex Angliæ Regem Franciæ in viam suam, et tandem, [5] vinctis manibus, super equos discesserunt ab invicem. Rex Franciæ equitavit ad Arde, Rex autem Angliæ ad Calesiam se convertit, ubi filiam Regis Franciæ duxit uxorem, pusiolam septennem vel octennem.

The King of France dines with the King of England, and they then separate.

Richard marries the daughter of the King of France.

---

[1] *per* in the printed texts.

[2] *patet* omitted in the printed texts; *videlicet*, instead of *patet*, in (1) MS. Corp. Chr. vii.; *patet* in (5) MS. Corp. Chr. vii.

[3] *similiter* in orig. and the printed texts; corrected from (1) and (5) MS. Corp. Chr. vii.

[4] *maxima* in orig., by inadvertence.

[5] *junctis* in the printed texts; the contraction may stand for either word in (1) and (5) MS. Corp. Chr. vii.

A.D. 1396.

Great expenditure of the King of England.

MS. Corp. Chr. vii. (1) & (5).

Fuit [1] autem iste Regum apparatus grandis, et sumptuosus in donariis et expensis; nam præter dona quæ Rex Angliæ dedit Regi Franciæ, aliisque proceribus illius regni, quæ superaverunt summam decem millium marcarum, Rex expendit, ut dicitur, trecenta millia marcarum et amplius, ea vice.

He loses part of his baggage in a storm.

Rediit igitur cito post in Angliam salvus, et uxor sua, sed aversa tempestate perdidit tentoria sua, et magnam partem supellectilis domus suæ.

Obituary of the year.

Hoc anno valefecit mundo Magister Willelmus Courtenay, Archiepiscopus Cantuariensis; cui successit, postulatione Communis Capituli, Thomas Arundel, frater Comitis Arundelliæ, regnique Cancellarius; qui mox Cancellariæ dimisit officium, et illius sollicitudinem, per Regis assensum, Magistro Edmundo [2] Stafforde commendavit.[3]

A.D. 1397.

Parliament at London. Bastard issue of the Duke of Lancaster legitimized.

Anno gratiæ millesimo trecentesimo nonagesimo septimo,[4] post Natale Domini factum fuit Parliamentum Londoniis, in quo Dux Lankastriæ legitimari fecit sobolem quam susceperat de Katerina Sywnforde.

Thomas Beaufort created Earl of Somerset.

In eodem Parliamento fuit ordinatum ut Justiciarii de cætero non habeant assessores. Item Thomas [5] Beuford, filius Ducis Lankastriæ et dictæ Katerinæ, (nam sic censuit Dux cognominari filios ejusdem Katerinæ, quos sibi genuerat,) creatus est Comes de Somersete.

Eo tempore concessa fuit Regi per clerum medietas unius decimæ, solvenda ad duos terminos ipsius anni.

The King recalls the banished Justiciars from Ireland.

Hoc anno Ricardus Rex Angliæ, contra juramentum quod præstiterat, revocavit de Hibernia Justiciarios, quos olim de consensu suo, proceres, propter defectus eorum notabiles, [6] constituerant exulare.

Rumour that the King has been chosen Emperor.

Eo tempore [7] increpuere rumores, licet vane, quod videlicet Rex Angliæ fuisset electus [8] Imperator; unde Rex elatus, ut fertur, ab eo tempore sapere cœpit altius quam solebat, vulgus apporiare, grandes summas pecuniæ de quibuslibet mu-

---

[1] *annus* in the printed texts.

[2] *Staffordo* in the printed texts.

[3] The following words are added here in the printed texts:—" *Eodem* " *anno decessit totius monasticæ reli-* " *gionis pater et speculum, Domi-* " *nus Thomas, Abbas Monasterii* " *Sancti Albani.*" This and a longer passage occur here in (1) and (5) MS. Corp. Chr. vii.

[4] " *qui est annus regni Regis Ri-* " *cardi, a Conquæstu Secundi, vice-* " *simus,*" inserted here in the printed texts.

[5] *Benforde* in the printed texts.

[6] *constituerunt* in the printed texts.

[7] *increbuere* in the printed texts; and (1) Corp. Chr. vii.; *increpuere* in (5) Corp. Chr. vii.

[8] *Imperatorem* in orig., by inadvertence.

MS. Corp. Chr. vii. (1) & (5). tuare; in tantum, quod nullus prælatus, nulla civitas, nullus civis notatus [1] locuples, in toto regno se potuit occultare, quin de sua pecunia mutuo Regi daret. A.D. 1397. His singular conduct thereon.

Anno præsenti, cum jam sibi regnum Angliæ summa videretur pace gavisurum, propter novas nuptias regales, et divitias per easdem [2] accumulatas, et treugas annorum triginta firmatas, et præsentiam tot nobilium Dominorum, quot et quales nulla externa regio poterat exhibere; repente Regis astutia cuncta turbantur, dum inopinate capit avunculum suum, Ducem Gloverniæ, vi et armis, nihil tale verentem, apud Plasshy in Estsexia, et usque ad Calesiam deduci fecit, carcerali custodiæ mancipandum. Comitem quoque Warwici , ipso die quo eum invitaverat ad convivium, fecit arestari, et protinus incarcerari, quamvis ei peroptimum vultum monstrasset eodem die, et insuper sibi bonum dominum futurum, et magnam amicitiam, promisisset. Comitem [3] quoque Arundeliæ, deceptum blandis persuasionibus, qui satis potens erat et se salvasse et suos amicos deliberasse, [4] Ducem Gloverniæ et Comitem Warwici, se reddentem pacifice, misit in insulam Vectam, pari modo in carcere detinendum.[5] The Duke of Gloucester, and the Earls of Warwick and Arundel, are suddenly seized and imprisoned. Et ne fieret communis vulgi commotio pro captione dictorum procerum, quam maxime verebatur, proclamari fecit per regnum quod ista Dominorum captio non erat facta pro [6] quibusque antiquis transgressionibus, sed pro novis commissis contra Regem, quæ propalarentur in Parliamento futuro. Sed hæc proclamatio ficta fuit, prout rei exitus comprobavit. Reason asserted by the King for this measure.

Rex vero, nescitur quid metuens, per idem tempus metuit ne Pontifices, aliive prælati, facerent processiones sive devotiones, pro causa præmissa, vel procerum ereptione tantorum. Et paulo post apud Notyngham fecit indictari dictos Dominos de proditione, subornavitque appellantes, qui eos appellarent in Parliamento futuro, scilicet, Edwardum Comitem Ruthlondiæ, Thomam Mounbray Comitem Marescallum, Thomam Holand Comitem Canciæ, Johannem Holand Comitem Huntyngdoniæ, [7] Thomam Beuford Comitem de Somersete, Johannem The King suborns accusers of the imprisoned peers.

---

[1] *locuplex* in (1) and (5) MS. Corp. Chr. vii., orig., and the printed texts.

[2] *accumelatas* in orig.

[3] *postea* in (1) MS. Corp. Chr. vii.

[4] *scilicet Ducem* in the printed texts.

[5] " *usque ad Parliamentum quo* " *diffinierat eos omnes morte plecten-* " *dos* " added in (1) MS. Corp. Chr. vii.

[6] *quibusdam* in Camden's text; *quibusquam* in Parker's text; *quibuscunque* in (1) MS. Corp. Chr. vii.; *quibusque* in (5) MS. Corp. Chr. vii.

[7] *Thomam* omitted, with an hiatus, in (1) MS. Corp. Chr. vii.

A.D. 1397. de Monte Acuto Comitem Sarum, Thomam Dominum de Spencer, et Willelmum Scrop Regis Camberlanum. Quibus sic gestis, fecit Rex proclamari per totum regnum quod Domini arestati proditores erant, et pro proditione detenti. MS. Corp. Chr. vii. (1) & (5).

Malefactors from Chester summoned to the King's aid.

Interea Rex, sibi metuens, convocavit ad tutelam sui corporis multos malefactores de Comitatu Cestriæ, qui noctium vigilias dierumque servarent, et dividerent, circa illum.

Parliament at London.

Circa Octabas Nativitatis Beatæ Mariæ, factum est Parliamentum Londoniis, ad quod venerunt omnes regni proceres armati, cum suis retinentiis, ducti timore Regis. Fuerunt autem præcipui prolocutores hujus Parliamenti milites valde cupidi, et ambitiosi, et tumidi, J. Bushi, Willelmus Bagot, et Henricus Grene. Hii importunis clamoribus petierunt, ut chartæ pardonationum inprimis revocarentur et annullarentur; super quibus requisiti, prælati de facili judicarunt chartas tales fore revocabiles; non attendentes quod [1] hujusmodi gratiæ revocatio personæ [2] Regis maxime repugnabat, cum misericordia sit solii regalis confirmatio, et qui tollit a Rege misericordiam tollit solii regalis firmamentum. Consequenter, Domini temporales, videntes [3] imperfectum cleri, censuerunt et ipsi [4] hujusmodi chartas annullandas, magis timore Regis dicti quam mentium ratione. Exactum etiam fuit a prælatis, ut constituerent laicum procuratorem pro eisdem, ut quia illi non poterant interesse judicio sanguinis, procurator eorum, si necesse foret, [4] hujusmodi negotio consentiret.

At demand of the Speakers of Parliament, the charters of pardon are annulled.

The Archbishop of Canterbury is banished.

Altero die, cum Archiepiscopus Cantuariensis, de Regis mandato et consilio, quem credebat amicissimum, se absentasset de Parliamento, (qui sibi juraverat quod nihil attentaretur in ejus præjudicium,) absente ipso, contra omnem justitiam adjudicatus fuit exilio; cum adjecto, quod non remaneret in regno ultra sex hebdomadas, ab eo die proximo computandas. Quo taliter condemnato, misit Rex clam ad Curiam Romanam pro translatione ejusdem; effecitque ut Rogerus de Waldene, regni pro tunc Thesaurarius, pro eo Archiepiscopus ordinaretur. Qui, quia cubile patris sui viventis ascendere præsumpsit, post biennium dejectus est auctoritate Papæ præfati.

Roger de Waldene is appointed Archbishop in his place.

Die Sancti Matthæi, datum est judicium contra Ricardum Comitem Arundeliæ, allegantem et exposcentem suffragia char-

---

[1] *hujus* in orig. and the printed texts; corrected from (1) MS. Corp. Chr. vii.

[2] *Rege* in orig.; corrected from the printed texts; *regiæ* in (1) MS. Corp. Chr. vii.

[3] *assensum cleri* in the printed texts.

[4] *hujus* in orig. and the printed texts; corrected from (1) MS. Corp. Chr. vii.

MS. Corp. Chr. vii. (1) & (5).

A.D. 1397.

tarum [1] et pardonatione Regis, sed nihil in hac parte proficientem; nam adjudicatus est tractioni, suspensioni, [2] exentrizationi, combustioni interiorum, decapitationi, et quarterizationi. Sed prolata sententia modificata est de Regis gratia; ut, condonatis pœnis cæteris, subiret [3] tantum capitalem sententiam; cujus executio mox facta est. Sed Comes nec cum responsis astitit, nec cum sententiam Domini tristem subiit, nec cum de loco judicii ad locum transivit supplicii, neque cum jam flexo poplite præstolabatur ictum gladii, vultu concidit, sed servans semper faciei colorem uniformem, non plus palluit quam si fuisset ad epulas invitatus. Præcessit autem eum, et sequebatur, satis [4] feralis turba Cestrensium, armata securibus, gladiis, arcubus et sagittis. Educebant eum, et urgebant ad mortis metam, Comites Marescallus et Kanciæ,—quorum alter gener ejus erat, alter nepos ex filia—, et Comes Huntyndoniæ, frater Regis.

The Earl of Arundel is condemned to death.

His resolute bearing.

Intuens ergo suos affines et necessarios, Comites scilicet Marescalli et Kanciæ, perurgere negotium decollationis suæ,—"Vere," inquit, "decuisset vos præcipue absentes fuisse, "et ab isto negotio subtraxisse; sed veniet in brevi tempus "quando tot mirabuntur de vestris infortuniis, quot de meis "casibus nunc mirantur." Deinde data lictori venia, rogavit ne torqueret eum diutius, sed ictu unico caput ejus amputaret; tentavitque suis digitis mucronis aciem quo fuerat feriendus;—"Satis," inquit, "acutus est, fac cito quod fac"turus es"; qui eum ictu unico decollavit; cujus corpus, cum capite, inter Augustinenses Londoniis est humatum.

His rebuke to the Earl Marshal and the Earl of Kent.

Post cujus mortem, Rex diversis imaginibus in somnis est turbatus; videbatur nempe umbra Comitis, mox ut dormire cœpisset, ante oculos suos volitare, minarique sibi, et eum indicibiliter deterrere, quasi diceret cum Poeta,—

The King is conscience-stricken, upon the Earl's death.

"Nunc quoque factorum venio memor umbra tuorum,
"[5] Insequor et vultus [6] ossea forma tuos."

Quibus Rex pavefactus imaginibus, [7] [cum] præ timore medios somnos interrumperet, maledixit diei in quo novit

[1] *et* omitted in (1) MS. Corp. Chr. vii.

[2] *exenterationi* in (1) and (5) MS. Corp. Chr. vii.

[3] *tamen* in the printed texts.

[4] *ferialis* in Camden's text.

[5] *Jus quoque* in orig. and the printed texts; corrected from (1) and (5) MS. Corp. Chr. vii.

[6] *cum ossea* in orig. and the printed texts; corrected from (1) and (5) MS. Corp. Chr. vii. A quotation from the *Ibis* of Ovid, ll. 145, 6.

[7] Omitted in orig. and the printed texts; supplied from (1) Corp. Chr. vii.

A.D. 1397. Comitem memoratum. Auxit quoque mentis insaniam, quod audivit vulgus commune Comitem reputare pro Martyre, peregrinationesque fieri ad corpus ejus: unde die decimo sepulturæ ejus Rex misit, circa decimam noctis horam, Duces et Comites, qui corpus ejus effodi facerent, et aspicerent si caput corpori esset junctum, prout fama communis erat. Qui, effosso corpore, cum famam mendacem reperissent, omnia Regi renunciarunt. Ille non contentus experimentis hujusmodi, jussit ut fratres signa deponerent, et quæ circa corpus ejus fixa erant, et locum sepulturæ suæ sub pavimento protinus occultarent.

MS. Corp. Chr. vii. (1) & (5).

The multitude venerate the Earl as a Martyr.

The King commands the Earl's body to be examined.

The Earl of Warwick confesses his criminality.

Post mortem Comitis Arundeliæ, prædictus fuit Comes Warwic ad standum judicio Parliamentali; sed defuit illi constantia quæ Comitem Arundeliæ comitabatur. Nempe requisitus quid respondere vellet ad equitationes factas cum Duce Gloverniæ et Comite Arundeliæ contra Regem, timore ductus mortis et latæ sententiæ in Comitem Arundeliæ, mox fatebatur cum lacrymis se proditorem eo facto; data igitur mortis sententia contra ipsum, quam mox temperavit misericordia Regis, condonans sibi veniam atque vitam: qui mox missus est ad insulam Euboniæ, quæ pertinebat Domino Willelmo Scrop, ubi sub custodia carcerali residuum transigeret vitæ suæ.

He is banished to the Isle of Man for life.

The Duke of Gloucester, by the King's order, is suffocated.

Interea, quia non videbatur tutum Regi ut Dux Gloverniæ responsis astaret [1] publice, propter favorem populi, qui ei nimis afficiebatur, Rex jussit Comiti Marescallo, ut eum occulte occideret; qui, missis iniquitatis ministris, fecit eum suffocari, superjectis culcitris et lectis, pluma refertis, super os ejus: sicque mortuus est ille vir optimus, Regis filius et Regis patruus, in quo posita fuere spes et solatium totius regni communitatis. Postea Rex astute fecit illud Parliamentum differri usque post Natale Domini, quod reincipitur, vel potius, continuaretur apud Salopiam in confinibus Walliarum.

The further sitting of Parliament postponed.

A.D. 1398. Anno millesimo trecentesimo nonagesimo octavo, [2] et Regis Ricardi vicesimo primo, post Natale in Parliamento continuato Salopiæ, [3] [procuravit] Rex subtiliter, fecitque concedi, de consensu omnium statuum regni, ut potestas Parliamenti remaneret penes certas personas, septem vel octo, quibus liceret determinare, dissoluto Parliamento, certas petitiones in eodem Parliamento porrectas, pro tunc minime expeditas. Cujus concessionis colore personæ sic deputatæ processerunt expost

The King prevails upon Parliament to delegate its powers.

[1] *princeps* in the printed texts.

[2] This and the four following words are omitted in the printed texts: they are added in a somewhat later hand in orig.

[3] Omitted in orig.: supplied from (1) and (5) MS. Corp. Chr. vii. and the printed texts.

MS. Corp. Chr. vii. (1) & (5). ad alia generaliter Parliamentum illud tangentia, et hoc de voluntate Regis, in derogationem status Parliamenti, et incommodum totius regni et perniciosum exemplum. Rex autem super hoc facto, ut videretur habere colorem et auctoritatem, fecit rotulos Parliamenti [1]mutari et deleri, contra effectum concessionis prædictæ. Tunc assumpsit Rex sibi nomen Principis Cestriæ, et Comitem de Derby creavit Ducem Herfordiæ, Comitem Marescallum Ducem Norfolchiæ, Comitem de Ruthlonde Ducem Albemar[l]iæ, Comitem Canciæ Ducem Southreyæ, Comitem Huntyngdone Ducem Excestriæ, Comitissam de Norfolke Ducissam Northfolchiæ, Comitem de Somersete Marchionem ibidem, Dominum de Spencer Comitem Glowcestriæ, Dominum de Nevile Comitem Westmerlonde, Dominum Willelmum Scrope Comitem de Wyltescheire, Dominum Thomam [2]Percy, Senescallum Regis, Comitem Wygorniæ: proinde Rex mutavit arma sua, addiditque scuto suo arma Sancti Edwardi, Regis et Confessoris.

A.D. 1398.

He orders the Rolls of Parliament to be altered.

He creates new titles.

Adds to his shield the arms of Edward the Confessor.

Eo tempore Rex contulit novis creatis suis Ducibus et Comitibus magnam partem terrarum Ducis Glovernіæ, Comitumque Arundeliæ et Warwyc.

Bestows part of the lands of the Duke of Gloucester and others.

In hoc Parliamento, continuato apud Salopiam, [3]Rex, Dominorum consensu, Johannem Dominum de Cobham misit in exilium ad insulam de Gernesey, et Dominus Reginaldus de Cobham condemnatur, quia fuit unus ex deputatis sibi pro suo consilio et tutela per Dominos anno suo undecimo; annullaturque [4]Parliamentum tentum eodem anno.[5] Et ut robur obtinerent perpetuæ firmitatis ordinationes et judicia facta, lata in præmisso Parliamento, impetravit Rex litteras Apostolicas, in quibus graves censuræ proferebantur contra quoscunque qui dictis Statutis in aliquo contravenire præsumpserint; quas promulgari fecit Londoniis ad Crucem Sancti Pauli, et aliis celeberrimis regni locis.

Proceedings against Sir John and Sir Reginald de Cobham.

Proceedings annulled, of the Parliament of the eleventh year of his reign.

Papal sanction thereto.

Circa præsens tempus appellavit Dux Herfordiæ Ducem Northfolchiæ, de quibusdam verbis per eum dictis, quæ in Regis [6]dedecus redundabant. Ob quam causam indictum fuit eis duellum apud Coventre. Tandem cum listas intrassent

The Duke of Hereford accuses the Duke of Norfolk, and a duel is arranged.

[1] *mittari et deliri* in orig., by inadvertence.

[2] *Dercy* in the printed texts.

[3] From this word down to *Gernesey, et*, the context is omitted in (5) MS. Corp. Chr. vii.: in (1) MS. Corp. Chr. vii. it is inserted in a somewhat later hand.

[4] *per* occurs here in orig. and the printed texts; but is not found in (1) and (5) MS. Corp. Chr. vii.

[5] "*Rex tamen, concessa vita Domino de Cobham, misit eum in exilium ad insulam de Gerneseya.*" —added in (1) MS. Corp. Chr. vii.

[6] *deditus* in orig., by inadvertence.

A.D. 1398. The King interferes, and banishes the Duke of Hereford for ten years. The Duke of Norfolk is condemned to perpetual banishment. *MS. Corp. Chr. vii. (1) & (5).*

tam animose quam magnifice, Rex in manu sua causam suscepit, et fecit proclamari quod Dux Herfordiæ debitum suum honorifice adimplesset. Sed tamen, velut immediate postea, Rex, sine causa quacunque legitima, dictum Ducem Herfordiæ ad decennium relegari fecit, et mandavit, contra justitiam et jura militaria, et consuetudines hujus regni. Ducem quoque Northfolchæ perpetuo damnavit exilio, immisericorditer statuens, sub pœnis gravibus, quod nullus rogaret, vel apud ipsum Regem intercedere præsumeret, pro gratia facienda Ducibus supradictis. Facta sunt hæc ea die ad annum, quo idem Dux Northfolchæ Ducem Glovernniæ fecerat suffocari.

Henry Beaufort made Bishop of Lincoln. The Bishop of Lincoln refuses translation.

Hoc anno, Papa Johannem Lincolniensem Episcopum transtulit ad Episcopatum Cestriæ, tunc vacantem, et dedit Episcopatum Lincolniæ Henrico Bewford, uni de filiis Domini Johannis Ducis Lancastriæ et [1] Katerinæ de Swy[n]forde, ob Ducis reverentiam et amorem. Episcopus vero Lyncolniæ veteranus noluit hanc admittere translationem; sed, ea spreta, contulit se Cantuariam, et in Ecclesia Christi inter monachos finem vitæ fecit. Confessor Regis, quidam Frater de Ordine Prædicatorum, de Episcopatu Landafensi translatus est ad Episcopatum Cestrensem.

The King consults the clergy as to arbitrary translations made by the Pope.

Rex eo tempore fecit convocari clerum, ut determinaret, si liceret Papæ tales facere translationes pro arbitrio [2] suæ voluntatis. Ad quod fuit responsum, non directe, sed modo supplicationis porrectæ Regi ex parte cleri, ut dignaretur Papæ scribere, ut a talibus translationibus [3] temperaret pro commodo totius Ecclesiæ Anglicanæ. Rex vero, cum audisset responsum tale, velut offensus [4] licentiæ Papæ, juravit quod si clerus restitisset constanter Papæ in isto negotio, ipse manus apposuisset in auxilium eorundem.

A nuncio from the Pope demands the repeal of certain Statutes.

Eo tempore venit in Angliam Domini Papæ nuncius, Petrus de Bosco, Aquensis Episcopus, ad commonendum Regem ut permitteret ligeos suos provisiones acquirere de manu Papæ, et revocaret Statutum editum contra Provisores, et illud breve "Quare impedit," multaque similia. Sed quod minus obtinuit de suo negotio, Rex accumulavit suo marsupio, donans ei jocalia magni pretii et valoris.

Discovery of the treasure of Helena, mother of

Sub hoc anno Romæ repertus est thesaurus Helenæ, matris Constantini Imperatoris, sub quodam pariete ruinoso: ipsa vero moneta aurea signata fuit imaginibus dictæ dominæ,

---

[1] *Kakerinæ* in orig., by inadvertence.

[2] *suo* in orig., by inadvertence.

[3] *teptaret* in orig.; corrected from (1) and (5) MS. Corp. Chr. vii.: *cessaret* in the printed texts.

[4] *tantæ licentiæ* in (1) MS. Corp. Chr. vii.

MS. Corp. Chr. vii. (1) & (5).

habens in circulo nomen ejus scriptum, et valuit una petra viginti solidos de nostra moneta: cum quo thesauro postea Papa fecit reædificari Capitolium et castellum Sancti Angeli. A.D. 1398. Constantine, at Rome.

[1] Hoc anno fere per totum regnum Angliæ lauri veteres aruerunt, et expost, contra multorum opinionem, reviruerunt. The laurels wither, and revive.

Anno gratiæ millesimo trecentesimo nonagesimo nono, [2] et Regis Ricardi vicesimo secundo, in die Circumcisionis Domini, prope Bedefordiam, aqua profundissima, quæ decurrit inter villas de Suelleston et [3] Harewode, repente restitit et se divisit, sic [4] [quod] per tria milliaria alveus siccus remansit, præbens quibuslibet ingressum siccum. Quod prodigium visum est pluribus significare proprii divisionem, et a Rege defectionem; quæ contigit eo anno. A.D. 1399. Prodigy near Bedford. Signification thereof.

Eo tempore, Rogerus Comes Marchiæ, dum nimis fidit in virtute propria, ab Hibernicis in Hibernia est [5] peremptus. Cujus morte cognita, Rex statuit vindicare personaliter mortem ejus, Hiberniensesque domare, non attendens quantum odium sibi accumulaverat ligeorum suorum, et quam amarum animum vulgus commune gerebat contra eum. Fecit igitur præparationem maximam per totum tempus Quadragesimæ, et sic deinceps usque ad suum transitum, extorquens pecunias, exigens equos et quadrigas, victualia pro profectione sua rapiens, nihilque solvens; unde factus est suis subditis odibilis et invisus. The Earl of March is slain in Ireland. The King resolves to avenge his death. Becomes hateful to his subjects, for his rapacity.

Per idem tempus venit in Angliam Episcopus [6] Calcidonensis, cum litteris Apostolicis [7] comminatoriis, ut regni fideles de bonis conferrent Imperatori Constantinopolitano, qui infestabatur nimium per Tartaros, et ducem eorum vocatum "Morectum." Ut autem proniores efficerentur regnicolæ ad offerendum huic negotio, concessit Papa benefactoribus, vere contritis et confessis, plenam remissionem; involvitque amaris censuris omnes impedientes [8] hujusmodi negotio conferre vo- The Pope aids in obtaining contributions for the Emperor of Constantinople.

---

[1] This passage, in (1) MS. Corp. Chr. vii., is given at the beginning of the following year.

[2] This and the four following words are omitted in the printed texts: they are added in orig. in a somewhat later hand.

[3] *Harlewode* in (1) MS. Corp. Chr. vii.; *Harlewode* in (5) MS. Corp. Chr. vii.

[4] Omitted in orig.; supplied from the printed texts.

[5] This took place in the year 1398.

[6] *Colcidenensis* in orig.; corrected from the printed texts.

[7] *commonitoriis* in (1) MS. Corp. Chr. vii.; *comminatoriis* in (5) MS. Corp. Chr. vii.

[8] *hujus* in orig., (5) MS. Corp. Chr. vii., and the printed texts; corrected from (1) MS. Corp. Chr. vii.

A.D. 1399. lentes, attendens quod licet Imperator esset schismaticus, Christianus tamen erat; et si ipse per incredulos opprimeretur, imminebat toti Christianitati ruina; habens in mente illud poeticum,— MS. Corp. Chr. vii. (1) & (5).

[1] "Tunc tua res agitur, paries cum proximus ardet."

Death of the Duke of Lancaster.

Hoc tempore obiit Johannes Dux Lankastriæ; cujus corpus in Ecclesia Sancti Pauli Londoniis est humatum.

The King changes the sentence of the Duke of Hereford to perpetual banishment.

Post cujus mortem, Rex Dominum Henricum, filium ejus, quem relegaverat ad decennium, exulare decrevit in perpetuum; revocans suas patentes litteras generales, quas sibi prius concesserat, quod in absentia ipsius, dum fuerat relegatus, generales attornati sui possent prosequi pro liberatione sibi facienda de quibuscunque hæreditatibus sive successionibus ipsum extunc contingentibus, et quod homagium suum respectuari posset pro fine rationabili faciendo. Quo facto, constabat manifestius Regem [2] [non] sincere diligere Ducem Herfordiæ, nec eum relegasse nisi pro dissensionibus quæ potuissent oriri inter familias suas et Ducis Northfolchiæ, ut prætensum fuerat, sed occasione bona Ducibus occupandi, ut multi dicebant.

Death of the Duchess of Norfolk.

Circa præsens tempus obiit nobilis fœmina, Domina Margareta Ducissa Northfolchiæ; cujus corpus in ecclesia Fratrum Minorum Londoniis tumulatur.

The King borrows large sums of money.

Interea Rex cepit mutuo grandes pecuniarum summas de quampluribus Dominis, tam temporalibus quam spiritualibus, aliisque personis regni, promittens eis bona fide, sub patentibus litteris, quod pecunias illas sic mutuatas resolveret termino limitato; quas tamen nunquam postea reddidit creditoribus supradictis.

He extorts money, on certain pretences, from seventeen Counties.

Eodem anno grandiores summas exegit pecuniarum a septemdecim regni Comitatibus, [3] metu mortis, imponens eis quod contra eum steterunt cum Duce Gloverniæ, Comitibus Arundeliæ et Warwic, etc; quare paratus erat super eos equitare, tanquam super hostes publicos. Quamobrem recepit a dictis Comitatibus novam securitatem sub jurisjurandi firmamento. Quo facto, misit certos Episcopos, cum aliis viris honorabilibus, ad dictos Comitatus, qui inducerent tam Dominos spirituales quam temporales, et omnes dictorum Comitatuum personas mediocres, ut se Regi submitterent, et semetipsos recognoscerent proditores per litteras sigillis signatas eorundem. Hac occasione coacti sunt Regi concedere clerus, et commune vulgus, Dominique temporales, dictorum Comita-

---

[1] Properly "*Nam tua, etc.*" Horace, *Epist.* I. 18, l. 84.

[2] Inserted from (1) and (5) MS. Corp. Chr. vii.; omitted in orig. and the printed texts.

[3] *metum* in the printed texts.

MS. Corp. Chr. vii. (1) & (5).

A.D. 1399.

tuum, importabiles summas pecuniæ, pro benevolentia sua recuperanda. Cupiens, ut fertur, populum regni sui suppeditare et opprimere, direxit patentes litteras ad omnes regni Comitatus, et per terrores induxit, ut ligei sui quicunque, tam temporales quam spirituales, juramenta insueta præstarent in genere, [1]quæ verisimiliter causare possent destructionem plebis suæ finalem, coegitque ligeos suos ipsa juramenta sub litteris eorum, et sigillis, roborare. Ad albas chartas insuper eosdem ligeos apponere sigilla sua compulit, ut, quotiens grassari vellet in eos, facultatem haberet eosdem singillatim, vel insimul, opprimendi. Fecit præterea, ut Vicecomites per totum regnum nova juramenta præstarent ultra solita; quod videlicet obedirent omnibus mandatis regiis, quotienscunque directa fuissent eisdem sub Magno Privatoque Sigillis, ac etiam litteris illis directis sub signeto suo. Et in casu quo iidem Vicecomites scire possent aliquos de ballivis suis, cujuscunque conditionis essent, aliquod malum dicere sive loqui, publice vel occulte, quod cedere posset in dedecus aut scandalum personæ Regis, ipsos [2]imprisonarent, donec de Rege aliud susciperent in mandatis. Unde contigit quod quamplures ligeorum suorum malitiose accusati, quod debuissent dixisse quicquam publice vel occulte, quod cedere posset in vituperium, scandalum, sive dedecus, personæ Regis, capti fuerunt et imprisonati, et ducti coram Constabulario et Marescallo Angliæ in curia militari; non excusandi aliter, nisi per eorum corpora commissa monomachia se justificarent et defenderent, non obstante quod accusatores et appellatores eorum essent juvenes fortes et sani, et illi sic accusati pro magna parte senes impotentes, [3]mutilati, et infirmi: unde non solum destructio magna regni, [4]sed omnium [5][et] singularum personarum communitatis ejusdem verisimiliter timebatur.

Other acts of tyranny on part of the King.

Circa festum Pentecostes, Rex relinquens regnum, ut præfertur, turbatum multipliciter, navigavit in Hiberniam, cum suis Cestrensibus et quibusdam regni magnatibus, Ducibus videlicet de [6]Almarle, de Excestria, aliis quoque multis; duxitque secum nobiles pueros, filios Ducum Gloverniæ et Herefordiæ, quorum affines præcipue verebantur. Episcopos

The King embarks for Ireland.

How attended.

[1] *suo* in orig. and the printed texts: corrected from (1) and (5) MS. Corp. Chr. vii.

[2] *incarcerarent* in the printed texts.

[3] *mutulati* in orig.

[4] *hæc* in orig.; corrected from (1) and (5) MS. Corp. Chr. vii., and the printed texts.

[5] Omitted in orig.; supplied from the printed texts.

[6] *Albamarla* in (1) MS. Corp. Chr. vii.; *Almarle* in (5) MS. Corp. Chr. vii.

A.D. 1399. etiam traxit secum multos, cum Abbate Westmonasterii, qui, quotiens vellet Parliamenta facere, prout prius constituerat, cum consensu octo personarum, præsto forent ad confirmandum pro parte sua quæ fuerant statuenda. Thesaurum præterea et reliquias, aliaque jocalia, regnique divitias, ab antiquis dimissas in archivis regni pro honore [1] regum, secum abstulit, in Hiberniam profecturus, sine consensu statuum regni sui. Cumque venisset in Hiberniam, videbatur primo quidem prosperari, et super inimicos suos confortari. Non tamen exinde multum lætabantur regnicolæ, qui semper de eo sentiebant deterius, et per eum adhuc gravius opprimi metuebant.

MS. Corp. Chr. vii. (1) & (5).

His intention to supplant Parliament.

Treasures carried with him to Ireland.

At first successful in Ireland.

The Duke of Lancaster prepares to invade England.

Intera Dux Henricus, olim Herfordiæ, sed nunc Lankastriæ, paterno jure, graviter ferens relegationem suam, sed multo gravius exilium suum et exhæredationem, et considerans Regem jam injustum cunctis [2] ligeis propter causas præfatas, nacta opportunitate de Regis absentia, Angliam redire disposuit, ad petendum hæreditatem suam; assumptisque secum Domino Thoma de Arundele, quondam Archiepiscopo Cantuariensi, et filio Comitis Arundeliæ, et hærede, qui jamdudum sibi adhæserant, mare intravit cum familia mediocri, quippe qui secum non amplius habuit quam, ut usu vulgari [3] [loquar], quindecim lanceas, licet [4] in multo fortiorem manum potuisset habuisse; tantum fidebat de sua justitia populique favore. Noluit tamen recto cursu terram ingredi, nec repente; sed nunc apparuit patriotis in una parte regni, nunc in alia; ut videret, si contra eum juxta littora resistentia pararetur.

His adherents.

He hovers about the coasts.

The Duke of York takes counsel how to oppose the Duke of Lancaster.

Audiens Dominus Edmundus, Dominus Dux Eboraci, Regis patruus, cui custodia regni commissa fuit in Regis absentia, quod Dux Lankastriæ jam mare teneret, essetque paratus ad ingrediendum regnum, vocatis regni Cancellario, Domino Edmundo Stafford, Episcopo Cicestrensi, et Thesaurario, Willelmo Scrope Comite de Wylteshere, et militibus de Regis Consilio, Johanne Busschi, Willelmo Bagot, Henrico Grene, et Johanne Russchel, quæsivit super isto negotio quid esset agendum. Qui consuluerunt, ut de Londoniis se transferret ad Sanctum Albanum, præstolaturus ibidem manum bellicam quæ posset Duci resistere venienti; sed quam inane fuit eorum in hac parte consilium, rei exitus declaravit. Nam advenientes illuc de multis provinciis protestabantur se Duci

---

[1] *regni* in the printed texts.

[2] *suis ligeis* in the printed texts.

[3] Omitted in orig., (5) MS. Corp. Chr. vii., and the printed texts: supplied from (1) MS. Corp. Chr. vii.

[4] *in* omitted in (1) and (5) MS. Corp. Chr. vii.

MS. Corp. Chr. vii. (1) & (5).

A.D. 1399.

Lancastriæ nolle nocere, quem noverant injuriose tractatum fuisse. Dicti vero nequam consiliarii, Johannes Bussy, Willelmus Bagot, Henricus Grene, cum Thesaurario, Willelmo Scrope, cognoscentes jam communitatem adhærere velle Duci Lankastriæ, relicto regni Custode atque Cancellario, fugerunt ad castrum Bristolliæ festinanter; et Dux Lancastriæ, circa festum Sancti Martini Translationis, applicuit prope locum ubi quondam fuit villa de Raveneshere, nemine resistente. Cui occurrit Comes Northumbriæ, Dominus Henricus Percy, et Dominus Henricus, ejusdem filius, Comes Westmerlonde, Dominus Radulphus Nevyle, aliique Domini, qui timebant Regis tyrannidem, plures valde. Factusque est in brevi exercitus quasi sexaginta millium pugnatorum, qui omnes uno voto statuerunt inprimis persequi Regis malos consiliarios antedictos. Venerunt Bristoldum celeriter, et [1] obsederunt castrum, quia paraverunt restitisse; ubi tandem capti sunt Thesaurarius Willelmus [2] Le Scrop, Johannes Bussy, Henricus Grene, qui statim in crastino, ad clamorem communium, sunt decapitati: solus ex eis Willelmus Bagot evasit, in Hiberniam navigando; non enim cum sociis suis Bristolliam se contulerat, sed apud Cestriam [3] fugerat, ut se occultaret.

The members of the Council take to flight.

The Duke of Lancaster lands, and is joined by many nobles.

Certain members of the Council are taken, and hanged.

Ricardus Rex, cum audisset in Hibernia de Ducis adventu, mox curavit filium Ducis Glovernisæ et filium Ducis Lankastriæ in castro de Trym recludere, quod est in Hibernia, satis forte; et confestim ad navigium convolavit, cum Ducibus Albemarlæ, Exoniæ, et Southreyæ, et Episcopis Londoniensi, Lincolniensi, et Carleolensi, multisque aliis, ut Duci occurreret cum armata manu, priusquam ipse auxiliarios congregasset.

King Richard, with certain of the nobles, returns to England.

[4] [Sed] cum Angliam attigisset, et cognosset de Ducis apparatu, pugnandi dimisit animum, pro certo tenens quod populus contra eum congregatus citius mori vellet quam cedere, tam propter ejus odium quam timorem. Dimisit igitur familiam, monens per Senescallum, Dominum Thomam Percy, ut se reservarent ad tempora meliora. Ipse vero Rex, quærens divortia, huc illucque contulit multis diebus, semper eum Duce cum exercitu insequente. Tandem apud castellum

He determines not to fight, but dismisses his household, and takes to flight.

---

[1] *obsedendum* in orig., by inadvertence; corrected from (1) and (5) MS. Corp. Chr. vii. and the printed texts.

[2] *De* in Camden's text.

[3] *fugat et* in orig. and the printed texts; *fugerat et occultarat* in (1) MS. Corp. Chr. vii.: corrected from (5) MS. Corp. Chr. vii.

[4] Omitted in orig.; supplied from (1) and (5) MS. Corp. Chr. vii., and the printed texts.

A.D. 1399. de Conewey constitutus, petiit habere colloquium cum Domino Thoma Arundelle, quem expulerat de Archiepiscopatu Cantuariæ, et Comite Northumbriæ, cum nulla spes esset ulterius fugiendi. Quibus indicavit se velle regno cedere, si sibi victus honorificus, vitæque securitas octo personis quas nominare vellet, fide interposita, donaretur. Quibus concessis et firmatis venit ad castrum de Flynt; ubi habito brevi colloquio cum Duce Lancastriæ, mox ascensis equis venerunt ad castellum Cestriæ ea nocte, cum exercitu, qui Ducem secutus fuerat, [1] numeroso valde. Reddidit autem se Rex Duci vicesimo die mensis Augusti, et quadragesimo septimo die ab ingressu Ducis in Angliam: thesaurus Regis, cum equis et aliis ornamentis, et universa domus supellectili, venit ad manus Ducis; sed familiares Regis, magnates, domini, et mediocres, per Wallicos et Northumbrenses despoliati sunt. Rex vero perductus est Londonias, conservandus in Turri usque ad Parliamentum proximo celebrandum.

MS. Corp. Chr. vii. (1) & (5).

Offers to resign the crown, on certain conditions.

Surrenders to the Duke of Lancaster.

He is placed in the Tower of London.

Interim directa sunt brevia ad personas regni, qui de jure debeant interesse Parliamento, sub nomine Regis Ricardi, ut convenirent Londoniis, apud Westmonasterium, in crastino Sancti Michaelis. Quibus convenientibus, ipso die Sancti Michaelis, coram Archiepiscopo Cantuariensi, Thoma de Arundele, Archiepiscopo Eboracensi, Ricardo Le Scroop, et Johanne Episcopo Herfordensi; necnon Domino Henrico, Duce Lancastriæ, Henrico Comite Northumbriæ, Radulpho Comite Westmerlondiæ, Hugone Domino de Burnele, Domino Thoma de Berkeley, Abbate Westmonasterii, Priore de [2] Cantuaria, [3] Dominis de Roos, de [4] Wylby, de Bergenneye, W. [5] Thirnyngge et J. Makeham, Justiciariis; T. Stoke et Johanne Burbache, Legum Doctoribus; T. [6] Herpingham et T. Gray, militibus; Willelmo de Ferby et Dionysio Lopham, notariis publicis; in Turri Londoniarum, Rex Ricardus gratanter, ut apparuit, et vultu hilari, perlegit distincte formam cessationis suæ, et absolvit ligeos suos a juramento fidelitatis et homagii, et relaxavit ab omnibus aliis juramentis quibuscunque, et suis dominiis renunciavit et cessit, juravit, talia dixit, et protulit in legendo, et manu propria [7] se subscripsit, prout in forma cessa-

A Parliament at Westminster.

In presence of certain parties, Richard formally resigns the crown.

[1] *numerosus* in the printed texts.

[2] *Cantuarie* in orig., by inadvertence.

[3] *Domino* in the printed texts.

[4] *Wyluby* in (1) MS. Corp. Chr. vii.; *Wiluby* in (5) MS. Corp. Chr. vii.

[5] *Thering* in (1) MS. Corp. Chr. vii.

[6] *Erpyngham* in (1) and (5) MS. Corp. Chr. vii.

[7] *se* omitted in the printed texts.

MS. Corp. Chr. vii. (1) & (5). tionis plenius continetur. Et mox adjunxit, quod [1] desideravit ut Dux Lancastriæ succederet sibi in regno; sed quia hoc in potestate sua non erat, Archiepiscopum Eboracensem et Episcopum Herfordensem pro tunc suos constituit procuratores, ad declarandum et intimandum cessationi [2] et renunciationi hujusmodi omnibus statibus dicti regni.[3] A.D. 1399. Expresses a desire that the Duke of Lancaster shall succeed him.

In crastino, in Magna Aula Westmonasterii, sede regali tunc vacua, absque præsidente quocunque, procuratores Regis Ricardi, Archiepiscopus [4] scilicet Eboracensis et [5] Episcopus Herfordensis, renunciationem dicti Regis, et cessionem, omnibus statibus regni tunc adunatis, ibi publice declararunt. Quam quidem renunciationem et cessionem singuli singillatim, super hoc requisiti, unanimiter et concorditer admiserunt. His proxies read his renunciation of the crown.

Tunc fuit expositum publice, quod fuit expediens ac utile regno prædicto, pro omni scrupulo et sinistra suspicione tollendis, quod plura crimina et defectus per dictum Regem circa malum regimen regni sui frequentius perpetrata, propter quæ, ut idem Rex asseruit in cessione sua, facta per eum, et esset ipse merito deponendus, [6] a populo legerentur, quodque essent populo declarata. Lecti sunt igitur articuli, numero triginta duo, qui omnes violationes juramenti regalis finaliter concludebant. Et quoniam videbatur cunctis regni statibus, super dictis articulis singillatim ac etiam communiter [7] interrogatis, quod illæ causæ criminum erant sufficientes et notoriæ ad deponendum eundem Regem, ordinati sunt Commissarii ex parte statuum et communitatis ejusdem regni, ad ferendum depositionis sententiam contra dictum Regem, sub forma quæ sequitur:— Articles of accusation read against Richard.

"In Dei nomine, Amen. Nos, Johannes Episcopus Assa-"vensis, J. Abbas [8] Glastoniensis, Thomas Comes Gloucestriæ, "Thomas Dominus de Berkeleye, Thomas de Erpyngham, Form of the sentence of deposition.

---

[1] *de* is inserted before *desideravit* in orig.; by inadvertence.

[2] From this word down to *sede*, the context is omitted in the printed texts.

[3] "*et in signum suæ intentionis et* "*voluntatis hujusmodi, annulum auri* "*de signeto suo patente de digito suo* "*tunc extraxit, et digito dicti Ducis* "*imposuit, desiderans hoc ipsum, ut* "*asseruit.*"— added in (1) MS. Corp. Chr. vii., p. 44.

[4] *scilicet* omitted in the printed texts.

[5] *Episcopus* omitted in the printed texts.

[6] *a* omitted in (5) MS. Corp. Chr. vii.; *publice legerentur* in (1) MS. Corp. Chr. vii.

[7] *interrogatus* in orig.; corrected from the printed texts.

[8] *Glostoniensis* in orig.; *Glasconienses* in the printed texts.

A.D. 1399. "Thomas Gray, milites, Willelmus Thirnyng, Justiciarius, per "pares et proceres regni Angliæ spirituales et temporales, et "ejus regni communitates, omnes status ejusdem regni repræ-"sentantes, Commissarii ad infra scripta spiritualiter deputati, "pro tribunali sedentes, [1]attentis perjuriis multiplicibus, [2]et "crudelitate, aliisque quampluribus criminibus dicti Ricardi, "[3]citra regimen suum in regnis et dominiis supradictis, pro "tempore sui regiminis commissis et perpetratis, ac etiam "dictis statibus palam et publice [4]propositis exhibitis et "recitatis, quæ adeo fuerunt et sunt publica et [5]notoria, "manifesta et famosa, quod nulla poterant aut poterunt ter-"giversatione celari, necnon confessione postdicti Regis, re-"cognoscentis et reputantis, ac veraciter, ex certa etiam "scientia, indicantis, se fuisse et esse insufficientem penitus et "irrationabilem, ad regimen et gubernationem regnorum et "dominii prædictorum, et partium eorundem, ac, propter "demerita [6]notoria, non immerito deponendum, ac per ipsum "Ricardum prius emissa, ac de voluntate et mandatis sui "coram dictis statibus publicata, eisque notificata et exposita "in vulgari, præhabita super hiis et omnibus in ipso negotio "actitatis coram statibus antedictis, et nobis, diligenti vice, "nomine, et auctoritate, nobis in hac parte commissa, ipsum "Ricardum, ex abundanti et ad cautelam, ad regimen et "gubernationem dictorum regnorum et dominii, juriumque et "partium eorundem, fuisse et esse inutilem, inhabilem, et "insufficientem penitus, et indignum, ac propter præmissa, et "eorum prætextu, ab omni dignitate et honore regiis, si quid "dignitatis et honoris hujusmodi in eo remanserit, merito "deponendum pronunciamus, decernimus, et declaramus; et "etiam simili cautela deponimus, per nostram definitivam "sententiam in hiis scriptis.—'Omnibus et singulis Dominis, "'Archiepiscopis, Episcopis, et Prælatis, Ducibus, Marchioni-"'bus, et Comitibus, Baronibus, Militibus, [7]vassallis, [8]valvas-"'soribus, ac cæteris hominibus dictorum regnorum et "'dominii, et aliorum locorum, ad dicta regna et dominia "'spectantium, subditis ac ligeis suis quibuscunque ipsorum,

MS. Corp. Chr. vii. (1) & (5).

[1] *attentos* in the printed texts.

[2] *ac* in the printed texts.

[3] *contra* in the printed texts.

[4] *propositionibus* in the printed texts.

[5] *notaria* in orig.: by inadvertence.

[6] *notaria* in orig.

[7] *vassallibus* in the printed texts.

[8] *quibuscunque, ac* in the printed texts.

MS. Corp. Chr. vii. (1) & (5). A.D. 1399.

" 'de cætero inhibentes expresse, ne quisquam ipsorum de " 'cætero præfato Ricardo, tanquam Regi, vel domino, regno- " 'rum aut dominii prædictorum, pareat quomodolibet, vel " 'intendat; volentes præterea dicti status, quod vel desit, " 'quod valeat aut debeat [1] circa præmissa requiri, superinde " 'singillatim interrogati personas easdem prius per Commis- " 'sarios nominatos, constituerunt procuratores suos, commu- " 'niter et divisim, ad resignandum et reddendum dicto Regi " 'homagium et fidelitatem prius sibi facta, et ad præmissa " 'omnia hujus depositionem et renunciationem tangentia, si " 'oportuerit, intimandum.' "

The Duke of Lancaster claims the throne.

Et confestim, ut constabat de præmissis, et eorum occasione, regnum Angliæ, cum pertinentiis suis, vacare, præfatus Henricus, Dux Laucastriæ, de loco suo surrexit, et stans erectus ut videri posset a populo, et muniens se signo Crucis in facie et in pectore, invocato Christi nomine, regnum Angliæ sic vacans, ut præmittitur, cum corona ac omnibus membris et pertinentiis, vendicavit in lingua materna, sub hac forma verborum:—

Form of the claim.

"In Dei nomine, Amen. Ego Henricus de Lankastria, " vendico regnum istud, cum corona et omnibus membris " illi pertinentibus, tanquam per regium sanguinem veniens " de Rege Henrico, et per justitiam quam Deus de sua gratia " mihi misit, cum adjutorio consanguineorum meorum et " amicorum, ad recuperandum illud; quod regnum erat in " [2] punctu perditionis, propter defectum gubernationis et legum " violationem."

The Lords accede to the claim.

Post quam quidem vendicationem, tam Domini spirituales quam temporales, et omnes regni status, concesserunt unaniminiter ut Dux præfatus super eos regnaret.

The Archbishops place him on the throne.

Tunc Archiepiscopus Cantuariensis, apprehendens manum ejus dextram, posuit eum in sede regali, assistente sibi Archiepiscopo Eboracensi, et universo populo applaudente. Et confestim Dominus Archiepiscopus, assumpto themate, prædicavit; cujus thema fuit, "Vir dominabitur in populo"— [3] Regum ix°, etc.

A Parliament is proclaimed; and the

Post hæc, de mandato novi Regis, fuit proclamatum publice in Magna Aula, quod die Lunæ proxima post festum Sancti Michaelis, Parliamentum [4] teneri ac celebrari deberet; et quod

[1] *contra* in the printed texts.

[2] *puncto* in the printed texts.

[3] 1 *Samuel* ix. 17, according to our version.

[4] *ibidem teneri* in (1) MS. Corp. Chr. vii.

A.D. 1399. die Lunæ extunc proximo sequente, videlicet in festo Sancti Edwardi, Coronatio Regis fieret apud Westmonasterium. Quibus ita peractis, Rex de sede sua surgens, et populum vultu hilari et benigno respiciens, recessit ad Albam Aulam, ubi eo die convivium solemne celebravit. MS. Corp. Chr. vii. (1) & (5).

Intended coronation of the new King.

His deposition is announced to Richard.

Die Mercurii proxima sequente, dicti procuratores, ut præmittitur, deputati ad præsentiam dicti Ricardi nuper Regis, infra Turrim existentis, prout eis injunctum fuerat, accesserunt, et, per os Domini Willelmi Thirnyng, admissionem renunciationis, ac modum, causam, et formam, [1] [sententiæ] depositionis hujusmodi eidem Ricardo notificarunt, et vice omnium regni statuum, homagium et fidelitatem, eidem Ricardo nuper Regi factam, ut præmittitur, reddiderunt et resignarunt: ita quod nullus dictorum statuum sive populi ab hoc tempore et deinceps sibi portaret fidem, nec obedientiam, tanquam regi suo. Ad quæ solum respondit istud, quod non respexit post talia;—"Sed post hæc omnia," inquit, "spero "quod cognatus meus vult esse mihi bonus dominus et "amicus."

His answer thereto.

The issue of King Henry.

Rex Henricus in hoc Parliamento fecit secundum filium suum, dictum "Thomam," Angliæ Senescallum: procreaverat siquidem masculini sexus ex filia Domini Humfridi Boun, Comitis Herfordiæ, juniore, quatuor liberos, et duas fœminas; primogenitus vocabatur "Henricus," secundus "Thomas," tertius "Johannes," quartus "Humfridus."

---

[1] *sive* is inserted here in orig., for *sententiæ*, as in (1) and (5) MS. Corp. Chr. vii.: both *sive* and *sententiæ* are omitted in the printed texts.

De Tempore Regis Henrici, post Conquæstum Quarti.

MS. Corp. Chr. vii. (1) & (5).

Die Translationis Sancti Edwardi, Regis et Confessoris, coronatus est Rex Henricus Quartus apud Westmonasterium per manus Domini Thomæ, Archiepiscopi Cantuariensis, ipso videlicet die quo fuerat in exilium relegatus anno revoluto; non sine divino miraculo, ut putatur; et in auspicium uberioris gratiæ sibi futuræ, prout creditur, unctus est illo [1] cœlesti [2] unguine, quod olim Beata Maria, Mater Dei, commisit Beato Thomæ, Martyri, Archiepiscopo Cantuariæ, dum esset in exilio, conservandum, prædicens eidem, quod Reges Anglorum qui ungerentur hoc unguento pugiles essent Ecclesiæ, et benigni. Hoc unguentum, in aquila aurea et ampulla lapidea conservatum, latuit per multa tempora, sed tandem miraculose manifestatum, dum Dominus Henricus, primus Dux Lancastriæ, bella [3] bellaret regis sui in partibus transmarinis. Ipsi nempe tradita fuit prædicta aquila per quendam sanctum virum, qui illam invenerat revelatione divina: qui dedit eam nobilissimo Principi Edwardo, primogenito Edwardi illustris Regis Angliæ, ut in ea unctione, post mortem patris, ungeretur in Regem. Qui posuit in Turri Londoniarum unguentum præfatum, recludens in cista multis firmata [4] serruris; latuitque ibi, vel per oblivionem vel per negligentiam, usque ad tempus Ricardi Regis, filii Principis memorati.

A.D. 1399. Coronation of Henry IV. at Westminster.

Account of the holy ointment used at his Coronation.

Anno Domini [5] millesimo trecentesimo nonagesimo nono, prædictus Rex Ricardus curiose [6] perscrutatus [res] a progenitoribus sibi relictas, inopinate reperit aquilam et ampullam, et scripturam, sive prophetiam, Beati Thomæ Martyris, cum eisdem. Et cum didicisset virtutem talem unctionis, rogavit Dominum Thomam, Cantuariensem Archipræsulem, ut eum denuo ungeret hoc unguento. Qui hoc facere omnino recusavit, dicens sibi sufficere quod semel per manus suas sacram susceperit in Coronatione pristina unctionem; quæ habere non

Desire of King Richard to have been reanointed with it.

---

[1] "*unguentum fictitium;*" marginal note in MS. Arundel, p. 503.

[2] *unguento* in the printed texts.

[3] *gereret* in the printed texts.

[4] *securis* in the printed texts: this word is omitted, with an hiatus, in (1) MS. Corp. Chr. vii.

[5] *prædicto millesimo* in the printed texts.

[6] *persecutators a* in orig.; corrected from (1) and (5) MS. Corp. Chr. vii. and the printed texts.

A.D. 1399. debuit [1] iterationem. Hanc aquilam, cum ampulla, Rex Ricardus portavit, in Hiberniam profecturus, et denuo rediens in hanc terram. Quam petenti Archiepiscopo apud Cestriam tradidit, dicens [2] sibi jam patenter clarescere quod non fuit voluntatis divinæ ut ungeretur illo [3] unguine, sed alteri deberi tam nobile sacramentum. Archiepiscopus vero, reservans tanta jocalia sub veneranda custodia, ea tenuit usque ad tempus Coronationis Regis moderni, qui primus Regum Angliæ unctus est tam pretioso liquore.

MS. Corp. Chr. vii. (1) & (5).

Henry IV. the first anointed with it.

The King's eldest son created Prince of Wales.

Durante Parliamento, creavit Rex filium suum primogenitum Henricum, cum consensu omnium regni statuum, Principem Walliæ, addens Ducatum Cornubiæ et Cestriæ Comitatum. Expost in eodem Parliamento creavit eum Ducem Aquitanniæ, et hæredem proximum regni Angliæ.

The acts of the Parliament of Shrewsbury are annulled, and those of the eleventh year of Richard II. maintained.

In hoc Parliamento fuit ordinatum ut Statuta, etc., facta in Parliamento tento in festo Exaltationis Sanctæ Crucis [4] [vicesimo] primo anno Ricardi Regis apud Westmonasterium, et postea dilato [5] Salopiam, (in quo certa potestas commissa fuit per auctoritatem dicti Parliamenti certis personis ad procedendum in certis articulis in Rotulo Parliamenti; qua occasione diversa Statuta, judicia, ordinationes, et confirmationes, erronea, facta fuerunt in exhæredationem finalem, destructionem, et extirpationem plurimorum honorabilium domorum, et aliorum ligeorum regni, et hæredum eorum,) in perpetuum, cum suis circumstantiis universis, [6] annullentur, revocentur, [7] irrita habeantur, et cassentur. Item, ut Parliamentum, tentum apud Westmonasterium anno Ricardi Regis undecimo, firmiter teneatur pro honore et commodo totius regni. Item, ut domini, [8] aliæque personæ, qui fuerunt forisjudicati in Parliamento anno vicesimo primo Ricardi Regis, et eorum hæredes qui mortui sunt, restituantur integraliter suis possessionibus, sine alia prosecutione aut liberatione facienda, excepto quod dicti domini et alii nihil habebunt de exitibus receptis medio tempore.

Judgment upon persons banished in that Parliament reversed.

[1] "*ridicule utrique*;" marginal note in MS. Arundel p. 503.

[2] *se* in orig. and the printed texts; *sibi* in (1) and (5) MS. Corp. Chr. vii.

[3] *unguento* in the printed texts.

[4] Omitted in orig.; supplied from (1) and (5) MS. Corp. Chr. vii. and the printed texts.

[5] *Solopiam* in orig. and (1) and (5) MS. Corp. Chr. vii.; corrected from the printed texts.

[6] *annulletur*, and the other verbs in the singular number, in (1) and (5) MS. Corp. Chr. vii., and in orig.; corrected from the printed texts.

[7] *irritum* in orig.; corrected from the printed texts.

[8] *aliique* in orig., by inadvertence.

MS. Corp. Chr. vii. (1) & (5).

A.D. 1399.

The Isle of Man is given to the Earl of Northumberland.

In eodem Parliamento, Rex dedit Comiti Northumbriæ insulam Euboniæ, tenendam de Rege per servitium deportationis gladii cum quo intravit Angliam: dedit et Comiti Westmerlondiæ Richemundiæ Comitatum.

Item, judicium datum fuit contra appellantes Ducis Glowcestriæ, tali modo:—

Judgment against the accusers of the Duke of Gloucester.

"Domini in præsenti Parliamento, Regis assensu, judicant "et decernunt, quod Duces Albemarlæ, Surreyæ, et Excestriæ, "qui modo sunt præsentes, et fuerunt appellantes, amitterent "Ducum nomina et honores exinde, pariter et dignitates. "Et quod Marchio de Dorsete, qui præsens est, nomen amittat "Marchionis, et Comes de Gloucestre, qui præsens est, "nomen amittat pro se et hæredibus suis, sicut et superius "nominati. Et ut omnia castella, prædia, dominia, et cætera "quæ habuerunt de hiis, quæ fuerunt eorum quos appellaverant, a die arestationis Ducis Glowcestriæ et aliorum dominorum, vel expost, aliquo tempore, simpliciter, et absque "gratia et misericordia ulla, perdant. Et ut omnia alia castella, "prædia, dominia, possessiones, et libertates, quæ tenuerant "de dono Regis ipso die vel postea, stent in Regis gratia ab "hac hora; et quod omnes litteræ patentes et chartæ quas "habuerunt, vel aliquis illorum habet, dictorum nominum, "castellorum, dominiorum, possessionum, et libertatum, sursum reddantur in Cancellariam, ibidem cancellanda. Et "quod omnino consistant in statu quem habuerunt nomine et "possessione, ante dictum diem arestationis prædictæ. Et "quod ipsi, nec aliquis illorum, det libratas vel signa, nec "faciat retinentiam hominum, nisi officiariorum intrariorum "in suis domibus, et officiariorum extra, ad gubernandum "hospitia, terras, et possessiones eorum, et aliorum intrariorum, prout rationabiliter pertinet dictarum statui personarum. Et ulterius, Domini temporales, Regis assensu, judicant et decernunt, quod si isti postdicti domini, Dux de "Almarle et cæteri, sive illorum aliquis, unquam adhæreat "Ricardo, qui fuit Rex et est depositus, ferendo consilium, "adjutorium, vel confortamen sibi, contra dictam depositionem, judicium, ordinationem, vel affirmationem, in præsenti "Parliamento, tangentem personam dicti Ricardi, ut sint in "pœna proditionis, et pro talibus habeantur et teneantur. "Et insuper, quia fuit, et est, clamor et tumultus magnus in "communi populo, quod quidam dictorum Dominorum famuli "fecerunt grandes extortiones, injurias, et oppressiones in "communi populo, per causarum manutenentiam, Domini "supradicti, Regis assensu, judicant et decernunt, quod fiant "proclamationes, etc., quod si ullus velit conqueri de "dictis Dominis, vel de aliquo de sua familia, qui cum illis

A.D. 1399. "est, aut erat hiis temporibus, scilicet de extortionibus, injuriis, vel oppressionibus, sibi factis per eosdem, veniat, et gravamen insinuet, et remedium fiet ei." MS. Corp. Chr. vii. (1) & (5).

Discontent of the multitude, that their lives are spared.

Post judicium datum contra Dominos prædictos, ortum est murmur maximum in communi populo contra Regem et Archiepiscopum Cantuariensem, Comitemque Northumbriæ, aliosque de Regis Consilio, quod vitas salvassent hominum, quos vulgus sceleratissimos et morte dignissimos reputabat.

Ambassadors sent to various countries, announcing the King's accession.

Rex, ut demonstraret cunctis gentibus in circuitu constitutis, quo jure, quo titulo, quo favore, coronam regni susceperit, misit ad Curiam Romanam ambassiatores, Episcopum Herfordensem, Magistrum Johannem Trevenant, J. Cheyne militem, et J. Cheyne scutiferum: in Franciam misit Episcopum Dunelmensem, Magistrum Walterum Skyrlow, et Comitem Wygorniæ, Dominum Thomam Percy. In Hispanniam Episcopum Assavensem, Magistrum Johannem Trevor, et Dominum Willelmum Par militem, destinavit. In Almanniam misit Episcopum Bangorensem, cum aliis quorum nomina non tenemus.

The Scots invade England, and destroy the Castle of Werk.

Scoti per tempus Parliamenti nacta occasione de Dominorum absentia Borealium, et quia partes Angliæ Boreales per illud tempus premebantur grandi pestilentia, partes illas hostiliter intraverunt, et castrum de Werk, quod deputatum fuerat custodiæ Domini Thomæ Gray militis, qui pro tunc in Parliamento stetit pro commoditate gentis suæ, ceperunt et per tempus aliquod tenuerunt; quod tandem despoliaverunt et funditus dejecerunt, aliaque multa mala fecerunt in terra.

Death of the Duke of Norfolk.

Thomas de Mounbray, quondam Dux Northfolchiæ, diem clausit extremum in terra peregrinationis; cujus mors fuisset toti regno defluenda merito, si in Ducis Gloverniæ necem [1] minime concessisset.

Death of the Duchess of Gloucester.

Item, hoc anno cessit in fata Domina Ducissa Gloverniæ; quæ, parum [2] fausto omine, filium suum et hæredem amiserat, "Humfridum" vocabulo, subtractum sibi pestilentia, cum fuisset [3] de Hibernia revocatus.

Miracle at Rome.

Sub hoc tempore Romæ imagines Crucifixi et Beatæ Virginis Mariæ humorem [4] consanguineum sudaverunt. Quo tempore nobiles pene totius Italiæ, cum plebe communi, nova devotione tacti, induti pannis lineis, cum crucibus [5] [rubeis] insertis in eisdem, ferentes cruces in manibus et vexilla habentes,

Several Companies of Flagel-

---

[1] *inime* in orig., by inadvertence.

[2] *infausto* in orig. and Camden's text; *ante infausto* in (1) and (5) MS. Corp. Chr. vii.

[3] *de* omitted in the printed texts.

[4] *sanguineum* in the printed texts.

[5] Supplied from (1) MS. Corp. Chr. vii.: omitted in orig. and the printed texts.

MS. Corp. Chr. vii. (1) & (5). etiam imaginem Crucifixi deportatam coram eis, fecerunt processiones, circumeuntes stationes die noctuque, et, nudatis corporibus usque [1]umbilicum, flagellabant se, cantantes pios cantus in vulgari et in Latino; sed devotius et frequentius, inter cæteros,— A.D. 1399. lants arise in Italy.

[2]"Stabat Mater dolorosa,
Juxta crucem lacrymosa,
Dum pendebat Filius;"—

et clamabant sæpissime misericordiam et pacem in suo vulgari. Fuerunt autem in una Comitiva quadraginta millia; in alia vero, viginti millia; in alia quoque, decem milia. Ut autem una Comitiva complevit Romæ suam devotionem, accessit et alia, faciens per omnia sicut prior; et non dormierunt in lectis pro tempore peregrinationis suæ, nec carnes aut lacticinia comederunt, et diebus Sabbati generaliter jejunaverunt.

Anno gratiæ millesimo quadringentesimo, [3]Comites Canciæ, Salesburiæ, et Huntyngdoniæ, ingrati Regis beneficiis, qui vitas eorum salvaverat, contra vota cunctorum regni communium, ac multorum procerum, congregantes iniquitatem sibi, per conventicula facta variis locis, et conjurationes, statuerunt super Regem irruisse repente in castello de Wyndeleshore, sub simulatione ludorum natalitiorum, et eum, cum filiis suis, crudeliter peremisse; Regemque Ricardum, requisitum, regno restituisse, et per tanta facinora nomina Ducum atque possessiones, quibus privati fuerant, recuperasse. A.D. 1400. Conspiracy of certain nobles, to slay the King, at Windsor. Sed Rex gratiose prænoscens præstructos dolos, de loco recessit, et Londonias se contulit festinanter. He is informed of their designs, and departs therefrom. Illi vero, scilicet Comes Canciæ et Comes Sarum, putantes Regem latere suam conspirationem, Dominica proxima post festum Circumcisionis Domini, id est, in Octabis Innocentium, in ipsius noctis crepusculo præfatum facinus perficere sunt [4]ingressi; perveneruntque ad castellum cum armata manu circiter quadringentorum virorum. Sed cum cognovissent Regem præmunitum, conturbati sunt valde, diverticula requirebant, veneruntque cursu velocissimo ad Sunnyngges, quoddam prædium juxta Radyngiam, ubi Regina tunc [5]temporis morabatur. Ingressusque Comes Canciæ, cum prædicto Comite Sarum, dissimulata tristitia in præsentia familiæ Reginæ, sibi occurrentis, elevata ad frontem dextra, They visit the wife of the late King, at Sunning.

---

[1] *umbilicam* in orig., by inadvertence.

[2] The beginning of the *Prose*, or *Sequence*, of the Mass for the Dead, in the Roman Church.

[3] "*qui est annus regni Regis Henrici, a Conquæstu Quarti, primus,*" inserted here in the printed texts.

[4] *aggressi* in the printed texts.

[5] *tempore* in orig.: corrected from (1) and (5) MS. Corp. Chr. vii. and the printed texts.

A.D. 1400.

Declaration made by the Earl of Kent.

MS. Corp. Chr. vii. (1) & (5).

signavit se;—"Benedicite," inquit, "quid accidit quod Dominus Henricus de Lancastria sic a facie mea fugit, qui "tantum de sua strenuitate et militia se extollebat?" Et mox subjunxit,—"Domini," ait, "et amici, noveritis quod "Henricus de Lancastria, me persequente, fugit ad Turrim "Londoniarum, cum filiis suis et amicis. Et meæ intentionis "est adire Ricardum, qui fuit, et est, et erit, verus Rex "noster; quia jam evasit de carcere, et jacet ad Pontem "Fractum cum centum millibus defensorum."[1]

He deprives certain persons of King Henry's cognizances.

Ut autem fidem faceret dictis, detraxit signa Regis, scilicet collaria, de collis quorundam quos vidit ibi habentes signa talia, cum despectu, dicens non esse gestandum de cætero tale signum. Detraxit insuper de brachiis domicellorum signa crescentium, et abjecit. Sicque lætificata Regina, licet inaniter, recessit, tendens primo Wallyngfordiam, deinde Abyndoniam, commonens populum per omnes vias, ut arma caperent et occurrerent regi suo Ricardo. Pervenit tandem Cirecestriam cœca nocte: viri vero dictæ villæ, suspectum habentes tantum apparatum, et putantes, prout erat, rumores eorum mendaces, præstrinxerunt omnes aditus et exitus hospitii eorundem. Cumque media nocte tentassent latenter discedere, villani, arcubus et sagittis armati, eos egredi non sinebant. Comites vero cognoscentes sibi imminere periculum, et ipsi ad arma convolant, putantes villanos levi negotio superandos. Pugnatum est igitur, hic et ibi, a noctis medio usque ad horam diei tertiam. Tandem fatigati, manus dederunt communibus, obnixe precantes ut salverentur a morte, donec cum Rege colloquium habuissent. [2][Quod factum fuisset], si non quidam presbyter de eorum familia ignem misisset in quasdam domos villæ, hac intentione, ut, occupatis communibus circa extinctionem ignis, Domini possent habere evadendi occasionem; sed frustra, nam communes, relictis domibus in conflagrationis periculo, majori furia concitabantur ad vindicandum in dictos Dominos incendii damna prædicti: perduxerunt igitur eos de Abbathia, et in ipso noctis crepusculo decollaverunt.

The Earls of Kent and Salisbury are taken and beheaded by the people of Cirencester.

The Earl of Salisbury, a favourer of the Lollards.

Comes Sarum, qui Lollardorum fautor in tota vita fuerat, et imaginum vilipensor, [3]contemptor Canonum, Sacramentorumque derisor, sine Sacramento confessionis, ut fertur, vitam finivit.

---

[1] "*Ideo qui Regem Ricardum diligitis, et Reginam, vos armate et "me sequimini, contrahentes vobiscum "de patria quos potestis.*" added in (1) MS. Corp. Chr. vii.

[2] Omitted in orig. and the printed texts: supplied from (1) MS. Corp. Chr. vii.

[3] *contempsor* in orig., by inadvertence.

MS. Corp. Chr. vii. (1) & (5).

A.D. 1400.

The Earl of Holland flies from London.

Comes Huntyngdone, Dominus Johannes Holand, non erat cum prædictis Dominis apud castellum de Wyndeshore, sed expectavit Londoniis rei finem. Qui, cum novisset rem versam contra vota, fugere nitebatur in scapha, sed vento flante contrario repulsus est. Quamobrem equo vectus, pervenit Estsexiam, cum quodam milite dicto "J.[1] Schevele." Tentavit igitur per mare fugisse ab illis partibus; sed quotiens voluit mare ingredi, totiens repulsus est vi ventorum, donec omnino desperans de Neptuni suffragiis, destitit ab inceptis. Tandem reversus in terram ad domum cujusdam amici [2]sui, dum sederet in cœna cum milite supradicto, captus est per communes patriæ, et ductus primo ad villam de Chelmesfordia, deinde ad [3]fortalitium de Plesshi, custodiendus ibidem tanquam loco securiori. Quo confluentibus regionis communibus, die Sancti Mauri, circa solis occasum, productus est, et in loco quo Dominus eorum, Dux Gloverniæ, quondam [4]arestatus fuit per Regem Ricardum, decapitatus est, confessus prius lacrymabiliter, se peccasse in Deum suum multipliciter, et in Regem suum, quia sciens consilia dictorum Dominorum, Regem exinde minime præmunisset.

He is taken prisoner, and executed at Plesshy.

Per idem tempus Dominus Thomas Le Spencer, qui dicebatur "Comes Gloucestriæ," dum fugisse proposuerat, repente captus, ductus est Bristoldum, ubi juxta vota communium decollatus est. Capti sunt quamplures alii hujus conspirationis conscii, et morte multati sunt, quidam Oxoniis, quidam Londoniis. Damnati sunt nempe Londoniis clerici, J. [5]Mawde et Willelmus Ferby, qui tractione, suspensione, et capitis detruncatione, finierunt vitam. Bernardus Brokays et [6]J. Schevele milites, alii quoque plures, acceperunt similem mortis sortem. Episcopus Karleolensis, impetitus [7]est de conjuratione; damnatus est, sed [8]vitæ Regis misericordia reservatus.

The Earl of Gloucester and others are executed.

The Bishop of Carlisle is condemned, but his life is spared.

Ricardus, quondam Rex Angliæ, cum audisset hæc infortunia, mente consternatus semetipsum extinxit inedia voluntaria, ut fertur, clausitque diem extremum apud castrum de Ponte

The late King said to have starved himself to

---

[1] *Johanne* in the printed texts.

[2] *qui, dum* in orig. and the printed texts; corrected from (5) MS. Corp. Chr. vii.

[3] *portalicium* in the printed texts.

[4] *erestatus* in orig., by inadvertence.

[5] The word "*Maudeleyn*" is inserted here in orig. and the printed texts, before *Mawde*, probably from the fact that "——*Maudelene*" only is given here in (1) MS. Corp. Chr. vii., and that *Maudeley* is inserted in the margin of (5) MS. Corp. Chr. vii.

[6] *Johannes* in the printed texts.

[7] *est* omitted in (1) MS. Corp. Chr. vii. and the printed texts.

[8] *tamen Regis* in the printed texts.

A.D. 1400. death, at Pontefract. Fracto, die Sancti Valentini. Cujus corpus per loca celeberrima quæ interjacent a dicto castello usque Londonias, ubi contigit pernoctare, monstratum est post Officium Mortuorum, et in crastino post Missam peractam. Cumque in ecclesia Sancti Pauli Londoniis celebratæ fuissent exequiæ, Rege præsente et Londoniarum civibus, confestim corpus reportari jubetur ad Langley, tumulandum in ecclesia Fratrum Prædicatorum; perfeceruntque ibidem supremum officium Episcopus Cestrensis, Abbas Sancti Albani, et Abbas de Waltham, sine magnatum præsentia, sine populari turba; nec erat qui eos invitaret ad prandium post laborem. MS. Corp. Chr. vii. (1) & (5.).

His body is shown on its way to London.

He is buried at Langley.

A fatal epidemic. Eodem anno, sub æstivo tempore, fuit epidemia quæ multos hac luce privavit.

Some Scottish ships taken by the men of Lynn. Eo tempore per viros de [1]Lennia captæ sunt quædam naves Scotorum, quarum Amirallus fuit Dominus Robertus Logon, miles Scoticus, qui pactus fuerat destruxisse navigium Anglicanum, et præcipue piscantes apud Aberdenam.

The Orkney Islands ravaged. Sub eodem tempore nostrates insulas [2]Orkatrium quasdam deprædati sunt.

The King ravages Scotland, and returns. Mox etiam Rex, congregato exercitu, profectus est in Scotiam; sed Scotis se subtrahentibus, nec facientibus belli copiam, Rex, vastata patria, reversus est.

Rebellion in Wales, under Owen Glendower. Interia Wallici, nacta occasione de Regis absentia, duce quodam Oweyno de Glendour, rebellare cœperunt. Hic primo apprenticius fuit apud Westmonasterium, [3]deinde scutifer Regis moderni; sed orta discordia inter eum et Dominum Reginaldum Grey de Ruthyn, pro terris quas asseruit sibi jure hæreditario pertinere, cum rationes suas et allegationes parvipensas cerneret, primo in dictum Dominum de Grey hostilia commovit arma, vastans possessiones ejus per incendia, et ferro perimens plures de sua familia nimis crudeliter et inhumane. Quem proinde Rex prosequi statuens, tanquam pacis patriæ turbatorem, cum armata manu Walliam est ingressus; sed Cambri, cum duce suo, montes Snowdoune occupantes, [4]intentatæ vindictæ se protinus subtraxerunt. Rex vero, combusta regione et quibusdam peremptis, quos sors pro tunc gladiis [5]evaginatis obtulerat, cum præda jumentorum et animalium remeavit.

Cause of the rising.

The King ravages part of Wales, and returns.

---

[1] *Lemnia* in the printed texts.

[2] *Orcadum* in the printed texts; *Orkadum* in (1) MS. Corp. Chr. vii.

[3] *de* in orig.; corrected from (5) MS. Corp. Chr. vii. and the printed texts.

[4] *intentata vindicta* in the printed texts.

[5] *ænigmatis* in the printed texts.

MS. Corp. Chr. vii. (1) & (5).

A.D. 1400.

Obituary of the year.

Hoc anno obiit Magister Radulphus Ergam, Episcopus Bathoniensis; cujus loco, Regis intuitu, electus est Magister Henricus Boowet.[1]

The Emperor of Constantinople visits England, and is honourably entertained.

Sub eodem tempore, Imperator Constantinopolitanus venit [2] Angliam, postulaturus subsidium contra Turkos; cui occurrit Rex, cum apparatu nobili, ad Le Blakeheth, die Sancti Thomæ Apostoli, suscepitque, prout decuit, tantum heroem, duxitque Londonias, et per multos dies exhibuit gloriose, pro expensis hospitii sui solvens, et eum respiciens tanto fastigio donativis.

The Bishop of Carlisle is deprived of his bishopric.

Papa transtulit Episcopum Karleolensem ad Episcopatum [3] unde nec fructus perciperet nec proventus: cui successit in Pontificatum [4] Lugubaliæ Magister Willelmus Strikeland.

A.D. 1401.

Parliament at London.

A Statute passed, enjoining capital punishment on the Lollards.

A false priest burnt at Smithfield.

Anno Domini millesimo quadringentesimo primo, [5] post Epiphaniam factum est Parliamentum Londoniis; in quo Statutum fuit editum de Lollardis, ut ubicunque deprehenderentur suam pravam [6] dogmatizare doctrinam, [7] caperentur, et Diœcesano Episcopo traderentur. Qui si perseverarent pertinaciter opiniones suas defendere, degradarentur, et jurisdictioni sæculari committerentur: practizataque fuit hæc lex in [8] quodam pseudo-presbytero, qui apud Smythefeld, multis aspectantibus, est combustus.

The son of Bajazet is slain in battle.

The Emperor of Constantinople leaves England.

Rex de Letto peremit in bello [9] Balsak, filium Balthasardan illustris, quem "Admiratum" vocant, destruxitque Hierusalem et in circuitu regionem; et quia gratiose vicit eum, et inopinabiliter, conversus est ad Christianitatis ritum, cum sexaginta millibus hominum sectæ suæ. Hiis auditis rumoribus, Imperator [10] effectus lætior recessit ab Anglis, honoratus a Rege donariis pretiosis.

Death of the Earl of Warwick.

Hoc anno, sexto Idus Aprilis, obiit Dominus Thomas de Bello Campo, Comes Warwyci; qui sævam fortunam expertus fuerat sub Rege Ricardo.

---

[1] A passage in (1) and (5) MS. Corp. Chr. vii. is omitted here.

[2] *in Angliam* in the printed texts.

[3] A blank in orig.; *alium* in the printed texts. Thomas Merkes, an adherent to the cause of King Richard, was deprived in 1399; and William Strickland succeeded him in that year.

[4] *Ligubaliæ* in orig. and the printed texts.

[5] "*qui est annus regni Regis Henrici, a Conquæstu Quarti, secundus,*" inserted in the printed texts.

[6] Omitted in the printed texts.

[7] *amplexantes caperentur* in the printed texts.

[8] *quodam* omitted in the printed texts.

[9] *Bassak* in (1) and (5) MS. Corp. Chr. vii.

[10] *effectus* omitted in the printed texts.

A.D. 1401. Obituary of the year.

Eodem anno debita naturæ solvit Magister [1] J. de Botelesham; qui ex Fratre de Ordine Prædicatorum factus [2] Episcopus Bethlemitanus, ac deinde Roffensis, per [3] Urbanum Papam; cui successit J., ejusdem cognominis clericus, de familia Domini Cantuariensis.

MS. Corp. Chr. vii. (1) & (5.)

Queen Isabella returns to France.

Sub hoc tempore, conditionibus jam inter regna firmatis, et omnibus profectioni Reginæ necessariis præparatis, revecta est Ysabella, quondam Regina Angliæ, ad patrem patriamque suam Franciæ, nondum annorum plene duodecim.

Damage inflicted on the English by Glendower.

Hoc tempore Owcynus de Glendore, cum suis Wallencibus, damna gravia infert Anglis.

The King escapes a plot to maim or slay him.

Cum, nocte quadam, Rex iturus esset cubitum, Deo protegente, evasit letale periculum; siquidem in stramento lecti sui, cujusdam proditoris ingenio, positum fuerat quoddam ferrum fabrefactum ad modum tricuspidis, habens tres [4] longos aculeos subtiles atque rotundos, punctuum aculeis acutissimis sursum erectis; tali ingenio, ut cum Rex decubuisset et mole corporali stramenta pressisset, per eosdem aculeos vulneratus fuisset, vel forsitan interfectus. Sed, Deo volente, Rex [5] inopinate persensit instrumentum mortiferum, et periculum devitavit.[6]

A.D. 1402. Appearance of a comet.

Anno gratiæ millesimo quadringentesimo secundo, [7] cometa apparuit mense Martio, primo inter Corum et Septentrionem, videlicet in Circio, flammas emittens, postremo comas in Boream transferens; præsignans fortassis effusionem humani sanguinis circa partes Walliæ et Northumbriæ [8] expost futuram.

Lord Reginald de Grey is taken by Owen Glendower.

Eo tempore Owenus de Glendore vastavit terras Domini Reginaldi de Grey; cui occurrens idem Dominus, putans eum levi negotio superandum, [5] inopinate versa [9] Martis alea, captus est, et de suis plurimi trucidati; quod infortunium Wallicos extulit in superbiam, et insolentiam auxit eisdem.

Circa festum Pentecostes conjuraverunt quidam mortem Regis, asserentes Regem Ricardum vivere et quantocius in

[1] William de Bottlesham, Bishop of Rochester, died in 1400; John de Bottlesham in 1404.

[2] *est Episcopus* in the printed texts.

[3] *Urbanam* in orig., by inadvertence.

[4] *laqueos* in (1) MS. Corp. Chr. vii.; *longos* in (5) MS. Corp. Chr. vii.

[5] *inopinate* in the printed texts.

[6] A passage in (5) MS. Corp. Chr. vii. is omitted here.

[7] *qui est annus regni Regis Hen-"rici, a Conquæstu Quarti, tertius,"* inserted here in the printed texts. A passage in (1) MS. Corp. Chr. vii. is omitted here.

[8] *et post* in orig.; corrected from (1) and (5) MS. Corp. Chr. vii. and the printed texts.

[9] *mortis* in the printed texts.

MS. Corp. Chr. vii. (1) & (5).

A.D. 1402.

palam venturum, et suos fideles digne remuneraturum. Hujus conspirationis in parte metus evanuit, capto quodam presbytero apud Ware, qui scripserat nomina multorum in matricula, qui futuræ turbationis auctores vel adjutores fuissent. Iste, juxta conceptum proprium, nomina plurimorum inscripserat, qui nullatenus conscii fuerant hujus pacti; prout expost patuit sua confessione. Nempe cum requisitus fuisset de certis personis coram eo constitutis, quarum nomina ipse irrotulasset, si novisset eas, respondit quod non; et cum interrogatus fuisset quare tales irrotulasset, dixit, quia opinabatur eos voluisse fecisse contra Regem, si complices invenissent, quia per Regem Ricardum ditati quondam fuerant, et promoti. Hac occasione liberati sunt plurimi qui fuere suspecti, et sacerdos tractus et suspensus est.

Ineffectual conspiracy against the King; promoted by a priest, who is taken and executed.

Non multo post, Prior quondam de Lawne, qui pro malo Prioratus sui regimine a beneficio et statu suo privatus erat, sortem similem est expertus, non quia deprehensus aliquid actitasse, sed quia confessus se maligni consilii fuisse conscium, et hoc utique concelasse. Hic erat quondam canonicus apud Dunstapliam, dictus "Walterus de Baldok," qui, malo omine, relicto claustro, pervenit ad Regis Ricardi Curiam, et ibidem [1] limitatus diutissime cum fortuna, tandem dono Regis de Lawne obtinuit Prioratum.

The former Prior of Lawne is similarly punished, for being privy to the plot.

Eo tempore, sat iniquo sidere, [2] [quidam] ex Ordine Minorum de proditione pensantes, priusquam procedere potuissent, capti sunt. Quorum unus interrogatus quid facere voluisset, si Rex Ricardus viveret et adesset, respondit constanter, se pro eo velle decertasse contra quemlibet usque ad mortem: data proinde contra eum sententia, tractus et suspensus est, in habitu suæ religionis. Sed [3] confratres ejus, non ferentes tantum dedecus, [4] obtinuerunt ut corpus defuncti supremis exequiis curaretur.

A Minorite Friar executed for treason.

Suspensus est etiam eo tempore miles Rogerus de Clarindon, filius, ut dicebatur, nothus quondam nobilis Principis Edwardi, filii Regis Edwardi, Tertii a Conquæstu; et, cum eo, suus armiger et valectus; eo quod accusati de proditione, defecerunt in purgatione.

Roger de Clarendon, bastard son of Edward, Prince of Wales, is executed.

Diabolica species apparuit in Estsexia apud Danbury, in festo Corporis Christi, hora Vesperarum, in similitudine Fratris

Appearance of the Devil at Dunbury in Essex.

---

[1] *linitatas* apparently in orig.; *limitatus* in the printed texts.

[2] Omitted in orig. and (5) MS. Corp, Chr. vii.: supplied from (1) MS. Corp. Chr. vii. and the printed texts.

[3] *conferens* in orig. by inadvertence; corrected from the printed texts.

[4] *æstimaverunt* in the printed texts.

A.D. 1402. The church suffers from lightning. Minoris intrantis ecclesiam, et insolentissime debacchantis; unde terrorem parochianis incussit indicibilem. Eadem hora, cum tempestatis turbine et tonitruo perhorrendo, fragore fulgurumque, et [1]coruscationum globis collucentibus, [2]summitas [3]totius ecclesiæ confracta est, et medietas cancelli confracta et dissipata. MS. Corp. Chr. vii. (1) & (5).

Eight Minorite Friars executed. Post dies aliquot capti sunt octo Fratres de Minorum Ordine, et ad judicium publicum dedecorose tracti, ubi examinati et convicti quod contra Regem fecissent, Londoniis tracti, suspensi, et decapitati sunt.

The men of Hereford defeated by Owen Glendower, and Edmund Mortimer taken prisoner. Eo tempore Owenus de Glendore, cum comitiva Cambrensium, assuetis intendens irruptionibus, pene totam militiam Herfordensis Comitatus provocavit ad arma. Cujus Comitatus viris congregatis, Edmundus de Mortuo Mari præbuit ducatum; sed cum perventum fuisset ad actum, proditione mediante, [4]et Edmundus captus et cæteri victi sunt, occisis de [5]nostratibus amplius quam mille viris: ubi perpetratum est facinus sæculis inauditum, nam fœminæ Wallencium, post conflictum, genitalia peremptorum absciderunt, et membrum pudendum in ore cujuslibet mortui posuerunt, testiculosque a mento dependere fecerunt; nasosque præcisos in culis presserunt eorundem; nec patiebantur corpora peremptorum sine grandi pretio supremis exequiis commendari. Atrocities practised on the bodies of the slain.

A daughter of King Henry is married to the son of the Emperor of Germany. Hoc anno misit Rex filiam suam, cum grandi apparatu, ad Coloniam Agrippinam; cui occurrit filius Imperatoris in apparatu, qui, ut decuit nomen tanti fastigii, nec [6]par erat in occursum venire tantæ virgini. Ibi, tamen juvenis, duxit, more regionis, [7]virginem in uxorem.

Glendower prevails against the English, by magic devices, it is surmised. Rex Angliæ, [8]circa festum Assumptionis Sanctæ Mariæ, collectis exercitibus, profectus est in Walliam, ad persequendum Owenum de Glendor; sed nihil profuit [9]tantus armorum strepitus, cum Wallicus in nota latibula se recepit; quin potius, ut putatur, arte magica Regem pene perdidit, cum exercitu quem ducebat, per pluvias, nives, et grandines, ut creditur, arte diabolica concitatas. In Vigilia vero Nativitatis Sanctæ

---

[1] *choruscatione* in Camden's text.

[2] *summitastoli* in (1) and (5) MS. Corp. Chr. vii.; *sravitas* (?) in orig.; *concavitas* in the printed texts.

[3] *toti ipsius* in orig.; corrected from the printed texts.

[4] *et* omitted in the printed texts.

[5] *magnatibus* in orig. and the printed texts; corrected from (1) and (5) MS. Corp. Chr. vii.

[6] *paruerat* in the printed texts.

[7] *virginiem* in orig., by inadvertence.

[8] *ante festum* in the printed texts.

[9] *tanti* in orig.; corrected from (1) and (5) MS. Corp. Chr. vii. and the printed texts.

MS. Corp. Chr. vii. (1) & (5). Mariæ, cum Rex in loco amœnissimo fixisset tentoria, ibi nihil [1]formidabile, sed summa requies, sperabatur, repente in ipsius noctis prima vigilia flaverunt venti, et descendit pluvia tam excessiva, ut ipsum Regis tentorium dejicerent, et ejusdem lanceam everterent impetu vehementi, et in Regis armatura defigerent. Fuisset ipsa Regi nox ultima, si non quievisset armatus; nec meminerunt Anglici, licet assueti rebus bellicis, se unquam tantum vexatos, periculis tantis expositos, in ulla expeditione fuisse. Fuerunt plures, si fas sit credere, qui dicerent hæc adversa arte Fratrum Minorum contra Regem fuisse commentata, qui parti Wallici favere dicebantur. Sed absit hoc ab hominibus tam sanctam professis regulam, ut cum dæmonibus tantam contraherent familiaritatem, et [2]ponerent in gloria sua maculam nullo sæculo detergendam. Rex autem, necessitate cogente, redivit in Angliam, post incensam patriam et prædatam.[3]

A.D. 1402.

The English suffer greatly from rain and storm.

Magical devices attributed to the Minorite Friars, by some.

Eo tempore Scoti, fastu solito concitati, satis hostiliter Angliam sunt ingressi; putabant nempe cunctos dominos Transhumbranos in Walliarum partibus regiis obsequiis fuisse detentos; sed Comes Northumbriæ, Dominus Henricus Percy, et Henricus ejus filius, Comesque de Dunbarre, qui dudum, relictis Scotis, fidem fecerat Regi Angliæ, cum armata manu et copia sagittariorum, Scotis repatriare volentibus, post prædas et incendia, restiterunt subito, et repente præcludentes eis viam, sic quod oportebat Scotos subsistere et capere locum pugnæ. Elegerunt ergo montem juxta villam de Wollor, vocabulo "Halweden Hil," in quo se cum suis armatis et arcitenentibus collocarunt. Quod nostrates cernentes, relicta via in qua constiterant contra Scotos, montem Scotis oppositum conscenderunt. Nec mora, nostri sagittarii, in vallo constituti, sagittas miserunt ad Scotorum cuneum, ut eos ad descensum quomodolibet provocarent. E contra, arcitenentes Scotici in nostros sua spicula dirigunt toto nisu. Qui tamen, ut senserunt gravitatem, et velut imbriferam tempestatem, sagittarum nostræ partis, fugerunt. Comes Duglas, cernens suorum fugam, nam et ipse [4]campi-ductor Scotorum, ne belli desertor videretur esse, arrepta lancea, cum turba suorum animose descendit, confidens nimirum in armatura propria complicium-que suorum, jam per triennium elaborata, et super arcite-

The Scots invade England.

They are defeated by the Earl of Northumberland and the Earl of Dunbar, at Homildon Hill.

---

[1] *formidans* in orig. and the printed texts; corrected from (1) and (5) MS. Corp. Chr. vii.

[2] *poneret* in the printed texts.

[3] A passage in (1) and (5) MS. Corp. Chr. vii. is omitted here.

[4] *erat campi-ductor* in the printed texts.

A.D. 1402. nentes irruere nitebatur. Quod videntes sagittarii, retrocedendo sagittabant, tam vivide, tam animose, tam graviter, ut ipsos armatos omnino penetrarent, cassides terebrarent, gladios perforarent, lanceas [1]finderent, et omnem armaturam levi negotio transverberarent. Ipse quoque Duglas [2]Comes quinque vulneribus confossus est, non obstante sumptuosissima armatura. Reliqui de Scotis qui nondum de monte descenderant, conversi retrorsum, a sagitta volante fugerunt. Sed fuga nihil profuit, dum insequerentur arcitenentes, quin se reddere cogerentur Scoti, metu spiculorum mortiferorum. Comes quoque Duglas captus est; sed ex hiis qui fugerant multi capti sunt, sed multi rapacitate Twedæ fluminis submersi fuere, dum vada nescirent, ad numerum, ut asseritur, quingentorum. In hac pugna nullus dominus, nullus miles aut scutifer, hostibus ictum intulit, sed solummodo Deus Omnipotens arcitenentibus Anglorum victoriam miraculose contulit, proceribus et armatis effectis belli spectatoribus otiosis.

MS. Corp. Chr. vii. (1) & (5.)

The Earl of Douglas is wounded, and taken prisoner.

The victory solely due to the English archers.

Other Scottish nobles, there captured or slain.

[3]Eo die flos Scoticanæ militiæ captivitati subactus est. Nempe cum Comite Duglas, Murdak de Fif, primogenitus Ducis Albaniæ, [4]qui hæres apparens regni Scotiæ, captus fuit. Experti quoque sunt similem sortem Comes de Murryf, Comes de Angus, Comes de Orkeney, et Barones Dominus de Montegomerito, Dominusque de Erskyn, Dominus de Grame, cum multis aliis militibus ad numerum octoginta, præter scutiferos et valectos, quorum numerum ignoramus. Interfecti sunt Barones ibidem, Dominus de Gurdone et Dominus Johannes de Swyntone, infidus utrique [5]regno. Commissum fuit bellum istud die Exaltationis Sanctæ Crucis.

Conclusions put forth in secret, by the Lollards.

Eo tempore Lollardi docuerunt Conclusiones execrabiles; in occulto tamen, propter metum judiciorum: quæ sunt istæ.—

Quod septem Sacramenta non sunt nisi signa mortua, nec valent in forma qua eis utitur Ecclesia.

Item, quod virginitas et presbyteratus non sunt status approbati a Deo, sed status conjugii optimus est, et ordinatus a Deo. Quapropter omnino virgines et presbyteri, religiosique populi, si salvari desiderant, debent conjugari, vel esse in voluntate et proposito conjugandi; alias sunt homicidæ, et destruunt sanctum semen unde consurgeret secunda Trinitas; et sic impediunt numerum salvandorum pariter et damnandorum.

---

[1] *funderent* in the printed texts; *frangerent* in (1) and (5) MS. Corp. Chr. vii.

[2] *Comes* omitted in the printed texts.

[3] *Eodem* in the printed texts.

[4] *et hæres* in the printed texts.

[5] *regio* in orig.; *regi* in the printed texts: corrected from (1) and (5) MS. Corp. Chr. vii.

MS. Corp. Chr. vii. (1) & (5).

A.D. 1402.

Item, si vir et fœmina convenerint in una voluntate nubendi, ipsa voluntas sufficiens est conjugium sine majori obedientia Ecclesiæ facienda; et sic conjuncti plures quam nos cognoscamus, prout dicunt.

Item, quod Ecclesia nihil est aliud quam synagoga Sathanæ; et ideo nolunt adire illam ad honorandum Dominum, neque percipiendum Sacramentum aliquod, et præcipue Sacramentum Altaris; quia, ut asserunt, non est nisi buccella panis mortui, et turris, sive pinnaculum, Antichristi.

Item, si haberent puerum modo natum, non baptizaretur per manus presbyterorum apud Ecclesiam; quia puer iste est secunda Trinitas, non contaminata peccato, et pejor esset si deveniret in manus eorundem.

Item, quod non habemus aliquem diem sanctificatum vel sanctum, sed nec diem Dominicum; sed quilibet dies est ejusdem libertatis ad operandum, comedendum, et bibendum.

Item, quod non est Purgatorium post hanc vitam, neque quod oportet agere majorem pœnitentiam pro ullo peccato, quanquam vilissimo; sed tantum, ut committentes illud deserant et apud se pœniteant; quia, ut dicunt, in fide stat quicquid est; sicut Mariæ Magdalenæ dixit Christus,—[1] "Fides "tua te salvam fecit."

Sir Louis de Clifford, a supporter of the Lollards, informs against them.

Has Conclusiones Lodewycus de Clifford miles, qui jamdudum Lollardis fautor extiterat, diu sub terminorum involucris palliatas, sed jam denudatas, Archiepiscopo Cantuariensi patefecit; ut videlicet se ostenderet, non ex pertinaci malitia, sed simplicitate cordis et ignorantia, communicasse cum impiis. Dedit etiam nomina Cantuariensi dictas dogmatizantium pravitates.

Full remission for benefactors, on a certain day, obtained from Rome by the people of Ely.

Elyenses per hoc tempus pares esse cupientes Norwicensibus, qui in festo Trinitatis, et Buriensibus, qui in festo Sancti Edmundi, indulgentias impetrant a Sede Apostolica, obtinuerunt peregre adventantibus et ecclesiæ suæ benefacientibus in festo Trinitatis, a primis ipsius Vesperis usque ad posteriores Vesperas feriæ Martis in hebdomada Trinitatis, vere contritis et confessis, plenam remissionem.

Death of Edmund Mortimer.

His marriage to the

Eo tempore, Edmundus [2]Mortymer obiit, juvenis quem retulimus ante captum ab Oweno Glendor, vel tædio diræ captivitatis, vel metu mortis, vel ex alia qua nescitur causa: conversus retrorsum, cum Owennio contra Regem Angliæ se

---

[1] *Luke* vii. 50.

[2] *Mortifer* in orig. and (5) MS. Corp. Chr. vii.; corrected from the printed texts: *de Mortuo Mari* in (1) MS. Corp. Chr. vii.

A.D. 1402. daughter of Glendower. sentire professus est, dum nuptias satis humiles, et suæ generositati impares, contrahit cum filia dicti Oweni. MS. Corp. Chr. vii. (1) & (5).

Sinister event at the birth of Glendower. Hujus, ut fertur, nativitatis exordia dira comitata sunt prodigia: quia nocte qua in lucem profusus est, in [1]hippodromo paterno omnes equi patris sui reperti sunt in alto cruore stetisse, usque ad tibiarum demersionem; quod tunc interpretati sunt plurimi sinistrorsum.

Parliament at London. Parliamentum Londoniis factum in crastino Sancti Michaelis per septem hebdomadas perduravit: cujus finalis effectus fuit concessio decimæ et medietas a clero, et a burgis decima, et quintadecima de regni communitate.

A.D. 1403. Henry marries the widow of John, Duke of Bretagne. Anno Domini millesimo quadringentesimo tertio, post festum Purificationis, [2]Regina venit in Angliam, de Minori Britannia ad Majorem, de ducatu ad regnum, de gente feroci ad populum pacificum, et, utinam, fausto pede. Hæc fuerat prius conjugata nobili viro, Domino Johanni de Monte Forti, Duci Britanniæ, de quo tulit utriusque sexus liberos: sed de Rege Angliæ Henrico, cui jam nupsit, omnino nullos. Vicesima vero sexta die mensis Januarii, Londoniis, apud Westmonasterium, fuit magnifice coronata.[3]

Marvellous appearances near Bedford and Biggleswade. Æstate secuta, juxta villas de Bedford et de [4]Bykkelesward frequenter visa sunt monstra, mane et meridie, de sylvis emergentia, sub colore vario, in similitudinem hominum bellatorum, quæ sibimet occurrentia videbantur inire dira bella. Quæ etsi conspici poterant a remotis, appropinquantibus inveniri minime potuerunt; sicque dicta fantastica vel fatalis apparitio sæpius delusit plurimos, accedere cupientes.[5]

Henry Percy, the Younger, rises against the King; and is joined by the Earl of Worcester. Eodem tempore Dominus Henricus Percy junior, cui fortuna semper hactenus blandita fuerat, et in quo spes erat reposita totius populi, repente hostis Regis apparuit. Cui contra cunctorum opinionem, [6]junxit se Dominus Thomas Percy, Comes Wygorniæ, patruus Henrici prædicti.[7] Hic, repente deserens domum Principis, Regis primogeniti, cujus Rex curam sibi commiserat in speciali, recessit ad nepotem, augens eidem vires et animum rebellandi. Quorum ut excusabilis esset

---

[1] *ypodromo* in orig.; *hypodromo* in the printed texts.

[2] A passage in (1) MS. Corp. Chr. vii. is omitted here.

[3] A passage in (1) MS. Corp. Chr. vii. is omitted here.

[4] *Bikeleswade* in (1) MS. Corp. Chr. vii.; *Bykkeliswade* in (5) MS. Corp. Chr. vii.; *Byckelesworth* in the printed texts.

[5] A passage in (1) MS. Corp. Chr. vii. is omitted here.

[6] *jux* in orig.; *junxit* in the printed texts.

[7] "*vir de quo nunquam aliquid* "*sinistri perante ferebatur*," added in (1) MS. Corp. Chr. vii.

MS. Corp. Chr. vii. (1) & (5).

A.D. 1403.

conjuratio, scripserunt provincialibus ubilibet [1]constitutis, propositum quod assumpserant non esse contra suam ligeantiam, [2]et fidelitatem quam Regi fecerant, nec [3]ab aliunde exercitum congregasse, nisi pro salvatione personarum suarum, et reipublicæ meliori gubernatione. Quia [4]census et talliagia [5]Regis concessa pro salva regni custodia, convertebantur, ut dixerunt, in usus indebitos, et inutiliter consumebantur: præterea querebantur, quod, propter æmulorum [6]delationes pessimas, Rex eis infensus fuerat, ut non auderent personaliter venire ad ejus præsentiam, donec Prælati, regnique Barones, Regi supplicassent pro eisdem, ut coram Rege permitterentur declarare suam innocentiam, et per pares suos legaliter justificari. Plures igitur, visis hiis litteris, collaudabant tantam virorum solertiam, et extollebant fidem quam erga rempublicam prætendebant.

Grounds alleged by them for their rising.

Sed Rex, ut fraudem comperit, turbatus nimirum, cogitabat quibus mediis communitati posset satisfacere, et eorum ficta commenta pessundare. Scripsit ergo personis quibus ipsi scripserant, dicens se [7]mirari quam maxime quod cum Comes Northumbriæ et Henricus, ejus filius, percepissent partem maximam summarum sibi concessarum per clerum seu communitatem Angliæ, pro tuitione Marchiæ Scotiæ, ut posset evidenter ostendere, unde concepissent materiam tantæ, non solum querimoniæ, sed detractionis manifestæ. Scripsit insuper, quod intellexerat Comitem Northumbriæ, filium quoque suum, necnon et Comitem Wigorniæ, certificasse multis se non audere, propter æmulatiorum [8]delationes, ad Regis venire præsentiam, sine mediatione prævia prælatorum et procerum; quare supplicabant, ut partes interponerent ut de Regis gratia venire possent, ad allegandum pro se, et sua innocentia declaranda. Quamobrem scripsit eidem Comiti, etc., sub sigillo regio, [9][quod] [10]possent accedere sine damno, salvoque recedere, sine periculo sive dolo.

The King's answer to their complaints.

He makes them offer of a personal interview.

Sed effrænata temeritas, [11]spreto lenimento regali, rigorem

---

[1] *et* inserted here in orig.; omitted in (1) and (5) MS. Corp. Chr. vii. and the printed texts.

[2] *ut* in orig.; corrected from the printed texts.

[3] *ad* in orig.; corrected from the printed texts.

[4] *sensus* in the printed texts.

[5] *Regi* in (1) and (5) MS. Corp. Chr. vii.

[6] *dilationes* in the printed texts.

[7] *mirare* in orig. and (5) MS. Corp. Chr. vii.

[8] *dilationes* in the printed texts.

[9] Omitted in orig. and the printed texts: supplied from (1) and (5) MS. Corp. Chr. vii.

[10] *possunt* in the printed texts.

[11] *spreta lenitate* in the printed texts.

A.D. 1403. rebellionis induit, et Salopiam properavit, sperans, ut putatur, in auxilio Oweynii Glendor et Edmundi de Mortuo Mari, quorundamque Cestrensium et Wallicorum. At Rex, ut persensit induratam juvenilem malitiam, nam pater ejus non excesserat limites patriæ suæ, decernit occurrendum [1] fore festinanter Henrico, patruo quoque suo, Domino Thomæ Percy, priusquam conflassent exercitum fortiorem. Nempe hii et eorum complices [2] publicari fecere per patrias Regem Ricardum vivere, et apud eos [3] [esse]; cujus nomine, sive causa, bella sumpserant contra Regem. Quem si videre vellent incunctanter, accederent armis instructi, et in castro Cestriæ viderent infallibiliter dictum Regem. Quæ quidem, quamvis dolosa, denunciatio, varios [4] in multorum mentibus motus effecit, et fluctuare coegit plurimos, ut ignorarent cui parti foret tutius adhærendum. Multi revera afficiebantur Regi Ricardo, et præcipue qui familiares ejus quondam fuerant, et ab eo donati feodis vel aliis donativis.

Percy hastens to Shrewsbury, to join Glendower.

MS. Corp. Chr. vii. (1) & (5).

He gives out that King Richard is still alive.

Rex Henricus præmissa prudenter attendens, cum esset manu fortis et audax, congregavit quos potuit, instigante cum Comite de Dunbarre, Scoto, maxime; qui monuit omnino ne moras necteret, commemorans illud Lucani,—

The Earl of Dunbar instigates the King to immediate action.

"Tolle moras, nocuit semper [5] differre paratis,
"Dum trepidant nullo [6] firmatæ robore partes."[7]

[8] Fecit Rex ut Scotus monuit, et [9] inopinate pervenit ad partes ubi rebelles bacchabantur. Henricus autem, subito conspecto vexillo regio, cum jam instaret effringere villam Salopiæ, mox destitit ab infestatione villanorum, dicens suis; —"Desistere nos," inquit, "oportet ab inceptis, et arma vertere "in eos qui contra nos veniunt. Videtis certe signum re-"gium, nec vacat quærere, licet vellemus, divortium. State "proinde corditer, quia dies hic aut nos omnes promove-"bit, si vincimus, [10] aut de [11] fastu regali liberabit, si victi "[12] simus. Nam pulchrius est in bello cadere pro republica, "quam post bellum mori, hostis nostri sententia."

Speech of Henry Percy, on the King's approach.

---

[1] *fere* in orig.; corrected from the printed texts.

[2] *pupplicaris* in orig., by inadvertence.

[3] Omitted in orig.; supplied from the printed texts.

[4] *in* omitted in the printed texts.

[5] *deferre deparatis* in orig.; *differre semper paratis* in the printed texts.

[6] *firmitate* in orig., by inadvertence.

[7] A passage in (1) MS. Corp. Chr. vii is omitted here.

[8] *Facit* in the printed texts.

[9] *inopinato* in the printed texts.

[10] *aut* omitted in the printed texts.

[11] *statu* in orig. and the printed texts; corrected from (1) and (5) MS. Corp. Chr. vii.

[12] *sumus* in the printed texts.

MS. Corp. Chr. vii. (1) & (5). A.D. 1403.

Conveniunt in [1]hoc votum subito qui sequebantur Henricum, ad numerum quatuordecim millium lectissimorum hominum, qui se perstituros ad flatum ultimum cum Henrico promittunt. Præoccupaverant autem illis campum magis accommodum: [2]Rex vero constitit cum suis, tenens campum ad eorum oppositum.[3] Cumque partis utriusque pugnatores signum belli præstolarentur, Abbas Salopiæ et Clericus de Privato Sigillo pro parte Regis legatione fungebantur, ut offerrent Henrico pacem et perdonationem, si desisteret ab inceptis. Quorum persuasionibus Henricus effectus mansuetior, cum illis direxit ad Regem patruum suum, Dominum Thomam Percy, qui sibi tantæ turbationis causas exprimeret, emendas exigeret cum effectu. [4]Ferunt autem quod cum Rex omni rationi condescendisset, et humiliasset se secus quam personam regiam decuisset, idem Dominus Thomas Percy, cum redisset ad nepotem, contraria referens responsis [5]regiis, exacerbavit mentem juvenis, et ad bellum impulit, etiam non volentem.

The King offers terms to Henry Percy.

Ambiguous conduct of Sir Thomas Percy.

Igitur arcitenentes Henrici prœlium inchoarunt, nec erat ad terram jaculis locus, sed in corpora ferrum omne ruit; caduntque de parte Regis ad instar [6]foliorum decidentium brumali tempore, post [7]pruinam. Nec minus regii sagittarii suum peregere negotium, sed imbrem asperrimum spiculorum in adversarios emisere.[8] Cadunt proinde utrinque plurimi, velut cum poma ruunt in Autumno, cum moventur ab Africo, multaque simul millia de loco belli fugiunt, putantes Regem sagittis occisum. Ipse vero campi-ductor Henricus partis adversæ, Comesque Duglas Scotus, quibus animosiores nullus unquam reperisset, spretis jaculis emissis de parte Regis, spretis armatorum consertis cuneis, contra solam personam regiam vires excitant, arma vertunt; ipsum pro decem millibus computantes, stratis requirunt obviis, infestis lanceis et gladiis perscrutantes.[9] Comes de Dunbarre, cum comperisset istorum propositum, Regem subtraxit a statione sua [10][prima]. Quod factum

Fierceness of the combat.

Danger of the King.

---

[1] *hunc* in orig.; corrected from the printed texts.

[2] *Pax* in the printed texts.

[3] A passage in (1) MS. Corp. Chr. vii. is omitted here.

[4] *Fuerunt* in orig.; corrected from the printed texts.

[5] *regis* in the printed texts.

[6] *filiorum* in orig., by inadvertence; corrected from the printed texts.

[7] *primam* in orig.; *prunam* in the printed texts.

[8] A passage in (1) MS. Corp. Chr. vii. is omitted here.

[9] A passage in (1) MS. Corp. Chr. vii. is omitted here.

[10] Supplied from (1) MS. Corp. Chr. vii.

A.D. 1403. salutare fuit Regi ea vice, quia et signifer regius a furentibus est prostratus, vexillumque dejectum, circumstantes occisi. Inter quos, Comes Staffordiæ et Dominus Walterus Blont, miles regius, cecidere; Princepsque, Regis primogenitus, pertentans prœliandi primitias, ictu sagitttæ vulneratus in facie. MS. Corp. Chr. vii. (1) & (5).

Prince Henry is wounded in the face.

Sir Henry Percy is slain.

Interea Dominus Henricus Percy, dum præcedit suos in prœlio, dum [1]inconsulte penetrat hostes suos, [2]inopinate concidit interemptus, dubium cujus manu; quo cognito, fugere partes adversæ defensores, quibus fugiendi copia est permissa. Sed Comes de Dowglas captus est[3] hic, bina vice hoc anno: pugnans adversus Anglicos adversam semper expertus est fortunam.[4] Nam [5]primo bello trajectus caput, amisit oculum, in secundo verenda transfixus perdidit paulo minus loculum, et sub jugum venit captivitatis secundæ. Captus est etiam Comes Wygorniæ, Dominus Thomas Percy, inventor, ut dicitur, totius mali, et causa præsentis infortunii; cum Domino Ricardo Vernoun, [6]Baroneque de Kynderton, cum multis aliis.[7] De parte Regis ceciderunt decem milites, multi scutiferi, plures valecti, et ad numerum trium millium sunt graviter vulnerati. Ex parte rebellium corruit major pars militum et scutiferorum Comitatus Cestriæ, ad numerum ducentorum, præter domicellos et pedites, quorum numerum non tenemus. Commissum fuit hoc prœlium in Vigilia Sanctæ Mariæ Magdalenæ; quo nunquam, [8][ut] putatur, ullum acrius gestum fuit.

Douglas is taken prisoner; and many others.

Numbers of the slain.

Executions at Shrewsbury.

Die Lunæ sequente, nam Sabbato commissum fuit antedictum bellum, judiciali sententia decollati sunt apud Salopiam Comes Wygorniæ, Baro de Kyndertone, et Dominus Ricardus de Vernona.

The Earl of Northumberland is stopped in his march.

Die etiam Lunæ secuta proximo, dum Comes Northumbriæ in manu robusta et brachio extenso versus filium suum properat, vel versus Regem, ut putatur, pro redintegrando pacis negotio, Comitem Westmerlondiæ et Robertum Watertone ne progrederetur habuit impedimento. Hii [9]nempe, exercitu grandi collecto, obviare sibi subito disponebant. Qui neutrum

[1] *inconsulto* in the printed texts.

[2] *inopinato* in the printed texts.

[3] A passage in (1) MS. Corp. Chr. vii. is omitted here.

[4] This passage is not found in (1) MS. Corp. Chr. vii.

[5] *proximo* in orig., *in proximo* in the printed texts; corrected from (5) MS. Corp. Chr. vii.

[6] *et Baroque de* in orig.: corrected from the printed texts.

[7] "*capti sunt ibidem viri nobiles et* "*potentes*," added in (1) MS. Corp. Chr. vii.

[8] *ut* omitted in orig.; supplied from (1) and (5) MS. Corp. Chr. vii. and the printed texts.

[9] *nempte* in orig., by inadvertence.

MS. Corp. Chr. vii. (1) & (5).

A.D. 1403.

horum putans sibi benevolum, fræna reflexit, rediens ad castellum proprium de [1] Werkwortha.[2]

Returns to Warkworth.

Truce with France.

Eo tempore, nuncii missi in Franciam reportarunt inducias et vacationem usque ad diem primum mensis Martii, videbanturque magnam rem fecisse in tanta rerum turbatione.

The Earl of Northumberland meets the King at York; and is placed in safe keeping.

Compositis rebus Salopiæ, Rex progreditur Eboracum, ubi constitutus litteraliter mandavit [3] Comiti Northumbriæ, ut sibi occurreret. Dimissa turba, venit Comes ad Regis monita, in crastino Sancti Laurentii, cum parva familia; non tamen susceptus est familiaritate solita, sed potius more supplicis gratiam requirentis. Cui Rex vitam condonavit, et victui necessaria, decernens conservandum secura custodia.[4]

The King is prevented by want of means from proceeding against the Welch.

Proposition for despoiling the Bishops of their horses and money.

Grant made by the clergy.

Reversus Rex de partibus Borealibus, disposuit adire Walliam, ad [5] compescendum insolentiam Wallicorum, qui multa damna irrogaverant patriæ post recessum suum. Sed tamen retinuit eum rei [6] familiaris inopia, eo quod destitutus esset pecunia pro exercitu conducendo. Astitere sibi tunc milites et scutiferi [7] magis Dionæi quam Martii, Lavernæ quam Palladis, qui censuerunt Episcopos qui tunc illic forte convenerant, equis et auro spoliandos, domumque pedites remittendos, ut familiarium Regis egestas ipsorum abundantia levaretur. Affuit tamen [8] gratiose Dominus [9]   , qui respondisse fertur, unus pro omnibus, satis alacriter, milites improbos non spoliaturos de suis aliquem; nisi prius ausus temerarios [10] luerent duris ictibus, et spolia verberibus nundinarent. Rex interea se gerens moderatius, aucupabatur quodammodo benevolentiam Prælatorum; unde contigit quod Dominus Cantuariensis, convocato clero, sibi de una decima, cum consensu Præsulum, provideret.

The Bretons burn Plymouth.

Britones Armorici, [11] duce Domino de [12] Castellis, villam de Plummouth invadunt impune et succendunt.[13] Mox classis Occidua, sub ducatu Willelmi de Wylford, scutiferi, in parti-

---

[1] This word is omitted in (1) MS. Corp. Chr. vii.

[2] A passage in (1) MS. Corp. Chr. is omitted here.

[3] *communitati* in the printed texts.

[4] A passage in (1) MS. Corp. Chr. is omitted here.

[5] *concupiscendum* in orig.; corrected from the printed texts.

[6] *familiares* in orig.; corrected from the printed texts.

[7] *magis idonei, Martis lavernæ* in the printed texts; *magis idonei quam Martii lavernæ* in orig.; corrected from (1) and (5) MS. Corp. Chr. vii.

[8] *gratiosus* in the printed texts.

[9] This hiatus occurs in orig.

[10] *lucerent* in orig.; corrected from the printed texts.

[11] *sociati Gallicis, villam de* in (1) MS. Corp. Chr. vii.

[12] *Castel.* in the printed texts.

[13] A passage in (1) MS. Corp. Chr. vii. is omitted here.

A.D. 1403. Successes of the English Western fleet.

MS. Corp. Chr. vii. (1) & (5).

bus prædictæ Britanniæ cepit naves quadraginta, refertas ferro, oleo, [1]sopo, et vino de Rupella, ad numerum mille doliorum. Redeundo vero, cremavit naves quadraginta, et apud Penarch applicans, idem Willelmus, cum suis, combussit villas et prædia ad spatium sex leukarum. Villam quoque Sancti Matthæi ultricibus flammis dedit, et tria millia in gyro dictæ villæ.[2]

The French plunder the Isle of Wight; but are put to flight.

[3]Paucis diebus ante Natale Domini, Galli, stipati bellatorum turba, ascenderunt terram in Vecta insula, jactantes se celebraturos Natalis [4]festum illic, etiam invito Rege. Cumque mille de Gallis intrassent insulam, et greges ac armenta fugassent, ut ad mare reverterentur cum præda non modica, superveniente subito auxiliatorum copia, coacti sunt prædas dimittere, et ad navigia cum [5]dedecore festinare, non sine damno suorum. Sicque contigit, ut qui prius instanter ab incolis petierant rerum redemptionem, vix evadere potuerunt publicam interventionem.

A.D. 1404. The Earl of Northumberland is restored to his dignities.

Anno Domini millesimo quadringentesimo quarto, in Parliamento tento Londoniis post Octabas Epiphaniæ, Comes Northumbriæ restitutus est suæ dignitati pristinæ, bonisque, mobilibus et immobilibus, integraliter, et hæredes sui.

Grant in Parliament; unusual nature thereof.

In hoc Parliamento, concessa fuit Regi taxa insolita, et incolis tricabilis et valde gravis. Cujus modum præsentibus inseruissem, nisi concessores ipsi, et auctores dicti tallagii, in perpetuum latere posteros maluissent; nempe sub ea tantum conditione concedebatur, ne traheretur posterius in exemplum, nec servarentur ejus evidentiæ in [6]Thesauraria regia, nec in Scaccario, sed scripturæ vel recordationes ejusdem, protinus post datum compotum, cremarentur; nec emitterentur brevia, seu commissiones, contra collectores vel inquisitores hujus negotii de melius inquirendo.

The French demand tribute from the Isle

Gallici circa tempus illud venerunt ante Vectam insulam cum magna classe, miseruntque de suis quosdam, qui peterent, nomine Regis Ricardi et Isabellæ Reginæ, tributum vel [7]spe-

---

[1] *sepum* in (1) MS. Corp. Chr. vii.; *sepo* in (5) MS. Corp. Chr. vii.

[2] A passage in MS. Corp. Chr. vii. is omitted here.

[3] The whole of this passage, to the beginning of 1404, is derived solely from (5) MS. Corp. Chr. vii.

[4] *festi* in (5) MS. Corp. Chr. vii. and orig.; corrected from the printed texts.

[5] *decore* in orig.; corrected from (5) MS. Corp. Chr. vii. and the printed texts.

[6] *Thesauria* in orig.; corrected from the printed texts.

[7] This word is very indistinct in (1) and (5) MS. Corp. Chr. vii., but it has the appearance of *pecuniale*.

MS. Corp. Chr. vii. (1) & (5).

A.D. 1404.

ciale subsidium ab insulanis. Qui responderunt, Regem Ricardum [1][fuisse] defunctum, Reginam, quondam suam conjugem, remissam pacifice ad parentes et patriam, sine conditione tributi. Quapropter responderunt finaliter, se subsidium non daturos; sed si belli voluntas tenet Gallos, jusserunt ut [2]ascenderent, sine [3]cujusvis impedimento, et daretur illis spatium refocillationis post ingressum insulæ sex horarum, et, expleto tempore supradicto, daretur [4]infallibiliter eis bellum.[5] Quo audito, Galli, nullo perfecto negotio, recesserunt.

of Wight, in the name of King Richard and Queen Isabella; which is refused.

Per idem tempus, Dominus de [6]Castellis, Britannicus, [7]fatis se trahentibus, cum multitudine Gallorum et Britonum, apud Dortmouth cum intolerabili fastu terram scandit, putans fortunam secuturam, sicut prius apud Plummouth; sed secus accidit quam sperabat. Nam ab hiis quos maxime habebat contemptui, scilicet ruralibus, est peremptus: et qui post ipsum terram scanderunt, mox oppressi a rusticis, capti sunt protinus, vel occisi. Fœminæ quoque fraudari non debent hujus facti præconio, quæ fundarum missilibus hostes diris straverunt ictibus. Unde contigit plures a fœminis, plures a rusticis, sterni vel captivari. A rusticis [8]vero occidebantur multi [9][quia nescierunt] eorum linguam, quamvis grandes pro sua redemptione summas obtulissent; sed rurales rudes, alia pro aliis interpretantes, putabant eos comminari, quando pro vita sollicite supplicabant. Capti tamen sunt eo die [10] tres domini et milites nominati viginti; [11]pessumdedit [12]quia Deus eo die arrogantiam superborum, et esse fecit victoriam rusticorum.[13] Prosecuti sunt igitur captivos suos rustici ad Regis usque præsentiam, postulantes aliquod commodum prædæ suæ: cum quibus Rex ipse libenter convenit, [14]et, eorum [crumenis

The French land at Dartmouth; and their leader is slain.

Prowess of the English women.

Many of the French slain, through our ignorance of their tongue.

The King rewards the peasants, and retains

---

[1] Omitted in orig.; supplied from the printed texts.

[2] *scanderent* in (5) MS. Corp. Chr. vii.; *ascenderent* in (1) MS. Corp. Chr. vii.

[3] *cujusquam* in the printed texts.

[4] *infalsibiliter* in orig., by inadvertence; corrected from the printed texts.

[5] A passage in (1) MS. Corp. Chr. vii is omitted here.

[6] *Castel.* in the printed texts.

[7] *satis* in orig.; corrected from the printed texts. A passage in (1) MS. Corp. Chr. vii. is omitted here.

[8] *vero* omitted in the printed texts.

[9] Omitted in orig.; supplied from (1) and (5) MS. Corp. Chr. vii. and the printed texts.

[10] "*id est, quinto decimo die mensis* "*Aprilis, si bene recolui,*" added in (1) MS. Corp. Chr. vii.

[11] *pessimi dedit* in orig.

[12] *que* in the printed texts.

[13] A passage in (1) MS. Corp. Chr. vii. is omitted here.

[14] *et eorum sufferre metallo* in orig.; corrected from (5) MS.Corp.Chr.vii. and the printed texts.

A.D. 1404. sufflarcinatis fulvo] metallo, abire permisit ad propria, retinens captivos penes se, graviori censu in posterum redimendos.[1] MS. Corp. Chr. vii. (1) & (5).

the French prisoners.

Conditional grant by the clergy.

Mense Aprili concessa fuit Regi per clerum una decima conditionaliter; sed ne quis provisor de cætero capiat bona vel careagia de ecclesiasticis contra voluntatem [2]eorum. Sed tamen, appensa pecunia, neglecta mox fuit conditio interposita.

Translation of the body of Saint John of Bridlington.

Anno præsenti, quinto Idus Martii, [3]clarescentibus miraculis circa corpus Sancti Johannis, quondam Prioris Canonicorum de Brydelyngtone, de mandato Domini Papæ, translatum fuit corpus ejusdem Sancti Johannis per manus honorabilium virorum, scilicet Eboracensis Archiepiscopi, et Dunelmensis atque Karleolensis Episcoporum.

Ravages committed by Owen Glendower.

Per omne tempus æstatis præsentis, Owenus Glendor, cum suis Wallicis, prædatur, incendit, et destruit regiones sibi contiguas, et nunc dolis, [4]nunc insidiis, nunc aperto Marte, multos captivat, plurimos perimit Anglicorum, castellaque nonnulla capta complanat, quædam sibi conservat integra pro tutela. Johánnes [5]Trevor, Episcopus Assavensis, cernens rem prosperari in manu Wallici, conversus est in [6]virum pravum, factus transfuga ad Howenum.[7]

The Bishop of St. Asaph joins him.

Capture of English ships by the Flemings.

[8]Eodem tempore Flandrenses et Britones ceperunt quasdam naves nostratum, onustas mercibus, et nautas gladio vel suspendio peremerunt.

The Countess of Oxford spreads a report that King Richard is alive; and distributes his cognizances.

Per idem tempus, Comitissa vetula quondam Oxoniæ, mater Roberti de Veer, Ducis Hiberniæ, quem exulatum diximus et mortuum Lovarnæ, fecit per se suosque familiares divulgari, per omnes fines Estsexiæ, Regem Ricardum vivere, et in proximo fore venturum et honorem pristinum vendicaturum. Fecitque fabricari cervos argenteos et auratos plurimos, signa videlicet quæ Rex Ricardus conferre solebat suis militibus, scutiferis, et amicis; ut hiis, vice Regis, distributis, facilius allicerentur in vota sua milites illius patriæ, cæterique valentes.

---

[1] Some matter in (5) MS. Corp. Chr. vii. is omitted here.

[2] At this point the manuscript (5) Corp. Chr. vii. is continued (p. 153) in a somewhat later hand.

[3] "*crebrescentibus miraculis apud* "*Prioratum Canonicorum Regula-* "*rium de Bridlyngtone*,"—(1) MS. Corp. Chr. vii.

[4] *et insidiis* in (1) and (5) MS. Corp. Chr. vii.

[5] *Grenor* in the printed texts; which it somewhat resembles in the Arundel MS.

[6] So in the printed texts; but *archū* in (1) MS. Corp. Chr. vii., *archum* in (5) MS. Corp. Chr. vii., and *archū* in orig.; possibly for *archiepiscopum*.

[7] A passage in (1) MS. Corp. Chr. vii. is omitted here.

[8] *Eo* in the printed texts.

MS. Corp. Chr. vii. (1) & (5). Urgebat namque plurimos ad putandum quod Rex Ricardus viveret, famaque cotidie ferebatur e Scotia Regem Ricardum, inibi constitutum, expectare solummodo tempus accommodum, quo, cum forti brachio Francorum atque Scotorum, posset recuperare regnum. A.D. 1404. Reports from Scotland to a like effect.

Auxit errorem istum cujusdam Serlonis, quondam cubicularii Regis Ricardi, commentum, qui falso finxerat Privatum Sigillum nomine dicti Regis Ricardi, et destinaverat litteras consolatorias, simul et [1] commonitorias, multis in regno de dicti Regis Ricardi quondam familiaribus, in quibus et continebatur ejus incolumitas, et ipsius in brevi cernenda prosperitas. Hac occasione multi dederunt fidem dictis et scriptis ipsius Dominæ Comitissæ, [2] in tantum ut crederent ejus mendaciis et religiosi quidam, Abbates illius patriæ, qui expost, eo quod cum Comitissa sensisse videbantur, de mandato Regis tenti sunt et carceribus mancipati. Comitissa vero, confiscatis bonis suis omnibus, artæ custodiæ [3] mancipatur. Clericus vero, qui præmissa fallaciter auribus multorum instillaverat, [4] tractione et suspendio muneratur; nam et ipse diligenter eundo per patrias, præeminentes personas nitebatur ad credendum allicere, Regem Ricardum non solum vivere, sed in proximo palam cunctis fore, adjiciens se dictum Regem nuper allocutum fuisse, loco tali, tali denique apparatu. Serle, a former Chamberlain of King Richard, aids the imposture. The Countess is imprisoned, and Serle is hanged.

In festo [5] Sancti Johannis Baptistæ, vocante Rege, Comes Northumbriæ venit ad Pontem Fractum, nepotes suos et filiorum suorum filios secum ducens. Quo facto mitigavit corda complurium, qui [6] putabant eum rebellionis juvenibus præbuisse consilium. Venit et cum Comite Dominus Willelmus de Clifford, miles, trahens secum Serlonem invisum [7] toti regno, (de quo supra fit sermo), quem parum ante ceperat cautelose. Quo facto, penes Regem meruit excusari, [8] quod ultra placitum tenuisset Berwyci castrum; [9] propter quod reus læsæ majestatis extiterat. The Earl of Northumberland obeys a summons to Pontefract. Sir William de Clifford brings Serle thither.

---

[1] *consonatorias* in the printed texts.

[2] Some matter in (1) MS. Corp. Chr. vii. is omitted here.

[3] *mancipantur* in the printed texts.

[4] *tractatione* in the printed texts.

[5] *Nativitatis Sancti* in (1) MS. Corp. Chr. vii.

[6] *cantabant* in orig.; corrected from (1) and (5) MS. Corp. Chr. vii. and the printed texts.

[7] *tanti* in orig.; corrected from (1) and (5) MS. Corp. Chr. vii. and the printed texts.

[8] *per ultra* in orig.; corrected from the printed texts.

[9] "*aliasque fecisset; propter quæ*" "*peccasse putabatur.*" — variation in (1) MS. Corp. Chr. vii.

A.D. 1404.

MS. Corp. Chr. vii. (1) & (5).

Confession of Serle as to the death of the Duke of Gloucester; and the alleged existence of King Richard.

Viso Serlone, fervebat omnis ætas in domo regia sciscitari, scire, vel audire, quibus modis, quibus mediis, quibusve sociis, illum inclytum Regis filium, Regis avunculum, Ducem Gloverniæ, jugularit. Ille vero, jam actum de se non ignorans, hoc solum fatebatur, quod dignus fuit mille [1] mortibus propter hoc scelus. Qua confessione, simul et [2] pœnitudine, multorum ita demulsit animos, ut gratis promitterent se pro ejus anima presbyteros [3] conducturos, qui suffragia spiritualia [4] quotis diebus ferrent. Requisitus cur dementare voluerat multos, ut putarent Regem Ricardum vivere, respondit se hoc odio Regis fecisse, ut alienaret ab ipso corda suorum; retulitque se beatum fuisse potuisse in aula Regis Franciæ, quam in aula Regis Scotiæ, si non defuisset gratia. Sed cum bene sibi fuisset in domo Regis Franciæ, audito quod Rex Ricardus viveret, in Scotiam se transtulit, ut probaret si veridica fama foret. Quo cum pervenisset, et invenisset [5] quamdam personam similem, sed non ipsum quem quærebat, nihilominus tamen, ut illuderet Scotis et Anglis, affirmavit hunc esse Ricardum Regem proculdubio, præservatum ab æmulis divino miraculo. Sed expost, cum comperisset commentatam fallaciam patefaciendam, et ipse jam incurrisset rei familiaris inopiam, pervenit Berwicum ad dictum Willelmum Clifford, putans se per ipsum pecuniali [6] subsidio relevandum, quo redire in Franciam potuisset. Sed in hac parte sua spe frustratus est; nam Willelmus [7] [ipsum] captum detinuit, usus consilio satis callido, ut Regis gratiam nundinaret hujusmodi mercimonio. Igitur Serlo finali judicio tractus est in qualibet villa præcipua inter Pontem Fractum et Londonias, inchoans pœnas meritas in ipsa villa regia de Ponte Fracto.[8]

His detention by Sir William Clifford.

Particulars of his execution.

Parliament at Coventry.

Eo tempore, Rex indigens, ut fertur, pecunia, convocavit regni proceres ad [9] consilii Parliamentum tenendum Conventræ, circa festum [10] Sanctæ Fidis Virginis, non considerato quod ipso anno, tempore Quadragesimali Parliamentum cele-

---

[1] *martibus* in orig.; corrected from the printed texts.

[2] *plenitudine* in orig. and the printed texts; corrected from (1) and (5) MS. Corp. Chr. vii.

[3] *conductores* in orig. and the printed texts.

[4] *quot* in (1) and (5) MS. Corp. Chr. vii.

[5] The language somewhat varies here from that in (1) MS. Corp. Chr. vii.

[6] *præsidio* in the printed texts.

[7] Supplied from (1) and (5) MS. Corp. Chr. vii.

[8] A passage in (1) MS. Corp. Chr. vii. is omitted here.

[9] *consilii* omitted in the printed texts.

[10] *Sancti* in the printed texts.

MS. Corp. Chr. vii. (1) & (5).

A.D. 1404.

braverat apud Westmonasterium; quod inutiliter, ut multis videbatur, per duodecim hebdomadas fuerat protelatum. Direxit ergo brevia Vicecomitibus, ne quosquam pro Comitatibus eligerent quovismodo milites, qui in jure regni vel docti fuissent vel apprenticii; sed tales omnino mitterentur ad hoc negotium, quos constaret ignorare cujusque juris methodum; factumque est ita. Qui convenientes in [1] unum et in id ipsum, cum propositum fuisset pro parte Regis quo premebatur rei familiaris incommodo, instantibus prope Scotis et Wallicis, procul Britonibus, Flandricis, et Gallicis, selecti milites Parliamentales pro relevando Rege non aliud invenire potuere remedium, quam confiscandi Christi per totum regnum patrimonium; scilicet, ut Ecclesia generaliter de bonis [2] temporalibus privaretur. Hinc orta est inter clericos et laicos grandis altercatio, militibus [3] regiis asserentibus se pro Rege, atque cum Rege, profectos sæpius [4] contra rebelles et hostes, non solum sua expendisse profusius, sed corpora quoque multis periculis exposuisse, sive laboribus, clericis interim domi otiose sedentibus et in nullo Regi suffragantibus.

Proposal by the Knights of Parliament to confiscate the property of the Church, for the King's necessities.

Altercation between the clerks and the laymen.

Contra quæ Dominus [5] Cantuariensis [6] respondit, clerum semper tantum Regi contulisse quam laici, dum decimas ipsi frequentius darent Regi quam ipsi quintas-decimas; et insuper, tenentes sui non minori numero Regem sequebantur ad bella vel pericula, quam tenentes feodi laicalis. Et super hæc omnia, nocte dieque Missas [7] [et] orationes facerent pro eodem, et [8] omnium sibi famulantium prosperitate. Et cum ad hæc Prolocutor militum vultu voceque prætendisset publice se preces Ecclesiæ parvipendere;—"Jam," inquit Dominus Cantuariensis, "video manifeste quorsum tendit regni fortuna, "exclusis vilipensisque suffragiis, quibus Divinitas placari "solet. Certe nunquam fuit diu regnum stabile quod vacavit "a precibus et devotione. Attamen tu, qui vilipendis cleri "religionem, [9] ne te putes impune direpturum Ecclesiæ pos-"sessionem, quia, si vivit Cantuariensis, malo tuo rapies "quicquam de suis." Erat autem Prolocutor miles dictus

The Archbishop of Canterbury threatens Sir John Cheyne, the Speaker.

---

[1] *onū* in orig.; corrected from the printed texts.

[2] *temporibus* in orig.; corrected from the printed texts.

[3] *regis* in the printed texts.

[4] *citra* in orig. and the printed texts; corrected from (1) and (5) MS. Corp. Chr. vii.

[5] *Thomas Arundele* is inserted here in orig., in a later hand.

[6] *Archiepiscopus* is inserted in a later hand.

[7] Supplied from the printed texts.

[8] *omnem* in the printed texts.

[9] *nec* in the printed texts.

A.D. 1404. "Johannes [1] Cheyne," qui, ut fertur, militiam sortemque Christi deserens, in sortem Martis apostatando transierat. Nam, prout dicunt, diaconus fuerat ordinatus, nulla tamen, ut resiliret, dispensatione [2] licentiatus. Archiepiscopus inter hæc Regem nutantem considerans, surrexit; genu flexo coram Rege, rogavit ut attenderet primitivum propositum suum, quod cuilibet servaret jura propria pro posse suo; attenderet et [3] juramentum quod non invitus præstiterat, videlicet quod Ecclesiam et ministros ejus honoraret, foveret, et [4] manuteneret; attenderet et periculum juramenti, sive dedecus, violati; et Ecclesiam gaudere [5] permitteret suis privilegiis et libertatibus, quibus gavisa est antecessorum suorum temporibus; vereretur offendere Regem per Quem reges regnant; vereretur et censuras quas incurrunt qui res ecclesiasticas deprædantur; [6] quos omnes constat excommunicationis sententia innodari.

The Archbishop appeals to the King.

MS. Corp. Chr. vii. (1) & (5).

The Archbishop censures the Knights of Parliament for their cupidity.

Hiis a Cantuariensi prolatis, Rex præcepit ei repetere sedem suam, asserens voluntatis suæ fore Ecclesiam in adeo bono statu dimittere [7] sicuti eam invenerat, vel potius meliori. Archiepiscopus concionatus militibus dixit;—"Vos," inquit, "et vestri similes, consilium dedistis Domino nostro Regi "moderno, et antecessoribus suis, ut confiscarent bona cella-"rum quæ Gallici vel Normanni possiderent in Anglia, di-"centes eis per hæc divitias accumulandas in magna copia, "et quidem, prout valent, multa fulvi metalli millia; sed "tamen constat hodie Regem non [8] esse ditiorem dimidia "quidem marca, vobis vel extorquentibus vel emendicantibus "de manu sua, et vobismet appropriantibus dicta bona. "Unde potest conjici vos [9] non pro Regis utilitate, sed pro "vestra cupiditate, temporalia nostra petere. Quia procul-"dubio, si Rex, quod absit, vestro satisfecisset execrando "proposito, non esset opulentior uno quadrante sequenti "anno. Et certe prius hoc caput exponam gladio, quam "Ecclesia destituatur minimo jure suo."

Milites hac sententia, simul et Metropolitani repercussi constantia, [10] conticuere: Archiepiscopus vero, ut Argus, sibimet

---

[1] *Cleyne* in (5) MS. Corp. Chr. vii. and orig.; corrected from (1) MS. Corp. Chr. vii. and the printed texts.

[2] *licensiatus* in orig.

[3] *in juramentum* in the printed texts.

[4] *defenderet* in the printed texts.

[5] *promitteret* in the printed texts.

[6] *quo* in orig. and the printed texts; corrected from (1) and (5) MS. Corp. Chr. vii.

[7] *secuti* in orig., by inadvertence.

[8] *esse* omitted in the printed texts.

[9] *omnino* in orig.; corrected from the printed texts.

[10] *Cantuarie* in orig.; corrected from the printed texts.

MS. Corp. Chr. vii. (1) & (5).

A.D. 1404.

ex omni parte [1]prospiciens, cum comperisset milites [2]perstituros in petitione temporalium, Dominos temporales quosdam allexit in partem suam, qui constanter affirmaverunt Sanctam Ecclesiam nunquam sua voluntate suis temporalibus spoliandam; et in hac parte reddentes Archiepiscopo et Prælatis gratiam, pro gratia quam sibi prius præstiterant, quando milites petierunt ad opus Regis restitui quæcunque dicti Domini de corona tenebant, vel dono Regis nunc vel antecessorum suorum, Regum Edwardi et Ricardi; cui scilicet petitioni Dominus Cantuariensis obnixius restitit, et Prælati: sic [3]et factum est, ut de exactione temporalium nulla fieret mentio in posterum.

The Archbishop is supported by certain temporal Peers; in return for his support on another occasion.

Sed et milites ipsi qui importune perstiterant in hoc errore, Domino Cantuariensi supplicabant, ut illis ignosceret fatentibus malitiam et reatum suum, et gratias agentibus quod animositate sua sub hac tempestate respirasset Ecclesia; commemorantes illud ethnici, ita dicentis;

The Knights of Parliament ask pardon of the Archbishop.

> [4]" —— Tu sub principe [5]duro,
> " Temporibusque malis, ausus es esse bonus."[6]

Præter multa quæ concessa fuerunt Regi in hoc Parliamento, laici concesserunt duas quintas-decimas, ea conditione ut Dominus de Furnival, etc. reciperent omnem [7]censum illum, et expenderent in werris Regis. Revocatæ sunt etiam patentes Regis præconcessæ personis variis de sustentatione sua annua per Reges Edwardum et Ricardum,[8] militibus Parliamentalibus ea censentibus, licet id in Regis dedecus redundaret. Clerus concessit Regi unam decimam et dimidiam, non obstante quod medietas unius decimæ ultimo præconcessæ in festo Sancti Martini fuerat persoluta.

Other proceedings in Parliament.

Eo tempore tanta repente, ruptis limitibus, irrupit aquarum influentia in terra Domini [9]Cantuariensis et aliorum in Kancia, quanta nunquam fuerat illic ante visa; qua submersa sunt animalia numero et pretio excessivo. Nec solummodo [10]deflevit Anglia damna talia, sed, ut fertur, Selandia, Flan-

Great inundation in Kent.

Similar inundations in Zealand,

[1] *perspiciens* in the printed texts.

[2] *perstituturos* in orig., (5) MS. Corp. Chr. vii., and the printed texts.

[3] *quod factum* in the printed texts.

[4] A quotation from Martial, *Epigr.* xii. 6.

[5] *diro* in the printed texts.

[6] A passage in (1) MS. Corp. Chr. vii. is omitted here.

[7] *sensum* in the printed texts.

[8] A passage in (1) MS. Corp. Chr. vii. is omitted here.

[9] *Edintuariensis* in orig.; but corrected in a later hand.

[10] *defluit* in orig.; corrected from the printed texts. The text in (1) MS. Corp. Chr. vii. varies here, and is much fuller.

A.D. 1404. dria, et Holandia, per undarum excrementa innumerabilia sensit dispendia eo anno. MS. Corp. Chr. vii. (1) & (5.)

Flanders, and Holland.

Death of William Wickham.

His foundations at Winchester and Oxford.

Hoc in tempore vir grandævus Dominus Willelmus Wikham, Wyntoniensis Episcopus, vivere [1] mundo desiit; cujus sumptibus et industria cotidie clerus Anglicanus augmentatur et crescit. Nam in Wyntonia constituit Collegium novellis grammaticis, et in Oxonia subtilioris scientiæ clericis fundavit domum. Exhibentur autem in utroque loco [2] centum personæ de sumptibus provisis per eundem.[3]

Death of Boniface IX. Accession of Innocent VII.

Mense Octobris, primo die mensis, obiit Romæ Papa Bonifacius Nonus; cui successit Episcopus [4] Bononiensis, et vocatus est "Innocentius Septimus," alias dictus "Cosmatus "Gentilis;" vir per omnia dignus nomine et gradu tanto.

A.D. 1405.

The sons of the Earl of March stolen, but restored.

Anno Domini millesimo quadringentesimo quinto, [5] circa festum Sancti Valentini, rapti sunt filii Comitis Marchiæ, et abducti, sed cito post recepti de castro de Wyndeleshores. Faber ferrarius qui claves finxerat, per quas patebat ingressus ad eos, truncatione manuum atque capitis est multatus.

Lady de Spencer seized and placed in confinement.

Domina de Spencer, relicta Domini Thomæ de Spencer, nuper occisi Bristolliæ, dum fugit, ut [6] fertur, ad Howenum Glendor, cum filio octenni, capta est, et cunctis thesauris spoliata; perque regios ad Regem reducta, custodiæ artioris subiit nocumenta.[7]

The Peers decline making a grant to the King.

Post festum Purificationis, Rex, accersitis Londonias regni Baronibus, tractabat cum eisdem de regni regimine, deque pecuniali subventione sibi [8] ferenda; sed proceres regiis votis tunc minime paruere.

A similar proposition is made, with the like result.

In Quadragesima vero sequente, Rex convenire fecit apud Sanctum Albanum clerum regnique Barones pro præmisso negotio; sed, proceribus renitentibus, nil actum fuit; discesseruntque cuncti, velut in concordi discordia penes Regem, in Vigilia Palmarum.[9]

Sub hiis diebus Comes Marescallus, Thomas Mounbray,

---

[1] *munda* in orig., by inadvertence.

[2] *centum viginti personæ* in (1) MS. Corp. Chr. vii.

[3] A passage in (1) MS. Corp. Chr. vii. is omitted here.

[4] *Banoniensis* in orig.; corrected from the printed texts.

[5] The context in (1) MS. Corp. Chr. vii., in reference to this narrative, varies here.

[6] *præfertur* in orig.; corrected from (5) MS. Corp. Chr. vii. and the printed texts.

[7] A passage in (1) MS. Corp. Chr. vii. is omittted here.

[8] *ferendo* in orig. and (5) MS. Corp. Chr. vii.; corrected from the printed texts.

[9] A passage in (1) MS. Corp. Chr. vii. is omitted here.

MS. Corp. Chr. vii. (1) & (5).

A.D. 1405.

armis instructus, accessit ad Archiepiscopum Eboracensem, Magistrum Ricardum Le Scrop, dubium an voluntate motus propria, an Pontifice sollicitatus ut veniret; eoque tempore Dominus de Bardolf, [1] Thomas, adivit Comitem Northumbriæ, Dominum Henricum Percy, eo animo ut molestarent Regem, ut expost apparuit manifeste. Sed Archiepiscopus atque Comes Marescallus non diu celavere propositum, quin mox palam facerent intentum suum. De Comitis [2] nempe Northumbriæ, Dominique de Bardolf, ut fertur, confisi solatio, cives [3] Eboraci, cum multis aliis, evocaverunt in magno numero, ut starent cum ipsis pro regni commodo communiumque salute; et [4] ut promptiores redderentur ad præsens negotium, fixerunt articulos in ostiis monasteriorum et ecclesiarum urbis, scriptos in Anglicis, pro quibus oportuit eos voluntarie in armis esse.[5] Lectis ergo articulis, milites, armigeri, plebs urbana et rustica, intellecto pio proposito, in magno valde numero Pontificem constipavere, quem cunctis commendabant et ætatis gravitas, et vitæ præcedentis sanctitas, et incomparabilis litteraturæ scientia, et cunctis amabilis ipsa persona.

The Archbishop of York and Earl Marshal rise for the redress of grievances.

Comes Westmarlandiæ, qui cum filio Regis, Johanne, tunc prope fuit, audito rumore præcedentium, congregatis copiis, festinat occurrere Pontificali turbæ, priusquam multiplicata facile vinci non posset. Sed frustra; nam manus Archiepiscopalium multo fortior erat gente sua.[6] Misit ergo qui peterent causam tantæ conglobationis, et cur contra pacem regiam adessent armati. Archiepiscopus respondit, se nil moliri contra pacem regiam, quinimmo cuncta pro pace tranquillitateque facere, armari vero sive vallari hominibus, tantum ob metum regium, ad quem alloquendum tutum non [7] haberet accessum sine multitudine assentatorum. Propositum vero suum Regis et regni fore commodum, si forte noscere vellent illud; demonstravitque scedulam qua articuli continebantur. Quam cum legisset [8] Comes Westmarlandiæ, verbo vultuque laudavit palam Præsulis pium sanctumque propositum, spondetque se velle prosequi, cum suis, propositum

The Earl of Westmoreland expostulates.

The Archbishop's answer.

The Earl proposes a conference.

---

[1] This name is omitted, with an hiatus, in (1) MS. Corp. Chr. vii.

[2] *nempte* in orig., by inadvertence.

[3] *Eborasi* in orig.

[4] *ut* omitted in the printed texts.

[5] A passage in (1) MS. Corp. Chr. vii. is omitted here.

[6] "*quamobrem cœpit agere cum* "*eodem.*"—added in (1) MS. Corp. Chr. vii.

[7] *habere* in orig.; corrected from (1) and (5) MS. Corp. Chr. vii. and the printed texts.

[8] "*filius Regis et Comes West-* "*mariæ . . . laudavere palam,*" in (1) MS. Corp. Chr. vii.

A.D. 1405. Archipræsulis; unde petit ut accedat cum paucis in medium, secum habiturus colloquium, et ipse cum paucis obviaret sibi, adæquato numero personarum. MS. Corp. Chr. vii. (1) & (5).

Antistes gavisus credit verbis [1]Consulis; persuadet Comiti Marescallo, etiam nolenti, secum procedere ad locum colloquio deputatum. Ad quem cum pari numero convenissent, cum perlecta fuisset charta de articulis, mox Comes et qui cum eo erant præbuerunt assensum dictis, et favorem.

Tunc Comes, astutior cæteris,—"Ecce!" inquit, "finis "optatus assumpti laboris; jamdiu est quod populus perse- "veravit in armis; renunciet ex vestris aliquis genti vestræ, "ut domum redeant, arma deponant, et solitis occupationibus "operam dent consuetam. Nos interim, in signum concordiæ, "bibamus pariter, cernente populo partis utriusque." Nec mora, datis dextris, miles emittitur de parte Præsulis, qui renunciet pacem populo, jubeat unumquemque, depositis armis, sua revisere, quoniam jam partes in unam sententiam [2]convenere. Illi vero, videntes signa pacifica proceresque combibentes, fessi ex insueta militia, læti lora vertere; sic quod factum est ut, illis recedentibus, cresceret ex condicto paulatim adversorum numerus; nec prius intellexit Archiepiscopus se seductum, quam per manus fuit Comitis arestatus, [3]cum multis aliis per eundem. Quibus omnibus indemnitas est promissa, sed nullatenus observata; quia tam Præsul, quam Comes, decollatus fuit postea, [4]veniente Rege ad Eboracum in crastino Pentecostes. Quo facto, potuit illud [5]febricitantis Brudelyntone vaticinium fore verum, prædicentis satis obscure præsens factum, sub hiis versibus:—

The Archbishop and Earl Marshal are treacherously seized by the Earl of Westmoreland.

They are beheaded at York.

"Pacem tractabunt, sed fraudem subter arabunt,
"Pro nulla marca salvabitur ille hierarcha."[6]

The Archbishop is venerated as a Martyr.

Archiepiscopo decapitato, qui satis constanter necem tulit, martyrio pulchro [7]finitus, ut vulgares opinabantur, qui etiam asseverabant miracula quædam facta fuisse, tam in campo quo decollatus quam in loco quo sepultus est; illico vulgus promiscuum cœpit obnixe colere cineres [8]Antistitis jam de-

---

[1] *Comitis* in the printed texts.

[2] *convenire* in orig.; corrected from the printed texts.

[3] "*Comes Marescallus etiam arestatus fuit in eodem loco, et quidam "alii, ad numerum—personarum.*"— in (1) MS. Corp. Chr. vii.

[4] This passage is not found in (1) MS. Corp. Chr. vii.

[5] *fabricitantis* in Camden's text.

[6] The preceding is somewhat varied in (1) MS. Corp. Chr. vii., and a long passage is omitted.

[7] *finitis* in orig.; corrected from the printed texts.

[8] *Antistis* in orig., by inadvertence.

(5) MS. Corp. Chr. vii.

functi, quem dilexerant perante viventem; donec per quosdam regales [1]prohibiti Præsulis monumentum revisere metuebant. Corpus vero Domini Thomæ Mounbray, Comitis Marescalli, permissione Regis sepultum est in ecclesia Cathedrali, multis dolentibus vicem ejus. Sed caput ejus, fixum in stipite, stetit supra muros urbis longo tempore, expositum fervori atque pluviæ. Quod tandem cum Rex annuisset ut consepeliretur corpori, ferunt inventum fuisse in nullo fluxum, in nullo marcidum, nec penitus decoloratum, sed eundem prætulisse decorem quem vivens obtinuerat.

A.D. 1405.

Visits to his tomb are forbidden.

Disposal of the remains of the Earl Marshal.

Rex post hæc, civibus Eboracensibus multatis ad libitum, qui cum Archiepiscopo senserant, promovit exercitum ad persequendum Comitem Northumbriæ et Dominum Thomam Bardolf, omne præparamentum belli secum contrahens, et exercitum triginta septem millium pugnatorum. Comes Northumbriæ, comperto Regis proposito, Berwicum se transtulit.

The King marches against the Earl of Northumberland.

Eo tempore, nuncii Regis Daciæ, Norwagiæ, et Suaviæ, venientes in Angliam, petiere Regis filiam in conjugium domino suo. Horum præcipuus fuit Episcopus Solucensis, qui cum scriptore præsentis Chronicæ de vita Sancti Albani, cujus peroptime novit, [2]et communicavit historiam, eo quod in Danemarchia Martyr noster celebris habeatur.

The King of Denmark asks the King's daughter in marriage.

Interea Rex firmans faciem contra Comitem Northumbriæ, venit Berwycum; Comes vero a facie formidinis ejus fugit in Scotiam, et Dominus de Bardolf cum eo; quos Dominus David Fleming, Scotus, in fide sua suscepit. Rex autem, cum cognovisset fugam Comitis, mandavit hiis qui erant in castello, ut illud sibi redderent. Quod cum illi præcise negarent, intendit [3]gunnam magnam, cujus unico jactu dejecit partem unius turris, et inclusos tantum terruit, ut mallent objicere se sponte gladiis quam expectare secundum jactum. Redditum est ergo castrum Regi, et de [4]defendentibus partim fuere decollati, partim carceribus mancipati. Quo recepto et pro votis disposito, castrum de Alnewyk et cætera castra Comitis reddita sunt faciliter in manus Regis.

The Earl of Northumberland flies to Scotland.

Berwick Castle is surrendered to the King.

He captures Alnwick and other Castles.

Quibus successibus Rex elatus, redivit incunctanter Walliam; ubi, e contrario, nil sibi cessit prosperum, sed velut [5]infortunitate omnia gerebantur. Quapropter, nullo profecto negotio, reversus est, currus, carectas, et plaustra perdens, numero quinquaginta, prout fertur, cum thesauro maximo et

Misfortunes overtake the King in Wales, through great inundations.

---

[1] At this word, (1) MS. Corp. Chr. vii. ends abruptly, at page 48.

[2] This passage seems imperfect.

[3] *gemmam* in orig., but corrected to *gunnam* in a later hand.

[4] *defensoribus* in the printed texts.

[5] *infortunate* in the printed texts.

A.D. 1405. coronis suis, per aquarum inundationes supervenientes improvise. (5) MS. Corp. Chr. vii.

He demands succour of the clergy.

Venit ergo Wygorniam, et accersitis Archiepiscopo et aliis Episcopis, patefecit eis infortunium quod acciderat, petens sibi succurri per eosdem; cui respondit Archiepiscopus, se cum clero super isto negotio tractaturum.

French forces arrive, in aid of Owen Glendower.

Medio tempore, Gallici venientes in succursum Wallici, id est, Howeni Gleyndor, cum centum quadraginta navibus applicuerunt in portum de Mylleford, amissis primo, præ penuria recentis aquæ, pene omnibus equis suis. Dominus de Berklee et Henricus Pay combusserunt ex eisdem navibus quindecim in eodem portu. Dicti vero Gallici obsederunt urbem Kaermerdyn, et ceperunt, concessis prius defensoribus omnibus bonis mobilibus, cum licentia se transferendi quocunque vellent.

They experience great losses.

Sub eodem tempore captæ sunt naves quatuordecim per supradictos Dominum de Berklee, et Dominum Thomam de Swynburne, ac Henricum Pay, dum velificarent versus [1] Walliam ad auxiliandum Howeno; in quibus Senescallus Franciæ et alii octo capitanei capti fuere.

Royston burnt.

Villa de Royston conflagravit in die Translationis Beati Martini.

The Earl of Arundel marries the daughter of the King of Portugal.

Comes Arundeliæ duxit Londoniis in uxorem filiam Regis Portingaliæ notham, satis magnifice, præsentibus Rege Angliæ et Regina, in crastino Sanctæ Katerinæ.

The King's daughter is proclaimed Queen of Denmark.

In festo Conceptionis Sanctæ Mariæ, Domina Regis filia, præconis voce, proclamata est Regina Daciæ, Norwagiæ, [2] et Suaviæ, sive Suesiæ, in præsentia nunciorum qui eam venerant petituri.

A.D. 1406.

Death of Roger de Waldene, Bishop of London.

Anno Domini millesimo quadringentesimo sexto,[3] Dominus Rogerus de Waldene debitum naturæ solvit; qui varia fortuna vectus, expertus est sub brevi tempore quam sit

" —— Inconstans, incerta, volubilis ipsa,
" Errans, instabilis, vaga, quæ, dum stare putatur,
" Occidit, et falso mentitur gaudia vultu."

His varying fortunes.

Nempe per hanc, ex pauperculo factus est regni Thesaurarius, et mox Cantuariensis Archiepiscopus, quo jure mundus novit, vivente [4] Domino Thoma de Arundelia. Et illico dejectus et privatus per longa tempora, tandem levatur iterum in Londoniarum thronum venerandum, quo tamen non est per-

---

[1] *Galliam* in the printed texts.

[2] *et* omitted in the printed texts.

[3] " *qui est annus regni Regis Henrici, a Conquæstu Quarti, septimus,*" inserted here in the printed texts.

[4] *Domino* omitted in the printed texts.

(5) MS. Corp. Chr. vii.

A.D. 1406.

missus gaudere per [1]annum. Huic successit Dominus [2]Nicholaus Bobwyth.

The slayers of the Archbishop of York excommunicated.

Hoc in tempore Dominus Papa peremptores Ricardi Scroop, quondam Eboracensis Archiepiscopi, publice excommunicavit.

Prolonged sitting of Parliament.

Eo tempore inchoatum est Parliamentum, quod protelabatur inutiliter fere per annum. Quia postquam Parliamentales milites distulissent diu concedere Regi subsidium, in fine tamen fracti concessere taxam petitam, communitatis damno. Nam propter hanc dilationem expensæ militum æquiparabant pene subsidium postulatum. Per clerum autem nova taxa Regi conceditur, levanda de presbyteris stipendiariis et Fratribus Mendicantibus, ac aliis religiosis qui annalia celebrabant; ut horum quilibet dimidiam marcam Regi daret, in relevationem cleri, sed qui semper onus portaverat pro eisdem.

The Earl of Northumberland flies to Wales.

Per idem tempus Comes Northumbriæ et Dominus de Bardolf, monitu David Flemyng, fugerunt in Walliam. Patefecerat nempe illis conspirationes Scotorum, qui conspiraverant illos tradere Regi suo pro quorundam captivorum commutatione.

Civil war in Scotland, and truce with England, on land.

Ob quam causam David a Scotis occiditur, et Scoti provocantur ad intestina bella, in tantum ut, invalescente discordia, treugas annales petere cogerentur. Quibus firmatis in terra, Scoti misere per æquora filium Regis sui, et hæredem, ut coalesceret et informaretur in Francia de facetia linguaque Gallica.

The son of the King of Scotland is taken at sea, and delivered to King Henry.

Quem quidam nautæ de Cley in Norfolchia cepere [3]fortuito, et quemdam Episcopum, Comitemque de Orkeney, quibus commissus fuerat a patre suo; et ad Angliam deduxerunt, Regique dederunt. Rex vero resolutus in jocos dixit;—"[4]Certe si grati fuissent Scoti, hunc misissent mihi juvenem instituendum, nam et idioma [5]Franciæ ego novi:" missique sunt ad Turrim Londoniarum dictus juvenis et Comes Orkadum, Episcopo per fugam lapso.

Great losses of the French, at sea.

Eo tempore, dum Galli properant in succursu Howenii Gleyndor, cum ratibus triginta et octo, captæ sunt ex eis octo naves armatis refertæ, reliquis in Walliam evadentibus meticulose. Non multo post captæ sunt naves quindecim, portantes vinum et ceram, per mercatores nostros ad maris custodiam deputatos.

The Pope bestows the Archbishopric of York, against the King's will.

Papa contulit Archiepiscopatum Eboracensem Magistro Roberto Alum, Cancellario Oxoniensi, tunc in Curia existenti; sed Rex Angliæ indignatur, et contradicit.

---

[1] He was Bishop of London rather *more* than a year.

[2] *Richardus* in the printed texts.

[3] *fortuitu* in orig.; corrected from the printed texts.

[4] *Certi* in orig.; corrected from the printed texts.

[5] *Franscia* in orig.

A.D. 1406.

The young Queen of Denmark is escorted to Lynn.

Hac æstate Rex et Regina perduxerunt [1] puellam, virginem Regis filiam, ex priore conjuge procreatam, ad villam de Lenna, ut inde transfretaret in Daciam, ad sponsum suum Regem. Hanc comitabantur nobiles, inter quos Episcopus Bathonensis erat, et Dominus Ricardus, frater Ducis Eboraci. Qui redeuntes, expleto negotio, parum vel nihil boni de patria retulerunt. (5) MS. Corp. Chr. vii.

Death of Henry de Spencer, Bishop of Norwich.

Circa finem Autumni, Dominus Henricus de Spencer, Episcopus Norwicensis, ingreditur viam patrum; vir qui et militis suo tempore consummavit officium, et pontificale non neglexit debitum: cujus loco monachi Norwycenses elegerunt Alexandrum, commonachum et Priorem suum.

The Duke of York restored to his former rank.

Adhuc durante Parliamento, restitutus est Dux Eboraci dignitati pristinæ, qui putabatur a multis obiisse in carcere.

Marriage of the Earl of Kent.

Comes Canciæ duxit in uxorem filiam Domini de Mediolano.

Death of Pope Innocent VII.

Compact of the Roman Cardinals, for putting an end to the schism.

Hoc anno, Die Sancti Clementis, Apostolica [2] Sede vacante per obitum [3] F. Re. Innocentii [4] Papæ, septem Cardinales, considerantes Christianæ religionis infamiam contractam ex pestifero schismate, quod tantis, proh dolor! temporibus perduravit, convenerunt: voverunt Deo ac ejus matri Mariæ, et Sanctis Apostolis, Petro et Paulo, totique [5] cœlesti curiæ juraverunt, et ad invicem unus alteri, et e converso se obligando solemniter promiserunt, quod si quis eorum assumptus foret ad apicem Summi Apostolatus, renunciaret effectualiter juri suo et Papatui, si et quando Antipapa qui est, et pro tempore fuerit, consimiliter renunciaret ac cederet, et Anticardinales sic convenire ac [6] concordare vellent cum eisdem dominis et Sacro Collegio, sic quod ex, [7] et pro, hiis duobus Collegiis sequeretur juste canonica electio unius Romani Pontificis; ac etiam promitterent se facturos et curaturos, quod si quis ex dominis absentibus vel extra Collegium per eos assumeretur in Papam, eandem faceret obligationem. Quodque nullus eorum a prædictis promissione, voto, et obligatione, absolutionem peteret vel impetraret. Et ad majorem præmissorum firmitatem, quilibet ex dominis de Collegio supradicto manu sua [8] se subscripsit.

Election of Pope Gregory XII.

Elegerunt itaque Dominum [9] Angelum tituli Sancti Marci, Presbyterum Cardinalem Constantinopolitanum, et vocaverunt

---

[1] Omitted in the printed texts.

[2] *Sede* omitted in the printed texts.

[3] So in orig., (5) MS. Corp. Chr. vii., and the printed texts.

[4] So in orig. and the other texts; probably an error for "*Papæ Septimi*, " *Cardinales, considerantes, etc.*"

[5] *cœlestique* in orig., by inadvertence.

[6] *concorditer* in orig.; corrected from the printed texts.

[7] *et pro* omitted in the printed texts.

[8] *se* omitted in the printed texts.

[9] *Anglicum* in the printed texts.

(5) MS. Corp. Chr. vii. "Gregorium Duodecimum;" qui eodem die, post electionem, votum, sacramentum, et promissionem, prout superius continetur, in præsentia dictorum Cardinalium et testium, se manu propria subscripsit:— A.D. 1406. Oath made by him, in conformity with the above agreement.

"Ego Gregorius, hodie, die ultimo mensis Novembris, anno "Domini millesimo quadringentesimo sexto assumptus in "Romanum Pontificem, juro, voveo, et promitto, ac confirmo "omnia supradicta, etc." Coronatus est autem die Sancti Andreæ Apostoli, vir annorum circiter octoginta.

Four ships of Lynn are swallowed up by a whirlpool, on their voyage to Bordeaux. Circa festum Sancti Martini, cum rates Anglicæ versus Burdegalim cursum tenderent, et infrequentatum mare nostris hactenus attentarent, quatuor naves de villa de Lenna, navigantes incautius, inciderunt subito in Charybdim quæ dicitur esse in mari Hispanico, et, cernentibus sociis, absorpti sunt. Nam illic dicitur esse mare vertiginosum, quod occultis gurgitibus naves sorbet. Ter enim in die stringit fluctus et ter vomit. Aquas itaque—"accipit ut vomat, vomit ut accipiat," unde [1] Naso;—

"Evomit epotas dira Charybdis aquas."

Doctæ sunt ergo reliquæ priorum periculo vela reflectere de tam pernicioso pelago, venereque [2] salvæ Burdegalim, sed numero diminuto.

Grant by the laity to the King. Appropinquante Natali Dominico, exactum est instantius ut Regi provideretur de pecuniali subsidio. Sicque tandem concessa fuit ei quinta-decima de communi populo.

A.D. 1407. Misfortunes overtake the Duke of Orleans in Gascoigne. Anno Domini millesimo quadringentesimo septimo, soluta est obsidio facta villarum de Burgh et de Bloy in Wasconia, facta per Ducem Aurelianensem; qui cum quinquaginta millibus venerat ad subvertendum illas. Sed Deo dispensante, Qui superbos humiliat, nulla dies per octo hebdomadas illuxit ei sine tempestate pluviarum, nivis, et grandinis, mixtæ cum ventis et [3] fulmine, quæ tam homines ad mortem compulit quam jumenta. Quibus infortuniis fertur sex millia hominum perdidisse; et qui, in adventu suo, supra fortunam suam nimis ambitiosus, fecerat deportari supra caput suum a quatuor militibus pannum aureum, jam revertens inglorius, gaudebat ab imbribus jam cessare cœlum. A punishment for his extreme vanity.

Great capture of French ships. Per idem tempus Henricus Pay et quidam de Quinque Portubus, cum navibus quindecim, in mari Britannico centum viginti naves anchorantes, onustas ferro, sale, oleo, vinoque de Rupella, ceperunt.

Death of Richard Mitford, Bishop of Salisbury. Episcopus Sarum, Ricardus Mitford, sæculo valefecit.

[1] See *Remed. Amor.* l. 740.

[2] *salvo* in the printed texts.

[3] *sublinine* apparently in orig.; corrected from the printed texts.

A.D. 1407. Statements circulated that King Richard is alive. Eo tempore fixæ sunt scedulæ multis in locis Londoniis, quibus continebatur [1][quod] Rex Ricardus viveret, et in proximo venturus esset, in magnificentia et gloria, accipere sibi regnum. Sed non multo [2][post] captus est, et punitus, ausus tam temerarii stultus commentor; [3]ex mendacio multorum conceptam lætitiam temperavit. (5) MS. Corp. Chr. vii.

The inventor of the report punished.

Great pestilence. Hac æstate ex [4]aeris corruptione tanta pestis humanis est infusa corporibus, quanta non est visa per annos plurimos in hac terram; ita, ut ita dicam,—

"[5]Letiferis calidi spirarunt æstibus Austri,
"Pestis et in magnæ dominatur mœnibus urbis."—

Disastrous effects thereof in London and the country towns. Nam et Londoniis consumpsit infra breve tempus ad triginta millia sexus utriusque; in villis vero ruralibus pervenit ad miseros damno graviore colonos, ut multæ domus, quondam frequentibus lætæ familiis, penitus vacuarentur.

Ineffectual negotiations between the Pope and Anti-Pope. Eo tempore, prout videbatur, in unam convenere sententiam Papa Romanus et Antipapa per litteras directas ad invicem; attamen nondum finis.

Captures by the French, and by the garrison of Calais. Sub hoc tempore Gallici ceperunt munitionem de Eye, et destruxerunt, ac bona inibi reperta rapuerunt; unde dolentes stipendiarii Calesiæ ceperunt et [6]ipsi castrum de Pouile, et ibidem bona reperta copiosa valde Calesiam comportarunt.

Defeat of the King of Naples by the supporters of Pope Gregory. Prope medium mensis Junii, cum Papa Gregorius se parasset ad proficiscendum Savonam, juxta condictum inter ipsum et Antipapam, gratia unionis [7]faciendæ in Ecclesia Dei, repente, dæmonis instinctu, supervenit Rex Neapolis, et ante portam Sancti Laurentii consedit cum exercitu; unde Dominus Papa confugit, cum Cardinalibus, in castellum Sancti Angeli; et accersito nobili viro Paulo Ursino, jussit ut cum manu forti militari valida opem ferret. Qui, commissa pugna, peremit septem millia de hostibus Ecclesiæ, nobilibus multis captis. Rex vero mœrore plenus aufugit, et inglorius Neapolim repedavit. Hac occasione retardatum est negotium unionis et pacis in Ecclesia [8]Sancta Dei.

---

[1] *quod* omitted in orig.: supplied from (5) MS. Corp. Chr. vii. and the printed texts.

[2] Omitted in orig.: supplied from the printed texts.

[3] *et ex* in the printed texts.

[4] Ovid, *Metam.* vii. ll. 532, 553.

[5] *aieris* in orig., by inadvertence.

[6] *ipsum* in orig.; corrected from (5) MS. Corp. Chr. vii. and the printed texts.

[7] *faciendo* in orig.; corrected from (5) MS. Corp. Chr. vii. and the printed texts.

[8] *Sancti* in orig.; corrected from (5) MS. Corp. Chr. vii., and the printed texts.

(5) MS. Corp. Chr. vii.

A.D. 1407.

Death of Sir Robert Knollis.

Circa festum Assumptionis Beatæ Virginis, Dominus Robertus Knollis diem clausit extremum: cujus arma regnum Franciæ sensit et expavit infesta, Ducatus Britanniæ verebatur Armoricæ, atque pertimuit gens citerioris Hispaniæ. Qui præter laudem quam sibi peperit in gestis martiis, construxit pontem ultra flumen de [1] Medewey juxta Roffam, provexitque domum Fratrum Carmelitarum Londoniis, fundavitque Collegium Sæcularium Clericorum apud Pontem Fractum, et alia multa laudabilia consummavit.

Bridge built by him over the Medway; and other benefactions.

Death of Guy de Mone, Bishop of St. David's

Eodem anno Gwido de Mone, Menevensis Episcopus, præsentis lucis sensit eclipsim; qui, dum vixit, magnorum malorum causa fuit.

Promotions to vacant Bishoprics.

Sub eodem tempore, Magister Henricus Bowet, ad instantiam Regis, translatus est ab Episcopatu Batoniensi ad Archipræsulatum Eboracensem, et Magister Robertus [2] Alum, cui Papa providerat de Archiepiscopatu Eboracensi, thronum conscendit Saresberiensem, [3] vacantem per mortem Magistri [4] Henrici [5] [de] [6] Chichele. Magister vero [7] Ricardus de Clifford de Pontificatu Wygorniensi transiit ad Sedem Londoniensem; Thomas quoque Peverelle ab Episcopatu Landavensi transfertur ad Cathedram Wygorniensem.

The Prince of Wales takes the Casle of Aberystwith; but it is recaptured.

Hac æstate Dominus Henricus, Princeps Walliæ, cepit per obsidionem castrum de Abrustwythe; sed non multo post Howenus Glendor fraudulenter illud intravit, et novos custodes imposuit.

Parliament at London.

Mense Novembri facto Parliamento Londoniis, facta fuit levatio pecuniæ [8] de toto regno.

A.D. 1408.

Severity of the winter. Mortality among certain kinds of birds.

Anno Domini millesimo quadringentesimo octavo,[9] fuit [10] hyems asperrima ex nivium abundantia, durans per menses Decembris, Januarii, Februarii, atque Martii; unde contigit pene cunctas volucres de genere maviscorum, vel merulārum, fame frigoreque perire.

Eo tempore, Rege tenente Consilium grande Londoniis,

---

[1] *Modewey* in orig. and the printed texts; *Medewey* in (5) MS. Corp. Chr. vii.

[2] *Alun* in orig. and the printed texts: corrected from (1) MS. Corp. Chr. vii.

[3] *vacante* in the printed texts.

[4] *Henrici* omitted in the printed texts and (5) MS. Corp. Chr. vii.

[5] *de* omitted in orig. and the printed texts: supplied from (5) MS. Corp. Chr. vii.

[6] *Clichole* in orig.; *Clickhole* in the printed texts: corrected from (5) MS. Corp. Chr. vii.

[7] *Ricardus* omitted in (5) MS. Corp. Chr. vii.

[8] *de* omitted in the printed texts.

[9] "*qui est annus regni Regis Henrici, a Conquæstu Quarti, octavus,*" inserted in the printed texts.

[10] *yemps* in orig.

A.D. 1408. cum regni magnatibus, Comes Northumbriæ Dominusque Thomas de Bardolf, fatis iniquis urgentibus, in Angliam [1]rediere. Qui, post longam equitationem, cum pervenissent ad villam de [2]Thrisk, proclamari fecerunt, ut quisquis libertatem cuperet, arreptis armis, eos alacriter sequeretur. Igitur secuti sunt eos plurimi, putantes sibi cuncta pro votis [3]accidere. [4]Vicecomes vero de Euerwyk, cum militibus patriæ, illis occurrens, juxta [5]Heselwode commisso gravi prœlio, Comitem interemit; cujus caput illico præcisum est. Dominus de Bardolf, ex vulneribus [6]acceptis saucius, captus est vivus, sed cito postea defecit in mortem. Acta sunt hæc, quantum ad bellum, undecimo Kalendas Martii; completaque putabatur prophetia quæ præmissa prænunciaverat sub hoc [7]involucro;—

(5) MS. Corp. Chr. vii.

The Earl of Northumberland and Sir Thomas Bardolf return to England.

They are defeated by the Sheriff of York, and the Earl is slain.

"[8]Stirps [9]Persitina periet confusa ruina."

Nempe dominus iste [9]stirps fuit cunctorum de nomine Percy superstitum, et aliorum plurimorum variis cladibus finitorum. De cujus infortunio vulgus non parum doluit, recolens viri magnificentiam, favorem, et gloriam, applicans sibi Lucani carmen lugubre, sic dicentis;—

"Sed nos nec sanguis, nec tantum vulnera nostri
"Affecere senis, quantum gestata per urbem
"Ora ducis; quæ transfixo [10]deformia pilo
"Vidimus.—"

Indignities offered to the Earl's remains.

Nam caput ejus, veneranda decoratum canitie, pilo superpositum, per urbem Londoniarum publice deportatum, super Pontem confusibiliter est locatum.

The Bishop of Bangor taken prisoner.

Pontifex Bangorensis, captus cum prædictis dominis, donari vita meruit, eo quod inermis captus fuit.

Informers in the North of England.

Post mortem prædictorum procerum, vires assumpsit invidia, succrevitque delatorum turba in Boreali patria, quæ patriotas accusare studuit de impenso favore dictis [11]dominis.

---

[1] *redire* in orig; corrected from (5) MS. Corp. Chr. vii. and the printed texts.

[2] *Trisk* in orig.; *Thrisk* in (5) MS. Corp. Chr. vii. and the printed texts.

[3] *accedere* in the printed texts.

[4] *Vicecomites* in orig.; corrected from (5) MS. Corp. Chr. vii. and the printed texts.

[5] *Horselwood* in the printed texts.

[6] *acceptus* in orig. and (5) MS. Corp. Chr. vii.; corrected from the printed texts.

[7] *in hoc* is added here in orig., by inadvertence.

[8] *Strips* in orig.

[9] So in all the texts.

[10] *de fortuna pilo* in orig.; corrected from (5) MS. Corp. Chr. vii. and the printed texts.

[11] *dominus* in the printed texts.

(5) MS. Corp. Chr. vii.

A.D. 1408.

Quorum clamore Rex excitus, perrexit Eboracum ad faciendum judicium transgressorum; ubi cum multos damnasset, plurima confiscasset, patriam pacificasset, suspenso Abbate de Hales, qui cum præfatis dominis armatus steterat, rediit ad partes Australes.

The King proceeds to York; causes the Abbot of Hales to be hanged.

In crastino Sanctæ Mariæ Magdalenæ, in Consilio cleri [1] celebrato Londoniis, assistentibus Doctoribus Universitatum [2] Oxoniæ et Cantabrigiæ, tractatum est de censu et obedientia Papæ subtrahendis vel non subtrahendis; quia contra votum et juramentum præstitum, se subtraxit a loco ubi, juxta pacta de cessione pro parte sua, procedendum fuerat ad unionem in Ecclesia faciendam.

A Council held at London, in reference to breach of his compact by Pope Gregory.

Eo tempore Dux [3] Aurelianorum, dum scortis, stupris, incestibus vacat, et adulteriis, in regno Franciæ, peremptus est a quodam milite, cujus uxorem adulterare consuevit. Dux Burgundiæ, quia præsumpsit factum defendere militis, proscriptus et multis affectus incommodis, Franciam dereliquit; sed expost captus et incarceratus, solutus est sub pacto Calesiæ capiendæ.

The Duke of Orleans slain.

The Duke of Burgundy imprisoned, but released on condition of taking Calais.

In Vigilia Nativitatis Beatæ Mariæ, [4] tanta fuit inundatio pluviæ, quantam senes veterani antea non viderunt.

Great fall of rain.

[5] Dominus Thomas Comes Canciæ, dum obsidet castrum de Briaut in Britannia, spiculo balistæ vulneratus in capite, cepit tamen castrum et destruxit funditus; nec multo post, putrefacto cerebro, mortem incurrit.

The Earl of Kent is wounded in Bretagne; and dies.

Circa festum Omnium Sanctorum, venit in Angliam Cardinalis Burdegalensis, vir potens in opere et sermone, missus a Collegio Cardinalium ad informandum Regem regnique clerum de inconstantia Papæ [6] Gregorii, prout prius edocuerat Regem Franciæ, et incolas regni ejus; quatenus hii duo Reges, qui censebantur in orbe præstantissimi, manus apponerent adjutrices, ad inducendum dictum Gregorium ad servandum juramentum præstitum, ut, ipsorum duorum Regum auctoritate, magnifica unio fieri posset in Ecclesia. Cui negotio Rex Franciæ [7] libens annuerat; et solemnes Gregorio nuncios destinaverat, licet tergiversanti et indurato. Quamobrem Rex

A Cardinal arrives in England, to represent the bad faith of Pope Gregory.

The King of France takes cognizance of such representations, and determines

---

[1] *celebrati* in orig.; corrected from (5) MS. Corp. Chr. vii. and the printed texts.

[2] The University of Cambridge is named first, in the printed texts.

[3] So in (5) MS. Corp. Chr. vii.; *Aurelianensii* in orig.; *Aurelianensis* in the printed texts.

[4] *tanto* in orig.; corrected from (5) MS. Corp. Chr. vii. and the printed texts.

[5] *Sanctus Thomas, Comes* in Parker's text; *Sanctus Edmundus, Comes* in Camden's text.

[6] *Gregorius* in orig., by inadvertence; corrected from the printed texts.

[7] *lubens* in the printed texts.

A.D. 1408. Franciæ, secutus consilia [1] Doctorum Universitatum Parisiorum et Bononiensium, Aurelianorum, Tholosanorum, et Montis Pesulani, ad evitandum pœnas fautoris schismatis, neutri de Papatu contendenti decrevit obedire, donec pax haberetur in Ecclesia Dei. Rex Angliæ, cum intellexisset propositionem Cardinalis, exhiberi sibi jussit omnem humanitatem, offerens sumptus sibi largifluos, quamdiu cuperet in Anglia [2] perhendinare. (5) MS. Corp. Chr. vii.

to recognize neither claimant of the Papacy.

The Cardinal is handsomely entertained in England.

A.D. 1409. Anno Domini millesimo quadringentesimo nono,[3] post Epiphaniam convocavit Dominus Cantuariensis regni clerum Londoniis, ad eligendum personas idoneas quæ proficiscerentur Pisas ad Consilium Generale. Inter quas [4] electæ sunt Magister Robertus [5] Alum, Saresberiensis Episcopus [6] .

Persons chosen to appear at the General Council of Pisa.

[7] Præmiserat [8] autem Rex Angliæ ambassiatores ad Papam Gregorium et Cardinales, Dominum Johannem Colvyle, militem, et Magistrum Nicholaum Rixtone, clericum, cum litteris exhibendis eisdem. Et quidem in littera Papæ directa, inter cætera scribit ita;—

English embassy sent to Pope Gregory.

"Beatissime Pater, si Sedis Apostolicæ dignaretur attendere providentia, quanta quasi per universum orbem pericula prætextu schismatis emersere, et præcipue de strage populi Christiani, quæ ultra ducenta millia personarum, ut asseritur, ex guerrarum fremitibus in [9] diversis mundi partibus exortarum, et jam pridem ad numerum triginta millium, ratione dissensionis habitæ super Episcopatu Leodiensi inter duos, unum scilicet auctoritate Domini veri Pontificis, et alium auctoritate Antipapæ titulo, contendentium, in bello campestri, quod dolenter referimus, fuerant interfecti; pro facto jam dicto anxiaretur in spiritu, et in isto dolore torqueretur in mente, dictanteque bona conscientia, potius Apostolicæ Sedis honorem relinqueret, quam hujusmodi detestanda convitia de cætero sub dissimulationis chlamyde toleraret, exemplum sumens de vera matre, quæ coram Rege Salomone contendens, cessionem potius elegerat, quam filii, sectionem. Et quamvis ex illa nova creatione

Letter to him from the King of England.

[1] *dictorum* in orig.; corrected from (5) MS. Corp. Chr. vii. and the printed texts.

[2] *commorari* in the printed texts.

[3] "*qui est annus regni Regis* "*Henrici, a Conquæstu Quarti,* "*nonus,*" inserted in the printed texts.

[4] *electæ* in orig. and (5) MS. Corp. Chr. vii.; *electi* in the printed texts.

[5] *Alin* in orig. and the printed texts; corrected from (5) MS. Corp. Chr. vii.

[6] This hiatus occurs in orig.

[7] *et præmiserat* in the printed texts.

[8] *ante Rex* in the printed texts.

[9] *diversarum* in orig.; corrected from the printed texts.

(5) MS. Corp. Chr. vii. "novem Cardinalium, contra juramentum vestrum, ut aliorum "verbis utamur, ultimo per vos facta, de qua vehemens ad-"mirationis causa consurgit, possit aliquatenus, præsertim "prout verisimile est censendum, intentionem vestram ad "finem schismatis non intendere; absit tamen a sæculo "semper, quod Sedes vestra circumspecta de tanta mentis "inconstantia notaretur ab aliquo, unde novissimus error, "priore deterior, haberetur." A.D. 1409.

Hæc descripsimus de Epistola quam Rex direxit Papæ, ut cunctis liqueat quam sobrie, quam modeste, tentavit Papam inducere ad votum juramentumque solvendum, ne per eum stare videretur quominus in Ecclesia unitas reformaretur.

In Epistola vero directa Cardinalibus, inter cætera scripsit sic;—

Letter to the Cardinals, from the King of England.

"Cupientes ostendere quem zelum habuimus, et habemus, "ut pax detur Ecclesiæ, de consensu statuum regni nostri, "Domino Summo Pontifici litteras nostras transmisimus, "juxta seriem copiæ præsentibus interclusæ, effectualiter "exequendas. Vestrum itaque venerabilem cœtum affectuose "precamur, quatenus, si contingat eundem Gregorium, inter-"essendo Generali Consilio apud Pisas, et cedendo Papatui, "juxta votum et juramentum per ipsum vicibus iteratis "emissum, adquiescere, votis vestris et nostris, prout cupimus "et tenemus, ipsum facturum, pro statu suo totaliter ordinare "velitis, ut præcipue Deus exinde placetur, et tam ipse Gre-"gorius quam nos, qui non immerito suum honorem et com-"modum ex affectu diligimus, vobis, et singulis vestrum, "merito teneamur ad gratiarum uberes actiones."

A.D. 1410.

Election, at Pisa, of Pope Alexander V.

Anno Domini millesimo quadringentesimo decimo, juxta condictum convenere Pisas Domini Cardinales utriusque Collegii, videlicet Gregorii et Benedicti, ut super reformatione unionis tractarent tam effectualiter quam finaliter; occurrentibus ad eundem locum pene totius orbis Latini prælatis et [1]viris venerabilibus electis ad suffragandum Cardinalibus in hac causa; sic quod factus est ibidem numerus [2] mitrarum. Qui, invocata Spiritus Sancti gratia, consenserunt in unam personam, ac elegerunt unum qui caput esset totius Ecclesiæ, duobus aliis abdicatis; vocaveruntque nomen ejus "Alexandrum Quintum," licet Gregorius et Benedictus, qui se de Consilio prædicto sponte subtraxerant, procaciter obgrunnirent.

---

[1] *ceris* in orig.; corrected from the printed texts.

[2] This hiatus occurs in orig. and with *maximus* in the printed texts.

(5) MS. Corp. Chr. vii.: it is filled

A.D. 1410.

Privileges granted by Pope Alexander to the Priory of Saint Bartholomew, in Smithfield.

Hic Alexander, in primordio suæ creationis, concessit omnibus vere confessis et contritis, qui manus adjutrices apponerent Ecclesiæ, sive Prioratui, Sancti Bartholomæi Canonicorum de Smethfeld, Londoniis, scilicet Die Cœnæ Domini, Die Parasceues, sive Sancto Sabbato Paschæ, ac etiam in festo Annunciationis Beatæ Virginis, a primis Vesperis usque ad secundas Vesperas, et quolibet istorum dierum, plenam remissionem omnium peccatorum.

(5) MS. Corp. Chr. vii.

Promotions to office.

Creati sunt hoc anno Dominus Thomas Beufort in regni Cancellarium, et Dominus Henricus Scroop in Thesaurarium.

A layman burnt in Smithfield, for heresy.

Facto Parliamento Londoniis, sub diebus Quadragesimæ, quidam laicus, arte faber, dum pertinaciter defendit hanc hæresim, quod videlicet non est Corpus Christi quod sacramentaliter tractatur in Ecclesia, sed res quædam inanimata, pejor bufone vel aranea, quæ sunt animalia animata, nec vellet opinionem istam deserere, traditus est judicio sæculari.

Prince Henry attempts to convert him.

Cumque damnatus esset, et in Smethfeld includendus dolio, Dominus Princeps Henricus, Regis primogenitus, qui tunc affuit, ad eum accessit, consuluit, monuit, ut resipisceret; sed neglexit perditus nebulo tanti Principis monita, et elegit potius se comburendum quam Sacramento vivifico deferre reverentiam. Quapropter [1]dolio includitur, affligitur a devorante flamma, mugitque miserabiliter inter incendia. Clamore cujus horribili Dominus Princeps motus, jussit ignis materiam ab eo subtrahi, ardorem longius amoveri. Consolatur pene mortuum, promittens nunc etiam victurum se et consecuturum veniam, ac singulis diebus vitæ suæ, si resipisceret, de fisco regio tres denarios percepturum; sed miser, refocillato spiritu, respuit tantæ dignationis oblationem, non dubium quin maligno spiritu induratus. Quamobrem jussit Dominus Princeps eum iterum recludi dolio, gratiam nullam consecuturum de reliquo; unde contigit quod illic ad favillas arsit [2]ardelio, miserabiliter mortuus in peccato suo.

At the last moment, he refuses to recant.

Attempt in Parliament to despoil the Church.

In hoc Parliamento, milites Parliamentales, (vel, ut dicamus verius, "Satellites Pilatales,") in maligno positi, nulli commoditati regni studentes, ad unum solummodo scelus vacant, ut Ecclesiam Dei per Angliam spoliarent, hujuscemodi scedulam Regi dantes;—

Representation as to the vast pecuniary resources

"Excellentissimo Domino nostro Regi, et omnibus Proceribus
"in præsenti Parliamento constitutis, omnes communes fideles
"demonstrant humiliter, dicentes veraciter, quod Dominus
"noster Rex potest habere de bonis temporalibus per Epi-

[1] *doleo* in orig.

[2] *ardalio* in (5) MS. Corp. Chr. vii., orig., and the printed texts.

(5) MS. Corp. Chr. vii. "scopos et Abbates, ac Priores, occupatis, ac superbe vastatis "in regno, quindecim Comites, mille quingentos milites, sex "millia ducentos armigeros, et centum xenodochia, plura "quam [1]nunc sunt, bene et fideliter sustentata de terris et "tenementis nunc inutiliter et superbe vastatis." A.D. 1410. of the Church.

Sed cum niterentur ostendere, de quibus locis tam grandes summæ levari possent, unde præmissi dotarentur, sive ditarentur, defecerunt scrutantes scrutinio, et, dum diligunt vanitatem, quæsivere mendacium. Serenissimus autem Princeps, abominatus tantam Lollardorum malitiam, probibuit ne de cætero præsumerent talia commentari. Cumque cœtus execrabilis Lollardorum militum videret se non posse progredi in præmeditata malitia, petierunt cum instantia, ut clerici convicti de cætero non traderentur ergastulis Episcoporum, sed carceribus regiis et temporalium Dominorum: sed nec hoc quidem consecuti sunt. Petierunt etiam, ut Statutum factum de Lollardis, in quo cavetur, ut ubicunque forent deprehensi dogmatizare doctrinas erroneas, caperentur sine brevi regio, et proximo Regis carceri manciparentur, vel mutaretur vel modificaretur. Et acceperunt responsum, se non habituros hujus petitionis propositum, quin potius Statutum super hujusmodi negotio aggravandum.

Fallacy of such representations; which are opposed by Prince Henry.

Attempt to render the clergy amenable to secular jurisdiction.

Vain attempt for amelioration of the Statute against the Lollards.

Rex vero in præsenti Parliamento petiit, ut quotannis, dum viveret, sine Parliamento tenendo, decerneretur sibi de clero una decima, et de laicis una quinta-decima; sed non obtinuit. Protelatum est ergo Parliamentum ab Octavis Sancti Hillarii fere in medium mensis Maii. Tandem de laicis concessa fuit illi una quinta-decima, non sine grandi murmure communitatis.

Vain attempt by the King to obtain a grant for life.

Hoc tempore Dominus Thomas Beuford, Comes [2]Surrey, concessit in fata.

Death of John de Beaufort.

Circa [3]nonum mensis diem Aprilis incensa est villa de Sancto Audomaro, cum Abbathia; ubi reconditus fuit apparatus execrabilis per Ducem Burgundiæ, qui pactus fuerat villam Calesiæ vel destruere vel Gallorum arbitrio subjugare. Ibi machinarum hactenus nullibi conspectarum multitudo maxima, ibi vasorum venena continentium, quæ projicienda præordinaverat in dictam villam, magna nimis abundantia servabatur. Collegerat siquidem serpentes, scorpiones, bufones, et alia venenorum genera, et incluserat in parvis cadis, ut dum

The town and Abbey of Saint Omer burnt.

Abominable provisions made there

[1] *non sunt* in orig., for *nunc sunt*, as in (5) MS. Corp. Chr. vii.: *non* omitted in the printed texts.

[2] John de Beaufort, Earl of Somerset, there can be little doubt, is the personage meant; though the same error is found in all the texts.

[3] *novem* in orig.; corrected from (5) MS. Corp. Chr. vii. and the printed texts.

A.D. 1410. [1]computruissent illic [2]noxiorum carnes animantium, et in (5) MS. Corp. Chr. vii.

for the capture of Calais.

tabem resolutæ fuissent, facta obsidione circa Kalesiam, cados emissos e machinis in villam projiceret; qui, dum confracti fuissent jactus violentia, fœtore pestifero strangularent inclusos, armatos contactu inficerent, et ubique vicos venena sparsa fœdarent. Interea juvenis quidam, ductus auri cupiditate, vel affectæ villæ regiæ, petiit a rectoribus, quid mercedis meretur, qui villam e tanto metu vacuaret, et omnem apparatum, quem formidabant, accenderet. At illi summam fulvi metalli taxant, qua contentus digreditur adolescens, et immisso igne non solum combussit dictam materiam, sed pene, cum Monasterio, totam villam.

The town and Abbey designedly burnt.

Death of Pope Alexander V.; accession of John XXIII.

Alexander Papa Quintus, electus in Consilio Pisis celebrato, diem clausit extremum; cui successit Balthazar, Bononiensis Archiepiscopus, consensu utriusque partis Cardinalium; qui vocatus est "Johannes [3]Vicesimus-tertius."

A.D. 1411.

Anno Domini millesimo quadringentesimo undecimo, hostis humani generis, invidens [4]crementis orbis Christiani, non solum grave scandalum, sed et magum scandalum, intulit Christianis. Siquidem Rex de Krakou, tactus affectu Christianæ professionis, baptizatus est in nomine Sanctæ et individuæ Trinitatis. Qua de causa, cuncti noti et amici sui qui remanserunt in perfidia Saresenica, se elongaverunt ab eo, et conspiraverunt ut ipsum perveterent, aut certe bello delerent. Quorum ut comperit molitiones, tanquam Christicola a vicinis Christianis contra hostes suæ fidei subsidium expetivit. Erant autem sibi contermini proceres et rectores de Le Pruws, qui, priusquam Christianus effectus esset, consuevere terras suas invadere, et exinde prædas optimas martio jure referre. Sed jam ratione religionis cessare necesse fuit. Nihilominus, Prusienses heroes, comperto quod affines sui persequerentur eum, ut afflictum magis affligerent, non verentes Dominum vindicem, bellum sibi crudeles indicunt, quamvis ipse ab eis suffragia contra Sarascenos primitus implorasset. Itaque constitutus inter [5]incudem et malleum, quo se verteret ignorabat; sed tandem animatus, ut creditur, et indutus virtute ex alto, quo majus imminebat periculum se convertit. Et licet hostes præstarent et numero et apparatu, invocato Rex neophytus

The people of Prussia harass the King of Cracow.

He defeats them.

---

[1] *corripuissent* in Camden's text; *computruissent* in Parker's text.

[2] *noctiorum* in orig.

[3] Sometimes also known as "John XXII."

[4] *incrementis* in the printed texts.

[5] *cudem* in orig. and (5) MS. Corp. Chr. vii.; corrected from the printed texts.

(5) MS. Corp. Chr. vii. Christi nomine commisit cum Prusiensibus, et fecit stragem magnam. Quo successu non solum sibi subegit hostes, sed et omnem regionem eorundem; in hoc tamem pie consulens subjugatis, ut permitteret eos suis avitis gaudere privilegiis, et mercimonia, prout soliti fuerant, exercere. A.D. 1411. Shews leniency to them.

Hoc anno, Burdegaliæ ex dysenteria pene quatuordecim millia hominum [1]periere; tantumque pestis invaluit in Aquitania et Wasconia, quod vindemiatores et uvarum calcatores in patria defecerunt. Dysentery at Bordeaux; and consequences thereof.

Johannes Prendergest, miles, et Willelmus Longe [2]de , pelagus præservantes a piratis, mare pacatum reddidere; sed non toleravit hoc malevolorum supercilium, quin viros accusarent de furtis, de rapinis, de prædationibus rerum inconcessarum. Quapropter miles Westmonasterii petivit asylum: non domum, [3][vel] tugurium, ubi caput reclinare posset, obtinere potuit, metu Regis [4]advocantis; sed in vestibulo Sancti Petri, explicatis tentoriis, sibi necesse fuerat repausare, adhibitis lateri suo custodibus, propter timores nocturnos qui sibi ab æmulis parabantur. Remansit interim Willelmus, collega [5]suus, in pelago, donec Admiralius qui [6]pro tunc fuit, naves armasset, et ad eum personaliter accessisset, et impunitatem sibi, fide interposita, spopondisset. Qua conditione, relictis navibus, secutus est eum; sed tamen, non obstantibus præmissis pollicitationibus, reclusus est in Turri Londoniarum. John Prendergest and William Long clear the seas of pirates; but are persecuted, in consequence.

Dominus Cantuariensis, dum nititur visitare Universitatem Oxoniarum, repulsam passus est. Visitatorial rights asserted over Oxford.

Guerra mota est inter Ducem Burgundiæ et Ducem Aurelianensem, filium Ducis Aurelianensis nuper occisi factione Ducis Burgundiæ supradicti; suffragantibus Duci Aurelianensi Regibus Navariæ et Arragoniæ, [7]Ducibus Bituriæ et Britanniæ, cum Wasconis et Aquitannis, necnon Comitibus de Huys et de Armanak, et multis aliis. Dux Burgundiæ, cui favit Rex Franciæ, et ejus primogenitus, dictus "Rector Franciæ," cum multis aliis, videns partem contrariam robore fortem, populositate numerosam, diffidens suis viribus, misit ambassiatores in Angliam, petens per eos Regis suffragia contra Ducem Aure- War between the Duke of Burgundy and Duke of Orleans. Embassadors sent to England by the Duke of Burgundy.

---

[1] *perire* in orig.

[2] *de* and the hiatus are omitted in the printed texts: they occur in (5) MS. Corp. Chr. vii.

[3] *tigurium* in orig.; *tigurium, vel* in the printed texts; *vel tigurium* in (5) MS. Corp. Chr. vii.

[4] Omitted in the printed texts.

[5] *sua* in orig., (5) MS. Corp. Chr. vii., and Parker's text; corrected from Camden's text.

[6] *pro* omitted in the printed texts.

[7] *Ducis* in orig.; corrected from (5) MS. Corp. Chr. vii. and the printed texts.

A.D. 1411. lianensem, offerens plurima, pluraque promittens, inter quæ nuptias filiæ suæ promisit Principi, simul cum maxima summa fulvi metalli. Cui Rex fertur dedisse tale responsum;— (5) MS. Corp. Chr. vii.

Advice given to him by the King of England.

"Consulimus ne cum hoste vestro præsumatis in hac causa "congredi, qui juste vos infestare videtur, pro nece per vos "procurata parentis sui; sed quantum in vobis est, animum "juvenis exasperati mitigare studete, satisfactionem rationa- "bilem, juxta consilium partis utriusque, promittentes. Quod "si nec sic a persecutione cessare decreverit, secedite in "partes tutiores vestri dominii, et illic vires aggregate, quæ "sufficiant ad repellendum suam violentiam. Si vero post "hæc bellum contra vos moverit, ad congrediendum cum eo "justius movebimini; et in tali causa favorem vobis quem "petitis, exhibebimus."

A force of English is sent to Paris, and is welcomed by the Duke of Burgundy.

Transmissi sunt ergo Comes de Arundelle, Comes de Kyme, Dominus de Cobham Johannes Oldcastelle, et quidam alii, cum armata manu et arcitenentibus in numero copioso; qui cum summa gratulatione recepti sunt per Ducem Burgundiæ, sufficienterque conducti. Sed cum moram Parisius diuturnam protraxissent, et jam macellarii carnes solito carius venderent, statuerunt nostrates egredi, et, si fortuna faveret, ab hoste quærere victum sibi. Jacuit tunc non procul Aurelianensis Comes in loco quodam forti, cum privata familia, prope villam de [1]Seynclo, in qua magna pars exercitus sui constituta fuit, quasi media via inter utrosque. Profecti sunt ergo Anglici pabulatum, proque sua necessitate providendum; cumque villam de Seynclo proponunt invadere, comperiunt pontem fractum ab hoste. Cui tabulas, licet strictas, longas tamen, hostes superstraverant, ut egredientes ab ingressu villæ nostros arcerent, et, si necesse foret, juxta qualitatem negotii reverti possent. Pugnatum est ergo, et Franci fugati; qui, dum meticulose fugiunt, per artitudinem tabularum cadentes, in flumine demerguntur. Occisi feruntur ibidem mille trecenti, cæterisque in villam[2] ad Ducem fugientibus, casumque referentibus cum ploratu. Qui, confestim fugiens e diversa parte, saluti suæ consuluit. Nostri proinde villam de Seynclo deprædantur, captivos multos secum trahunt, Parisius revertuntur.

The English defeat the Orleanists at St. Cloud.

[3]Regales et nobiles, cum vidissent manum magnam quam exercuerat Dominus super hostes per manum nostratum, Deum pro successu novo laudavere, nostrisque gratias retulere. Sed

---

[1] Meaning, *Saint Cloud.*

[2] The word *fugerunt* is inserted here in orig., and *fuerunt* in (5) MS. Corp. Chr. vii., by inadvertence.

[3] *Reguli* in the printed texts.

(5) MS. Corp. Chr. vii.

quia captivos secum traxerant, [1]qui rei læsæ majestatis extiterant, eosdem captivos Galli mox judicialiter punire tentabant; contradicunt nostrates, eo quod, pacta redemptione, salvassent eos juxta leges armorum, et timebant perdere summas pactas. Quapropter, bile repleti, dum nituntur salvare quos tueri ceperant, de Parisiensibus plures morte plectunt. Sed tandem, recepta pecunia pacta pro redemptione captivorum de fisco Regis et civibus, permisere Francos gaudere suorum mortibus. Quorum quidam decapitantur, quidam tormentis variis, juxta morem patriæ, mori coguntur.

A.D. 1411. The English, for a sum of money, give up their prisoners to the King of France.

Parliamentum celebratur Londoniis in crastino Animarum.

Parliament at London.

Anno Domini millesimo quadringentesimo duodecimo, Dux Aurelianensis, qui se putabat insuperabilem, accepta plaga per Anglos inflicta, mox dispersiquivit media, per quæ Regem Angliæ, necnon et proceres, ac commune vulgus, in affectum sibi posset allicere. Initoque consilio super isto negotio, scripsit Procuratorium sub hiis verbis:—

A.D. 1412. Envoys sent to England by the party of the Duke of Orleans.

"Johannes, Regis Francorum filius, Dux Bituriæ et Al-
" verniæ, Comes Pictaviæ, Stamparum, Boloniæ, et Alverniæ,
" etc., Karolus Dux Aurelianensis et Valesii, Comes Blesensis
" et Belli Montis, et Dominus Conciati, Johannes Dux Bur-
" boniæ, Comes Clari Montis et Forestarum, et Dominus
" Belli Joci, et Johannes Comes Alekoniæ, de Armanak, et de
" Pertica, et Dominus Filgeriarum,—notum vobis facimus
" universis, quod nostrum quilibet de probitate et fidelitate,
" circumspectione et prudentia, Falconeti, etc., ad plenum con-
" fisi, ipsos et eorum quemlibet, præsentium tenore, nostros
" procuratores fecimus certos, indubitatos, et irrevocabiles, ac
" nuncios et legatos speciales, ad tractandum, et concordan-
" dum, et concludendum, cum serenissimo Principe, Domino
" Henrico, Dei gratia, Rege Angliæ, et illustrissimis ejus
" natis, etc., super restitutione et traditione reali Ducatus
" Aquitanniæ, cum suis juribus et pertinentiis universis, quæ
" ad serenissimum Dominum Regem Angliæ hæreditario jure,
" ut asseritur, pertinent, per nos eidem fiendis, etc."

Powers given to the Envoys.

Postquam legati suum Procuratorium exhibuissent, obtulerunt quæ in subscriptis Articulis denotantur:—

Particulars of their offers and demands.

Primo, obtulerunt sua corpora exponenda pro servitio Domini Regis Angliæ in omnibus suis causis et actionibus, salva semper eorum fidelitate, scientes quod aliter requirere nollet. Secundo, obtulerunt filios suos, filias, neptes, nepotes, et universaliter omnes consanguineos suos, pro conjugiis faciendis, ad complendum juxta dispositionem Regis Angliæ.

[1] *qui* omitted in Camden's text.

A.D. 1412. Tertio, obtulerunt castra, villas, thesauros, et alia bona, in obsequium præfati Domini Regis. Quarto, obtulerunt amicos, fere omnes nobiles Franciæ, clericos famosos, cives honestos, qui eis assistunt, ut de facto patebit. Quinto, obtulerunt Ducatum Aquitanniæ integre, eodem modo quo ejus prædecessores obtinuerunt, nihil excipiendo de pertinentibus ad præfatum Ducatum; ita quod parati [1][sunt] recognoscere terras quas tenent a præfato Domino Rege, et tradere in manu sua quas possunt, et residuas pro juribus conquiescant. Ipsi vero petunt recipere, quod Dominus Rex Angliæ et successores ejus eisdem Dominis assistant, contra Ducem Burgundiæ, scilicet de crimine commisso in personam Ducis Aurelianensis. Secundo, petunt quod Dominus Rex Angliæ assistat contra Ducem Burgundiæ et suos fautores, usque ad reparationem omnium bonorum quæ habuerunt illius et suorum occasione causæ. Tertio, petunt quod assistat contra Ducem Burgundiæ pro restitutione damnorum, et reparatione offensarum, amicorum, vassallorum, et subditorum suorum. Quarto, petunt quod eis assistat pro pace regnorum, quantum poterit, etc. (5) MS. Corp. Chr. vii.

Hoc anno, libra piperis quatuor solidis vendebatur.

The King sends aid to the Duke of Orleans, and withdraws his support from the Duke of Burgundy.

Circa festum Assumptionis [2]Beatæ Mariæ, cum Rex, decreto sui Consilii, statuisset opem præstare partibus Ducis Aurelianensis, misit filium natu secundum, Thomam Ducem Clarentiæ, necnon Edwardum Ducem Eboraci, Dominumque Thomam Comitem Dorcetanum, plurimosque valentes, cum manu valida, ut Duci præfato ferrent auxilium contra Ducem Burgundiæ, nondum [3]reversis in Angliam cunctis qui jamdudum cum Comite Arundeliæ transfretaverant ad roborandum partes Burgundionis: unde succrevit multis admiratio, qualiter tam repentina facta sit mutatio, ut sub temporis tantilli spatio contingeret, Anglos velut duo contraria confovere.

The English lay waste Normandy. Conference between the Duke of Clarence and the Duke of Orleans.

Profecti sunt tamen prænotati proceres, et in Neustria applicuere; ubi cum Dux Aurelianensis, juxta condictum, tempore statuto non occurrisset, incenderunt villas suas, prædati sunt vicos, et municipia multa cepere. Tandem, licet [4]sero, convenerunt ad colloquium [5]Duces Clarensis et Aurelianensis, habitusque est tractatus inter eos, ut nostrates desis-

[1] Omitted in orig.; supplied from (5) MS. Corp. Chr. vii. and the printed texts.

[2] *Sanctæ* in the printed texts.

[3] *reversus* in orig.; corrected from the printed texts.

[4] *cero* in orig. and (5) MS. Corp. Chr. vii.

[5] *Ducis Clarientiæ* the printed texts.

(5) MS. Corp. Chr. vii. terent ab hostili equitatione, et [1]a prædationibus temperarent. Quo concesso, recesserunt Duces nostri in Aquitanniam, illic hyematuri; Aurelianensis ad propria se convertit. Medio tempore, Dominus de Heyle, Marescallus Franciæ, cum multis magnatibus, hominibusque de armis, ad numerum quatuor millium pugnatorum, obsedit quoddam municipium in Aquitannia, quod erat in custodia Domini Johannis de Blount militis; qui cum trecentis auxiliariis fugavit et subdidit totum exercitum Gallicorum, captis de nominatis viris duodecim, et aliis generosis ad numerum centum viginti. A.D. 1412. Sir John de Blount defeats the Marshal of France.

Anno Domini millesimo quadringentesimo tertio-decimo, Rex Henricus tenuit Natale apud Eltham, valetudine gravi pressus, sic quod quandoque mortuus videbatur. Resumpsit tamen vires, [2]Deo volente, et dies Natalitios jocunditate, qua potuit, celebravit. A.D. 1413. The King is taken ill at Eltham; but recovers.

Post Natale, convocavit regni proceres ad Parliamentum tenendum Londoniis, in crastino Purificationis Beatæ Mariæ; sed tamen finem Parliamenti non expectavit, fato præventus die vicesima mensis Martii, cum gloriose regnasset annis tresdecim et dimidio, præter quinque dies: sepultusque est in Ecclesia Christi Cantuariæ. He dies; and is buried at Canterbury.

[1] *ea* in orig., by inadvertence. | [2] *de* in orig., by inadvertence.

De Tempore Regis Henrici, post Conquæstum Quinti.

A.D. 1413. His son, Henry, is crowned. Great storm of snow at that time.

Eodem anno coronatus [1] est Londoniis Henricus, primogenitus Regis Henrici, nuper defuncti, quinto Idus Aprilis, Dominica in Passione Domini. Quo die fuit tempestas nivis maxima, cunctis admirantibus de temporis asperitate, quibusdam novelli Regis fatis impingentibus aeris turbulentiam, velut ipse futurus esset in agendis frigidus, in regimine regnoque severus; aliis mitius de persona Regis sapientibus, et hanc aeris intemperiem interpretantibus omen optimum, quod ipse videlicet nives et frigora vitiorum faceret in regno cadere, et serenos virtutum fructus emergere, ut posset effectualiter a suis dici subditis;—"Jam enim [2] hyems transiit, imber abiit "et recessit." (5) MS. Corp. Chr. vii.

Virtuous conduct of the new King.

Qui revera, mox ut initiatus est regni infulis, repente mutatus est in virum alterum, honestati, modestiæ, ac gravitati, studens, nullum virtutum genus omittens, quod non cuperet exercere. Cujus mores et gestus omni conditioni, tam religiosorum quam laicorum, in exempla fuere.

Parliament at London.

Post festum Paschæ tenuit Rex Parliamentum solemne Londoniis, in quo subsidium petiit et accepit.

The Duke of Clarence returns from Acquitaine.

Circa præsens tempus rediit Dominus Thomas Dux Clarentiæ, frater Regis, de partibus Aquitanniæ; quem directum diximus in auxilium Ducis Aurelianensis contra Ducem Burgundiæ.

Part of the city of Norwich burnt.

Sub hiis diebus, magna pars civitatis Norwicensis, cum tota domo Fratrum Prædicatorum Ordinis Sancti Dominici, et omnibus eisdem pertinentibus, necnon et duobus Fratribus Ordinis ejusdem, repentinis ignibus conflagravit.

Funeral of Henry IV.

In festo Sanctæ Trinitatis celebratæ sunt solemnes exequiæ Regis Henrici, a Conquæstu Quarti, Cantuariæ, præsente Rege Henrico, filio suo et hærede.

Decree as to the Feasts of St. George and St. Dunstan.

Eo tempore, decretum fuit per cleri Consilium, Londoniis apud Sanctum Paulum celebratum, ad instantiam maxime Regis nunc, ut festivitas Sancti Georgii Martyris ut duplex festum de cætero celebretur. Quod etiam [3] de festo Sancti Dunstani Dominus Cantuariensis censuit faciendum.

Death of Alexander,

Alexander Episcopus Norwicensis, qui de veterano Priore loci prædicti Pontifex factus fuerat, curis sæculi valefecit; cui

---

[1] *est* omitted in the printed texts.
[2] *hiemps* in orig.
[3] *die Sancti* in the printed texts.

(5) MS. Corp. Chr. vii. successit, per electionem, Magister Ricardus de Curtunaco, dignus qui genere, moribus, et scientia, conquadraret hunc gradum. A.D. 1413. Bishop of Norwich.

Threatenings of the Lollards. Eo tempore Lollardi, qui doctrinam Evangelicam et Apostolicam, atque Propheticam, depravabant, fixerunt scedulas in valvis Ecclesiarum Londoniis, quæ continebant centum millia parata ad insurgendum contra cunctos qui non saperent sectam suam. [1]Invitabantur nempe viribus et ingenio cujusdam qui dicebatur "Johannes Oldcastelle," qui, ob reverentiam nuptiarum quas contraxerat cum affine nobilis viri Domini de Cobham, cognomen dicti dominii est sortitus. Erat iste Johannes fortis viribus, operi martio satis idoneus, sed hostis Ecclesiæ pervicacissimus; Regi, propter probitatem, carus et acceptus, sed tamen propter hæreticam pravitatem valde suspectus. Sir John Oldcastle their leader, by courtesy called "Lord Cobham."

Charges in Convocation against Sir John Oldcastle. Eo tempore facta Londoniis cleri Convocatione per Dominum Cantuariensem, maxime jam causa prædicti Johannis, repertum fuit quod idem Johannes fuit, et est, [2]principalis receptator et fautor, protector et defensor, Lollardorum, et quod præsertim in Diœcesibus Londoniensi, Roffensi, et Herefordensi, ipsos Lollardos, ab Ordinariis sive Diœcesanis locorum minime licenciatos, contra Constitutionem Provincialem inde factam, ad prædicandum transmisit, eorumque prædicationibus nefariis interfuit, et contradictores, si quos repererat, minis et terroribus, ac brachii sæcularis potestate, compescuit: asserens inter cætera, quod Cantuariensis Archiepiscopus et ejus Suffraganei non habuerunt, nec habent, potestatem aliquam hujusmodi Constitutionem faciendi; aliterque sentiit et sentit, ac dogmatizat et docet, de Sacramentis Altaris et Pœnitentiæ, peregrinationibus et adorationibus imaginum, ac clavibus, quam Romana Ecclesia docet et affirmat. Quare, ex parte totius cleri, Dominus Cantuariensis fuerat requisitus, ut [3]de et super præmissis contra eundem Johannem procedere dignaretur. Qui tamen, ob reverentiam Domini Regis, cujus ad tunc idem Johannes familiaris extiterat, et ob honorem ordinis militaris, una cum omnibus Suffraganeis tunc præsentibus, et magna parte cleri, accessit ad præsentiam Domini Regis, tunc in prædio suo de Keningtoune existentis, declarans ei defectus ejusdem. Ad instantiam tamen Domini Regis, cupientis eum sine dedecore revocare, suspensum fuit negotium magno tempore. Sed cum Dominus Rex circa reduc- Representations made to the King thereon. The matter is postponed for a time.

[1] *Invitebantur* in orig. and (5) MS. Corp. Chr. vii.

[2] *principale* in orig.; corrected from the printed texts.

[3] *desuper præmissis* in the printed texts.

A.D. 1413.

The Archbishop of Canterbury attempts to cite Oldcastle.

(5) MS. Corp. Chr. vii.

tionem ejus longum tempus trivisset inaniter, significavit Domino Cantuariensi [1][se] circa eum inutiliter laborasse. Dominus ergo Cantuariæ dictum Johannem de et super præmissis personaliter responsurum coram eo ad certum terminum decrevit evocandum; ac nuncium suum, cum litteris citatoriis, ad dictum Johannem transmisit, tunc in castro suo de Coulynge degentem, mandans dicto nuncio, ut dictum castrum dicti Johannis nullo modo ingrederetur, nisi [2]licentiatus; sed per mediationem cujusdam Johannis Butaler, [3]hostiarii Cameræ Domini nostri Regis, ipsum Dominum Johannem requireret, quatenus [4]aut daret dicto nuncio licentiam ingrediendi; ut citaret eundem, seu saltem extra castrum suum prædictum faceret sui copiam, ut sic citatione posset apprehendi.

Oldcastle declines to be served with the citation.

Qui tamen Johannes Oldcastelle dicto Johanni Butiler, ex parte Domini Regis sibi præmissa exponenti, publice respondit quod nullo modo citari voluit, nec citationem ipsius aliqualiter tolerare.

The Archbishop causes him to be publicly cited.

Hiis auditis, Dominus Cantuariensis decrevit eum citandum per edictum, in valvis Roffensis ecclesiæ, sibi vicinæ, publice affigendum; ut compareret coram eo undecimo die mensis Septembris, super præmissis, et aliis hæreticam pravitatem concernentibus, personaliter responsurus. Quo die adveniente, Dominus Cantuariensis in Capella [5]majori infra castrum de Ledis, quod tunc inhabitabat, sedens pro tribunali, audita et recepta relatione, quod idem Dominus Johannes se incastellavit et fortificavit in castro suo prædicto, ac opiniones suas defendit, claves Ecclesiæ et potestatem Archiepiscopalem multipliciter contemnendo, fecit eum citari publice ac præconizari.

He is excommunicated, as contumacious.

Qui cum diu expectatus nullo modo compareret, prout [6]merito contumacem excommunicavit in scriptis. Et quia dictus Johannes in defensionem erroris sui contra claves Ecclesiæ se incastellavit et fortificavit, Dominus Cantuariensis decrevit iterato citare dictum Johannem, si posset apprehendi,

And is again cited.

vel alias per edictum, sicut prius, ut compareret coram eo die Sabbati proximo post festum Sancti Matthæi Apostoli et Evangelistæ proximo futuro; causam rationabilem, si quam habet, quare contra eundem ad graviora procedi non debeat, tanquam publicum hæreticum, schismaticum, et hostem et adversarium universalis Ecclesiæ; quare etiam pronunciari

---

[1] Omitted in orig.; supplied from (5) MS. Corp. Chr. vii. and the printed texts.

[2] *licensiatus* in orig.

[3] *hosticiarii* in orig.; corrected from (5) MS. Corp. Chr. vii. and the printed texts.

[4] *ut* in the printed texts.

[5] *mari* in orig.; corrected from the printed texts.

[6] *initio* in the printed texts.

(5) MS. Corp. Chr. vii. non debeat, ac auxilium brachii sæcularis contra eum solemniter invocari, personaliter responsurus, facturus, et recepturus, circa omnia et singula præmissa, quod justitia suadebat. A.D. 1413.

Oldcastle is taken in custody, and appears before the tribunal.

Adveniente termino præfixo, [1] Domino Cantuariensi sedente pro tribunali in Capitulo Sancti Pauli Londoniis, assidentibus sibi Dominis Ricardo Londoniensi et Henrico [2] Wintoniensi, Episcopis, Dominus Robertus Murley, miles, Custos Turris Londoniarum, secum præfatum Dominum Johannem adduxit; nam parum ante per regios ministros comprehensus fuerat, et in Turri clausus. Cui Dominus Cantuariensis recitavit processum memoratum; quomodo videlicet in Convocatione cleri detectus et delatus extiterat, quomodoque citatus et propter suam contumaciam excommunicatus; unde Dominus Cantuariensis gratiose se obtulit, et paratum fore promisit, ad absolvendum eum: sed ille absolutionem Domini Cantuariæ petere noluit, sed, divertens ad alia, dixit quod libenter recitaret coram Domino Cantuariensi fidem quam tenet. Extraxitque de sinu suo [3] quandam scedulam indentatam, quam tradidit Domino Cantuariensi postquam legisset.

He refuses absolution offered by the Archbishop of Canterbury, and reads a profession of his faith.

The Archbishop puts further questions to him.

Qua scedula perlecta, Dominus Cantuariensis dixit;—"Ecce! "Domine Johannes, in hac scedula vestra plura bona continentur, ac satis Catholica; sed habetis terminum istum ad "respondendum super aliis, errores et hæreses sapientibus, "quibus per contenta in hac scedula non est plene [4] responsum. Et propterea, vos oportet ad eadem respondere qualiter sentitis, et fidem vestram plenius declarare, "videlicet an [5] teneatis, credatis, et affirmetis, quod in "Sacramento Altaris, post consecrationem rite factam, remaneat panis materialis, vel non. Item, an teneatis, credatis, "et affirmetis, quod in Sacramento Pœnitentiæ necessarium "fuerit, quod habens copiam sacerdotis confiteatur de peccatis "suis presbytero per Ecclesiam ordinato?"

He refuses to make further answer; whereupon the Archbishop warns him.

Qui respondit expresse, se nolle aliter prædicta declarare quam in dicta scedula sua continetur. Cui compatiens, Dominus Cantuariensis dixit,—"Caveatis, Domine Johannes, quia "[6] [si] ad hæc vobis [7] objecta clare non respondeatis in termino "legitimo vobis jam dato, poterimus vos denunciare et de-

---

[1] *Dominus Cantuariensis* in the printed texts.

[2] *Wintoniensis* in orig., by inadvertence; corrected from the printed texts.

[3] *quandam* omitted in the printed texts.

[4] *responsurum* in orig.; corrected from the printed texts.

[5] *teneatis* omitted in the printed texts.

[6] Omitted in all the texts.

[7] *injecta* in the printed texts.

A.D. 1413. "clarare hæreticum." Sed dictus Johannes aliter respondere contempsit. (5) MS. Corp. Chr. vii.

The Archbishop expounds the doctrines of the Church, on certain pionts; and calls upon him to make answer thereon.

Tunc Dominus Cantuariensis declaravit ei quid Sancta Romana Ecclesia, sequens dicta Beatorum Augustini, Hieronymi, et Ambrosii, et aliorum Sanctorum, determinavit; quas determinationes oportet quoscunque Catholicos observare. Ad quæ dictus Johannes respondit, quod voluit credere et observare quicquid Sancta Ecclesia determinavit, ac quicquid [1] Deus voluit se credere et observare; sed quod Dominus Papa et Cardinales, Archiepiscopi, Episcopi, cæterique prælati Ecclesiæ, haberent potestatem talia determinandi, noluit ad tunc aliqualiter affirmare. Unde Dominus Cantuariensis, sibi compatiens, sub spe melioris deliberationis, [2] datis sibi in Anglicis certis articulis, rogavit ut in die Lunæ proximo sequente plene et clare suum daret responsum super eisdem.

Oldcastle is again summoned.

Quo die Lunæ, videlicet vicesimo-quinto die mensis Septembris, coram Domino Cantuariensi et [3] antedictis Episcopis, adjuncto illis Bangorensi Episcopo, Domino Benedicto, comparuit Dominus Robertus Murlee, Custos Turris Londoniensis, ac præfatum Dominum Johannem secum duxit, ac coram Domino Cantuariensi et toto clero, pro tunc congregato, statuit. Cui Archiepiscopus affabiliter et suaviter recitavit acta prioris diei, et quomodo excommunicatus fuerat, et est; ac rogavit et requisivit eundem, ut peteret ac admitteret in forma debita Ecclesiæ absolutionem. Quod se dictus Johannes facturum negavit, sed a Deo solo absolutionem petiturum. Consequenter Dominus Cantuariæ suavi et modesto modo rogavit et requisivit eundem, quatenus de et super contentis in dicta scedula determinationem Ecclesiæ eidem transmissam de sibi oppositis clarum daret responsum.

He refuses to ask absolution of the Church.

He is called upon to answer the charges.

His answer as to the Sacrament of the Eucharist, and other matters of faith.

Et [4] primo super Sacramentum Eucharistiæ.—Ad quem articulum, inter cætera, respondit, quod sicut Christus hic in terra degens habuit in se divinitatem et humanitatem, divinitatem tamen velatam et invisibilem sub humanitate, quæ in eo aperta et visibilis fuerat; sic in Sacramento Altaris est verum corpus et verus panis, videlicet quem videmus, et corpus Christi sub eadem velatum, quod non videmus. Ad fidem circa Sacramentum hujusmodi in scedula prædicta per Dominum Cantuariensem transmissa sibi, perque Sanctam Romanam Ecclesiam et Doctores Sanctos determinatam, expresse negavit, dicens

[1] *Deus* omitted in the printed texts.

[2] *datis* omitted in the printed texts.

[3] *antedictos Episcopos* in the printed texts.

[4] *primum* in the printed texts.

(5) MS. Corp. Chr. vii. quod determinatio Ecclesiæ facta est contra Sacram Scripturam, [1]et postquam [2]Ecclesia dotata est, et venenum infusum in [2]Ecclesia, et non ante. Quod etiam ad Sacramentum Pœnitentiæ et Confessionis,—dixit et asseruit, quod si quis esset in aliquo gravi peccato constitutus, a quo ipse surgere nesciret, expediret, et bonum esset, sibi adire aliquem sanctum et discretum sacerdotem pro consilio ab eo habendo. Sed quod confiteretur peccatum suum proprio curato seu alteri presbytero, etiamsi haberet copiam ejusdem, non est necessarium ad salutem, quia sola contritio peccatum hujusmodi delere posset, et ipse peccator purgari. A.D. 1413.

Circa adorationem Sanctæ crucis.—Dixit et asseruit, quod solum corpus Christi quod pendebat in cruce, debuit adorari; quia illud corpus solum fuit, et est, adorandum. Et interrogatus quem honorem faceret imagini ipsius crucis, respondit verbis expressis, quod illum honorem solum faceret sibi, quod bene mundaret eam et poneret in bona custodia. [3]Quo autem ad potestatem clavium, Dominum nostrum Papam, et Archiepiscopos, et alios prælatos:—dixit quod Dominus noster Papa est verus Antichristus, hoc est caput ejusdem; Archiepiscopi et Episcopi, necnon alii prælati, sunt membra, et Fratres cauda ejusdem. Quibus Papæ, Archiepiscopis, et prælatis, non est obediendum, nisi quatenus fuerint imitatores Christi et Petri, in vita, moribus, et conversatione. Et quod ipse est successor, qui est vita melior, moribus purior, et nullus alius. Ulterius dixit idem Johannes alta voce, manibus expansis, alloquendo circumstantes;—"Isti qui judicant et volunt damnare me, "seducunt vos omnes et seipsos, et vos ducent ad infernum, "et ideo caveatis ab eis."

Oldcastle warns the bystanders against his judges.

Quibus omnibus per eum sic dictis, Dominus Cantuariensis iterum ac sæpius flebili vultu dictum Dominum Johannem alloquebatur, verbis quibus potuit exhortando, ut ad unitatem rediret Ecclesiæ, crederet et teneret quod Ecclesia Romana credit et tenet. Qui respondit expresse, se aliter non credere quam superius expressit. Videns ergo Dominus Cantuariensis se in nullo posse proficere, cum magna cordis amaritudine processit ad prolationem sententiæ diffinitivæ, in hunc modum:

The Archbishop again exhorts him; but to no purpose.

"In Dei nomine, Amen. Nos, Thomas, permissione divina "etc., in quadam causa, sive negotio, hæreticæ pravitatis, de "et super diversis articulis, super quibus Dominus Johannes "Oldcastelle, miles, Dominus de Cobham, coram nobis in

The Archbishop adjudges him to be guilty of heresy.

[1] *et* omitted in the printed texts.
[2] *Ecclesiam* in the printed texts.
[3] *Quod* in Camden's text.

A.D. 1413. "ultima Convocatione cleri [1]nostri Cantuariensis Provinciæ, "in Ecclesia Sancti Pauli celebrata, post inquisitionem diligentem ibidem inde captam, reperimus eundem [2]Dominum "Johannem fore et esse hæreticum, hæreticis credentem, ac "in fide et observantiis Sacrosanctæ Romanæ et universalis "Ecclesiæ errantem, et præsertim circa Sacramenta Eucharistiæ et Pœnitentiæ; ad quod, tanquam iniquitatis et tenebrarum filius, in tantum obduravit cor suum, ut non intelligat "vocem pastoris sui, nec velit monitionibus allici, nec reduci "blanditiis; unde pensatis ipsius delictis et culpis, per ipsius "damnabilem pertinaciam aggravatis, [3]nolentes quod is qui "nequam est fiat nequior, et alios inficiat sua labe, de consilio et assensu magnæ discretionis et sapientium virorum "venerabilium nobis assistentium, præfatum Dominum Johannem Oldcastelle, militem, Dominum de Cobham, de et "super hujusmodi detestabili reatu convictum, et ad Ecclesiæ "unitatem pœnitentialiter redire nolentem, hæreticum, ac in "iis quæ tenet, docet, determinat, et prædicat, Sacrosancta "Romana et universalis Ecclesia, et præsertim in articulis "subscriptis, errantem judicamus, declaramus, [4]et concedimus, sententialiter et diffinitive, in hiis scriptis, relinquentes "eundem ex nunc, tanquam hæreticum, judicio sæculari. "Ipsumque nihilominus hæreticum, omnesque alios et singulos, qui eundem de cætero in sui favorem erroris receptaverint, defensaverint, seu sibi consilium, favorem, vel auxilium, in hac parte præbuerint, tanquam fautores, receptatores, et defensores hæreticorum, excommunicamus, et excommunicatos denunciamus in hiis scriptis." (5) MS. Corp. Chr. vii.

The Archbishop obtains further time for him, from the King, in order that he may relent.

Hiis [5]ita peractis, Dominus Cantuariensis Regem certificavit super præmissis, vivæ vocis oraculo, postulans ut Dominus Rex dignaretur dicto Johanni, damnato juridice, gratiose concedere [6]quadraginta dies ad inducias. Nam tam Rex quam Pontifex non ejus interitum, sed vitam, cupiebant affectualiter, et pro salute sua laboravere non segniter. Unde factum est, ut ad Turrim [7]reduceretur, ubi, sub induciarum spatio sibi concessarum, posset resipiscere, et gratiam, tam ecclesiasticam quam regiam, promereri. Sed ista specialis indul-

---

[1] *nostre* in orig. and (5) MS. Corp. Chr. vii.

[2] *Dominum* omitted in the printed texts.

[3] *volentes* in the printed texts.

[4] *concedamus* in orig., by inadvertence.

[5] *itaque* in orig. and the printed texts; corrected from (5) MS. Corp. Chr. vii.

[6] 50 in Camden's text; *quadraginta* in (5) MS. Corp. Chr. vii., and Parker's text.

[7] *adduceretur* in the printed texts.

(5) MS. Corp. Chr. vii. gentia facta fuit sibi malignandi copia, dum citra præfixum terminum elapsus e custodia, congregavit iniquitatem sibi, nil aliud cogitans quam de vindicta. Revera, clam destinatis litteris ad sequaces suos, tam milites quam armigeros, qui non pauci fuere, hortabatur, ut et ipsi scriberent ad amicos suos, ut et ipsi se ad vindictam mutuo concitarent. Igitur per omne tempus illud quod fluxit ab evasione ejus usque ad [1] Circumcisionem Domini, vel Epiphaniam, discurrebant undique Lollardorum nuncii, qui rurales et quoscunque poterant, promissis amplis stipendiis, allectarent, quatenus in certum diem, eis denunciandum, parati forent ad standum viriliter, et actus martios peragendum. Multis ignaris quærentibus causam, pro qua vel in qua certare deberent, responsum fuit non esse curandum, dummodo stipendia larga reciperent, et pro rebus bene gestis affluenter remunerandos proculdubio se sperarent. Sed de hiis omnibus in ordine præsentis historiæ post hæc plenius referemus.

A.D. 1413. He escapes from the Tower, and summons his friends to his aid.

Hoc anno plures Angli peste percussi, vel epidemia, vivere desiere.

A pestilence in England.

Item, hoc anno levatum fuit corpus quondam Ricardi Regis Angliæ, quod humatum fuerat juxta ecclesiam Fratrum Prædicatorum de Langelee, et deportatum Londonias, ac apud Westmonasterium regaliter tumulatum; non sine maximis expensis Regis nunc, qui fatebatur se sibi tantum venerationis debere, quantum patri suo carnali.

The body of King Richard II. is removed from Langley to Westminster.

Anno Domini millesimo quadringentesimo decimo-quarto, Rex tenuit Natale solemniter apud Eltham, ubi Lollardi, facta conjuratione, Regem [2] inopinate, cum fratribus suis et amicis, cepisse, vel occidisse, statuerant. Sed Deus Omnipotens noluit innocentem nocentium perire manibus, neque periclitari; sed immisit timorem suum in corda quorundam conspiratorum, qui Regem monuere vitare periculum, et jam structas insidias declinare. Unde factum est, ut sine strepitu Rex modeste se transferret ad Palatium suum prope Westmonasterium, ubi et locus tutior et frequentia populi major fuit.

A.D. 1414. Conspiracy of the Lollards, to seize or slay the King; who is warned, and escapes.

Lollardi vero, cum jam completa esset eorum malitia, effutire parabant quæ mente conceperant, gestientes experiri fortunam quam suis votis fore propitiam putavere. Veneruntque sub ipso noctis conticinio in campum [3] [qui] dicebatur Sancti Ægidii, prope Londonias, ubi ferebatur eorum campi-ductor, Johannes Oldcastelle, Dominus de Cobham, suos satellites

The Lollards meet in Saint Giles's Fields.

[1] *Circumsicionem* in orig.
[2] *inopinato* in the printed texts.
[3] Omitted in orig.; supplied from (5) MS. Corp. Chr. vii. and the printed texts.

A.D. 1414. opperiri: videres per semitas, perque vicos, per compita, concurrentium turbas, pene de cunctis regni Comitatibus sollicitatas magnis promissis, confluere ad diem et horam jam instantem. Qui requisiti quamobrem sic festinabant, et velut [1]anheli currebant, responderunt se properare ad Dominum de Cobham, qui eos conductos suis stipendiis accivisset. Rex vero, non ignarus omnium præmissorum, sub ejusdem noctis articulo jussit suos in armis esse paratos, tunc primum suis intimans, quid facere decrevisset. Fuerunt tunc plures cum Rege qui laudaverunt in diem clarum protelandum negotium, quo decernere possent qui cum Rege, vel contra Dominum, stare vellent. Alii vero consuluere Regem debere præstolari, donec ad eum multitudo convenisset exercitus, ne, cum paucis hostes aggrediens, pejorem, quod absit, reportaret calculum. Sed neutris adquievit Rex, eo maxime quod audisset Lollardorum fore propositum, si prævaluissent, primitus destruendi Monasteria de Westmonasterio, de Sancto Albano, de Sancto Paulo, et cunctorum Fratrum Londoniis constituta. Quamobrem Rex, tantis malis se objiciens, ingessit periculo, contra vota suorum in campum progrediens, paulisper transacta nocte media, ubi et constitit præstolaturus quid ventura pariat dies proxima; ubi contigit, ut multi de remotis partibus ad castra hostilia prius intrarent per errorem, castra regia, ubi requisiti quid quærerent, responderunt, dominum suum de Cobham. Quapropter contra spem capti sunt, et carceribus mancipati.

(5) MS. Corp. Chr. vii.

The King takes measures to defeat their designs.

Pervenit rumor iste ad duces partis adversæ, scilicet quod Rex cum manu valida occupasset arva contermina, et de suis plurimos captivasset. Consternatique sunt peramplius, quod neminem viderunt de Londoniis adventare, unde putabant millia ruitura in auxilium eorundem. Præceperat autem Rex ut civitatis portæ clauderentur, et per armatos servarentur artius, ut nullis pateret egressus nisi hiis quos scirent ad signa regia properare. Et revera, nisi Rex usus fuisset hac calliditate, nocte illa, prout fertur, exivissent de servis et apprenticiis, simul cum quibusdam de civibus, eorundem magistris, ad quinquaginta millia contra Regem. Qui vero de Lollardis adunati [2]fuere, ut audivere Regem jam in eodem campo suas acies statuisse, non habentes ultra spiritum, fugæ præsidia petiere; quos regales insequentes, quosdam cepere, quosdam peremere. Quo vero diverterit dux eorum, minime scire potuit, licet Dominus Rex spopondisset publica voce præconis cuicunque prodenti eum, de

Alleged designs of the servants and apprentices of London.

The Lollards take to flight.

[1] *haneli* in orig., and (5) MS. Corp. Chr. vii.

[2] *fuere* repeated in orig., by inadvertence.

(5) MS. Corp. Chr. vii.

A.D. 1414.

Proof of the popularity of their opinions.

suo [1]marsupio mille marcas, et civitatibus, sive pagis, qui illum detegerent, maximas libertates; unde potest conjici pene totam patriam ejus dementiam amplexatam fuisse, cum nullus inveniretur, qui respectu tanti lucri eum voluerit publicare. Capti sunt tamen de suis asseclis plurimi, qui dicebantur conspirasse generaliter in destructionem Regis et Procerum, Prælatorum, religiosorum possessionatorum, Fratrum Mendicantium, atque civium; qui, super hiis convicti, non solum tractioni et furcarum suspensioni, sunt addicti, sed post infelicia fata cremati.

Capture and execution of many followers of Oldcastle.

Inter quos, quidam de Dunstapalia, negotio braciator, dives admodum, dictus "Willelmus Murlee," qui artius secutus opiniones Johannis Oldcastelle, orthodoxorum plurimos, supra cunctos sectæ suæ perfidæ, molestaverat. Hic cum in campo fuisset, et Regis præsentiam cognovisset, meticulose civitatem repetiit, latebrasque quæsivit. Præordinaverat utique, prout fertur, eo die suscepisse de manu Johannis Oldcastelle ordinem militarem; cujus rei argumenta fuere dextrarii duo se sequentes, auro phalerati, et deaurata calcaria quæ sinu suo recondiderat, exinde detracta quando captus fuerat. Quod et evenit parvo peracto spatio post fugam suam. Tractus ergo, suspensus, et combustus, finem quem meruit est sortitus. Repertus est autem rotulus Præcentoris Sancti Albani, continens cuncta monachorum nomina dicti loci, in manica sua, quem vel ipse vel sui furtim abstulerant; quos, [2]ut fertur, eliminasse proposuerat, et eorum locum, velut dominus et Comes Hertfordensis pagi, dono ducis sui Johannis Oldcastelle, obtinuisse. Fuerunt et plures alii, tam sacerdotes quam laici, qui capti, convicti sunt, et damnati, exituque [3]fiunt consimili; quorum plurimi nec quidem pœnitere curabant. De hiis prophetatum est apud Anglos per longa tempora antequam ista contingerent, sub hiis verbis:—

W. Murlee, of Dunstaple, a follower of Oldcastle, is hanged and burnt.

His alleged designs against St. Alban's.

Other followers of Oldcastle similarly punished.

"Inter petrosum fontem montemque [4]nodosum,
"Corruet Anglorum [5]gens perfida fraude suorum."

Ancient prophecy in reference to them.

[1] *marcipio* in orig., (5) MS. Corp. Chr. vii., and the printed texts.

[2] *prout* in the printed texts.

[3] *fuit* in orig., corrected from (5) MS. Corp. Chr. vii. and the printed texts.

[4] In Elmham's Metrical *Life of Henry V.* (printed in this Series) p. 99, this Prophecy is given at greater length, and more in accordance with the rules of Prosody:—
"*Cum fuerint anni completi mille*
"*trecenti,*
"*Et decies deni, post partum Vir-*
"*ginis almæ,*
"*Inter nodosum montem fontem-*
"*que petrosum,*
"*Corruet Anglorum gens perfida*
"*fraude suorum.*"

[5] *gentes* in the printed texts.

A.D. 1414. Constat veraciter inter hæc duo loca gentem perfidam contra Regem venisse, fraudeque suorum illic corruisse; quia quidam de suis Regi nunciaverunt eorum conspirationes. (5) MS. Corp. Chr. vii.

Death of Thomas Arundel, Archbishop of Canterbury. [1] Hoc anno cecidit eminentissima turris Ecclesiæ Anglicanæ, et pugil invictus, Dominus Thomas de Arundelia, morti solvens debita decimo Kalendas Martii. Cui successit in Archiepiscopatum [2] Magister Henricus Chichele, Confessor Regis. Promotions in consequence. Magister Stephanus [3] de Patryngtone, Frater de Ordine Carmelitarum, vir eruditus in Trivio et [4] Quadrivio, factus est [5] Episcopus Menevensis.

Henry Percy is received into the King's favour, and restored to the Earldom of Northumberland. Rex compatiens Henrico Percy, [6] adolescentulo, qui per avum suum, Henricum Percy, Comitem Northumbriæ, ductus fuit in Scotiam, post mortem patris sui, perempti in bello apud Salopiam, cum adhuc esset parvulus, jussit suis necessariis ut pro ejus evocatione sollicitarentur; eum non solum honorare statuens ejus revocatione, sed ut [7] sublimaret Comitis Northumbrorum nomine et dignitate.

Envoys from the King of France, and Duke of Burgundy. Eo anno, ad Parliamentum tentum Leycestriæ venere nuncii Regis [8] Franci Ducisque Burgundiæ, [9] [licet non pari voto. Nam Dux Burgundiæ] contra Ducem Aurelianensem fortificari petiit, promittens, ut fertur, plura quam præstare potuit. Envoys sent to them. Missi sunt ergo per Regem Angliæ solemnes nuncii ad utrumque: inter quos duo Pontifices, scilicet Dunelmensis et Norwycensis, legationis [10] principes extitere. Frequenter enim et hii in Franciam, et Francorum legati directi sunt in Angliam; sumptusque maximi consumpti sunt utrobique, spe pacis omnino sopita.

The King begins the foundation of three Monasteries. Hoc anno cœpit Rex Henricus fundare tria Monasteria religiosorum juxta prædium suum, "apud Schene" vulgariter [11] appellatum; unum de Ordine monachorum Cartusiensium; aliud, monachorum qui "Cœlestini" vocarentur, qui profitentes Regulam Sancti Benedicti, quam servare se dicunt ad litteram, et ulterius se astringunt ad reclusionem perpetuam;

---

[1] Archbishop Arundel died in February 1413.

[2] This and the following word are omitted in (5) MS. Corp. Chr. vii.; and *Ricūs* is inserted in a later hand.

[3] *de* omitted in the printed texts.

[4] *Quatrivio* in orig. and (5) MS Corp. Chr. vii.

[5] Patrington was made Bishop of St. David's in 1415.

[6] *adulescentulo* in orig. and (5) MS. Corp. Chr. vii.

[7] *sublimiaret* in the printed texts.

[8] *Franciæ* in the printed texts.

[9] Omitted in orig. and the printed texts; supplied from (5) MS. Corp. Chr. vii.: *qui* occupies its place in the printed texts.

[10] *principis* in orig.

[11] *appellatur* in orig. and (5) MS. Corp. Chr. vii.; corrected from the printed texts.

(5) MS. Corp. Chr. vii. tertium, [1]Brigittinorum, qui Sancti Augustini profitentur Regulam, quæ, cum aliis adjectis cæremoniis, vocatur ab eis "Regula Salvatoris:" hiis non licet habere proprium, non quidem obolum, nec pecuniam tangere quovismodo. In hoc Monasterio, juxta Regulam, debent esse sorores sexaginta, sacerdotes tresdecim, diaconi quatuor, octo fratres laici; quibus omnibus computatis, tantus erit numerus personarum, quantus erat tresdecim Apostolorum et septuaginta duorum discipulorum Christi. Hii non lineis, sed laneis, semper utuntur. Qui duo Conventus habebunt unam ecclesiam in communi, moniales habebunt superius sub tecto, fratres inferius ad terram. Et sunt utrique Conventus separatim inclusi: quibus post professionem non licebit egredi, nisi de Domini Papæ licentia speciali. Isti duo Conventus debent habere ex Regula sufficientem dotationem ad sustentationem personarum et servientium, ac supportationem onerum tanti monasterii, ita quod absque indigentia et mendicitate, tam in anno sterili quam fertili, possint sufficienter et quiete subsistere. Postea vero, si totus mundus possessiones et prædia eis offerret, quicquam omnino recipere non liceret. Ante festum Omnium Sanctorum annuatim computari debent et præsciri victualia, et necessaria, anni subsequentis; et quæcunque tunc remanent de victualibus seu pecunia anni tunc instantis, in crastino Omnium Sanctorum debent pauperibus erogari. Si vero aliquando victualia sequentis anni [2]videntur non sufficere, tunc de pecunia aut victualibus imminentis anni [3]addatur sequenti anno quantum necesse est, et non plus, si [4]Abbatissa et generalis ejusdem loci Confessor periculum animæ suæ voluerint evitare. Et expost, quicquid remanserit, egenis dari debet. Abbatissa, cum consensu sororum et fratrum, eligere [5]debet unum de tresdecim sacerdotibus in Confessorem generalem Monasterii; cui omnes fratres obedire debent, et contra præceptum ejus omnino nihil facere. Nullus sæcularium virorum, seu mulierum sæcularium, seu religiosorum, ingredietur claustra Monasterii monialium. Hos ritus, et plures alios, observant hujus novellæ religionis professores, quos ad præsens omittimus, ad alia festinantes.

A.D. 1414.

Rule of the Brigittines.

Ambassiatores nostri, Dunelmensis et Norwicensis Episcopi, jam secundo de Francia redeuntes, Gallicos dolis hactenus

The ambassadors give

[1] *Brigatinorum* in orig.; corrected from (5) MS. Corp. Chr. vii. and the printed texts.

[2] *videntes* in orig.; corrected from (5) MS. Corp. Chr. vii., and the printed texts.

[3] *additur* in the printed texts.

[4] *Abbetissa* in orig.

[5] *debent* in orig., (5) MS. Corp. Chr. vii., and the printed texts.

A.D. 1414. inservisse [1] declarant. Quamobrem Rex, irritatus, cachinnos eorum temperare decrevit, et in [2] derisores animadvertere belli jure, et quantæ sit dementiæ [3] suscitasse canem dormientem factis ostendere. (5) MS. Corp. Chr. vii.

notice of the treachery of the French. The King resolves to punish them

Circa festum Michaelis, jussit Rex venire Londonias ad Consilium cunctos regni proceres et prælatos, consultaturus de negotiis arduis tangentibus regnum suum. Quo quidem tempore Cantuariensis celebravit ibidem grande Consilium, in quo tractatum est de privilegiis exemptorum per Romanos Pontifices indultorum, quibus gavisi sunt hactenus, annullandis. Hoc initium signorum fecit novus Metropolitanus, ut manifestaret bilem suam. In hoc Consilio sunt electi, qui pro parte cleri Angliæ proficiscerentur ad Generale Consilium celebrandum, apud Constantiam, Germaniæ civitatem. Quo pene, per laudabilem sollicitudinem Regis Romanorum et Hungariæ, viri Christianissimi, qui, electus in Imperatorem Almanniæ, recusavit coronam suscipere, donec sibi constaret indubitanter, quis esset præficiendus in Papam, totius Christianitatis prudentissimi Pontifices et Prælati, cum aliis clericis, velut innumeris, confluxere. Utque de aliis taceamus, de regno Angliæ missi sunt ad Consilium viri valde venerabiles, Saresberiensis, Bathoniensis, Herfordensis, Episcopi, et, cum hiis, Abbas Westmonasterii, Prior Wygorniæ, et plures alii pollentes ingenio, religione famosi. Horum cœtum honoravit multipliciter præsentia Comitis Warwicensis. Hiis ergo et Collegiis Cardinalium, quondam Gregorii et [4] Petri de Luna, cum aliis prælatis et doctoribus [5] præcipuis Christianitatis, apud Constantiam, Gregorius renunciavit Papatui, ita duntaxat ut idem faceret Petrus de Luna, qui in Arragonia, et Johannes, qui in Roma, nomen sibi Papatus [6] assumpserant: sed Johannes noster aliquandiu tergiversavit, donec monitus et inductus per Imperatorem, se renunciaturum, sicut et cæteri, aliquando concessit. Quo facto, factum est indicibile gaudium inter omnes qui aderant, putantes jam finem dissidii imponendum.

Great Council held at London.

Representatives of the Clergy at the Council of Constance.

The Earl of Warwick accompanies them.

The three claimants of the Papacy resign their pretensions.

A.D. 1415. Sed, proh dolor! ubi sperabatur perfectionis et pacis initium, jam novæ dissensionis surrepsit exordium. Nam Papa Johannes, infirmitate simulata, nocte repente recessit, cum Duce Austriæ, ad quandam civitatem dicti Ducis; se tamen excusavit litteraliter penes Imperatorem, quod propter aerem,

Pope John suddenly leaves Constance.

---

[1] *declarat* in the printed texts.
[2] *derisiores* in orig.
[3] *sussitasse* in orig.
[4] *Petre* in orig., by inadvertence.
[5] *præcipue* in orig.; corrected from (5) MS. Corp. Chr. vii. and the printed texts.
[6] *assumpserat* in orig., (5) MS. Corp. Chr. vii., and the printed texts.

(5) MS. Corp. Chr. vii. sibi nocivum, reliquisset Constantiam; sed nihilominus quandocunque Imperator duceret eum [1] accersendum, paratus foret ad Consilium sine mora regredi, ad consummandum et implendum quæcunque promiserat. Cum vero post dies aliquot visum fuisset Imperatori et Consilio ut [2] suam exhiberet inter eos præsentiam, per nuncios rogaverunt, ut venire non deferret ad Consilium, prout promiserat se facturum; quod plane negavit se facere, et occulte disfiguratus fugit cum Duce Austriæ in terram suam. Misit ergo Imperator ad Ducem, mandans ut eum reduceret, vel saltem reduci permitteret, ad Consilium memoratum. Quod cum Dux supersedisset facere, Imperator terras ejus ingressus est, coegitque Ducem se submittere, Papamque reducere in eodem habitu quo eum abduxerat fugitivum. Reductus est ergo, coramque Consilio demonstratus, non indumentis religiositatis redimitus, sed, brigantinorum more, semivestitus, gestans ad latus [3] sagittas breves, [4] qualibus utuntur equites illarum partium, qui "Malendrini" dicuntur. Derisus igitur a toto cœtu, tam religioso quam sæculari, missus est in carcerem, sub arta custodia conservandus. Moxque cuncta bona sua mobilia direptioni patuere; fertur enim, quod despoliatus sit de septuaginta quinque millibus librarum auri et argenti; quibus auditis in Anglia, pecunia collecta ad opus ejus, et apud Sanctum Paulum in cista reposita, diruptis seris, extracta est, melioribus usibus destinata.

A.D. 1414.

Notwithstanding his promises, he refuses to return.

The Duke of Austria screens him; but is compelled by the Emperor to give him up.

Pope John is presented in his disguise, imprisoned, and his property plundered.

"In nomine Sanctæ et individuæ Trinitatis, Patris, et Filii, "et Spiritus Sancti, Amen. Sacrosancta Generalis Synodus "Constantiensis, in Spiritu Sancto congregata legitime, invo- "cato Christi nomine, solum Deum præ oculis habens, visis ar- "ticulis in hac causa contra Dominum Johannem Papam, Vice- "simum-tertium, formatis, habita matura deliberatione super "eisdem, per hanc sententiam diffinitivam, quam proferimus "in his scriptis, pronunciat, decernit, et declarat, recessum "per præfatum Johannem Papam, Vicesimum-tertium, ab hac "civitate Constantiensi, in dicto sacro Consilio Generali, clan- "destine et de nocte, hora suspecta, in habitu dissimulato et "indecenti factum, fuisse et esse illicitum, Ecclesiæ Dei et "dicto Consilio scandalosum, vacationis et unionis ipsius "Ecclesiæ turbativum et impeditivum, schismatis inveterati "nutritivum, a voto, promissione, et juramento, per Domi- "num Johannem Papam Deo et Ecclesiæ, et huic Sacro Con- "silio præstitis, deviativum, ipsumque Dominum Johannem

Sentence of deprivation against the three claimants of the Papacy, promulgated by the Council of Constance.

[1] *accerciendum* in orig. and (5) MS. Corp. Chr. vii.

[2] *suum* in orig.

[3] *sagatas* in orig.

[4] *qualibet* in orig.; *qualiter* in the printed texts; corrected from (5) MS. Corp. Chr. vii.

A.D. 1415. "Papam simoniacum notorium, honorum, bonorumque et "jurium, nedum Romanæ, sed aliarum Ecclesiarum, et plu- "rium aliorum piorum, dilapidatorem notorium, malumque "spiritualium et temporalium Ecclesiæ administratorem et "dispensatorem, fuisse et esse, suis detestabilibus inhonestis- "que moribus, et vita, Ecclesiam Dei et populum Christia- "num notorie scandalizantem, ante ejus assumptionem ad "[1]Papatum, et post, usque ad ista tempora, ipsumque per "præmissa Ecclesiam Dei et populum Christianum notorie "scandalizasse et scandalizare; postque monitiones debi- "tas et caritativas, iteratis et crebris vicibus eidem factas, "in præmissis malis pertinaciter perseverasse, seque ex hoc "notorie incorrigibilem reddidisse; ipsumque, propter præ- "missa et alia crimina, in processu dictæ causæ contra eum "deducta et contenta, tanquam indignum, inutilem, et dam- "nosum, a Papatu et omni administratione spirituali et tem- "porali amovendum, privandum, et deponendum, fore: et dicta "Synodus amovet, privat, et deponit, universos et singulos "Christicolas, cujuscunque status, dignitatis, vel conditionis, "ut existant ab ejus obedientia, fidelitate, et juramento abso- "lutos, declarando; inhibendo insuper universis Christi fide- "libus, ne eundem de cætero Papam nominent, nec illi "tanquam Papæ adhæreant, seu quoquomodo obediant. Et "nihilominus ex certa scientia, et de plenitudine potestatis, "supplet dicta sancta Synodus omnes et singulos defectus, si "qui forsan in præmissis, vel aliquo præmissorum, inter- "venerint, etc. Item decernit, statuit, ordinat, dicta sancta "Synodus, pro bono unionis Ecclesiæ Dei, quod nullo un- "quam tempore reeligantur in Papam Dominus Baltazar "Cossa, nuper Johannes Papa Vicesimus-[2]tertius, nec Petrus "de Luna, [3]Benedictus Tertius-decimus, nec Angelus Corrario, "Gregorius Duodecimus, in suis obedientiis sic nominati; et "si contrarium fieret, id sit ipso facto irritum et inane; [4]nul- "lusque, cujuscunque dignitatis et præeminentiæ, etiamsi im- "periali, regali, cardinalatus, vel pontificali, dignitate, præ- "fulgeat, eis, vel eorum alicui, contra hoc decretum, ullo "unquam tempore obediat seu adhæreat, sub pœna fautoriæ "dicti schismatis et maledictionis æternæ; ad quas contra "præsumptiones, si quæ in posterum fuerint, etiam cum "invocatione brachii sæcularis rigide procedatur." (5) MS. Corp. Chr. vii.

Sub hoc tempore, cum jam Rex Angliæ comperisset Francos

[1] *perpetuum* in the printed texts.

[2] *quartus* in the printed texts; *tertius* in (5) MS. Corp. Chr. vii.

[3] *Clemens* in orig., (5) MS. Corp. Chr. vii., and the printed texts, erroneously.

[4] *nullus cujuscumque* in the printed texts.

(5) MS. Corp. Chr. vii.

A.D. 1415.

fallaciis et fraude, fictisque promissionibus, eum inaniter sollicitasse, naves conduxit, arcitenentes et armatos elegit, machinas et [1] missilia, ac omnem apparatum bellicum, præparavit, quibus posset hostes efficacius infestare: jussitque ut omnes secum profecturi parati forent in festo Nativitatis Sancti Johannis Baptistæ, apud Hamptone.

The King prepares for war with France.

Quo tempore accesserunt ad eum novi recentesque legati Francorum, inter quos præcipuus fuit Archiepiscopus Senonensis, vir verbosus et arrogans, sed parum disciplinatus, prout ostendit expost; nimis petulanter se gerens in præsentia Regis et procerum in peroratione suæ legationis. Finaliter tamen Rex legatorum sprevit oblationes et promissa, quæ nec rationi fuere consona, nec sibi honorifica; et Londonias remisit eos.

French ambassadors arrive.

Their proposals are rejected.

Dum Rex suorum procerum, qui cum eo transfretare debebant, apud Southamtoniam præstolaretur adventum, tres viri potentes, in quibus præ cæteris confidebat, in ejus necem conjuraverunt. Quorum nomina si vellem supprimere, fama flagitii divulgaret, etiam me tacente. Dicam ergo quod me dicturum doleo, parricidarumque nomina non celabo. Primus et præcipuus Dominus Henricus Le Scrop, in cujus fide sive constantia totus animus regius requievit. Qui sub hypocrisi cuncta gerenda foris suppallians, et

Conspiracy, while the King is at Southampton.

Names of the conspirators.

"[2] Astutam vapido gestans sub pectore vulpem,"

in cunctis agendis agninam simplicitatem publice præferebat.—

"[3] Edidicit," nempe, "simulare fidem, vultusque minaces
"Protegere, et blando fraudem prætexere risu;
"Plenus sævitiæ, lucrique cupidine fervens,
"Doctus et unanimes odio turbare sodales."

Hic tantæ fuit æstimationis penes Regem, ut si quando consilia privata vel publica tractabantur, hujus diffinitione terminabantur. Prætendebat namque tantam gravitatem in vultu, tantam in gestu modestiam, tantam in affatu religionem, ut quicquid ipse dictasset, velut oraculum e cœlo lapsum Rex oportere fieri judicaret. Si legatio solemnis emittenda foret in Franciam, ingenio vel persona Henrici Le Scrop exequi necesse putabat. Ille proinde tractabat cum hostibus, ipse domino suo Regi hostis occultus, mulcebatque Regem vanis sponsionibus; delusit Consilium promissis inanibus, referens utrisque alia pro aliis, fronte favens suis, mente vero Gallis. Cumque Rex innocens, propter magnam confidentiam,

The treachery of Sir Henry Le Scrop.

[1] *missalia* in orig., by inadvertence.
[2] Persius, *Sat.* v. 117.
[3] Claudian, *In Rufinum*, ll. 98–101.

A.D. 1415. hujus se arbitrio in pluribus commisisset, et ei multa donaria specialia tribuisset, ille tantis beneficiis retributor iniquus, dominum suum, cum jam in procinctu foret profectionis suæ, parata classe et aggregatis militum copiis, repente vita privare moliebatur. Spoponderat ista Francis, ut fertur, pacta sibi pro proditione pecunia; qui, jam ad sua regressi, lætificavere suos, asserentes Regem Angliæ, mutato proposito, vel ad sua regressum, vel certe, quod verius putavere, peremptum. Habuit consortes proditionis Ricardum Comitem Cantabrigiæ, fratrem scilicet Ducis Eboraci, et Thomam Grey, militem Borealem. Quem quidem Ricardum Comitem Rex creaverat, et multis bonis ditaverat, et præ cæteris honoraverat ratione generis et parentelæ. Sed nulla impensa benevolentia, nullum collatum beneficium, proditores prævertere poterant, quin in necem tanti benefactoris mutuo se armarent. [1] Attamen priusquam conceptum facinus possent ad effectum perducere, Deo volente, detecti sunt, et judicio parium suorum condemnati decapitationis sententiam subire; Rege alias pœnas, de jure debitas, perdonante, (præterquam Henrico Scrop, qui dicitur fuisse tractus), qui etiam [2] deflevisse vices eorum fertur. Quamobrem nonnulli propter Regis modestiam, compassionem, et pietatem, laudes Augusti in eum transferunt, quondam editas a Nasone, eo quod

(5) MS. Corp. Chr vii.

He is joined by the Earl of Cambridge and Sir Thomas Grey.

They are executed.

The King's clemency commended.

"[3] Sit piger ad pœnas princeps, ad præmia velox,
"Quique dolet quoties cogitur esse ferox."

Rising of the Lollards.

Eodem tempore, velut ex condicto, et tanquam proditionis præfatæ conscientia, Lollardi stimulati, e latebris emersere et in Regem blasphemias evomuere, loquentes grandia, minasque spargentes in scriptis, quæ fixerunt in valvis ecclesiæ [4] et ecclesiarum Londoniis in multis locis, talibus se cohortantes:—"Jam," inquiunt, "princeps presbyterorum abiit, jam "hostis noster abcessit, jam nobis arrisit tempus accommo-"dum, qno nostras impune licebit injurias vindicare;" sicque se mutuo confortantes, scripserunt ad invicem multa millia in sua vota venisse.

Oldcastle utters threats of vengeance.

Interea campi-ductor et caput eorum, Johannes Oldcastelle, cum latuisset prope Malverniam, et accepisset a falso nuncio Regem Angliæ transfretasse, ex ejus absentia concepta audacia, verba comminatoria misit ad Dominum de Bergeyne; dicens in capite ejus ulcisci velle sibi et suis illatas injurias ab eodem. Qui, prudenter sibi præcavens, cum circa noctis

[1] *Atque* in the printed texts.

[2] *rex deflevisse* in the printed texts.

[3] Ovid, *Epist. Pont.* I. 2. 123.

[4] The name of a church is evidently omitted here.

(5) MS. Corp. Chr. vii. medium hæc audisset, illico secretis egit nunciis, ut mane diluculo occurrerent armati sibi apud castrum suum de Haneley, ex Wigornia, [1] Persora, et Teukesburia, prope quinque millia arcitenentium et armatorum. Quo comperto, dictus Johannes Oldcastelle more solito latebras requisivit: cepit tamen idem herus quendam presbyterum dicti Johannis Oldcastelle, et quosdam alios ex suis complicibus, quos, sic artatos, quæstionibus examinavit, ut patefacerent locum quo dictus Johannes arma sua, cum pecuniis, occultasset. Quæ cuncta congesta sunt in quadam domo inter duos parietes, sic erectos, ut nullus sine indice dictæ structuræ fallaciam percepisset. Illic inventa sunt signa sua cum vexillo, in quibus depingi sumptuose fecerat calicem, et hostiam in forma panis. Ibi etiam conspicienda fuere crux Christi cum flagris, lancea cum clavis, quæ depinxerat in vexillis ad seducendum simplices, si quando contigisset erigere signa suffultum populari dementia: sed cognito apparatu disposito contra se, demisit cornua quæ arroganter erexerat, suppressit minas fastuosas, et eo celerius atque meticulosius latebras, ut prius, repetiit, eo quod audivit Henricum Scrop et suos complices apud Hamptoniam proditionis suæ pœnas meritas exsolvisse.

A.D. 1415

Preparations alleged to have been made by him, for the rising.

He retires to his concealment.

Nec multo post captus est quidam inveteratus Lollardus, Willelmus Cleydone, qui in tantam dementiam ruerat confidentia suæ sectæ, ut etiam filium proprium sacerdotem constitueret, et Missam celebrare faceret in domo sua, die quo conjux ejus, a puerperio surgens, purganda ad ecclesiam processisset. Hic ergo captus, examinatus, legitimeque convictus de hæresi, Londoniis est combustus.

William Cleydon, a Lollard, burnt at London.

Rex Angliæ, punitis justissime, ut præmittitur, proditoribus, ascensis navibus, mare sulcans, applicuit in Normanniam, in loco vocato [2] "Ke de Caus," nemine resistente. Traxit autem secum classem mille et quingentarum carinarum, ad negotia martia sufficienter instructam; ut dum ipse cum suis villam de Hareflu obsideret per aridam, classis in pelago, coram villa constituta, villanis omne præsidium victualium præcluderet, et solatia quævis arceret. Nacta vero tellure feria quarta in Vigilia Assumptionis Sanctæ Mariæ, sequenti Sabbato obsidionem posuit circa villam, quam continuavit per quinque septimanas honorifice, usque ad Dominicam proximam ante festum Sancti Michaelis; qua die Dominica villa fuit reddita tali modo:—

King Henry lands in Normandy.

Besieges Harfleur.

It surrenders.

Feria nempe tertia proxima ante dictam Dominicam, domini Gallici, qui fuere Custodes ipsius villæ, scilicet de Gaucort, Dominus de Estutevyle, Dominus de Hakevyle, et Dominus de

Particulars of the surrender.

---

[1] *persora* in the printed texts.

[2] Meaning, *Chef de Caux*.

A.D. 1415. Clere, non ferentes crebras quassationes murorum et ædificiorum infra villam, aliaque pericula perpessa per gunnas regias, (nam ab ipsis evolantia saxa, ingenti verberis ictu, obvia fregere quæque ruentes, nec tantum corpora pressa necabant, sed totos cum sanguine dissipant artus, et singula cesserunt ictibus arma,) conturbati et conterriti, coacti sunt nocte media quendam servum-ad-arma ad Ducem destinare Clarentiæ, Domini Regis fratrem, qui illorum vice precaretur obnixe dictum Ducem, quatenus dignaretur, ob honorem Dei, Regi supplicare, ut eis concederet facultatem tractandi cum quibuscunque personis, quas Dominus Rex duceret ad istud negotium emittendas. Nec mora, Dux exequitur villanorum vota; cujus interventu, et ob honorem Dei præcipue, Rex inclinatus eorum precibus, misit Comitem de Dorcet, Dominum Filium Hugonis, et Dominum Thomam Erpynham, ad cognoscenda desideria obsessorum. Qui petiere suppliciter, ut Rex, caritatis intuitu, cessaret ab eorum debellatione, ab ea hora noctis mediæ usque ad Dominicam proximam post festum Sancti Michaelis, nisi contingeret Regem, vel Dolphinum, ejus primogenitum, per bellum obsidionem dissolvere. Alias, parati forent Regi villam reddere, salvis vita et bonis omnibus eorundem. Rex vero remandari jussit eisdem, quod nisi villam in crastino redderent, nulla conditione interposita, non tractarent amplius de materia memorata. Instabant adhuc Gallicani domini, et Regis referendarios deprecabantur, ut apud Regem insisterent quatenus inducias illis concedere dignaretur, ab illa hora [1][usque ad horam] proximam post [2][nonam] Dominicæ subsequentis. Qua hora promiserunt se cum [3]viginti duobus militibus et scutiferis ad Regem accessuros, cum viris honoratioribus infra dictam villam constitutis; quos omnes obsides darent Regi usque ad Dominicam supradictam; et ulterius, prædicti proceres spopondere se juraturos super Corpus Dominicum, coram omni populo, quod si Rex Francus, vel filius ejus et hæres, Dolphinus, non accederent ad deliberandum eos infra horam dictæ Dominicæ prænotatam, ipsi se redderent sine conditione aliqua Regi Angliæ, ad faciendum de corporibus et bonis eorum juxta suæ beneplacitum voluntatis. Ita duntaxat, ut permitteret eos dirigere nuncios Regi Franco et Dolphino, qui eis prætaxata pacta referrent. (5) MS. Corp. Chr. vii.

Cumque Rex acceptasset hanc oblationem, dedit eorum legatis litteras de salvo conductu; quorum principalis fuit

[1] Omitted in orig.; supplied from (5) MS. Corp. Chr. vii. and the printed texts.

[2] Omitted in orig. and the printed texts; supplied from (5) MS. Corp. Chr. vii.

[3] *propriis militibus* in the printed texts.

(5) MS. Corp. Chr. vii. Dominus de Hakevyle; quem sequebantur viri valentes ad numerum duodecim personarum. In crastino, scilicet feria quarta mane, dicti domini, cum viginti duobus militibus et armigeris, ac civibus notabilibus, exivere de villa: quibus occurrit processio solennissima, antecedens [1]Eucharistiam, cum multis honorabilibus dominis, militibus, et armigeris, et populi frequentia magna valde. Ubi expleto receptoque publice [2]jurejurando, cuncti Gallici sunt introducti ad regale tentorium, ubi et comederunt die illo: Dominum tamen Regem non viderunt. Post prandium disjuncti sunt, et diversis dominis commendati, qui eos tractarent honorifice, usque ad reditum suorum legatorum, quos destinaverant ad Regem Francum; qui, fidenter promissa complentes, rediere statuta Dominica, hora præfixa, sine quovis suffragio per Regem Francum, seu Dolphinum, obsessis oblato. Quapropter, qui intra villam erant, cuncti se sine conditione Regis gratiæ summisere; remansereque captivi Regi Angliæ toti domini, cum militibus et armigeris, atque generosis, qui missi sunt a Rege Franco ad custodiam villæ. Rex autem constituit illic Capitaneum Dominum Thomam, Comitem Dorcetanum, dans ei manum [3][validam] defensorum. A.D. 1415.

The surrender is accepted.

The Earl of Dorset appointed Captain.

Durante obsidione regali, plures ex esu fructuum et algore noctium, fœtoreque cadaverum diversarum pecudum, quas mactavere per castrorum circuitum, et non operuerant cespitibus sive terra, nec injecerant in aquis fluviatilibus, ut earum putridas exhalationes tollerent, fluxu ventris vel dysenteria periere. Inter quos et imprimis vir venerandissimus, Magister Ricardus de Cortiniaco, Norwicensis Episcopus, Domino Regi fidissimus, diem clausit extremum; cui successit in Episcopatu Dominus [4] Wakeringge; Comesque Southfolchiæ, Dominus Michael Atte Poole, simili sorte functus est. Cujus loco, ne familia sua gubernatore careret, creavit Dominus Rex filium ejus Comitem Southfolchiæ; sed et ejus [5]filum sæva nimis Atropos præcidit in bello, de quo inferius dicturi sumus.

Deaths in the English army from dysentery.

Death of Richard Courtney, Bishop of Norwich, and of Michael, Earl of Suffolk.

Eodem tempore redierunt in Angliam, adversa cogente valetudine, Dux Clarentiæ, Comes Marchiæ, Comes Arundeliæ, et Comes Marescallus, cum multis aliis ægrotantibus morbo præfato. Sed Arundeliensis, ut fertur, [6]impotionatus, non multo post in fata concessit.

Other nobles, through illness, return to England.

Rex Angliæ, compositis rebus apud Hareflu, prout Regem

---

[1] *Eucharistia* in the printed texts.

[2] *jusjurando* in orig., (5) MS. Corp. Chr. vii., and the printed texts.

[3] Omitted in orig.; supplied from (5) MS. Corp. Chr. Cambr. and the printed texts.

[4] His surname was "John."

[5] *filium* in orig. and the printed texts.

[6] *veneno, non* in the printed texts.

A.D. 1415. decuit, et victorem, terrestrem viam versus Kalesiam, cum paucis admodum, arripere statuit; non amplius, ut fertur, quam octo millibus arcitenentium et armatorum; [1] quorum magna pars infirmitate contracta apud Hareflu, prout supra retulimus, vexabatur. Cum hac tam parva manu mirum est quod densissimam ausus sit aggredi Francorum sylvam; sed multo plus mirandum quod eam perforavit, tot obicibus præmunitam. Galli nempe per totum tempus obsidionis villæ de Hareflu electos quosque de semetipsis, et conterminarum regionum fortissimos et audacissimos viros, adunaverunt, et auxiliarios undique conduxerunt, ut numerus eorum, prout fertur, excresceret ad centum quadraginta millia pugnatorum.

(5) MS. Corp. Chr. vii.

The King proceeds towards Calais.

Sufferings of the English, on their march.

Hii ergo se præparaverunt ad diem, tempus, et horam, qua Regem possent invadere, et pusillum gregem suum, jam fame, fluxu, ac febribus, tenuatum. Cumque pene [2] bis denis diebus Rex equitasset per regnum Franciæ, et hostes [3] ubique subtraxissent victualia, priusquam accederet ad castrametandi loca, defecit panis in exercitu, sic quod plures, loco panis, avellanis nucibus et assis carnibus uterentur; potus aqua fuit cunctis inferioris fortunæ viris in exercitu, spatio pene decem et octo dierum. Hiis lautitiis, hiis opsoniis, athletæ Regis Angliæ nutriti sunt et pasti, qui cum tot gigantum millibus fuerant congressuri. Adde, quod ab itinere fatigati, a vigiliis macerati, a frigoribus nocturnis debilitati, mirum quod subsistere potuere. Sed animavit debiles, invalidis dedit vires, Qui voluit fortes pessundare per infirmos. Nempe cum Rex, non sine difficultate maxima, pertransisset flumina interposita, quia Franci pontes destruxerant, per quos iter compendii habuisse poterat, mox glomerati festinavere cum suis militibus præcludere viam per quam de necessitate debeat transire Kalesiam; et vicesimo quarto die mensis Octobris, in quadam villa substitere. Rex tamen imperterritus iter arreptum constanter aggreditur, et eo usque procedit quo uterque exercitus velut infra spatium milliarii ipsa eadem consedit nocte. Erat tamen facies utriusque exercitus varia, disparque vultus; Gallis refocillatis, victualibusque refertis, Anglis fatigatis, infirmis, inediaque confectis; quibus etiam nec copia aquæ fuit. Certum tamen erat Anglis in crastino se pugnaturos, et cum tota nobilitate Franciæ manus conserturos. Quapropter ipsam noctem non tantum duxerunt insomnem corpora confovendo, quantum votis et confessionibus animabus propriis consulendo. Jactitaverant nempe Galli se nemini velle parcere, præterquam dominis et ipsi Regi;

The French destroy the bridges on their route.

The armies encamp near each other.

Contrast between the armies.

Threats of the French.

---

[1] *quarum* in the printed texts.

[2] *bis Dominus Rex* in the printed texts.

[3] *ubi* in orig.; omitted in the printed texts: corrected from (5) MS. Comp. Chr. vii.

(5) MS. Corp. Chr. vii. reliquos immisericorditer perempturos, vel membris irrestaurabiliter [1] mutilaturos. Qua de causa nostri magis concitati, animos erexerunt, et contra casus omnes [2] se mutuo confortarunt. Igitur, A.D. 1415.

> " [3] Postera vix [4] summo spargebat lumine montes
> " Orta dies, [5] tuba cum sonitum procul ære canoro
> " Increpuit"—

de castris regiis, accelerantque nostrates pervenire ad sui ducis præsentiam, parati dupliciter ad provocandum Martem, scilicet audacia et conscientiæ puritate.

King Henry marshals his troops.

Rex cernens suos alacriter advenisse, mox agmina producit in campum tritico recenter satum, ubi vix standi paulisper, vel progrediendi, facultas fuit, propter salebras solique mollitiem. Nec segnius summo mane Galli in eundem campum emittunt primam aciem, viribus instructam fortibus, armis ornatam fulgentibus, equitibus hinc inde ex utroque latere præcedentibus in equis generosis et nobilibus, quibus, ut ita dicam,

The French prepare for battle.

> "[6] Aurea pectoribus demissa monilia pendent;"

qui insuper,

> "[7] Tecti auro, fulvum mandunt sub dentibus aurum."

Commencement of the battle of Azincourt.

Non tamen voluere Franci, propter loci lutositatem, procul in campum procedere, sed videre cupiebant quod Angli, quorum paucitatem maximo contemnebant, facere proponebant. Inter utrumque cuneum campus late patuit, ad spatium, prout fertur, pene mille passuum; sed non utrinque pari procurrunt agmina motu, quia, Gallis immobiliter primam servantibus stationem, Anglis necesse fuit, si cum hoste vellent conserere, spatium medium armis onustos pedibus emetiri. Rex interea, Gallorum perpendens astutias, quod sic perstabant immobiles in uno loco, ne peditando per campum lutosum fatigarentur,

King Henry exhorts his troops.

> " Sublimi vectus equo volat agmina circum,
> " Hortaturque duces, [8] et animos ad prœlia firmat."

" O fidissimi," inquiens, " socii, vadimus in campum

> " 'Ad magnum virtutis opus, summosque labores.—' "

" En! ipsam diem quam flagitavit sæpius vestra virtus; " totas ergo vestras effundite vires. Experiamini quid lancea, " quid securis, quid gladius, quid sagitta, [9] valent, in manu

---

[1] *mutulaturos* in orig.

[2] *de* in orig., by inadvertence.

[3] *Æneid*, xii. 113, 4.

[4] So in orig., (5) MS. Corp. Chr. vii., and the printed texts; incorrectly, for "*summos*."

[5] An adaptation of Virgil's *Æneid*, ix. l. 503.

[6] *Æneid*, vii. 278.

[7] *Æneid*, vii. 279.

[8] So in all the texts, for *animosque*.

[9] *Valeat* in the printed texts.

A.D. 1415. " potentis. Quisquis ergo census, honores, aut præmia cupit, (5) MS. Corp. Chr. vii.
" isthic reperiet hæc; nempe

" '—Medio posuit Deus omnia campo.' "

Sic [1] fatus jussit convelli signa;—" Quia " inquiens, " hostes " injuriosi iter nostrum præcludere tentant, adeamus illos, in " nomine Trinitatis, et optima hora totius anni." Et, erectis vexillis, jussit suis ordinate procedere, a dextris [2] vero et sinistris fecit sagittarios anteire. Qui conspicientes eos qui pridie conjuraverant in mortes vel mutilationes eorum, accensi indignatione [3] nimia, omnis lassitudinis, omnis incommodi vel infirmitatis, obliti sunt, et, ut ita fatear,—

" [4]—— Turgescit in eis vitrea bilis,"
iraque—
" —— Vires animumque ministrat."

Mirumque in modum, qui sero debilem arcum nequivit tendere, jam fortissimum valuit sine difficultate pro voto trahere.

The French meet the advance of the English.

Galli videntes nostros campum cum summo labore emensos fuisse, rati jam tempus arrisisse quo fatigatos invaderent, quos putabant nullo negotio captivandos, horribiliter in campum ruunt, præmissis equitibus qui nostros arcitenentes pectoribus dextrariorum præferratis obruerent, et suorum caballorum pedibus conculcarent. Sed, Deo volente, secus accidit quam sperabant. Quia sagittarii, hinc inde occurrentes equitibus, tot simul emisere jacula, ut illa procella grandinea primitus

Successes of the English archers.

equites dissiparent. Nam, regente Deo, nusquam cassa manus, nusquam sine vulnere fugit missile, nullaque fuit requies mittentis dextræ, sed et omne sedet telum, quia nulli fuere [5] sine cædibus ictus. Ut ergo primum sonipedes ferro transfixi sunt, sessores, conversis frænis, in sua agmina præcipites corruere, omnesque equites qui evaserant campo cessere. Exhinc, ut acies convenere, ingens nostratum clamor ad sidera tollitur, et impletur quodammodo vocibus [7] vastus aer. Tunc iterato volat undique telorum nubes, et [8] ferrum ferro sonat, dum jacula constanter emissa cassides feriunt, laminas, et loricas. Cadunt proinde de Gallis plurimi, sagittis terebrati, hinc quinquageni, hinc pariter sexageni.

---

[1] *satus* in orig., by inadvertence.

[2] *vero* omitted in the printed texts.

[3] *injuria* in the printed texts.

[4] Adapted from Persius, *Sat.* iii. 8, and Virgil, *Æn.* ix. 764.

[5] *sagittarius* in orig.; corrected from (5) MS. Corp. Chr. vii. and the printed texts.

[6] *si* in orig. and (5) MS. Corp. Chr. vii.; corrected from the printed texts.

[7] *vastis* in orig. and (5) MS. Corp. Chr. vii.; corrected from the printed texts.

[8] *ferro ferro* in orig. and (5) MS. Corp. Chr. vii.; *ferrc fere* in the printed texts.

(5) MS. Corp. Chr. vii. Rex ipse, non tantum Regis, quantum militis, exequendo vices, primus in hostes advolat, crudeles ictus infert et tolerat, exempla suis audendi fortia præbens in persona propria, stricto securi oppositas acies dissipando. Nec secus militares viri, æmulantes acta regia, totis viris collaborabant oppositam illam sylvam Francorum frementium ferro prosternere; donec tandem via vi facta, Galli non tantum cessere, quam mortui cecidere. Et revera Franci, cum prostratos in acie belli cernerent quos autumabant [1] indomabiles, eorum mox A.D. 1415. Personal valour of King Henry. The French are utterly defeated.

"[2] Obstupuere animi; gelidusque per ima cucurrit
" Ossa tremor,"—

tantus, ut immobiles et sine sensu starent; dum nostri secures ab eorum extorquerent manibus, et eos mactarent, velut pecudes, cum eisdem. Perdidit inde modum cædes, et velut nulla secuta est pugna; sed jugulis bellum geritur, nec valent Angli tot prosternere, quot perire possunt de adversa parte.

Sic ergo pene Franciæ periit omne decus, per manus paucorum quos parum ante summo despectui habuere. Illic interempti sunt Duces de Alasoun, de Braban, et de Baar, cum quinque Comitibus, et [3] Constabulario Franciæ et aliis nominatis dominis, ad numerum pene centum. De militibus et armigeris, quatuor millia sexaginta novem feruntur occisa. Numerus vulgi non fuit ab armorum nunciis computatus. Capti sunt ibidem Duces Aurelianensis et Burbonensis, Comites vero de Ew et de Wendone, et Arturus frater Ducis Britanniæ, qui se dicit "Comitem Richemundiæ," et quidam Burdegaldus, miles honoratissimus regni Franciæ, et alii, ut ferunt, ad numerum septingentorum. De parte Regis cecidere Dominus Edwardus Dux Eboraci, et Dominus Michael Comes Southfolchiæ, quatuor milites et unus armiger, dictus "David "Game," et de communibus viginti octo. Numbers of the French nobility slain. French nobles captured. Losses of the English.

Dum Rex et sui bello detinerentur contra Gallorum multitudinem pugnando comminus, vispiliones Francorum, invadentes a tergo, dimissas sarcinas rapuerunt et protinus abduxerunt; in quibus cum reperissint coronam regiam, inani gaudio lætificavere suos, [4] in tantum ut signa solemniter pulsari facerent, et Canticum laudis, "Te Deum laudamus," cum summo tripudio decantari. Ementiti enim fuerant Regem captum sine mora venturum. Sed post pusillum, cum ex tristi nuncio cognovissent veritatem rei gestæ, versus est in luctum chorus eorum, et gaudium in mœrorem. The English baggage pillaged, and the English crown captured. Great expectations of the French therefrom.

---

[1] *immobiles* in the printed texts.
[2] Virgil, *Æneid*, ii. 120.
[3] *Constabularia* in orig., by inadvertence.
[4] *ita tamen ut* in the printed texts.

A.D. 1415. Rex autem omnes hos eventus prosperos ascribens Deo, gratias infinitas egit Ei, Qui sibi dedit inopinatam victoriam, et ferocissimos hostes subegit. Pernoctavit igitur in eodem loco, et in crastino, scilicet die Sabbati, versus Kalesiam iter inceptum [1]continuavit. Deinde sexto-decimo die Novembris applicuit sero apud Doveriam, in maxima nivis intemperie; vicesima vero tertia die dicti mensis venit Londonias, ducens secum Duces et nobiles quos dudum captivaverat; quorum nomina superius sunt expressa. Quali gaudio, quali tripudio, quali denique triumpho, sit [2]acceptus a Londoniensibus, dicere prætermitto. Quia revera curiositas apparatuum, nimietas expensarum, varietates spectaculorum, tractatus exigerent merito speciales. (5) MS. Corp. Chr. vii.

King Henry returns thanks to God.

His triumphal reception in London.

Obsequies, in London, of the Duke of York and others slain at Azincourt.

Primo die mensis Decembris, jussu Regis, affuere Londoniis Pontifices et Abbates in magno numero, ut interessent solemnissimis exequiis Domini Edwardi, quondam Ducis Eboraci, et aliorum, tam Francorum quam Anglorum, qui interierant in partibus transmarinis. Ad has etiam exequias venit ab Hareflu Capitaneus dictæ villæ, Regis avunculus, Comes de Dorcet; qui parum ante fecerat equitationem in regionem conterminam, et fugaverat octingentos ante se captivos, quos infra dictam villam strictæ custodiæ mancipavit.

Successes of the Earl of Dorset.

Successes of the King of Portugal.

Hoc anno Rex Portyngaliæ, fretus auxilio mercatorum Angliæ quam maxime, et Alemannorum, vicit Agarenos in terra Regis Betinarinorum, multis eorum millibus ad [3]generum [4]Cereris destinatis. Cepitque civitatem eorum amplissimam, supra mare sitam, vocatam "Sunt" eorum lingua; cinctam muro viginti millium passuum, prout ferunt.

A.D. 1416. Anno Domini millesimo quadringentesimo sexto-decimo, tenuit Rex Natale juxta Londonias apud Lambhitham; quo tempore delati sunt sibi rumores de conflictu habito inter Anglos et Gallos juxta villam de Hareflu, in quo plures Gallici sunt occisi.

News of a victory near Harfleur.

Dolphins in the Thames.

Circa festum Purificationis septem delphini luserunt in Tamisia, quarum quatuor sunt occisæ: prænosticabant, ut quidam volunt, tempestatem maximam ventorum et imbrium, continuo subsecutam.

Fight between the Earl of Dorset and the Count of Armagnac.

Feria quarta Quatuor Temporum in initio Quadragesimæ, Comes de Dorcet pugnavit cum Comite de Armanak, Duce Gallorum; in quo conflictu cecidere plurimi de utraque parte, quia dictus Comes gentem nostram invaserat improvise.

---

[1] *continiavit* in orig.

[2] *exceptus* in orig. and (5) MS. Corp. Chr. vii.

[3] *I.e.* Pluto.

[4] *Sereris* in orig. and (5) MS. Corp. Chr. vii.

(5) MS. Corp. Chr. vii.

A.D. 1416

Fugati [1]tamen sunt Franci, et illo die nostratibus terga dedere, uno solo [2][usi] solatio, quod vispiliones eorum, dum cum nostris manus consererent, equos Anglorum et sarcinas rapuerunt. Oportebat ergo nostros, prout erant in armis, reverti pedites ad villam de Hareflu, per multa milliaria regionis. Itaque peditando juxta littus maris, ut hostes suos semper ante faciem suam, non a tergo constitutos, haberent, incedebant armis onusti per totam quintam feriam, noctemque sequentem: mane vero sexta feria, nostrates levantes oculos, viderunt in montibus Gallos recollectos, cum duce eorum, Comite de Armanak, paratos ad invadendum eos. Misit ergo Comes de Armanak quendam armorum nuncium ad Comitem Dorcetanum, qui diceret;—"Ecce! conclusus es inter nos et "mare, nec tibi superest evadendi facultas; quapropter, ne "pereas ore gladii, redde te mihi, tractaboque te juxta nobili"tatem tuorum natalium, prout decet, rationabiliter redimen"dum." Ad hæc ille;—"Renuncia sibi qui te misit, nun"quam fuisse moris Anglorum hosti se reddere ante præludia "Martis et Bellonæ. Nec me reperiet ita vecordem, ut manus "illi dem quem potest Deus tradere in manus meas."

The English baggage plundered.

The Count of Armagnac demands the surrender of the English.

The Earl of Dorset answers in the negative.

Hiis auditis, Comes de Armanak furibunde cum suis equitibus pernici gressu per declivum montis descendere conabatur. Quos [3]accipientes nostri sagittarii, vel præverterunt jaculis vel peremerunt. [4]Exin crevit pugna inter reliquos, et utrobique gladiis et securibus diu res martia gerebatur. Tandem, Deo miserante, gens jejuna, lassa, famelica, somnique penuria fatigata, vicit Dei virtute manifesta: [5]nam cum non essent plures ex Anglicis in hoc conflictu quam mille quingenti, gloriose vicerunt, et ad fugam coegerunt, quindecim millia Gallicorum, duce illorum prope capto. Ferunt quod, non obstante sacro Quadragesimali tempore, ipsoque inviolabili jejunio Quatuor Temporum, carnes assaverant in castris suis, et meretriculas introduxerant, ut, post suffarcinationem ventris, Veneris se [6]spurcitiis macularent.

The English again defeat the French.

Alleged impiety of the French.

Circa præsens tempus oboli Januensium, quia debito carebant pondere, prohibiti sunt ab Anglis in mercaturis accipi sive dari.

The Genoese half-pence prohibited in England.

Septimo die mensis Maii venit Imperator Londonias, deductus in magnificentia et gloria per Regem et regni nobiles; et hospitatus est in Palatio Regis juxta Westmonasterium,

The Emperor visits London.

---

[1] *tum* in the printed texts.

[2] Omitted in orig.; supplied from (5) MS. Corp. Chr. vii. and the printed texts.

[3] *excipientes* in orig.

[4] *Exinde* in the printed texts.

[5] *et* is inserted here in orig.; in (5) MS. Corp. Chr. vii. it is indistinct, but to all appearance *etjam*.

[6] *spursiciis* in orig. and (5) MS. Corp. Chr. vii.

A.D. 1416. Rege recepto apud Lambhitham. Rex autem cupiens deferre omnem humanitatem Regi Romanorum, suspendit ad tempus cuncta Parliamenti negotia, ducens eum secum Wyndeleshoram ad festum Sancti Georgii, [1]honorans illic eum et tantæ fraternitatis titulo, et religionis illius nobili vestimento; signumque regale imposuit collo suo, quod Imperator expost semper gessit in omni conventu publico vel privato. (5) MS. Corp. Chr. vii.

Honours paid to him by King Henry.

The Duke of Holland visits England.

Ante festum Ascensionis, Dux Holandiæ venit in Angliam, cum apparatu maximo, ad habendum colloquium cum Rege nostro, Regeque Romanorum.

A succession of thunder and lightning.

In festo Trinitatis et per [2]consequens biduum, audita sunt horrida tonitrua, omnemque modum excedentia, et velut sine interpolatione durantia; quæ præcesserunt terrifica fulmina sine cessatione coruscantia, quæ multos straverunt et occiderunt, arbores succenderunt, et ædificia diruerunt.

The French collect a fleet.

Per totum tempus æstivale putabatur, quod mediatione Imperatoris fuisset pax inter regna firmata; sed, tergiversantibus Gallis, suspensum fuit pacis negotium, eo maxime quod Galli conduxerant classem magnarum navium, karicarum et [3]galearum, quæ regnum Angliæ molestaret. Contra quos Dominus Johannes Dux Bedfordiæ, frater Regis, missus fuit cum manu potenti. Qui in die Assumptionis Beatæ Virginis, commisit cum eis, et cepit tres karicas et unam hulkam, et quatuor balingarias. Tres vero karicæ fugere; una vero de tribus inter syrtes confracta submersa fuit. Alia magna karica submersa fuit coram Southamptone, cum qua perierunt octingenti viri, quales "[4]*legharneys*" vulgo vocamus.

The Duke of Bedford captures some French ships; and others are wrecked.

Alliance between the Emperor and the King of England.

Imperator et Rex Angliæ fœdus ad invicem pepigere, videlicet, quod ipsi et successores sui, boni et firmi, et stabiles in perpetuum, amici erunt, alligati, obligati, et confœderati, pro se et hæredibus ac successoribus suis, contra homines, cujuscunque gradus, status, dignitatis, aut conditionis existat; et contra omnes homines qui vivere aut mori possunt, exceptis Sacrosancta Romana Ecclesia, et Romanorum Pontifice, etc.

King Henry shows readiness to treat of peace.

Rex Angliæ, ut ostenderet se ex corde pacem cupere, personaliter transfretavit Kalesiam, ne Gallis ullam calumniandi ministraret materiam; quia dixerant non stare per eos quin ei offerrent largam pacis viam. Ubi cum Imperatore constitutus, cum nihil ab eis audisset procurari nisi dolos et fraudem solitam, commenta [5]sprevit eorum, et inter Imperatorem Ducemque

Effects a reconciliation

---

[1] *honoratus* in the printed texts.
[2] *sequens* in (5) MS. Corp. Chr. vii. and the printed texts.
[3] *galiarum* in orig.
[4] *light harneys* in the printed texts.
[5] *spirent* in orig.; corrected from (5) MS. Corp. Chr. vii. and the printed texts.

(5) MS. Corp. Chr. vii. Burgundiæ, qui dissidebant, fecit concordiam atque pacem. Quibus ita gestis, Dux fecit homagium Imperatori. Post hæc, Dux Gloverniæ, frater Regis minimus, cum magna Regis familia, deduxit Imperatorem, donec venisset ad villam de Doredrauth; ubi cunctos Anglos remuneravit imperialiter, a maximo ad minimum. A.D. 1416. between the Emperor and the Duke of Burgundy.

Benedictus Wleman, civis Londoniarum, qui sparserat scedulas in multis locis, errore plenas, captus, tractus, suspensus, et decollatus est, die Sancti Michaelis. Benedict Wleman executed.

Parliamentum, quod diximus intermissum propter præsentiam Regis Romanorum, tentum fuit Londoniis circa festum Sancti [1] Lucæ; in quo Dominus Thomas Beuford, Comes de Dorcet, creatus est Dux Exoniæ, concessis sibi de fisco regio annuis mille libris, et quadraginta libris de villa Exoniæ supradicta, quas Dominus Rex de eadem villa percipere consuevit. In hoc Parliamento requisiti proceres si ista sibi placerent, responderunt quod optime, si donum regium tam exile non esset, nec correspondens meritis et virtutibus tanti viri. Parliament at London. The Earl of Dorset created Duke of Exeter, and honoured with a grant.

Concessæ fuere duæ decimæ per clerum Regi, sub unius anni spatio persolvendæ.

Anno Domini millesimo quadringentesimo septimo-decimo, Rex celebravit Natale apud Kenelwitham; quo tempore, structæ sunt illi insidiæ, prout fertur, per quendam scutiferum, complicem Johannis Oldcastelle dictum. A.D. 1417. Alleged plot against the King.

In crastino Natalis Domini sparsæ sunt scedulæ Lollardorum venenosæ, impingentes contra cunctos status Ecclesiæ, fere in qualibet magna domo vel hospitio villarum de Sancto Albano, de Northamtona, de Radingia, auctorem nullo sciente. Tracts of the Lollards dispersed in certain towns.

"Ad laudem, et gloriam, et honorem, Omnipotentis Dei, "ad pacem et unitatem universalis Ecclesiæ, ac totius populi "Christiani, ut electio futuri Romani et Summi Pontificis, "proxime celebranda, firmiori auctoritate et plurium roboretur assensu, et ne, attento statu Ecclesiæ super dicta electione, in posterum ulla retractio, ullusve scrupulus, in mentibus hominum resideat, sed ex illa sequatur unio certa, "vera, plenissima, et perfecta; Sacrosancta Generalis Synodus "Constantiensis, communi utilitate pensata, de speciali et "expresso consensu, ac voluntate concordi, Sanctæ Romanæ "Ecclesiæ Cardinalium in eadem Synodo personaliter existentium, et Collegii eorundem, ac omnium nationum præsentis Consilii, ordinat, statuit, et decernit, quod hac vice "duntaxat ad eligendum Romanum Pontificem summum, una "cum Cardinalibus, sex Prælati, vel aliæ honorabiles personæ Resolution of the Council of Constance, for the election of a Pope.

[1] *Lucie* in orig.; corrected from (5) MS. Corp. Chr. vii.

A.D. 1417. "ecclesiasticæ in sacris ordinibus constitutæ, de qualibet nati- (5) MS. Corp. Chr. vii.
"one in eadem Synodo pro nunc existente et nominata, quos,
"seu quas, quælibet ipsorum nationum pro se adhuc infra dies
"duxerit eligendos, seu eligendas, ipsis Cardinalibus adjun-
"gantur; quibus omnibus eadem Sancta Synodus eligendi
"Romanum Pontificem, secundum formam hic expressam,
"quatenus opus est, tribuit potestatem; videlicet, quod ille,
"absque ulla exceptione, ab universali Ecclesia Romanus
"Pontifex habeatur, qui a duabus partibus Cardinalium, in
"Conclavi existentium, et a cujuscunque nationis duabus par-
"tibus eisdem Cardinalibus adjungendorum, et tunc adjecto-
"rum, electus fuerit et receptus: quodque non valeat electio,
"nec electus pro Summo Pontifice habeatur, nisi duæ partes
"Cardinalium, in Conclavi existentium, et cujuslibet nationis
"duæ partes, cum Cardinalibus ad eligendum adjungendo-
"rum, et tunc adjunctorum, consentiant, et consenserint, in
"Romanum Pontificem eligendum. Statuit insuper, et ordinat,
"ac decernit, quod vota quorumcunque in electione hujusmodi
"emittenda, sint nulla, nisi, ut præmittitur, duæ partes
"Cardinalium, et duæ partes cujuslibet nationis adjungen-
"dorum, et tunc adjunctorum, prædictorum, principaliter, aut
"per accessionem, in unum concurrant. Hoc etiam adjecto,
"quod prælati et alii, cum ipsis Cardinalibus, ad electionem
"hujusmodi adjungendi, et tunc adjuncti, omnes et singulas
"Constitutiones etiam pœnales, circa electionem Romani
"Pontificis editas, atque consuetudines observare consuetas,
"quemadmodum ipsi Cardinales, observare teneantur, et
"ad illarum observantiam astringantur. Teneantur insuper
"jurare, et jurent, dicti electores, Cardinales et alii, ante-
"quam ad electionem procedant, quod in hujusmodi electionis
"negotio attendentes quod eis imminebit, cum de citatione
"agetur Vicarii Jesu Christi, successoris Beati Petri, univer-
"salis Ecclesiæ rectoris, gregis Dominici directoris, puris
"et sinceris mentibus, et quam credent publicæ utilitati
"universalis Ecclesiæ proficere, omni cujuscunque nationis
"peregrinæ, aut alio inordinato affectu, odio, gratia, vel
"favore, abjectis, procedent, ut eorum ministerio de utili
"et idoneo universali Ecclesiæ provideatur pastore. Ordinat
"insuper, statuit, et decernit, eadem Sancta Synodus, quod
"infra decem dies ex nunc continue numerandos, quos decem
"dies omnibus et singulis Sanctæ Romanæ Ecclesiæ Cardi-
"nalibus, præsentibus et absentibus, et cæteris electoribus
"supradictis, attenta Romanæ Ecclesiæ vacatione notoria, ad
"intrandum Conclave in hac civitate Constantiensi, in Majori
"Domo communitatis civitatis ejusdem, ad hoc jam ordi-
"nata, præfigit et assignat, præfati electores, Cardinales et

(5) MS. Corp. Chr. vii. "alii supradicti, intrent ipsum Conclave, ad electionem hujus- A.D. 1417.
"modi celebrandum, cæteraque faciendum, observandum, et "prosequendum, quemadmodum in cæteris, præter præmissa, "de Cardinalibus et aliis in electione Romani Pontificis jura "decernunt; quæ omnia præmissa observata vult eadem Sancta "Synodus in suo robore permanere. Hanc autem formam, "et hunc modum, electionis approbat, ordinat, statuit, pro "hac vice, et, ad omnem scrupulum removendum, vel summo-"vendum, omnes et singulos in eadem Synodo præsentes et "venturos qui eidem Synodo adhærebunt, ac omnes actus "legitimos in eadem Synodo agendis active et passive, qua-"tenus opus est, habilitat, et habiles esse declarat, cæteris "ejusdem Sacri Consilii decretis semper salvis, supplens "omnes defectus, si qui forsan intervenerint in præmissis; "Apostolicis et in Generalibus Consiliis editis Constitutioni-"bus, et aliis in contrarium facientibus, non obstantibus qui-"buscunque."

Particulars of the election of a Pope, by order of the Council of Constance.

Ultimo die mensis Octobris, Episcopus Wyntoniensis accessit [1] [ad] Consilium, peregrinaturus Hierosolymam, post electionem Summi Pontificis celebratam; ubi tantum valuit ejus facunda persuasio, ut et excitaret Dominos Cardinales ad concordiam, et ad [2] electionem Summi Pontificis se ocius præpararent. Quamobrem mox præparata fuit domus, quæ "Conclave" vocaretur, et [3] esset cum lectis stratis honorifice pro Dominis Cardinalibus, et electoribus adjungendis eisdem. Ordinatum nempe fuerat decreto Consilii, ut eligerentur ex omni natione quæ convenerat sex personæ, ad intrandum Conclave cum Cardinalibus, prout superius est expressum. Unde de Anglia ingressi sunt Conclave Episcopi Londoniensis, Bathoniensis, Norwicensis, Lichefeld, Abbas [4] Eboracum, et Magister Thomas de Poltone, Decanus [4] Eboracum. Quælibet autem natio scripsit nomina personarum suarum in scedula, et cera involvit. Præordinatæ proinde personæ Conclave sunt ingressæ, die Quatuor Coronatorum. Quibus intromissis, quædam persona laica attulit omnes scedulas, cera circumductas, ad Vicecancellarium in Conclave. Qui, nudatis brachiis usque ad cubitum, posuit omnes scedulas super mensam. [5] Exin decretum factum est, quomodo reclusi ederent in Conclavi; statutumque fuit ut haberent panem et vinum, et uno die unicum genus carnium, et altero unum genus [6] piscium, et singulis diebus unum genus potagii, prout dies exigebat.

---

[1] Omitted in orig.; supplied from (5) MS. Corp. Chr. vii. and the printed texts.

[2] *dilectionem* in the printed texts.

[3] *essent* in the printed texts.

[4] *Eboracensis* in the printed texts; *Eborac*ᴰ in (5) MS. Corp. Chr. vii.

[5] *Exinde* in the printed texts.

[6] *pissium* in orig.

A.D. 1417.

The Electors are shut up in Conclave.

(5) MS. Corp. Chr. vii.

Tunc Imperator et tresdecim Duces, ac majores civitatis Constantiæ, juravere super Librum, quod fideliter custodirent Conclave ab impeditoribus, et né alia cibaria intromitterentur quam statuta fuere. Quo facto, Imperator personaliter perscrutatus est domum totum, et duabus seris ostium post se clausit. In ostio domus illius factum [1]fuerat foramen quadratum, habens in longitudine et latitudine pedem unum, per quod immitti deberent cibaria inclusorum, omniquaque die dum in Conclavi fuerunt. Abbas Sancti Edmundi de Bury, et Prior Sancti Johannis de Klerkenewelle, fuerunt assignati ad prægustandum cibaria Anglicorum. Mox vero ut servitum fuit inclusis, dictum foramen clausum fuit tribus seris.

The Cardinal Colonna is chosen Pope, as Martin V.

Igitur illis conferentibus de injuncto negotio, quidam nominavere Wyntoniensem, quidam Londoniensem, Episcopos; nonnulli vero Cardinalem Franciæ; nihilque fuit actum primo die vel secundo. Die vero Sancti Martini, primo mane, Episcopus Londoniensis venit, et inter omnes Cardinales protulit ista verba;—"Ego, Ricardus Episcopus Londoniensis, accedo "ad Dominum meum, Cardinalem de Columna." Audito præsenti sermone, repente cuncti præsentes, per Dei gratiam, in eandem consensere personam. Et illico exuerunt eum vestibus suis omnibus, et novis eum revestierunt, ac super altare posuerunt, et deosculati sunt manus ejus et pedes. Hiis ita gestis, confestim unus eorum qui inclusi fuerant, fregit foramen in pariete, et clamavit,—"Habemus Papam, Martinum;" et tunc exiverunt omnes in Magnam Ecclesiam, cantantes, "Te Deum, "laudamus."

Ceremonies of his consecration.

In crastino Papa fuit factus presbyter, et die sequenti fuit sacratus Episcopus, et celebravit Missam suam primam; cui Missæ interfuerunt centum quadraginta mitrati. Sequenti Dominica, Dominus Papa fecit mane diluculo solemnem processionem, transiens per Australem partem ecclesiæ versus Occidentalem; ubi constitutus fuit quidam clericus, habens canabum et stuppam, et combussit ea, dicens:—

"Ecce! pater sancte, sic transit gloria mundi."

His Coronation.

Posthæc, eodem die fuit factum quasi quoddam solarium pro Coronatione Papæ, in altitudine habens viginti pedes. Prior Sancti Johannis de Klerkenwelle tenuit diadema Papæ in officio Coronationis. Ipso die, post prandium, Papa equitavit per medium civitatis Constantiæ, quem sequebantur in equis omnes Episcopi mitrati [2]et Abbates. Equus Papæ phaleratus cum rubeo eskarleto, equi vero cunctorum Episcoporum phalerati fuere candido panno bissino; et Imperator in hac equitatione tenuit frænum Papæ. Cum autem pervenisset

Procession through the City of Constance.

[1] *fuerit* in orig., by inadvertence. | [2] *et* omitted in the printed texts.

(5) MS. Corp. Chr. vii. Papa ad locum fori, illic obviavere sibi omnes Judæi civitatis, qui porrexerunt sibi, sicut mos est, cæremonias ac legem suam; quas acceptas Papa projecit post tergum suum, dicens;— "Recedant vetera, nova sunt omnia." Papa, prout dicunt, prius vocabatur "Paulinus," natus de illa nobili et antiqua gente, Paulina Romæ." A.D. 1417. The Jews of the city meet the Pope.

King Henry lands at Touque in Normandy, and captures the place.

Hoc anno, circa finem mensis Julii, Rex Henricus, cum magna classe mare sulcans, decimo navigationis die salvus applicuit in Normannia, scilicet in festo Sancti Petri ad Vincula, [1] in loco vocato "Touque," ubi villa fortis est, et castrum nobile, quod reddere per annum solet octo millia [2] coronatorum. Quo in loco quingenti equites hostiliter occurrerunt ei, transitum prohibere volentes; sed perempto per arcitenentes eorum capitaneo, et ejus collega capto, cæteri meticulose fugerunt. Nec multo post, redditum fuit Regi dictum castrum, et qui remanere volebant, [3] accepere gratiam remanendi; volentes abire tulerunt secum de gratia regia pecunias et supellectilem, relinquentes arma et instrumenta bellica, necnon et victualia, dicto castro. Consimili modo reddita fuit Regi villa de Aumberes, cum castello; qua tempestate monachus quidam solivagus, captus a quodam de familia Regis, despoliatus est. Quod [4] [ut] Rex comperit, sollicite quæsivit a monacho, si personam recognosceret quæ tulerat ab eo res suas. Qui cum diceret bene se personam noscere, si videret eam, tandem post aliquos in conspectu ductos, notavit unum, dicens illum bona sua rapuisse. Quem Rex illico vehementer redarguit, dicens illum morte dignum, qui, cum aliunde satisfacere potuisset suæ necessitati, ad res religiosorum manus extenderet; modo tamen gavisurum perdonationis titulo, si nihil tale committat de cætero. Fecitque virum reddere monacho [5] quæ tulerat prius ab eo, monacho mandans ut domum repeteret, et consuetum servitium, cum fratribus suis, intrepidanter Deo rependeret; asserens se non illuc advenisse modo vispilionis, ut res religiosorum raperet, sed potius more regis, ut eorum bona a [6] direptione servaret. Nec mora, proclamari fecit per exercitum, ne quis religiosum, clericum vel presbyterum, nec ullum penitus ecclesiasticum, despoliare, seu quovismodo

He takes cognizance of the case of a monk who has been despoiled.

Proclamation made that the religious

[1] *vocato in loco* in the printed texts.

[2] *coronarum* in the printed texts.

[3] *accipere* in orig.; corrected from the printed texts.

[4] Omitted in orig., supplied from (5) MS. Corp. Chr. vii. and the printed texts.

[5] *quis* in the printed texts.

[6] *direptionibus* in the printed texts.

A.D. 1417. molestare, præsumeret, nec ad res ecclesiasticas animo rapiendi manus mittere, sub pœna suspensionis et laquei. Qua proclamatione per plebanos vulgata, videres rusticos, indumentis clericorum sumptis, vagari per exercitum, negotia tractare foralia, impune accedere et recedere, Anglis astu pie deceptis. Nec valebant Anglici rei veritatem agnoscere, [1] rusticis coronas sibi radentibus, ut Anglos fallerent efficacius aspectu capitum [2] albatorum. Consequenter, insuper fecit Rex proclamari, ne quia fœminam conjugatam, viduam, sive virginem, contra voluntatem auderet opprimere, vel bona diripere plebeiorum qui se Regi summiserant, sub pœna prætaxata.

(5) MS. Corp. Chr. vii.

shall be exempt from spoliation.

The country people assume disguises, in consequence.

Proclamation against other acts of violence.

The King marches to Caen, and lays siege to it.

Tertio-decimo die mensis Augusti, Rex recessit cum exercitu de villa de Touque, et pernoctavit apud villam Sancti Salvatoris de Tybe. Crastino die Sabbati, pernoctavit apud villam de Granvyle, ubi commoratus est die Dominica, videlicet, in festo Assumptionis Beatæ Mariæ. Die Lunæ pernoctavit apud Abbathiam de Fontenes, et in die Martis pervenit ad villam de Stutevyle: die vero Mercurii consedit cum exercitu coram villa de Caen, ex parte Australi, prope Monasterium Sancti Stephani; Dux Clarentiæ ex parte Boreali, juxta Monasterium monialium Sanctæ Trinitatis; Comes Marescallus sedit ex parte sinistra Regis, et Dominus de Mautrevers juxta eum. Juxta quem Domini Talbot et Umfrevile sunt locati, et consequenter [3] [Domini] de Nevyle et [4] Wylby. Ex parte Regis dextera considens, Comes de Warwyk, et Dominus Johannes Gray, juxta quos Comites de Huntyngdone et de Sarum, et Dominus [5] Johannes Grenecornewayle.

The French propose burning the Abbey of St. Stephen.

Dum sic esset dispositus regalis exercitus, et [6] Abbathia Sancti Stephani foret Francis [7] conjuncta, videntes qui in Monasterio pro tutamento [8] fuere, se impares regiis viribus, locum deserere festinabant; et diripientes tam victualia quam alia loci jocalia, latenter in villam commigraverunt, notabiles sacrilegio manifesto; ubi constituti tractabant inter se qualiter dictum monasterium flammis absumerent, et turres ecclesiæ complanarent; per quas multa mala fieri posse non dubita-

[1] *rustici* in the printed texts.

[2] *abrasorum* in the printed texts.

[3] Omitted in orig.; supplied from (5) MS. Corp. Chr. vii., and the printed texts.

[4] *Willoughby* in the printed texts; *Wylluby* in (5) MS. Corp. Chr. vii.

[5] *Johannis Grecornwayle* in the printed texts.

[6] *Abbethia* in orig.

[7] *conjuncti* in orig.; *communita* in (5) MS. Corp. Chr. vii. and the printed texts.

[8] *fore* in the printed texts.

(5) MS. Corp. Chr. vii.

A.D. 1417.

bant. [1]Audivit hæc insusurrari inter Francos [2]quidam monachus ejusdem loci, qui metuens sui monasterii destructionem, confidenter dedit se periculo, et sub illius noctis [3]conticinio, manibus reptans et genibus, et [4][per] hostes, per ignes, per arma, per gladios, tandem pervenit ad locum ubi Dux Clarentiæ, frater Regis, obsidionis suæ vigilias observabat. Et impetrato aditu, vidit [5]ubi recubuerat armatus ad unguem in horto quodam super herbam, supposito capiti suo saxo. Cui confestim, flexis genibus, flebiliter supplicavit, ut [6]loci sui ruinæ succurreret, qui jam diruendus erat, nisi maturius subveniret.—"Vobis," [7]ait, "specialius convenit nostrum servare monasterium, qui de Regum linea descendistis [8]qui "locum nostrum [9]fundaverunt, extruxerunt, atque dotaverunt. "Quapropter incunctancter utamini [10]me duce prævio; et "ego [11]vos inducam, et gaudere faciam loco nostro." Nec mora, fecit Dux ut monuit, et, arreptis scalis, pervenit ad eam partem quam monachus bene novit immunitam; nam pauci, sed invalidi, relicti fuerant, magis ad ostentationem quam ad defensionem loci: quos adventu suo territos vel captivavit vel abire permisit, reputans eos indignos gladio suo propter rusticitatem et vilitatem personarum. Unum tamen decollari jussit, qui confessus fuerat se res Monasterii, scilicet ferramenta fenestrarum et hujusmodi, compilasse, dicens ei;—"Si nos," [12]ait, "nostros propter talia sacrilegia justa morte [13]multavimus, "multo plus tu pœnam mereris, qui patriæ propriæ sacella spo-"liare non times." Dux ergo tali modo potitus loco, introduxit Regem in crastino, gaudentem nimirum quod a [14]telis et turribus Monasterii valebat intueri quæcunque gerebantur in villa, et illic figere vel locare gunnas suas, quas Galli "*canones*" vocant, quibus validius villam infestare posset.

A monk of the place gives notice to the Duke of Clarence.

The Duke captures the Monastery, and rescues it from destruction.

The Monastery is found to command the town.

Posthæc denunciatur dies et hora quibus fieri deberet insultus ad villam. Interea, sonante terrifico lituorum et tuba-

The place is assaulted.

---

[1] *Audiunt* in the printed texts.

[2] *quod quidam* in the printed texts.

[3] *silentio* in the printed texts.

[4] Omitted in orig.; supplied from (5) MS. Corp. Chr. vii. and the printed texts.

[5] *ut* in the printed texts.

[6] *loco suo succurreret* in the printed texts.

[7] *autem specialius* in the printed texts.

[8] *in locum* in the printed texts.

[9] *quem fundaverunt* in the printed texts.

[10] *me* omitted in the printed texts.

[11] *vobis* in orig.; corrected from (5) MS. Corp. Chr. vii. and the printed texts.

[12] *et* in the printed texts.

[13] *multaveris* in the printed texts.

[14] Perhaps an error for *tegulis*, "tiles."

A.D. 1417. rum [1]classico, obsessi, semet cohortantes, ad muros alacriter cucurrere, telis armati, gladiis et missilibus, jaculis et petrariis, ut vim vi repellant. De parte Regis, ut ita dicam, (5) MS. Corp. Chr. vii.

[2]"Induit adversis contraria pectora telis
"Miles, ut æternum sanguine nomen emat."

Valour of Sir Edward Spring.

Inter milites, Dominus Edmundus Springeus, qui dudum cum aliis militiæ cingulo donatus fuerat, muros [3]Cadoniæ armatus ascendit, et vulnera

"——[4] alterna datque capitque manu."
"[5]Sicut aper, longe sylvis [6]latratibus actus,
"Fulmineo celeres dissipat ore canes;
"Mox tamen ipse perit,"—

His dreadful death.

sic et iste vir egregius, dum multos muris dejicit, dum plures ense perimit, dum Martis acta peragit, lapsus pede corruit in foramen muri, ubi sedendo pugnans peremptus est; quem mox inhumaniter, ut erat armatus, adhuc spirantem, [7]ganeones, circumjectis ignibus, cremaverunt. Non tamen destitere regales inimicis insistere, sed bili concitata propter infortunium tanti socii,—fuerat nempe cunctis amabilis—insurrexerunt acrius, et [8]exarserunt contra tam improbos [9]pollinctores, fatigantes illos sic ex parte, quod videbatur ipsis qui tuebantur oppidum ex parte altera necessarium, ut, statione sua relicta, ad eam partem accurrerent qua Rex oppugnabat villam.

The Duke of Clarence scales the walls.

Sicque rarescente in dicta parte defensore, Dux Clarentiæ, factis instrumentis in loco qui putabatur tutissimus, muros scandit, et, post terga Gallorum desiliens, eos adeo repente terruit, ut ignorarent utrum juvaret potius procedere contra Regem, an reverti et manus erigere contra Ducem. Facta est igitur strages magna Gallorum, obviantibus a fronte regalibus, instantibus a tergo Clarentianis, omnemque illis adimentibus spem salutis.

The English capture the town.

Talique modo Rex villa potitus est, castello nondum rebellibus vacuato. Quapropter Rex gunnarum jactu sic castrum debilitavit, ut impossibile videretur inclusis se defendere locum posse. Proinde impetrato tractatu, obtinuerunt a Rege libertatem abeundi, relictis armis

---

[1] *classio* in orig., by inadvertence.

[2] Ovid, II *Amor.* x. 31, 32.

[3] *Cadomi* in (5) MS. Corp. Chr. vii.

[4] Ovid, *Fasti*, ii. 234, slightly altered.

[5] Ovid, *Fasti*, ii. 231–3.

[6] So in orig. (5) MS Corp. Chr. vii., and the printed texts; erroneously for *Laurentibus*.

[7] *ganenones* in orig., by inadvertence; *tormentarii* in the printed texts.

[8] *exarxerunt* in orig., by inadvertence.

[9] *pollinitores* in orig. and the printed texts.

(5) MS. Corp. Chr. vii. [1]et victualibus, auro et argento, atque jocalibus, in castello. Sed ne inanes et vacui omnino recederent, Rex indulsit eis ut milites quidam certam summam fulvi metalli secum ferrent, armigeri quoque taxatam, et alii limitatam, tollerent, et non amplius, sub pœna perditionis summarum concessarum, pariter et vitarum. Fœminas vero permisit ornamenta vel quæque mobilia secum ferre, et indemnes abire. Quæ magnas auri summas, ut fertur, in utribus abstulere. Hiis omnibus ingrati Franci beneficiis regiæ munificentiæ pessime responderunt, et invidentes ejus commodis, aurum et argentum, et quicquid in castrum ad tuendum deportatum fuerat, igne combusserunt; ut post recessum patuit eorundem.

A.D. 1417. Terms are granted to the garrison of the castle.

The French make an ungrateful return for the King's generosity.

Post deditionem castri Caen, quod obtinuerat conditionaliter, [2]si Rex Francus vel Dolphinus, aut Comes de Armanak, bello non dissolverent obsidionem infra nonum-decimum diem mensis Septembris, reddiderunt se pacto [3]consimili civitas et ecclesia Baiocensis, cum aliis multis villis.

Bayeux surrenders to the English.

Cum hæc agerentur in Neustria, Lollardi, duce Johanne Oldcastelle, insanire cœperunt in Anglia; qui Scotos concitavit tam prece quam repromissa pecunia, ut intrarent hostiliter regnum, in Regis absentia, levi negotio, ut asseruit, subjugandum. Ferunt quod Willelmum Duglas, Scotum, apud Pontem Fractum allocutus [4]fuerit, grandem promittens auri summam, si gentem suam sollicitaret, et eum qui false dicebatur apud eos "Rex "Ricardus," venire cum eis faceret, et se ostentare tanquam Regem. Scotus vero, "[5]auri sacra fame" coactus, non multo post contribules suos cum magno strepitu venire fecit ad obsidendum castellum, cum villa, de Rokesburgh. Quo cum venisset, suffossores immiserunt ad subvertendum muros.

Alleged treaty of Sir J. Oldcastle with the Scots.

The Scots besiege Roxburgh.

Contigit eo tempore Ducem Exoniæ, Dominum Thomam Beuford, ad Brydelingtoniam venisse peregrinandi gratia; qui confestim, audito rei nuncio, properavit ad partes, eundo colligens armatos et arcitenentes, hostibus occurrere festinando. Ex alia parte, Custos regni, Dominus Johannes, frater Regis, Dux Bedfordiæ, cum aliis regni nobilibus, magnum conflans [6]exercitum, ad easdem pervenit partes. Quod Scoti per exploratores comperientes, expectare non audentes diutius,

The Dukes of Exeter and Bedford hasten to meet the Scots,

who take to flight.

[7]"Turpia fœmineæ terga dedere fugæ."—

Nec mirum, quia plusquam centum millia virorum convenisse ferebantur ad repellendum eos. Et ne rurales æstimarentur, et

The Duke of Exeter's opinion of his troops.

---

[1] *et* omitted in the printed texts.
[2] *scilicet si* in the printed texts.
[3] *consilii* in the printed texts.
[4] *fuerat* in the printed texts.
[5] In allusion to *Æneid*, iii. 57.
[6] *exercititum* in orig., by inadvertence.
[7] Ovid, *Fasti*, vi. 522.

A.D. 1417. inexperti, qui cum dictis heroibus venerant, vir valde venerabilis, Dux Exoniæ, palam asseveravit se scivisse ex illis cohortibus delegisse quadraginta millia virorum bellicosorum, qui virtute præstarent et animis, æque cum valentioribus quasi regni totius, non obstante quod maxima multitudo cum Rege in Normannia militabat.

(5) MS. Corp. Chr. vii.

Oldcastle conceals himself at St. Alban's.

Eo tempore Dux Lollardorum, Johannes Oldcastelle, dum diversis in locis requirit latibula, prope [1] Sanctum Albanum in domo cujusdam rustici, habentis ibidem idoneam mansionem, [2] in dominio Abbatis delituit multis diebus. Quo audito, familiares Abbatis, illuc nocte properantes, illum quidem non invenerunt, sed quosdam de suis specialibus asseclis tenuerunt, et ad carcerem adduxerunt. Ipse vero dux perfidorum, hoc audito rumore, vehementer ingemuit, dicens suum grande propositum enervatum, captis præcipuis consociis votorum suorum. In præfato loco reperti fuerunt libri in Anglicis scripti litteris, et nonnulli libri quondam nobiliter et imaginibus Sanctorum diversorum decorati; quarum imaginum capita, juxta formam falsæ doctrinæ suæ, nebulones abraserant, et in Letaniis omnium Sanctorum nomina, una cum nominibus Beatæ Virginis, aboleverant, usque ad hunc versum, "Parce nobis, Domine." Inventa sunt insuper illic quædam scripta plena blasphemiæ in Beatam Mariam, quæ propter horrorem scribere supersedi. Librum tali rasura [3] deformatum, misit Domino nostro Regi dictus Abbas Sancti Albani, cum quibusdam aliis deliramentis repertis ibidem; et Dominus Rex [4] eundem librum Archiepiscopo Cantuariensi remisit, [5] ut in sermonibus faciendis ad Crucem Sancti Pauli Londoniis ostenderetur; ut vel sic civibus innotesceret quanta furia Lollardi vehebantur, qui, non dico imagines, sed nec ipsa Sanctorum nomina, in suis membranis inseri permittebant.

Indications of his opinions found in the place of his concealment.

Hatred of the Lollards for the effigies and names of Saints.

Successes of King Henry in France.

Rex Angliæ, per idem tempus impiger, in partibus transmarinis cepit plures civitates et villas muratas, cum castris et munitionibus plusquam centum.

Death of the Bishop of Salisbury, at Constance

Hoc anno, quarto die mensis Septembris, obiit Magister [6] Alum, Episcopus Sarum, apud Constantiam, Consilio nondum finito.

Siege and capture of the town of Falaise.

Mense [7] Decembri Rex Henricus obsedit Falesiam, villam munitissimam, refertam defensoribus, superbam suis opibus,

[1] The word *apud* is inserted here in orig., by inadvertence.

[2] *in* omitted in the printed texts.

[3] *deformatam* in orig., by inadvertence.

[4] *eundum* in orig.

[5] *et* in orig.

[6] *Robertus Alin* in the printed texts.

[7] *Decembrio* in orig. and (5) MS. Corp. Chr. vii.; *Decembris* in the printed texts.

(5) MS. Corp. Chr. vii. instauratam machinis, confidentem mœniis, ut nec quidem portas contra Regem [1] in initio claudere dignabantur; villa tamen levi negotio, terrore gunnarum, reddita fuit Regi. Sed castrum cum magno fastu detentum fuit, fere usque ad festum Purificationis, medio tempore multis hinc inde jactis convitiis. Tandem obstinatione deposita, pœnituit obsessos tamdiu perseverasse in pertinacia, et humilius sapiendo Regis gratiam flagitabant. Non enim ferre valebant horridos saxorum volatus, quos crebro circa se cernebant emissos, cuilibet formidandos; et proinde maluere semel vitam servare quoquo pacto, quam cotidie quasi mortem metuendo mori. Igitur post [2] certas conditiones, assecuraverunt [3] Regem, se propriis suis sumptibus damna castri villæque ruinas reparaturos, præter illas quas solverent redemptionis suæ summas; quas idcirco illis imposuit, propter suæ fastuosæ detentionis diuturnitatem, quæ fuit causa ruinæ magnæ dicti castelli. A.D. 1417. The castle is surrendered.

Circa præsens tempus captus fuit in Anglia ille vaniglorius, [4] "inveteratus dierum" malorum, primicerius Lollardorum, dux et princeps perfidorum, Johannes Oldcastelle, quondam dictus "Dominus de Cobham," in terris Domini de Powisia, non sine periculo læsioneque quorundam qui ceperunt eum, sed nec ipse sine vulnere tentus fuit. Sir John Oldcastle is captured, and wounded.

Sub eodem tempore vocati fuerant ad Parliamentum Londonias omnes status regni, ut de pecuniali suffragio Regi ferendo consulerent, qui laborabat in partibus ultramarinis. Cumque domini et personæ Parliamentales audissent quod captus fuisset hostis publicus, placuit cunctis Parliamentum non dissolvendum donec interrogatus et auditus fuisset in eodem Parliamento. Missus est igitur Dominus de Powysia, qui deduceret eum manu forti. Qui et adduxit eum Londonias in lectica saucium, una cum clerico, omnium secretorum suorum conscio. Nec mora, cum constitutus fuisset in præsentia regni Rectoris, Ducis de Bedfordia, et statuum Parliamenti, lectum fuit indictamentum coram eo de hostili insurrectione contra Regem in Campo Sancti Ægidii, et aliis offensis læsæ majestatis, qui partim tanguntur superius in locis suis. Quæsitum fuit ab eo qualiter se voluit excusare, et ostendere quare non merito sit adjudicandus morti; qui mox aliunde quærens [5] diffugia, assumpta parabola, cœpit prædicare de Dei He is brought to London by Lord Powis. Is brought before Parliament. His address to Parliament.

---

[1] *inimitio* in orig.; corrected from (5) Corp. Chr. vii.; *initio* in the printed texts.

[2] *cartas* in orig., by inadvertence.

[3] *regi* in the printed texts.

[4] In allusion to an expression found in *Daniel*, Chapters vii., xiii., and xxii.

[5] *diffiugia* in orig., by inadvertence.

A.D. 1417. misericordia, et quicunque mortales Dei imitatores esse vellent, deberent semper misericordiam [1]superexaltare judicio; vindictam fore solius Dei; [2]quæ ab ejus cultoribus non debuit exerceri, sed soli Deo relinqui; et alia plura commemoravit, redimendo tempus, donec Summus regni Justiciarius Regis Vicarium monuit, ne pateretur eum inaniter tempus terere, et assistentes regni proceres molestare. Jussit ergo regni Rector, ut responderet conformiter ad objecta; qui se videns constanter urgeri, tandem post brevem meditationem, soluto silentio, respondit, dicens: — "Mihi autem," inquit, "pro minimo est, ut a vobis judicer, aut ab humano "die;" et iterum impertinenter garrulare cœpit, donec Summus Justiciarius jussit ut responderet finaliter, et doceret, si posset, quare mori non debuit. Qui confestim, cum summa superbia et abusione, respondit se non habere judicem inter eos, vivente ligeo domino suo in regno Scotiæ, Rege Ricardo. Quo responso accepto, quia non opus erat testibus, sine mora jussus est trahi et [3]suspendi super furcas, atque comburi, pendens in eisdem. Ubi cum plures personæ honorabiles huic spectaculo interessent, Domino Thomæ Erpingham, prout dicunt, novissima verba locutus est, adjurans eum, ut si cerneret eum resurgere die tertia, pacem procuraret sectæ suæ. Tanta perditus fuit dementia, ut putaret se post triduum a mortuis resurrecturum.

(5) MS. Corp. Chr. vii.

The Duke of Bedford commands him to answer the charges made against him.

He alleges that King Richard is still living.

He is put to death.

A.D. 1418. Anno Domini millesimo quadringentesimo decimo-octavo, tenuit Rex Natale in Normannia apud Baiocas; circa quod tempus redditum fuit sibi castrum de Falesia, et civitas de Abrincis, id est "Averance," se summisit.

Surrender of Avranches.

Post festum Paschæ, missi sunt per Regem ad obsidendum Monasterium de Bekke Herlewyn, Dominus Thomas Dux Clarentiæ; ad obsidendum villam de Cherburgh, Dominus Humfridus Dux Gloverniæ; ad obsidendum castrum de Daunfrount Dominus Ricardus Comes Warwici; ad obsidendum Castrum Nully Lovesque, Dominus Comes de Kymo.

Other places besieged.

In die Sancti Georgii Rex apud Cadomum, in castello, celebravit solemniter idem festum.

King Henry at Caen.

Circa festum Trinitatis, ad jussum Regis, profectus est in Normanniam Dominus Thomas Dux Exoniæ, Regis avunculus, cum quindecim millibus, prout dicitur, bellatorum.

The Duke of Exeter sets out for Normandy.

Mense Junii Burgundiones nocte Parisium intraverunt, et Comitem de Armanak morte turpissima [4]mutilaverunt. Nam,

The Count of Armagnac, and others,

---

[1] *superaltare* in orig., by inadvertence.

[2] *qui* in orig. and the printed texts.

[3] *suspensi* in orig., by inadvertence.

[4] *mutulaverunt* in (5) MS. Corp. Chr. vii., orig., and the printed texts.

(5) MS. Corp. Chr. vii.

ut ferunt, eum crudeliter excoriaverunt, [1]et expost crudelissim peremerunt. In illa ferali seditione jugulati feruntur plures nobiles, scilicet Cardinalis [2]de Baar, Archiepiscopus Remensis, Episcopus Meulx, Episcopus Constantiensis, Episcopus de Liseux, Abbas Sancti Dionysii, Abbas de Jormayle, Cancellarius Franciæ, Præpositus Parisiorum, et plures alii, ad numerum quatuordecim millium personarum. Nec satiari potuit effrænata furia tanta cæde virorum, quin et in fœminas grassaretur. Nempe feruntur jugulata quinque millia fœminarum. A.D. 1418. murdered by the partisans of the Duke of Burgundy.

Sub eodem tempore Rex obsedit nobilem villam vocatam "Loveres," quam fortiter expugnatam compulit ad deditionem sub certis conditionibus utrobique pactis. Reddita est ergo Regi villa in Vigilia Sancti Johannis Baptistæ. Die vero Lunæ sequente movit Dominus Rex exercitum versus Pount de la Arche. Eodem tempore, Dux Exoniæ obsedit civitatem Ebroicensem, (Everoyse). Siege and capture of Louviers. Siege of Evreux.

Ipso anno, infra Octavas Assumptionis Beatæ Mariæ, Jesus Christus, ut putatur, ob honorem gloriosæ Matris suæ, quam propensius veneratur Rex Angliæ, dedit ei in locis variis tres miraculosas victorias in provincia Normannorum. Three victories granted to the King, for his piety.

Prima fuit, quod centum de suis Anglicis, die Martis infra dictas Octavas, ceperunt tres magnos dominos apud locum vocatum "Kylbeuef," et personas alias octoginta, et [3]trecentos fugere compulerunt. Secunda fuit, die Jovis quadringenti nempe de hostibus intraverunt suburbana civitatis Ebroicensis; et undecim ex Anglis fugaverunt eos, et ceperunt ex eis quatuor, et duodecim peremerunt, captis quadraginta dextrariis eorundem. Tertia fuit, die Sabbati sequente, summo mane, hostes revera voluerunt cepisse villam quam Rex ceperat in prima equitatione sua præsentis anni, dictam "Loveres;" sed capitaneus dictæ villæ, cum centum de nostris, exivit animose contra mille, et, Deo volente, vicit eos; et tradidit in manus hominum nostræ partis centum et octoginta personas generosas ex hostibus per omnia benedictus Deus. Particulars of those victories

[4]Pridie Kalendas Augusti, capta fuit inopinato villa de Pounteyse, prope Parisium, probitate Capitanei de la Bouche, summo mane, qui nocte non procul a villa delitescens inter vineas, cum nonnullis de Domini Regis familia, in vigilia matutina repente scalarum scansione muros ascendit; ubi post diutinam dimicationem, occisis multis de defensoribus, et A.D. 1419. Capture of Pontoise by the Captal de la Bouche.

---

[1] *et* omitted in the printed texts.

[2] *de* omitted in the printed texts.

[3] *ter centum* in the printed texts.

[4] At this point there is an hiatus in the History; as it passes on to the latter part of the year 1419.

A.D. 1419. pluribus vulneratis, cum cives cernerent numerum invictum crescere inter eos, oppressi vecordia, portis apertis, fugerunt quo sors quemque trahebat. Fuerunt utique in ea villa præfortes homines constituti pro defensione mille, qui ferebant lanceas atque scuta, et balistariorum duo millia; qui omnes sub festinatione versus Parisium fugere contendebant; sed intercepti sunt et præoccupati per Comitem de Huntyndonia, qui et ipse destinatus fuit ad istud negotium, ut ipse ex una parte [1] [mille cives occupasset, dum alii ex parte] altera muros ascendere [2] molirentur, sed tamen retardatus fuerat in marisco, non inveniens exitum usque ad solis ortum. Occisa est ergo illa pene multitudo per Comitem, villa per nostros detenta. In qua recondita fuerant omnis generis victualia ad duos annos; de cujus amœnitate, divitiis, et utilitate, Rex scripsit quod inter omnia quæ gessit in transmarinis partibus, opus magis utile non peregit. Hæc autem gesta sunt expirantibus treugis, in crastino postquam Franci Regem suis falaciis delusissent, et pacis vias quas [3] Rex obtulerat refutassent: ferunt quod dicta villa fuit instaurata sufficienter victualibus pro duobus annis.

(5) MS. Corp. Chr. vii.

Great stores found there.

Die Lunæ proxima post festum Sancti Matthæi Apostoli, castrum Gisorcii recuperatum fuit per Anglos; et die Sabbati proximo post idem festum, recuperatum fuit castrum de Galiard per eosdem.

Castle of Gisors taken by the English; Cheateau Galiard retaken.

Dux Burgundiæ, vocatus ad [4] Dolphini colloquium, et suorum perfidorum complicium, proditiose peremptus est, licet perante pariter omnes pari sacramento se [5] constrinxissent, quod nullus alterum læderet eorundem qui ad colloquium convenissent. Filius Ducis Burgundiæ, qui et hæres ejusdem, patris cupiens vindicare jugulationem, destinatis humiliter ad Regem nostrum multis personis honorabilibus, præstitit sacramentum per eosdem de fidelitate servanda sibi.

The Duke of Burgundy slain by the Dauphin.

The Duke's son makes terms with the English.

Episcopus [6] Surreyensis, Domini Wyntoniensis Suffraganeus, celebravit solemnes Ordines apud [7] S .

---

[1] Omitted in orig.; supplied from (5) MS. Corp. Chr. vii.: *aut altera muros* in the printed texts.

[2] *moliretur* in the printed texts.

[3] *res* in orig., (5) MS. Corp. Chr. vii., and the printed texts.

[4] *Dolfini* in (5) MS. Corp. Chr. vii. and orig.

[5] *constrixissent* in orig. and the printed texts.

[6] *Surrexensis* in orig.; *Surreyensis* in (5) MS. Corp. Chr. vii. and the printed texts.

[7] The name is omitted in orig. and the printed texts; in (5) MS. Corp. Chr. vii. the following is added—"*Sanctum Albanum; vocatus* "*ab Abbate, vicesimo tertio die men*-"*sis Septembris.*"

(5) MS. Corp. Chr. vii. Hoc anno noverca Regis, Anna Regina, per quosdam infamata de quodam maleficio, quod in læsionem Regis commentata fuisset, amotis cunctis suis famulis, commendata est custodiæ Pellam; qui, adhibitis sibi [1]novem servientibus, introduxit eam in castrum de Peveneseye, sub ejus providentia gubernandam. A.D. 1419. The widow of the late King Henry is imprisoned on suspicion.

Circa festum Omnium Sanctorum, Ducissa Clarentiæ, cum multis aliis dominabus Angliæ, [2]Neustriam transfretavit. The Duchess of Clarence crosses over to Normandy.

Balthazar Cossa, nuper dictus "Johannes Papa Vicesimus-"tertius," decreto Concilii Constantiensis, degradatus et incarceratus, propter humilem summissionem qua se summisit Papæ Martino, liberatur a carcere, et ad Cardinalatus restituitur dignitatem. Balthazar Cossa is restored to the Cardinalate.

Dominus Humfridus, Dux Glovernię, frater Regis minimus, factus est Custos regni Angliæ, loco fratris suis Domini Johannis, Ducis Bedfordiæ; qui vocatus a Rege, navigavit in Neustriam cum valida bellatorum [3][manu,] postquam gloriose regimen regni tenuerat per duos annos. Duke of Gloucester made guardian of the realm. Duke of Bedford crosses over to Normandy.

Hoc anno, sexto-decimo die Maii, nostri pugnaverunt cum Gallicis, qui venerant ad dissolvendum obsidionem villæ de Freney, quam Comes Saresberiensis obsedit: et occiderunt ex eis pene quinque millia, captis sexcentis, cum Marescallo de Rows, et multis aliis nobilibus et honoratis viris. Ductores ex parte nostra fuere Comites Huntyngdoniæ et [4]Marescalli, J. Grecornewayle, et Philippus Le [5]Beche. [6]Capta sunt in hoc conflictu multa signa nobilium; inter quæ Willelmus Duglas perdidit vexillum suum, occisis de Scotis suis plusquam centum. Signum Willelmi Duglas Rex jussit extendi in ecclesia Sanctæ Mariæ Rotomagi. A.D. 1420. Defeat of the French by the Earl of Huntingdon and Earl Marshal.

Dux Burgundiæ per hoc tempus sollicitat, ut pax et concordia fiat inter Reges, [7]sub certis modo et forma, atque conditionibus; quarum talis est effectus:— The Duke of Burgundy proposes terms of peace.

Inprimis, quod Rex noster acciperet, et habebit, in conjugem puellam præclarissimam, Dominam Katerinam, Regis Francorum, Karoli, filiam: et quod per eum modum illustrissimos consanguineos suos, Regem Franciæ et Reginam, efficiet sibi patrem et matrem, et eosdem ut patrem et matrem suos habebit, et pro talibus venerabitur præ cunctis aliis per- The purport of the proposed terms

---

[1] *nomen* in orig.; corrected from the printed texts.

[2] *in Neustriam* in (5) MS. Corp. Chr. vii. and the printed texts.

[3] Omitted in orig.; supplied from the printed texts

[4] *Marchiæ* in the printed texts.

[5] *Leche* in orig. and the printed texts; corrected from (5) MS. Corp. Chr. vii.

[6] *capti* in the printed texts.

[7] *modo et forma sub certis conditionibus*, in the printed texts.

A.D. 1420. sonis mundi; et quod non impediet quin consanguineus suus, Rex Franciæ, teneat et possideat, quoad vixerit, coronam et dignitatem regalem Franciæ, et proventus, more solito, ad sustentationem sui status et onerum regni; et præfata consanguinea sua, serenissima Regina Franciæ, contoralis ejusdem Regis Franciæ, etiam teneat, quamdiu vixerit, statum et dignitatem Reginæ, secundum morem regni prædicti, etc. (5) MS. Corp. Chr. vii.

Quæ præmissa illustrissimus Rex Angliæ se observaturum, facturum, et impleturum, offert, dummodo per partem Regis Franciæ ista promittantur, concordentur, et fiant. Similiter, inprimis, quod immediate post obitum ejusdem consanguinei sui, et extunc deinceps, corona et regnum Franciæ, cum eorum juribus et pertinentiis universis, manebunt et erunt ipsius Henrici et hæredum suorum in perpetuum. Item, quod pro eo quod præfatus serenissimus consanguineus suus Franciæ tenetur, ut plurimum, adversa valetudine, sic quod non potest commode vacare disponendis regni negotiis, idcirco ad vitam ejusdem consanguinei sui Franciæ, facultas disponendi rempublicam regni prædicti, et exercitium, cum consilio nobilium et prudentum ejusdem regni, eidem serenissimo consanguineo obedientium, qui commodum et honorem ipsius regni dilexerint, penes ipsum Dominum Regem Henricum sint et maneant, ita ut ipsam per seipsum, et etiam per alios, quos cum consilio præfatorum nobilium ad hoc duxerit deputandos, regere possit et gubernare, secundum exigentiam justitiæ et æquitatis. Item, quod proceres, magnates, et nobiles, ac status regni prædicti, tam spirituales quam temporales, necnon civitates et notabiles [1] comitates, ac cives et burgenses villarum ejusdem regni, præfato consanguineo suo pro tempore obedientes, præstabunt juramenta quæ sequuntur:—

Oath to King Henry, to be made by the estates of France.

Inprimis, quod eidem Domino Regi Henrico, facultatem et exercitium disponendi et regendi dictam rempublicam gerenti, ac jussionibus suis humiliter et obedienter in omnibus exercitium regiminis dicti regni concernentibus, et per omnia, parebunt et intendent. Item, quod ea quæ inter præfatum consanguineum et consanguineam ejusdem Regis et ipsum Regem, cum consilio eorum [2] quos iidem consanguineus et consanguinea, et ipse Dominus Rex ad hoc duxerit adhibendos, appunctata [3] fuerint et concordata, ipsi proceres et magnates, etc., quatenus eos simul, et singulos eorum, concernere poterit, in omnibus et per omnia, bene et fideliter observabunt, et pro posse suo facient ab aliis quibuscunque observari.

[1] *communitates* in the printed texts.

[2] *quod* in the printed texts.

[3] *fuerunt* in the printed texts.

(5) MS. Corp. Chr. vii. Item, quod continue ab obitu, et post obitum, dicti consanguinei sui Franciæ, erunt ipsi fideles homines et ligei præfati Regis Henrici ac hæredum suorum, ac ipsum pro domino suo ligeo ac supremo, ac vero Rege Franciæ, absque oppositione, contradictione, seu difficultate, recipient et admittent, ac pro tali obedient; et quod præterquam dicto consanguineo nulli unquam post hæc, tanquam Regi et Regenti regni Franciæ, obedient, nisi eidem Regi Henrico et hæredibus suis. A.D. 1420.

Item, quod non erunt in consilio, auxilio, vel assensu, quod præfatus Rex Henricus perdat vitam aut membrum, seu capiatur mala captione, aut quod patiatur damnum seu diminutionem in persona, statu, honore, seu rebus; verum si quid tale contra eum moliri seu machinari noverint, illud pro posse suo impedient, et eidem Regi quam celerius [1] poterunt per seipsos, seu [2] nuncio vel litteris, intimabunt.

Assurances to be made on part of the King of France.

Item, quod præfatus serenissimus consanguineus suus Franciæ, super præmissis omnibus et singulis, ac aliis quibuscunque, inter ipsum consanguineum et præfatum Regem in hac parte concordandis, eidem Regi Henrico dabit et faciet, ac dari et fieri faciet, suas litteras patentes, suo Magno Sigillo sigillatas, nec non litteras patentes approbatorias et confirmatorias præfatæ serenissimæ Principissæ, consortis suæ, ac illustris consanguinei sui, Ducis Burgundiæ, et aliorum procerum et magnatum dicti regni, eidem consanguineo suo Franciæ nunc vel in futurum obedientium, quorum litteras in ea parte ab eodem consanguineo dictus Rex exigere voluerit, sub ita claris, apertis, et securis, modo, forma, et verbis, sicut per Consilia partium poterit advisari; necnon omnimodas rationabiles securitates quas in hac parte velit idem Rex Henricus [3] [exigere]. Et offert Dominus Henricus, quod simili modo pro parte sua dabit et faciet super eisdem suas litteras patentes, approbatorias et affirmatorias præclarissimorum fratrum suorum, et aliorum de sanguine suo regali, [4] pro eorumque et magnatum sibi obedientium, necnon omnimodas securitates rationabiles quas dictus consanguineus exigere velit in hac parte.

Assurances on part of the King of England.

The articles of peace are assented to

Duce Burgundiæ suadente, Rex Francus et Regina, contoralis ejus, necnon et magnates et proceres qui astabant eidem

[1] *poterint* in (5) MS. Corp. Chr. vii., orig., and the printed texts.

[2] *nuncios* in the printed texts.

[3] Omitted in orig. and the printed texts; supplied from (5) MS. Corp. Chr. vii.

[4] The text is apparetny defective here.

A.D. 1420. Regi, gratanter admiserunt præscriptos articulos, et eos se observaturos fideliter promiserunt. Ac proinde Rex Angliæ cœpit equitare cum exercitu versus Regem [1]Franciæ, qui perhendinavit apud Troys in Campania de Ponteys, octavo die mensis Maii, transiens per villam Sancti Dionysii, ubi et obtulit et devotiones fecit. Deinde transiit juxta fossata Parisiorum, populo civitatis inspectante, et, ut apparuit, valde gaudente; pervenitque ad pontem de Charentone, super quem turris habetur fortissima, et ex utraque parte turris est pons elevabilis et tractabilis, sic quod nullus accedere potest ad turrim, si isti pontes fuerint elevati. In hoc loco Rex dimisit Dominum Willelmum Gascoyne, cum forti manu, ad pontis custodiam, donec rediret; sicque fecit in omnibus locis in quibus tales pontes habebantur.

by the King of France. (5) MS. Corp. Chr. vii.

King Henry proceeds to meet the King of France.

Precautions taken by King Henry.

He arrives at Troyes; where the Treaty is duly ratified.

Tandem vicesimo die mensis Maii pervenit ad Troys, ubi cum summa reverentia Pontifices qui fuerunt in villa, et Cancellarius Franciæ, cum toto clero, et omnes qui aliquem gradum tenebant circa Regem Franciæ, Dux Burgundiæ, cum multis proceribus et militibus, facti sunt in obviam Domino nostro Regi, ad spatium milliarii extra civitatem. In crastino, partes convenerunt ad ecclesiam Sancti Petri, Rex, videlicet, cum quadraginta personis dominorum, militum, et armigerorum, ad istud negotium specialiter assignatorum; Ducissa quoque Clarentiæ intravit, cum Domino nostro Rege. Regina vero [2]Franca venit illuc cum Duce Burgundiæ et quadraginta personis de suo Consilio, et cum ea filia sua, Domina Katerina Ducissa de Baire, et Regina Angliæ mox futura. Obviaverunt igitur Rex et Regina in medio ipsius ecclesiæ, et ascenderunt pariter ad majus altare; ubi coram utrisque partibus recitabantur omnes articuli et appunctuationes præmissæ concordiæ; quæ, partibus consentientibus, sigillatæ fuere sigillis amborum Regum, et partes juratæ de concordia sine fraude. Quibus ita gestis, Dominus Rex et Katerina fecerunt assecurationem, fide interposita, per manus eorundem. Post hæc, Dux Burgundiæ juravit publice, quod esset obediens Domino nostro Regi, tanquam Regenti Franciæ, durante termino vitæ Regis Franci, et quod post ejus decessum, deveniret illico ligeus homo Regis nostri. Proinde mox pax proclamata fuit, primo in parte Regis Franci, in lingua Gallica, et expost in parte Regis nostri, in lingua nostra: ubi tunc recitati fuerunt articuli istius concordiæ, et publicati per totam civitatem et exercitum Anglicanum.

---

[1] *Francia* in orig., by inadvertence.

[2] *Francia* in orig.; corrected from (5) MS. Corp. Chr. vii. *Franciæ* in the printed texts.

(5) MS. Corp. Chr. vii.

A.D. 1420.

Tertio die mensis Junii, scilicet in crastino Trinitatis, Rex noster Henricus duxit in uxorem Dominam Katerinam, et assignavit sibi ministros domus suæ, valentes personas Anglicanas; nec remansit in ejus obsequio quisquam Gallicus, exceptis tribus mulierculis generosis, et duabus ancillis, quæ famularentur magistræ suæ.

King Henry marries Katherine, daughter of the King of France.

Acta sunt hæc anno gratiæ millesimo quadringentesimo vicesimo, et [1]regni Regis [2]Franciæ quadragesimo, et Regis Anglorum octavo.

Quarto-decimo die mensis Junii, facta fuit Londoniis solemnis processio, in qua et Sermo de præmissis publice dicebatur apud Crucem Sancti Pauli: ubi insuper divulgabatur, quod Sigillum Regis Angliæ confringeretur, et insculptio nova fieret in eodem, quæ nomen Regis præferret; adjecto titulo quod Rex noster in suis apicibus "Rex Angliæ," vocaretur, et "Regens," vel "Rector, Franciæ," et hæres apparens regni prædicti.

Procession at London, and Sermon at St. Paul's Cross.

A new Seal to be made.

[3]Nuptiis itaque inter Dominum Regem Angliæ et Dominam Katerinam, filiam Regis Franciæ, ut præscribitur, solemniter celebratis, et pace reformata, Rex Angliæ, utpote Rector et hæres Franciæ, se disposuit ad civitates, sibi et coronæ Franciæ rebelles, pro suis viribus [4]subjugandas. Cepit civitates de Saunz et de Botreus, per deditionem continuo sibi redditas; deinde ad civitatem fortissimam de Melone, cum suis exercitibus, se transtulit, et eandem per obsidionem fortissimam vallavit. Fuerunt namque in ipsa obsidione Reges Angliæ, et Franciæ, et Scotiæ, Ducesque Burgundiæ, Bavariæ, Clarentiæ, Bedfordiæ, et Excestriæ, Comites vero Marchiæ, Warwici, Huntyngdoniæ, de Somersede, etc.; et alii domini, barones, milites, et armigeri, genere præclari, et armis validi, quorum nomina memoriæ non occurrunt. Duravit ipsa obsidio quatuordecim hebdomadibus et quatuor diebus; videlicet a festo Sanctæ Mariæ Magdalenæ usque ad festum Omnium Sanctorum proximum sequens, non sine cotidiano pene, et valido, conflictu obsidentium cum obsessis, [5]læsione, mutilatione, et interitu plurimorum. Interierunt namque de obsidentibus, ut asseritur, plures quam mille et septingenti viri: [6]fuerat namque dicta obsidio Anglicis omnium obsidionum quas antea habuerant magis nociva. Tandem deficientibus et absumptis

King Henry subdues certain rebellious cities of France.

Siege of Melun,

and surrender thereof.

---

[1] *rex in* in orig.; corrected from (5) MS. Corp. Chr. vii. and the printed texts.

[2] *Franci* in the printed texts.

[3] *Nunciis* in the printed texts.

[4] *subjugandis* in orig. and the printed texts.

[5] *læsioni* in orig., by inadvertence.

[6] *fuerunt* in orig.; corrected from (5) MS. Corp. Chr. vii. and the printed texts.

A.D. 1420. cunctis victualibus obsessorum, [1]Regum Angliæ et Franciæ se gratiæ reddiderunt; de quibus plures quam quadringenti de valentioribus castrorum diversorum custodiæ sunt commissi, reliqui vero Regis Angliæ pietate sunt dimissi. Habita igitur de suis rebellibus tam mortifera quam gloriosa victoria, Reges prædicti, cum magna parte eorum exercitus, Parisius accesserunt, ibidem dies Natalitios et maximum Parliamentum solemniter celebraturi. (5) MS. Corp. Chr. vii.

The Kings of England and France enter Paris.

A.D. 1421. Anno Domini millesimo quadringentesimo vicesimo primo, regni vero Henrici Quinti, Regis Angliæ, hæredis et Regentis Franciæ, [2][nono], tenuit idem Rex Natale Domini Parisius, in quodam loco munitissimo ("Castrum Sancti Antonii" vocitatum, in latere ejusdem civitatis [3]situatum); ubi in civitatem poterat respicere, et rebelles eidem, si necesse fuerit, de facili cohibere; non tamen sine vigilia sui exercitus et custodia satis forti.

King Henry lodged at the Castle of Saint Antoine.

Expletis diebus Natalitiis, et solemni Parliamento ibidem, Rex Angliæ Rothomagum transiit; ibique, cum suis Normannis et Anglicis ligeis, aliud Parliamentum similiter celebravit. Disposítis dehinc sufficienti securitate et custodia, ut sibi videbatur, tam pro regno Franciæ quam Ducatu Normanniæ, Angliam properavit, et per Picardiam et Kalesiam pertransiens, in Vigilia Purificationis Beatæ Mariæ Doveryam, deinde Cantuariam, cum Regina sibi noviter nupta, [4]et parva familia, [5]pervenit. [6]Habuit itaque secum solummodo Ducem Bedfordiæ, Comitem Warwyci, Dominum Johannem Cornewayle, militem, reliquis in partibus transmarinis pro tutela perquisitorum et patriæ derelictis. Transactis quoque Cantuariæ paucis diebus, Londonias accessit; ubi a clero et populo ludicis et vario apparatu, ut decuit, cum maximo gaudio receptus fuit. Dicta quoque Regina, Dominica Prima Quadragesimæ proximo sequente, [7]præmissis equitationibus et processionibus congruis, ad Westmonasterium a Turri Londoniarum conducta,

Parliament held at Rouen.

King Henry returns to England.

Is joyfully received in London.

The Queen is crowned at Westminster.

---

[1] *regnum* in Camden's text.

[2] Omitted in orig. and (5) MS. Corp. Chr. vii.; supplied from the printed texts.

[3] *cituatum* in orig. and (5) MS. Corp. Chr. vii.: *situm* in the printed texts.

[4] This and the two following words are omitted in the printed texts.

[5] *advenit* in the printed texts.

[6] Instead of this passage, the only words in the printed texts are "*Domino Johanne Cornewayle, militе, reliquis,*" *etc.* In (5) MS. Corp. Chr. vii. the words "*Cornewayle militem*" are followed by "*et alios numero non excessivo, et de infirmioribus et impotentioribus sui exercitus reliquis,*" *etc.*

[7] *præmissa* in the printed texts.

(5) MS. Corp. Chr. vii. et ibidem ministerio Cantuariensis Archiepiscopi, et aliorum quibus competit, solemniter coronata. A.D. 1421.

The King and Queen perform a pilgrimage to various holy places.

Coronatione itaque Reginæ, cum omni solemnitate et lætitia, ut decuit, celebrata, et competenti familia eidem et ejus hospitio deputata, Rex cum Regina per diversa loca solemnia et celebria Sanctorum pertransiens, et peregrinationes suas et vota adimplens, festum Paschæ apud Leycestriam tenuit; festum vero Sancti Georgii non ipso ejus die, sed usque [1] Dominicam post Ascensionem Domini, apud castrum [2] suum de Wyndeshore tenendum more solito, prorogavit.

Parliament at London.

[3] Quo [4] quidem tempore Parliamentum, per ipsum primitus limitatum, Londoniis fuerat inceptum, et infra mensem feliciter expeditum. Nempe præter decimam a clero, et quintamdecimam a populo, Domino Regi, in suarum guerrarum sustentationem et subsidium, [5] concessas, multa alia sunt in clero et populo [6] ad Regis placitum reformata; et præcipue in Ordine Nigrorum Monachorum, illuc in maximo numero Regis edicto insimul congregato. Fuerant utique ibidem etiam sexaginta Abbates et Priores Conventuales, etiam trecenti et amplius monachi, doctores, et procuratores. Delatum namque fuerat regiæ majestati a quibusdam falsis fratribus, [7] Abbates, cum sociis, multum [8] [deviasse]; religionem monasticam a suis primævis institutionibus et observantiis fore dilapsam, et necessario per [9] eandem, et non aliter, posse reformari. Quæ quidem credibilior fuerat, eo quod major pars prælatorum ac seniorum ejusdem Ordinis defecisset, et effrænata juventus ejus tempore, successisset; unde idem Rex, cum quatuor solummodo personis valentibus, ad eosdem, in Capitulo Westmonasterii insimul [10] congregatos, satis humiliter intravit, et præmissa humili salutatione, collationem ad hoc idoneam, per Episcopum Excestriæ, Magistrum videlicet Edmundum Lacy, Sacræ Theologiæ Professorem, auditurus consedit. Post cujus terminationem ipsemet eisdem alloquebatur de pristina religione monachorum, et ob hoc

Reforms made in the Order of Black Monks, (or Benedictines).

Causes of the late lapse in the Order.

The King attends the Chapter at Westminster, and

[1] *ad Dominicam* in the printed texts.

[2] *suum* omitted in the printed texts.

[3] *Quodam* in (5) MS. Corp. Chr. vii. and orig.; corrected from the printed texts.

[4] *quidam* in orig.

[5] *conceditur* in the printed texts.

[6] *a* in orig., by inadvertence.

[7] *vel* occurs here in orig., by inadvertence: the word *Abbates* is erased in (5) MS. Corp. Chr. vii.

[8] *plusquam extiterat* in (5) MS. Corp. Chr. vii. and orig., instead of this word, as in the printed texts.

[9] *eundem* in the printed texts.

[10] *congregatis* in orig. and the printed texts.

A.D. 1421.

exhorts the monks.

suorum antecessorum et aliorum in fundatione et dotatione (5) MS. monasteriorum devotione, ac de modernorum negligentiis et Corp. Chr. indevotione. Tradiditque eisdem quosdam articulos inde [1] per vii. eosdem corrigendos; suppliciter exorans ut ad pristinam religionem se retraherent, pro ipso, et statu regni ejus et Ecclesiæ, indesinenter orarent; satis animose et corditer affirmans, [2] ut si talia agerent, seipsos nullum hostem penitus verituros, et se in eorum orationibus specialiter confidere.

Certain heads of reform in the Order, assented to.

Quibus quidem articulis, et aliis, per dictum Episcopum et alios ex parte regia approbatis, per Abbatem Sancti Albani, Sacræ Theologiæ Professorem, et alios valentiores et sapientiores dictæ congregationis, diligenter [3] discussis, [4] facta fuerat super eisdem [5] reformatio, prout tempus, status, et imbecillitas hominum, videretur permittere, per Capitulum Provinciale proximum approbandum, et per Dominum Apostolicum confirmandum. Quam qui voluerit aspicere, in Monasterio Sancti Albani, et aliis pluribus locis ejusdem religionis, poterit invenire.

Every third benefice to be presented to a clerk of Oxford or Cambridge, for a limited time.

Statutum etiam fuerat in eodem Parliamento, ad instantiam maximam Domini Regis, ut asseritur, per clerum, ut tertium [6] [beneficium] collationi seu præsentationi prælatorum et monasteriorum [7] pertinens, a modo per septennium vacaturum, conferretur alicui clerico Universitatis Oxoniæ seu Cantabrigiæ, secundum modum et formam in quodam Statuto inde plenius specificato.

Privileges granted to parts of certain counties belonging to the Crown.

Ad petitionem insuper Domini Regis, obtentum fuerat quod portio hæreditaria de [8] Comitatibus Northamtoniæ, Herfordiæ, et Estsexiæ, ipsum concernens, paribus gauderent libertatibus, aliis per Edwardum Tertium, Regem Angliæ, Ducatui de [9] Lancastria primitus concessis. Plura quoque alia fuerant statuta, quæ nostræ notitiæ non occurrunt, inter Parliamentalia Statuta plenius annotata.

The Duke of Clarence proceeds,

Præterea, Dominus Thomas, frater Regis, Dux Clarentiæ, cum exercitu Anglicano satis valido, in Franciam progreditur.

---

[1] *sibi tradit* occurs here in (5) MS. Corp. Chr. vii. and orig., by inadvertence; the word "*articulos*" is followed by "*ut expost se per eosdem* "*corrigerent*," in the printed texts.

[2] *et* in orig. and the printed texts.

[3] *discusset* in orig., by inadvertence; corrected from the printed texts.

[4] *facere* in the printed texts.

[5] *reformationem* in the printed texts.

[6] Omitted in orig.; supplied from (5) MS. Corp. Chr. vii. and the printed texts.

[7] *pertinentem*, or *pertinentium*, in (5) MS. Corp. Chr. vii. and orig., by inadvertence.

[8] *Comitibus* in the printed texts.

[9] *Lancastrie* in orig. and (5) MS. Corp. Chr. vii.: corrected from the printed texts.

(5) MS. Corp. Chr. vii.

A.D. 1421.

Regis et regni rebelles subjiciens, et eorum bona sibi et suis diripiens, pervenit ad castrum fortissimum in partibus de Meyns, "Beuforde" nominatum; ubi a duobus Scotis, per suos exploratores, seu feriarios, interceptis, relatus sibi fuerat exercitus Dolphini, ad numerum quatuor [1] millium pugnatorum, per quatuor inde leucas prope civitatem de [2] nominatam residere; unde supra modum exhilaratus, et secus quam decuit tantum principem, festinus [3] transmisit nuncios ad capitaneos sui exercitus per patriam dispersos, ut ipsum illuc sequerentur indilate. Ipse quoque Dux, cum paucis ultra numerum non supputatum, inde progrediens pervenit ad quendam fluvium et mariscum, quos cum maxima difficultate, et non sine suorum tam hominum quam equorum amissione, pertransiens, divisim et absque militari ordine incedens, in manus suorum inimicorum se injecit; a quibus ipse et alii plurimi de suis valentioribus fuerant interfecti, plurimi quoque intercepti, gravibus redemptionibus redimendi. Multi quoque plures cecidissent, nisi [4] nox eorum conflictum præpedisset. Latebant tamen suos adversarios quos occiderunt, donec per duos [5] haraldos, per ipsum ibidem interceptos et super hoc stricto juramento oneratos, [6] scrutinio facto corporum occisorum, continuo inde certificati plenius [7] extitissent. Imposuerunt dictum Ducis corpus in quodam vehiculo, ad Dolphinum, qui tunc temporis Turonis aderat, cum cæteris captivis deducendis; sed filius dicti Ducis nothus, coadunato reliquo exercitu, illud de eorum manibus viriliter eripuit, et ad suam conjugem, Ducissam, in Normanniam transmisit, in Ecclesia Christi Cantuariæ postea tumulatum. Cecideruntque ibidem Dominus de Ros et germanus ejus, Dominus Gilbertus Humfrevile, factus Comes de Kyme, et Dominus Johannes Gray, factus [8] similiter per eundem Comes de Tankervile in Normannia. Capti quoque fuerant ibidem Comes Dominus de Huntyndone, Dominus Comes de Somersede, et frater ejus, Dominus [9] Fitz-Walter, et Dominus Willelmus Bower.

with an army, to France.

He is slain.

His body is rescued, and sent to the Duchess, in Normandy.

Other nobles slain.

[10] Ceperant namque dicti Regis adversarii, in ejus absentia,

Further successes of

[1] *milia* in (5) MS. Corp. Chr. vii. and orig.; corrected from the printed texts.

[2] *de* and the hiatus are omitted in the printed texts; they occur in (5) MS. Corp. Chr. vii.

[3] *festinos* in the printed texts.

[4] *vox* in the printed texts.

[5] *haroldos* in orig. and the printed texts; corrected from (5) MS. Corp. Chr. vii.

[6] *scrutinii* in (5) MS. Corp. Chr. vii. and orig.

[7] *extiterunt* in the printed texts.

[8] *scilicet* in the printed texts.

[9] *Fyewater* in orig. and (5) MS. Corp. Chr. vii.; corrected from the printed texts.

[10] *Ceperunt* in the printed texts.

A.D. 1421. quandam civitatem munitam, primitus sibi redditam; ejus (5) MS. Corp. Chr. vii. capitaneo Anglicano, cum omnibus aliis, gladio trucidatis. De quibus victoriis elati, tantam conceperunt audaciam, ut timeretur de rebellione et redditu cæterorum superius sibi redditorum; unde supplicarunt attentius Domino Regi sui fideles et ligei, ut ad illas partes cum valida armatorum manu quantocius festinaret.

the Dauphin's supporters.

King Henry returns to France.

Rex igitur, omnibus regnum Angliæ et guerras Scotiæ concernentibus pro suo beneplacito dispositis, cum valida armatorum et arcitenentium manu, ad mille et amplius supputatis, ad partes Gallicanas rediit, mortem sui fratris et cæterorum pro suis viribus vindicaturus. Sed noluit Dolphinus cum eo confligere, licet aliter eidem suis nunciis intimasset, et majorem exercitum, ut asseritur, [1] habuisset, et eidem juramento astrinxerat, si daretur opportunitas, cum Rege nostro Angliæ voluisse confligere. Sed se in longinquis tunc partibus tenuit, et patriam undique devastavit; unde asseritur majorem suorum stipendiariorum armatorum partem ab [2] eodem recessisse, nec ei diutius militare voluisse. Rex itaque, postquam per terras per ipsum Dolphinum primitus vastatas, cum magno detrimento sui exercitus, inaniter prosecutus fuisset, civitatem de Mewz, super fluvium, et partibus de Bry, suis rebellibus plenam, cum suis exercitibus obsedit; ubi per conflictum et victualium inediam, magna ejus multitudo consumpta vel infirmata fuit, magna quoque ejus pars in Angliam rediit, denuo minime reditura.

The Dauphin declines to engage in combat.

King Henry lays siege to Meaux, and experiences great losses.

The Duke of Burgundy besieges Saint Richer.

Per idem tempus Dux Burgundiæ civitatem Sancti [3] Richarii, munitissimam, sibi et coronæ Franciæ rebellem, adjutorio Anglicorum, obsidione vallavit; sed ad ejus dotationem ex causis subsequentibus non pervenit. Nam Pikardi et Gallici, undique congregati, dictam obsidionem dissolvere nitebantur, majori armatorum super eum numero irruente. Quorum adventum paulo prius per suos exploratores præsciens, [4] tria propria tentoria combussit, et se fugere simulavit; unde ejus adversarii amplius efferati, eum persequi non desistunt: sed inter ipsum et insidias ejusdem retropositi intercepti, mille et octingenti de eisdem occisi, ac captivati, cæteris per fugam dilapsis. Sic itaque prædicta obsidione dissoluta, ipse Dux pro tanta victoria Deo gratias retulit, et suas peregrinationes et vota ob hoc promissa indilate persolvit; non enim poterat cum suo exercitu pro tunc amplius obsidere, propter

He defeats the French, and abandons the siege.

---

[1] *habuisse* in (5) MS. Corp. Chr. vii. and orig.

[2] *eo* in the printed texts.

[3] *Richardi* in the printed texts.

[4] Probably an error for "*sua*."

(5) MS. Corp. Chr. vii.

crematione suorum tentoriorum, ut præscribitur; quia magna pars sui exercitus ab eo recesserat ante conflictum, et sui adversarii, taliter provocati, super eum accrescere poterant tota die. A.D. 1421.

A.D. 1420.

The energies of the Emperor Sigismund are directed against the prevalence of heresy.

Postquam vero Christianissimus et excellentissimus Hungariæ, Boemiæ, ac Romanorum, Rex Sygismundus, ad Romanum Imperium electus, sua præsentiali sollicitudine Ecclesiam Dei cum Generali Consilio stabilisset, et verum Domini Vicarium, et successorem Petri, Martinum [1] scilicet Quintum, in eadem præfecisset, rediit ad sua regna et dominia propria, pro inimicis fidei debellandis, et hæresi Lollardorum, [2] quæ [3] tepore et manutenentia sui fratris senioris in regno Boemiæ invaluerat, pro suis viribus distrahendis. Collecta itaque armatorum maxima multitudine, universitatem et civitatem de [4] Prake, in qua ultra cæteras dicta hæresis originem sumpserat, et suas radices fixerat et dilataverat, etiam sibi rebellem, obsidione fortissima circumcinxit. Videntes igitur obsessi se tantæ potentiæ non posse resistere, summiserunt [5] totaliter ejus imperio, fatentes se fore ejus ligeos, et ejus consilio, ordinationi, et imperio, parituros, dummodo maximam partem sui exercitus, quæ totam eorum patriam devastaverat, [6] remitteret, et cum suo solo familiari exercitu cum eisdem inde amicabiliter pertractaret; eisdem victualia et dona, in signum suæ promissionis et futuræ fidelitatis, omittentes, et suos ambaciatores honorifice suscipientes; quorum promissionibus nimis credulus, et effusionem sanguinis Christiani evitare desiderans, fortissimam partem suorum exercituum remisit, et reliquo suo familiari exercitu, ut optaverant, rei exitum expectavit. Videntes igitur fallaces et falsidici tempus suis desideriis arrisisse, irruperunt etiam subito in ejus exercitum, feceruntque inde stragem maximam, antequam Imperator cæteris poterat subvenire. Tandem resumpto spiritu vivaciori, per medium illorum trina vice se ingessit, plurimos peremit, et cæteros reintrare coegit: et cum reliquo exercitu ad propria rediit, fortior denuo rediturus, et sui injuriam vindicaturus. Coadunato namque suorum Principum, Ducum, et militum, et aliorum armatorum et arcitenentium, et balistariorum, validissimo exercitu, cum Archiepiscopis Coloniensi, Magutunensi, et Treverensi, et aliis, ob hoc, exhortatione et auctoritate Apostolica cruce-signatis,

Siege of Prague.

Insidious offer made to the Emperor by the citizens.

Part of his army slaughtered in consequence.

He finally triumphs over the heretics.

---

[1] *scilicet* omitted in the printed texts.

[2] *qui* in orig. and the printed texts.

[3] *tempore* in orig.; corrected from the printed texts.

[4] *Prage* in the printed texts.

[5] *se totaliter* in the printed texts.

[6] *remittendi* in orig.; *remittendis* in (5) MS. Corp. Chr. vii.; corrected from the printed texts.

dictos hæreticos persequi non cessavit, et eosdem aut unitati fidei et Ecclesiæ revocavit, aut gladio vel ignibus tradidit devorandos. (5) MS. Corp. Chr. vii.

A.D. 1421. Birth of Prince Henry, (Henry VI.) Hoc etiam anno, Domina Katerina, Regina Angliæ, peperit filium suum primogenitum, apud castrum suum de Wyndeshore, die Sancti Nicholai Episcopi et Confessoris; et vocatum est nomen "Henricus." Susceperunt namque eum de sacro fonte Dominus Johannes Dux Bedfordiæ, ejus avunculus, et pro tunc Custos Angliæ, et Dominus Henricus, Domini Regis avunculus, Wyntoniensis Episcopus, et Domina Jakelina Ducissa Holandiæ, pro tunc in Anglia moram trahens, ministerio Domini Henrici, Cantuariensis Archiepiscopi, cum ea quæ decuit solemnitate, et lætitia [1] cunctorum præcipue Anglicorum, non sine maximis donativis, [2] ad valorem et amplius computatis.

Parliament at Westminster. Hoc insuper anno, primo die mensis Decembris, coadunatum est Parliamentum apud Westmonasterium per Dominum Regem, Domino Duce Bedfordiæ, pro tunc Custode Angliæ, eidem præsidente. Grant made by the laity. In quo fuerat una quinta-decima a laico populo Domino Regi, in suarum guerrarum subsidium, concessa, ad festum Purificationis Beatæ Virginis et Sancti Martini eidem persolvendum; sed nihil a clero ea vice, pro eo quod decima, per eundem in ultimo Parliamento conditione tali concessa, nondum fuerat plene persoluta; sub ea etiam conditione, quod prima medietas dictæ [3] quintæ-decimæ solveretur de pecunia [4] consimili, et alia tunc currente. Ordinatum etiam fuerat, quod talis moneta cum reliquo usque dictum festum Purificationis indifferenter curreret, dummodo foret argentum verum vel aurum, nec tonsione vel lotione enormiter diminutum. Ordinances as to the currency.

Hoc etiam anno, mense Aprili,[5] transfretavit Regina Angliæ in Normanniam, cum manu valida, sub conductu Domini Johannis, fratris Regis, Ducis Bedfordiæ; et Dominus Humfridus, frater ejusdem, Custos Angliæ subrogatur.

A.D. 1422. The siege of Meaux continued. Anno Domini millesimo quadringentesimo vicesimo secundo, tenuit Dominus Rex Angliæ, Regens et hæres regni Franciæ, Natale Domini, cum suo pauco Anglorum exercitu sibi relicto, in obsidione civitatis de Mews, in partibus de Brye, quam obsederat [6] a mense anno proximo præcedente. Duravit quoque eadem obsidio usque quintum diem mensis Maii proximo subsequentem; It surrenders. quo quidem die reddita fuerat civitas memorata, cum omnibus eidem pertinentibus, dispositioni et

---

[1] *et* is inserted here in orig., by inadvertence.

[2] *ad magnum valorem computatis,* in the printed texts.

[3] *quinta-decimæ* in (5) MS. Corp. Chr. vii. and orig.

[4] *conservata* in the printed texts.

[5] This took place, A.D. 1422.

[6] *per quoddam spatium anni proximi præcedentis,* in the printed texts.

(5) MS. Corp. Chr. vii.

A.D. 1422.

Disposal of the prisoners and the spoil.

gratiæ Domini Regis. Rex vero admisit ad gratiam omnes inclusos, præter Scotos, Hibernicos, et falsos Anglicos, et alios sibi antea juratos, [1] præter , de valentioribus ad Angliam [2] sub conductu Comitis Devoniæ [3] transmissis, et ibidem diversis carceribus mancipatis, gravibus, ut creditur, summis pecuniæ redimendis; salvis etiam Domino Regi [4] omnimodis armatura, victualibus, et re pretiosa, in eadem civitate repertis.

The Dauphin besieges (Cosne,) a town of the Duke of Burgundy.

Interea Dolphinus, cum Comite de Armanak et Scotis, et aliis sibi adhærentibus, et exercitu satis valido, quandam civitatem muratam Ducis Burgundiæ obsedit. Obsessi igitur, ob inopiam victualium in arto positi, miserunt eidem Duci, ac etiam Domino Regi Angliæ, hæredi et Regenti Franciæ, pro succursu; alias urbem prædictam eosdem eidem Dolphino necessario reddituros. Misit igitur Dominus Rex illuc cum suis exercitibus fratrem suum Dominum Johannem Ducem Bedfordiæ, Dominum Thomam Beuford, avunculum suum, Ducem Excestriæ, Comitem Marchiæ, Comitem Warwici, et alios Comites et Barones, et milites, quorum nomina nostræ notitiæ non occurrunt, cum dicto Duce Burgundiæ, pro dicta obsidione amovenda, et bellis cum suis adversariis committendis. Sed Dolphinus, eorum adventu per suos exploratores recognito, more solito fugit, et ejus tentoria [5] Anglicorum direptioni dereliquit.

King Henry sends a force in aid of the besieged.

The Dauphin takes to flight.

King Henry is attacked by fever and dysentery.

Rex itaque diutina intemperie, quam ex nimio et diutino labore contraxerat, interim incidit in febrem acutam, cum dysenteria vehementi, quæ in tantum ejus vires consumpserant, quod medici eidem medicinas aliquas intrinsecas apponere non audebant, sed de ejus vita penitus desperabant. Cernens igitur Dominus Rex sibi mortem proximam imminere, convocatis suis Ducibus et aliis qui adesse poterant, pro regnis tam Franciæ quam Angliæ, ac Ducatu Normanniæ, sapienter disposuit, testamentum confecit, et debita sua de suis thesauris et jocalibus superabundantibus solvenda constituit; sumptisque [6] vivificis Corporis Dominici, et aliis [7] [quæ] ad Christianum pertinent, Sacramentis, in vera pœnitentia, fide recta, spe certa, et caritate perfecta, et bona memoria, huic sæculo et suis valefaciens, animam suam suo reddidit Creatori,

His death.

---

[1] *sed de* in the printed texts.

[2] *sunt conducti* in orig. and the printed texts; corrected from (5) MS. Corp. Chr. vii.

[3] *transmissi . . . mancipati . . . redimendi*, in the printed texts.

[4] *omnimodas* in orig.

[5] *Anglorum* in the printed texts.

[6] *vivifici* in the printed texts.

[7] Omitted in orig.; supplied from (5) MS. Corp. Chr. vii. and the printed texts.

A.D. 1422. [1] penultimo die mensis Augusti, postquam regnasset novem annis, quinque mensibus, et quatuordecim diebus: sibique similem inter Christianos Reges vel Principes non reliquit; unde ejus mors, non solum regnicolis Angliæ et Franciæ, verum toti Christianitati, non [2] immerito est deflenda. (5) MS. Corp. Chr. vii.

His character and great virtues depicted.

Fuit itaque pius in animo, rarus et discretus in verbo, providus in consilio, prudens in judicio, modestus in vultu, magnanimus in actu, constans in agendis, in peregrinationibus frequens, et eleemosynis largus; Deo devotus, et Ecclesiæ prælatos et ministros promovens et honorans; belliger quoque, insignis, et fortunatus: qui in cunctis congressibus bellicis semper victoriam reportabat. In ædificiis construendis et monasteriis fundandis, magnificus, in donis munificus, inimicos fidei et Ecclesiæ super omnia persequens et impugnans.

Grief of his subjects for his death.

Hæc et ejus gesta notabilia ejus subditi animo revolventes, de tam subitanea et terribili mutatione dextræ Excelsi plurimum formidabant, ac indicibiliter condolebant; nec mirum, cum pro tam potentissimo Rege et Domino sapiente, et omnibus bonis moribus adornato, reciperent pro eorum Rege et Domino ejus filium nondum annalem, invalidum et improvidum, ad regendum tot et tanta regna et dominia sibi [3] hæreditaria pertinentia; illud "Væ," Salomonis metuentes, "[4] cujus terræ "rex puer est, etc.;" nisi Ejus bonitatis clementia subveniat, qui æque mirabilia operatur in minimis ut in magnis, cujus manus non est abbreviata quin faciat bonum, dummodo in ejus et nostris oculis, ad modum nostri Regis, humiles efficiamur et parvuli, et in nostris actibus et bonis consiliis indivisi.

Probable disadvantages of the rule of an infant sovereign.

The King of France solemnly confirms the agreement made by him with King Henry; and dies soon after.

Rex itaque Franciæ Karolus, audita morte sui generi Angliæ prænotati, post solemnes exequias et Missas in sua Capella pro ejus anima solemniter celebratas, accersito ejus edicto, suorum prælatorum et aliorum dominorum, qui concordiæ nuper [5] pridium inter regna Franciæ et Angliæ consenserant, numero copioso, fecit eandem concordiam coram ipsis perlegi, et tam suo quam illorum juramento super Corpus Dominicum et Sancta Dei Evangelia denuo confirmari. Deinde dolore et desolatione contabescens, tertio-decimo die subsequenti et ipse instabili luci [6] sæculi valefecit. Sed et

[1] Correctly, "*ultimo*;" 31st August.

[2] *merito* in orig. and the printed texts; corrected from (5) MS. Corp. Chr. vii.

[3] *hæreditarie* in the printed texts.

[4] *Eccles.* x. 16.

[5] *pᵗdiū* in orig. and in (5) MS. Corp. Chr. vii.: its meaning seems doubtful.

[6] *sæcylo* in orig., by inadvertence.

(5) MS. Corp. Chr. vii. [1]omnes pene Francigenæ, qui ejusdem Regis Angliæ [2]æquum et discretum regimen, post tam turbulentam et improbam aliorum tyrannidem, experti fuerant, planctu maximo condolebant; præcipue Parisienses et Rothomagenses, ejusdem Regis corpus in funeralibus obsequiis legitime, et oblationibus, pro eorum viribus multipliciter honorantes, offerentes auri summas maximas pro ejus corpore inter eosdem tumulando, pro eorum honore et solamino singulari. Sed hoc fieri non poterat, pro eo quod testamentarie primitus legaverat se apud Westmonasterium tumulandum; quod postmodum, ut sequitur, satis honorifice est completum. A.D. 1422. Honours paid to King Henry's memory by the French. Their desire to have him buried in their country.

Congregato interea apud Parisium et Rotomagum Magno Consilio utriusque regni, Dominoque Johanne fratre Regis, [3]Duce Bedfordiæ, et Custode Ducatus Normanniæ, ac Domino Duce Burgundiæ, Regente Regis et regni Franciæ, prout idem Rex Angliæ vivens ordinaverat, constitutis; necnon Comite Salusburiensi, Comiteque Suthfolchiæ, et aliis pluribus proceribus, ad tutelam castrorum et villarum inibi [4]relictis; reliqui pene Comites et Domini, cum Regis corpore et Regina, ad Calesiam, deinde in Angliam, redierunt, præmissis Regis thesauris et jocalibus, in Turri Londoniensi conservandis. Provisions made for the government of France. The body of King Henry is brought over to England.

Regiis quoque exequiis apud Cantuariam, et Sanctum Paulum Londoniis, et Westmonasterium, ut tantum Principem decuit, solemniter celebratis, inceptum fuerat Parliamentum auctoritate et brevibus Henrici, Regis Angliæ, Sexti, dicti Regis filii, pridem [5]summonitum apud Westmonasterium, præsidente eidem ejus avunculo Domino Humfrido, Duce Gloucestriæ, prius Custode Angliæ, commissione dicti Regis. Infra quod Parliamentum, solemnes exequiæ Regis ab omnibus statibus, ut præscribitur, fuerant celebratæ. A Parliament summoned at Westminster.

Cujus Regis mortui apparatus si scire libeat, talis erat.—Superposita namque fuerat cistæ, in qua corpus ejus habebatur, quædam imago staturæ et faciei Regis mortui simillima, chlamyde purpurea satis longa et larga, cum furrura de ermyn induta, sceptrum in una manu, et pila rotunda aurea, cum cruce infixa, in altera; corona aurea in capite, super capellum [6]regium, et sandaliis regiis in pedibus, impositis. Et taliter elevatur in curru, ut a singulis videri potuisset, ut per hoc Funeral obsequies of King Henry V.

[1] *omnis* in the printed texts.

[2] Apparently *parium* in orig.; corrected from the printed texts.

[3] *Ducis* in orig.; corrected from (5) MS. Corp. Chr. vii. and the printed texts.

[4] *relictarum* in orig. and the printed texts, by inadvertence.

[5] *summoniti* in the printed texts.

[6] *regni* in the printed texts.

A.D. 1422. mœror et dolor accresceret, et ejus amici et subditi pro ejus anima Dominum tenerius exorarent. Fertur etiam mille torticios magnos per venerabiles personas circa ejus corpus delatos, et pannos aureos et sericos pro eodem oblatos. Adducti etiam fuerant ad majus altare Westmonasterii tres dextrarii, cum eorum [1]sessoribus, ut moris est, armis Regis Angliæ et Franciæ optime armatis, et sessores inibi inde expoliati. Arma vero integre ablata, vexilla insuper, circa corpus defuncti ferebantur, arma Sancti Georgii, Angliæ, et Franciæ, ac imaginum Sanctæ Trinitatis, Sanctæ Mariæ, [2]continenter. (5) MS. Corp. Chr. vii.

He is buried in Westminster Abbey.

Sicque corpus dicti Regis usque ad Monasterium deducitur, et, ministerio prælatorum et procerum regni, inter Reges Angliæ ibidem, inter feretrum Sancti Edwardi et Capellam Sanctæ Virginis, loco quo reliquiæ ibidem fuerant reconditæ, honorifice fuerat tumulatum: ac Parliamentum continuatum.

The Duke of Gloucester is appointed, by Parliament, Protector of England.

In quo quidem Parliamento, [3]ex assensu omnium statuum ejusdem, idem Dux Defensor, seu Protector, Angliæ, in absentia sui fratris senioris, Ducis videlicet Bedfordiæ, fuerat ordinatus ac nominatus; omniaque regni officia et beneficia[4] ejus dispositioni sunt commissa.[5]

---

[1] *cessoribus* in orig.

[2] *continentur* in the printed texts.

[3] *et* in orig.; corrected from the printed texts.

[4] The words *præter beneficia* are inserted here in orig. and (5) MS. Corp. Chr. vii.; by inadvertence.

[5] Here occur the words, in page 182 of (5) MS. Corp. Chr. vii., in a hand of the 16th century,—"*Hiis* "*istis verbis finitur Historia Thomæ* "*de Walsingham*," and, in a later hand, "*qui ex hoc opere suam Histo*-"*riam compilavit.*"

APPENDIX.

APPENDIX. (A).

VARIATIONS IN THE PRINTED TEXTS OF WALSINGHAM'S "ENGLISH "HISTORY" FROM THE TEXT OF MS. ARUNDEL NO. VII.

After "suscepit," *line* 9, *page* 119, *Vol.* 1, *the following is added,* (*Camden's Edition, p.* 95):—

— et in die S. Matthiæ Apostoli coronantur Dominus Edwardus, [1]Rex Angliæ, et Domina Isabella, Regina, apud Westmonasterium, ab Episcopo Wintoniensi, commissione Archiepiscopi Cantuariensis speciali, in finibus transmarinis per biennium, exceptis septem septimanis, exulantis, propter iram Domini Regis Edwardi, nuper defuncti, quam certis de causis incurrebat. Cui quidem coronationi interfuerunt Dominus Carolus et Dominus Ludovicus de Claro Monte, fratres Regis Franciæ, Dux quoque Brabantiæ, et Comes de Fens, et cæteri magnates utriusque Franciæ et Angliæ, et Domicella de Artoys, miræ pulchritudinis juvencula.

Eodem anno, Dominus Rex reddidit Gilberto de Claro terram suam, redemptione facta pro tempore minoris ætatis.

Sed hoc anno prius, octavo Calendas Februarii, Edwardus desponsavit Isabellam, filiam Regis Franciæ, apud Bolon Super Marc; quibus nuptiis celebrandis interfuerunt quatuor Reges, videlicet, Philippus Rex Franciæ, Rex Navarræ filius Regis Franciæ, Rex Almaniæ, et Rex Siciliæ; Regina Franciæ Maria, mater Margaretæ Reginæ Angliæ, Regina Angliæ Domina Margareta, Edwardi Primi sponsa, Regina Navarræ, cum copiosa dictorum regnorum multitudine.

After "Cantia oriundus," *line* 26, *page* 190, *Vol.* 1, *a passage is added in Camden's Edition, p.* 128,—"Hoc anno, in festo Sancti Bricii —— libere concessit; *which in the text of the Arundel MS. is transferred to ll.* 18–22, *p.* 191, *Vol.* 1. *The words* "libere concessit"—*are followed in Camden's Edition* (*p.* 128) *by this passage:*—

Rex Angliæ, excitatus et inductus per matrem suam, fuit occasio matrimonii prædicti inter Davidem prædictum et sororem Regis, ac etiam per Rogerum de Mortuo Mari, ad resig-

[1] The punctuation and orthography (Camden's Edition) are corrected throughout.

nandum omne jus et vendicationem, etc. —— *Continuing as in ll. 13–26, page* 192, *Vol.* 1; *to which locality the passage (derived from Roger of Chester,) has, in the Arundel MS., been transferred.*

In p. 129 *of Camden's Edition, the following is substituted for the text of the Arundel MS., Vol.* 1, *pp.* 191, 192: "In festo "Sancti Hillarii (*p.* 191, *l.* 2) —— in die Pentecostes rediit" (*p.* 192, *l.* 28).

Anno Domini millesimo trecentesimo vicesimo octavo, et Regis Edwardi, Tertii a Conquæstu, secundo, post quindenam Sancti Michaelis tenuit Rex Parliamentum apud Sarum; in quo fecit tres Comites, scilicet Dominum Johannem de Eltham, fratrem suum, Comitem Cornubiæ, et Dominum Rogerum de Mortuo Mari, Comitem Marchiæ et Walliæ, et Pincernam Hiberniæ Comitem de Ormonde. Ad quod Parliamentum Comes Lancastriæ, Dominus de Wake, et alii quidam nobiles, non venerunt, licet prope venerant armati; de quo Rex fuit offensus: qui tamen postmodum in æstate, se gratiæ Regis, procurante Archiepiscopo, submiserunt.

Eodem anno obiit Dominus W. de Norwico, die Sancti Vincentii Martyris.

Item, eodem anno, circa festum Ascensionis, Rex Angliæ transiivit mare, fratre suo, Comite Cornubiæ, custode in regno relicto; et fecit homagium suum Regi Franciæ Carolo pro toto Ducatu Aquitaniæ et Comitatu Pontinæ; super quibusdam protestationibus, videlicet, quod non admisit homagium pro terris quas pater suus Carolus sibi vendicavit, quousque esset sibi satisfactum de damnis et expensis, etc.

Eodem anno, die Veneris post Purificationem Beatæ Mariæ, Simon Archiepiscopus Cantuariensis tenuit Concilium Provinciale Londoniis, in quo ordinavit aliqua, licet modicum ponderanda; scilicet quod in die Parasceue, et in Commemoratione Omnium Animarum, ab omni servili opere cessaretur. Item, ipse et omnes Episcopi præsentes excommunicarunt, et excommunicatos denunciarunt, omnes illos qui Walterum de Stapleton, Exoniæ Episcopum, interfecerunt, seu manus violentas quomodolibet injecerunt, et omnes qui eis operam, assensum, vel consilium, præbuerunt. Item Archiepiscopus statuit, de consensu Consilii, quod festum Conceptionis Beatæ Mariæ solemniter celebretur.

In pp. 129, 130 *of Camden's Edition the following is inserted between the context of the Arundel MS., lines* 2 *and* 3, *page* 193, *Vol.* 1.

Eodem anno, Petrus de Corbario, de Ordine Fratrum Minorum, de consilio et auxilio Ludovici, Ducis Bavariæ, in civitate Romana in Papam se fecit coronari. Deinde idem Petrus Antipapa eundem Ludovicum in Regem Romanorum, contra statutum Ecclesiæ, coronavit. Iste Antipapa Cardinales et alios officiarios, quos verus Papa solebat habere, creavit.

Anno gratiæ millesimo trecentesimo vicesimo-nono, qui est annus regni Regis Edwardi Tertii tertius, Episcopus Londoniensis fuit accusatus de eo quod quidam confingentes patrem Regis vivum, et quod ipse et alii conspiraverunt eum liberare, et ad statum regni reducere; inter quos etiam Robertus Taunton, eadem de causa, carceri mancipatur; et eadem de causa Edmundus, Comes Cantii, et propter quasdam confessiones suas, et quasdam litteras secum inventas, anno præterito decollabatur, licet nullæ illarum confessionum vel litterarum, etsi veræ essent, deberent causam tribuere morti suæ. Ista recognitio facta fuit coram Roberto Houel, Coronatore de hospitio Domini Regis, et postea coram senioribus et proceribus illius terræ, apud Wincestriam sexto-decimo die Martii, anno quarto.—Nimirum quia Edmundus Comes Cantii cognovit, quod Apostolicus sibi præceperat, sub pœna suæ maledictionis, quod vires suas et diligentiam adhiberet ad liberandum Edwardum, suum fratrem, jam olim Regem Angliæ, et quod ipse hac de causa sua sustineret expensa. Et dixit quod quidam Frater Prædicator Conventus Londoniarum ipsum convenit apud Reussington prope Londonias, et ipse dixit se excitasse dæmonium; quibus sibi pro certo affirmat, quod Edwardus, suus frater, jam olim Rex Angliæ, vivit. Et dixit, quod Archiepiscopus Eboracensis ad illum misit per quendam capellanum, Dominum Æyn, epistolam fidelitatis; et fidelitas fuit talis, quod ipse ad illum misit pro liberatione fratris sui ad quina centena hominum, et eo amplius, quantum habuit et quantum potuit reddere. Et dixit, quod Dominus Ingeram Berenger aiebat ad illum Londini, a Domino Wilhelmo de Souch, quod niteretur quantum potuit ad liberationem sui fratris. Et dixit quod Dominus Wilhelmus de Cliff ad ipsum venit in eodem mandato per tales instructiones, quod ipse sinat compositionem fieri inter Wockingum et Gildefordum; et sibi dixit se velle oppugnare civitatem Herefordensem; propterea quod ejus neptis de fratre, de familia Spencer, qui fuit in eadem civitate de Gildeford, et ipse Dominus Wilhelmus, secum confabulatus est de affinitate inter filium Ricardum, Comitem de Arundel, et ejus filiam; et dixit ulterius, quod hoc illi foret maximus honos qui unquam illi potuit accidere, et quod ipse nervos intenderet quantum potuit, ad hoc faciendum. Et dixit quod Dominus Wilhelmus de Werham, clericus fratrum suorum, et Frater Thomas de Brounfeld, forent illi qui sibi magis gratum facerent, et allicerentur ad has res supradictas faciendas. Et dixit quod Dominus Robertus de Taunton ab Archiepiscopo Eboracensi in præcepto habuit has res supradictas, et ipse dixit quod habuit in paratu quinque millia hominum ad hoc negotium supradictum complendum. Et quod idem Dominus Robertus, et duo Fratres Prædicatores qui sunt extra eorum Ordinem, quorum unus fecit se appellari "Edmundum Savage," et alter "Johannem," isti fuerunt factores istius negotii. Et dixit quod Dominus Fouke filius Waryn ad ipsum venit Westmonasterii, et ipsum rogavit, et ipsum exhortatus est, hanc rem incipere, et ad hoc faciendum; et sibi dixit quod hoc foret maximus honos qui sibi unquam contigit, et illi dixit quod sibi opem præberet quantum potuit. Et dixit quod Dominus Ingeram Berenger ad ipsum venit a Domino Johanne Peche, qui fuit de hoc consilio, et ad hoc voluit adunari quantum potuit. Et dixit quod Dominus Henricus Beamond et Dominus Thomas Rosselin ad ipsum locuti sunt Lutetiis in cubiculo Ducis Brabantiæ, quod parati erant venire in Angliam in auxilium horum prædictorum, et quod illi se instigarunt ad has res conficiendas. Et quod applicuerunt versus partes Scotiæ per Abbatem de Donalder de Maar, quod ipse foret paratus pro eorum auxilio ad tuendum partes suas quantum ille potuit; sed tempus de illorum adventu fuit transactum. Et dixit quod Dominus Richardus de Ponfret, confessor Dominæ N., ad illum venit ad Reusington in Coronationem, et postea ad Arundel, ab Archiepiscopo Eboracensi, pro his rebus supradictis. Et dixit quod monachus de Quarier et Johannes Ciminge, ejus cognatus, habuerunt similiter cymbam paratam ad deducendum fratrem suum, et ipsum a sua turri de Arundel. Et dixit quod patefecit has res supradictas E. de Mounchiver et Georgio de Percy; et dixit quod literæ quas misit ad Dominum Buges de Baiouse et Johannem Euroille, firmatæ sunt de suo sigillo, quas ipsis misit; et quod una litera scripta fuit manu uxoris suæ. Et dixit quod Ingeram Berenger, Mauchein Musarder, et Johannes Cyminge, opem tulerunt, et nervos intenderunt, ad has res faciendas. Et dixit quod Dominus Ingeram Berenger ad ipsum venit ab Arundel in cubiculum super capellam; et dixit quod Episcopus Londoniarum ipsi succurreret in liberationem sui fratris, quantum potuit. Et istas res cognovit esse veras, et sic fatetur se non vacare culpa. Ideo ponit se in misericordia.

Hoc anno, circa mediam Quadragesimæ vacavit ecclesia Sarum per mortem Magistri Rogeri de [1] Mortivans; cui eccle-

---

[1] Roger de Martival, who died A.D. 1330.

siæ Papa providit de Roberto Wivil, qui scripsit speciales literas Reginæ; viro utique competenter illiterato, et minime personato, quem si Papa vidisset, nunquam eum, ut creditur, ad tantum apicem promovisset.

Item, hoc anno mortuus fuit Johannes Episcopus Bathoniensis; et licet Magister Radulphus de Salopia fuisset concorditer electus, confirmatus, et consecratus per Simonem Cantuariensem Archiepiscopum, post tamen de Curia Romana se redemit, ut rata essent facta de ipso, non sine magna pecuniæ quantitate.

Hoc anno Papa fecit graves processus contra Ducem Bavariæ, electum Imperatorem, et contra sibi adhærentes, et, pro sustinenda guerra contra eum, omnes fructus beneficiorum vacantium per quadriennium reservavit.

In p. 131 *of Camden's Edition the following is inserted after* "tenuerunt"*—between the context of lines* 25 *and* 26, *page* 193, *Vol.* I.:—

Anno gratiæ millesimo trecentesimo tricesimo, qui est annus regni Regis Edwardi, a Conquæstu Tertii, quartus, P. Antipapa vicesimo quinto die Augusti conversus ad fidem Catholicam; et fecit confessionem suam coram Domino Papa Johanne et Cardinalibus in pleno Consistorio, et Papa ipsum absolvebat.

Hoc anno concessit Papa decimas Regi Angliæ omnium bonorum ecclesiasticorum in Anglia per quadriennium, medietate sibi retenta[n]s.

Causæ vero antedicti Comitis Marchiæ, quæ imponebantur eidem, sequuntur. Prima, quia dicebatur quod ipse fuit consentiens quod pater Regis in castro Berkley suffocatus; ex qua causa Dominus Johannes Matravers, et Dominus Thomas de Gorney senior, qui fuerunt deputati custodiæ dicti patris Regis ibidem, et quidam alii, se retraxerunt ad partes transmarinas, et propterea Dominus Simon de Bedford fuit suspensus. Secunda causa imposita fuit, quod impedivit honorem Regis et regni apud Stannop Park, ubi Scoti fugerunt; qui capi et interfici faciliter potuissent, si ipse, qui fuit major de Consilio Regis, Anglicos cum Scotis tunc congredi fecisset. Item, quod ipse, receptis viginti mille libris a Scotis, illos tunc promisit evadere, et turpem pacem postmodum inter Scotos et Regem juvenem fieri procuravit, et super hoc chartam Regis eisdem fecit fieri; et etiam illud vile matrimonium, contractum inter sororem Regis Angliæ et David, filium Roberti de Brus, fieri consuluit et procuravit. Item, quod male consumpsit totam pecuniam inventam in thesauris Regis et Domini N. [H?] de Spencer, et omnia bona regni, postquam Angliam Regina intravit; ita quod ipse et Regina abundabant, et Dominus Rex fuit egenus. Item, quod appropriavit sibi custodias et maritagia pinguia per totam Angliam, et fuit malus consiliarius Regi et Reginæ matri, et nimis secretus cum ea;—at de aliis taceamus.

In pp. 131, 132 *of Camden's Edition the following is inserted between the context of lines* 3 *and* 4, *page* 195, *Vol.* I.:—

Anno gratiæ millesimo trecentesimo tricesimo primo, qui est annus regni Regis Edwardi, a Conquæstu Tertii, quintus, tenuit Dominus Rex solemniter Natale apud Welliam, usque Epiphaniam; ubi fiebant multa mirabilia sumptuosa.

Archiepiscopus vero Cantuariensis, visitans Diœcesim Bathoniæ, tunc tenuit Natale apud Wembliscumbe, qui postmodum mandavit se velle inchoare visitationem suam in Ecclesia Exoniæ; et postmodum in civitate Exoniæ, die Lunæ proxima post festum Ascensionis Domini. Quod ne fieret, Episcopus Exoniensis appellavit; qua appellatione non obstante, dicto die Lunæ accessit idem Archiepiscopus ad civitatem Exoniæ; sed non fuit sibi permissum ecclesiam, neque claustrum, intrare, armata multitudine resistente.

Hoc anno, circa festum Nativitatis Beatæ Mariæ, fuit Consilium Provinciale Londini congregatum; sed, propter discordiam inter Archiepiscopum et suos Suffraganeos, sine effectu aliquo terminatum.

Item, Parliamentum tunc ibidem sine aliqua utili expeditione finitur. Rex tamen habuit quintam-decimam a populo, et decimam a civibus et burgensibus, sibi per unum annum concessum.

Eodem anno, quidam maligni, fulti quorundam magnatum præsidio, Regis adolescentiam spernentes, et regnum perturbare intendentes, in tantam turbam creverunt, nemora et saltus occupaverunt, ita quod toto regno terrori essent. Rex militarem manum congregans, et contra impios viriliter agens, quosdam captos carceribus intrusit, quosdam excapitavit, et regni perturbatio quievit.

In p. 132 *of Camden's Edition, there are inserted before the words* "Rex Angliæ cum militia, etc.," *in line* 36, *page* 195, *Vol.* 1., *the words*:—

Anno gratiæ millesimo trecentesimo tricesimo secundo, qui est annus regni Regis Edwardi, a Conquæstu Tertii, sextus,—

In pp. 132, 133, *of Camden's Edition, the following is inserted after* "interfectis"—*between the context of lines* 20 *and* 21, *page* 196, *Vol.* I.:—

Numerus vero occisorum et fugatorum, per æstimationem, se extendebant ad sexaginta millia.

Facta igitur voluntate Regis de his qui fuerant in villa et castro, et relicta custodia nomine suo in ipsis, quia dixit illa sua esse jure hæreditario, et ex conquæstu antecessorum suorum, dimisit Edwardum de Baliol, cum aliis nobilibus qui secum erant, ad custodiam totius regni Scotiæ, et ipsemet Rex Angliæ, cum modica familia, loca devota Angliæ, ad quæ sua devotio eum duxit, peregre est profectus. Prælati vero totius regni Scotiæ in Franciam fugerunt, et aliqui ad Summum Pontificem, de eorum infortunio adjutorium et remedium requirentes. Sed uniusque suo desiderio sunt frustrati,

Hoc anno, parum ante festum Sancti Michaelis, vacavit Ecclesia Dunelmiæ per mortem Domini Ludovici de Bellomonte, de cujus successore infra proximo anno patet.

Anno gratiæ millessimo trecentesimo tricesimo tertio, qui est annus regni Regis Edwardi, Tertii a Conquæstu, septimus, circa festum Sancti Calixti Papæ, vacavit Ecclesia Cantuariensis per mortem Magistri Simonis de Mepham, qui septimo Calendas Novembris Cantuariæ est sepultus; in cujus locum, Capitulum Cantuariense Magistrum Johannem Stretford, Wintoniensem, elegit Episcopum. Sciverat enim quod Dominus Rex scripsit Summo Pontifici, et ipse fuit bene in gratia Papæ. Cui Papa providit de dicto Archiepiscopatu primo die Decembris, non virtute postulationis Capituli Cantuariensis, sed proprio suo motu.

Eodem anno, primo die Decembris transtulit Papa Magistrum Adam de Orelton de Ecclesia Wigorniæ ad Ecclesiam Wintoniæ, ad preces Regis Franciæ. Cujus translationem Dominus Rex Angliæ non habebat acceptam, imponens sibi quod tunc ipse fuit nuncius ipsius Regis Angliæ ad Regem Franciæ, et quod ipse plus placuit Regi Franciæ, quam Regi Angliæ negotia utilia procuravit; et quod idem Rex Franciæ scripsit Papæ pro ipso ad Ecclesiam Wintoniensem transferendo. Item, ex eo Rex Angliæ fuit magis offensus, quod ipse pro alio Domino Papæ scripsit pro Episcopatu eodem, sibique visum fuerat, quod preces suæ pro Episcopatibus et dignitatibus in Anglia citius audiri debent quam preces Regis Franciæ supradicti. Ideo retinuit Dominus Rex temporalia Episcopatus Wintoniensis in manibus suis usque ad diem Veneris post Exaltationem Sanctæ Crucis; quo die, Archiepiscopus et cæteri Episcopi in Parliamento Londoniis rogaverunt pro ipso, ita quod mandavit sua temporalia sibi reddi.

Hoc anno, cito post festum Sancti Michaelis, Capitulum Dunelmensis ecclesiæ elegit unum monachum ejusdem ecclesiæ, nomine "Richardum de Bury," qui cito postmodum per Archiepiscopum Eboracensis ecclesiæ fuerat confirmatus, et ante festum Natalis Domini in ecclesia Eboracensi solemniter consecratus; non obstante fama per totam Angliam volante, quod contra Regis voluntatem erat promovendus. Item, Papa commendavit ipsum Episcopatum Domino Richardo de Bury, clerico dicti Domini Regis, ad preces ipsius Domini Regis; quam famam rei exitus postmodum comprobavit. Nam idem Dominus Richardus, cito post festum Natalis Domini, obtentis litteris Apostolicis super sua provisione, se fecit, auctoritate Apostolica, in Monasterio de Chertsey per Dominum Wintoniensem Episcopum consecrari; et a Domino Rege obtinuit sibi temporalia ipsius Episcopatus integra liberari, quod prius dicto monacho facere denegavit. Quo viso et intellecto, idem monachus electus et consecratus ad claustrum, sine Episcopatu Episcopus, est reversus, et cito postea expiravit.

Hoc anno, Dominus Edwardus de Baliol, Rex Scotiæ, tenuit Parliamentum cito post festum Sancti Michaelis; ad quod venerunt nobiles regni Angliæ terras et possessiones ibidem habentes; et, finito Parliamento, sunt in pace reversi.

Hoc anno, tenuit Rex Angliæ Nativitatem Domini apud Wallingforde, cum Regina peregrinante, et, finitis festis, dimisit eam apud Woodstock, ad pariendum; et ipse, post Purificationem Beatæ Mariæ, transtulit se versus Eboracum, ad tenendum Parliamentum ibidem; quod in die Lunæ in secunda hebdomada Quadragesimæ inchoavit. Ad quod Parliamentum vocatus fuit Edwardus, Rex Scotiæ; sed non venit, propter insidias inimicorum suorum, in insulis juxta Scotos latitantibus; propter quod misit excusatores solemnes, scilicet Dominos N. [H?] de Bello Monte et W. de Monte Acuto, et quosdam alios milites seu barones. Hoc anno, Rex, etc.

In p. 134 of Camden's Edition, the following is inserted between the context of lines 9 and 10, page 197, Vol. I.:—

Hoc anno vocavit Rex Angliæ prælatos et magnates, quod infra sex dies post Translationem Sancti Thomæ venirent ad eum apud Notingham, pro consilio et aliis tractatibus habendis ibidem; et tunc ordinavit Parliamentum Londoniis, et Archiepiscopus convocavit clerum ibidem ad Sanctum Paulum die Lunæ post festum Exaltationis Sanctæ Crucis. Et quia nova venerunt ad Parliamentum, quod Scoti omnes insurrexerunt et ceperunt Dominum Richardum Talebot et sex alios milites, et multos pedites occiderunt, Rex promisit se iturum versus Scotos, pro Scotorum malitia refrænanda. Populus concessit sibi decimum-quintum denarium de temporalibus, et de civitatibus et burgis decimum denarium; et clerus concessit unam decimam. In dicto Parliamento, Dominus Rex concessit quod iret in Terram Sanctam propriis sumptibus, sed certum tempus inchoandi iter non expressit. Sed ordinavit mittere Archiepiscopum Cantuariensem ad Papam et ad Regem Franciæ, ut possent de tempore concordari; ita quod illi duo Reges possent, cum suis potentiis, simul arripere dictum iter.

Anno gratiæ millesimo trecentesimo tricesimo quarto, qui est annus regni Regis Edwardi, a Conquæstu Tertii, octavus, Johannes Archiepiscopus Cantuariensis in festo Sancti Dionysii intravit ecclesiam suam Cantuariæ, et solemne convivium more solito celebravit; et in festo Apostolorum Simonis et Judæ transivit mare versus Regem Franciæ, cum aliis nunciis, sicut prius fuerat ordinatum.

Hoc anno, circa festum Sancti Martini, Dominus Edwardus Le Boun fuit submersus in Marchia Scotiæ, dum voluit liberari domicellum suum, fugantem prædam animalium; ita quod neuter evasit.

Item, hoc anno, in nocte Sancti Clementis, per nimiam inundationem maris per totum regnum Angliæ, et maxime in Thamisia, fuerunt rupti muri maritimi, et animalia infinita submersa; et terræ fructiferæ in salsuginem sunt conversæ, adeo quod ad fertilitatem solitam per multa tempora non speratur posse redire.

Item, hoc anno, quarto die Decembris, obiit Johannes Papa Vicesimus-secundus, in Palatio suo Annivoniæ, et in ecclesia Beatæ Mariæ, eidem palatio contigua, est sepultus; in qua ipse fuit Episcopus ante Cardinalatus honorem. Vacavit Sedes Apostolica per quindecim dies.

Rex Angliæ tenuit festum Natalis Domini apud Rokesburgh; et vicesimo die mensis Decembris fuit electus in Papam Frater Jacobus, Titulo Sanctæ Priscæ Presbyter Cardinalis, qui fuit monachus Ordinis Cisterciencis, et Magister in Theologia, de Comitatu Sluxensi, juxta partes Tholosanas, oriundus; et die Dominica post Epiphaniam tunc sequente, fuit coronatus apud Fratres Prædicatores Avinioni.

Archiepiscopus Cantuariensis rediit circa Epiphaniam, et, statim post Purificationem, ecclesiam, civitatem, et Diœcesim, suas Cantuariæ visitavit.

Et cito post Epiphaniam, Rex Franciæ misit nuncios Regi Angliæ, scilicet, Episcopum Abricensem et quendam, pro pace Scotorum; qui usque in diem Lunæ Mediæ Quadragesimæ in Angliam expectarunt; et tunc apud Notingham concessæ fuerunt treugæ usque ad festum Sancti Johannis proxime tunc futurum, ut interim fieret Parliamentum super illis et aliis tangentibus statum regni.

Between lines 28 *and* 20, *page* 197, *Vol.* I., *and instead of the words* "Hoc anno," *the following is inserted in Camden's Edition, page* 135 :—

Anno gratiæ millesimo trecentesimo tricesimo [1] quinto, qui est annus regni Regis Edwardi, a Conquæstu Tertii nonus,—

In p. 135 *of Camden's Edition, the following is inserted after* "duxit," *between lines* 14 *and* 15, *page* 198, *Vol.* I. :—

In hoc Parliamento apud Londonias statutum fuit, quod nulla lana crescens in Anglia exeat, sed quod ex ea fierent panni in Anglia; et quod omnes operatores pannorum, undecunque in Angliam venientes, reciperentur; et quod loca opportuna assignarentur eisdem, cum multis libertatibus et privilegiis, et quod haberent vadia Regis quousque commode de sua arte lucrari possent. Item statutum fuit, quod nullus uteretur panno extra Angliam operato, et in posterum deferendo, Rege, Regina, et eorum liberis, duntaxat exceptis. Item, quod nullus uteretur pellibus transmarinis, nisi haberet in redditibus centum libras; quorum Statut[or]um nullus sequebatur effectus, nec aliquis ea servari curavit.

In p. 136 *of Camden's Edition, the following is inserted after* "gratia," *between lines* 12, *and* 13, *page* 200, *Vol.* I. :—

Et sic mediantibus nunciis Papæ et Regis Franciæ, multi tractatus pacis inutiles habebantur, et multæ treugæ ex parte Scotorum, subdole agentium, concessæ fuerunt; sed nihil efficaciter expeditum, quia, illis pendentibus, Comitem de Arcell interfecerunt. Rex autem non permisit Johannem Archiepiscopum Cantuariensem ab ipso longe distari.

Anno gratiæ millesimo tricentesimo tricesimo [2] sexto, qui est annus regni Regis Edwardi, a Conquæstu Tertii, decimus, habuit Rex decimam a burgensibus, quindecimam ab aliis, decimam a clero; et circa Pentecosten habuit Parliamentum Northamptoniæ; ubi dimisit prælatos et alios tractare, et ipse secrete equitavit versus Scotiam, cum paucis admodum, usque Berewike; et inde, assumptis secum paucis armatis, equitavit ad villam Sancti Johannis, ubi invenit suos, qui de suo stupebant et mirabantur adventu; et ibi dictam villam fecit muniri fossatis et muris, et suos Comites misit cum Rege Scotiæ per patriam, si possent invenire Scotos resistentes; sed nulli audebant eos expectare, sed per montes, paludes, et nemora, latitabant.

---

[1] This date is manifestly wrong; "*septimo*" would be the correct reading.

[2] Correctly, "*octavo*."

Hoc anno, Dominus Rex in singulis Ecclesiis Cathedralibus fecit capi totam pecuniam collectam et repositam, in subsidium Terræ Sanctæ. Item, hoc anno Papa revocavit sexennalem concessam in subsidium Terræ Sanctæ, pro eo quod Rex Franciæ versus Terram Sanctam minus distulit iter suum, et voluit quod solutum redderetur; sed in Anglia nihil fuit redditum, quia fuit per clerum Regi concessum.

After line 12, *page* 200, *Vol.* I., *the texts of the Arundel MS. and the printed Editions, with the exception of merely verbal variations, correspond, down to the end of the work.*

APPENDIX. (B).

PASSAGES IN THE MANUSCRIPT BIBL. REG. 13 E. IX. WHICH HAVE BEEN OMITTED IN THE COMPILATION OF WALSINGHAM'S "ENGLISH "HISTORY," MS. ARUNDEL, No. VII.

After "migrasse," *line* 23, *page* 13, *Vol.* I.

Rex Francorum ducit Uxorem.

fol. 178 a. Eodem anno Philippus, Rex Francorum, defuncta prima uxore sua, filia Regis Arragonum, secundam accepit, Mariam nomine, sororem Ducis Brabantiæ.

Moritur Rex Navarriæ.

Eodem tempore, Henricus, Navarrorum Rex, moritur, unica filia hærede relicta. Cujus uxor Regina postea nupsit Edmundo, germano Edwardi, Regis Angliæ; qui de ea tres filios procreavit, primogenitum, Thomam Comitem Lancastriæ, secundum, Henricum de Lancastria, tertium vero, "Johannem" dictum.

After "honoratum," *line* 4, *page* 14, *Vol.* I.

fol. 178 b. Walterus de Mertona, quondam Regis Henrici Cancellarius, hoc anno Episcopus fit Roffensis.

After "interfecit," *line* 10, *page* 15, *Vol.* I.

Obitus Episcopi Herefordensis.

fol. 178 b. Hoc anno obiit Johannes de Bretton, Herefordensis Episcopus, qui, admodum peritus in juribus Anglicanis, librum scripsit perutilem de eisdem. Cui successit Magister Thomas de Cantilupo, Doctor in Sacra Theologia, vir nobilis genere, sed multo moribus melior, animique virtute.

After "mortuus est," *line* 36, *page* 19, *Vol.* I.

fol. 180 a. Frater Johannes de Derlingtona, quondam Confessor Regis Henrici, ex collatione Papali efficitur Archiepiscopus Dublinensis; qui nondum a collectione decimarum, per Summum

Pontificem sibi imposita, totaliter expeditus, per annos aliquot in Anglia moram traxit.

After " transferuntur," *line* 5, *page* 26, *Vol.* I.

Antonius Bekko Episcopus.

Hoc anno, defuncto Roberto De Insula, Dunelmensi Episcopo, fol. 181 b.
Antonius de Bekko igitur eligitur in successorem, et ab Archiepiscopo Eboracensi consecratur.

After " summam," *line* 28, *page* 26, *Vol.* I.

Frater Johannes, Dublinensis Archiepiscopus, per tempus fol. 181 b.
istud, cum versus Ecclesiam iter arripuisset, correptus infirmitate gravi, ultimam diem clausit; cujus corpus in Domo Fratrum Prædicatorum Londoniis est humatum.

After " coronari," *line* 2, *page* 28, *Vol.* I.

—— in Regem Siciliorum. fol. 182 a.

Hoc anno obiit Willelmus Wykewane, Eboracensis Archiepiscopus, in Galliis, apud Pontiniacum; cui successit Johannes Romanus, Sacræ Theologiæ Doctor eximius, in Romana Curia consecratus.

After " non deesse," *line* 26, *page* 29, *Vol.* I.

Rex Angliæ transit in Arragoniam. fol. 182 b.

Eodem anno Rex Angliæ profectus est in [1] Arragoniam, ut consanguineum suum, Karolum, filium Karoli, quondam Regis Siciliæ, ab Alfonso, Rege Arragoniæ, detentum in carcere, liberaret.

After " gravi multa," *line* 20, *page* 31, *Vol.* I.

Statuta Westmonasterii Tertia. fol. 183 a.

Hoc anno tenuit Rex Parliamentum Londoniis; in quo edita sunt Statuta quæ dicuntur " Westmonasterii Tertia." In quo etiam Parliamento, pro expulsione Judæorum, concessa est Regi a populo quinta-decima pars bonorum.

After " liberatis," *line* 14, *page* 53, *Vol.* I.

Obiit Gilbertus, Comes Gloverniæ. fol. 187 b.

Hoc anno Gilbertus, Comes Gloverniæ, dies suos clausit, relictis ex uxore sua, Johanna, filiabus tribus, et filio unico minoris ætatis, nomine Gilberto.

Willelmus etiam de Walentiis, Comes Penbrochiæ, moritur, et in ecclesia monachorum Westmonasterii sepelitur. Cui successit in Comitatu filius suus Aymerus.

---

[1] Apparently writted *Arroganiam* in orig., but indistinct.

After "frustratus," *line* 5, *page* 55, *Vol.* I.

fol. 188 a. *Occiditur Comes Holondiæ.*

Florentius, Comes Holondiæ, per hoc tempus, qui filium suum Regi Angliæ nutriendum tradidit, cui etiam Rex filiam suam Elizabeth connubio jungere disponebat, quemdam spurium volens hæredem substituere, a propria gente necatur.

After "reunitum," *line* 19, *page* 62, *Vol.* I.

fol. 189 b. *Obiit Episcopus Sarum.*

Sub hoc tempore obiit Nicholaus de Longa Spata, Sarisburiensis Episcopus; cui successit Simon de Gandavo, vir magnæ sapientiæ et eximiæ sanctitatis.

fol. 193 a. *After* "transfertur," *line* 11, *page* 77, *Vol.* I.

[1] Hoc anno obierunt duo Comites, Humfridus Comes Herefordiæ et Estsexiæ, et Willelmus de Bello Campo, Comes Warwici.

After "processit," *line* 29, *page* 79, *Vol.* I.

fol. 193 b. *Rex venit ad Sanctum Albanum.*

Priusquam Rex iter istud arripuisset, venit personaliter ad Sanctum Albanum, comitantibus eum Episcopo Norwicensi et Comite de Saveya, cum multis aliis; ubi, in Die Animarum, audita Missa solemni de Beato Martyre, cui totus Conventus interfuit solemniter revestitus, prostravit se sub Martyre, protensam faciens devotionem.

Deinde erigens se, coram omni populo talia loquebatur:— "Idcirco præsentem Martyrem visitavi, ut ejus ope protegar "ab insidiis adversariorum meorum, Scotorum videlicet, con- "tra quos me modo oportet bellum instaurare. Sed et ab "isto sacro Conventu, et omni populo, precor instantius devo- "tionibus et orationibus adjuvari."

Mox concessum fuit Regi et Reginæ, Abbate jubente, et toto Conventu approbante, ut una Missa cotidie de Sancto Albano celebraretur, præcipienda vicissim de fratre in fratrem; ad quam secunda Collecta foret pro Rege, quæ sic incipit,— "Deus, in cujus manu." Quæ Collecta etiam foret habenda in Missa Majori et Missa Virginis gloriosæ.

After "orationes," *line* 7, *page* 80, *Vol.* I.

fol. 194 a. *Regina venit ad Sanctum Albanum.*

Eo tempore Regina accessit ad Monasterium Sancti Albani, et obtulit Martyri duas pallas auro textas. Ubi perhendinavit per tres hebdomadas cum familia magna nimis.

---

[1] Written in the margin of folio 193 a., in, apparently, a somewhat later hand.

Ante recessum suum, ingressa Capitulum, suscepit beneficium fraternitatis, sive sororitatis, cum maxima devotione.

After "nesciebatur," *line* 11, *page* 80, *Vol.* I.

Hoc anno obiit Henricus, Archiepiscopus Eboracensis. Cui successit Thomas de Colebrugge, Doctor in Theologia. fol. 194 a.

After "factum est," *line* 18, *page* 84, *Vol.* I.

Rex vero in Angliam est regressus. fol. 195 a.

After "inglorius," *line* 3, *page* 99, *Vol.* I.

Karolus, Comes Valesii, cum Frederico, occupatore Siciliæ, tractatu sine omni effectu habito, in Gallias rediit isto anno. fol. 198 a.

After "custodiam," *line* 7, *page* 99, *Vol.* I.

Obitus Comitis Herefordiæ. fol. 198 a.

Hoc anno obiit Humfridus de Boun, Comes Herefordiæ; cui successit filius suus, Humfridus; qui postea duxit Elizabeth, Regis filiam, Comitissam Holandiæ, marito suo primo orbatam.

After "unus solus," *line* 18, *page* 100, *Vol.* I.

De Terris Comitis Marescalli. fol. 198 b.

Comes Marescalli, fratri suo Johanni offensus, captans Regis benevolentiam, omnes terras suas Regi donavit; ita ut ei, adjectis mille libratis terrarum, redonarentur ad vitam.

After "transferri," *line* 16, *page* 106, *Vol.* I.

Hoc anno obiit Magister Thomas de Colebrugge, Archiepiscopus Eboracensis; cui successit Willelmus de Grenefeld, Doctor in utroque Jure, Canonico et Civili. fol. 200 a.

After "diversa loca," *line* 15, *page* 113, *Vol.* I.

Eo tempore obiit Dominus Oliverus, Præsul Lincolniæ. fol. 201 b.

After "potuerunt," *line* 8, *page* 114, *Vol.* I.

Captio et Mors [1] *Willelmi Waleys.* fol. 201 b.

Eo tempore quidam miles de Scotia, Willelmus Waleys, prædo et homicida, ac proditor Regis Angliæ, captus est ac transmissus Londonias; ubi suspensus et truncatus est. Cujus caput juxta caput fratris sui Willelmi, super Pontem Londoniæ, est affixum.

After "concederetur," *line* 23, *page* 120, *Vol.* I.

Eodem anno obiit Dominus Thomas de Buctone, Exoniensis Episcopus. fol. 203 a.

---

[1] An error for "*Johannis,*" John, the brother of William Wallace; whose execution has been previously mentioned in Bibl. Reg. 13 E. ix.

After "sunt finita," *line* 7, *page* 122, *Vol.* I.

fol. 203 b. *Nuptiæ inter Anglos et Hibernos.*

Hoc anno, in festo Sancti Michaelis, Gilbertus, Comes Gloucestriæ, filiam Comitis de Woluestere, de Hibernia, desponsavit; et Johannes, filius Comitis de Woluestere, sororem Comitis Gloucestriæ duxit in crastino, apud Waltham.

Before "Hoc anno," *line* 1, *page* 124, *Vol.* I.

fol. 204 a. *Eclipsis Solis.*

Hoc anno facta est solis eclipsis circa horam vespertinam, septimo-decimo Kalendas Octobris.

After "patris sui," *line* 3, *page* 124, *Vol.* I.

fol. 204 a. *Obitus Episcopi Batoniensis.*

Hoc anno obiit Dominus Walterus de Haselschaghe, Batoniensis et Wellensis Episcopus; cui per electionem Dominus Johannes de [1]Drokelesforde electus apud Bathoniam, Domini Regis Sub-Thesaurarius.

After "spoliatus," *line* 22, *page* 146, *Vol.* I.

fol. 209 a. *Provisio de Episcopatu Dunelmensi.*

Hoc anno Papa providit Ecclesiæ Dunelmensi de Domino Lodowico de Bello Monte; qui, licet fuit nobilis genere, fuit tamen mediocriter litteratus, et claudus utroque pede, sicut multi Francigenæ. Quem si Papa vidisset, forsitan non creasset.

After "exordium," *line* 14, *page* 153, *Vol.* I.

fol. 210 b. *Novi Episcopi.*

Isto anno venerunt in Angliam a Romana Curia Magister Thomas de Cobham, quondam [2]Cantuariensis, electus per Dominum Papam in Wygorniensem; et Magister Adam de Orletone in Herefordensem, creati Episcopi.

After "destiterunt," *line* 24, *page* 160, *Vol.* 1.

fol. 212 b. *De malitia Roberti Walkefare, Militis.*

Per idem tempus, miles quidam de Northfolchia, dictus "Robertus Walkfare," promptus ad scelera, stipatus caterva satellitum dæmonicorum, Sancti Albani subintravit Monasterium, Cameram Abbatis suscipiens pro hospitio suo, compliciumque suorum. Oderat enim Abbatem longo tempore; propter Priorem de Bynham, quem injuste fovit contra Abbatem suum, et rebellem esse fecerat suo nequam consilio, et ecclesiæ

---

[1] Properly, *Drokenesforde*.

[2] This is apparently the meaning of *Cant*^{o}.

de Bynham manifestum dilapidatorem: quem, propter tales causas, Abbas Sancti Albani privaverat, et custodiæ mancipaverat carcerali.

Hic ergo inveteratum odium effutire gestiens, nostrum Monasterium, prout præfertur, ceperat pro hospitio, studens ubi damnum posset inferre in recessu suo. Considerans itaque quod in secretiori camera quædam loci jocalia servabantur, seris et repagulis diruptis ferreis ostiorum, interiora cameræ furtive cum suis ingreditur; et loricas ferreas et alia arma Abbatis, quibus servitium suum pro Baronia sua in werra Regis faceret, asportavit. Qui, cum suis omnibus, præter illos qui de tanto publice pœnituere facinore, ultore Beato Martyre, fecit miserabilem vitæ finem.

After "regressi," *line* 3, *page* 167, *Vol.* I.

Obiit Episcopus Coventrensis. fol. 214 a.

Hoc anno obiit Episcopus Coventrensis, Walterus de Langetone; et provisum fuit, ad preces Regis, Domino Rogero de Northburgh, clerico Regis, per Papam, virtute reservationis prius factæ per Papam.

Before "Missi sunt," *line* 1, *page* 175, *Vol.* I.

[1] *Obiit Eymerus, Comes Penbrok.* fol. 216 a.

Circa tempus istud, missus est ad Regem Franciæ Dominus Aymerus, Comes Penbrochiæ, ad tractandum de pace prælocuta; qui in ultramarinis, in quadam villa juxta Sanctum Richerum, inopinato languore detentus, inter brachia domesticorum subito expiravit.

After "consecutus est," *line* 11, *page* 177, *Vol.* I.

Obiit Northwycensis Episcopus. fol. 216 b.

Sub hiis diebus obiit Episcopus Northwycensis, monachus, in Cancia, de Francia revertendo. Cui loco monachi Northwycenses Magistrum Robertum de Baldok, Regis Cancellarium et Archidiaconum Midelsexiæ, elegerunt. Sed Papa, prius facta inde reservatione, cassata electione præfata, providit eidem ecclesiæ de Domino Willelmo Aermiyne, ad preces Isabellæ Reginæ Angliæ; quia fuit nuncius illo anno sæpius inter Regem Angliæ et Reginam.

Provisio Karleolensis.

Item, Papa providit Magistro Johanni de Ros de Episcopatu Karleolensi.

---

[1] *Obitus* in orig., by inadvertence.

After "voluntatem," *line* 21, *page* 188, *Vol.* I.

fol. 219 b. *Insania Villanorum de Sancto Albano.*

De Sancto Albano villani, per idem tempus, contra suos dominos surrexerunt, et obsidentes Abbathiam, diversas libertates contra fas extorserunt; ut in Gestis Abbatis Hugonis plenius continetur.

Hoc anno fuit Magister Jacobus de Berkley concorditer electus in Episcopum [1] [Exoniensem], in Vigilia Sancti Nicholai, et Dominica Mediæ Quadragesimæ fuit Cantuariæ consecratus.

After "partes suas," *line* 11, *page* 189, *Vol.* I.

fol. 219 b. Hoc anno obiit Jacobus, Exoniensis Episcopus, cui successit per provisionem Johannes de Grandissono; quamvis idem Jacobus fuisset concorditer electus ibidem.

After "Rege suo," *lines* 2, 3, *page* 190, *Vol.* I.

fol. 220 a. Item, Thomas Rondulf obiit, Comes Moraviæ.

After "oriundus," *line* 26, *page* 190, *Vol.* I.

fol. 220 a. Eodem tempore obiit Magister Thomas Cobham, Episcopus Wygorniæ; cui successit, per provisionem Papæ, Adam, Episcopus Herefordiæ, tunc præsens in Curia pro negotiis Regis Angliæ. Et mox Papa providit Ecclesiæ Herefordiæ de Magistro Thoma de Cherletone, in Curia tunc præsente.

In Bibl. Reg. 13 *E. ix. the following matter is substituted for the context between the words* "In festo," *line* 1, *page* 191, *and* "Anno gratiæ," *line* 18, *page* 221, *Vol.* I.

fol. 221 a. Anno gratiæ millesimo trecentesimo vicesimo octavo, qui est annus regni Regis Edwardi, a Conquæstu Tertii, secundus, tenuit Rex Natale Londoniis, cum matre sua et multis nobilibus regni sui.

De Concilio Provinciali.

Eodem anno, die Veneris post Purificationem Beatæ Mariæ, Simon, Archiepiscopus Cantuariensis, tenuit Consilium Provinciale Londoniis: in quo ordinavit quod in Die Parasceues et in Die Commemorationis Animarum ab omni servili opere cessaretur. Item, ipse et omnes præsentes Episcopi excommunicaverunt, et excommunicatos denunciaverunt, omnes illos qui Walterum de Stapultone, Episcopum Exoniæ, interfecerunt, seu in eum manus violentas quomodolibet injecerunt;

[1] Omitted in the MS.

et omnes qui eis opem, assensum, vel consilium, præbuerunt. Item, Archiepiscopus statuit, de consensu Consilii, quod festum Conceptionis Beatæ Mariæ principaliter celebretur.

Rex transit mare.

Eodem anno, circa Festum Ascensionis, Rex Angliæ transivit mare, fratre suo, Comite Cornubiæ, Custode regni relicto; et fecit homagium suum Regi Franciæ pro toto Ducatu Aquitanniæ et Comitatu Pontinæ; super quibusdam protestationibus. Quod homagium recepit Rex Franciæ, sub aliis protestationibus; videlicet, quod non admisit homagium pro terris quas pater suus Karolus, ut præmittitur, equitavit, quousque esset sibi satisfactum pro damnis et expensis.

Parliamentum Sarum.

Eodem anno, circa Festum Sancti Michaelis, tenuit Rex Parliamentum Sarum; in quo fecit tres Comites, scilicet Dominum Johannem de Eltham, fratrem suum, Comitem Cornubiæ, et Dominum Rogerum de Mortuo Mari, Comitem Marchiæ Walliæ, et Pincernam Hiberniæ, Comitem de Ormund.

Ad hoc Parliamentum Comes Lancastriæ, et Dominus De Wake, et multi alii, non venerunt, licet prope venissent armati; unde Rex juvenis multum fuit offensus. Hii tamen postmodum, procurante Archiepiscopo, se gratiæ regiæ submiserunt.

Annalis Conclusio.

Transiit annus iste frugifer satis, et fructifer; Ecclesiæ Sanctæ pacificus; regno honorabilis, et tamen molestus et suspiciosus, propter dissensiones inter Regem et proceres, quæ parvo tempore duraverunt; Franciæ et Scotiæ pacificus et quietus.

Anno gratiæ millesimo trecentesimo vicesimo nono, qui est annus regni Regis Edwardi, a Conquæstu Tertii, tertius, tenuit Rex Natale Walyngfordiæ; cui festo interfuit mater sua et plures nobiles de exteris regionibus, in magna gloria et apparatu.

Nuptiæ illaudabiles.

Hoc anno, David, filius Roberti le Brus, [1] Johannam, sororem Regis Edwardi præsentis, duxit uxorem.

Eodem anno, circa Mediam Quadragesimam, tenuit Rex Parliamentum Wyntoniæ; ubi, procurante Regina et Rogero de Mortuo Mari, Comes Canciæ, patruus Regis, dictus "Ed-

[1] *Johannem* in orig.

"mundus de Wodestoke," decollatus fuit, propter quasdam confessiones suas, et quasdam litteras secum inventas; licet nullæ illarum confessionum vel litterarum, etsi veræ fuissent, deberent causam tribuere morti suæ.

Fuerunt eo tempore multi accusati de eo quod, confingentes patrem Regis vivum, conspiraverunt eum liberare et ad statum regni reducere; licet hoc falsum et phantasma foret, sicut rei exitus comprobavit. Et qui super hoc accusati fuere, super manucaptione dimissi sunt, ut Episcopus Londoniensis, W. de Souche, et [1] nulli alii. Quidam vero carceri mancipati sunt, ut Robertus de Tauntone et quidam alii. Solus Comes, pro omnibus, est occisus: et eo minus deploratus fuit, quod malam habuit familiam, quæ res popularium, eundo per patriam, auctoritate propria occuparunt, et parum vel nihil solverunt eisdem.

Vacatio Ecclesiæ Sarum.

Hoc anno vacavit ecclesia Sarisburiensis per mortem Magistri Rogeri de Mortinans; cui Ecclesiæ Papa providit de Roberto de Wyvyle, qui scripsit speciales litteras Reginæ; viro igitur [2] competenter illiterato et minime personato: quem si Papa vidisset, nunquam eum, ut creditur, ad tantum apicem promovisset.

Ipso anno obiit Johannes Episcopus Bathoniæ; et licet Magister Radulphus de [3] Salopia fuisset concorditer electus, confirmatus, et consecratus per Symonem, Cantuariensem Archiepiscopum, postea tamen de Curia Romana se redemit, ut rata essent facta de ipso, non sine grandis pecuniæ interventu.

Processus contra Ducem Bavariæ.

Sub eodem anno, Papa fecit graves processus iterato contra Ducem Bavariæ, electum in Imperatorem, et adhærentes sibi; et pro sustinenda guerra contra eum omnes fructus beneficiorum vacantium per quadriennium reservavit.

Annalis Conclusio.

Transiit annus frugifer et fructifer; Anglis, Gallicis, atque Scotis, jocundus et lætus.

fol. 221 b. Anno gratiæ millesimo trecentesimo tricesimo, qui est annus regni Regis Edwardi, a Conquæstu Tertii, quartus, tenuit Rex Natale apud Eltham, cum multis nobilibus regni sui.

---

[1] Qy. if not *multi*?

[2] *competer* in orig., by inadvertence.

[3] *Solopia* in orig.

Hoc anno, Robertus Le Brus, qui se fecerat Regem Scotorum, lepra percussus obiit, septimo Idus Junii,

Ipso anno natus est Regi Edwardo primogenitus suus, "Edwardus" dictus, septimo-decimo Kalendas Junii.

Parliamentum apud Notyngham, et captio Rogeri de Mortuo Mari.

Eodem anno, die Veneris proxima post Festum [1] Sancti Lucæ Evangelistæ, fuit Parliamentum apud Notyngham, ubi captus fuit de nocte, in camera Reginæ, matris Regis, Dominus Rogerus de Mortuo Mari, per Dominum Willelmum de Monte Acuto et alios, ipso Rege præsente; et statim fuit missus dictus Comes ad Turrim Londoniarum, usque ad Parliamentum; quod fuit parum ante festum Sancti Andreæ. In quo, apud Westmonasterium, in Vigilia Sancti Andreæ, fuit idem Comes judicatus ad mortem per pares suos. Non tamen venit coram eis, nec habuit responsionem; nec mirum, quia a morte Comitis Thomæ de Lancastria usque ad mortem istius Comitis, omnes nobiles ad mortem traditi, sine responsione et communicatione legitima voluntarie perierunt; et, ut patet ex præcedentibus, quod quisque juris in alterum statuit, usus extitit eo jure; ut eadem [2] mensura qua aliis mensi fuerant, esset remensum eisdem.

Comes Marchiæ, Rogerus, suspenditur.

Igitur in Vigilia Sancti Andreæ fuit dictus Comes Marchiæ suspensus apud Elmus super communi furca latronum; ubi pendebat per biduum, et postea fuit sepultus Londoniis apud Fratres Minores; sed per multa tempora postea fuit translatus ad Wygomore. Causæ vero mortis ejus quæ imponebantur eidem, fuerunt infra scriptæ:

De causis Mortis ejus.

Prima, quia dicebatur quod fuit consentiens quod pater Regis in castro de Berkeleye fuerat suffocatus: ex qua causa, Dominus Johannes Matravers et Dominus Thomas de Gorneye, senior, qui fuerunt deputati custodiæ patris Regis ibidem, et quidam alii, se subtraxerunt ad partes transmarinas: et postea Dominus Simon de Berforde fuit suspensus.

Secunda causa imposita fuit, quod ipse impedivit honorem Regis et regni apud Stanne Park; ubi Scoti fugerunt, qui capi et interfici faciliter potuissent, si ipse, qui fuit major de Consilio Regis, Anglos cum Scotis congredi tunc fecisset.

---

[1] *Sancte* in orig., by inadvertence. | [2] In allusion to *Matt.* vii. 2.

Tertia causa imposita fuit ei, quod ipse recepit viginti millia librarum a Scotis, et illos tunc permisit evadere, et turpem pacem postmodum inter Scotos et Regem juniorem fieri procuravit; et super hoc chartam Regis eisdem fecit fieri, et illud vile matrimonium contractum inter sororem Regis Angliæ et David, filium Roberti le Brus, fieri [1] consuluit et procuravit.

Quarta causa imposita fuit, quod male consumpsit totam pecuniam inventam in thesauris Regis et Domini Hugonis Despenser, et omnia bona regni, postquam Regina Angliam intravit, suæ dispositioni subjecit; ita quod ipse et Regina abundabant, et Dominus Rex egebat.

Quinta causa fuit, quod appropriavit sibi custodias et maritagia nobiliora per totam Angliam; et quod fuit malus consiliarius Regis et Reginæ matris, et nimis secrete cum ea,—ut de aliis taceamus.

Decimæ concessæ Regi per Papam.

Hoc anno concessit Papa decimas Regi Angliæ omnium bonorum ecclesiasticorum per quadriennium, medietate sibi retenta.

Hoc anno, cito post Pascha, Rex Angliæ, cum Episcopo Wyntoniensi et Domino Willelmo de Monte Acuto, transivit mare sicut mercator sive harnesus, et vix habuit secum quindecim equites; et fecit proclamari Londoniis quod ivit in peregrinationem, et fecit Custodem regni Dominum Johannem de Eltham, fratrem suum; et rediit ante finem mensis Aprilis. In cujus reditum fuit torneamentum apud Dortforde.

Eodem anno, parum ante Festum Sancti Michaelis, fecit Rex pulcherrima hastiludia Londoniis, in Chepe; ubi Regina juvenis cecidit de quadam machina, sed tamen sine læsione corporum suorum; de quo plurimi mirabantur.

Annalis Conclusio.

Transiit annus iste frugibus opulentus, et fructibus; sed Sanctæ Ecclesiæ Anglicanæ nocivus, propter exactiones, tam regales quam Papales; popularibus lætus et jocundus, propter quorundam, ut putabatur, proditorum pœnas; Francis et Scotis sub silentio paceque transactus.

Novus annus et festum Natale apud Welles.

Anno gratiæ millesimo trecentesimo tricesimo primo, qui est annus regni Regis Edwardi, a Conquæstu Tertii, quintus,

[1] *consulit* in orig.

tenuit Rex Natale solemniter apud Welliam usque Epiphaniam; ubi fiebant multa mirabilia sumptuosa. Archiepiscopus Cantuariensis, tunc visitans Diœcesim Bathoniensem, mandavit se velle inchoare visitationem suam in ecclesia Exoniensi; quod ne fieret, Exoniensis Episcopus appellavit. Qua appellatione non obstante, accessit idem Archiepiscopus ad civitatem Exoniæ; sed non fuit sibi permissum ecclesiam, neque clausum, intrare, armata multitudine resistente.

Concilium Provinciale cassatur.

Hoc anno, circa festum Nativitatis Sanctæ Mariæ, fuit Consilium Provinciale Londoniis congregatum; sed propter discordiam inter Archiepiscopum et suos Suffraganeos, sine effectu fol. 222 a. aliquo terminatum.

Parliamentum tunc ibidem factum sine aliqua utili expeditione finitur. Rex tamen habuit quintam-decimam a populo, et decimam a civibus et burgensibus, sibi per unum annum concessam.

Edwardus de Baylol vendicat regnum Scotiæ.

Eodem anno, circa festum Sancti Laurentii, venit in Angliam Dominus Edwardus de Baylol, dicens se jus habere in regnum Scotiæ. Cui adhæserunt Dominus Henricus de Bello Monte, David Comes de Asseles, Gilbertus Umfrevyle, Ricardus Taleboth, et multi alii nobiles, asserentes se jus habere ad terras vel possessiones in dicto regno, vel ratione juris hæreditarii, vel ratione uxorum suarum, volentes ingredi Scotiam per regnum Angliæ; quod Rex noluit permittere, contemplatione sororis suæ, nuptæ David filio Roberti De le Brus; unde ipsi, egressi Angliam, intraverunt mare, et per mare ingressi sunt Scotiam, circa festum Sancti Laurentii, juxta Abbathiam de Dounfermelyn; ubi statim in littore maris resistentiam habuerunt; sed pedites Anglici, pauci numero, citius ad terram applicantes, omnes Scotos qui ibi fuerant fugaverunt, et plures interfecerunt, antequam viri armati ad terram poterant applicare. Postea vero, infra paucos dies, habuerunt conflictum prope Abbathiam et locum vocatum "Gledesmor," ubi duo millia Anglicorum vicerunt quadraginta millia Scotorum, præ multitudine et pressura seipsos opprimentium; de quibus Scotis, quinque Comites et alii multi interfecti et oppressi fuerunt; et hoc totum non sua virtute, sed gratia divina, ipsi Anglici factum esse dixerunt, et Deum propterea laudaverunt.

Annalis Conclusio.

Transiit annus iste opulentus, fœcundus fructuum diversi generis; Anglis et Francis otiosus; Scotis asper et bellicosus.

Guerra continuatur in Scotia.

Anno gratiæ millesimo trecentesimo tricesimo secundo, qui est annus regni Regis Edwardi, a Conquæstu Tertii, sextus, tenuit Rex Natale apud Westmonasterium.

Hoc anno continuata fuit [1] guerra in Scotia, ut præmittitur, inchoata per Dominum Edwardum Baillol et alios nobiles supradictos; et circa festum Sancti Johannis Baptistæ, multi alii nobiles in Anglia, et viri bellicosi, ad eos voluntarie et sumptibus propriis [2] accesserunt, et villam et castrum de Berwyk obsederunt. Rex autem Angliæ, considerans multa vituperia sibi et antecessoribus suis per Scotos illata, et quod concordia, facta inter ipsum et Scotos, fuit inita per proditionem, et ipso in minori ætate notorie constituto, et in custodia matris suæ existente, quæ consilio Domini Rogeri de Mortuo Mari, proditoris sui, per omnia regebatur, contra consilium matris suæ, collecta multitudine armatorum, ad Berwik viriliter et potenter accessit, et ibi aliquandiu permansit: ubi tenentes castrum et villam habuerunt cum eo multos dolosos tractatus, ut ab extra adjutorium expectarent, sicut exitus declaravit.—Sed hæc de Regis Angliæ profectione, acta sunt anno sequenti.

Edwardus de Baylol coronatur.

Eodem anno gratiæ quo supra, idem Edwardus de Bayllol, filius Johannis de Baillol, apud Scone in Regem Scotiæ coronatur, quinto Kalendas Octobris.

Hoc anno concessa est Regi quinta-decima de communi plebe.

Obiit Episcopus Dunelmensis.

Eodem anno, parum ante festum Sancti Michaelis, vacavit Ecclesia Dunelmensis per mortem Domini Lodowici de Bello Monte.

Annalis Conclusio.

Transiit annus iste frugifer et fructifer; Francis pacificus, Anglis sollicitus; sed Scotis quam maxime inquietus.

Novus [annus], et Festum Natale.

Anno gratiæ millesimo trecentesimo tricesimo tertio, qui est annus regni Regis Edwardi, a Conquæstu Tertii, septimus, tenuit Rex Natale .[3]

[1] *guera* in orig.

[2] *ad eos* repeated before this word in orig.; by inadvertence.

[3] The locality is omitted.

Victoria Regis apud Berwicum.

Hoc anno, in festo Sanctæ Margaretæ Virginis, venerunt Scoti in magna multitudine de tota Scotia congregata, volentes obsidionem Berwici removere, si possent. Quibus Rex Angliæ, cum suo exercitu, peditando, et ipso Rege exercitum præcedente, et omnes bono vultu et audaci animo confortante, ita viriliter se habebat, quod post aliqualem numerum occisorum, cum manu ad manum pugnaverunt, universi Scoti sunt in fugam conversi. Quos Rex Angliæ et suus exercitus occidendo et fugando per quinque milliaria sequebantur, ita quod vix e Scotis evaserunt aliqui magni aut valentes; sed tantum pedites et agrestes. Ceciderunt autem ibi de Scotis octo Comites, mille et trecenti equites, et de popularibus triginta quinque millia, vel, ut quidam volunt, quadraginta millia de universis. Adduxerat autem hos Scotos contra Anglicos in tribus aciebus, quidam miles, vocatus "Willelmus Keth," ad locum juxta Berwicum, qui dicitur "Boothulle," juxta Halidone, sicut ante promiserat, fidem servans in hoc, quanquam foret alias infidelis. In hoc certamine sagittarii Angliæ laudem perpetuam et memoriam merebantur, per quos præcipue ista victoria facta fuit. Miserant interea subdole Scoti quosdam de suis in Angliam, qui obsederunt castrum de Bamburgh, ubi tunc temporis Regina Angliæ morabatur; si sic fol. 222 b. fortassis potuissent solvere obsidionem; sed ista victoria gratiose adepta, dimissa obsidione de Bamburgh, ad latibula nota fugerunt: "gratiose" nempe dixerim, quia, quod mirabile dictu est, non ceciderunt ex Anglicis nisi unus miles, unus armiger, et duodecim pedites. Quibus visis, oppidani de Berwico villam, cum castro, Regi Angliæ reddiderunt.

Villa Berwici redditur Regi Angliæ.

Facta ergo voluntate Regis de hiis qui fuerunt in villa vel castello, et relicta nomine suo in ipsis custodia, quia dixit illa sua fore jure hæreditario et ex conquæstu antecessorum suorum, dimisit Edwardum de Bayllol, cum aliis nobilibus qui secum aderant, ad custodiam totius regni Scotiæ; et ipsemet Rex Angliæ, cum modica familia, loca devota Angliæ, ad quæ sua devotio eum duxit, peregre est profectus.

Fuga Scotorum.

Eo tempore, prælati regni Scotiæ fugerunt in Franciam; quorum aliqui ad Summum Pontificem accesserunt, conquerentes Regi Franciæ et Summo Pontifici de eorum infortunio, adjutorium et remedium flagitantes: sed hucusque suo desiderio sunt frustrati.

Circa festum Sancti Kalixti Papæ, obiit Magister Simon de Mepham, quondam Cantuariensis Archiepiscopus; cujus loco Capitulum Magistrum Johannem de Stratforde, Wyntoniensem Episcopum, postulavit, faciendo de necessitate virtutem. Sciebant nempe monachi, quod Dominus Rex scripserat Summo Pontifici pro eodem, et ipse fuit bene in gratia Papæ. Cui Papa providit quidem de Archiepiscopatu, non virtute postulationis Capituli Cantuariæ, sed proprio suo motu.

Translatio facta per Papam.

Eodem anno, primo die Decembris, transtulit Papa Magistrum Adam de [1] Orleton de Ecclesia Wygorniensi ad Ecclesiam Wyntoniensem, ad preces Regis Franciæ; cujus translationem Dominus Rex Angliæ moleste tulit, imponens sibi quod ipse fuit tunc nuncius ipsius Regis Angliæ ad Regem Franciæ, et quod ipse plus placuit Regi Franciæ quam Regi Angliæ, et propria negotia utiliter procuravit; et quod ideo Rex Franciæ scripsit Papæ pro ipso, ut ad Wyntoniensem Ecclesiam transferretur. Et ideo retinuit Dominus Rex temporalia Episcopatus Wyntoniæ in manibus suis, usque diem Veneris post Exaltationem Sanctæ Crucis; quo die Archiepiscopus et cæteri Episcopi in Parliamento Londoniis rogaverunt pro ipso; ita quod Rex mandavit sua temporalia sibi reddi.

Electus Dunelmensis cassatur.

Hoc anno, cito post festum Sancti Michaelis, Capitulum Dunelmiæ elegit unum monachum ejusdem Ecclesiæ, nomine [2] , qui cito postmodum Eboraci fuerat confirmatus, et ante festum Natalis Domini in ecclesia Eboracensi solemniter consecratus; non obstante fama per totam Angliam volante, quod Papa ipsum Episcopatum Domino Ricardo de Bury, clerico Domini Regis Angliæ, contulisset, ad preces ipsius Regis; quam famam veram fuisse rei exitus postmodum comprobavit. Nam idem dictus Ricardus, cito post festum Natalis Domini, obtentis litteris Apostolicis super sua provisione, se fecit, auctoritate Apostolica, in Monasterio de Chertcseye per Dominum Wyntoniensem Episcopum consecrari, et a Domino Rege obtinuit sibi temporalia ipsius Episcopatus integre liberari; quod prius dicto monacho facere denegavit. Quo viso et intellecto, idem monachus, electus et consecratus, ad claustrum, sine Episcopatu Episcopus, est reversus, et cito postea expiravit.

---

[1] Apparently *Orbeton*, in orig.

[2] The name is omitted: *Robert de Greystanes* was the monk whose election was thus set aside.

Parliamentum Regis Scotiæ.

Eodem anno, Dominus Edwardus de Bayllol, Rex Scotiæ, tenuit Parliamentum suum cito post festum Sancti Michaelis; ad quod venerunt nobiles regni Angliæ, terras et possessiones ibidem habentes, et, finito Parliamento, in pace sunt reversi.

Annalis Conclusio.

Transiit annus præsens copiosus frugibus, fructibus satis abundans; Gallicis lætus et hilaris; Anglicis votivus et honorabilis; Scotis nocivus, damnosus, et luctuosus.

Novus [annus], et Festum Natale.

Anno gratiæ millesimo trecentesimo tricesimo quarto, qui est annus regni Regis Edwardi, a Conquæstu Tertii, octavus, tenuit Rex Natale Walyngfordiæ, cum Regina prægnante; et, finito festo, dimisit eam apud Wodestoke, ad pariendum; et ipse, post Purificationem Beatæ Mariæ, transtulit se versus Eboracum, ad tenendum Parliamentum ibidem; quod die Lunæ in secunda [1] hebdomade Quadragesimæ inchoavit.

Parliamentum Eboraco.

Ad quod Parliamentum vocatus fuit Rex Edwardus Scotiæ; sed non venit, propter insidias inimicorum suorum, in insulis juxta Scotiam latitantium: propter quod, misit excusatores solemnes, scilicet Dominum Henricum de [2] Bello Monte et Willelmum de Monte Acuto, et quosdam alios milites seu barones.

Homagium Regis Scotiæ.

Eodem anno, in festo Sanctorum Gervasii et Prothasii, Edwardus de Balliolo, verus Rex Scotiæ, fecit homagium Regi Angliæ Edwardo apud Novum Castrum super Tynam, in præsentia trium Episcoporum, Comitum, et Baronum, et copiosæ plebis.

Eodem fere tempore, Rex Angliæ recepit homagium Ducis Brytanniæ pro Comitatu Richemundiæ.

Consilium apud Notyngham.

Circa festum Translationis Sancti Thomæ, vocavit Rex prælatos et magnates, ut infra sex dies post dictum festum veni-

[1] *ebdomada* in orig.

[2] *Bollo* in orig., by inadvertence.

rent ad eum, ad Notyngham, pro consilio et aliis tractatibus habendis ibidem. Et tunc ordinavit Parliamentum Londoniis;
fol. 223 a. et Archiepiscopus convocavit clerum ibidem ad Sanctum Paulum, die Lunæ post festum Exaltationis Sanctæ Crucis. Et quia nova venerunt ad Parliamentum, quod Scoti omnes insurrexerunt et ceperunt Dominum Ricardum Talbot et sex alios milites, et multos pedites occiderunt, Rex promisit se iturum versus Scotiam, pro Scotorum malitia refrænanda. Quamobrem populus concessit sibi quintum-decimum denarium de temporalibus, et de civitatibus et burgis decimum denarium; et clerus concessit unam decimam. In dicto Parliamento, Rex concessit quod iret in Terram Sanctam propriis sumptibus, sed tempus certum inchoandi itineris non expressit. Sed ordinavit mittere Archiepiscopum Cantuariæ ad Regem Franciæ, ut possent de tempore concordare; ita quod illi duo Reges possent, cum suis potentiis, simul arripere dictum iter.

In festo igitur Apostolorum Simonis et Judæ, Archiepiscopus transivit mare versus Regem Franciæ, cum aliis nunciis, sicut prius fuerat ordinatum.

Rex hyemat in Scotiæ partibus.

Eodem anno, Rex, post festum Sancti Michaelis, se transtulit versus Marchiam Scotiæ, et in illis finibus hyemavit; atque sub hyeme gelida Galwediam intrans, totam patriam usque ad mare Scoticum devastavit. Audito autem quod Comes de Assellcs fuit proditiose conversus ad Scotos, iratus est; et cum didicisset quod Dominus Henricus de Bello Monte in quodam castro fuit obsessus per Scotos, obsidionem fecit celeriter amoveri.

Inundatio damnosa.

Hoc anno, in nocte Sancti Clementis, per nimiam inundationem maris per totum regnum Angliæ, et maxime in Tamisia, fuerunt rupti muri maritimi, et animalia infinita submersa; et terræ fructiferæ in salsuginem sunt conversæ, ita quod ad fertilitatem solitam per multa tempora non speratur posse redire.

Obiit Johannes Papa.

Hoc anno, quarto die Decembris, obiit Johannes Papa Vicesimus-secundus, in Palatio suo Avinioniæ, et in ecclesia Beatæ Mariæ, eidem palatio conjuncta, est sepultus; in qua idem fuerat Episcopus ante Cardinalatus honorem.

Benedictus Papa.

Vacavit autem Sedes Apostolica diebus quindecim: vicesimo vero die ejusdem mensis, fuit electus in Papam Frater Jacobus, Tituli Sanctæ Priscæ Presbyter Cardinalis; qui prius fuit monachus et Abbas Cisterciensis Ordinis, et Magister in Theologia, de Comitatu Fuxensi, juxta partes Tholosanas, oriundus; deinde in propria Diœcesi Episcopus; tandem Cardinalis, et demum Apostolicus est effectus, et "Benedictus Duodecimus" est vocatus. Qui mox ad Professores diversorum Ordinum Constitutiones edidit, eorum regulas concernentes.

Annalis Conclusio.

Transiit annus iste frugifer et fructifer, quoad Anglos; Gallicis quietus, lætus, et hilaris; Anglicis honorabilis, sed [1]tam varius, propter infortunia, sive damna, per aquarum fluxum contingentia; Scotis lamentabilis et dolorosus.

Novus annus, et treugæ [2]concessæ Scotis.

Anno gratiæ millesimo trecentesimo tricesimo quinto, qui est annus regni Regis Edwardi, a Conquæstu Tertii, nonus, fuit Rex ad Natale apud Rokesburgh, cum valido exercitu Anglicorum. Hoc anno concessæ fuerunt treugæ Scotis, usque ad Natale Sancti Johannis Baptistæ, proximo futurum, duraturæ.

Parliamentum Eboraci.

Eo tempore apud Eboracum factum fuit Parliamentum super illis treugis, et aliis statum regni tangentibus; in quo fuerat ordinatum quod Rex, Comites, et Barones, cum suis exercitibus, irent in Scotiam, et mare Scoticum pertransirent. Quod cito postea factum est.

Acta in Scotia.

Sed Scoti, bellum campestre expectare nolentes, finxerunt se pacem habere velle. Et postmodum, circa festum Sancti Michaelis venerunt ad pacem quidam, inter quos præcipuus fuit Comes de Asselles; alii vero qui pacem petierant, venire noluerunt. Ob quam causam, postmodum captus fuit Comes de Moryf apud Edyngburgh, et in Anglia carceri mancipatus.

Eodem tempore, Dominus Ricardus Talboth pro duobus millibus marcarum redemptus fuit.

---

[1] Probably, an error for *tamen*. | [2] *concessis* in orig., by inadvertence.

Comes de Asselles, volens se ostendere vere reversum ad Anglicos, equitavit contra Scotos ad obsidionem cujusdam castri, et, subito dissipata comitiva sua, cum paucis equitans in [1]hostes incidit, magna multitudine circumdatus ex omni parte. Et cum se reddere nullo modo vellet, sed pugnare constanter eligeret, cum tresdecim personis mediocribus est occisus.

Post festum Sancti Michaelis, Rex morabatur in Marchia Scotiæ, in qua nuncii Papæ et Regis Franciæ, illuc missi, pro Scotis expectabant, ut aliquam pacem, vel saltem longam treugam, licet nobis inutilem, providerent.

Annalis Conclusio.

Transiit annus iste frugifer et fructifer, aura salutifer, rerum venalium uber et commodus, Anglis lætus, Gallis quietus, sed Scotiæ turbulentus.

Anno gratiæ millesimo trecentesimo tricesimo sexto, qui est annus regni Regis Edwardi, a Conquæstu Tertii, decimus, tenuit Rex Natale [2].

Hoc anno revocata est decima sexennalis concessa per Papam in subsidium Terræ Sanctæ.

fol. 223 b. Eodem anno, Rex Edwardus in singulis Ecclesiis Cathedralibus capi fecit totam pecuniam collectam in subsidium supradictum.

Regina Philippa peperit secundum filium.

Eodem anno, Domina Philippa Regina peperit filium suum secundum, dictum "Willelmum," apud Hatfeld; qui, non diu vivens, sepultus est apud Eboracum.

Obiit Johannes de Eltham, frater Regis.

Eodem anno, in Vigilia Exaltationis Sanctæ Crucis, apud villam Sancti Johannis in Scotia, Dominus Johannes de Eltham, frater Regis Edwardi præsentis, et quondam Comes Cornubiæ, debita naturæ solvit; qui expost, in Vigilia Epiphaniæ, apud Westmonasterium, in Capella Sancti Thomæ Martyris est sepultus.

Novus Dux Cornubiæ.

Eodem anno, circa festum Sancti Gregorii in Quadragesima, Rex Edwardus, in pleno Parliamento apud Londonias, de Comitatu Cornubiæ fecit Ducatum, quem contulit primogenito suo Edwardo, una cum Cestriæ Comitatu. Ordinavit etiam

[1] *hostos* in orig., by inadvertence. | [2] The locality is omitted.

ibidem sex Comites, videlicet Henricum de Lancastre, juniorem, Comitem de Derby, Willelmum de Monte Acuto Comitem Sarisburiensem, Hugonem de Audelee Comitem Gloverniæ, Willelmum de Clyntone Comitem Huntyndoniæ, Robertum de Ufford Comitem de Southfolchia.[1]

Statuta Parliamenti.

Statutum est autem in eodem Parliamento, quod nullus uteretur panno extra Angliam operato, exceptis Rege, Regina, et liberis eorundem; et quod nullus uteretur pellura transmarina, nisi valentes centum libras reddituum annuatim.

Eodem anno, magnus classis per totam æstatem et autumnum in pluribus partibus detinebatur.

Cardinales.

Eodem anno, circa festum Sancti Andreæ, venerunt duo Cardinales, ad tractandum de pace et aliis negotiis, in terram istam, videlicet, Dominus Petrus Hispanus et Bernardus de Monte Favenciæ.

Fœdus fœdum.

Hoc anno Rex Edwardus cum Lodowico de Bavaria, regnum Alemaniæ occupante et se Imperatorem appellante, fœdus iniit fructuosum.

Obiit Abbas Sancti Albani, Ricardus secundus.

Hoc anno obiit Ricardus de Walyngford, Abbas Sancti Albani, decimo Kalendas Junii, vir in astrologiæ scientia cunctos tunc viventes in Anglia antecedens; qui horologium construxit in ecclesia sua, quod cunctis temporis moderni peritis est admirationi. Cui successit, per electionem, Dominus Michael Mentemor, Bachalarius in Theologia.

Circa Gulam Augusti, hoc anno, directi sunt nuncii ad Regem Franciæ ex parte Regis Angliæ, videlicet, Dominus Ricardus de Bury, Episcopus Dunelmensis, Dominus Willelmus Trussel, et quidam alii, ad tractandum de pace inter regna, et conveniendum Regem Franciæ, eo quod injuste fovit partem Scotorum contra Regem Angliæ, dominum eorundem. Quibus adhuc in Francia existentibus, directa est per Regem Franciæ magna navium multitudo, cum armatorum numerositate, in Scotorum auxilium perfidorum. Quamobrem Rex Anglorum, tunc existens in Scotia, misit pro toto suo navigio festinanter. Et præterea misit brevia sua ad omnes Comites et

[1] Only *five* creations are here enumerated, unless the Earldom of Chester is included.

Barones regni sui, aliosque magnates, Ecclesiæque prælatos, et Londonienses, ut forent apud Notyngham in quindena Sancti Michaelis, una secum tractaturi de gubernatione regni, et auxilio sibi conferendo; quia nullo modo voluit, ut fatebatur, quiescere, donec Scotos ad subjectionem debitam coegisset.

Obsidio Castri de Dunbar.

Eo tempore fuit obsessum castrum de Dunbar, in Scotia, per Dominum Willelmum de Monte Acuto, Comitem Sarisburiensem, et alios magnates regni Angliæ; quos Rex ibidem dimiserat pro custodia illius terræ, dum interim ipse redisset in Angliam pro regni negotiis exequendis. Cumque cognovisset quod Scoti dictum castrum obsidione vallassent, illuc celeriter properavit. In itinere vero quosdam de suis amisit, et ipse periculum vix evasit, eo quod cum paucis equitare solebat; aliquando ubi cum octo, aliquotiens ubi cum sex, viris incedens.

Annalis Conclusio.

Transiit annus iste frugibus abundus, fructibusque jocundus; Angliæ et Franciæ suspectus et subdolus; sed Scotis tristis, odibilis, et molestus.

After "ubique," *line* 3, *page* 223, *Vol.* I.

fol. 224 a. *Rex intrat mare, cum Regina.*

Circa festum Translationis Sancti Thomæ, Dominus Rex, cum Philippa Regina, prægnante, et duabus filiabus suis, et exercitu copioso, intravit mare, ut tractaret cum Duce Brabantiæ et aliis alligatis suis, de aggrediendo regnum Franciæ, sibi jure successorio per mortem celebris memoriæ Domini Karoli, Regis ultimi, fratris germani Dominæ Isabellæ, matris dicti Domini Regis Edwardi, devolutum, et per Dominum Philippum de Walesio, filium patrui dicti Domini Karoli, injuste hactenus occupatum.

Favente igitur Neptuno, immo numine divino, prospere pervenit ad portum de Le Swyne; ubi unanimiter Flandrenses occurrerunt ei, offerentes se paci ejus, et fidelitati. Indeque transiens pervenit ad terram Brabanciæ; cui occurrit Dux Brabanciæ, cognatus ejus, et ipsum suscepit cum gaudio et honore.

After "deliberatus est," *line* 22, *page* 224, *Vol.* I.

fol. 224 b. *De Parliamento Londoniis celebrato.*

Eodem anno, celebrato Londoniis Parliamento, aliisque negotiis rite dispositis, indixit Anglicis tributum quintæ partis bonorum suorum, et lanas ovium occupavit; nonam garbam de omni gleba Angliæ suis expeditionibus deputavit: de quorum proventu dominos vicinarum villarum respondere fecit.

After "incrementum, etc.," *line* 24, *page* 225, *Vol.* I.

Eclipsis Solis. fol. 224 b.

In die Translationis Sancti Thomæ, Archiepiscopi Cantuariensis, isto anno, fuit eclipsis solis, immediate post meridiem; et duravit per duas horas. Eclipsabatur enim usque ad quartam partem.

After "effectus," *line* 19, *page* 226, *Vol.* I.

Ipso anno obiit Ricardus de Benteworthe, Episcopus Londoniensis, regni Cancellarius; cui successit Magister Radulphus de Stratford, nepos Archiepiscopi Cantuariensis. fol. 224 b.

After "est sepulta," *line* 8, *page* 228, *Vol.* I.

Annalis Conclusio. fol. 225 a.

Transiit annus iste frugifer et fructifer; lætus Anglicis, et gloriosus; tristis Gallicis, et dolorosus; Scotis sub silentio in pace volutus.

After "subjugata," *line* 7, *page* 254, *Vol.* I.

Annalis Conclusio. fol. 225 b.

Transiit annus iste frugifer et fructifer, et necessariis bonis uber; initium laborum et dolorum Britanniæ; Angliæ commendabilis, honorabilis, lucrativus; Franciæ et Scotiæ sub magna expectatione decursus.

After "demonstrare," *line* 6, *page* 264, *Vol.* I.

De morte Regis Siciliæ. fol. 227 b.

Per idem tempus obiit Robertus, Rex Siciliæ; post cujus mortem, Laurentius, filius Regis Hungariæ, dicti Roberti consanguineus, super idem regnum coronatur.

Obiit Comes Sarum.

Obiit etiam isto tempore Willelmus de Monte Acuto, Comes Sarum, Rex Manniæ et Marescallus Angliæ. De cujus elegantia, strenuitate, sapientia, et animositate, digne scribere, speciales actus requirit. Successit ei, dono Regis, in officium Marescalciæ, Dominus Thomas Beuchampe, Comes Warwici.

After "contulisset," *line* 9, *page* 265, *Vol.* I.

Filia nata Regi. fol. 228 a.

Edwardo Regi nata est filia, nomine Maria; quæ fuit postea copulata Duci Britanniæ, sed præmature de medio est sublata.

After " triplo major," *line* 11, *page* 266, *Vol.* I.

fol. 228 a. *Obiit Episcopus Dunelmensis.*

Hoc anno obiit Ricardus de Bury, Episcopus Dunelmensis; cui successit Thomas de Hatfeld, Regi Secretarius, mediantibus Regis litteris ad Papam; in magnam Regis et regni confusionem. Nam cum ante Rex et nobilitas instititissent pro electionibus libere faciendis et confirmandis, jam Rex, directe contra suas litteras et vota procerum, hunc fieri Episcopum
fol. 228 b. flagitavit. Papa vero, non invitus, hanc petitionem Regi concessit, sed quibusdam de Cardinalibus calumniantibus dictum Thomam fore levem et laicum, ita respondit;—" Vere," inquit, " si Rex pro asino supplicasset, obtinuisset ad vota, ista " vice."

Eodem anno obiit Episcopus Herefordensis, Thomas Cherltone; cui successit J[ohannes] Trellik.

Obiit etiam Episcopus Eliensis, Simon de Monte Acuto; cui successit, ex collatione Papæ, Thomas de Lyle, Frater Prædicator.

After " sunt salvati," *line* 16, *page* 274, *Vol.* I.

fol. 230 a. *Obiit Magister Johannes Ufford.*

Hoc anno obiit Magister Johannes de Ufford, Cancellarius regni, electus et confirmatus in Archiepiscopum Cantuariæ, non tamen confirmatus; cui successit per electionem Magister Thomas de Bradwardyn.

After " morientibus," *line* 19, *page* 274, *Vol.* I.

fol. 230 a. *Obiit Abbas Sancti Albani.*

Eodem anno obiit Michael, Abbas Sancti Albani; cui successit Thomas De la Mare, quondam Prior de Thinemuta.

After " die Septembris," *line* 37, *page* 281, *Vol.* I.

fol. 231 b. —— vel, ut quidam volunt, vicesimo primo die mensis ejusdem, quasi in, etc.

After " Episcopus," *line* 18, *page* 288, *Vol.* I.

fol. 233 a. —— cui successit Dominus Robertus de Stratton.

After " Mendicantium," *line* 21, *page* 294, *Vol.* I.

fol. 234 b. *Obiit Armachanus Episcopus.*

Eodem anno obiit Armachanus prædictus Avinione, die Sancti Edmundi Regis; cujus ossa succedenti tempore in Hiberniam sunt delata, et in Dundalk, ubi natus fuerat, sunt sepulta;

quo in loco innumera, ad laudem Dei fiunt miracula. Iste composuit libros diversos de Quæstionibus Armenorum, de Pauperie Christi, Sermonesque insignes; ex quibus, et aliis suis tractatibus, constat veraciter, quod erat probatissimus scriba in regno cœlorum.

Obiit Episcopus Roffensis.

Obiit eodem anno J[ohannes] Episcopus Roffensis, et J[ohannes] Trelek, Episcopus Herefordensis.

After " in vanum," *line* 15, *page* 315, *Vol.* I.

Obiit hoc anno Magister Thomas Tryllyk, Roffensis Episcopus; cui, ex provisione Domini Papæ, successit Thomas de Brumptone, Doctor in Decretis et monachus Northwicensis, qui aliquandiu Pœnitentiarius erat Papæ. fol. 240 b.

After " delictum," *line* 3, *page* 331, *Vol.* I.

—— aliquod fatentur se fecisse contra Ducem; sed quasi pro bono pacis, et honore tam Regis quam Ducis, ad leniendum corda, et ad commitigandum indignationem utriusque, advenerunt in hac vice. fol. 243 b.

Dux vero videns eos sub tali forma Regi submisisse, hac submissione civium nimium delectabatur, rancorem omnem deponens animi, et velut amplectens corditer præmissam Londoniensium humiliationem spontaneam, corruit ad pedes Regis, deprecans ut susciperet causam suam, sub forma quam Londonienses expresserunt, et rogans ut hii qui incarcerati fuerant propter aliquod dedecus sibi illatum, Regis gratia laxarentur. Si qui vero judicio aliquod membrum vel vitam propter hujuscemodi causam forent perdituri, ut Rex eis ex sua gratia vitam redonaret, et membra.

Ipse etiam Dux condonavit civibus quicquid contra eum in aliquo deliquerunt, et recepit eos in plenam gratiam suam, præsente Rege, affirmans cum juramento se futurum eorum amicum, et eorum commoditatibus invigilaturum, sicut suis propriis; et in signum non fictæ pacis, osculatus est ibidem omnes et singulos coram Rege; sicque sunt cum pace cives in sua dimissi. Qui revertentes, Deum in suis collaudavere mirabilibus, et Beato Anglorum Protomartyri, Albano, gratias reddiderunt, eo quod ejus Passionis die ista pax, contra spem, sit facta; cujus orationibus in instanti necessitate se fatebantur adjutos. Cujus etiam patrocinium in hac causa perante devotissime implorarunt. Nam quis crederet Ducem, cujus heri potestati subjecta fuerat tota tellus, hodie sine manifesto miraculo ad tantam humilitatem posse perduci?

Feria autem sexta proxima sequente, Dux et communes civitatis Londoniarum ad Westmonasterium convenerunt; ubi præconis voce proclamata est concordia inita, et pax, inter Ducem et cives; quo facto, omnes gaudentes ad propria recesserunt.

Rex juvenis facit pacem.

Rex vero juvenis, ex innata sibi bonitate, pacem inter subjectos suos ubique cupiens, in ingressu suo Ducem et Episcopum Wyntoniensem reduxit ad pacis concordiam et unitatis. Sed et ubicunque cognovit in regno suo aliquod exortum fore [1]dissidium, querelas in manu sua suscepit, promittens se utrobique facturum finem commodum et fructuosum. Felix auspicium in tantæ ætatis puero, ut ipse, nullo impellente, sollicitaretur circa pacem, nullo docente, sciret pacem populo suo prodesse!

Nec prætereundum, quod mox ut insignitus est nomine regio, Dominum Petrum de la Marc militem, qui, pro fidelitate sua erga Regem et regnum, in Parliamento facto apud Westmonâsterium ultimo anno Regis Edwardi prædicti, qui pro tunc erat miles pro communitate electus, cum nollet taxis in dicto Parliamento petitis consentire, ad castellum de Notyngham, ibidem incarceratus, in tuta custodia tenebatur, deliberare studuit. Et ut tutior esset omnino contra suos æmulos, per patentem remisit, et relaxavit, eidem omnia, quæcunque nomine Regis possent ab eo exigi, vel eidem imponi. Qui mox, gratias acturus Regi, iter maturavit ad illum.

Videres populum per civitates et vicos cum summo gaudio egredi in occursum ejus, et non minori plausu quam olim Beato Thomæ, ab exilio revertenti, dicere,—"Benedictus, qui "venit in nomine Domini." Londonienses autem et ipsi, eum suscipientes, alacriter in donis variis et exenniis respexerunt.

Villa de Rye incenditur per Gallicos.

In festo Apostolorum Petri et Pauli, Gallici in Aurora cum quinquaginta navibus, majoribus et minoribus, invaserunt villam de Rya, ad numerum quinque millium; et modico labore villam ceperunt, quanquam villani, ex confidentia virium suarum, statuissent, et firmiter promisissent, quod nullus a dicta villa bona sua mobilia elongaret; ut saltem amore rerum temporalium, animosius persisterent in conflictu. Qui tamen effecti similes filiis [2]Ephrem, intendentes et mittentes arcum, conversi

---

[1] *discidium* in orig.

[2] *Effrem* in orig. The allusion is to *Psalm* lxxviii. 9.

in die belli. Unde contigit eorum vecordia villam prædictam capi, cum omnibus bonis suis.

Abbas autem de Bello, audito rumore tam flebili, adunatis expeditis hominibus suis, consilium habuit ut arceret eos a depopulatione et deprædatione villarum et agrorum, et ne eis pateret aditus in patriam longius evagari. Cumque noctem circa talia duxisset insomnem, quibusdam ex inimicis pabulatum exeuntibus, unus captus fuit per unum de servientibus Abbatis de Bello. Qui requisitus ab Abbate de Francorum proposito, dixit quod proposuerunt custodisse dictam villam per decem dies.

Abbas de Bello, præcavens ne plura damna villis eis vicinis, et supra mare positis, irrogarent, transtulit se et suos ad villam de Wynchelsee, quæ situata est juxta villam de Rya; quam villam, ut dictus captivus retulit, eadem die proposuerunt hostiliter invasisse; sed cum vidissent Abbatem et suos in fol. 244 a. dicta villa de Wynchelsee adunatos, desperantes de ulteriori progressu in patriam, ceperunt incendere villam de Rya ex omni parte; et infra quinque horas eam totaliter in cineres redegerunt, cum ecclesia quæ ibidem mirandæ pulchritudinis habebatur. Quatuor de ditioribus captivis abductis, de villanis occiderunt sexaginta sex, non amittentes de Francorum numero ultra octo. Postquam, ut diximus, incendissent villam de Rya, modicum ante solis occasum redierunt ad naves, quadraginta duo dolia vini, quæ ibidem repererunt, secum suis navibus transportantes; et ita locum illum desolatum relinquentes, se, cum præda quam ceperant, alto pelago commiserunt.

Tertio Nonas Julii, corpus illustris Regis Edwardi apud Westmonasterium est humatum, cum honore.

Indignatio Londoniensium contra R. Belknap, Justiciarium.

Per eosdem dies Rex Londoniis suam præsentiam exhibuerat, recordatus sui promissi; quem cives in donis variis liberaliter respexerunt, a quo etiam meruerunt, cum honore quo decuit, salutari. Et non multo post, dominorum et magnatum universali decreto, statutus est dies Coronationis regiæ, videlicet sexto-decimo die mensis Julii; quod est septimodecimo Kalendas Augusti; ad quam invitantur tam ecclesiastici quam sæculares viri, ut tantum officium veneratione debita peragatur.

Interim proceres, ad quos ex antiquo jure in Coronatione regia aliqua spectabat administratio, decerni sibi sua officia petierunt. Judices, habito respectu ad uniuscujusque jus hæreditarium, ne lis aliqua oriretur in die tantæ solemnitatis, prudenter unicuique quod suum fuerat, decreverunt. Si aliqua vero talis causa pro tunc discuti non poterat, distulerunt eam usque post Coronationem regiam, ordinatis certis personis qui digne tales administrationes facerent, salvo jure utriusque partis.

Londonienses autem quod suum erat exegerunt, videlicet officium Pincernariæ. Dominus vero Robertus Belknappe, Justiciarius principalis Domini Regis in Banco Communi, minus circumspecte respondens dixit eis, — "Domini," ait, "multa sunt inter pincernas officia. Nam quibusdam incumbit haurire vina, quibusdam deferre, quibusdam delata servare, quibusdam in aula circumsedentibus ministrare, quibusdam autem vasa, puta urceos, ollas, cyphosque, mundare; et ideo frustra petitis decerni vobis officium, nisi specificetis illud." Cives vero, hoc audito, mox indignati responderunt se vasa mundare non debere, vasa de propriis meliora ipso habere, quod in ejus capite probare vellent. Itaque cum summa indignatione comminantes eidem, recesserunt; occidissentque eum si in Civitate potuisset postea deprehendi. Verum quia eum comprehendere non valebant, in dedecus personæ suæ effigiaverunt simile sibi caput, et statuerunt super Aquæductum in Foro venalium; quod in adventu Regis et plebis evomeret ore vinum.

Magnifica Regis Equitatio die præcedente Coronationem suam.

Die præcedente diem Coronationis regiæ, magnates et plebs numerosa regni Londoniis confluxerant, ut supra taxavimus, et post horam nonam proceres regni, cum Londoniensibus, aliisque multis quos amor Regis attraxerat, equis vecti sublimibus, ad Turrim, ubi pro tunc Rex fuerat, properarunt.

Dispositisque tunc ibidem qui præcederent et qui sequerentur, equitare cœperunt versus Westmonasterium per frequentissimos vicos Civitatis: quæ nimirum Civitas tot pannis aureis et argenteis, tot holosericis, aliisque adinventionibus quæ animos intuentium oblectarent, ornata fuerat, ut putares te ibidem vel Cæsarianos triumphos cernere, vel Romam, ut quondam fuerat, in præcellente decore. Tantus itaque populus adventarat, ut eos vici celeberrimi capere non valerent, sed, ut ita dicam—

——"Gradibus evecti ad culmina Crucis
"Quamplures, avidique suum cognoscere Regem,
"Edita murorum longa statione coronant."

Igitur in tanta equitatione præcessere cives Baiocenses, antecedentibus in una secta tibiis et tubis, et tympanis, aliisque exquisitis musicorum generibus. Hos sequebatur una de Custodiis civitatis, quas "Wardas" appellant, et ipsi in secta sua et maxima melodia. Quos sequebantur Alemanni Regis stipendiarii, et ipsi aliis dissimiles in vestitu. Deinde secuta est et alia Custodia civitatis, priori similis in apparatu; quam sequebantur Wasconenses, et ipsi vario superioribus habituum colore fulgentes. Mox etiam cives Londonienses, qui residui fuerant, secuti sunt Wasconenses equitatione longissima, ita ut numerarentur ex eis in una secta ad tria millia et septingentos. Hos sequebantur Comites et Barones regni, cum suis militibus et armigeris, in amictu similes Regi suo. Nam indumenta omnium erant alba; qui color profecto Regis innocentiam figurabat. Capitaneus De la Buche, cum suis, inter Regem et Dominos in secta sua nobiliter equitabat. Tunc fol. 244 b. Angliæ Marescallus, qui pro tunc fuerat Dominus Henricus Percy—[*continued in line 4, page 331, Vol. I.*]

After "virgam officii sui," *line 5, page 340, Vol. I.*

——asserens se non posse propriis commode rebus præesse, fol. 246 b. et tantæ gravitatis officio. Ferunt eum non ob harc causam renunciasse virgæ, sed quia vidit Dominam de Segrave instare penes Regem pro eodem officio, eo quod contingebat eam jure hæreditario, et credidit adjudicandum illud sibi, noluit tali modo deponi, sed ratus est majus honorificum cedere, nemine compellente: cessit igitur, et ad sua discessit.

After "terram suam," *line 25, page 340, Vol. I.*

Scoti capiunt Thomam Musgrave, Custodem Castelli de Berwyco. fol. 246 b.

Post hæc modico interjecto tempore, quidam miles, Dominus Thomas Mosegrave, Custos castelli de Berwico, ductus cupidine vel transgrediendi facta Comitis, vel adquirendi sibi laudem, Scotiam cum electis militibus, sed admodum paucis, intravit. De cujus adventu Scoti certificati, tetenderunt insidias venienti, et ipsum, cum valentioribus, interceperunt, paucis de valectis et garcionibus per fugam elapsis. Qua occasione Anglici bona Scotorum, ubicumque potuerunt, dantes direptioni, non modicas molestias intulerunt. Siquidem naves oneratas cum bonis mercatorum Scotiæ, ubicumque locorum, vel tempestate pulsas, vel armis captas, apprehenderunt, aut inter se diviserunt, aut regiis usibus servaverunt. Itaque factum est ut Scoti illo anno ubique luerent inconsultæ temeritatis offensas.

After "prope centum," *line* 20, *page* 342, *Vol. I.*

fol. 247 a. [1]*Responsum Comitis Arundeliæ.*

Comes de Arundelle, Ricardus, cernens tot irruptiones in terris suis in Southsexia fieri per Gallicos, dimisit castellum de Lewes apertum pene sine custode, et recessit ab illa provincia; petentibusque hominibus suis de Lewes adjutorium, respondit non habituros ab eo, nisi conducerent propriis sumptibus quos ipse destinaret in succursum eorum. Eo namque pacto, dixit se velle eis mittere auxiliarios, scilicet, lanceas quadringentas.

Acta Ducis Lancastriæ.

Dux Lancastriæ, habens quoddam castellum, dictum "Cas-" tellum de Peveneseye," in illis partibus, cum peteretur ab hominibus suis mittere illuc custodiam, ne locus ille occuparetur a Gallis, summe despexit Gallicorum potentiam, ... [2]dicens suis :—"Etiam destruant," ait, "illud funditus, potes-" tatem habeo iterum reædificare illud."

Ipse autem Dux, dum hæc omnia agerentur, in partibus Borealibus jocis et venationibus indulsit, Gallorum parvipendens potentiam; æstimans fortassis, prout erat, quod non erant inter eos nobiles, sed vispiliones, qui nollent expectare conflictum, si Dux movisset exercitum contra eos.

Gallici repatriaverunt.

Cum jam Gallici hyemem instare conspicerent, patriam repetere festinabant, maxime propter galeyas in quibus erant, quæ hyemales intemperies hoc anno non poterant tolerare. Qui licet in multis locis tentassent irrumpere, nullicubi tamen ascenderunt, nisi illis in locis ubi nulla maris custodia fuerat constituta. Qui utique, si tantum valuissent audacia, quantam viguit inter eos armatorum copia, Anglia proculdubio irrecuperabile dispendium persensisset. Sed, per omnia benedictus Deus, qui Anglis conservavit suam memoriam, talibus terro-
fol. 247 b. ribus vocans ad pœnitentiam, ut saltem terroribus revocarentur ab errore viæ suæ, qui Ejus nesciebant perfrui lenitate.

Before "Parliamentum Londini," *line* 1, *page* 343, *Vol. I.*

fol. 247 b. Circa Festum Sancti Michaelis Archangeli, cum instaret piscationis tempus, quo Anglici, et præcipue homines de

---

[1] This passage is preceded by six lines in Bibl. Reg. 13 E. ix., fol. 247 a; which have been most carefully erased.

[2] The passage is rendered indistinct by numerous erasures.

Gernemutha, consueverunt pro alleco piscari, missæ sunt duæ bargiæ refertæ bellatoribus apte Gallicorum, quarum una fuerat de Bolonia, ad impediendum piscatores prædictos; quarum metu piscatores patriæ se continentes magnum incurrunt dispendium pro piscatione dimissa; sed et quædam vasa patriæ sunt per easdem bargias intercepta.

Tandem, licet sero, Northfolchi, tot malis [1] antidotum statuentes inferre, quinque naves replent bellatoribus, qui piscatores et patriam tuerentur ab incursibus piratarum. Quo cognito, illico Gallici, velut œstro agitati, patriam et consuetas latebras petere festinarunt; et ita demum piscatores, malorum timore sublato, consueto operi insistebant, patriæ necessitatibus providentes.

After "inclinaret," *line* 29, *page* 430, *Vol. I.*

Episcopus Northwicensis movet causam contra Priorem de Wymundham. fol. 266 a.

Circa dies istos, Henricus Le Spencer, Episcopus Northwicensis, vir litteris nec discretione præditus, juvenis effrænus et insolens, amicitias nec servare doctus nec locare, levavit contra amicum suum calcaneum suum, Priorem videlicet de Wymundham, Dominum Nicholaum de Radclif, Sacræ Paginæ Professorem; et cui gratiam debebat pro meritis, inquietudinem machinatus est.

Siquidem, cum, prout moris est, mandatum accepisset a Rege ad colligendum, in sua Diœcesi, decimas concessas regiis usibus in Parliamento ultimo Londoniis, ut prædicitur, celebrato; vel deputandum ad idem onus ex suis subditis collectorem, non sibi subditum cum voto, non voto professionis obnoxium, cum hujusmodi mandato onerare voluit, sed externum, et a sua obedientia omnimodis alienum; virum videlicet exemptum, et nulli, citra Romanam Curiam, subditum, præterquam Abbati Sancti Albani, ut patet per privilegia ipsius loci, infestare decrevit, Dominum, scilicet, Nicholaum prædictum, de ejus amicitia satis præsumentem, ob merita et beneficia præeminentia quibus sperabat sibi eundem Episcopum amicum maximum præparasse.

Huic ergo mandatur, ut diximus, collectoris officium, ut vel sic quicquam in eo jurisdictionis habere videretur, si mandatum susciperet; vel, si tantum laborem declinare decerneret, saltem donum aliquod prægrande ab eodem, vel pecuniam, taliter extorqueret. Credebat quippe unum ex hiis duobus proculdubio eventurum.

---

[1] *antitodum* in orig., by inadvertence.

Prior autem, modeste declinare cupiens utrumque inconveniens, cum reverentia qua decebat, et mandatum remisit eidem, et ipsum collectoris officium non debere suscipere, præsertim cum per privilegia Monasterii Sancti Albani quo modo a sua subjectione alienus existeret, intimavit. Ad hæc iracundiæ felle commotus Antistes instabilis, et velut alter Herodes insaniens, ad juramenta se contulit, affirmans se nec regalis majestatis intuitu, nec illius interventu, mandatum flectendum a dicto Priore de Wymundham, quin vel collector remaneret, vel Regi responderet de summa in illa provincia colligenda. Sed Qui cunctis legem mandavit, dicens "Non jurabis, ne " forte perjures," pontificale juramentum stare non permisit; sed perjurum, ut expost claruit, et esse pertulit, et incomposito desiderio, non sine magna amaritudine mentis, dimovit.

Revera Prior, cernens Præsulis animum erectum taliter ad ejus inquietationem, prudenter declinavit a patria, et ad Monasterium Sancti Albani perrexit, malens cedere Prioratui quam seipsum et locum suum contra fas tanta sollicitudine irretire. Episcopus vero, nihilominus incepta prosequi, et Justiciarios et apprenticios regni, legisque doctores, allicere, conducere, et in partem suam trahere, promissionibus et muneribus laboravit.

Prior ergo, cum ad Sanctum Albanum pervenisset, et tantos motus Abbati plenius intimasset, mox Abbas, ut cunctis luceret Episcopum nullam jurisdictionem habere in ipsum Priorem, vel in fratres apud cellam suam de Wymundham commorantes, Priorem cessare jussit ab officio Prioratus, et eundem Archidiaconum Monasterii esse præcepit. Sed nec quidem Pontifex et ejus conductitii a prædicti negotii prosecutione cessaverunt; sed constanter asseverabant eundem Priorem electum esse, et ideo deponi nec posse nec debere. E contra, advocati
fol. 266 b. pro parte Abbatis allegabant Abbatem plenam habere potestatem in ponendis et removendis cellarum suarum Prioribus, et non solum Abbatem, sed Priorem Monasterii, Abbathia vacante, cum consilio Conventus eandem potestatem habere dicebant; et ideo talis conditionis Priores astringi ad tam grande officium non posse nec debere probabant. Sed nec ista agebant ad quietem, tanta erat partis adversæ fulvo metallo cœcata multitudo, tam graviter accensa indignatio, ut nulla ratio, nulla allegatio, nulla probatio, adversos ducere posset ad orbitam veritatis; quin potius, magis ac magis nocere cupientes, secreto quoddam breve, sub obtentu juris regalis, fusa pecunia, emercarentur ad distringendum bona Prioratus pro Regis subsidio, defectu Prioris minime relevato.

Interea, prosecutores negotiorum Abbatis, hæc cognoscentes, et ipsi in contrarium breve regium consequuntur ad Vicecomitem, ut supersedeat, et quiescat ab executione prioris scripti sibi directi, usque ad certum tempus.

Dolet igitur Episcopus, et Pontificales advocati turbantur in istis, et totis animis eriguntur ad infirmandum breve prædictum. Pergunt idcirco latenter, ut dolo deciperent quos ratione manifeste nequibant, et occulte aliud breve, quod "Distringas" dicitur, priori simile, petunt et accipiunt; nocituri proculdubio immaniter, si non magis nostrates fuissent in nostris negotiis vigilantes. Sed, quod—[1] "Vigilantibus, et "non dormientibus, jura subveniunt," in præsenti negotio experti sumus.

Enimvero, cum pro instanti negotio et domi orationes fierent, et Londoniis sollicitudo magna procuratorum nostrorum, adepti sunt diligenti vigilantia, contra communem modum regalis Curiæ, et aliud breve regium, quod merito tantæ commotionis turbinibus finem daret, in hæc verba:—

"Rex Thesaurario et Baronibus suis de Scaccario, salutem. "Licet in certificatorio venerabilis patris Henrici, Episcopi "Norwicensis, ad Scaccarium misso, inter alia contineatur "quod idem Episcopus loco sui Priorem de Wymundham, "ad subsidium nobis per clerum nostrum regni Angliæ "ultimo concessum, in Archidiaconatu Norwicensi et North-"folk, in Episcopatu prædicto, ad opus nostrum levandum, "assignavit; quibusdam tamen certis de causis, coram Con-"silio nostro motis et propositis de avisiamento ejusdem, "vobis mandamus quod prædictum Priorem, prætextu certifi-"cationis prædictæ, seu levationis subsidii prædicti, non "molestetis in aliquo, seu gravetis, sed cuicunque processui "coram vobis in dicto Scaccario, contra dictum Priorem, ex "causa prædicta facto seu faciendo, supersedeatis omnino. "Mandavimus enim præfato Episcopo, quod de levatione sub-"sidii prædicti hac vice disponat; ita quod nobis inde citra "terminos in mandato nostro limitatos respondeatur, ut est "justum."

After "manus suas," *line* 23, *page* 439, *Vol. I.*

Charta regia quod Abbas Sancti Albani, nec Priores Cellarum, fient Taxatores nec Collectores Subsidii. fol. 268 b.

Hoc anno concessit Rex, cum avisiamento Consilii sui, quasdam libertates Monasterio Sancti Albani, et chartam exinde confectam sigillari fecit Magno Sigillo; cujus tenor fuit:—"Omnibus ad quos, etc., salutem. Sciatis quod, ob devo-

[1] A well known legal maxim.

"tionem specialem quam erga Sanctum Albanum, Protomar-"tyrem regni nostri Angliæ gloriosum, necnon ad ejus "Monasterium in villa Sancti Albani situatum, quod de fun-"datione progenitorum nostrorum, quondam Regum Angliæ, "et nostro patronatu, existit, gerimus et habemus, nos, de "gratia nostra speciali, concessimus, pro nobis et hæredibus "nostris, dilecto nobis in Christo, Thomæ De la Mare, "Abbati Monasterii prædicti, necnon Prioribus Cellarum "eidem Monasterio subjectarum, quod idem Abbas et Priores, "ac successores eorundem Abbatis et Priorum, in perpetuum "hanc habeant libertatem, videlicet, quod nullus eorum fiat "collector, taxator, assessor, decimarum, quintadecimarum, "subsidii, collectæ, aut cujuscunque rei concessæ, aut con-"cedendæ, nobis, seu hæredibus nostris, Regibus Angliæ, "per clerum aut communitatem regni nostri Angliæ; nec "receptor denariorum inde provenientium aliquo tempore in "futurum, contra suam, seu ipsorum, voluntatem; ut præfati
fol. 269 a. "Abbates et Priores, ac etiam monachi, in Monasterio et "cellis prædictis morantes et moraturi, talibus non implicati "negotiis, Altissimo suum debitum impendere valeant quie-"tius famulatum. In cujus rei testimonium, etc. Teste "Rege, apud Westmonasterium, vicesimo primo die Augusti."

After "patefaciunt," *line* 32, *page* 440, *Vol. I.*

fol. 269 a. *Notabilis Compositio pro Vacatione Abbathiæ Sancti Albani.*

Sub eisdem diebus adquisita est et alia Charta; quod, vacante sede Abbathiæ, Prior et Conventus habeant et teneant custodiam Abbathiæ, omnium videlicet temporalium illius, tam eorum quæ de dotatione et fundatione ejus existunt, quam omnium aliorum temporalium eidem Abbathiæ per prædictos nunc Abbatem et Conventum, et prædecessores suos, legitime adquisitorum; ac etiam per eosdem Abbatem et Conventum, et successores suos, ex nunc, de licentia Regis et hæredum suorum, legitime adquirendorum. Et quod Prior et Conventus inde plenam et liberam administrationem habeant, et inde disponere et ordinare possint; prout Abbas dicti loci, pro tempore existens, inde posset ordinare et disponere, sede plena; salvis feodis militum et advocationibus ecclesiarum, cum acciderint temporibus advocationum prædictarum. Ita tamen, quod omnes redditus et servitia annua de feodis prædictorum, in vacationibus illis, provenientia, remaneant Priori et Conventui prædictis; et salvis Regi, et hæredibus ejus, escaetis quas accidere contigerit temporibus prædictis; quæ quidem escaetæ, postquam rite profectus fuerit, remaneant Abbati, Priori, et Conventui, et eorum successoribus: reddendo Regi et hæredibus suis annuatim, pro custodia Abbathiæ prædictæ, necnon omnium prætactorum, in forma prænotata et recompensatione mille marcarum quæ in singulis vacationibus Regi persolvi solebant, et ratæ earundem, quinquaginta marcas sterlingorum singulis annis ad Scaccarium Regis et hæredum suorum, ad terminos Paschæ et Sancti Michaelis, per æquales portiones. Et quod prædicti Prior et Conventus, et successores eorundem, in singulis vacationibus Abbathiæ prædictæ, in perpetuum habeant et teneant custodiam Abbathiæ prædictæ, et omnium temporalium ejusdem, tam eorum quæ de dotatione et fundatione Abbathiæ prædictæ existunt, quam omnium aliorum temporalium eidem Abbathiæ per prædictos nunc Abbatem et Conventum, et prædecessores suos, legitime adquisitorum, et etiam per eosdem ex nunc, de licentia Regis et hæredum suorum, legitime adquirendorum. Et quod Abbas, Prior, et Conventus, ac successores eorundem, sint quieti de quibuscunque decimis Regi vel hæredibus suis, in quibuscunque vacationibus futuris Abbathiæ prædictæ, per clerum regni Angliæ seu Cantuariensis Provinciæ, concedendis Regi vel hæredibus suis.

Concessit etiam Rex, de avisiamento Consilii sui, et ordinavit, quod dictus redditus quinquaginta marcarum annuarum, coronæ suæ et hæredibus suis [Regibus] Angliæ remaneat annexus in perpetuum; absque eo quod aliqua remissio seu perdonatio ejusdem redditus, in toto vel in parte, per fol. 269 b. se vel hæredes suos, vel eorum aliquem, fiat aliquo tempore futuro, Abbati, Priori, et Conventui, dictæ Abbathiæ, seu eorum aliquibus vel alicui; et absque eo quod per se, vel per hæredes suos, aut ipsorum aliquem, redditus prædictus in toto, vel in parte, per remissionem et perdonationem hujusmodi, aut per alienationem, assignationem, seu dimissionem quamcunque, a dicta corona separaretur quomodolibet in futurum. Et si forte per Abbatem, Priorem, et Conventum, dictæ Abbathiæ, qui pro tempore fuerint, vel aliquos aut aliquem eorundem, aliqua remissio seu perdonatio dicti redditus, in toto vel in parte, a Rege, vel ab aliquo hæredum suorum, impetrata et acceptata fuerit, quod ex tunc præsens concessio regia nullius sit roboris vel virtutis. In cujus rei, etc. Teste Rege, apud Westmonasterium, sexto die Septembris anno regni sui quarto.

Si quem videre delectat plenius tenorem istius chartæ, munimenta scrutetur Domini Abbatis, inter quæ magis plene processum ejusdem poterit reperire.

After "duraturam," *line* 34, *page* 448, *Vol. I.*

Archiepiscopus Cantuariensis, et regni Cancellarius, in festo fol. 271 b. Omnium Sanctorum, rogatus ab Abbate, accessit ad Sanctum

Albanum, ubi celebravit solemniter ipso die divina, una cum Episcopo Bangorensi. Qui ratificavit omnes indulgentias collatas altari reliquiarum, et in posterum conferendas. Et insuper concessit quadraginta dies indulgentiæ frequentatoribus illius loci.

After " elucebit," *line* 29, *page* 483, *Vol. I.*

fol. 279 a. *Præsumptio Villanorum de Barnet, etc.*

Viri de Barnet, de Watforde, et de Rikemersworth, Albanensium instigationibus inducti et animati, chartas consimilium libertatum pro villis suis, pari forma ut Albanenses, de liberis venationibus, piscationibus, et molis manualibus erigendis, intrantes penticium Abbatis, cum arcubus et sagittis, bisacutis, bipennibus, gladiis, et fustibus, extorserunt.

Et de Barnet quidam viri quemdam librum confectum de
fol. 279 b. rotulis curiarum expetierunt, cum multa protervia, comburendum: quia in ipso inveniendum erat, quod omnes pene domus de Barnet tenebantur per rotulos; cum ipsi fallaces et falsi chartas liberas confecissent temporibus pestilentialibus, unus alteri, quando pene nullus senescallus aut cellerarius superat, vel saltem curarat de hujusmodi rebus transitoriis et caducis. Et hunc quidem librum Dominus Abbas, timore perterritus, ipsis tradendum promisit, infra tres hebdomadas, fide-jubente pro eo Henrico Fowik, et quibusdam aliis ex amicis.

Acta sunt hæc a viris de Barnet et de præmissis villis, partim die Sabbati, partim die Dominico, partim die Lunæ, post refectionem.

De Redburniensibus.

Redburnienses consequenter et ipsi, astricti villanis de Sancto Albano simili conjuratione, ipso die Sabbati advenerunt; plebs quidem viribus invalida, sed repleta malitia, postulatura chartam de venationibus, aucupationibus, et piscationibus, liberis exercendis, et de nullis debitæ aut consuetæ servitutis officiis vel operibus manerio de cætero impendendis. Contraxerant autem cum ipsis, ad proloquendum pro eisdem, sub terribili comminatione mortis, si supersedere decernerent, vicinos eorum, homines generosos, Edmundum Crescy, Willelmum Eyle, Thomam Nortone, et quosdam alios valectos villæ. Quibus Abbas satis competens dedit responsum, affirmans se paratum esse ad concedendum eis chartam manumissionis, secundum formam quam Rex concesserat. Aliis vero petitionibus eorum se dixit nescire pro tunc respondere, sed deliberare velle cum Consilio suo, quid de hiis esset agendum; revenirentque sequenti die Jovis, et daret responsum tam rationabile quo merito contentari deberent. Illi vero abeuntes adierunt villanos, qui tunc, ut præmittitur, dejectionibus domorum vacabant; et commixti sunt inter eos, et didicerunt opera eorum, facturi secundum nequitiam eorum; et factum est illis in scandalum.

Nam cum venissent in ipso noctis crepusculo ad Redburnam, mox proclamari fecerunt, sub pœna dejectionis domorum suorum, ut tam qui ad lectos et quietem concessirent, quam qui vigilantes reperti sunt, illico convenirent ad molendinum quod "Bettespol Mulle" vocatur, prostraturi fossatam quæ circumdabat, ex parte stratæ regiæ, pratum Prioris de Redburna, quod vocatur "Pondesmede;" quod falso asserebant pertinuisse communibus præfatæ villæ quondam, et ab eisdem per vim et potentiam alienatum fuisse. Nec mora; invenit stultos stultitia, et congregatus est [1]ad istud perpetrandum magnus numerus fatuorum; multisque manibus adunatis, in brevi dejecta est fossa in multis locis, et complanata, arboresque omnes dejectæ et asportatæ, quæ consitæ fuerant super fossam. Itaque demonstraverunt palam tempore tranquillitatis non eis malitiam adversus dominos suos, sed audaciam operandi nequitiam, defuisse. Ministrabat illis audaciam insolentia et superbia villanorum de Sancto Albano aliqualem, qui affirmabant se confœderatos fuisse villis triginta duabus, quæ omnes exsurgerent in adjutorium illis, si necessitas emersisset.

Redburnenses ergo fatui ipsum Regem, nec totum regnum quidem, putabant posse resistere tantæ virtuti:—Hæc de Redburniensibus.

After "profuturis," *line* 17, *page* 64, *Vol. II.*

Hac æstate, in die Passionis Sancti Albani, celebravit Archiepiscopus Cantuariensis Missam Majorem solemniter apud Sanctum Albanum, non tamen cum pallio; et exhibuit eum splendido Abbas eo die, eo quod rogaverat eum interesse festo. fol. 293 b.

After "prædictorum," *line* 8, *page* 78, *Vol. II.*

[2]*Copia Bullæ Indulgentiæ concessæ per Papam Clementem Hospitali Beatæ Mariæ Leycestriæ, ad instantiam commendabilis memoriæ Henrici Ducis Lancastriæ.* fol. 296 b.

"Clemens Episcopus, servus servorum Dei, ad perpetuam "rei memoriam. Piis desideriis devotorum, illis præsertim "qui salutem respiciunt fidelium animarum, gratum nos decet "præbere consensum; cum itaque, sicut accepimus, ad

[1] *ad apud istud* in orig., by inadvertence.

[2] "*Ista Bulla utilis est, sed inconveniens(?) huic loco.*"—Marginal Note in Bibl. Reg. 13 E. ix.—It belongs, in fact, to an earlier date.

"Ecclesiam Hospitalis Beatæ Mariæ Leycestriæ, Lincolniensis "Diœcesis, in festivitatibus Beati Michaelis Archangeli, ac "per octo præcedentes et octo sequentes festivitates easdem "dies, magna confluat Christi fidelium multitudo: Nos, volentes "Ecclesiam ipsam munere prosequi gratiæ specialis, et a fide-"libus ipsis in spiritualium largitione munerum exhibere nos "liberales, Magistro, seu Priori, dicti Hospitalis, qui est, "et erit, pro tempore, auctoritate Apostolica, tenore præsen-"tium indulgemus, ut fidelium prædictorum qui ad eandem "Ecclesiam festivitatum ipsarum, et præcedentibus ac se-"quentibus octo diebus eisdem, causa devotionis se duxe-"rint conferendos, possint confessiones audire, et, auctoritate "prædicta, eis ab omnibus peccatis quæ sibi confitebuntur, "injuncta eis pœnitentia salutari, de absolutionis beneficio pro-"videre. Nulli ergo omnino homini liceat hanc paginam nostræ "concessionis infringere, vel ei, ausu temerario, contraire. "Si quis autem hoc attentare præsumpserit, indignationem "Omnipotentis Dei et Beatorum Petri et Pauli, Apostolorum "ejus, se noverit incursurum. Data Avinione, nono Kalendas "Martii, Pontificatus nostri anno decimo."—[1] Summa Indulgentiæ, ccclxxvii anni et xl dies.

After "impertimur," *line* 8, *page* 80, *Vol. II.*

fol. 297 a. [2] "Notum sit omnibus vestræ dominationi ac dominationi om-"nium dominorum, ac sanctitati totius Italiæ, quod nos, Magis-"ter Ordinis Sancti Johannis de Rodes, recepimus expressas "litteras a nostris exploratoribus qui pro salute nostræ fidei "habitant Babiloniæ, quod currente anno Domini millesimo "trecentesimo octogesimo quinto, die vicesimo quinto Januarii, "in partibus extraneis Babiloniæ, in uno loco qui vocatur "'Gyeralasi,' una vilissima mulier peperit unum filium, cujus "pater non reperitur, sed [3] eis [4] præcise, mater cujus nomen "est 'Sathanas' de stirpe 'Danathos. Qui puer obscurus "est, et tenebrosus, et habet physionomiam talem, quod ipse "nec clarus est nec lucidus in suo aspectu. Formam habet "terribilem, lucentes oculos, acsi essent lucernæ. Insuper "nostri præfati exploratores dicunt se vidisse dictum puerum, "quod habet oculos pro duobus. Item dicunt, quod cum puer "esset in ætate duorum mensium, loquebatur acsi fuisset

---

[1] A rubric superadded.

[2] There is a Note running down the margin of folio 297 in Bibl. Reg. 13 E. ix.—"*Totum istud Capitulum frivolum est et absurdum,* "*et alieno ingenio hic insertum; et* "*idcirco abradendum usque huc.*"

[3] Qy. if not *ei.*

[4] Written *precisi* in orig.

" perfectæ ætatis, nuncians populo se fore Dei filium. Item fol. 297 b.
" scribunt nostri exploratores, quod videntur in isto puero " omnes scientiæ mundi: cujus statura, de sua ætate, est " optime formata. Item dicunt, quod in nativitate hujus pueri " virtutes cœlestes fecerant diversorum miraculorum signa, " ostendendo diversa. Nam in dicta hora suæ nativitatis, in " media nocte existente magna serenitate temporum ac aeris " luciditate, subito apparuit aeris obscuritas, quæ duravit " ultra spatium quatuor mensium, sic quod nunquam apparuit sol in partibus Babiloniæ; et quamvis sit ibi tempus " aliqualiter clarefactum, videtur tamen quod non possit pristinam claritatem recuperare. Item dicunt, quod ab illo " tempore, et citra, non fuit visa aliqua stella in partibus " illis. Item, in nocte nativitatis ipsius apparuit in aere " magnus ignis, qui taliter coloravit aerem quo videbatur aer " quasi sanguinei coloris. Bene per tres horas descendit ille " ignis, ut terra, super domum nativitatis hujus pueri, et " statim extinctus est sine aqua. Multa alia signa tunc apparuerunt; nam in tertia die post ejus nativitatem, fuit " tempus obscurum, et descenderunt ad terram in loco pluviæ " multi lapides. Ultra quam pluviam, nocte sequente, usque " ad diem, fuerunt multi visi serpentes valde terribiles, per " aerem volantes. Ob cujus causam interrogatus puer prædictus de significatione pluviæ et tot lapidum pretiosorum, " ac illorum serpentium, respondit, quod illi lapides pretiosi " significabant vitam æternam, seu Paradisum, sibi adhærentibus dandum, serpentes vero æternum cruciatum sibi contrariis contribuendum. Item, in nocte nativitatis ejus apparuit hoc signum, quod unus de altioribus montibus totius " Babiloniæ divisus est in duas partes; in cujus medio inventa " columna semialba et semirubea, in qua columna tales " litteræ in lingua Latina repertæ fuerunt sculptæ;—'Nunc " 'venit hora meæ nativitatis, et mundi recessus ac destruc- " 'tionis,'—in vulgari '*Sicut e le vonu lora de lune nascimente* " '*vel pertinente dicto mundo.*' Quam quidem columnam, ac " litteras in eadem sculptas, dicti magistri exploratores dicunt " se vidisse ac legisse, non solum ista sed omnia suprascripta, sic et infrascripta. Item dicunt præfati, puerum " multa miracula facere solo verbo, scilicet mortuos suscitare, " infirmos sanare, cœcos illuminare; et noveritis, quod omnes " illi de Babilonia adorant puerum tanquam Deum, et in " ipsum veraciter credunt, in tantum quod si reperitur aliquis nolens præfato puero credere, aut suæ legi adhærere, " statim Sarraceni præfati ducunt eum ante puerum, qui " unico verbo statim eos ad terram facit cadere mortuos. " Item dicunt istum puerum se velle omnes scripturas anti-

" quas declarare, seu prophetias, quæ per aliquos non possunt " intelligi. Item dicunt, quod fuit vivus venerabilis Doctor " in Theologia, Ordinis Minorum qui est de Viterbio, qui " tantam fidem adhibuit isti puero, quod ipse prædicavit " suam legem multis de populis, asserendo multis rationibus " ipsum fore Omnipotentem Dei Filium, credens hoc esse " verum, propter unam vocem quam asserit de cœlo venisse " per duas horas ante ipsius nativitatem; et dicunt nostri " exploratores istam vocem audisse in hac forma;—'Sitis " 'omnes parati ad recipiendum dilectum filium meum, et " 'beati qui verbum suum sequentur;' quod et dicunt ista " vox fuit ita terribilis et tanti timoris, quod fuit bene audita " per trecenta milliaria. Quapropter nostri exploratores præ- " dicti, videntes talia signa, credunt ipsum firmiter esse " illum expectatum in fine mundi quem nos Christiani 'Anti- " 'christum' appellamus; et credunt firmiter illum puerum " esse puerum unius sacerdotis de Legione, et de qua dicunt " prophetiæ, quod debet venire in mundum ad destruendum " partem fidei Catholicæ. Et auditis talibus novis, nolentes " tam altis verbis de facili fidere, fecimus congregari Capitulum " nostrum, seu Consilium, et conclusimus quosdam de sociis " nostris mittere in Babiloniam, quod nos certificarent de tot " mirabilibus. Qui reversi nunciarunt se cum prædictis ex- " ploratoribus fuisse, et dictum puerum se vidisse, ac illum " vere taliter esse sicut nobis per præfatos nostros exploratores " alias extitit intimatum et notificatum. Qui etiam viderunt " illum lapidem qui erat in monte; ubi sculptæ fuerant supra- " dictæ litteræ, et multa alia mirabilia et innumerabilia, de " quibus esset sermo nimis prolixus narrare. Quapropter nos " considerantes quod milites concordant se cum nostris ex- " ploratoribus, [1]rogant vos instanter et devote, ut omnia præ- " fata publicari faciatis populis omnibus Italiæ; sic quod " quilibet custodiat se a peccatis et pravis operibus, quia " firmiter credimus finem mundi jam instare, etc."

After "Secundi sextus," *line* 34, *page* 83, *Vol. II.*

fol. 298 b. Hoc in tempore Dominus De la Spar, Aquitannicus, rediit de carcere et captivitate Hispanorum, per longam moram inter eosdem misere protelatam.

Rediit et eo tempore Dominus Johannes Karpele de eadem captivitate, miles strenuus: qui ambo capti fuerant cum Domino Johanne Comite Penbrochiæ, eo tempore quo idem Comes suscepit a Rege Edwardo de Wyndeshores Wasconiam defendendam contra Regis Franciæ populosum exercitum, qui

---

[1] Apparently an error for "*rogamus.*"

tunc universam terram illam crudeliter lacerabat. Captus est idem Comes in die Sanctæ Etheldredæ Virginis, juxta multorum opiniones, propter injuriam quam intulit ecclesiæ supradictæ Virginis, in causa inter eandem ecclesiam et ecclesiam Sancti Edmundi Regis de Bury, priusquam recederet de terra ista, supradicta virgine suas injurias in eum et suos, ac etiam totam Angliam, vindicante. Præter captivitatem autem multorum militum et armigerorum, et aliorum hominum, et mortem eo tempore in conflictu prostratorum, perdidit viginti millia marcarum euscoparum ad continuandum werram Wasconiæ supradictam. Dicta vero pecunia quæ collecta fuerat de Sancta Ecclesia Anglicana, fuit Regi, ut creditur, minime fructuosa, quia—

"Non habet eventus sordida præda bonos."

Memoratus autem Comes, ductus in Hispanniam, satis inhumane tractabatur ab Hispanis. Qui, non ferens supercilium Hispanorum, clam misit ad Bertrandum Cleykyn, eo tempore Franciæ Constabularium, rogans ut eum de inhumanorum prædonum manibus liberaret. Erat nempe ipse Bertrandus tantæ fortunæ, ut cunctæ res gerendæ in Francia et Hispania ejus consilium expectarent. Hic ergo, missis litteris, Comitem a Bastardo qui se Regem vocavit Hispaniæ, Henrico, recepit, in partem solutionis pecuniæ sibi debitæ ab eodem. fol. 299 a.

Assignata autem redemptionis suæ summa, cœpit idem Comes usque ad mortem ægrotare, et erat languor gravissimus, ita ut de ejus vita Gallici desperarent. Qui formidantes ne, antequam sua redemptio solveretur, inter eos spiritum efflaret, eum sub omni festinatione Calesiam vivum vehere satagebant. Sed frustra, nam inter illos in fata concessit; ac per hoc Gallici redemptionis ejus summa, non sine magna tristitia, caruerunt. Captus vero fuit, ut præmittitur, anno Domini millesimo trecentesimo septuagesimo secundo.

Quod Castellum capitur in [1] Acquitannia.

Brittrigaldus De la Bret, quidam ex Dominis Acquitanniæ, dum in hac terra dispendiosam tam sibi quam Anglicis moram trahit, homines suo subjecti dominio infestati per Gallicos, eisdem vicem reddere cupientes, congregata manu valida ad quoddam castellum regale prope [2] Richemadour profecti sunt, et insultum facientes eidem, post dirum conflictum illud jure bellico sunt adepti, centum viris armatis,

---

[1] *Acquitancia* in orig.

[2] This hiatus occurs in orig.

quales "lanceas" usu vulgari vocamus, prius in conflictu captis vel occisis.

Eo tempore, cum Januenses Scotiam suis mercibus instaurare cupiunt, navis illorum, quæ "carica" vocabatur, onusta diversis pretiosis rebus, in Comitatu[1] prope villam de Fourneys tempestate collisa et confracta est. Homines ergo prædicti Comitatus, ut sunt ingenii mobilis et levi capite, rati se posse tollere quicquid vellent a naufragis, et præcipue [qui] cursum direxerant ad hostes suos, quæque pretiosa diripiebant, sibi clamantibus Januensibus frustra fidem et suffragium regionis, et leges regni. Et cum nihil proficerent, et nostrates insolentius agerent, Londonias accesserunt, suasque injurias coram Regis Consilio depondituri; ubi tantam misericordiam invenerunt, ut dirigerentur cum eis, ex parte Regis, quidam qui eorum damna resarciri facerent, et eos facerent cum pace remeare.

After "rite rexisset," *line* 4, *page* 115, *Vol. II.*

fol. 306 a. *De Visitatoribus.*

Per idem tempus, Abbas de Burgo Sancti Petri, visitator constitutus in ultimo Generali Capitulo celebrato, misit suos Commissarios, duos videlicet de commonachis suis, ad visitandum Monasterium Sancti Albani, instructos sufficienti mandato ad dictam visitationem peragendam; quam et perfecerunt uno die, nihil ibidem reperientes quale voluerant aut sperabant.

After "eum facti," *line* 25, *page* 116, *Vol. II.*

fol. 306 b. *De Eclipsi Solis.*

Eodem anno, die sexta-decima mensis Augusti, sero et per noctem sequentem audita sunt in Anglia perhorrenda tonitrua, et visa fulgura terribilia, quæ mortales multipliciter terruerunt.

In crastino vero post meridiem, quasi per horam, facta est eclipsis solis, et conjunctio simul, aspicientibus eas multis.

After "tumulari," *line* 22, *page* 130, *Vol. II.*

fol. 309 a. *De quibusdam insolitis.*

Hoc anno, dum Conventus Sancti Albani interesset adhuc Matutinis, quæ in honorem Translationis Beati Martyris Thomæ, et Archiepiscopi Cantuariensis, celebrantur cito post mediam noctem, corruit coquina Abbatis, et irrestaurabiliter est confracta. Cujus lapsus tunc adeo, prout credimus, et

---

[1] This hiatus occurs in orig.—"*Cumbriæ*" is probably the word omitted.

Beato Martyre est provisus quando nullus pernoctavit in eadem domo. Nunquam enim sine pueris vel hominibus esse solebat in nocte. fol. 309 b.

Septimo die sequente, circa horam tertiam, audita sunt tonitrua et visa fulgura—(*as in page* 130, *line* 26, *of this Volume*).

After "prisones," *line* 31, *page* 136, *Vol. II.*

Captivatio Domini Mediolanensis. fol. 310 b.

Hoc anno, Barnabo Dominus Mediolani a [1] genero suo captus est, et mancipatus carceri, propter tyrannidem quam exercere non destiterat; et tota regio ejus præfato genero parebat voluntarie, eo quod videbatur civitatem et regionem a gravibus subjectionibus liberasse.

Nempe præter tributa multa quæ remisit, diversis in locis delevit maximam canum multitudinem, quos pascendos susceperant, non solum divites sed ipsi pauperes, et pene nihil habentes propriæ sustentationi; quique tamen illud modicum quod habebant, dare canibus cogebantur. Ob quam causam Barnaboni captivatio, et ejus genero totius dominii deditio, facilius succedebat.

After "hac plaga," *line* 32, *page* 142, *Vol. II.*

De exercitu Regis Franciæ prostrato in Portyngalia. fol. 312 a.

Sub hiis diebus, Hispani audientes quod Dux Lancastriæ fixum teneret in animo regnum Hispaniæ vendicare, et ad illud negotium exercitus et arma, naves et necessaria, præparasset, missis legatis Regi Franciæ, deprecantur auxilium, ut ipse illis, juxta fœdera inter illa regna firmata, in tam arta necessitate aliquale subsidium provideret. Quibus Rex Franciæ in sua petitione deesse reputans indecorum, misit armatos ex Gallicis et Britonibus viros præelectos, ad numerum sexcentorum.

Qui illuc quidem feliciter pervenientes, sed infeliciter se gerentes, dum nimis confidunt in virtute propria, et bacchantur in patria, dispendium magnum et inevitabile repente senserunt. Revera Anglici, qui cum Rege fuerunt Portingaliæ, adunatis Ulixibonensibus et aliis patriotis, occurrunt Gallicis insolentibus, etiam in Portingalia prædas et incendia, ac [2] cædes crudeles, agentibus, et tam animose committunt cum eisdem prœlia, quod totum prædictum numerum dissipaverunt, pro-

[1] *genere* in orig.

[2] *sedes* in orig.

straverunt, ceperunt, vel occiderunt. Quo facto, luctus et desperatio crevit Hispanis, et ira ac indignatio Britonibus atque Gallicis, postquam hæc domi infortunia cognoverunt.

After " cum Rege," *line* 28, *page* 156, *Vol. II.*

fol. 315 a. *De Visitatoribus.*

Eo tempore, mense Maio, circa decimum diem mensis, venerunt duo monachi de Monasterio de Eynesham, vice Abbatis sui, nuper in ultimo Generali Capitulo constituti Visitatores in Lincolniensi Diœcesi, ad visitandum præsens Monasterium. Qui peracto negotio redierunt, nihil, quod tantum locum deceret, reportantes.

After " susceptus est," *line* 28, *page* 182, *Vol. II.*

fol. 320 a. *Quid Scoti egerunt apud Tynemutham.*

Eodem tempore Scoti intraverant, et pene totum Comitatum de Tynemutha vastaverant, prædati fuerant, et succenderant, nemine resistente; et cum ad villam de Tynemutha venissent, petierunt loqui pacifice cum cellerario et hiis qui in castello erant. Egressus ergo cellerarius, cum cœpisset pacifice cum eis agere de redimenda villa, cum appendiciis, ab incendio, subito vispiliones latenter ingressi domos, imposuerunt ignem in tectis, et repente incendium per totam villam colluxit. Quod cernens quidam de castellanis, emisit de balista et percussit quemdam garcionem Comitis de Murrez, ita ut mortuus crederetur. Fit ergo clamor Scotorum ingens, et cellerarium perfidiæ arguunt, eum perimere statuentes. Sed interventu quorundam Scotorum, eum diligentium, ereptus est, et domum redire permissus, ea conditione ut læsum Scotum secum duceret, et curam ipsius haberet, sanumque in Scotiam ad dominum suum, domus suæ sumptibus, destinaret.

Sicque Scoti ab illo loco recesserunt.

fol. 322 a. *After* " negotii supradicti," *line* 39, *page* 192, *Vol. II.*

In reditu Domini Archiepiscopi de sua visitatione, misit Abbas Sancti Albani Priorem Monasterii ad villam de Dunstaple, ad Dominum Archiepiscopum, ut invitaret eum ad
fol. 322 b. capiendum recreationem in Monasterio Sancti Albani, et pernoctandum ibidem. Quibus Archiepiscopus gratanter annuit, et in Monasterio cœnavit et pernoctavit, ad sumptus Abbatis, et mane recessit gratias agens infinitas. Non tamen visitare petiit, aut aliquid, quod nostra privilegia læderet, atten-

tavit; nec in adventu suo, vel recessu, pulsata sunt signa Monasterii, aut ecclesiarum parochialium ipsius villæ.

After "discesserunt," *line* 6, *page* 195, *Vol. II.*

Obiit Abbas de Waltham. fol. 322 b.

Sub eisdem diebus, obiit Dominus Nicholaus, quondam Abbas de Waltham, videlicet, nono-decimo Kalendas Januarii; cujus loco electus est Dominus Willelmus Neel, olim capellanus ejusdem Domini Nicholai.

After "incommodo generali," *line* 5, *page* 197, *Vol. II.*

Subsidium de Tynemutha. fol. 323 a.

Eodem tempore, Dominus Rex, sollicita mediatione Ducum Lancastriæ et Gloverniæ, necnon Comitis Northumbriæ, ac intuitu precum venerabilis patris Domini Thomæ, Abbatis de Sancto Albano, quam maxime, ut putatur, concessit quingentas libras ad resarciendum ruinam quæ apud Tynemutham contigerat, in porta Prioratus, anno proximo præcedente. Ad quod opus maturandum, dictus Dux Lancastriæ de thesauro proprio dedit centum libras, et Dominus Comes Northumbriæ contulit centum marcas.

Visitatores.

In Vigilia Sancti Basilii, Archiepiscopi, Abbas de Thorneya, decretus Visitator in Diœcesi Lincolniensi, misit duos de suis commonachis, discretos viros, cum procuratorio sufficienti, qui apud Sanctum Albanum, vice sua, visitationis officium exercerent; qui, admissi cum reverentia debita, injunctum sibi negotium suaviter peregerunt.

After "murmurarent," *line* 32, *page* 199, *Vol. II.*

Acta apud Sanctum Albanum. fol. 324 a.

Hoc anno, in Die Ascensionis Dominicæ, Dominus Thomas Arundel, Archiepiscopus Eboracensis, rogatus celebravit Missam Magnam in Ecclesia Sancti Albani, et interfuit processioni et deportationi Martyris eodem die, et ad mensam præsidebat in Aula Abbatis,

In hebdomada Pentecostes Sabbato, Dominus Simon, Episcopus Akadensis, celebravit Ordines ad majus altare in Ecclesia nostra, vocatus ab Abbate nostro, et in crastino interfuit precibus, et celebravit Missam solemniter ad idem altare, et fuit in choro ad utrasque Vesperas revestitus.

After "adventu suo," *line* 29, *page* 202, *Vol. II.*

fol. 324 b. Eo tempore obiit Edmundus Brounfeld, Episcopus Landafensis.

After "horresco," *line* 21, *page* 208, *Vol. II.*

fol. 325 b. *Consilium apud Notyngham.*

Rex igitur apud Notyngham tenuit super hiis Consilium, ubi fuere congregati cum Rege, Duces, Comites, et Barones, Vicecomites, et plures aliarum civitatum procuratores et cives; et, inter cæteros, vocati sunt Londonienses, non ut venirent more solito ad Parliamentum pro communitate quatuor electi de civitate, sed ut ipse Major adesset, cum Vicecomitibus Londoniarum, Aldermannis, et ditioribus ac valentioribus civitatis.

Profecti sunt ergo de civitate, dubii quorsum tenderet hæc evocatio, majores, ut diximus, qui re vel nomine aliis præstare videbantur. Cumque pervenissent Notyngham, ibi repererunt Vicecomites et tribunos, urbium rectores, jurisperitos, et villarum comprovincialium eminentiores, qui, si necesse foret, possent juratas facere per bis senos.

In place of the passage in page 211, *Vol. II., commencing* (*l.* 24), "Eodem tempore, cum Dux Glovernise," *and ending, page* 212, "*l.* 16, defuit ei disciplina."—*the following is the context in the closing page of Bibl. Reg.* 13 *E. ix.*—

fol. 326 b. ***Dux Gloverniæ, profecturus in Hibernia, revocatur.***

Eo tempore, Dux Glovernise, accepta a Rege grandi summa pecuniæ, juxta condictum, disposuit se transfretare in Hiberniam cum forti exercitu pugnatorum; de cujus adventu cuncti reguli illius terræ tantum sunt territi, ut de deditione tractarent, talia conferentes;—"Adest," inquiunt, "invictus heros, "sapiens et prudens dominus, miles audax, strenuus, et fortunatus, non de vulgari progenie procreatus, sed regis "proles et regis avunculus, cui non dedecet quemquam confœderari. Occurramus ei cum pace, offeramus nos et "nostra; et forsitan indulgebit nobis bona nostra et consuetudines nostras antiquas; vel si hoc non fecerit, saltem "vivamus sub eo, more Wallicorum, qui satis alta pace "gaudent, quotiens pacifici volunt esse."

Placuit hoc consilium cunctis regulis qui palustria colunt, sylvestria, vel montana, quorum regiones nullum dominum extraneum hactenus sunt expertæ, propter inaccessibilitatem et locorum notoriam difficultatem. Sed illis metum dempsit illico Ducis repentina revocatio, qui, quorundam levium in regno consilio, impeditus fuit a fructuoso proposito.

Ordines apud Sanctum Albanum.

Hoc anno, mense [1] Septembris, celebravit Ordines apud Sanctum Albanum, in capella Sanctæ Mariæ, jussu Abbatis, Dominus Milo, Episcopus Clunenensis.

De infirmitate Regis Franciæ periculosa.

Eodem anno Rex Franciæ Karolus gravem infirmitatem incurrit phrenesis, ut putatur, dum expeditionem moveret in Britanniam, ad infestandum Ducem, ut dicitur, minus juste. Nempe cum pervenisset Floriacum, ubi corpus quiescit legislatoris monachorum, Beati, videlicet, Benedicti, et ingressus ecclesiam sanctis reliquiis insignitam, scrinium, in quo ossa Sancti sunt recondita, cepit, sine humano ingenio, tremere et moveri. Cumque Rex hoc vidisset, et visum horruisset, quæsivit quid prætenderet tale signum. Cui loci custos,— "Domine mi, Rex," inquit, "progenitores vestri, illustres "Reges Franciæ, quotiens in longinquam provinciam vel ad "bella fuerant egressuri, hunc locum, devotionis gratia, visi-"tarunt. Quibus si quodlibet infortunium immineret, per "signum commotionis reliquiarum in hoc feretro conditarum, "præsciverunt damna vel dispendia affutura; unde frequenter "mutantes propositum, infortunia devitabant. Nunc ergo "pensate, mi domine, quid vobis expediat, et non contem-"natis quod ostendit Dominus vobis signum."

Rex tamen, nihili pendens verba monentis, statuit peragere cœptum iter; cumque foret in itinere, repente cœpit furere, et in quemlibet vicinius propinquantem irruere, multos perimere, plurimos vulnerare, donec ingeniose captus et constrictus esset. Perseveravitque in hac amentia, semet ipsum dilanians et discerpens, ac manus et brachia sua mordens, donec calor æstivus transisset. In hyeme vero cœpit paulatim infirmitas mitigari, et ipse redditus est suo sensui et sobrietati priori.

De morte Roberti, quondam Comitis Oxoniæ.

Circa præsens tempus, Robertus de Veer, quondam Comes Oxoniæ, qui per multos gradus saltaverat ad nomen Ducatus Hiberniæ, in Lovania diem clausit extremum, in mentis angaria, et rerum penuria miseranda. Qui equidem juvenis aptus fuit ad cuncta probitatis opera, si non defuisset ei in pueritia disciplina. Sed væ præsentis temporis pueritiæ! quæ permittitur sine doctore, sive magistro, pergere quocunque

---

[1] *Septembrio* in orig.

libet. Olim regni nobiles filios suos, a balbutiente ætate, tradiderunt militibus vel armigeris veteranis, ad informandum litteris et facetia, ut scirent omne genus inhonestatis cautius evitare. Nunc, quia res versa est in contrarium, adolescentes præsentis temporis, doctore carentes, gaudent vigiliis protractis ultra noctem mediam, et somnis usque meridiem, ludis pilæ et alcæ, horribilibus juramentis, et cæteris quæ non expediunt neque decent. Unde contingit, quod liberi ruricolarum plus proficiunt in facetia, [1] qui domi de parentibus audiunt, quam filii dominorum qui continue in carnalitate versari deberent.

(The concluding words of the MS. Bibl. Reg. 13 E. i.e. as now found in the British Museum.)

---

[1] *quam* in orig., by inadvertence.

APPENDIX. (C).

FINAL LEAF ORIGINALLY BELONGING TO THE ST. ALBAN'S MS. BIBL. REG. 13 E. IX. (IN THE BRITISH MUSEUM), WHICH IS NOW INSERTED IN MS. CORP. CHR. VII., PAGES 49 AND 50.

Annalis Conclusio. page 49. MS. Corp. Chr. vii.

Transiit annus iste frugifer abundanter, ut modius frumenti pro quatuor denariis venderetur, sed fructuum raritate notabilis; pacificus Anglis, Francis, et Scotis; regionibus ultra Danubium et Mare Magnum inquietus.

Anno gratiæ millesimo trecentesimo nonagesimo tertio, qui est annus regni Regis Ricardi, a Conquæstu Secundi, sextusdecimus, tenuit Rex Natale ad manerium suum in magnificentia et gloria magna valde.

Hoc anno tenuit Rex, cito post Natale, Parliamentum Wyntoniæ; ex quo nullus omnino fructus evenit, præterquam quod exegit dimidiam decimam et mediam quintam-decimam, ad expensas Ducum Lancastriæ et Gloverniæ, pro tractando de pace profecturorum.

Eodem tempore fuere rumores in regno quod Rex Franciæ, dum tripudiaret in aula sua cum quatuor militibus de familia sua, et esset disfiguratus in sylvestrem hominem, habens strictum vestimentum resina et pice refertum, ut lini stipula, quæ fixa erat in vestimento, hæreret fortius et tenacius, et repræsentaret sylvanum evidentius, nisi gratia affuisset, in cineres combustus fuisset; factione fratris sui, qui a tempore suæ infirmitatis aspiravit ad regnum. Nempe illo cum sociis ducente choream, quidam, ad hoc subrogatus, ex industria torticii submisit ignem in stipula; qui, ardens usque ad vestimentum, quod constrictum et consutum erat corpori, ubi invenit materiam picis et resinæ, inextinguibiliter arsit usque ad corpus. Videns tantum periculum, quædam domina occurrit et Regem rapuit de chorea. Rex vero hoc modo salvatus fuit, sed quatuor socii nullo ingenio potuerunt salvari, donec semiustis pellibus atque carnibus expirassent.

Translatio Banci et Curiarum Regiarum ad Eboracum.

Hoc anno Bancus Regius et Cancellaria transferuntur de Londoniis ad Eboracum, vel odio Londoniensium, ut fertur, vel favore Eboracensium; eo quod Cancellarius, qui fuit Archiepiscopus Eboraci, cuperet profectum civitatis suæ. Sed non longo tempore duravit hæc novitas; quia eadem facilitate qua transportabantur Eboracum, eadem Londoniis reportabantur.

Obitus Johannis Deveros, Regis Senescalli, et aliorum loco ejusdem substitutorum.

Isto anno, in festo Cathedræ Sancti Petri, obiit repente Dominus Johannes Devros, miles, Regis Senescallus et Doveriæ Constabularius, dum parasset se ad maris transitum cum Ducibus Lancastriæ et Gloverniæ, pro tractatu pacis prælocutæ. Cui successit, in officio Senescalli, Dominus Thomas Percy, qui fuerat prius Subcamberlanus regius: in Constabulariam Doveriæ Dominus de Bemond successit eidem, et Willelmus Scrop Regis Subcamerarius est effectus.

Creatio Novi Comitis Oxoniæ.

Eodem tempore, Dominus Albredus De Veer factus est Comes Oxoniæ, quippe qui fuit proximus in consanguinitate Roberto De Veer, qui in Lovania desiit superesse.

De Insula de Man, a Comite Sarum Domino Willelmo Scrop vendita.

Circa tempus præsens, Dominus Willelmus Scrop, miles providus et prædives, emit de Domino Willelmo de Monte Acuto, Comite Saresbiriæ, insulam Euboniæ cum corona. Est autem jus illius insulæ, ut quisquis illius fuerit dominus capitalis, "Rex" vocetur; cui etiam fas est corona aurea coronari. Hæc insula vulgari vocabulo "Insula Man" vocatur.

Profectus, apparatus, et effectus tractatus, Anglorum et Francorum.

Hoc anno Duces Lancastriæ et Gloverniæ profecti sunt in Franciam, tractaturi de pace finali totiens prolocuta; sed tamen nondum finis, quia Rege Franciæ infirmato, iterum non potuit finis esse, nec etiam Rex Angliæ ad quasdam conditiones quas Franci imposuerant, licet Rex Franciæ sanus affuisset et incolumis, voluit consensisse. Apparatus tamen non minor fuit in præparatione et ostentatione divitiarum, et in tentoriis mirabilis operis et amplitudinis utrobique. Nam etsi Franci magnifice sua tentoria in campo ultra Calesiam extendissent, quia et in campo tractatus futurus erat, Ducis tamen Lancastriæ apparatus omnium aliorum vicit incomparabiliter apparatum; ita ut aulam prægrandem, cum funiculis et campana notante diurnas horas et nocturnas, capellam, et cameras, varia quoque claustra et plateas diversas, pro reliquo suo populo hospitando, in quibus cotidie exercebantur fora et mercimonia, causæque curiales, non tam magnifice quam mirifice erexisset.

Fecerunt itaque Duces in illo loco longam moram, dona donantes varia, et recipientes plurima convivia; facientes opipara, sed non tamen reportantes pacis gaudia, nisi quod treugas reportaverunt tractatus tempore duraturas.

Henricus Percy, Junior, fit Custos Aquitanniæ. page 50.

Per idem tempus Dominus Henricus Percy, junior, constitutus Custos Burdegaliæ loco Ducis Lancastriæ, profectus est in Aquitanniam, sed tamen artatus est ab ingressu Burdegaliæ, qui venit vice Ducis Lancastriæ, cui Rex dudum donaverat Ducatum Aquitanniæ. Burdegalenses nempe, et primores illius patriæ, detrectabant ferre dominium cujusquam nisi Regis Angliæ, vel certe filii sui, si filium genuisset; et idcirco, nunc Henrico negabant ingressum, donec asseverasset se non vice Ducis Lancastriæ, sed vice Regis Angliæ, advenisse.

Visitatio Monasterii Sancti Albani, auctoritate Provincialis Capituli.

Eodem anno venerunt ad Sanctum Albanum duo monachi de Rameseia, commissarii Abbatis sui, cui visitationis officium fuit injunctum nuper in Capitulo Generali. Qui ostendentes commissionem, reverenter admittebantur ad visitationis officium exercendum; perfeceruntque visitationem omnium personarum in Vigilia festi Corporis Christi, post dictum sermonem ante prandium in duabus horis, et mane in Capitulo facta brevi collatione in laudem religionis et personarum Monasterii, Capitulum dimiserunt.

De tempestatibus mirabilibus et insuetis.

Mense Septembris in multis locis fulgura et coruscationes, cum tonitruis horribilibus, plurimos terruerunt, et gravia damna quibusdam intulerunt; nam ut prætermittamus loca plurima quæ damna senserunt, villam de Lollysworth, in Comitatu Cantabruggiæ, vehementius invaserunt, ita quod quamplures domos in eadem villa, cum frugibus ibi collectis, et in campo blada acervata, cremaverunt, et tanto fœtore cineres infecerunt, ut propius possessores accedere timuerunt.

Subsequenter mense Septembri apud Novum Mercatum, et juxta villam de Barwe, inundationes aquarum tantæ de nubibus ceciderunt, ut bina vice domos diruerent, et viris et mulieribus periculum demersionis pene inferrent.

Circa præsens tempus multa miraculorum signa fecit Divinitas circa corpus Baldewyni, quondam Abbatis de Bury, quæ merito et devotionem augerent provincialium, et affectum ad illius reliquias venerandum.

Eodem anno, in Estsexia, mensibus Septembris et Octobris, multi tacti pestilentia moriebantur.

APPENDIX. (D).

PASSAGES IN THE MANUSCRIPT, (1) CORP. CHR. VII. WHICH HAVE BEEN OMITTED IN THE COMPILATION OF THE LATTER PORTION OF WALSINGHAM'S "ENGLISH HISTORY," MS. ARUNDEL No. VII.

After "commendavit," *line* 14, *page* 222, *Vol. II.*

— successitque in Archipræsulatum Eboraci Frater de Ordine , provisione Papali, contra vota totius cleri Eboracensis. Eodem anno decessit totius monasticæ religionis speculum, Dominus Thomas, Abbas Monasterii Sancti Albani: cui successit, per electionem, Dominus Johannes Moot, Prior ejusdem loci; qui, juxta nova privilegia de Curia impetrata, ut videlicet eo ipso quod esset rite electus, esset et confirmatus, primus omnium eo privilegio usus; accepitque munus benedictionis ab Archiepiscopo Cantuariensi, Domino Thoma de Arundelia; non quia sic oportuit, sed quia per manus benedici præelegit. Qui benedixit eum in manerio suo de Saltwode. page 25. (1) MS. Corp. Chr. vii.

After "Boowet," *line* 3, *page* 247, *Vol. II.*

[1] Sub eodem tempore Abbas de Waltham sæculo valefecit. page 101.

After "devitavit," *line* 20, *page* 248, *Vol. II.*

Hoc anno Dominus Johannes Moot, Abbas Sancti Albani, rebus humanis exemptus est; cui successit, electus per viam scrutinii, Dominus Willelmus de Hethworthe, cellerarius dicti loci. page 101.

After "prædatam," *line* 16, *page* 251, *Vol. II.*

Eo tempore obiit Dominus Edmundus de Langley, Dux Eboraci, filius quondam illustris Angliæ Edwardi, Tertii page 103.

---

[1] The variation in the marginal references to the pages, arises from the fact that the pages of several manuscripts are promiscuously intermingled in MS. Corp. Chr. vii.

Conquæstu; cujus corpus, sine tumultu sive frequentia, apud Langley sepultum est, juxta corpus suæ conjugis, inter Fratres. —Hæc erat filia quondam Regis Castillæ Petri.

Before "Regina," *line* 13, *page* 254, *Vol. II.*

page 104. Post festum Purificationis, nuncii solemnes, qui destinati fuerant ad conducendum Reginam de Britannia, sospites redierunt, licet maris infortunia multotiens perpessi fuissent; occurrit ergo Rex Reginæ futuræ, cum nobilibus multis, apud Wyntoniam, ubi præstolabantur adventum Dominæ multitudo procerum et dominarum. Vicesima vero sexta die mensis ejusdem Londoniis, apud Westmonasterium, coronata fuit magnifice Domina memorata. Sicque translata fuit hera præfata de Minori Britannia ad Majorem, de ducatu ad regnum, de gente feroci et inculta ad populum pacificum et quietum, et, utinam, fausto pede.

After "coronata," *line* 20, *page* 254, *Vol. II.*

page 104. Eodem tempore egressa est a Sede Apostolica inusitata sententia, novitas inaudata, facula scintillans occasiones murmurationis et scandala per totum pene regnum Angliæ contra Sanctam Sedem; dum quisque, qui per graves labores et sumptus immodicos a dicta Sede gratias, beneficia, vel indulgentias impetraverat, tempore Papæ præsentis, vel in diebus prædecessoris sui, doluit se repente totam perdidisse operam et impensam, cernens inopinate quicquid impetraverat revocatum et irritum, cassatum penitus et annullatum; unde de [1] tanta levitate, quam vocant hii qui gravati sunt mutabilitatem vel inconstantiam, fiebant execrationes et obloquia pleno ore, et dissuasiones ad invicem ne quis impetraret quicquam de cætero, ubi nulla fuerat certitudo, sed quotiens Dominus Papa consulere vellet suo marsupio proprio, non dubitaretur erubesceret contravenire verbo vel scripto. Sic susurrabant in privato et publico, et sic impingebant adversus Dominum et adversus Christum ejus. Nos autem, quia putamus nihil inordinatum, nihil incultum, ab ipsa Sancta Sede posse procedere, committimus hanc materiam pertractandam discretioribus, ad alia festinantes.

After "cupientes," *line* 27, *page* 254, *Vol. II.*

page 104. Consequenter Comes Northumbriæ, cum filio, hostiliter intrans Scotiam, vastavit in gyro patriam, prædas et captivos

---

[1] This word is indistinct and uncertain in the original.

trahens, nemine succurrente. Post dies aliquot per aliam viam reversus est in regionem suam. Et mox rumores spargebantur per totam Angliam, quod illi præfixissent bellum Scoti in festo ad Vincula Sancti Petri; cujus belli fuisset occasio cujusdam castri per eundem obsessio dum dudum Scotiam penetravit. Cujus castri defensores dum nequirent se defendere, petierunt, ut ferebatur, inducias usque ad dictum festum. Quo die, si Scoti non facerent sibi belli copiam, castrum redderetur in manus suas; et rursum, si Scotos superari contingeret, illi castrum nihilominus redderetur. Ad hos rumores tota juventus evigilavit Angliæ, regnique nobilitas, cum ipso Rege, bello cupiens interesse: sed Comes denunciavit Regi non opus esse sibi sua præsentia, sed nec expedire ut se elongaret a patria; sed tantum voluit ut quibus placuit Domini accederent et Barones. Cumque plures se præparassent ad prænotatum negotium, repente totum patuit fuisse phantasma et frivolum, prout sequentia declarabunt.

After "partes," *line* 23, *page* 256, *Vol. II.*

Cumque Rex causaretur sibi deesse militares copias,—"Non "curetis," inquit, "quia qui vos diligunt, cum profecti fueri- "tis, vestigia vestra sequentur, cognoscetisque in hoc facto "vestros fideles, et eos qui vos ficte colunt." page 89.

After "oppositum," *line* 6, *page* 257, *Vol. II.*

Interea requisivit Henricus, quo confidebat præ cæteris, ubi foret, responsumque fuit quod relictus erat cum rebus aliis in parva villa juxta posita, quæ "Berwicus" ab incolis dicebatur. Ad quod nomen ita mox palluit, ut astantes duceret in stuporem, trahensque ab alto suspiria,—"Cerno," ait, "cerno quod modo meum aratrum ad sulcum pervenit ulti- "mum; nempe prædictum mihi fuit per fatidicum, cum ad- "huc in partibus essem propriis, apud Berwicum moriturum; "sed decepit me, proh dolor! nominis æquivocatio." Nec tamen suos segnius disposuit ad bellum, sed promittit ipsos eo die finem malorum consecuturos, si persisterent, et expost divites et gloriosos futuros de tanti fama facti. Secuti sunt eum nobiles ad hunc locum Comes Wygorniæ, Dominus Thomas Percy, de quo nunquam perante surrepserat ulla suspicio cujuscunque perfidiæ; sed inter Anglos, qui de levitate notantur apud exteros, hic solus de fidei præ cæteris integritate laudem promeruit. Itaque Regis Franciæ et Hispaniæ, alia- page 89.

rumque [1] nationum rectores et domini, ejus solo verbo, plus quam alterius chirographo; in tractatibus sive conventionibus fidem darent. Secutus est et Henrici propositum, Comes Doglas, Scotus, qui dudum captus fuerat in bello de Homeldon Hulle, vir per omnes bellicosus, cujus animositati, prudentiæ, sive fortitudini, pauci sub hiis diebus poterant adæquari. Baro quoque de Kyndertone et Dominus Hugo Brown, necnon Dominus Ricardus Vernoun, affuerunt He[n]rici conceptibus, cum decem aliis qui pares Baronibus extiterunt.

Cernens Rex acies contra se desposítas et arcitenentes præcipuos, disposuit et ipse suos alacritate qua Regem decuit, et ad prœlium confortavit.

Variation in ll. 18–21, *page* 257, *Vol. II, for* "Igitur arcitenentes . . . regii sagittarii.

page 90. Igitur arcitenentes Henrici, quibus meliores nusquam poterant inveniri, sagittando prœlium inchoarunt; qui densantes jacula excutere diem—

"Telis, nec jaculis artatus sufficit aer;
"Nec locus ad terram jaculis, in corpora ferrum
"Omne cadit, sæpe ignari [2] perimuntque caduntque;
"Casus agit virtutis opus."—

Nec minus regii sagittarii—

After "emisere," *line* 23, *page* 257, *Vol. II.*

page 90. "[3] Quantus ab occasu veniens pluvialibus Hædis,
"Verberat imber humum."—

Non tamen sufferre potuere regales horrida sagittarum nubila de parte Henrici evolantia, sed sociorum casu territi, qui in circuitu suo decidere subito, velut poma cadentia in Autumno, cum jam matura moventur ab Africo; multa simul millia de bello fugerunt, putantes Regem proculdubio sagittatum. Sed cum sagittarii sua jacula expendissent—

—— "Et spatiis utrinque æqualibus acti,
"Adventant, mediumque vident decrescere campum,
"Jam clypeus clypeis, umbone repellitur umbo,
"Ense minax ensis, pede pes, et cuspide cuspis."

Ipse vero campiductor, etc.

After "perscrutantes," *line* 32, *page* 257, *Vol. II.*

page 90. "Fulmineos veluti præceps cum comminus egit,
——strictisque erexit cornua setis."

---

[1] *nationes* in orig., by inadvertence.
[2] Apparently, *puniuntque* in orig.
[3] Virgil, *Æneid*, ix., ll. 668, 9.

After "captus est," *line* 11, *page* 258, *Vol. II.*

—— cujus animositatem et constantiam reliqui rebelles si imitati fuissent, non dubium quam plaga insanabilis facta fuisset eo die in populo Anglicano, hic bina vice, etc. page 90.

After "Werkwortha," *line* 2, *page* 259, *Vol. II.*

—— Quod affatim victualibus instauratum firmavit contra cunctos incursus hostium. page 90.

After "custodia," *line* 12, *page* 259, *Vol. II.*

Per id tempus heremita quidam, nomine "Willelmus de "Norham," qui multa futura prædixerat Regi Ricardo, dum Regi moderno prophetare nititur, et minus prudenter invehitur, notatus de mendacio apud Eboracum decollatur. page 41.

After "invadunt," *line* 31, *page* 259, *Vol. II.*

—— succendunt, et impune diripuerunt, duce quodam Britone, Domino de Castellis; cui reverso senex quidam Britannicus monuit cavere de canda, "quia non diu," inquit, "tolerabunt æquanimiter Angli tot illata sibi damna." Evenitque cito prophetia, ut lugeret Britannia quod Anglia perdidisset. Nam de classe Occidua profecti sunt viri virtutis sub ducatu cujusdem scutiferi, qui vocabatur "Willelmus de Wilford," in partes Britanniæ, ubi ceperunt naves majores et minores ad numerum quadraginta. page 41.

After "villæ," *line* 7, *page* 260, *Vol. II.*

—— sicque rebus gestis prospere, redierunt. page 41.

Sub hiis diebus, quidam peregrini Anglici in transmarinis partibus deviantes in vasta solitudine, sole ruente, coacti sub divo pernoctare, sed quia cognoverunt hæc omnia referta malis bestiis, non putabant tutum solo cubare. Quapropter ascenderunt arbores, quæ frondosæ fuerunt ibidem, gladios lanceasque secum trahentes. Cum ecce! noctis prima vigilia confluxerunt illic lupi, cum ursis plurimis, qui nitebantur arbores illas ascendere, allecti nimirum spe delectabilioris prædæ. Sed repulerunt feras viri, viriliter pro vita certantes contra bestias nocte tota.

Mane sauciæ recedentes dedere peregrinis copiam discedendi, qui longo pergentes itinere, tandem pervenerunt ad tugurium cujusdam solitarii, aquis paloque satis munitum; ubi clamantes foris diutius precantur ingressum. Quibus aperuit vir grandævus, et introduxit in casale suum. Quos cum vidisset viribus destitutos a labore nocturno præcedenteque vigilia, refecit pane, caseo, satis sedulo, atque vino. Cumque cognovisset eos Anglicos, monuit ipsos regratiari Deo pro sua salvatione, non tantum quia præservasset eos a bestiis, sed quia eripuisset eos ab infestis hostibus in terra propria et gladio devorante.—"Nam," inquit, "in visione Dei vidi, et "ecce! Angelus, vindicem exertum tenens gladium ultionis, "super terram vestram apparuit; non destiturus vindictam "facere, donec peccatores de terra conterat, et scelestos. Vos," inquit, "peregrinationis vota perficite, donec cognoveritis "pacem redditam terræ vestræ. Quia non in perpetuum "irascetur Dominus, neque in æternum comminabitur; sed "cum iratus fuerit, misericordiæ recordabitur."

Nec multo post secutum fuit bellum de Salopia, et turbatio grandis in patria, ut præfertur.

After "bellum," *line* 8, *page* 261, *Vol. II.*

page 42. Quorum alacritatem cernentes Gallici, crediderunt, prout erat, ipsos animatos alieno suffragio, et idcirco, nullo perfecto negotio, recesserunt.

Variation for "Per idem . . . peremptus," *ll.* 10–15, *page* 261, *Vol. II.*

page 42. Per idem tempus, Dominus de Castellis, Britonicus, inflatus de fortuna quæ sibi paulisper arriserat apud Plummouth, sic si composuisset cum̃ ea, recollecta juventute nobilium tam Gallicorum quam Britonum, [pergit] cum magna classe versus Angliam.

Sed—

"Hæc Dea non stabili quare sit levis orbe fatetur,
"Quæ summum dubio sub pede semper habet."

Nam

"[1]Passibus ambiguis Fortuna volubilis errat,
"Et manet in nullo certa tenaxque loco."

Quia

"Si modo læta manet, modo vultus sumit acerbos,
"[2]Et tantum constans in levitate sua est."

Hæc expertus est Dominus ipse de Castellis, dum audaciam supra vires induit, et apud Dortemouth in superbia et abusione

---

[1] This and the next three verses are a somewhat incorrect version of Ovid's *Tristia*, v. 8, ll. 15–18.

[2] *tũ* in orig.

terram scandit; nam ab hiis quos maxime habebat despectui, [1] scilicet, ruralibus, est peremptus.

After "rusticorum," *line* 26, *page* 261, *Vol. II.*

Mirabatur tamen quisque, et stupuit, cernens tantæ nobili- page 42.
tatis heroes infimorum hominum devenisse.

After "redimendos," *line* 2, *page* 262, *Vol. II.*

Prope medium mensis Aprilis, facta Londoniis per Dominum page 42.
Cantuariensem cleri convocatione, concessa fuit Regi una decima, conditione perutili, ut servetur; adjecta videlicet, ut Dominus Rex proclamari faceret in terra generaliter, ne quis provisor de cætero præsumat offendere privilegia vetusta, capiendo bona vel cariagia contra voluntatem possessorum. Sed si provisores privilegium istud offenderint, capiantur per ballivos, et custodiantur, vel Regi mittantur, per Regis justitiam puniendi. Evenit tamen postea ut, appensa pecunia, negligeretur conditio prius interposita.

After "Howenum," *line* 21, *page* 262, *Vol. II.*

— quamvis Dominus Cantuariensis obtulisset ex propriis page 42.
honorificum victum sibi; nam perante deploraverat bonorum suorum direptiones per Wallensium debacchationes; cujus rei consideratione, Rex eum misit in domo manere Principis, donec sibi providisset de remedio quo posset restitui, vel proprio beneficio vel alieno. Sed mens doli conscia præelegit hærere Wallico, pluripendens sui sanguinis originale principium quam fidem quam servare juraverat ad Henricum.

Eo tempore rediit classis antiqua, quæ conducta fuerat ad servandum maria contra piratas. Post cujus regressum, mox Flandrenses et Britones intrant pelagus, et ad nostrum nituntur dedecus, naves nostratum capientes aliquas, habentes merces plurimas, et nautas vel gladio vel suspendio trucidantes.

Per id temporis, serpens antiquus, qui per fœminam primitivæ suæ deceptionis et doli ministrare præsumpsit toxicum, per mulierem plenum fraudis adjunctum fecit disseminari mendacium.

After "Comitissæ," *line* 13, *page* 263, *Vol. II.*

— quæ monuit ut deponerent per maritima signa, quibus page 29.
evocari solebat patria, quotiens hostes nunciabantur adesse, ne

[1] *filiorum* occurs here in orig., in place of *scilicet*, by inadvertence.

veniente Rege Ricardo, fieret tumultus in populo, sive turbatio cujuscunque ignis inflammantis indicio. Credebant talibus mendaciis et religiosi quidam prælati, proh dolor! Abbates, ut fertur, Sancti Johannis de Colcestria et Sanctæ Osithæ, qui, eo quod cum Comitissa sentire videbantur, etc.

After "Ponte Fracto," *line* 29, *page* 264, *Vol. II.*

page 29. — Londoniis vero tandem factis digna[s] pœnas suscepit, tractus, suspensus, exenteratus, decapitatus, et in quartas divisus.

Per id tempus, Tamberlanus, quidam Tartarus de ditione Magni Cham, parentela velut infimus, arte faber ferrarius, sed fortuna repente levatus, cum esset sermone jocundus, discretione persuadibilis, et manu promptus, plures allexit ut se sequerentur contra Balthasardan, qui terras in Asia violenter occupaverat, et tam inibi quam Europa fecerat strages magnas. Cui inopinate paruit tota juventus regnorum Aquilonis, ipsum secuta de montibus [1] Caspiis usque in Palæstinam. Qui, quocunque locorum devenerit, permittebat incolis suis avitis gaudere legibus et cæremoniis, nullius leges vacuans, nullius sectam improbans, tantum se imperatorem altissimo Deo constitutum asserens, ut fallaces divitias in quibus confidunt homines sibi capiat, et eos exuat a curis supervacuis quæ nulli prosunt. Secuti sunt ergo eum multi de provinciis quas peragraverat, pauperes, ut suis stipendiis, quæ suis reddebat quotidie, ditarentur, divites, ut divitias per eum raptas sibi militando recuperarent; cujus in brevi tantum multiplicabatur [exercitus], ut amplius quam mille sexcentis millibus numeraretur. Unde contigit, quod cum civitates obsideret, quando [2] quadringentorum millium non doleret.

Hiis auditis, ille Magnus Cham, dominus regionis Catayæ, cœpit habere suspectum quem infimum et subjectum habuerat parum ante. Sed quia tantum robur non valebat evertere, curabat caute de suis finibus elongare, jubens ut in Persidem copias suas [3] curaret transponere, et sibi regiones opulentissimas subjugare; sicque vir vafer sub honoris titulo Tamberlanum emittens longius, sibi suoque populo pacem providit ad tempus; sperans eum periturum per extrema pericula, quem domare non potuit potestate domestica.

---

[1] *Caspeos* in orig., by inadvertence.

[2] This hiatus occurs in orig.

[3] *curabat* in orig.; corrected in the margin, in a later hand.

After "bonus," *line* 19, *page* 267, *Vol. II.*

Tempore Parliamenti prædicti, fuit in villa Coventriæ pesti- page 45.
lentia, velut particularis, quæ cotidie plures absumpsit; nec tamen terruit quos merito potuerat terruisse. De quibus, in persona Dei, propheta prædixit,—"[1] Perdidi populum meum, et "tamen ab iniquitate sua non sunt reversi." Nempe tunc aderant multi milites et armigeri, de familia Regis maxime, qui, Lollardorum erroribus instructi, inter cætera male sapiebant de Eucharistia, sive Missa. Quorum opiniones alias ostendimus ab Ecclesia fuisse damnatas. Horum irreverentia cum Domino Cantuariensi fuisset aliquotiens intimata, credere tamen distulit, donec illam cernere fide contigit oculata. Nempe quodam die, prout negotium exigebat, constitutus in platea publica, vidit sacerdotem viaticum deferentem moribundo, videlicet Sacramentum Corporis Salvatoris. Cui, prout religio Christiana requirit, prostratus ad terram venerationis obsequium, cum suis, Archiepiscopus exhibebat. Stabant in eodem vico milites plures et scutiferi confabulantes, et nescio quid tractantes. Qui cum sonitum nolæ præcedentis presbyterum audissent, et jam sacerdos, cum Corpore Christi, venisset ad locum quo turba stabat instabilis, mox omnes terga verterunt Corporis Dominici portitori, nec tantillam quidem reverentiam facientes, ut removerent caputia vel galeros. Vidit ista Cantuariensis, et tactus dolore cordis intrinsecus, quod in hominibus fidem Christianam professis tam obstinatam irreverentiam conspiciebat, cucurrit ad Regem, narrans ei suorum familiarium irreligiositatem, simul et Sacramenti vivifici vilipensionem,—"Dorsum," inquiens, "et non faciem, verterunt "Deo familiares et alumni regii, et non plus honoris impen"derunt Corpori Christi quam detulissent canino cadaveri. "O neglecta Christiana religio! O milites magnos et homi"nes nomine Christianos! Certe si tanta citius non extermi"netur abominatio, superveniet in brevi cleri regnique "desolatio."

Hæc Archiepiscopo cum magna mentis amaritudine proferente, commotus est Rex ipse, ut detestaretur publice tam notorios Christianæ religionis et fidei contemptores, instititque ut deducerentur ad rectam semitam transgressores.

After "Ricardum," *line* 25, *page* 267, *Vol. II.*

—Regemque modernum, ut exinde inopia regia relevaretur; page 45.
tanquam Rex ipse Regesque futuri se suaque tueri [possent] sola pecunia, nulla munificentia pro se laborantibus de cætero

---

[1] *Jerem.* xv. 7.

facienda; non considerata sententia versificationis egregii, sic dicentis,—

"Non murus, non arma, ditem tutantur avarum,"

sed,

"Est dare pro muro, solidique numinis instar."

Et idem,

"Non opus est vallo quos dextera dapsilis ambit."

Archiepiscopus cernens clerum non posse suffugere, nisi et ipse laicis correspondentem summam concessisset, convocato clero Londoniis in festo Sanctæ Katerinæ, cum communi consilio, concessit Regi unam decimam, non obstante quod medietas unius decimæ, etc.

Variation at "deflevit," *line* 34, *page* 267, *Vol. II.*

page 45. —— deflevit in hac parte Anglia sua damna; sed multo major vastitas facta est per oras maritimas, ut fertur, in Selandia, Flandria, et Holandia, per undarum influentias insuetas: fuerunt etiam qui affirmaverunt fluctus intumuisse contra Calesiam, ut in villam fluerent ultra muros.

Hoc anno cecidit firmissima columna Ecclesiæ Anglicanæ, Johannes de Botelesham, Roffensis Episcopus, Domini Cantuariensis alumnus, vir vitæ suæ prodigus, si instaret necessitas in causa Dei; cui successit[1] .

After "eundem," *line* 9, *page* 268, *Vol. II.*

page 46. Item, Magister Trevenaunt, Herefordensis Episcopus, sæculo valefecit; cui successit[1] .

Item, Magister Robertus Braybrok, Episcopus Londoniensis, ab hominibus est subtractus; cujus loco, Dominus Papa præposuit Dominum Rogerum de Waldene, nuper ab Archiepiscopatu dejectum.

Item,[1] Episcopus Wygorniensis, hoc anno concessit in fata, cui successit[1] .

Variation at "circa," *line* 14, *page* 268, *Vol. II.*

page 46. Hoc anno, nondum finitis diebus Festi Natalis, quidam temerarii, confictis clavibus posterulæ castri de Wyndeleshore, quidam de summo mane latenter et inopinate ingressi sunt cameram qua pueri Comitis Marchiæ dormiebant; quos assumptos secum duxerunt, volentes, ut dicebatur, eos offerre Oweno Glen-

[1] An hiatus in orig. Robert Mascall succeeded as Bishop of Hereford. The statement as to the death of a Bishop of Worcester in 1404, is erroneous.

dor, tanquam rectos hæredes regni Angliæ, ut vel sic conditio prosperaret Wallici quem noverant hostem Regi, vel ipsi aliquod grande perciperent ab eodem loco sceleris perpetrati. Sed fefellit eos eorum astutia: quia mox pueri, requisiti cum diligentia, recepti sunt, et qui abduxerant eos vel occisi vel in fugam acti.

After "nocumenta," *line* 23, *page* 268, *Vol. II.*

Ferunt Romipetæ quod per paucos dies ante mortem Bonefacii Papæ, [1] Antipapa Romam destinaverat nuncios honorabiles, qui vice sua docerent Curiam se paratum fore, si forte tali pacto posset Ecclesia reduci ad unitatem pristinam, de sua dignitate cessare; ita quod Dominus Papa idem faceret in persona sua; ut tunc, convocato Christianitatis clero, provideri posset Ecclesiæ legaliter et juridice de sacerdote summo. Quam conditionem Papa dicitur tulisse tam graviter, ut et nuncios convitiis multis afficeret, et Antipapam falsum vocaret excommunicatum. Quem etiam excommunicatum publice denunciasset ante hæc sæpius, ut dicebat, si consiliis adquievisset amicorum. Post quorum verborum prolationem, ambassiatores exacerbati clamaverunt libere dominum suum non esse excommunicatum, quin potius Christi verum Vicarium, cui oportuit exhiberi honorem summum. Et facta est magna seditio varie sentientium in Consistorio. page 46.

Dominus vero Papa, cum se recepisset in camera, tactus est infirmitate gravissima, quæ eum perduxit ad extrema. Nam per sex horas jugiter magna fatigatus molestia, tandem decessit a vita. Quo tempore Romæ, cunctis cernentibus, terribile portentum apparuit. Supra cameram in qua Papa languebat, illico moriturus, videbatur nempe nubes atra supra palatium Papæ descendere, quæ lucem diei sua fuscabat nigredine, et ibidem per tempus notabile, tanquam casura, jugiter permanere. Fuit igitur gravis expectatio, summaque cunctorum trepidatio, scire volentium finem portenti. Interim Papa moritur, et eodem instanti nubes rumpitur: de qua tot evolavere nigræ volucres, ad sternorum quantitatem grandiuscule, quod videbantur [2] aerem denigrare. Quibus visis, timor et tremor venere super hostes pacis, cunctis laudantibus oportere fieri protinus unitatem. Quapropter, cum eligeretur favore cunctorum Papa modernus, respondisse fertur, non se suscepturum dignitatem Papatus, nisi sub spe redintegrandi tunicam diu inconsutilem, quæ jam multis annis scissa permanserat manibus superborum.

---

[1] *Antipa* in orig.

[2] *aerō* in orig., apparently.

After "Palmarum," *line* 32, *page* 268, *Vol. II.*

page 46. Per id temporis [Rex Franciæ] viam inevitabilem carnis adiit; unde surrexit occasio dissensionis in Francia, Aurelianensium Duce præstante fomitem, qui [1] regum nomen jamdudum ambiverat totis viribus; sed obstitit ei multitudo nobilium, qui, vellet nollet, filium Regis mortui concorditer erexerunt.

After "armis esse," *line* 15, *page* 269, *Vol. II.*

page 47. Inprimis affirmabant, se velle Parliamentum Londoniis fieri, in quo desiderabant omnes conditiones, omnes status regni, posse gaudere suis libertatibus, et habere liberam electionem militum Parliamentalium de quolibet Comitatu; quia necesse est ut articuli sequentes emendentur, in evitationem adversitatis et obversionis, quæ verisimiliter ruituræ sunt in regno pro defectu recti, nisi Deus de sua gratia, et regni status, ea voluerit emendare. Inprimis igitur, ut malum regimen quod habetur in regno, corrigatur secundum cursum justitiæ et virtutis, et ut disponatur pro importabilibus oneribus quæ currunt super omnes status cleri, et ut emendentur injuriæ et derogationes factæ, tam statibus spiritualibus quam temporalibus, pro salvatione Sanctæ Ecclesiæ et libertate, quæ sint semper ante hæc ordinata et usitata ad beneplacitum Omnipotentis Dei.

Item, ut ordinetur remedium contra subjectiones, vel subactiones, et adnihilationes, in quo verisimile est regni Dominos [2] periclitari, tam in personarum quam in hæreditatum præjudicium, contra conditiones et status nativitatum vel genealogiarum suarum, et leges usitatas et antecessoribus suis factas.

Item, ut ordinetur emendatio contra gubernationes excessivas, et taxas importabiles atque subsidia, necnon extorsiones et oppressiones quæ fiunt generosis regni, mercatoribus et communibus, in extremam depauperationem et destructionem eorundem, qui fore deberent veri supportatores omnium statuum spiritualium et temporalium, si forent bene et rationabiliter gubernati; et ut voluntaria prodigalitas et inutiles expensæ, pro profectu singulari, de magnis bonis et divitiis quæ receptæ sunt de prædictis generosis mercatoribus et communibus, puniantur; et de eisdem bonis fiant emendæ, ad regni salvationem, et emendationem status sive conditionis fidelis communitatis. Ut, istis articulis et defectibus sic resarcitis et reformatis, et

[1] *regm.* This statement, as to the death of the King of France, is incorrect.

[2] This word is somewhat indistinct, and is doubtful.

emendatis ac ordinatis, in gubernatione et prosperitate, pace et unitate regni, inter nos ipsos, tunc ad faciendum vias et gubernationes ad resistendum hostibus exterius, per Dei gratiam, qui nunc et nos destruunt et mercatores nostros, procedamus; qui deberent esse quoddam de substantialioribus divitiis hujus regni; et alias vias multas, tam per aquas quam per terras providendas, quæ hactenus sunt omissæ pro defectu boni regiminis; quibus resisti potuit malitiæ eorundem.

Et si hæc adimpleri poterunt, habemus informationem plenam quod permissionem ab hiis qui sunt rebelles in Wallia, quod erunt læto corde sub regimine Regis Anglorum, prout fuerunt temporibus Regum Ricardi [et] Edwardi, sine defensione facienda.

Quapropter rogamus et requirimus, ad honorem Dei, vos omnes qui hæc estis audituri, ut sitis benevoli et adjutores huic proposito, pro salvatione vestra atque nostra, et bono statu et gubernatione nobilis regni hujus.

After " hierarcha," *line* 30, *page* 270, *Vol. II.*

Archiepiscopus autem ductus est ad castrum[1] , conservandus page 48.
donec Rex veniret, et diceret quod fieri vellet tam de Comite quam de illo. Rex eo tempore præparaverat magnam expeditionem facere super Wallicos, et progressus fuerat usque ad partes illas, multis vallatus millibus bellatorum. Sed cum audisset rumores istos, collocato illic quo Marchia tueretur, festinavit Eboracum, ut plebem compesceret a seditione, et insurrectores puniret. Cum vero prope castrum venisset quo servabatur Archiepiscopus, rogavit Antistes Comitem Westmerlandiæ, ut liceret ei obviam procedere domino suo Regi. Quod cum annuisset, hora qua Rex advenit, stans in turri, cum solus esset ibi destitutus ministris, vidit quemdam in curia sacerdotem, quem ad se advocans, rogavit ut ferret crucem suam coram eo. Qui libenter complens jussa Præsulis, tulit crucem; sed cum venisset ad januam, qui astabant rapuerunt de manibus ejus crucem; quod cernens Archiepiscopus, et ipse eluctando crucem violenter extorsit ab eis. Qui tandem conglobati, iterum crucem rapiunt ab eodem, et suis incomitatum exire compellunt. Cumque venisset ad Regis præsentiam, humi prostratus gratiam precabatur. Quem Rex allocutus breviter, reverti jussit in castrum, donec cum Consilio providisset quid agendum.

Interea Rex properat cum suis legionibus contra civitatem Eboraci, eo quod cum Archiepiscopo cives sensissent contra ipsum. Quibus tantum terrorem incussit, ut mox, apertis portis,

[1] This hiatus occurs in orig.

exirent obviam nudis pedibus, succincti pannis vilibus, discoopertis capitibus, mucrones sive restes gestantes in manibus, et cum singultibus et miserabilibus fletibus veniam postulantes. Quos turbulenter increpans, jussit ut reverterentur quilibet in domum suam, nihilque suorum mobilium alienare præsumerent, donec deliberasset quid de eis facere debuisset.

Archiepiscopum vero et Comitem Marescallum deduci fecit illuc, ut quos ad rebellionem concitaverant, hos mortis haberent ignominiosæ spectatores et testes.

Proinde feria secunda Pentecostes, dum Rex et Archiepiscopus Cantuariensis, qui illuc properaverat pro salute collegæ, jentaculum protelarent, Comes Arundeliæ et Dominus Thomas Beuforde, collateralis frater Regis[1] Justiciarius, accepta commissione, sederunt in judicio contra dictos Episcopum et Comitem Marescallum; et condemnaverunt eos sententia prædictorum, et Archiepiscopum quidem, damnatum velut apostatam et ordinis sui transgressorem, eo quod captus sit armatus, et Regis sui, necnon et regni, publicum proditorem. Ad quod verbum tantum respondit, se regni proditorem nullatenus extitisse; acceptaque tristi sententia, mox urgebatur ad mortem, ne, mediante prece cujusquam, Rex miseris indulgeret. Impositique jumentis vilibus et sine stramentis, cum turba multa ducti sunt extra civitatem, in campum satum hordeo tunc virenti. Cumque Comes Marescallus, utpote junior et ephebus, ac delicatior, manum lictoris horreret, Archiepiscopus confortans eum monuit forti animo [esse], cum esset damnatus inique, et constanter sufferre mortem momentaneam quam subiturus erat, ut asseruit, pro [2]nihilo; promittens sibi, sub periculo animæ suæ, quod solutus carnis onere spiritus gaudiis perennibus frueretur. Quibus monitis herus exhilaratus [3]cervicem exposuit spiculatori, sicque præcisa est, velut a texente, vita sua; et dum [4][adhuc] ordirer, succisus est, non sine lacrymis plurimorum.

Archiepiscopus vero magis constanter necem tulit, non procul a loco decollationis Comitis, juxta vulgarium opiniones martyrio perpulchro finitus; prædicant namque miracula quædam facta fuisse, etc.

---

[1] This hiatus occurs in orig.

[2] This is perhaps the word, though it resembles "*nistia*."

[3] *cervices* in orig.

[4] *adhuc* is inserted in the margin.

APPENDIX. (E).

Various Readings from the Text of the *“Ypodigma Neustriæ” of Thomas Walsingham, as given in Camden's Edition (Anglica, Normannica, Hibernica, etc.), Frankfort, 1603.

Camden's Ed. Page.				
548.	Page 216,	line 30,	*ante*	“aulicorum” for “Anglicorum.”
549.	,, 222,	,, 7,	,,	“adversa” for “aversa.”
550.	,, 223,	,, 27,	,,	“vetuit” for “metuit.”
551.	,, 226,	,, 11,	,,	“productus” for “prædictus.”
552.	,, 229,	,, 13,	,,	“populi” for “proprii.”
554.	,, 232,	,, 40,	,,	“cunctis” for “multis.”
,,	,, 233,	,, 9,	,,	“Thomas” for “Henricus.”
,,	,, 234,	,, 19,	,,	“debebant” for “debeant.”
556.	,, 247,	,, 9,	,,	“respiciens dignis tanto” for “respiciens tanto.”
557.	,, 249,	,, 22,	,,	“luctatus” for “limitatus.”
558.	,, 252,	,, 38,	,,	“civitas” for “Trinitas.”
,,	,, 253,	,, 12,	,,	“sancta Trinitas” for “secunda “Trinitas.”
559.	,, 255,	,, 3,	,,	“ad aliud” for “ab aliunde.”
,,	,, 255,	,, 32,	,,	“salvique” for “salvoque.”
560.	,, 257,	,, 31,	,,	“obvios” for “obviis.”
561.	,, 259,	,, 22,	,,	the hiatus after “Dominus” is filled up with “Cant.”
,,	,, 260,	,, 34,	,,	“pecuniale” for “speciale.”
562.	,, 262,	,, 20,	,,	“animum pravum” for “virum “pravum.”
,,	,, 264,	,, 9,	,,	“aliquot” for “quotis.”
263.	,, 265,	,, 7,	,,	“et sapientes in id,” for “et “in id.”
565.	,, 270,	,, 8,	,,	“dictis articulis” for “dictis.”
,,	,, 270,	,, 26,	,,	“patuit” for “potuit.”
566.	,, 272,	,, 19,	,,	“octo” for “septem.”
,,	,, 273,	,, 35,	,,	“viginti” for “triginta.”
567.	,, 274,	,, 16,	,,	“nuper” for “F. Re.”
569.	,, 280,	,, 2,	,,	“Lovanensium” for “Bononen-“sium.”
,,	,, 280,	,, 13,	,,	the hiatus after “Episcopus” is filled up with “cum aliis viris “doctis et prudentibus.”

* See page ix. of the Introduction to the present Volume.

Camden's Ed. Page.		
569.	Page 280, line 16, *ante*	"Ricardum" for "Nicholaum."
,,	,, 280, ,, 27, ,,	"contendentes" for "contendentium."
,,	,, 280, ,, 29, ,,	"profecto jam dicta sedes" for "pro facto jam dicto."
,,	,, 280, ,, 29, ,,	"justo" for "in isto."
,,	,, 281, ,, 9, ,,	"decerpsimus" for "descripsimus."
571.	,, 284, ,, 19, ,,	"magnum dispendium" for "magnum scandalum."
,,	,, 285, ,, 16, ,,	"id vetantis" for "advocantis."
572.	,, 287, ,, 9, ,,	"proditoribus" for "mortibus."
573.	,, 288, ,, 9, 10, ,,	"viribus conquestant" for "juribus conquiescant."
574.	,, 291, ,, 8, ,,	"innitebantur" for "invitabantur."
576.	,, 296, ,, 20, ,,	"condemnamus" for "concedimus."
577.	,, 297, ,, 21, ,,	"intra" for "juxta."
578.	,, 300, ,, 29, ,,	"quod Schene" for "apud Schene."
583.	,, 310, ,, 29, ,,	"millibus" for "militibus."
,,	,, 310, ,, 34, ,,	"tum" for "tamen."
585.	,, 314, ,, 25, ,,	"Belmarinorum" for "Betinarinorum."
,,	,, 316, ,, 32, ,,	"existant" for "existat."
588.	,, 321, ,, 24, ,,	"restellas suas" for "res suas."
589.	,, 322, ,, 25, ,,	"consedere" for "considens."
,,	,, 323, ,, 27, ,,	"a turribus" for "a telis et turribus."
,,	,, 324, ,, 21, ,,	"ex parte illa" for "ex parte."
590.	,, 325, ,, 13, ,,	"obtinuerunt" for "obtinuerat."
,,	,, 325, ,, 15, ,,	"vicesimum nonum" for "nonum decimum."
,,	,, 326, ,, 17, ,,	"picti nobiliter" for "nobiliter."
591.	,, 328, ,, 41, ,,	"mulctaverunt" for "mutilaverunt."
592.	,, 330, ,, 1, ,,	"nostratum" for "invictum."
,,	,, 330, ,, 9, ,,	"villæ" for "mille."
,,	,, 330, ,, 18, ,,	"recusassent" for "refutassent."

INDEX TO WALSINGHAM'S ENGLISH HISTORY.

INDEX TO WALSINGHAM'S ENGLISH HISTORY.

A.

B.

D.

E.

F.

G.

H.

I.

J.

K.

M.

N.

O.

P.

S.

T.

V.

W.

Y.

Z.

CPSIA information can be obtained
at www.ICGtesting.com
Printed in the USA
LVHW100508130422
716029LV00002B/30

9 783752 591736